OXFORD WORLD'S CLASSICS

IVANHOE

WALTER SCOTT (1771–1832) was born in Edinburgh of a Border family. After attending the High School and University of Edinburgh he followed his father into the profession of the law, becoming an advocate (barrister) in 1792. In 1799 he was appointed Sheriff-Depute for the county of Selkirk, and in 1806 a Clerk of the Court of Session—appointments which he retained until the end of his life. His first major publication was a collection of ballads entitled *The Minstrelsy of the Scottish Border* (1802–3). He became famous as a poet with *The Lay of the Last Minstrel* (1805), *Marmion* (1808), and *The Lady of the Lake* (1810). In 1814 he published his first novel, *Waverley*, set during the Jacobite rising of 1745. Its success encouraged him to produce more historical novels. With *Ivanhoe* (1820), a romance of medieval England, Scott moved from an early modern Scottish setting to a variety of countries and periods. Scott's work was widely acclaimed in Europe and America. He spent the income from his writings on establishing a house and estate at Abbotsford, near Melrose. He was awarded a baronetcy by the Prince Regent in 1818. Partnership in the printing firm of James Ballantyne and Co. involved him in a financial crash in 1826. His last years were darkened by illness and the need to continue his output of writing to pay off the debts incurred. His *Journal* of those years is the most moving of his works. He died at Abbotsford in 1832; his biography was written by his son-in-law, John Gibson Lockhart.

IAN DUNCAN is Barbara and Carlisle Moore Professor of English at the University of Oregon, and the author of *Modern Romance and Transformations of the Novel: The Gothic, Scott, Dickens* (1992). He has edited Conan Doyle's *The Lost World*, John Buchan's *The Island of Sheep*, and Sir Walter Scott's *Rob Roy* for Oxford World's Classics.

OXFORD WORLD'S CLASSICS

*For over 100 years Oxford World's Classics have brought
readers closer to the world's great literature. Now with over 700
titles—from the 4,000-year-old myths of Mesopotamia to the
twentieth century's greatest novels—the series makes available
lesser-known as well as celebrated writing.*

*The pocket-sized hardbacks of the early years contained
introductions by Virginia Woolf, T. S. Eliot, Graham Greene,
and other literary figures which enriched the experience of reading.
Today the series is recognized for its fine scholarship and
reliability in texts that span world literature, drama and poetry,
religion, philosophy and politics. Each edition includes perceptive
commentary and essential background information to meet the
changing needs of readers.*

OXFORD WORLD'S CLASSICS

SIR WALTER SCOTT

Ivanhoe

Edited with an Introduction and Notes by
IAN DUNCAN

OXFORD
UNIVERSITY PRESS

OXFORD
UNIVERSITY PRESS

Great Clarendon Street, Oxford OX2 6DP

Oxford University Press is a department of the University of Oxford.
It furthers the University's objective of excellence in research, scholarship,
and education by publishing worldwide in

Oxford New York

Athens Auckland Bangkok Bogotá Buenos Aires Cape Town
Chennai Dar es Salaam Delhi Florence Hong Kong Istanbul Karachi
Kolkata Kuala Lumpur Madrid Melbourne Mexico City Mumbai Nairobi
Paris São Paulo Shanghai Singapore Taipei Tokyo Toronto Warsaw

with associated companies in Berlin Ibadan

Oxford is a registered trade mark of Oxford University Press
in the UK and in certain other countries

Published in the United States
by Oxford University Press Inc., New York

This edition © Ian Duncan 1996
Chronology © Claire Lamont 1982

The moral rights of the author have been asserted

Database right Oxford University Press (maker)

First published as a World's Classics paperback 1996
Reissued as an Oxford World's Classics paperback 1998

All rights reserved. No part of this publication may be reproduced,
stored in a retrieval system, or transmitted, in any form or by any means,
without the prior permission in writing of Oxford University Press,
or as expressly permitted by law, or under terms agreed with the appropriate
reprographics rights organizations. Enquiries concerning reproduction
outside the scope of the above should be sent to the Rights Department,
Oxford University Press, at the address above

You must not circulate this book in any other binding or cover
and you must impose this same condition on any acquirer

British Library Cataloguing in Publication Data

Data available

Library of Congress Cataloging in Publication Data

Scott, Walter, Sir, 1771–1832.
Ivanhoe / Sir Walter Scott; edited with an introduction by Ian Duncan.
(Oxford world's classics)
Includes bibliographical references.
1. Great Britain—History—Richard I, 1189–1199—Fiction.   2. Knights and
knighthood—England—Fiction.   I. Duncan, Ian.   II. Title.   III. Series.
PR5318.A2D86 1996 823'.7—dc20 95–33167

ISBN 0–19–283499–1

5 7 9 10 8 6

Printed in Great Britain by
Clays Ltd, St Ives plc

CONTENTS

ACKNOWLEDGEMENTS

I AM grateful to the Trustees of the National Library of Scotland, Edinburgh, and the Pierpont Morgan Library, New York (accession no. MA 440), for permission to cite manuscript materials in their holdings. I should also like to thank the staff of those libraries and the Yale University libraries for their assistance, and the Whitney Humanities Center at Yale University for a grant from the A. Whitney Griswold Research Fund.

INTRODUCTION

THE popularity of *Ivanhoe* in the early months of 1820 moved one Scots reviewer to gloat over his countryman's success:

With a charm far beyond the power of *Michael* Scott, he has already made Scotland his own to its remotest isles; but now, with one mighty cast, he has brought England within the pale of his genius; and, with her interesting people, established her, too, a province of his empire. . . . In his first foreign enterprise, he is as much at home as he ever was in his native land; and, from what he has already done, he has in store, we have no doubt, much of wonder for our neighbours of the South that he should know more about them than they know about themselves; till, with Faulconbridge, they exclaim,

'How easy doth he take all England up!'

or, with Richard,

'As were our England in reversion his,
And he our subjects' next degree in hope!'[1]

The reviewer astutely reads the historical theme of *Ivanhoe*, the Norman conquest, as an allegory of its author's ambitions. Like a literary version of the Conqueror, Scott has achieved the most effective Scottish invasion of England since the Union, and reversed the relations between imperial centre and province. Unlike earlier, much-resented invasions (by a Jacobite army in 1745, by ambitious Scots infesting British government and the professions) this one succeeds because it represents a cultural rather than a political or economic colonization. The next hundred years would fully justify the reviewer's prediction. In *Ivanhoe* Scott furnished the English with their idea of an ancestral England as effectively as had Shakespeare in his history plays.

Scott well knew the risks and rewards of presuming to make 'the traditions and manners of Old England' his own. Both the

---

[1] *Edinburgh Monthly Review*, 3 (Feb. 1820), 163–4. The quotations are adapted from *King John*, IV. iii and *Richard II*, I. iv. Michael Scott, 13th-cent. scholar and supposed warlock, haunts Scott's *The Lay of the Last Minstrel* (1805).

'Dedicatory Epistle' to the first edition and the 1830 'Introduction' brood upon this border-crossing. Although most of his readers had surely always been English, Scott's literary reputation was built on Scottish ground; an earlier venture into Yorkshire (*Rokeby*, 1813) had accompanied the decline of his pre-eminence as a poet. Now, at the height of new fortune as an anonymous novelist, Scott wanted a bold stroke to win fresh readers in a market he feared was becoming glutted with the Scottish historical novels he had done so much to popularize in the five years since *Waverley* (1814). As he worked on the new romance in the summer and autumn of 1819, recovering from a near-fatal illness, he grew confident that it would be something 'uncommon', and his printer and publisher, James Ballantyne and Archibald Constable, caught the excitement.[2] After delays occasioned by over-extension at the printers and a difficulty with the paper supply, *Ivanhoe* finally appeared on 18 December. The first edition of 8,000 copies sold out early in the new year, despite the high price of thirty shillings for the three handsomely produced post-octavo volumes; by the end of 1820 the Ballantynes were printing a third edition, and at least five different theatrical versions had opened in London throughout the year. In the words of Scott's biographer, 'the publication of Ivanhoe marks the most brilliant epoch in Scott's history as the literary favourite of his contemporaries. With the novel which he next put forth, the immediate sale of these works began gradually to decline.'[3]

As it turned out, *Ivanhoe* marked the crux of Scott's reputation more problematically than Lockhart could have foreseen. The most popular novel of one of the best loved of British authors throughout the nineteenth century, in the twentieth it has come to represent the decay of an unfashionable literary monument. Today its dwindling popularity can no longer outweigh the neglect or disdain of professional readers. According to the standard modern criticism, *Ivanhoe* executes the fatal turn in Scott's career from a once influential historical realism (in the

---

[2] See *The Letters of Sir Walter Scott*, ed. H. J. C. Grierson (12 vols., 1932; hereafter *Letters*), v. 402, vi. 6.

[3] J. G. Lockhart, *Memoirs of the Life of Sir Walter Scott, Bart.* (1 vol. edn., 1896), ch. 46.

novels about the making of modern Scotland) to a tinsel-and-
tushery medievalism. Apologists for *Ivanhoe* have had to fall
back on the schoolmasterly philistinism that once seemed requisite for the appreciation of Scott, exhorting us with a dreary
heartiness not to think but to enjoy the book as an 'adventure
story'.

The first step in Scott's descent 'from the library to the
school-room' (Leslie Stephen), *Ivanhoe* flourished for a century
and a half in the fertile loam of popular culture, where its influence continues to be felt; less now through literal renditions in
other media (if Arthur Sullivan's 1891 opera gathers dust in the
archives, the 1953 movie with Robert Taylor and Elizabeth
Taylor retains some of its gleam), than in spin-offs of its characters and settings and events. Above all *Ivanhoe* revived the
ancient folk careers of Robin Hood and Richard the Lionheart,
both played in my childhood by the aptly named Richard
Greene, although the embers of Robin Hood's appeal may recently have been stamped out by Kevin Costner. *Ivanhoe*'s more
insidious influence, according to the authorities, may well be
found in the popular grasp of twelfth-century history. The stric-
tures of Edward Augustus Freeman, Regius Professor at Oxford,
upon Scott's howlers (the supposed Saxon provenance of
Coningsburgh Castle, the cocktail of pagan demons invoked by
Ulrica, a host of discrepancies about names and dates) might
seem irrelevant to the concerns of a romance, but they were
provoked by the readiness of fellow historians such as Augustin
Thierry to mistake that romance for real history.[4]

It is probably safe to say, though, that the career of *Ivanhoe* as
childhood reading or school text has by now run its course.
Faster, lighter technologies of narration have made Scott's seem
sluggish and encumbered, altogether too literary. The historical
dissertations and costume descriptions, the pastiche dialogue
with its registers of melodramatic declamation and facetious
banter, all no doubt bore the juvenile reader now. To be sure,

[4] E. A. Freeman, *The History of the Norman Conquest in England* (6 vols.,
1867–79), v. 839. On *Ivanhoe* and historiography, see Clare A. Simmons, *Reversing the Conquest: History and Myth in Nineteenth-Century British Literature*
(1990), 87–112; Ina Ferris, *The Achievement of Literary Authority: Gender, History and the Waverley Novels* (1991), 195–236.

once Scott's narrative takes off (by the Ashby tournament) all is
fleet and glittering. The heaviness of the preliminaries has much
to do with the author's labour in putting together a new kind of
fiction, even if its very success—its triumphant saturation of the
popular imagination—would seem eventually to have exhausted
it. But the generation that has forgotten *Ivanhoe* is well placed to
rediscover Scott's dashing *rifacimento* of national history and
popular culture. We may even enjoy the pseudo-antiquarian
clutter, as we recognize an ancestor of the archival comedy of
Umberto Eco. The literariness of the enterprise, the brilliance of
Scott's play with stock figures and situations, has caught us up
again.

While the first reviewers of *Ivanhoe* acknowledged its charm
and excitement, many also expressed a disquiet over something
inauthentic, not just an inaccuracy of historical detail but the
settlement of the Author of *Waverley* in a sub-literary neighbourhood—with the suspicion that this, not the mansion of a
respectable historicism, had been his address all along.[5] *Ivanhoe:
A Romance*. It was the first time Scott had actually given one of
his novels that label. The 'Dedicatory Epistle' that prefaces the
tale, the most carefully poised and detailed yet of Scott's theo-
retical statements about his art, uses the terms 'modern antique
romance' and (in a rather disparaging architectural analogy)
'modern Gothic'. Specifically, the rubric points us back to the
late-eighteenth-century Gothic romance of Ann Radcliffe,
'Monk' Lewis, and Horace Walpole, whose pseudo-antiquarian
'goblin tale' Scott mentions in the 'Epistle'. *Ivanhoe* rehearses
the Gothic novel's medieval setting, its scenery of castles and
monasteries, and its stock figures of despotic barons, corrupt and
fanatical prelates, and persecuted maidens. The example of the
Gothic novel had been crucial for Scott, but where his Scottish
novels had absorbed Gothic elements into a larger scheme of
historical romance, *Ivanhoe* appears to mark a ceremonial return
to Gothic: a re-Gothicization of historical fiction. In this *Ivanhoe*
rides a wave of neo- and retro-Gothic experiments, including

---

[5] e.g. [Francis Jeffrey], *Edinburgh Review*, 33 (Jan. 1820): its shift 'from the
reign of nature and reality, to that of fancy and romance' makes *Ivanhoe* 'a
fantastical pageant' rather than a novel (7–8); *Eclectic Review*, 13 (1820): 'no other
impression is left on the mind, than that of a pageant or a masquerade' (528).

some notably powerful and original inventions, that swept British fiction in the decade after Waterloo: Mary Shelley's *Frankenstein* (1818), Maturin's *Melmoth the Wanderer* (1820), and Hogg's *Private Memoirs and Confessions of a Justified Sinner* (1824) are only the most famous. *Ivanhoe* differs from all of these in its relative lack of concern with terror, psychopathology, the supernatural, and the uncanny. Indeed, where they Gothicize modern life, *Ivanhoe* enlightens the Gothic past. Ghosts, demons, and enchanters are almost shockingly absent from their natural habitat here in the forests and castles of the Middle Ages. 'Will future ages believe that such stupid bigotry ever existed!' exclaims Brian de Bois-Guilbert of the charges brought against Rebecca for witchcraft, and for once we sense that his judgement coincides with the author's.

The English setting is *Ivanhoe*'s other striking departure from mainstream Gothic convention. Scott's novel unfolds not upon the foreign political and religious territory of Renaissance Italy or Spain, but in England itself—an England invaded and colonized by foreign warlords. With this move, Scott brings into historical daylight the secret, scandalous national theme of Gothic. Its feudal and Catholic despotisms were reassuringly alien, set in another place and period; yet at the same time they were part of our own ancestral past, and their traces might yet linger in the recesses of modern life, in the private relations of sexuality and the family. Gothic thus came to signify a contradiction at the heart of the late-eighteenth-century ideological formation—in Benedict Anderson's influential phrase, the 'imagined community'[6]—of a British national culture. On the one hand the classical view, traditionally dominant, saw Gothic as an alien, barbaric darkness, the enemy of civilization; on the other, a new, romantic and nationalist revaluation of Gothic claimed it as the figure of an authentic, native, Northern and Germanic cultural origin.[7] Gothic identified a divided and contaminated national heritage, our own and not our own.

---

[6] Benedict Anderson, *Imagined Communities: Reflections on the Origin and Spread of Nationalism* (1983).

[7] See Samuel Kliger, *The Goths in England: A Study in Seventeenth and Eighteenth-Century Thought* (1952); Gary Kelly, 'Social Conflict, Nation and Empire: from Gothicism to Romantic Orientalism', *Ariel*, 20 (1989), 2, 3–18.

At a more refined stage, the question of Gothic informed the antiquarian controversy about the origins of romance which agitated the main literary-historical sources of *Ivanhoe*. Scott's precursors in the archaeology of native literature, romance revival editors such as Bishop Percy, Joseph Ritson, and George Ellis, disputed whether romance—our vernacular narrative tradition, the imaginative stock of Chaucer and Spenser and Shakespeare—came from the Norse scalds, or from the Celtic bards, or even (in an unsettling, diabolic reversal of Biblical origins) from an Oriental strain of marvellous fabulation, caught from the Saracen enemy confronted in the Crusades. Scott himself, following Ritson, accepted a verdict of mixed origins, a contaminated genealogy: it was impossible to disentangle a single source for our cultural traditions. He thus participates in an intellectual movement of the late Enlightenment that celebrated, rather than deplored, the ethnically and culturally heterogeneous formation of Britain out of Celtic, Phoenician, and Roman elements as well as Saxon and Norman, Latin and Germanic and Romance.[8]

Ivanhoe explores a crucial, transitional moment of this debated cultural historiography, between the last of the great alien invasions (Norman upon Saxon, or Romance upon Gothic) and the compound formation of a national identity represented linguistically by the appearance of English. *Ivanhoe* is set in about 1193–4: 'we may fairly infer', writes one of Scott's authorities, 'that the Saxon language and literature began to be mixed with the Norman about 1180; and that in 1216 the change may be considered as complete'.[9] Scott exemplifies this account of English origins in the rich miscellany of his literary sources for *Ivanhoe* (the Robin Hood ballads and popular romances, Chaucer, Spenser, and Shakespeare), in addition to representing

---

[8] Ritson summarizes the debate, rather fiercely, in his 'Dissertation on Romance and Minstrelsy', prefaced to *Ancient Engleish Metrical Romancëes* (sic) (1802), vol. i. pp. xix–xxxii. He concludes: 'After all, it seems highly probable that the origin of romance, in every age or country, is to be sought in the different systems of superstition which have, from time to time, prevail'd, whether pagan or Christian.' For a modern view of this question, see Howard Weinbrot, *Britannia's Issue: The Rise of British Literature from Dryden to Ossian* (1993), 477–571.

[9] George Ellis, *Specimens of Early English Poetry* (4th edn., 1811), i. 76.

an England inhabited by a hotchpotch of clans and societies and castes: Saxon serfs and gentry, Norman barons, monks, outlaws, Jews, and Templars. The Druidical remains that decorate the opening scene, and the reference to a Roman army, remind us that the Saxons too were *conquistadores*, and far from first in the series. And now England is open to horizons more exotic than Germany or France: Crusaders return from the East bearing cultural influences ranging from Provençal troubadour ballads and the cult of Courtly Love to the sinister Oriental despotism of the Templar, with his black slaves and his design of world domination. Even the critical presence of the Jews in *Ivanhoe* recalls the scholarly argument about a Hebraic origin of ancient British culture, in obedience to orthodox sacred history. This picture of the mixed nation works to dispel Gothic anxieties of genealogical contamination by bringing them out into the open. Everyone is an alien, no one is a 'native', in time all blend into one greater Englishness. The narrator duly reports the marriage of Ivanhoe and Rowena 'as a pledge of the future peace and harmony betwixt the two races, which, since that period, have been so completely mingled, that the distinction has become wholly invisible' (Chapter XLIV). Scott's readers would have recognized such a solution. It solemnizes the end of *Waverley*, when the wedding of hero and heroine symbolizes the cultural as well as genealogical union of Scotland and England into a single British nation; Scott had adapted the device from the Anglo-Irish 'National Tale' of Sydney Owenson and Maria Edgeworth.[10] Ostensibly, then, Scott imposes the comic solution of the national tale, the allegory of union, upon the Gothic ancestral scenery of *Ivanhoe* to create a new historical romance of English origins.

The historical setting of *Ivanhoe* also makes explicit the political theme of Gothic, which underlies the literary and philological arguments about cultural origins. The French Revolution had inflamed debates about the character of the English constitution in a domestic history consisting largely of invasions, usurpations, and revolutions. A mainly radical tradition located the origins of English liberty, parliamentary assembly, and common law in a

---

[10] See Katie Trumpener, 'National Character, Nationalist Plots: National Tale and Historical Novel in the Age of *Waverley*, 1806–1830', *ELH* 60 (1993), 685–731.

primitive Saxon constitution, derived from those virtuous ancestors described by Tacitus in the *Germania*,[11] but curtailed under
the Norman conquest and the imposition of feudalism. Hence
the so-called 'Norman yoke' thesis of British history, which
interpreted a persistence of the Conquest in the ongoing oppression of the English people by a usurping ruling class, and in
the reproduction of 'Gothic' (i.e. Norman) power relations
within domestic social structures. (The enclosure movement, for
example, represented a revival of the Norman forest laws.) When
Scott wrote *Ivanhoe*, however, the Norman yoke was losing its
usefulness for Radical polemic, largely because of the mobiliz-
ation of patriotic sentiment in the recent wars against revolution-
ary and Napoleonic France. Norman usurpers no longer typified
British landlords but a French imperial military machine poised
for a thoroughly modern conquest.[12]

Scott was perhaps the most influential author in the cultural
formation of a modern British nationalism that occupies this
period, and in *Ivanhoe* he undertakes a conservative capture of
the radical myth of the Norman yoke. The novel seeks out rather
than avoids the theme: Scott's insistence on a colonial antagon-
ism between Normans and Saxons a century and a quarter after
the Battle of Hastings is perhaps the most notorious of the
historical sins of *Ivanhoe*, and Scott has been blamed for relying
on a third-rate play (Logan's *Runnamede*) for so material a point.
The last stages of composition of *Ivanhoe* coincided with an
escalation of Radical reform agitation and government re-
pression, the most violent event of which was the 'Peterloo
massacre' of August 1819, when cavalry troops attacked a Manchester crowd. Scott supported the most draconian measures of

[11] Translations of Tacitus appeared in 1777 (by John Aikin) and 1793 (by
Arthur Murphy).

[12] See Christopher Hill, 'The Norman Yoke', in *Puritanism and Revolution:
Studies in Interpretation of the English Revolution of the Seventeenth Century*
(1962), 50–122, esp. 94–109; Asa Briggs, 'Saxons, Normans and Victorians', in
Collected Essays (1085), i. 215–35. On nationalism, see Gerald Newman, *The Rise
of English Nationalism: A Cultural History, 1720–1830* (1987); Linda Colley,
Britons: Forging the Nation, 1707–1837 (1992). On the somewhat different va-
lency of these themes in Scottish historiography see Colin Kidd, *Subverting
Scotland's Past: Scottish Whig Historians and the Creation of an Anglo-British
Identity 1689–c.1830* (1993).

government (he praised the judicious conduct of the Manchester officials), wrote a series of anti-Radical pamphlets (*The Visionary*, December 1819), and started organizing a loyalist militia in his district of the Borders. Fearful of 'a bloody and remorseless struggle between property and the populace' as the year drew to its close, he argued for the need to build a popular cultural resistance to Radical ideology.[13]

In so far as *Ivanhoe* participates in this political climate—and its composition is largely anterior to the crisis—it is more relaxed and generous than the fierce prognostications to be found in Scott's correspondence. 'Thematically his most contemporary novel to date', as Marilyn Butler has argued, *Ivanhoe* represents a politically divided (rather than organically harmonious) medieval England in order to draw the dynamics of compromise.[14] The characters find refuge from Norman tyranny in the greenwood, where the folk meet their king on terms of primitive simplicity. If Robin Hood's forest commonwealth is a type of that 'beautiful system invented first in the woods' (in the words of Montesquieu's commentary on Tacitus[15]), it appears to be a primitive monarchy, as in the hunting society of Scottish Enlightenment anthropology, rather than a republic; the outlaws are ready to swear fealty to a true English king when they recognize one among them. The vassal Wamba sings a subversive ditty about the 'Norman yoke', and at the same time is eager to give his life for his Saxon overlord. The detailed description of the two serfs in the opening pages, with Scott's notorious invention of the metal collar, insists on a Saxon yoke that preceded the Norman one in the domestic social order. 'The milder and more free spirit of the Saxon constitution' (Chapter I) consists after all in an 'organic' reciprocity of obligations and a familiar intimacy between the castes—not in any freedom from distinction and hierarchy. So Carlyle understood, when he took over Scott's serf's collar for the emblem of a kinder servitude than the intangible and inhuman bondage of the cash

[13] *Letters*, v. 486 (12 Sept. 1819).

[14] Marilyn Butler, *Romantics, Rebels, and Reactionaries: English Literature and its Background 1780–1830* (1982), 149–50.

[15] See *The Spirit of the Laws* (1748), trans. Thomas Nugent (1750), bk. 11, ch. 6.

nexus.[16] Other figures of slavery appear in the text, as we shall see. Gurth's celebrated linguistic critique, meanwhile (the Saxon names of domestic animals denote the peasant's labour in tending them, the Norman names denote the landlord's consumption of them), serves to divert a problem of class difference (workers and owners) into one of ethnic and cultural difference (Saxons and Normans), more easily resolved in an evolutionary blending. But, as contemporary reviewers were quick to notice, the critique retains its Radical charge.[17] The compound entity of modern English encodes the distinction between those who produce and those who consume, and the reader is left to decide how far it is open or closed in social practice. *Ivanhoe* remains a novel in which a popular uprising storms the castle of aristocratic tyrants, clergymen are all ruffians or hypocrites, and the only virtuous piety is professed by Jews.[18] Scott co-opts Radical themes, but he does not simply erase them, and they remain active in the text, open to application in different situations. *Ivanhoe* might have inspired Disraeli's Young England Toryism, the Oxford Movement of Pusey and Newman, and Victorian cults of chivalry, but it was also Ho Chi Minh's favourite reading in another greenwood.[19]

The symbolic topography of national origins in *Ivanhoe* ident-

[16] Thomas Carlyle, *Past and Present* (1843).

[17] e.g. *Edinburgh Monthly Review*, 3 (Feb. 1820), 168. While at work on *Ivanhoe* Scott asked John Ballantyne to send him Horne Tooke's philological treatise *The Diversions of Purley*: 'I must take care my *Saxon* characters speak proper language not unintelligible but not modern. They are rebels moreover and Horne Tooke is a good pilot in either character' (*Letters*, v. 426). Tooke's argument concerning the origins of language in the verb does not seem to have helped Scott with *Ivanhoe*, however.

[18] Some contemporaries complained about this: 'Timothy Touchstone', *A Letter to the Author of Waverley, Ivanhoe, &c. &c. &c., on the Moral Tendency of those Popular Works* (1820), argues that Scott's mockery of clergymen and the upper classes can only assist 'the principles of BLASPHEMY, TREASON, and REBEL-LION' (54); while *A Letter, containing some remarks on the tendency and influence of the Waverley Novels on Society, from a Clergyman of the Church of England to a Younger Brother* (1832) finds in sorrow that Scott's works are 'directly opposed to the spirit of the Gospel' (9).

[19] See Mark Girouard, *The Return to Camelot: Chivalry and the English Gentleman* (1981); and A. N. Wilson, *The Laird of Abbotsford: A View of Sir Walter Scott* (1980), 146–50; for Ho Chi Minh, a news item from *The Times*, 18 June 1991, reproduced in *The Scott Newsletter*, 20 (1992), 4.

ifies the feudal and religious institutions of Norman rule with the dungeons of Gothic fiction. The primeval forest surrounds the strongholds of Torquilstone and Templestowe, and neutralizes their sinister energy. Liminal spaces of ceremonial combat frame the action: they are at once closed, regulated by Gothic power, and open to the providential arrival of the knight-errant from the woods. These woods turn the *banditti* of Gothic romance (congruent with Gothic force even in Godwin's Radical updating of the genre, *Caleb Williams*) into freedom fighters and merry men. The opening sentence of *Ivanhoe* identifies the greenwood with the cultural ensemble Scott calls 'merry England'. Scott's main sources for this festive definition of national character are an antiquarian construction of popular culture, and Shakespearian comedy. The great forest of *Ivanhoe* represents both an ancestral common economy, violated by the Norman forest laws (notwithstanding that the author, as Sherriff-Depute of Selkirkshire, had sentenced many a poacher), and a common culture of the kinds of traditional feasts and games recorded by the antiquarian Joseph Strutt. This popular valency condenses in the figure of Robin Hood, the wood-sprite of folklore turned counter-cultural hero, celebrated in traditions of protest ballads and ancient festivals such as May games and mummers' plays.[20]

Although Robin Hood had been the subject of a recent antiquarian revival (in Joseph Ritson's edition of the ballads), Scott took his artistic cue from a speech in Shakespeare's *As You Like It*:

They say [the Duke] is already in the Forest of Arden, and a many merry men with him; and there they live like the old Robin Hood of England. They say many young gentlemen flock to him every day, and fleet the time carelessly as they did in the golden world. (I. i. 111)

Ivanhoe creatively imitates the greenwood of Shakespearian comedy, which provides not only a refuge to the virtuous and legitimate characters exiled from a tyrant's court, but a festive

[20] In a recent critical history of the tradition, *Robin Hood: A Complete Study of the English Outlaw* (1994), Stephen Knight argues that Robin Hood was 'in the air' when Scott was writing *Ivanhoe*, adducing treatments by John Keats and Thomas Love Peacock (*Maid Marian*, 1822), among others.

space of freedom in disguise and role-playing. Here, not so much underground as on holiday, the true nation abides, and kings and subjects discover themselves and one another in the play of primitive social forms and relations. King Richard observes the manners of his Anglo-Saxon subjects, and even learns their ballads, so that he can make the promise he will henceforth be truly a king of the English people rather than a Norman potentate. While the disguised king and knight-errant traverse this realm, its monarch is Robin Hood, who of all the figures in *Ivanhoe* is the one most completely absorbed by his mask. He is accordingly so businesslike, even impersonal, that he may disappoint readers expecting a more swashbuckling characterization.

The mythic dimension of the greenwood in *Ivanhoe* has been vividly described by Judith Wilt, in one of the few compelling recent accounts of the novel.[21] It remains to be noted that it presents an emphatically cultural solution to the political inequities of class and race that lacerate the novel's body politic. The strategy that will later be called 'passing', based on a performative understanding of identity as a set of forms that can be imitated and enacted, initiates a long-term healing of the wounds of conquest by cultural absorption and assimilation. King Richard learns how to play with his Saxon subjects, much as Ivanhoe has learnt the conventions of Norman chivalry. By this Ivanhoe sets himself apart from the rigid traditionalism of his father, which looks by comparison reactionary and futile. At the same time, the greenwood setting represents a natural, rather than political, matrix for the generation of a culture residing in the decorum of everyday life, a community's habits and courtesies and recreations, rather than in laws and institutions. Commerce succeeds conquest as Norman and Saxon blend by everyday usage and intercourse—by dealing with one another—into the larger, compound entity of English, the medium we are even now reading. The linguistic analogy is crucial because it fixes the culturalism of Scott's scheme. For Scott, let us remember, English was a foreign dialect, the language of imperial administration and literature rather than of daily speech. The famous synthetic style of *Ivanhoe* brings this condition home to

[21] Judith Wilt, *Secret Leaves: The Novels of Walter Scott* (1985), 37–48.

xix
INTRODUCTION

the English reader. Concocted from the literary ingredients of a national culture—Chaucer, Shakespeare, the English Bible—Scott's style nevertheless makes the English reader a stranger in his or her own language. An English reader, in other words, inhabits 'English' no more naturally than does (for instance) a Scot. Yet, as we read on—as we play the game—we grow used to it; it becomes 'second nature'.[22]

The performance of English in which we join as readers of *Ivanhoe* establishes a national identity that is not simply cultural, but imperial and colonial. Ivanhoe and Richard have acquired their culture-crossing skills on the Crusades, in the confrontation with an alien empire at the limits of Christendom. That rash, disastrous, but glamorous adventure provides an explicitly imperialist frame for the domestic history of conquest in which all subjects are strangers in relation to their place and origins, all are disinherited, all occupy a colonial subjectivity. The converse of this alienation is the proposition so neatly put in that Scott-soaked epitome of popular history, *1066 and All That*: 'The Norman Conquest was a Good Thing, as from this time onwards England stopped being conquered and thus was able to become top nation.'[23] The colonial origins of modern England, the mixing and tempering of its stock by foreign conquest, have produced its modern world-imperial fitness. The multiple valencies of a heterogeneous English equip it to absorb any cultural element.

If this imperial nationalism becomes more explicit in later, Victorian formulations (including Darwinian natural history), it works here as the solution to a specifically Scottish national predicament. I began by quoting a contemporary review of *Ivanhoe* that recognized in Scott's enterprise a Scottish conquest

[22] Scott's model of culture is in some respects close to the political aesthetic of Edmund Burke; for a discussion of these themes in a contemporary context, see James K. Chandler, *Wordsworth's Second Nature: A Study of the Poetry and Politics* (1984). On the language of *Ivanhoe* see Graham Tulloch, *The Language of Walter Scott* (1980), chs. 3 and 4; and C. R. Vanden Bossche, 'Culture and Economy in *Ivanhoe*', *Nineteenth-Century Literature*, 42 (1987), 46–72.

[23] W. C. Sellar and R. J. Yeatman, *1066 and All That* (1930), 17. Compare Scott's 'Essay on Romance': 'England, so often conquered, yet fated to receive an accession of strength from each new subjugation' (*Miscellaneous Prose Works* (1834), vi. 203).

of English culture. Recent studies by historians and cultural critics have illuminated the crucial Scottish role in the consolidation of an Anglo-British national ideology between the mid-eighteenth century and Victoria's reign. Scots patronage managed the spectacular expansion of the British empire, to the extent that empire became the primary field of advancement for ambitious Scots, while the curricular formation of 'English' in the academy and the poetic invention of a British national literature were both Scottish projects.[24] Scott's annexation of English culture in *Ivanhoe*, so shrewdly noted by the reviewer, is not the least influential episode in this complex movement.

But *Ivanhoe* also dwells on the limits and exclusions of this imperial cultural nationalism. Specifically, Jews and women inhabit a different history from the official, imperial one of expansion and synthesis. Far more than in his Scottish novels (which are informed by an intimate knowledge of primary materials, both oral and documentary) Scott relied on modern historians, in addition to his literary sources, for the depiction of medieval England in *Ivanhoe*. Among these, Sharon Turner's *History of the Anglo-Saxons, to the Norman Conquest* (1799–1805), with its important reassessment of Anglo-Saxon culture, insists most clearly on a programme of gradual, progressive, evolutionary synthesis, in which waves of foreign invasion invigorate rather than deplete the national stock. With his justification of both Saxon and Norman conquests in a Whig historiography of improvement, Turner may fairly be said to be one of the fathers of the imperial model of British history I have been discussing. The conclusion of *Ivanhoe* certainly gestures towards such a horizon, but it resides beyond the narrative itself, which provides a view of the conquest very different from Turner's account of continuity and accommodation. Scott's representation of the conquest as a social trauma, an unhealed wound in the body politic, derives not just from Radical polemic about the Norman yoke but from the Tory historical tradition of David Hume, reproduced in the early volumes of Robert Henry's *History of Great Britain* (1771–85), the other major historical source

---

[24] See Michael Fry, *The Dundas Despotism* (1992); Robert Crawford, *Devolving English Literature* (1992).

for *Ivanhoe*. Both Hume and Henry insist on the sheer violence of the Saxon and Norman conquests: Hume represents the Saxon conquest as a genocide, and Henry represents the Norman conquest as a rape. Scott sets this latter equation— disconcertingly—at the very centre of *Ivanhoe*, where it brings his Gothic setting into thematic focus.

In the captivity of the Saxons and Jews at the usurped castle of Torquilstone, Scott cites Henry's *History* to justify scenes in which Rowena and Rebecca are threatened with sexual force. At the nadir of these events Ulrica, the daughter of the castle, tells the horrid story of her rape by Norman barons who murdered her father and brothers. *Ivanhoe*'s Gothic setting, in other words, at last discloses a conventional Gothic plot of incarceration and violation. The episode culminates in the melodramatic death-agony of Front-de-Bœuf and Ulrica's recital of the war-song of her heathen ancestors atop the burning castle. Here *Ivanhoe* visits the Gothic version of history as a regression to traumatic origins, a repetition of primal violence that can only end in apocalyptic ruin. Ulrica's fate and the plight of Rowena and Rebecca represent the dismal persistence of 'conquest' in the politics of everyday life. Rowena understands immediately that the courtly-love blandishments of De Bracy are nothing more than a new-fangled mask for primitive coercion; in his earlier phrase (Chapter XV), 'the work of the Conquest should be completed'.

At the centre of *Ivanhoe*, then, Scott inverts the relation between Gothic and national tale, the constituent genres of his historical romance. Gothic fiction, as I have been suggesting, discloses a vision of national history opposite to the evolutionary synthesis of differences. The Gothic plot of the female body as object of totalitarian power expels any notion of reciprocity or consent, and with that the potent ideological category of feminine subjectivity, from the imperial allegory of the heroine as vessel of a union of races. The birth of the nation is founded on rape. As Katie Trumpener has argued, a Gothic destabilization of its conventions actually does occur in versions of the national tale written through the 1820s; it remains to be noted that Scott himself had prepared this development, most strikingly in his penultimate Scottish novel *The Bride of Lammermoor* (1819).

While the marriage of Ivanhoe and Rowena, unlike the tragically botched union in *The Bride of Lammermoor*, rehearses a comic national-tale conclusion, the novel's Gothic centre suggests the different history of a continuation of the politics of conquest around the female body. The forest games, in which national culture (rather than politics) constitutes a common public space of conversation, negotiation, and the suspension of differences in a traditional repertoire of roles and gestures, remain heartily masculine, from the bouts of deadly or playful violence to the bibulous jollity of the Black Knight and the Clerk of Copmanhurst. (There is an authentically drunken heaviness about the gaiety in these scenes.) Scott's romance of cultural origins shows the modern 'separation of spheres', the gendering of public and private life, to be founded on a primal violence—the threat of a force that reduces persons to bodies—rather than on any ethical fitness. After all the most intellectually formidable as well as most courageous character in *Ivanhoe* is the Jewess Rebecca.

Rebecca's perils dominate the second half of the tale, from the threatened rape to her forced unveiling before the Templars' inquisition. The inclusion of her father Isaac in the triad of ordeals at Torquilstone, where we see him stripped for torture, affirms an important thematic connection between women and Jews, who share the virtues of purity and resistance as well as the sacrificial vulnerability of the body. For many nineteenth-century readers the Jews were the main attraction of *Ivanhoe*. A remarkable number of the contemporary dramatic and chap-book adaptations, which probably reached a larger public than the novel itself, bear titles or subtitles like 'Isaac, the Jew of York', 'Rebecca, the Jew's Daughter', 'Rebecca, the Jewess', 'The Knight Templar and the Jew's Daughter'. (*The Monthly Magazine* even retitled the novel *Ivanhoe, or the Jew of York* in its review of February 1820.) 'Our ancestors were not more distinct from us', Scott argues in the 'Dedicatory Epistle', 'than Jews are from Christians', and he quotes Shylock's famous speech from *The Merchant of Venice*. The claim insists on the Jews' common humanity and at the same time holds on to a sense of their strangeness. *Ivanhoe* is an important text in the cultural dismantling of medieval stereotypes, even if some of those stereotypes remain in place, revalued rather than thrown away. Scott gives Isaac the stock avarice and cowardice of the stage Jew, but in order to represent the social conditioning he will be able to transcend—fitfully but authentically—when put to the test of love for his daughter. All readers adored Rebecca, one of the sublime heroines of nineteenth-century fiction, ancestress of the noble Jews who light up the Victorian national and cultural romances of Disraeli (*Coningsby*, 1844; *Tancred*, 1847) and George Eliot (*Daniel Deronda*, 1876). She, in particular, represents the Jews as figures far more potent than scapegoats whose rejection from the body politic guarantees its cohesion (although they are also that). They command purity of faith, magical goods (such as Ivanhoe's armour), and arts of healing. Their response to Christian persecution is to cleave all the more resolutely to their own traditions; Scott eschews the solution of conversion, ubiquitous in plots involving Jewish characters before his own. Such intransigence becomes heroic when Rebecca refuses the Grand Master's offer of her life in return for baptism.[25]

The Jews in *Ivanhoe* represent above all a superior authenticity of cultural value, which has everything to do with their condition of exile. They occupy an extreme position in the novel's scheme of alienated nationality. Their loss of a homeland obliges them to reconstitute Zion as a purely spiritual property: culture in the absolute degree, unbound by a political economy. More than Christianity, Judaism maintains by virtue of its worldly disinheritance a direct relation to the sacred origins of history and culture in the Holy Land. This becomes clear in the important relation between the Jews and the Templars, both stateless aliens who look towards a lost and fallen East. Jerusalem, the focus of imperialist ambitions in the novel, represents the vanity of a material and literal return to origins. Taking some

[25] On the Jews in *Ivanhoe*, see Edgar Rosenberg, *From Shylock to Svengali: Jewish Stereotypes in English Fiction* (1961), 73–115; Alide Cagidemetrio, 'A Plea for Fictional Histories and Old-Time "Jewesses"', in Werner Sollers (ed.), *The Invention of Ethnicity* (1989); Silvia Mergenthal, 'The Shadow of Shylock: Scott's *Ivanhoe* and Edgeworth's *Harrington*', in D. Hewitt and J. H. Alexander (eds.), *Scott in Carnival* (1993); Michael Ragussis, 'Writing Nationalist History: England, the Conversion of the Jews, and *Ivanhoe*', *ELH* 60 (1993), 181–215; and John Sutherland, *The Life of Walter Scott: A Critical Biography* (1995), 229–32.

historical liberties, Scott blames the Crusaders' failure to regain Jerusalem on the Templars' territorial designs in Palestine. The consequence for them, the opposite to the case of the Jews, is a kind of negative cultural contamination, as Brian de Bois-Guilbert exchanges his Christianity for the manners of Asiatic despotism.

The Templar's black slaves, the most sinister of his Oriental properties, eagerly assist in the preparations for the torture of Isaac and the burning of Rebecca. The almost heraldic quality of their outlandishness measures the humanity of the kindly aliens, the Jews. The narrator says that their appearance, 'so little known in England, appalled the multitude, who gazed on them as on demons employed about their own diabolical exercises' (Chapter XLIII); his description of their 'blubber lips' and 'white fangs' does little to dispel the illusion. With their strangeness blazoned on their bodies these Africans occupy the outside of the novel's gallery of 'race', where the enlightened law of cultural variation founded on a universal human nature, expounded in the 'Dedicatory Epistle', reverts to an infernal taxonomy of biological difference. In this outlook, Scott's representation suggests, the modern reader remains medieval: it would be over a dozen years before slavery was finally outlawed in the British Empire.

Rebecca and Bois-Guilbert are the true antagonists of *Ivanhoe*, and their splendidly high-flown confrontations express the novel's most ambitious openings of its national theme. Both speak prophetically for a global or universal collectivity that transcends not only local, medieval horizons but the very boundaries of the nation-state. The Templar dreams of a secular world dictatorship, in a malign combination of the incipient realities of empire in Scott's day and the fantasies about Masonic and Rosicrucian conspiracies that vexed the *anciens régimes* in the wake of the French revolution.[26] Rebecca, the voice of a lost and

[26] Malcolm Barber, *The New Knighthood: A History of the Order of the Temple* (1994), argues that *Ivanhoe* and *The Talisman* were largely responsible for popularizing the modern stereotype of the Templars as a sinister secret society bent on world domination. Scott himself was a Freemason, having been inducted into the Lodge St David, Edinburgh No. 36 (his father's lodge and that of his patron, the Earl of Dalkeith) in 1801. In 1823 Scott declined to be proposed as a candidate

sublimated Zion, commands a subtler ideological power. She imagines a utopian, ecumenical expansion of her religion into a universal faith, invoking 'the great Father who made both Jew and Gentile' and the more mysterious figure of 'the Comforter', properly the third person of the Trinity. In Scott's audacious turning of the conventional destiny of conversion, it is the Jewess who undertakes the imperial annexation of Christianity—but in cultural rather than doctrinal terms, as a code of feeling and behaving rather than of believing. Rebecca utters blasting critiques not only of the Templar's secular ambitions but, in her great scene with the wounded Ivanhoe at Torquilstone, the vanity of chivalry itself: in effect denouncing the obsolescence of the romance's nominal hero. As Alide Cagidemetrio argues,[27] Rebecca is the prophet of modernity in its 'feminine' ideological guise of domesticity, as opposed to the evil empire of Bois-Guilbert. Through their exchanges we glimpse the shadow of a post-national *imperium* that lies beyond the novel's official fiction of nationality.

Rebecca's exile in the last pages of *Ivanhoe* brings home the anomaly that the final marriage is an inter-cultural but not an inter-ethnic union, despite the rhetoric about racial blending. Although Ivanhoe has assumed the manners of Norman chivalry, he and Rowena are both Saxons. Scott's text continues to register the pressure of the categories—sexuality and race—that will mark the limits of 'culture', the fluid space of national identity formation, in nineteenth-century discourse. Reception history shows that readers have regretted the failure of an Ivanhoe–Rebecca liaison more than they have enjoyed the success of the Ivanhoe–Rowena one;[28] the effect is carefully crafted

for Grand Master of the Masonic Order of Knights Templar in Edinburgh, on the grounds of age and health.

[27] Cagidemetrio, 'Old-Time "Jewesses"'. For the novel and the modern feminine ideology of domesticity, see Nancy Armstrong, *Desire and Domestic Fiction: A Political History of the Novel* (1987).

[28] A number of contemporary dramatic and operatic versions of *Ivanhoe* contrived the union of Wilfred and Rebecca, including George Soane's *The Hebrew* (Drury Lane, Mar. 1820) and the Deschamps and De Wailly *Ivanhoe* (with music by Rossini) that Scott himself saw in Paris in 1826. Posthumous revisions include not only Thackeray's *Rebecca and Rowena: A Romance upon Romance* (1850) but also Thomas Plowman's 'travesty', *Ivanhoe Abroad; or,*

rather than inadvertent. Rebecca's stately withdrawal offers
something more critical than a pre-emption of nationalist racism
by the internalization of its decree of purity. In the final scene
she trounces a vain Rowena with the weapons of humility and
magnanimity, and leaves Ivanhoe to brood over her memory
'more frequently than the fair descendant of Alfred might
altogether have approved'. More Christian than the Christians
themselves, who are united in nothing but their anti-semitism,
the Jewess diminishes the English future from which she is shut
out. We cannot be surprised that so many readers of *Ivanhoe*
wanted to bring her into the fold. Critics who have found Scott
wanting in passion or enthusiasm have missed the point.[29] Aloof
from utopian or apocalyptic consolations, this romance leaves us
where it found us, in an untransfigured world.

Ivanhoe Settled and Rebecca Righted (1878). (Henry Adelbert White, *Sir Walter
Scott's Novels on the Stage*, 1927; see also Jerome Mitchell, *The Walter Scott
Operas*, 1977.)

[29] For this tradition see *Eclectic Review*, 13 (1820), 529–30; Thomas Carlyle,
London and Westminster Review, 28 (1838), repr. in John O. Hayden (ed.), *Scott:
The Critical Heritage* (1970), 345–73; E. M. Forster, *Aspects of the Novel* (1927),
ch. 2.

NOTE ON THE TEXT

SCOTT wrote *Ivanhoe* between June and November 1819; composition was interrupted by illness (mid-June) and by delays at the printers. The novel came out late in December 1819, bearing the publication date 1820. It went through two subsequent editions (1820 and 1821) in the three-volume format. In 1822 *Ivanhoe* was reissued in two volumes as the first title in the series *Historical Romances of the Author of Waverley*. From 1829 until just before his death in 1832, Scott edited all his novels for republication in a collected edition, writing new introductions and additional notes for them and correcting and revising the texts. This, the so-called 'Magnum Opus' edition (published by Archibald Constable's erstwhile partner, Robert Cadell), established the texts of the Waverley novels as they have been read since Scott's death.

Anyone seriously interested in *Ivanhoe* will want to consult Graham Tulloch's forthcoming volume in the new Edinburgh Edition of the Waverley Novels, based on the early editions collated with Scott's manuscripts and proofs. The present edition of *Ivanhoe*, like most other Scott titles in World's Classics, is based on the 1830 Magnum Opus text. It differs considerably in its details from the earlier editions (variants between 1820 and 1822 do not appear to be substantive), and so represents a different historical state of the text, with a different kind of cultural presence and influence.

Scott's revisions for Magnum Opus from the 1822 edition tend to affect detail rather than main event. Some are routine: the modernization and anglicization of spellings (chaunted, decypher, ingulph, leach, mellay, murther, phrenzied, relique, sylvan) to conform to a new house-style, an increased density of punctuation, a clarification of the syntax of long and tangled sentences, the elimination of verbal repetition by variation, and the identification (often supererogatory) of speakers in dialogue. Scott was notoriously careless about names and chronology, and expected his associates to help tidy up. Only in 1830 are traces of earlier names such as Edwina, Barbara, and Godstowe finally

absorbed into Elgitha, Urfried, and Templestowe, Rowena completely converted from Cedric's daughter to his ward, a reference to Richard II corrected to one to Richard I, Hubert's
great-grandsire who fought at Hastings turned into his
grandsire, and Henry II turned from prince John's grandfather
into his father. The traces of hesitation about chronology
throughout the different stages of the text (and many remain in
1830) are strategic rather than merely inattentive, however—an
aspect of the romance aesthetic of syncretism outlined in Scott's
'Dedicatory Epistle'. Ostensibly set in the summer of 1193,
Ivanhoe at once takes place within a generation's memory of the
Conquest, has Norman dandies wearing fashions of the reign of
William Rufus, features military costume, equipment, and cer-
emonies of the fourteenth and fifteenth centuries, and is steeped
in English literary diction from Chaucer to the seventeenth
century.

Some of the 1830 revisions seem fussy to modern taste, slow-
ing down the narrative pace and burdening exchanges with
superfluous detail. Many, though, represent an advance in clar-
ity and heft, and in some ways—despite the attractive roughness
of the first editions—the Magnum Opus *Ivanhoe* is the text to be
preferred. We often find Scott enhancing the vividness of a scene
by focusing on a particular gesture, as at the Ashby tournament.
Bois-Guilbert is now 'standing carelessly at the door of the
pavilion' when Ivanhoe comes to challenge him (Chapter VIII);
later in the same chapter, 'Fair and true he hit the Norman on
the visor, where his lance's point kept hold of the bars'. In
Chapter XII the Black Knight's overthrow of Front-de-Boeuf is
given a similar gestural precision. Elsewhere, we find Scott taking a firmer hold over the reader's interpretation of characters or
events, notably in the sensitive case of the Jews. In the scene
between Isaac and Gurth, Chapter XI, Scott's additions make
Isaac's exactions somewhat less grasping ('the sum demanded
was more reasonable than he had expected'), hint at a psychology
for the cartoon Jew which anticipates his later ascent to pathos
('panting and hesitating between habitual love of gain and a new-
born desire to be liberal in the present instance'), and emphasize
mitigating circumstances for the meanness above which the plot
will have him rise (explaining that the treatment of the Jews by

'those whom they termed Gentiles . . . certainly merited little hospitality at their hand'). Reciprocally, Gurth's vow to give Isaac 'one-fourth' of the sum he will ask for is softened to 'one-half'.

Scott's working copy of the 1822 *Ivanhoe*, containing corrections and insertions in his hand, makes up two volumes (xiii and xiv) of the so-called 'Interleaved Set' of the Waverley Novels, which he used to prepare the Magnum Opus edition. The National Library of Scotland acquired the Interleaved Set in 1986, after more than fifty years' absence from the public domain. *Ivanhoe* is catalogued as MSS 23013–14. Two nineteenth-century editions of the Waverley Novels, the Centenary (1871) and the Dryburgh (1892–4), were corrected rather cursorily against the Interleaved Set. The present World's Classics edition is the first modern *Ivanhoe* to take account of Scott's preparatory materials.

Scott wrote swiftly, with few traces of hesitation or revision, and he expected his printers (especially James Ballantyne, whose technical and artistic advice carried considerable weight), compositors, and proof-readers to establish punctuation, correct grammar and syntax, and clean up any inconsistencies and irregularities on the way to publication. The last of these tasks could well include rearranging phrases within a sentence and changing individual words for the sake of stylistic precision and balance. Such revisions often took place through dialogue with the author, who would himself make changes on proof. In short, Scott's manuscript represented only a preliminary stage—if the most substantial one—in a continuous, quasi-collaborative process, overseen by the author, through which the text would be shaped and dressed for publication; and Scott's modern editors have rightly declined to privilege the manuscript as the unique site of origins. The many discrepancies between manuscript and first edition, some but not all of which can be tracked at proof stage (where proofs survive—in the case of *Ivanhoe*, a few of the opening chapters), thus by no means constitute trespasses upon authorial intention. The same holds for the discrepancies between Scott's holograph revisions in the Interleaved Set and the published 1830 *Ivanhoe* (in this case, no proofs are known to have survived).

This state of affairs complicates rather than simplifies our reliance on the published text, however, if we are to present something more than a facsimile of 1830. To begin with, Scott had his manuscripts copied before they went to the printers, to disguise his hand and protect his incognito before 1827, and for legibility's sake thereafter (Cadell appears to have done much of the Magnum Opus transcription himself). Errors were bound to accumulate during what was almost always a furious rush to publication: Scott's extension of authorial function to his collaborators also meant a scattering rather than concentration of editorial surveillance, and the evidence suggests that proofs were not checked against the original. In short, some of the discrepancies between Scott's hand and published copy may after all represent corruptions rather than developments of authorial intention: they may simply be mistakes, misreadings of Scott's never very clear holograph, especially in the case of archaic usages or literary and historical allusions.

In the present edition of *Ivanhoe* I have adopted a conservative stance, retaining the 1830 text except where, in my judgement, the copyist or compositor has misread Scott's Interleaved Set holograph ('the land of the warriors whom he led', 'Sir Lazy Loon') or lost an allusion in the 1822 text (Isaac as a 'bottled spider', from *Richard III*; the epithet is uncorrected by Scott in the Interleaved Set). In many cases, Scott and/or his compositors added identifications of the speakers to passages of dialogue. While some of these might seem pedantic to present taste, I have only deleted Scott's insertion of one superfluous 'said the Grand Master', on the grounds that he seems to have overlooked 'exclaimed the Grand Master' tagging the same speech just a few lines further down (on the last line of the page in 1822). When in doubt, I have followed 1830; thus, it is not clear whether the approach to Cedric's manor should be along a 'wilder' (1822) or 'wider' (1830) avenue—both make different kinds of sense.

If errors slipped in between the Interleaved Set and the Magnum Opus edition, it follows that errors also slipped in between the manuscript and the early editions, not all of which were picked up in 1822 or 1830 (although some of the Interleaved Set revisions do indeed restore MS readings). Here I tread on ground less secure. For the present edition I have not attempted a serious collation of the manuscript and early editions; for that, the interested reader must consult Tulloch's Edinburgh *Ivanhoe*. On the supposition stated above, however, I have examined the manuscript in Scott's hand, constituting the second half of the novel, in the Pierpont Morgan Library, New York. (Too ill to write, Scott dictated the first half; its whereabouts is unknown.) I have restored readings only where later versions represented a loss of sense, rather than of mere felicity, and where it seemed probable from the context (i.e. illegibility) that Scott's hand was misread, most likely by the copyist. I have commented on some items of interest in the MS, such as Scott's original version of the fall of Athelstane and two unpublished notes, in my explanatory notes.

A useful account of the Magnum Opus edition can be found in Jane Millgate, *Scott's Last Edition: A Study in Publishing History* (1987). See also Iain Gordon Brown (ed.), *Scott's Interleaved Waverley Novels: An Introduction and Commentary* (1987), especially J. H. Alexander, 'Descriptive Guide to the Interleaved Set' (11–26), and Iain Gordon Brown, 'An Illustrated Commentary on the Interleaved Set', which reproduces several folios showing Scott's revisions and additions to *Ivanhoe* (plates 40–6).

EMENDATION LIST

The 1830 edition text is printed in the left-hand column and the emendation in the right. 'MS' marks the restoration of a reading from Scott's manuscript (1819), 'Interleaved Set' marks the restoration of a revision in Scott's hand that was altered or unincorporated in the 1830 edition, and '1822' marks the restoration of a reading from the 1822 edition, unemended in the Interleaved Set but altered in the 1830 edition. (All the 1822 readings I have adopted correspond with the first edition of 1820.)

p. 6	'Trick upon Trick'	'trick upon trick' (Interleaved Set)
p. 7	Ballengeigh	Ballengiech (Scott's spelling in Interleaved Set and *Tales of a Grandfather*, ch. 27)

p. 9	should thou	thou should (Interleaved Set and original)
p. 44	but-end	butt-end (1822)
p. 61	ourslves	ourselves (1822)
p. 82	then	than (1822)
p. 86	Chapter VIII	Chapter VII (numbering of subsequent chapters in vol. 1, i.e. VII–XXIII, has been corrected)
p. 91	bloated	bottled (1822; see editorial note)
p. 121	toll	tolls (1822)
p. 164	Anjoù	Anjou (1822)
p. 197	Anjoù	Anjou (1822)
p. 219	wine-but	wine-butt (1822)
p. 222	Jewess.	Jewess.' (1822)
p. 276	receding	recoiling (MS)
p. 286	to England	in England (1822)
p. 287	Anjoù	Anjou (1822)
p. 288	for he	'for he (1822)
p. 301	one or two	one to two (1822)
p. 333	chivalrous	chivalrously (MS)
p. 343	the silvan followers	his silvan followers (MS)
p. 354	sir lazy lover	Sir Lazy Loon (Interleaved Set)
p. 358	Nicodemus	Nicodemus,' (1822)
p. 364	said Locksley	said Locksley gravely (Interleaved Set)
pp. 390, 4	Cistertian	Cistercian (1822; so spelt elsewhere in 1830)
p. 391	Up on	Upon (1822)
p. 392	said the Grand Master	(erroneous insertion in Interleaved Set; speaker is identified a few lines later)
p. 407	desirest	desireth (MS)
p. 409	even	ever (MS)
p. 456	lordlings	lordings (MS and original)
p. 457	Robin, or the quarter-staff	Robin, the quarter-staff (MS)
p. 461	secret	second (MS)
p. 463	Athelstane, occasioned	Athelstane occasioned (MS)
p. 476	more or less	nor less (MS)
p. 480	communicated	enumerated (MS)
p. 483	Brian-de-Bois-Guilbert	Brian de Bois-Guilbert (1822)
p. 507	(*Scott's note*) band of warriors	land of the warriors (Interleaved Set)
p. 512	(*Scott's note*) black vault	Black Vault (Interleaved Set and original: placename)

SELECT BIBLIOGRAPHY

BIOGRAPHICAL, BIBLIOGRAPHICAL, AND OTHER REFERENCE WORKS

Brown, Iain Gordon (ed.), *Scott's Interleaved Waverley Novels: An Introduction and Commentary*, 1987.

[Cochrane, J. G.], *Catalogue of the Library at Abbotsford*, 1938.

Corson, James, C., *A Bibliography of Sir Walter Scott, 1797–1940*, 1943.

—— *Notes and Index to Sir Herbert Grierson's Edition of the Letters of Sir Walter Scott*, 1979.

Crockett, W. S., *The Scott Originals*, 1912.

Johnson, Edgar, *Sir Walter Scott: The Great Unknown*, 2 vols., 1970.

Lockhart, John Gibson, *Memoirs of the Life of Sir Walter Scott, Bart.*, 10 vols., 1839.

Millgate, Jane, *Scott's Last Edition: A Study in Publishing History*, 1987.

—— 'Making It New: Scott, Constable, Ballantyne, and the Publication of *Ivanhoe*', *Studies in English Literature*, 34 (1994), 795–811.

Rubenstein, Jill, *Sir Walter Scott: A Reference Guide*, 1978.

Scott, Walter, *The Letters of Sir Walter Scott*, ed. H. J. C. Grierson, 12 vols., 1932–7.

Sutherland, John, *The Life of Walter Scott: A Critical Biography*, 1995.

CRITICISM

Beiderwell, Bruce, *Power and Punishment in Scott's Novels*, 1992.

Butler, Marilyn, *Romantics, Rebels, and Reactionaries: English Literature and its Background, 1760–1830*, 1982.

Cagidemetrio, Alide, 'A Plea for Fictional Histories and Old-Time "Jewesses"', in Werner Sollors (ed.), *The Invention of Ethnicity*, 1989, 13–43.

Chandler, Alice, *A Dream of Order: The Medieval Ideal in Nineteenth-Century English Literature*, 1970.

—— 'Chivalry and Romance: Scott's Medieval Novels', *Studies in Romanticism*, 14 (1975), 185–200.

Cockshut, A. O. J., *The Achievement of Walter Scott*, 1969.

Cottom, Daniel, *The Civilised Imagination: A Study of Ann Radcliffe, Jane Austen, and Sir Walter Scott*, 1985.

Diedrick, James, 'Dialogical History in *Ivanhoe*', in J. H. Alexander and

David Hewitt (eds.), *Scott in Carnival: Selected Papers from the Fourth International Scott Conference, 1991*, 1993, 280–93.

Duncan, Ian, *Modern Romance and Transformations of the Novel: The Gothic, Scott, Dickens*, 1992.

Duncan, Joseph E., 'The Anti-Romantic in *Ivanhoe*', in D. D. Devlin (ed.), *Modern Judgments: Walter Scott*, 1969, 142–7.

Ferris, Ina, *The Achievement of Literary Authority: Gender, History, and the Waverley Novels*, 1991.

Garside, P. D., 'Scott, the Romantic Past, and the Nineteenth Century', *Review of English Studies*, 23 (1972), 147–57.

de Gategno, Paul J., *Ivanhoe: The Mask of Chivalry*, 1994.

Hart, Francis R., *Scott's Novels: The Plotting of Historic Survival*, 1966.

Hayden, John, O. (ed.), *Scott: The Critical Heritage*, 1970.

Hillhouse, James T., *The Waverley Novels and their Critics*, 1936.

Hodgell, Patricia C., *The Nonsense of Ancient Days: Sources of Scott's Ivanhoe* (Ph.D. diss., University of Minnesota), 1987.

Kaufmann, David, *The Business of Common Life: Novels and Classic Economics between Revolution and Reform*, 1995.

Kelly, Gary, *English Fiction of the Romantic Period, 1789–1830*, 1989.

—— 'Social Conflict, Nation and Empire: From Gothicism to Romantic Orientalism', *Ariel*, 20 (1989), 2, 3–18.

Kerr, James, *Fiction Against History: Scott as Storyteller*, 1989.

Lascelles, Mary, *The Story-Teller Retrieves the Past*, 1980.

Lukács, Georg, *The Historical Novel*, 1937, trans. Hannah Mitchell and Stanley Mitchell, 1962.

McMaster, Graham, *Scott and Society*, 1981.

Mergenthal, Silvia, 'The Shadow of Shylock: Scott's *Ivanhoe* and Edgeworth's *Harrington*', in J. H. Alexander and David Hewitt (eds.), *Scott in Carnival: Selected Papers from the Fourth International Scott Conference, 1991*, 1993, 320–31.

Mitchell, Jerome, *Scott, Chaucer, and Medieval Romance: A Study in Sir Walter Scott's Indebtedness to the Literature of the Middle Ages*, 1987.

Ragussis, Michael, 'Writing Nationalist History: England, the Conversion of the Jews, and *Ivanhoe*', *ELH* 60 (1993), 181–250.

Robertson, Fiona, *Legitimate Histories: Scott, Gothic, and the Authority of Fiction*, 1994.

Shaw, Harry E., *The Forms of Historical Fiction: Sir Walter Scott and His Successors*, 1983.

Sroka, Kenneth M., 'The Function of Form: *Ivanhoe* as Romance', *Studies in English Literature*, 19 (1979), 645–60.

Tulloch, Graham, *The Language of Walter Scott: A Study of his Scottish and Period Language*, 1980.

—— '*Ivanhoe* and Bibles', in J. H. Alexander and David Hewitt (eds.), *Scott in Carnival: Selected Papers from the Fourth International Scott Conference, 1991*, 1993, 309–19.

Vanden Bossche, Chris R., 'Culture and Economy in *Ivanhoe*', *Nine-teenth-Century Literature*, 42 (1987), 46–72.

Wallace, Tara Ghoshal, 'Competing Discourses in *Ivanhoe*', in J. H. Alexander and David Hewitt (eds.), *Scott in Carnival: Selected Papers from the Fourth International Scott Conference, 1991*, 1993, 294–308.

Welsh, Alexander, *The Hero of the Waveley Novels; With New Essays on Scott*, 1992 (1st pub. 1963).

Wilson, A. N., *The Laird of Abbotsford: A View of Sir Walter Scott*, 1980.

Wilt, Judith, *Secret Leaves: The Novels of Walter Scott*, 1985.

RELATED HISTORICAL AND CULTURAL STUDIES

Anderson, Benedict, *Imagined Communities: Reflections on the Origin and Spread of Nationalism*, 1983.

Barber, Malcolm, *The New Knighthood: A History of the Order of the Temple*, 1994.

Briggs, Asa, 'Saxons, Normans and Victorians', in *The Collected Essays of Asa Briggs*, 2 vols., 1985, 215–35.

Colley, Linda, *Britons: Forging the Nation, 1707–1837*, 1992.

Crawford, Robert, *Devolving English Literature*, 1992.

Freeman, Edward Augustus, *The History of the Norman Conquest of England, its Causes and its Results*, 6 vols., 1867–79.

Fry, Michael, *The Dundas Despotism*, 1992.

Girouard, Mark, *The Return to Camelot: Chivalry and the English Gentleman*, 1981.

Hill, Christopher, 'The Norman Yoke', in *Puritanism and Revolution: Studies in Interpretation of the English Revolution of the 17th Century*, 1958, 50–122.

Hobsbawm, E. J. and Ranger, Terence (eds.), *The Invention of Tradition*, 1983.

Johnston, Arthur, *Enchanted Ground: The Study of Medieval Romance in the Eighteenth Century*, 1964.

Kidd, Colin, *Subverting Scotland's Past: Scottish Whig Historians and the Creation of an Anglo-British Identity, 1689–c.1830*, 1993.

Knight, Stephen, *Robin Hood: A Complete Study of the English Outlaw*, 1994.

Newman, Gerald, *The Rise of English Nationalism: A Cultural History, 1720–1830*, 1987.

Poole, Austin Lane, *From Domesday Book to Magna Carta, 1087–1216*, 1951.

Rosenberg, Edgar, *From Shylock to Svengali: Jewish Stereotypes in English Fiction*, 1960.

Simmons, Clare A., *Reversing the Conquest: History and Myth in Nineteenth-Century Literature*, 1990.

A CHRONOLOGY OF
SIR WALTER SCOTT

1771   Born in Edinburgh, son of Walter Scott, W. S., and Anne Rutherford.

1772–3   Suffered from poliomyelitis which left him lame.

1779–83   Attended the High School, Edinburgh.

1783–6   Attended classes at Edinburgh University; 1786, apprenticed to his father.

1792   Admitted to Faculty of Advocates.

1796   *The Chase*, and *William and Helen*, translated from Bürger, issued anonymously.

1797   Married Charlotte Charpentier.

1799   *Goetz of Berlichingen*, translated from Goethe; *Tales of Terror*; appointed Sheriff-Depute of Selkirkshire.

1801   Contributed to M. G. Lewis's *Tales of Wonder*.

1802–3   *The Minstrelsy of the Scottish Border*.

1804   Moved to Ashestiel.

1805   *The Lay of the Last Minstrel*; entered into partnership with James Ballantyne & Co., printers; started *Waverley*.

1806   Appointed a Principal Clerk of Session.

1808   *Marmion*; edition of *The Works of John Dryden*; completed Joseph Strutt's *Queen-Hoo Hall*.

1810   *The Lady of the Lake*; resumed *Waverley*, but laid it aside again.

1812   Moved to Abbotsford.

1813   *Rokeby*; declined offer of Poet Laureateship.

1814   *Waverley*; edition of *The Works of Jonathan Swift*.

1815   *The Lord of the Isles*; *Guy Mannering*.

1816   *The Antiquary*; *The Black Dwarf* and *Old Mortality* (*Tales of My Landlord*, 1st series).

1817   *Rob Roy*.

1818   *The Heart of Midlothian* (*Tales of My Landlord*, 2nd series); accepted Baronetcy (gazetted 1820).

1819   *The Bride of Lammermoor* and *A Legend of Montrose* (*Tales of My Landlord*, 3rd series); *Ivanhoe*.

1820   *The Monastery*; *The Abbot*; his daughter, Sophia, married J. G. Lockhart.

1821   *Kenilworth*.

1822   *The Pirate*; *The Fortunes of Nigel*; *Peveril of the Peak*.

1823   *Quentin Durward*.

1824   *St. Ronan's Well*; *Redgauntlet*.

1825   *The Betrothed* and *The Talisman* (*Tales of the Crusaders*); began *Journal*.

1826   Financial collapse, caused by the bankruptcy of Archibald Constable & Co., and James Ballantyne & Co.; *Woodstock*.

1827   Acknowledged authorship of Waverley novels; *Life of Napoleon*.

1827–8 *Chronicles of the Canongate* (two series).

1828–31 *Tales of a Grandfather* (four series).

1829   *Anne of Geierstein*; Magnum series of Waverley Novels starts to appear.

1830   *Letters on Demonology and Witchcraft*; Magnum *Ivanhoe*.

1831   Voyage to Mediterranean in search of health.

1832   *Count Robert of Paris* and *Castle Dangerous* (*Tales of My Landlord*, 4th series).

        Died at Abbotsford, 21 September.

IVANHOE

A Romance

Now fitted the halter, now traversed the cart,
And often took leave,—but seem'd loath to depart![1]

PRIOR*

INTRODUCTION
TO
IVANHOE

THE Author of the Waverley Novels had hitherto proceeded in an unabated course of popularity, and might, in his peculiar district of literature, have been termed *L'Enfant Gâté** of success. It was plain, however, that frequent publication must finally wear out the public favour, unless some mode could be devised to give an appearance of novelty to subsequent productions. Scottish manners, Scottish dialect, and Scottish characters of note, being those with which the author was most intimately and familiarly acquainted, were the groundwork upon which he had hitherto relied for giving effect to his narrative. It was, however, obvious, that this kind of interest must in the end occasion a degree of sameness and repetition, if exclusively resorted to, and that the reader was likely at length to adopt the language of Edwin, in Parnell's Tale:—*

> ———' "Reverse the spell," he cries,
> "And let it fairly now suffice,
> The gambol has been shown." '

Nothing can be more dangerous for the fame of a professor of the fine arts, than to permit (if he can possibly prevent it) the character of a mannerist to be attached to him, or that he should be supposed capable of success only in a particular and limited style. The public are, in general, very ready to adopt the opinion, that he who has pleased them in one peculiar mode of composition, is, by means of that very talent, rendered incapable of venturing upon other subjects. The effect of this disinclination, on the part of the public, towards the artificers of their pleasures, when they attempt to enlarge their means of amusing, may be seen in the censures usually passed by vulgar criticism upon actors or artists who venture to change the character of their efforts, that, in so doing, they may enlarge the scale of their art.

There is some justice in this opinion, as there always is in such as attain general currency. It may often happen on the stage, that an actor, by possessing in a pre-eminent degree the external qualities necessary to give effect to comedy, may be deprived of the right to aspire to tragic excellence; and in painting or literary composition, an artist or poet may be master exclusively of modes of thought, and powers of expression, which confine him to a single course of subjects. But much more frequently the same capacity which carries a man to popularity in one department will obtain for him success in another, and that must be more particularly the case in literary composition, than either in acting or painting, because the adventurer in that department is not impeded in his exertions by any peculiarity of features, or conformation of person, proper for particular parts, or, by any peculiar mechanical habits of using the pencil, limited to a particular class of subjects.

Whether this reasoning be correct or otherwise, the present author felt, that, in confining himself to subjects purely Scottish, he was not only likely to weary out the indulgence of his readers, but also greatly to limit his own power of affording them pleasure. In a highly polished country, where so much genius is monthly employed in catering for public amusement, a fresh topic, such as he had himself had the happiness to light upon, is the untasted spring of the desert;—

'Men bless their stars and call it luxury.'*

But when men and horses, cattle, camels, and dromedaries, have poached the spring into mud, it becomes loathsome to those who at first drank of it with rapture; and he who had the merit of discovering it, if he would preserve his reputation with the tribe, must display his talent by a fresh discovery of untasted fountains.

If the author, who finds himself limited to a particular class of subjects, endeavours to sustain his reputation by striving to add a novelty of attraction to themes of the same character which have been formerly successful under his management, there are manifest reasons why, after a certain point, he is likely to fail. If the mine be not wrought out, the strength and capacity of the miner become necessarily exhausted. If he closely imitates the narratives which he has before rendered successful, he is doomed to 'wonder that they please no more.'* If he struggles to take a different view of the same class of subjects, he speedily discovers that what is obvious, graceful, and natural, has been exhausted; and, in order to obtain the indispensable charm of novelty, he is forced upon caricature, and, to avoid being trite, must become extravagant.

It is not, perhaps, necessary to enumerate so many reasons why the author of the Scottish Novels, as they were then exclusively termed, should be desirous to make an experiment on a subject purely English. It was his purpose, at the same time, to have rendered the experiment as complete as possible, by bringing the intended work before the public as the effort of a new candidate for their favour, in order that no degree of prejudice, whether favourable or the reverse, might attach to it, as a new production of the Author of Waverley; but this intention was afterwards departed from, for reasons to be hereafter mentioned.

The period of the narrative adopted was the reign of Richard I, not only as abounding with characters whose very names were sure to attract general attention, but as affording a striking contrast betwixt the Saxons, by whom the soil was cultivated, and the Normans, who still reigned in it as conquerors, reluctant to mix with the vanquished, or acknowledge themselves of the same stock. The idea of this contrast was taken from the ingenious and unfortunate Logan's tragedy of Runnamede,* in which, about the same period of history, the author had seen the Saxon and Norman barons opposed to each other on different sides of the stage. He does not recollect that there was any attempt to contrast the two races in their habits and sentiments; and indeed it was obvious, that history was violated by introducing the Saxons still existing as a high-minded and martial race of nobles.

They did, however, survive as a people, and some of the ancient Saxon families possessed wealth and power, although they were exceptions to the humble condition of the race in general. It seemed to the author, that the existence of the two races in the same country, the vanquished distinguished by their plain, homely, blunt manners, and the free spirit infused by their ancient institutions and laws; the victors, by the high spirit of military fame, personal adventure, and whatever could distinguish them as the Flower of Chivalry, might, intermixed with other characters belonging to the same time and country, interest the reader by the contrast, if the author should not fail on his part.

Scotland, however, had been of late used so exclusively as the scene of what is called Historical Romance, that the preliminary letter of Mr Laurence Templeton became in some measure necessary. To this, as to an Introduction, the reader is referred, as expressing the author's purpose and opinions in undertaking this species of composition, under the necessary reservation, that he is far from thinking he has attained the point at which he aimed.

It is scarcely necessary to add, that there was no idea or wish to pass off the supposed Mr Templeton as a real person. But a kind of continuation of the Tales of my Landlord had been recently attempted by a stranger,* and it was supposed this Dedicatory Epistle might pass for some imitation of the same kind, and thus putting enquirers upon a false scent, induce them to believe they had before them the work of some new candidate for their favour.

After a considerable part of the work had been finished and printed, the Publishers, who pretended to discern in it a germ of popularity, remonstrated strenuously against its appearing as an absolutely anonymous production, and contended that it should have the advantage of being announced as by the Author of Waverley. The author did not make any obstinate opposition, for he began to be of opinion with Dr Wheeler, in Miss Edgeworth's excellent tale of 'Manœuvring,' that 'trick upon trick'* might be too much for the patience of an indulgent public, and might be reasonably considered as trifling with their favour.

The book, therefore, appeared as an avowed continuation of the Waverley Novels; and it would be ungrateful not to acknowledge, that it met with the same favourable reception as its predecessors.

Such annotations as may be useful to assist the reader in comprehending the characters of the Jew, the Templar, the Captain of the mercenaries, or Free Companions, as they were called, and others proper to the period, are added, but with a sparing hand, since sufficient information on these subjects is to be found in general history.

An incident in the tale, which had the good fortune to find favour in the eyes of many readers, is more directly borrowed from the stores of old romance. I mean the meeting of the King with Friar Tuck at the cell of that buxom hermit. The general tone of the story belongs to all ranks and all countries, which emulate each other in describing the rambles of a disguised sovereign, who, going in search of information or amusement, into the lower ranks of life, meets with adventures diverting to the reader or hearer, from the contrast betwixt the monarch's outward appearance, and his real character. The Eastern tale-teller has for his theme the disguised expeditions of Haroun Alraschid with his faithful attendants, Mesrour and Giafar, through the midnight streets of Bagdad; and Scottish tradition dwells upon the similar exploits of James V, distinguished during such excursions by the travelling name of the Goodman of Ballengiech, as the Commander of the Faithful, when he desired to be incognito, was known by that of Il Bondocani.* The French minstrels are not silent on so popular a theme. There must have been a Norman original of the Scottish metrical romance of Rauf Colziar,* in which Charlemagne is introduced as the unknown guest of a charcoalman.[2] It seems to have been the original of other poems of the kind.

In merry England there is no end of popular ballads on this theme. The poem of John the Reeve, or Steward, mentioned by Bishop Percy, in the Reliques of English Poetry,[3] is said to have turned on such an incident; and we have besides, the King and the Tanner of Tamworth, the King and the Miller of Mansfield, and others on the same topic.* But the peculiar tale of this nature to which the author of Ivanhoe has to acknowledge an obligation, is more ancient by two centuries than any of these last mentioned.

It was first communicated to the public in that curious record of ancient literature, which has been accumulated by the combined exertions of Sir Egerton Brydges and Mr Hazlewood, in the periodical work entitled the British Bibliographer.* From thence it has been transferred by the Reverend Charles Henry Hartshorne, M.A., editor of a very curious volume, entitled

'Ancient Metrical Tales, printed chiefly from original sources, 1829.' Mr Hartshorne gives no other authority for the present fragment, except the article in the Bibliographer, where it is entitled the Kyng and the Hermite. A short abstract of its contents will show its similarity to the meeting of King Richard and Friar Tuck.

King Edward (we are not told which among the monarchs of that name, but, from his temper and habits, we may suppose Edward IV) sets forth with his court to a gallant hunting-match in Sherwood Forest, in which, as is not unusual for princes in romance, he falls in with a deer of extraordinary size and swiftness, and pursues it closely, till he has outstripped his whole retinue, tired out hounds and horse, and finds himself alone under the gloom of an extensive forest, upon which night is descending. Under the apprehensions natural to a situation so uncomfortable, the king recollects that he has heard how poor men, when apprehensive of a bad night's lodging, pray to Saint Julian, who, in the Romish calendar, stands Quarter-Master-General to all forlorn travellers that render him due homage. Edward puts up his orisons accordingly, and by the guidance, doubtless, of the good Saint, reaches a small path, conducting him to a chapel in the forest, having a hermit's cell in its close vicinity. The King hears the reverend man, with a companion of his solitude, telling his beads within, and meekly requests of him quarters for the night. 'I have no accommodation for such a lord as ye be,' said the Hermit. 'I live here in the wilderness upon roots and rinds, and may not receive into my dwelling even the poorest wretch that lives, unless it were to save his life.' The King enquires the way to the next town, and, understanding it is by a road which he cannot find without difficulty, even if he had daylight to befriend him, he declares, that with or without the Hermit's consent, he is determined to be his guest that night. He is admitted accordingly, not without a hint from the Recluse, that were he himself out of his priestly weeds, he would care little for his threats of using violence, and that he gives way to him not out of intimidation, but simply to avoid scandal.

The King is admitted into the cell—two bundles of straw are shaken down for his accommodation, and he comforts himself that he is now under shelter, and that

'A night will soon be gone.'

Other wants, however, arise. The guest becomes clamorous for supper, observing,

'For certainly, as I you say,
I ne had never so sorry a day,
    That I ne had a merry night.'

But this indication of his taste for good cheer, joined to the annunciation of his being a follower of the Court, who had lost himself at the great hunting-match, cannot induce the niggard Hermit to produce better fare than bread and cheese, for which his guest showed little appetite; and 'thin drink,' which was even less acceptable. At length the King presses his host on a point to which he had more than once alluded, without obtaining a satisfactory reply:

'Then said the King, "by Godys grace,
Thou wert in a merry place,
    To shoot thou should lere;
When the foresters go to rest,
Sometyme thou might have of the best,
    All of the wild deer;
I wold hold it for no scathe,
Though thou hadst bow and arrows baith,
    Althoff thou best a Frere."'

The Hermit, in return, expresses his apprehension that his guest means to drag him into some confession of offence against the forest laws, which, being betrayed to the King, might cost him his life. Edward answers by fresh assurances of secrecy, and again urges on him the necessity of procuring some venison. The Hermit replies, by once more insisting on the duties incumbent upon him as a churchman, and continues to affirm himself free from all such breaches of order:—

'Many day I have here been,
And flesh-meat I eat never,
    But milk of the kye;
Warm thee well, and go to sleep,
And I will lap thee with my cope,
    Softly to lye.'

It would seem that the manuscript is here imperfect, for we do not find the reasons which finally induce the curtal Friar to amend the King's cheer. But acknowledging his guest to be such a 'good fellow' as has seldom graced his board, the holy man at length produces the best his cell affords. Two candles are placed on a table, white bread and baked pasties are displayed by the light, besides choice of venison, both salt and fresh, from which they select collops. 'I might have eaten my bread dry,' said the King, 'had I not pressed thee on the score of archery, but now have I dined like a prince—if we had but drink enow.'

This too is afforded by the hospitable anchorite, who dispatches an assistant to fetch a pot of four gallons from a secret corner near his bed, and the whole three set in to serious drinking. This amusement is superintended by the Friar, according to the recurrence of certain fustian words, to be repeated by every compotator in turn before he drank—a species of High Jinks,* as it were, by which they regulated their potations, as toasts were given in latter times. The one toper says *fusty bandias*, to which the other is obliged to reply, *strike pantnere*, and the Friar passes many jests on the King's want of memory, who sometimes forgets the words of action. The night is spent is this jolly pastime. Before his departure in the morning, the King invites his reverend host to Court, promises, at least, to requite his hospitality, and expresses himself much pleased with his entertainment. The jolly Hermit at length agrees to venture thither, and to enquire for Jack Fletcher, which is the name assumed by the King. After the Hermit has shown Edward some feats of archery, the joyous pair separate. The King rides home, and rejoins his retinue. As the romance is imperfect, we are not acquainted how the discovery takes place; but it is probably much in the same manner as in other narratives turning on the same subject, where the host, apprehensive of death for having trespassed on the respect due to his Sovereign, while incognito, is agreeably surprised by receiving honours and reward.

In Mr Hartshorne's collection,* there is a romance on the same foundation, called King Edward and the Shepherd,[4] which, considered as illustrating manners, is still more curious than the King and the Hermit; but it is foreign to the present purpose.

The reader has here the original legend from which the incident in the romance is derived; and the identifying the irregular Eremite with the Friar Tuck of Robin Hood's story, was an obvious expedient.

The name of Ivanhoe was suggested by an old rhyme. All novelists have had occasion at some time or other to wish with Falstaff, that they knew where a commodity of good names* was to be had. On such an occasion the author chanced to call to memory a rhyme recording three names of the manors forfeited by the ancestor of the celebrated Hampden, for striking the Black Prince a blow with his racket, when they quarrelled at tennis;—

> 'Tring, Wing, and Ivanhoe,*
> For striking of a blow,
> Hampden did forego,
> And glad he could escape so.'

The word suited the author's purpose in two material respects,—for, first, it had an ancient English sound; and secondly, it conveyed no indication whatever of the nature of the story. He presumes to hold this last quality to be of no small importance. What is called a taking title, serves the direct interest of the bookseller or publisher, who by this means sometimes sells an edition while it is yet passing the press. But if the author permits an over degree of attention to be drawn to his work ere it has appeared, he places himself in the embarrassing condition of having excited a degree of expectation which, if he proves unable to satisfy, is an error fatal to his literary reputation. Besides, when we meet such a title as the Gunpowder Plot, or any other connected with general history, each reader, before he has seen the book, has formed to himself some particular idea of the sort of manner in which the story is to be conducted, and the nature of the amusement which he is to derive from it. In this he is probably disappointed, and in that case may be naturally disposed to visit upon the author or the work, the unpleasant feelings thus excited. In such a case the literary adventurer is censured, not for having missed the mark at which he himself aimed, but for not having shot off his shaft in a direction he never thought of.

On the footing of unreserved communication which the Author has established with the reader, he may here add the trifling circumstance, that a roll of Norman warriors, occurring in the Auchinleck Manuscript, gave him the formidable name of Front-de-Bœuf.*

Ivanhoe was highly successful upon its appearance, and may be said to have procured for its author the freedom of the Rules,* since he has ever since been permitted to exercise his powers of fictitious composition in England, as well as Scotland.

The character of the fair Jewess found so much favour in the eyes of some fair readers, that the writer was censured, because, when arranging the fates of the characters of the drama, he had not assigned the hand of Wilfred to Rebecca,* rather than the less interesting Rowena. But, not to mention that the prejudices of the age rendered such an union almost impossible, the author may, in passing, observe, that he thinks a character of a highly virtuous and lofty stamp, is degraded rather than exalted by an attempt to reward virtue with temporal prosperity. Such is not the recompense which Providence has deemed worthy of suffering merit, and it is a dangerous and fatal doctrine to teach young persons, the most common readers of romance, that rectitude of conduct and of principle are either naturally allied with, or adequately rewarded by, the gratification of our passions, or attainment of our wishes. In a word, if a virtuous and self-denied character is dismissed with temporal wealth, greatness, rank, or the indulgence of such a rashly formed or ill assorted passion as that of Rebecca for Ivanhoe, the reader will be apt to say, verily Virtue has had its reward. But a glance on the great picture of life will show, that the duties of self-denial, and the sacrifice of passion to principle, are seldom thus remunerated; and that the internal consciousness of their high-minded discharge of duty, produces on their own reflections a more adequate recompense, in the form of that peace which the world cannot give or take away.

ABBOTSFORD,
1st September, 1830.

DEDICATORY EPISTLE

TO

THE REV. DR DRYASDUST, F.A.S.*

Residing in the Castle-Gate, York

MUCH ESTEEMED AND DEAR SIR,

It is scarcely necessary to mention the various and concurring reasons which induce me to place your name at the head of the following work. Yet the chief of these reasons may perhaps be refuted by the imperfections of the performance. Could I have hoped to render it worthy of your patronage, the public would at once have seen the propriety of inscribing a work designed to illustrate the domestic antiquities of England, and particularly of our Saxon forefathers, to the learned author of the Essays upon the Horn of King Ulphus, and on the Lands bestowed by him upon the patrimony of St Peter.* I am conscious, however, that the slight, unsatisfactory, and trivial manner, in which the result of my antiquarian researches has been recorded in the following pages, takes the work from under that class which bears the proud motto, *Detur digniori.** On the contrary, I fear I shall incur the censure of presumption in placing the venerable name of Dr Jonas Dryasdust at the head of a publication, which the more grave antiquary will perhaps class with the idle novels and romances of the day. I am anxious to vindicate myself from such a charge; for although I might trust to your friendship for an apology in your eyes, yet I would not willingly stand convicted in those of the public of so grave a crime, as my fears lead me to anticipate my being charged with.

I must therefore remind you, that when we first talked over together that class of productions, in one of which the private and family affairs of your learned northern friend, Mr Oldbuck of Monkbarns, were so unjustifiably exposed to the public, some discussion occurred between us concerning the cause of the popularity these works have attained in this idle age, which, whatever other merit they possess, must be admitted to be hastily written, and in violation of every rule assigned to the epopeia. It seemed then to be your opinion, that the charm lay entirely in the art with which the unknown author had availed himself, like a second M'Pherson,* of the antiquarian stores which lay scattered around him, supplying his own indolence or poverty of invention, by the incidents which had actually taken place in his country at no distant period, by introducing real characters, and scarcely suppressing real names. It was not above sixty or seventy years, you observed, since the whole north of Scotland was under a state of government nearly as simple and as patriarchal as those of our good allies the Mohawks and Iroquois.* Admitting that the author cannot himself be supposed to have witnessed those times, he must have lived, you observed, among persons who had acted and suffered in them; and even within these thirty years, such an infinite change has taken place in the manners of Scotland, that men look back upon the habits of society proper to their immediate ancestors, as we do on those of the reign of Queen Anne, or even the period of the Revolution. Having thus materials of every kind lying strewed around him, there was little, you observed, to embarrass the author, but the difficulty of choice. It was no wonder, therefore, that, having begun to work a mine so plentiful, he should have derived from his works fully more credit and profit than the facility of his labours merited.

Admitting (as I could not deny) the general truth of these conclusions, I cannot but think it strange that no attempt has been made to excite an interest for the traditions and manners of Old England, similar to that which has been obtained in behalf of those of our poorer and less celebrated neighbours. The Kendal green,* though its date is more ancient, ought surely to be as dear to our feelings, as the variegated tartans of the north. The name of Robin Hood, if duly conjured with, should raise a spirit* as soon as that of Rob Roy; and the patriots of England deserve no less their renown in our modern circles, than the Bruces and Wallaces of Caledonia.* If the scenery of the south be less romantic and sublime than that of the northern mountains, it must be allowed to possess in the same proportion superior softness and beauty; and upon the whole, we feel ourselves entitled to exclaim with the patriotic Syrian—'Are not

Pharphar and Abana, rivers of Damascus, better than all the rivers of Israel?'*

Your objections to such an attempt, my dear Doctor, were, you may remember, two-fold. You insisted upon the advantages which the Scotsman possessed, from the very recent existence of that state of society in which his scene was to be laid. Many now alive, you remarked, well remembered persons who had not only seen the celebrated Roy M'Gregor, but had feasted, and even fought with him. All those minute circumstances belonging to private life and domestic character, all that gives verisimilitude to a narrative, and individuality to the persons introduced, is still known and remembered in Scotland; whereas in England, civilisation has been so long complete, that our ideas of our ancestors are only to be gleaned from musty records and chronicles, the authors of which seem perversely to have conspired to suppress in their narratives all interesting details, in order to find room for flowers of monkish eloquence, or trite reflections upon morals. To match an English and a Scottish author in the rival task of embodying and reviving the traditions of their respective countries, would be, you alleged, in the highest degree unequal and unjust. The Scottish magician, you said, was, like Lucan's witch,* at liberty to walk over the recent field of battle, and to select for the subject of resuscitation by his sorceries, a body whose limbs had recently quivered with existence, and whose throat had but just uttered the last note of agony. Such a subject even the powerful Erictho was compelled to select, as alone capable of being reanimated even by *her* potent magic—

> ————gelidas leto scrutata medullas,
> Pulmonis rigidi stantes sine vulnere fibras
> Invenit, et vocem defuncto in corpore quærit.*

The English author, on the other hand, without supposing him less of a conjuror than the Northern Warlock, can, you observed, only have the liberty of selecting his subject amidst the dust of antiquity, where nothing was to be found but dry, sapless, mouldering, and disjointed bones, such as those which filled the valley of Jehoshaphat.* You expressed, besides, your apprehension, that the unpatriotic prejudices of my countrymen would not allow fair play to such a work as that of which I endeavoured to demonstrate the probable success. And this, you said, was not entirely owing to the more general prejudice in favour of that which is foreign, but that it rested partly upon improbabilities, arising out of the circumstances in which the English reader is placed. If you describe to him a set of wild manners, and a state of primitive society existing in the Highlands of Scotland, he is much disposed to acquiesce in the truth of what is asserted. And reason good. If he be of the ordinary class of readers, he has either never seen those remote districts at all, or he has wandered through those desolate regions in the course of a summer tour, eating bad dinners, sleeping on truckle beds, stalking from desolation to desolation, and fully prepared to believe the strangest things that could be told him of a people, wild and extravagant enough to be attached to scenery so extraordinary. But the same worthy person, when placed in his own snug parlour, and surrounded by all the comforts of an Englishman's fireside, is not half so much disposed to believe that his own ancestors led a very different life from himself; that the shattered tower, which now forms a vista from his window, once held a baron who would have hung him up at his own door without any form of trial; that the hinds, by whom his little pet-farm is managed, a few centuries ago would have been his slaves; and that the complete influence of feudal tyranny once extended over the neighbouring village, where the attorney is now a man of more importance than the lord of the manor.

While I own the force of these objections, I must confess, at the same time, that they do not appear to me to be altogether insurmountable. The scantiness of materials is indeed a formidable difficulty; but no one knows better than Dr Dryasdust, that to those deeply read in antiquity, hints concerning the private life of our ancestors lie scattered through the pages of our various historians, bearing, indeed, a slender proportion to the other matters of which they treat, but still, when collected together, sufficient to throw considerable light upon the *vie privée**
of our forefathers; indeed, I am convinced, that however I myself may fail in the ensuing attempt, yet, with more labour in collecting, or more skill in using, the materials within his reach, illustrated as they have been by the labours of Dr Henry, of the late Mr Strutt, and, above all, of Mr Sharon Turner,* an abler hand

would have been successful; and therefore I protest, beforehand, against any argument which may be founded on the failure of the present experiment.

On the other hand, I have already said, that if any thing like a true picture of old English manners could be drawn, I would trust to the good-nature and good sense of my countrymen for insuring its favourable reception.

Having thus replied, to the best of my power, to the first class of your objections, or at least having shown my resolution to overleap the barriers which your prudence has raised, I will be brief in noticing that which is more peculiar to myself. It seemed to be your opinion, that the very office of an antiquary, employed in grave, and, as the vulgar will sometimes allege, in toilsome and minute research, must be considered as incapacitating him from successfully compounding a tale of this sort. But permit me to say, my dear Doctor, that this objection is rather formal than substantial. It is true, that such slight compositions might not suit the severer genius of our friend Mr Oldbuck. Yet Horace Walpole wrote a goblin tale which has thrilled through many a bosom;* and George Ellis could transfer all the playful fascination of a humour, as delightful as it was uncommon, into his Abridgement of the Ancient Metrical Romances.* So that, however I may have occasion to rue my present audacity, I have at least the most respectable precedents in my favour.

Still the severer antiquary may think, that, by thus intermingling fiction with truth, I am polluting the well of history with modern inventions, and impressing upon the rising generation false ideas of the age which I describe. I cannot but in some sense admit the force of this reasoning, which I yet hope to traverse by the following considerations.

It is true, that I neither can, nor do pretend, to the observation of complete accuracy, even in matters of outward costume, much less in the more important points of language and manners. But the same motive which prevents my writing the dialogue of the piece in Anglo-Saxon or in Norman-French, and which prohibits my sending forth to the public this essay printed with the types of Caxton or Wynken de Worde,* prevents my attempting to confine myself within the limits of the period in which my story is laid. It is necessary, for exciting interest of any kind, that the subject assumed should be, as it were, translated into the manners, as well as the language, of the age we live in. No fascination has ever been attached to Oriental literature, equal to that produced by Mr Galland's first translation of the Arabian Tales;* in which, retaining on the one hand the splendour of Eastern costume, and on the other the wildness of Eastern fiction, he mixed these with just so much ordinary feeling and expression, as rendered them interesting and intelligible, while he abridged the long-winded narratives, curtailed the monotonous reflections, and rejected the endless repetitions of the Arabian original. The tales, therefore, though less purely Oriental than in their first concoction, were eminently better fitted for the European market, and obtained an unrivalled degree of public favour, which they certainly would never have gained had not the manners and style been in some degree familiarized to the feelings and habits of the western reader.

In point of justice, therefore, to the multitudes who will, I trust, devour this book with avidity, I have so far explained our ancient manners in modern language, and so far detailed the characters and sentiments of my persons, that the modern reader will not find himself, I should hope, much trammelled by the repulsive dryness of mere antiquity. In this, I respectfully contend, I have in no respect exceeded the fair license due to the author of a fictitious composition. The late ingenious Mr Strutt, in his romance of Queen-Hoo-Hall,[5]* acted upon another principle; and in distinguishing between what was ancient and modern, forgot, as it appears to me, that extensive neutral ground, the large proportion, that is, of manners and sentiments which are common to us and to our ancestors, having been handed down unaltered from them to us, or which, arising out of the principles of our common nature, must have existed alike in either state of society. In this manner, a man of talent, and of great antiquarian erudition, limited the popularity of his work, by excluding from it every thing which was not sufficiently obsolete to be altogether forgotten and unintelligible.

The license which I would here vindicate, is so necessary to the execution of my plan, that I will crave your patience while I illustrate my argument a little farther.

He who first opens Chaucer, or any other ancient poet, is so much struck with the obsolete spelling, multiplied consonants, and antiquated appearance of the language, that he is apt to lay the work down in despair, as encrusted too deep with the rust of antiquity, to permit his judging of its merits or tasting its beauties. But if some intelligent and accomplished friend points out to him, that the difficulties by which he is startled are more in appearance than reality, if, by reading aloud to him, or by reducing the ordinary words to the modern orthography, he satisfies his proselyte that only about one-tenth part of the words employed are in fact obsolete, the novice may be easily persuaded to approach the 'well of English undefiled,'* with the certainty that a slender degree of patience will enable him to enjoy both the humour and the pathos with which old Geoffrey delighted the age of Cressy and of Poictiers.

To pursue this a little farther. If our neophyte, strong in the new-born love of antiquity, were to undertake to imitate what he had learnt to admire, it must be allowed he would act very injudiciously, if he were to select from the Glossary the obsolete words which it contains, and employ those exclusively of all phrases and vocables retained in modern days. This was the error of the unfortunate Chatterton.* In order to give his language the appearance of antiquity, he rejected every word that was modern, and produced a dialect entirely different from any that had ever been spoken in Great Britain. He who would imitate an ancient language with success, must attend rather to its grammatical character, turn of expression, and mode of arrangement, than labour to collect extraordinary and antiquated terms, which, as I have already averred, do not in ancient authors approach the number of words still in use, though perhaps somewhat altered in sense and spelling, in the proportion of one to ten.

What I have applied to language, is still more justly applicable to sentiments and manners. The passions, the sources from which these must spring in all their modifications, are generally the same in all ranks and conditions, all countries and ages; and it follows, as a matter of course, that the opinions, habits of thinking, and actions, however influenced by the peculiar state of society, must still, upon the whole, bear a strong resemblance to each other. Our ancestors were not more distinct from us, surely, than Jews are from Christians; they had 'eyes, hands, organs, dimensions, senses, affections, passions;' were 'fed with the same food, hurt with the same weapons, subject to the same diseases, warmed and cooled by the same winter and summer,'* as ourselves. The tenor, therefore, of their affections and feelings, must have borne the same general proportion to our own.*

It follows, therefore, that of the materials which an author has to use in a romance, or fictitious composition, such as I have ventured to attempt, he will find that a great proportion, both of language and manners, is as proper to the present time as to those in which he has laid his time of action. The freedom of choice which this allows him, is therefore much greater, and the difficulty of his task much more diminished, than at first appears. To take an illustration from a sister art, the antiquarian details may be said to represent the peculiar features of a landscape under delineation of the pencil. His feudal tower must arise in due majesty; the figures which he introduces must have the costume and character of their age; the piece must represent the peculiar features of the scene which he has chosen for his subject, with all its appropriate elevation of rock, or precipitate descent of cataract. His general colouring, too, must be copied from Nature: the sky must be clouded or serene, according to the climate, and the general tints must be those which prevail in a natural landscape. So far the painter is bound down by the rules of his art, to a precise imitation of the features of Nature; but it is not required that he should descend to copy all her more minute features, or represent with absolute exactness the very herbs, flowers, and trees, with which the spot is decorated. These, as well as all the more minute points of light and shadow, are attributes proper to scenery in general, natural to each situation, and subject to the artist's disposal, as his taste or pleasure may dictate.

It is true, that this license is confined in either case within legitimate bounds. The painter must introduce no ornament inconsistent with the climate or country of his landscape; he must not plant cypress trees upon Inch-Merrin, or Scottish firs among the ruins of Persepolis;* and the author lies under a corresponding restraint. However far he may venture in a more full detail of passions and feelings, than is to be found in the ancient compositions which he imitates, he must introduce nothing inconsistent with the manners of the age; his knights, squires, grooms, and yeomen, may be more fully drawn than in the hard, dry delineations of an ancient illuminated manuscript, but the character and costume of the age must remain inviolate; they must be the same figures, drawn by a better pencil, or, to speak more modestly, executed in an age when the principles of art were better understood. His language must not be exclusively obsolete and unintelligible; but he should admit, if possible, no word or turn of phraseology betraying an origin directly modern. It is one thing to make use of the language and sentiments which are common to ourselves and our forefathers, and it is another to invest them with the sentiments and dialect exclusively proper to their descendants.

This, my dear friend, I have found the most difficult part of my task; and, to speak frankly, I hardly expect to satisfy your less partial judgment, and more extensive knowledge of such subjects, since I have hardly been able to please my own.

I am conscious that I shall be found still more faulty in the tone of keeping and costume, by those who may be disposed rigidly to examine my Tale, with reference to the manners of the exact period in which my actors flourished: it may be, that I have introduced little which can positively be termed modern; but, on the other hand, it is extremely probable that I may have confused the manners of two or three centuries, and introduced, during the reign of Richard the First, circumstances appropriated to a period either considerably earlier, or a good deal later than that era. It is my comfort, that errors of this kind will escape the general class of readers, and that I may share in the ill-deserved applause of those architects, who, in their modern Gothic, do not hesitate to introduce, without rule or method, ornaments proper to different styles and to different periods of the art. Those whose extensive researches have given them the means of judging my backslidings with more severity, will probably be lenient in proportion to their knowledge of the difficulty of my task. My honest and neglected friend, Ingulphus,* has furnished me with many a valuable hint; but the light afforded by the Monk of Croydon, and Geoffrey de Vinsauff,* is dimmed by such a conglomeration of uninteresting and unintelligible matter, that we gladly fly for relief to the delightful pages of the gallant Froissart,* although he flourished at a period so much more remote from the date of my history. If, therefore, my dear friend, you have generosity enough to pardon the presumptuous attempt, to frame for myself a minstrel coronet, partly out of the pearls of pure antiquity, and partly from the Bristol stones and paste,* with which I have endeavoured to imitate them, I am convinced your opinion of the difficulty of the task will reconcile you to the imperfect manner of its execution.

Of my materials I have but little to say: they may be chiefly found in the singular Anglo-Norman MS, which Sir Arthur Wardour* preserves with such jealous care in the third drawer of his oaken cabinet, scarcely allowing any one to touch it, and being himself not able to read one syllable of its contents. I should never have got his consent, on my visit to Scotland, to read in those precious pages for so many hours, had I not promised to designate it by some emphatic mode of printing, as 𝕿𝖍𝖊 𝖂𝖆𝖗𝖉𝖔𝖚𝖗 𝕸𝖆𝖓𝖚𝖘𝖈𝖗𝖎𝖕𝖙; giving it, thereby, an individuality as important as the Bannatyne MS, the Auchinleck MS,* and any other monument of the patience of a Gothic scrivener. I have sent, for your private consideration, a list of the contents of this curious piece, which I shall perhaps subjoin, with your approbation, to the third volume of my Tale, in case the printer's devil should continue impatient for copy, when the whole of my narrative has been imposed.

Adieu, my dear friend; I have said enough to explain, if not to vindicate, the attempt which I have made, and which, in spite of your doubts, and my own incapacity, I am still willing to believe has not been altogether made in vain.

I hope you are now well recovered from your spring fit of the gout, and shall be happy if the advice of your learned physician should recommend a tour to these parts. Several curiosities have been lately dug up near the wall, as well as at the ancient station of Habitancum. Talking of the latter, I suppose you have long since heard the news, that a sulky churlish boor has destroyed the ancient statue, or rather bas-relief, popularly called Robin of Redesdale.* It seems Robin's fame attracted more visitants than was consistent with the growth of the heather, upon a moor worth a shilling an acre. Reverend as you write yourself, be

revengeful for once, and pray with me that he may be visited
with such a fit of the stone,* as if he had all the fragments of poor
Robin in that region of his viscera where the disease holds its
seat. Tell this not in Gath,* lest the Scots rejoice that they have
at length found a parallel instance among their neighbours, to
that barbarous deed which demolished Arthur's Oven.* But
there is no end to lamentation, when we betake ourselves to such
subjects. My respectful compliments attend Miss Dryasdust; I
endeavoured to match the spectacles agreeable to her commission, during my late journey to London, and hope she has
received them safe, and found them satisfactory. I send this by
the blind carrier, so that probably it may be some time upon its
journey.[6] The last news which I hear from Edinburgh is, that the
gentleman who fills the situation of Secretary to the Society of
Antiquaries of Scotland,[7] is the best amateur draftsman in that
kingdom, and that much is expected from his skill and zeal in
delineating those specimens of national antiquity, which are
either mouldering under the slow touch of time, or swept away
by modern taste, with the same besom of destruction which John
Knox used at the Reformation. Once more adieu; *vale tandem,
non immemor mei.** Believe me to be,

                    Reverend, and very dear Sir,

              Your most faithful humble Servant,

                                    LAURENCE TEMPLETON

TOPPINGWOLD, NEAR EGREMONT,
CUMBERLAND, NOV. 17, 1817.

IVANHOE

CHAPTER I

Thus communed these; while to their lowly dome,
The full-fed swine return'd with evening home;
Compell'd, reluctant, to the several sties,
With din obstreperous, and ungrateful cries.

POPE'S *Odyssey**

IN that pleasant district of merry England which is watered by
the river Don, there extended in ancient times a large forest,
covering the greater part of the beautiful hills and valleys which
lie between Sheffield and the pleasant town of Doncaster. The
remains of this extensive wood are still to be seen at the noble
seats of Wentworth, of Warncliffe Park, and around Rotherham.
Here haunted of yore the fabulous Dragon of Wantley;* here
were fought many of the most desperate battles during the Civil
Wars of the Roses; and here also flourished in ancient times those
bands of gallant outlaws, whose deeds have been rendered so
popular in English song.

Such being our chief scene, the date of our story* refers to a
period towards the end of the reign of Richard I, when his
return from his long captivity had become an event rather
wished than hoped for by his despairing subjects, who were in
the meantime subjected to every species of subordinate oppression. The nobles, whose power had become exorbitant during the reign of Stephen, and whom the prudence of Henry the
Second had scarce reduced into some degree of subjection to
the crown, had now resumed their ancient license in its
utmost extent; despising the feeble interference of the English
Council of State,* fortifying their castles, increasing the number
of their dependants, reducing all around them to a state of
vassalage, and striving by every means in their power, to place
themselves each at the head of such forces as might enable him to

make a figure in the national convulsions which appeared to be impending.

The situation of the inferior gentry, or Franklins, as they were called, who, by the law and spirit of the English constitution, were entitled to hold themselves independent of feudal tyranny, became now unusually precarious. If, as was most generally the case, they placed themselves under the protection of any of the petty kings in their vicinity, accepted of feudal offices in his household, or bound themselves, by mutual treaties of alliance and protection, to support him in his enterprises, they might indeed purchase temporary repose; but it must be with the sacrifice of that independence which was so dear to every English bosom, and at the certain hazard of being involved as a party in whatever rash expedition the ambition of their protector might lead him to undertake. On the other hand, such and so multiplied were the means of vexation and oppression possessed by the great Barons, that they never wanted the pretext, and seldom the will, to harass and pursue, even to the very edge of destruction, any of their less powerful neighbours, who attempted to separate themselves from their authority, and to trust for their protection, during the dangers of the times, to their own inoffensive conduct, and to the laws of the land.

A circumstance which greatly tended to enhance the tyranny of the nobility, and the sufferings of the inferior classes, arose from the consequences of the Conquest by Duke William of Normandy. Four generations had not sufficed to blend the hostile blood of the Normans and Anglo-Saxons, or to unite, by common language and mutual interests, two hostile races, one of which still felt the elation of triumph, while the other groaned under all the consequences of defeat. The power had been completely placed in the hands of the Norman nobility, by the event of the battle of Hastings, and it had been used, as our histories assure us, with no moderate hand. The whole race of Saxon princes and nobles had been extirpated or disinherited, with few or no exceptions; nor were the numbers great who possessed land in the country of their fathers, even as proprietors of the second, or of yet inferior classes. The royal policy had long been to weaken, by every means, legal or illegal, the strength of a part of the population which was justly considered as nourishing the most inveterate antipathy to their victor. All the monarchs of the Norman race had shown the most marked predilection for their Norman subjects; the laws of the chase, and many others, equally unknown to the milder and more free spirit of the Saxon constitution, had been fixed upon the necks of the subjugated inhabitants, to add weight, as it were, to the feudal chains with which they were loaded. At court, and in the castles of the great nobles, where the pomp and state of a court was emulated, Norman-French was the only language employed; in courts of law, the pleadings and judgments were delivered in the same tongue. In short, French was the language of honour, of chivalry, and even of justice, while the far more manly and expressive Anglo-Saxon was abandoned to the use of rustics and hinds, who knew no other. Still, however, the necessary intercourse between the lords of the soil, and those oppressed inferior beings by whom that soil was cultivated, occasioned the gradual formation of a dialect, compounded betwixt the French and the Anglo-Saxon, in which they could render themselves mutually intelligible to each other; and from this necessity arose by degrees the structure of our present English language, in which the speech of the victors and the vanquished have been so happily blended together; and which has since been so richly improved by importations from the classical languages, and from those spoken by the southern nations of Europe.

This state of things I have thought it necessary to premise for the information of the general reader, who might be apt to forget, that, although no great historical events, such as war or insurrection, mark the existence of the Anglo-Saxons as a separate people subsequent to the reign of William the Second; yet the great national distinctions betwixt them and their conquerors, the recollection of what they had formerly been, and to what they were now reduced, continued, down to the reign of Edward the Third, to keep open the wounds which the Conquest had inflicted, and to maintain a line of separation betwixt the descendants of the victor Normans and the vanquished Saxons.

The sun was setting upon one of the rich grassy glades of that forest, which we have mentioned in the beginning of the chapter. Hundreds of broad-headed, short-stemmed, wide-branched

oaks, which had witnessed perhaps the stately march of the
Roman soldiery, flung their gnarled arms over a thick carpet of
the most delicious green sward; in some places they were inter-
mingled with beeches, hollies, and copsewood of various descriptions, so closely as totally to intercept the level beams of the
sinking sun; in others they receded from each other, forming
those long sweeping vistas, in the intricacy of which the eye
delights to lose itself, while imagination considers them as the
paths to yet wilder scenes of silvan solitude. Here the red rays of
the sun shot a broken and discoloured light, that partially hung
upon the shattered boughs and mossy trunks of the trees, and
there they illuminated in brilliant patches the portions of turf to
which they made their way. A considerable open space, in the
midst of this glade, seemed formerly to have been dedicated to
the rites of Druidical superstition; for, on the summit of a hil-
lock, so regular as to seem artificial, there still remained part of a
circle of rough unhewn stones, of large dimensions. Seven stood
upright; the rest had been dislodged from their places, probably
by the zeal of some convert to Christianity, and lay, some prostrate near their former site, and others on the side of the hill. One
large stone only had found its way to the bottom, and in stopping
the course of a small brook, which glided smoothly round the
foot of the eminence, gave, by its opposition, a feeble voice of
murmur to the placid and elsewhere silent streamlet.

The human figures which completed this landscape, were in
number two, partaking, in their dress and appearance,* of that
wild and rustic character, which belonged to the woodlands of
the West-Riding of Yorkshire at that early period. The eldest of
these men had a stern, savage, and wild aspect. His garment was
of the simplest form imaginable, being a close jacket with sleeves,
composed of the tanned skin of some animal, on which the hair
had been originally left, but which had been worn off in so many
places, that it would have been difficult to distinguish, from the
patches that remained, to what creature the fur had belonged.
This primeval vestment reached from the throat to the knees,
and served at once all the usual purposes of body-clothing; there
was no wider opening at the collar, than was necessary to admit
the passage of the head, from which it may be inferred, that it
was put on by slipping it over the head and shoulders, in the

manner of a modern shirt, or ancient hauberk. Sandals, bound with thongs made of boars' hide, protected the feet, and a roll of thin leather was twined artificially round the legs, and, ascending above the calf, left the knees bare, like those of a Scottish Highlander. To make the jacket sit yet more close to the body, it was gathered at the middle by a broad leathern belt, secured by a brass buckle; to one side of which was attached a sort of scrip, and to the other a ram's horn, accoutred with a mouthpiece, for the purpose of blowing. In the same belt was stuck one of those long, broad, sharp-pointed, and two-edged knives, with a buck's-horn handle, which were fabricated in the neighbourhood, and bore even at this early period the name of a Sheffield whittle.* The man had no covering upon his head, which was only defended by his own thick hair, matted and twisted together, and scorched by the influence of the sun into a rusty dark-red colour, forming a contrast with the overgrown beard upon his cheeks, which was rather of a yellow or amber hue. One part of his dress only remains, but it is too remarkable to be suppressed; it was a brass ring, resembling a dog's collar, but without any opening, and soldered fast round his neck, so loose as to form no impediment to his breathing, yet so tight as to be incapable of being removed, excepting by the use of the file. On this singular gorget was engraved, in Saxon characters, an inscription of the following purport:—'Gurth,* the son of Beowulph,* is the born thrall of Cedric* of Rotherwood.'

Beside the swineherd, for such was Gurth's occupation, was seated, upon one of the fallen Druidical monuments, a person about ten years younger in appearance, and whose dress, though resembling his companion's in form, was of better materials, and of a more fantastic description. His jacket had been stained of a bright purple hue, upon which there had been some attempt to paint grotesque ornaments in different colours. To the jacket he added a short cloak, which scarcely reached half way down his thigh; it was of crimson cloth, though a good deal soiled, lined with bright yellow; and as he could transfer it from one shoulder to the other, or at his pleasure draw it all around him, its width, contrasted with its want of longitude, formed a fantastic piece of drapery. He had thin silver bracelets upon his arms, and on his neck a collar of the same metal, bearing the inscription, 'Wamba,* the son of Witless, is the thrall of Cedric of Rotherwood.' This personage had the same sort of sandals with his companion, but instead of the roll of leather thong, his legs were cased in a sort of gaiters, of which one was red and the other yellow. He was provided also with a cap, having around it more than one bell, about the size of those attached to hawks, which jingled as he turned his head to one side or other; and as he seldom remained a minute in the same posture, the sound might be considered as incessant. Around the edge of this cap was a stiff bandeau of leather, cut at the top into open work, resembling a coronet, while a prolonged bag arose from within it, and fell down on one shoulder like an old-fashioned nightcap, or a jelly-bag, or the head-gear of a modern hussar.* It was to this part of the cap that the bells were attached; which circumstance, as well as the shape of his head-dress, and his own half-crazed, half-cunning expression of countenance, sufficiently pointed him out as belonging to the race of domestic clowns or jesters, maintained in the houses of the wealthy, to help away the tedium of those lingering hours which they were obliged to spend within doors. He bore, like his companion, a scrip, attached to his belt, but had neither horn nor knife, being probably considered as belonging to a class whom it is esteemed dangerous to intrust with edge-tools. In place of these, he was equipped with a sword of lath, resembling that with which Harlequin operates his wonders upon the modern stage.

The outward appearance of these two men formed scarce a stronger contrast than their look and demeanour. That of the serf, or bondsman, was sad and sullen; his aspect was bent on the ground with an air of deep dejection, which might be almost construed into apathy, had not the fire which occasionally sparkled in his red eye manifested that there slumbered, under the appearance of sullen despondency, a sense of oppression, and a disposition to resistance. The looks of Wamba, on the other hand, indicated, as usual with his class, a sort of vacant curiosity, and fidgetty impatience of any posture of repose, together with the utmost self-satisfaction respecting his own situation, and the appearance which he made. The dialogue which they maintained between them was carried on in Anglo-Saxon, which, as we said before, was universally spoken by the inferior classes, excepting the Norman soldiers, and the immediate personal dependants of the great feudal nobles. But to give their conversation in the original would convey but little information to the modern reader, for whose benefit we beg to offer the following translation:

'The curse of St Withold* upon these infernal porkers!' said the swineherd, aiter blowing his horn obstreperously, to collect together the scattered herd of swine, which, answering his call with notes equally melodious, made, however, no haste to remove themselves from the luxurious banquet of beech-mast and acorns on which they had fattened, or to forsake the marshy banks of the rivulet, where several of them, half plunged in mud, lay stretched at their ease, altogether regardless of the voice of their keeper. 'The curse of St Withold upon them and upon me!' said Gurth; 'if the two-legged wolf snap not up some of them ere nightfall, I am no true man.* Here, Fangs! Fangs!' he ejaculated at the top of his voice to a ragged wolfish-looking dog, a sort of lurcher, half mastiff, half greyhound, which ran limping about as if with the purpose of seconding his master in collecting the refractory grunters; but which, in fact, from misapprehension of the swineherd's signals, ignorance of his own duty, or malice prepense,* only drove them hither and thither, and increased the evil which he seemed to design to remedy. 'A devil draw the teeth of him,' said Gurth, 'and the mother of mischief confound the Ranger of the forest, that cuts the foreclaws off our dogs, and makes them unfit for their trade!⁸ Wamba, up and help me an thou beest a man; take a turn round the back o' the hill to gain the wind on them; and when thou'st got the weather-gage,* thou mayst drive them before thee as gently as so many innocent lambs.'

'Truly,' said Wamba, without stirring from the spot, 'I have consulted my legs upon this matter, and they are altogether of opinion, that to carry my gay garments through these sloughs, would be an act of unfriendship to my sovereign person and royal wardrobe; wherefore, Gurth, I advise thee to call off Fangs, and leave the herd to their destiny, which, whether they meet with bands of travelling soldiers, or of outlaws, or of wandering pilgrims, can be little else than to be

converted into Normans before morning, to thy no small ease
and comfort.'

'The swine turned Normans to my comfort!' quoth Gurth;
'expound that to me, Wamba, for my brain is too dull, and my
mind too vexed, to read riddles.'

'Why, how call you those grunting brutes running about on
their four legs?' demanded Wamba.

'Swine, fool, swine,' said the herd, 'every fool knows that.'

'And swine is good Saxon,' said the Jester; 'but how call you
the sow when she is flayed, and drawn, and quartered, and hung
up by the heels, like a traitor?'

'Pork,' answered the swineherd.

'I am very glad every fool knows that too,' said Wamba, 'and
pork, I think, is good Norman-French; and so when the brute
lives, and is in the charge of a Saxon slave, she goes by her Saxon
name; but becomes a Norman, and is called pork, when she is
carried to the Castle-hall to feast among the nobles; what dost
thou think of this, friend Gurth, ha?'

'It is but too true doctrine, friend Wamba, however it got into
thy fool's pate.'

'Nay, I can tell you more,' said Wamba, in the same tone;
'there is old Alderman Ox continues to hold his Saxon epithet,
while he is under the charge of serfs and bondsmen such as thou,
but becomes Beef, a fiery French gallant, when he arrives before
the worshipful jaws that are destined to consume him. Mynheer
Calf, too, becomes Monsieur de Veau in the like manner; he is
Saxon when he requires tendance, and takes a Norman name
when he becomes matter of enjoyment.'*

'By St Dunstan,'* answered Gurth, 'thou speakest but sad
truths; little is left to us but the air we breathe, and that appears
to have been reserved with much hesitation, solely for the purpose of enabling us to endure the tasks they lay upon our
shoulders. The finest and the fattest is for their board; the love-
liest is for their couch; the best and bravest supply their foreign
masters with soldiers, and whiten distant lands with their bones,
leaving few here who have either will or the power to protect the
unfortunate Saxon. God's blessing on our Master Cedric, he
hath done the work of a man in standing in the gap;* but
Reginald Front-de-Bœuf is coming down to this country in per-

son, and we shall soon see how little Cedric's trouble will avail him.—Here, here,' he exclaimed again, raising his voice, 'So ho! so ho! well done, Fangs! thou hast them all before thee now, and bring'st them on bravely, lad.'

'Gurth,' said the Jester, 'I know thou thinkest me a fool, or thou wouldst not be so rash in putting thy head into my mouth. One word to Reginald Front-de-Bœuf, or Philip de Malvoisin, that thou hast spoken treason against the Norman,—and thou art but a castaway swineherd,—thou wouldst waver on one of these trees as a terror to all evil speakers against dignities.'

'Dog, thou wouldst not betray me,' said Gurth, 'after having led me on to speak so much at disadvantage?'

'Betray thee!' answered the Jester; 'no, that were the trick of a wise man; a fool cannot half so well help himself—but soft, whom have we here?' he said, listening to the trampling of several horses which became then audible.

'Never mind whom,' answered Gurth, who had now got his herd before him, and, with the aid of Fangs, was driving them down one of the long dim vistas which we have endeavoured to describe.

'Nay, but I must see the riders,' answered Wamba; 'perhaps they are come from Fairy-land with a message from King Oberon.'*

'A murrain* take thee!' rejoined the swineherd; 'wilt thou talk of such things, while a terrible storm of thunder and lightning is raging within a few miles of us? Hark, how the thunder rumbles! and for summer rain, I never saw such broad downright flat drops fall out of the clouds; the oaks, too, notwithstanding the calm weather, sob and creak with their great boughs as if announcing a tempest. Thou canst play the rational if thou wilt; credit me for once, and let us home ere the storm begins to rage, for the night will be fearful.'

Wamba seemed to feel the force of this appeal, and accompanied his companion, who began his journey after catching up a long quarter-staff which lay upon the grass beside him. This second Eumæus* strode hastily down the forest glade, driving before him, with the assistance of Fangs, the whole herd of his inharmonious charge.

CHAPTER II

A Monk there was, a fayre for the maistrie,
An outrider that loved venerie;
A manly man, to be an Abbot able,
Full many a daintie horse had he in stable:
And whan he rode, men might his bridle hear
Gingeling in a whistling wind as clear,
And eke as loud, as doth the chapell bell,
There as this lord was keeper of the cell.

CHAUCER*

NOTWITHSTANDING the occasional exhortation and chiding of his companion, the noise of the horsemen's feet continuing to approach, Wamba could not be prevented from lingering occasionally on the road, upon every pretence which occurred; now catching from the hazel a cluster of half-ripe nuts, and now turning his head to leer after a cottage maiden who crossed their path. The horsemen, therefore, soon overtook them on the road.

Their numbers amounted to ten men, of whom the two who rode foremost seemed to be persons of considerable importance, and the others their attendants. It was not difficult to ascertain the condition and character of one of these personages. He was obviously an ecclesiastic of high rank; his dress was that of a Cistercian Monk,* but composed of materials much finer than those which the rule of that order admitted. His mantle and hood were of the best Flanders cloth, and fell in ample, and not ungraceful folds, around a handsome, though somewhat corpulent person. His countenance bore as little the marks of self-denial, as his habit indicated contempt of worldly splendour. His features might have been called good, had there not lurked under the penthouse* of his eye, that sly epicurean twinkle which indicates the cautious voluptuary. In other respects, his profession and situation had taught him a ready command over his countenance, which he could contract at pleasure into solemnity, although its natural expression was that of good-humoured social indulgence. In defiance of conventual rules, and the edicts of popes and councils, the sleeves of this dignitary were lined and turned up with rich furs, his mantle secured at the throat with a golden clasp, and the whole dress proper to his order as much refined upon and ornamented, as that of a quaker beauty of the present day, who, while she retains the garb and costume of her sect, continues to give to its simplicity, by the choice of materials and the mode of disposing them, a certain air of co-quettish attraction, savouring but too much of the vanities of the world.

This worthy churchman rode upon a well-fed ambling mule, whose furniture was highly decorated, and whose bridle, accord-ing to the fashion of the day, was ornamented with silver bells. In his seat he had nothing of the awkwardness of the convent, but displayed the easy and habitual grace of a well-trained horseman. Indeed, it seemed that so humble a conveyance as a mule, in however good case, and however well broken to a pleasant and accommodating amble, was only used by the gallant monk for travelling on the road. A lay brother, one of those who followed in the train, had, for his use on other occasions, one of the most handsome Spanish jennets ever bred in Andalusia, which mer-chants used at that time to import, with great trouble and risk, for the use of persons of wealth and distinction. The saddle and housings of this superb palfrey were covered by a long foot-cloth, which reached nearly to the ground, and on which were richly embroidered, mitres, crosses, and other ecclesiastical em-blems. Another lay brother led a sumpter mule,* loaded prob-ably with his superior's baggage; and two monks of his own order, of inferior station, rode together in the rear, laughing and conversing with each other, without taking much notice of the other members of the cavalcade.

The companion of the church dignitary was a man past forty, thin, strong, tall, and muscular; an athletic figure, which long fatigue and constant exercise seemed to have left none of the softer part of the human form, having reduced the whole to brawn, bones, and sinews, which had sustained a thousand toils, and were ready to dare a thousand more. His head was covered with a scarlet cap, faced with fur—of that kind which the French call *mortier*, from its resemblance to the shape of an inverted mortar. His countenance was therefore fully displayed, and its expression was calculated to impress a degree of awe, if not of fear, upon strangers. High features, naturally strong and power-fully expressive, had been burnt almost into Negro blackness by constant exposure to the tropical sun, and might, in their ordi-nary state, be said to slumber after the storm of passion had passed away; but the projection of the veins of the forehead, the readiness with which the upper lip and its thick black moustaches quivered upon the slightest emotion, plainly inti-mated that the tempest might be again and easily awakened. His keen, piercing, dark eyes, told in every glance a history of diffi-culties subdued, and dangers dared, and seemed to challenge opposition to his wishes, for the pleasure of sweeping it from his road by a determined exertion of courage and of will; a deep scar on his brow gave additional sternness to his countenance, and a sinister expression to one of his eyes, which had been slightly injured on the same occasion, and of which the vision, though perfect, was in a slight and partial degree distorted.

The upper dress of this personage resembled that of his com-panion in shape, being a long monastic mantle; but the colour, being scarlet, showed that he did not belong to any of the four regular orders of monks. On the right shoulder of the mantle there was cut, in white cloth, a cross of a peculiar form.* This upper robe concealed what at first view seemed rather inconsist-ent with its form, a shirt, namely, of linked mail, with sleeves and gloves of the same, curiously plaited and interwoven, as flexible to the body as those which are now wrought in the stocking-loom, out of less obdurate materials. The fore-part of his thighs, where the folds of his mantle permitted them to be seen, were also covered with linked mail; the knees and feet were defended by splints, or thin plates of steel, ingeniously jointed upon each other; and mail hose, reaching from the ankle to the knee, effec-tually protected the legs, and completed the rider's defensive armour. In his girdle he wore a long and double-edged dagger, which was the only offensive weapon about his person.

He rode, not a mule, like his companion, but a strong hackney for the road, to save his gallant warhorse, which a squire led behind, fully accoutred for battle, with a chamfrom or plaited head-piece upon his head, having a short spike projecting from the front. On one side of the saddle hung a short battle-axe, richly inlaid with Damascene carving; on the other the rider's plumed head-piece and hood of mail, with a long two-handed sword, used by the chivalry of the period. A second squire held aloft his master's lance, from the extremity of which fluttered a small banderole, or streamer, bearing a cross of the same form with that embroidered upon his cloak. He also carried his small triangular shield, broad enough at the top to protect the breast, and from thence diminishing to a point. It was covered with a scarlet cloth, which prevented the device from being seen.

These two squires were followed by two attendants, whose dark visages, white turbans, and the Oriental form of their garments, showed them to be natives of some distant Eastern country.[9] The whole appearance of this warrior and his retinue was wild and outlandish; the dress of his squires was gorgeous, and his Eastern attendants wore silver collars round their throats, and bracelets of the same metal upon their swarthy legs and arms, of which the former were naked from the elbow, and the latter from mid-leg to ankle.* Silk and embroidery distinguished their dresses, and marked the wealth and importance of their master; forming, at the same time, a striking contrast with the martial simplicity of his own attire. They were armed with crooked sabres, having the hilt and baldric inlaid with gold, and matched with Turkish daggers of yet more costly workmanship. Each of them bore at his saddle-bow a bundle of darts or javelins, about four feet in length, having sharp steel heads, a weapon much in use among the Saracens, and of which the memory is yet preserved in the martial exercise called *El Jerrid*,* still practised in the Eastern countries.

The steeds of these attendants were in appearance as foreign as their riders. They were of Saracen origin, and consequently of Arabian descent; and their fine slender limbs, small fetlocks, thin manes, and easy springy motion, formed a marked contrast with the large-jointed heavy horses, of which the race was cultivated in Flanders and in Normandy, for mounting the men-at-arms of the period in all the panoply of plate and mail; and which, placed by the side of those Eastern coursers, might have passed for a personification of substance and of shadow.

The singular appearance of this cavalcade not only attracted the curiosity of Wamba, but excited even that of his less volatile companion. The monk he instantly knew to be the Prior of Jorvaulx Abbey,* well known for many miles around as a lover of the chase, of the banquet, and, if fame did him not wrong, of other worldly pleasures still more inconsistent with his monastic vows.

Yet so loose were the ideas of the times respecting the conduct of the clergy, whether secular or regular, that the Prior Aymer maintained a fair character in the neighbourhood of his abbey. His free and jovial temper, and the readiness with which he granted absolution from all ordinary delinquencies, rendered him a favourite among the nobility and principal gentry, to several of whom he was allied by birth, being of a distinguished Norman family. The ladies, in particular, were not disposed to scan too nicely the morals of a man who was a professed admirer of their sex, and who possessed many means of dispelling the ennui which was too apt to intrude upon the halls and bowers of an ancient feudal castle. The Prior mingled in the sports of the field with more than due eagerness, and was allowed to possess the best-trained hawks and the fleetest greyhounds in the North Riding; circumstances which strongly recommended him to the youthful gentry. With the old, he had another part to play, which, when needful, he could sustain with great decorum. His knowledge of books, however superficial, was sufficient to impress upon their ignorance respect for his supposed learning; and the gravity of his deportment and language, with the high tone which he exerted in setting forth the authority of the church and of the priesthood, impressed them no less with an opinion of his sanctity. Even the common people, the severest critics of the conduct of their betters, had commiseration with the follies of Prior Aymer. He was generous; and charity, as it is well known, covereth a multitude of sins,* in another sense than that in which it is said to do so in scripture. The revenues of the monastery, of which a large part was at his disposal, while they gave him the means of supplying his own very considerable expenses, afforded also those largesses which he bestowed among the peasantry, and with which he frequently relieved the distresses of the oppressed. If Prior Aymer rode hard in the chase, or remained long at the banquet,—if Prior Aymer was seen, at the early peep of dawn, to enter the postern of the abbey, as he glided home from some rendezvous which had occupied the hours of darkness, men only shrugged up their shoulders, and reconciled themselves to his irregularities, by recollecting that the same were practised by many of his brethren who had no redeeming qualities whatsoever to atone for them. Prior Aymer, therefore, and his character, were well known to our Saxon serfs, who made their rude obeisance, and received his '*benedicite, mes filz,*'* in return.

But the singular appearance of his companion and his attendants, arrested their attention and excited their wonder, and they could scarcely attend to the Prior of Jorvaulx' question, when he demanded if they knew of any place of harbourage in the vicinity; so much were they surprised at the half monastic, half military appearance of the swarthy stranger, and at the uncouth dress and arms of his Eastern attendants. It is probable, too, that the language in which the benediction was conferred, and the information asked, sounded ungracious, though not probably unintelligible, in the ears of the Saxon peasants.

'I asked you, my children,' said the Prior, raising his voice, and using the lingua Franca, or mixed language, in which the Norman and Saxon races conversed with each other, 'if there be in this neighbourhood any good man, who, for the love of God, and devotion to Mother Church, will give two of her humblest servants, with their train, a night's hospitality and refreshment?'

This he spoke with a tone of conscious importance, which formed a strong contrast to the modest terms which he thought it proper to employ.

'Two of the humblest servants of Mother Church!' repeated Wamba to himself,—but, fool as he was, taking care not to make his observation audible; 'I should like to see her seneschals,* her chief butlers, and her other principal domestics!'

After this internal commentary on the Prior's speech, he raised his eyes, and replied to the question which had been put.

'If the reverend fathers,' he said, 'loved good cheer and soft lodging, few miles of riding would carry them to the Priory of Brinxworth, where their quality could not but secure them the most honourable reception; or if they preferred spending a penitential evening, they might turn down yonder wild glade, which would bring them to the hermitage of Copmanhurst, where a pious anchoret would make them sharers for the night of the shelter of his roof and the benefit of his prayers.'

The Prior shook his head at both proposals.

'Mine honest friend', said he, 'if the jangling of thy bells had not dizzied thine understanding, thou mightst know *Clericus clericum non decimat;** that is to say, we churchmen do not exhaust each other's hospitality, but rather require that of the laity, giving them thus an opportunity to serve God in honouring and relieving his appointed servants.'

'It is true,' replied Wamba, 'that I, being but an ass, am, nevertheless, honoured to bear the bells as well as your reverence's mule; notwithstanding, I did conceive that the charity of Mother Church and her servants might be said, with other charity, to begin at home.'

'A truce to thine insolence, fellow,' said the armed rider, breaking in on his prattle with a high and stern voice, 'and tell us, if thou canst, the road to——How call'd you your Franklin, Prior Aymer?'

'Cedric,' answered the Prior; 'Cedric the Saxon.—Tell me, good fellow, are we near his dwelling, and can you show us the road?'

'The road will be uneasy to find,' answered Gurth, who broke silence for the first time, 'and the family of Cedric retire early to rest.'

'Tush,* tell not me, fellow!' said the military rider; ''tis easy for them to arise and supply the wants of travellers such as we are, who will not stoop to beg the hospitality which we have a right to command.'

'I know not,' said Gurth, sullenly, 'if I should show the way to my master's house, to those who demand as a right, the shelter which most are fain to ask as a favour.'

'Do you dispute with me, slave!' said the soldier; and, setting spurs to his horse, he caused him make a demivolte* across the path, raising at the same time the riding rod which he held in his hand, with a purpose of chastising what he considered as the insolence of the peasant.

Gurth darted at him a savage and revengeful scowl, and with a fierce, yet hesitating motion, laid his hand on the haft of his knife; but the interference of Prior Aymer, who pushed his mule betwixt his companion and the swineherd, prevented the meditated violence.

'Nay, by St Mary, brother Brian, you must not think you are now in Palestine, predominating over heathen Turks and infidel Saracens; we islanders love not blows, save those of holy Church, who chasteneth whom she loveth.*—Tell me, good fellow,' said he to Wamba, and seconded his speech by a small piece of silver coin, 'the way to Cedric the Saxon's; you cannot be ignorant of it, and it is your duty to direct the wanderer even when his character is less sanctified than ours.'

'In truth, venerable father,' answered the Jester, 'the Saracen head of your right reverend companion has frightened out of mine the way home—I am not sure I shall get there to-night myself.'

'Tush,' said the Abbot, 'thou canst tell us if thou wilt. This reverend brother has been all his life engaged in fighting among the Saracens for the recovery of the Holy Sepulchre; he is of the order of Knights Templars,* whom you may have heard of; he is half a monk, half a soldier.'

'If he is but half a monk,' said the Jester, 'he should not be wholly unreasonable with those whom he meets upon the road, even if they should be in no hurry to answer questions that no way concern them.'

'I forgive thy wit,' replied the Abbot, 'on condition thou wilt show me the way to Cedric's mansion.'

'Well, then,' answered Wamba, 'your reverences must hold on this path till you come to a sunken cross, of which scarce a cubit's length remains above ground; then take the path to the left, for there are four which meet at Sunken Cross, and I trust your reverences will obtain shelter before the storm comes on.'

The Abbot thanked his sage adviser; and the cavalcade, setting spurs to their horses, rode on as men do who wish to reach their inn before the bursting of a night-storm. As their horses' hoofs died away, Gurth said to his companion, 'If they follow thy wise direction, the reverend fathers will hardly reach Rotherwood this night.'

'No,' said the Jester, grinning, 'but they may reach Sheffield if they have good luck, and that is as fit a place for them. I am not so bad a woodsman as to show the dog where the deer lies, if I have no mind he should chase him.'

'Thou art right,' said Gurth; 'it were ill that Aymer saw the Lady Rowena; and it were worse, it may be, for Cedric to quarrel, as is most likely he would, with this military monk. But, like good servants, let us hear and see, and say nothing.'

We return to the riders, who had soon left the bondsmen far behind them, and who maintained the following conversation in the Norman-French language, usually employed by the superior classes, with the exception of the few who were still inclined to boast their Saxon descent.

'What mean these fellows by their capricious insolence?' said the Templar to the Cistercian, 'and why did you prevent me from chastising it?'

'Marry, brother Brian,' replied the Prior, 'touching the one of them, it were hard for me to render a reason for a fool speaking according to his folly;* and the other churl is of that savage, fierce, intractable race, some of whom, as I have often told you, are still to be found among the descendants of the conquered Saxons, and whose supreme pleasure it is to testify, by all means in their power, their aversion to their conquerors.'

'I would soon have beat him into courtesy,' observed Brian; 'I am accustomed to deal with such spirits: our Turkish captives are as fierce and intractable as Odin* himself could have been; yet two months in my household, under the management of my master of the slaves, has made them humble, submissive, serviceable, and observant of your will. Marry, sir, you must beware of the poison and the dagger; for they use either with free will when you give them the slightest opportunity.'

'Ay, but,' answered Prior Aymer, 'every land has its own manners and fashions; and, besides that beating this fellow could procure us no information respecting the road to Cedric's house, it would have been sure to have established a quarrel betwixt you and him had we found our way thither. Remember what I told you; this wealthy Franklin is proud, fierce, jealous, and irritable; a withstander of the nobility, and even of his neighbours, Reginald Front-de-Bœuf, and Philip Malvoisin, who are no babes to strive with. He stands up so sternly for the privileges of his race, and is so proud of his uninterrupted descent from

Hereward, a renowned champion of the Heptarchy,* that he is universally called Cedric the Saxon; and makes a boast of his belonging to a people from whom many others endeavour to hide their descent, lest they should encounter a share of the *vae victis*,* or severities imposed upon the vanquished.'

'Prior Aymer,' said the Templar, 'you are a man of gallantry, learned in the study of beauty, and as expert as a troubadour in all matters concerning the arrets of love;* but I shall expect much beauty in this celebrated Rowena, to counterbalance the self-denial and forbearance which I must exert, if I am to court the favour of such a seditious churl as you have described her father Cedric.'

'Cedric is not her father,' replied the Prior, 'and is but of remote relation; she is descended from higher blood than even he pretends to, and is but distantly connected with him by birth. Her guardian, however, he is, self-constituted as I believe; but his ward is as dear to him as if she were his own child. Of her beauty you shall soon be judge; and if the purity of her complexion, and the majestic, yet soft expression of a mild blue eye, do not chase from your memory the black-tressed girls of Palestine, ay, or the houris of old Mahound's paradise,* I am an infidel, and no true son of the church.'

'Should your boasted beauty,' said the Templar, 'be weighed in the balance and found wanting,* you know our wager?'

'My gold collar,' answered the Prior, 'against ten butts of Chian wine;—they are mine as securely as if they were already in the convent vaults, under the key of old Dennis the cellarer.'

'And I am myself to be judge,' said the Templar, 'and I am only to be convicted on my own admission, that I have seen no maiden so beautiful since Pentecost was a twelvemonth. Ran it not so?—Prior, your collar is in danger; I will wear it over my gorget in the lists of Ashby-de-la-Zouche.'

'Win it fairly,' said the Prior, 'and wear it as ye will; I will trust your giving true response, on your word as a knight and as a churchman. Yet, brother, take my advice, and file your tongue to a little more courtesy than your habits of predominating over infidel captives and Eastern bondsmen have accustomed you. Cedric the Saxon, if offended,—and he is noway slack in taking offence,—is a man who, without respect to your knighthood, my high office, or the sanctity of either, would clear his house of us, and send us to lodge with the larks, though the hour were midnight. And be careful how you look on Rowena, whom he cherishes with the most jealous care; an he take the least alarm in that quarter we are but lost men. It is said he banished his only son from his family for lifting his eyes in the way of affection towards this beauty, who may be worshipped, it seems, at a distance, but is not to be approached with other thoughts than such as we bring to the shrine of the Blessed Virgin.'

'Well, you have said enough,' answered the Templar; 'I will for a night put on the needful restraint, and deport me as meekly as a maiden;* but as for the fear of his expelling us by violence, myself and squires, with Hamet and Abdalla, will warrant you against that disgrace. Doubt not that we shall be strong enough to make good our quarters.'

'We must not let it come so far,' answered the Prior; 'but here is the clown's sunken cross, and the night is so dark that we can hardly see which of the roads we are to follow. He bid us turn, I think, to the left.'

'To the right,' said Brian, 'to the best of my remembrance.'

'To the left, certainly, the left; I remember his pointing with his wooden sword.'

'Ay, but he held his sword in his left hand, and so pointed across his body with it,' said the Templar.

Each maintained his opinion with sufficient obstinacy, as is usual in all such cases; the attendants were appealed to, but they had not been near enough to hear Wamba's directions. At length Brian remarked, what had at first escaped him in the twilight; 'Here is some one either asleep, or lying dead at the foot of this cross—Hugo, stir him with the butt-end of thy lance.'

This was no sooner done than the figure arose, exclaiming in good French, 'Whosoever thou art, it is discourteous in you to disturb my thoughts.'

'We did but wish to ask you,' said the Prior, 'the road to Rotherwood, the abode of Cedric the Saxon.'

'I myself am bound thither,' replied the stranger; 'and if I had a horse, I would be your guide, for the way is somewhat intricate, though perfectly well known to me.'

'Thou shalt have both thanks and reward, my friend,' said the Prior, 'if thou wilt bring us to Cedric's in safety.'

And he caused one of his attendants to mount his own led horse, and give that upon which he had hitherto ridden to the stranger, who was to serve for a guide.

Their conductor pursued an opposite road from that which Wamba had recommended, for the purpose of misleading them. The path soon led deeper into the woodland, and crossed more than one brook, the approach to which was rendered perilous by the marshes through which it flowed; but the stranger seemed to know, as if by instinct, the soundest ground and the safest points of passage; and by dint of caution and attention, brought the party safely into a wider avenue than any they had yet seen; and, pointing to a large low irregular building at the upper extremity, he said to the Prior, 'Yonder is Rotherwood, the dwelling of Cedric the Saxon.'

This was a joyful intimation to Aymer, whose nerves were none of the strongest, and who had suffered such agitation and alarm in the course of passing through the dangerous bogs, that he had not yet had the curiosity to ask his guide a single question. Finding himself now at his ease and near shelter, his curiosity began to awake, and he demanded of the guide who and what he was.

'A Palmer,* just returned from the Holy Land,' was the answer.

'You had better have tarried there to fight for the recovery of the Holy Sepulchre,' said the Templar.

'True, Reverend Sir Knight,' answered the Palmer, to whom the appearance of the Templar seemed perfectly familiar; 'but when those who are under oath to recover the holy city, are found travelling at such a distance from the scene of their duties, can you wonder that a peaceful peasant like me should decline the task which they have abandoned?'

The Templar would have made an angry reply, but was interrupted by the Prior, who again expressed his astonishment, that their guide, after such long absence, should be so perfectly acquainted with the passes of the forest.

'I was born a native of these parts,' answered their guide, and

as he made the reply they stood before the mansion of Cedric;—
a low irregular building, containing several court-yards or
enclosures, extending over a considerable space of ground, and
which, though its size argued the inhabitant to be a person of
wealth, differed entirely from the tall, turretted, and castellated
buildings in which the Norman nobility resided, and which
had become the universal style of architecture throughout
England.

Rotherwood was not, however, without defences; no habitation, in that disturbed period, could have been so, without the
risk of being plundered and burnt before the next morning. A
deep fosse, or ditch, was drawn round the whole building, and
filled with water from a neighbouring stream. A double stockade,
or palisade, composed of pointed beams, which the adjacent
forest supplied, defended the outer and inner bank of the trench.
There was an entrance from the west through the outer stockade,
which communicated by a drawbridge, with a similar opening in
the interior defences. Some precautions had been taken to place
those entrances under the protection of projecting angles, by
which they might be flanked in case of need by archers or
slingers.

Before this entrance the Templar wound his horn loudly; for
the rain, which had long threatened, began now to descend with
great violence.

CHAPTER III

Then (sad relief!) from the bleak coast that hears
The German Ocean roar, deep-blooming, strong,
And yellow-hair'd, the blue-eyed Saxon came.

THOMSON's *Liberty**

IN a hall, the height of which was greatly disproportioned to its
extreme length and width, a long oaken table formed of planks
rough-hewn from the forest, and which had scarcely received
any polish, stood ready prepared for the evening meal of Cedric
the Saxon. The roof, composed of beams and rafters, had
nothing to divide the apartment from the sky excepting the
planking and thatch; there was a huge fireplace at either end of
the hall, but as the chimneys were constructed in a very clumsy
manner, at least as much of the smoke found its way into the
apartment as escaped by the proper vent. The constant vapour
which this occasioned, had polished the rafters and beams of the
low-browed hall, by encrusting them with a black varnish of
soot. On the sides of the apartment hung implements of war and
of the chase, and there were at each corner folding doors, which
gave access to other parts of the extensive building.

The other appointments of the mansion partook of the rude
simplicity of the Saxon period, which Cedric piqued himself
upon maintaining. The floor was composed of earth mixed with
lime, trodden into a hard substance, such as is often employed in
flooring our modern barns. For about one quarter of the length
of the apartment, the floor was raised by a step, and this space,
which was called the dais, was occupied only by the principal
members of the family, and visitors of distinction. For this purpose, a table richly covered with scarlet cloth was placed trans-
versely across the platform, from the middle of which ran the
longer and lower board, at which the domestics and inferior
persons fed, down towards the bottom of the hall. The whole
resembled the form of the letter T, or some of those ancient
dinner-tables, which, arranged on the same principles, may be
still seen in the antique Colleges of Oxford or Cambridge. Mass-

ive chairs and settles of carved oak were placed upon the dais, and over these seats and the more elevated table was fastened a canopy of cloth, which served in some degree to protect the dignitaries who occupied that distinguished station from the weather, and especially from the rain, which in some places found its way through the ill-constructed roof.

The walls of this upper end of the hall, as far as the dais extended, were covered with hangings or curtains, and upon the floor there was a carpet, both of which were adorned with some attempts at tapestry, or embroidery, executed with brilliant or rather gaudy colouring. Over the lower range of table, the roof, as we have noticed, had no covering; the rough plastered walls were left bare, and the rude earthen floor was uncarpeted; the board was uncovered by a cloth, and rude massive benches supplied the place of chairs.

In the centre of the upper table, were placed two chairs more elevated than the rest, for the master and mistress of the family, who presided over the scene of hospitality, and from doing so derived their Saxon title of honour, which signifies 'the Dividers of Bread.'*

To each of these chairs was added a footstool, curiously carved and inlaid with ivory, which mark of distinction was peculiar to them. One of these seats was at present occupied by Cedric the Saxon, who, though but in rank a thane, or, as the Normans called him, a Franklin, felt, at the delay of his evening meal, an irritable impatience, which might have become an alderman, whether of ancient or of modern times.

It appeared, indeed, from the countenance of this proprietor, that he was of a frank, but hasty and choleric temper. He was not above the middle stature, but broad-shouldered, long-armed, and powerfully made, like one accustomed to endure the fatigue of war or of the chase; his face was broad, with large blue eyes, open and frank features, fine teeth, and a well formed head, altogether expressive of that sort of good-humour which often lodges with a sudden and hasty temper. Pride and jealousy there was in his eye, for his life had been spent in asserting rights which were constantly liable to invasion; and the prompt, fiery, and resolute disposition of the man, had been kept constantly upon the alert by the circumstances of his situation. His long yellow hair was equally divided on the top his head and upon his brow, and combed down on each side to the length of his shoulders; it had but little tendency to grey, although Cedric was approaching to his sixtieth year.

His dress was a tunic of forest green, furred at the throat and cuffs with what was called minever; a kind of fur inferior in quality to ermine, and formed, it is believed, of the skin of the grey squirrel.* This doublet hung unbuttoned over a close dress of scarlet which sate tight to his body; he had breeches of the same, but they did not reach below the lower part of the thigh, leaving the knee exposed. His feet had sandals of the same fashion with the peasants, but of finer materials, and secured in the front with golden clasps. He had bracelets of gold upon his arms, and a broad collar of the same precious metal around his neck. About his waist he wore a richly studded belt, in which was stuck a short straight two-edged sword, with a sharp point, so disposed as to hang almost perpendicularly by his side. Behind his seat was hung a scarlet cloth cloak lined with fur, and a cap of the same materials richly embroidered, which completed the dress of the opulent landholder when he chose to go forth. A short boar-spear, with a broad and bright steel head, also reclined against the back of his chair, which served him, when he walked abroad, for the purposes of a staff or of a weapon, as chance might require.

Several domestics, whose dress held various proportions betwixt the richness of their master's, and the coarse and simple attire of Gurth the swine-herd, watched the looks and waited the commands of the Saxon dignitary. Two or three servants of a superior order stood behind their master upon the dais; the rest occupied the lower part of the hall. Other attendants there were of a different description; two or three large and shaggy greyhounds, such as were then employed in hunting the stag and wolf; as many slow-hounds of a large bony breed, with thick necks, large heads, and long ears; and one or two of the smaller dogs, now called terriers,* which waited with impatience the arrival of the supper; but, with the sagacious knowledge of physiognomy peculiar to their race, forbore to intrude upon the moody silence of their master, apprehensive probably of a small white truncheon which lay by Cedric's trencher, for the purpose of repelling the advances of his four-legged dependants. One grisly old wolf-dog alone, with the liberty of an indulged favourite, had planted himself close by the chair of state, and occasionally ventured to solicit notice by putting his large hairy head upon his master's knee, or pushing his nose into his hand. Even he was repelled by the stern command, 'Down, Balder,* down! I am not in the humour for foolery.'

In fact, Cedric, as we have observed, was in no very placid state of mind. The Lady Rowena, who had been absent to attend an evening mass at a distant church, had but just returned, and was changing her garments, which had been wetted by the storm. There were as yet no tidings of Gurth and his charge, which should long since have been driven home from the forest; and such was the insecurity of the period, as to render it probable that the delay might be explained by some depredation of the outlaws, with whom the adjacent forest abounded, or by the violence of some neighbouring baron, whose consciousness of strength made him equally negligent of the laws of property. The matter was of consequence, for great part of the domestic wealth of the Saxon proprietors consisted in numerous herds of swine, especially in forest land, where those animals easily found their food.

Besides these subjects of anxiety, the Saxon thane was impatient for the presence of his favourite clown Wamba, whose jests, such as they were, served for a sort of seasoning to his evening meal, and to the deep draughts of ale and wine with which he was in the habit of accompanying it. Add to all this, Cedric had fasted since noon, and his usual supper hour was long past, a cause of irritation common to country squires, both in ancient and modern times. His displeasure was expressed in broken sentences, partly muttered to himself, partly addressed to the domestics who stood around; and particularly to his cupbearer, who offered him from time to time, as a sedative, a silver goblet filled with wine—'Why tarries the Lady Rowena?'

'She is but changing her head-gear,' replied a female attendant, with as much confidence as the favourite lady's-maid usually answers the master of a modern family; 'you would not wish her to sit down to the banquet in her hood and kirtle? and no lady within the shire can be quicker in arraying herself than my mistress.'

This undeniable argument produced a sort of acquiescent umph! on the part of the Saxon, with the addition, 'I wish her devotion may choose fair weather for the next visit to St John's Kirk;—but what, in the name of ten devils,' continued he, turning to the cupbearer, and raising his voice, as if happy to have found a channel into which he might divert his indignation without fear or control—'what, in the name of ten devils, keeps Gurth so long a-field? I suppose we shall have an evil account of the herd; he was wont to be a faithful and cautious drudge, and I had destined him for something better; perchance I might even have made him one of my warders.'[10]

Oswald the cupbearer modestly suggested, 'that it was scarce an hour since the tolling of the curfew;' an ill-chosen apology, since it turned upon a topic so harsh to Saxon ears.

'The foul fiend,' exclaimed Cedric, 'take the curfew-bell, and the tyrannical bastard by whom it was devised, and the heartless slave who names it with a Saxon tongue to a Saxon ear! The curfew!'* he added, pausing, 'ay, the curfew; which compels true men to extinguish their lights, that thieves and robbers may work their deeds in darkness!—Ay, the curfew;—Reginald Front-de-Bœuf and Philip de Malvoisin know the use of the curfew as well as William the Bastard himself, or e'er a Norman adventurer that fought at Hastings. I shall hear, I guess, that my property has been swept off to save from starving the hungry banditti, whom they cannot support but by theft and robbery. My faithful slave is murdered, and my goods are taken for a prey—and Wamba—where is Wamba? Said not some one he had gone forth with Gurth?'

Oswald replied in the affirmative.

'Ay? why this is better and better! he is carried off too, the Saxon fool, to serve the Norman lord. Fools are we all indeed that serve them, and fitter subjects for their scorn and laughter, than if we were born with but half our wits. But I will be avenged,' he added, starting from his chair in impatience at the supposed injury, and catching hold of his boar-spear; 'I will go with my complaint to the great council; I have friends, I have

followers—man to man will I appeal the Norman to the lists; let
him come in his plate and his mail, and all that can render
cowardice bold; I have sent such a javelin as this through a
stronger fence than three of their war shields!—Haply they think
me old; but they shall find, alone and childless as I am, the blood
of Hereward is in the veins of Cedric.—Ah, Wilfred, Wilfred!'*
he exclaimed in a lower tone, 'couldst thou have ruled thine
unreasonable passion, thy father had not been left in his age like
the solitary oak, that throws out its shattered and unprotected
branches against the full sweep of the tempest!' The reflection
seemed to conjure into sadness his irritated feelings. Replacing
his javelin, he resumed his seat, bent his looks downward, and
appeared to be absorbed in melancholy reflection.

From his musing, Cedric was suddenly awakened by the blast
of a horn, which was replied to by the clamorous yells and
barking of all the dogs in the hall, and some twenty or thirty
which were quartered in other parts of the building. It cost some
exercise of the white truncheon, well seconded by the exertions
of the domestics, to silence this canine clamour.

'To the gate, knaves!' said the Saxon, hastily, as soon as the
tumult was so much appeased that the dependants could hear his
voice. 'See what tidings that horn tells us of—to announce, I
ween, some hership* and robbery which has been done upon my
lands.'

Returning in less than three minutes, a warder announced,
'that the Prior Aymer of Jorvaulx, and the good knight Brian de
Bois-Guilbert, commander of the valiant and venerable order of
Knights Templars, with a small retinue, requested hospitality
and lodging for the night, being on their way to a tournament*
which was to be held not far from Ashby-de-la-Zouche, on the
second day from the present.'

'Aymer, the Prior Aymer? Brian de Bois-Guilbert?'—muttered Cedric; 'Normans both;—but Norman or Saxon, the
hospitality of Rotherwood must not be impeached; they are
welcome, since they have chosen to halt—more welcome would
they have been to have ridden further on their way—But it were
unworthy to murmur for a night's lodging and a night's food; in
the quality of guests, at least, even Normans must suppress their
insolence.—Go, Hundebert,' he added, to a sort of major-domo

who stood behind him with a white wand; 'take six of the attendants, and introduce the strangers to the guests' lodging. Look
after their horses and mules, and see their train lack nothing. Let
them have change of vestments if they require it, and fire, and
water to wash, and wine and ale; and bid the cooks add what they
hastily can to our evening meal; and let it be put on the board
when those strangers are ready to share it. Say to them,
Hundebert, that Cedric would himself bid them welcome, but he
is under a vow never to step more than three steps from the dais
of his own hall to meet any who shares not the blood of Saxon
royalty. Begone! see them carefully tended; let them not say in
their pride, the Saxon churl has shown at once his poverty and
his avarice.'

The major-domo departed with several attendants, to execute
his master's commands. 'The Prior Aymer!' repeated Cedric,
looking to Oswald, 'the brother, if I mistake not, of Giles de
Mauleverer, now lord of Middleham?'

Oswald made a respectful sign of assent. 'His brother sits in
the seat, and usurps the patrimony, of a better race, the race of
Ulfgar of Middleham; but what Norman lord doth not the same?
This Prior is, they say, a free and jovial priest, who loves the
wine-cup and the bugle-horn better than bell and book: Good;
let him come, he shall be welcome. How named ye the Templar?'

'Brian de Bois-Guilbert.'

'Bois-Guilbert?' said Cedric, still in the musing, half-arguing
tone, which the habit of living among dependants had accustomed him to employ, and which resembled a man who talks to
himself rather than to those around him—'Bois-Guilbert?
that name has been spread wide both for good and evil. They say
he is valiant as the bravest of his order; but stained with their
usual vices, pride, arrogance, cruelty, and voluptuousness; a
hard-hearted man, who knows neither fear of earth, nor awe of
heaven. So say the few warriors who have returned from Palestine.—Well; it is but for one night; he shall be welcome too.—
Oswald, broach the oldest wine-cask; place the best mead,
the mightiest ale, the richest morat, the most sparkling cider,
the most odoriferous pigments,[11] upon the board; fill the largest
horns—Templars and Abbots love good wines and good
measure.—Elgitha, let thy Lady Rowena know we shall not

this night expect her in the hall, unless such be her especial pleasure.'

'But it will be her especial pleasure,' answered Elgitha, with great readiness, 'for she is ever desirous to hear the latest news from Palestine.'

Cedric darted at the forward damsel a glance of hasty resentment; but Rowena, and whatever belonged to her, were privileged and secure from his anger. He only replied, 'Silence, maiden; thy tongue outruns thy discretion.* Say my message to thy mistress, and let her do her pleasure. Here, at least, the descendant of Alfred still reigns a princess.' Elgitha left the apartment.

'Palestine!' repeated the Saxon; 'Palestine! how many ears are turned to the tales which dissolute crusaders, or hypocritical pilgrims, bring from that fatal land! I too might ask—I too might enquire—I too might listen with a beating heart to fables which the wily strollers devise to cheat us into hospitality—but no— The son who has disobeyed me is no longer mine; nor will I concern myself more for his fate than for that of the most worthless among the millions that ever shaped the cross on their shoulder, rushed into excess and blood-guiltiness, and called it an accomplishment of the will of God.'

He knit his brows, and fixed his eyes for an instant on the ground; as he raised them, the folding doors at the bottom of the hall were cast wide, and, preceded by the major-domo with his wand, and four domestics bearing blazing torches, the guests of the evening entered the apartment.

CHAPTER IV

With sheep and shaggy goats the porkers bled,
And the proud steer was on the marble spread;
With fire prepared, they deal the morsels round,
Wine rosy bright the brimming goblets crown'd.

. . . . .

Disposed apart, Ulysses shares the treat;
A trivet table and ignobler seat,
The Prince assigns——

Odyssey, Book 21*

THE Prior Aymer had taken the opportunity afforded him, of changing his riding robe for one of yet more costly materials, over which he wore a cope curiously embroidered. Besides the massive golden signet ring, which marked his ecclesiastical dignity, his fingers, though contrary to the canon, were loaded with precious gems; his sandals were of the finest leather which was imported from Spain; his beard trimmed to as small dimensions as his order would possibly permit, and his shaven crown concealed by a scarlet cap richly embroidered.

The appearance of the Knight Templar was also changed; and, though less studiously bedecked with ornament, his dress was as rich, and his appearance far more commanding, than that of his companion. He had exchanged his shirt of mail for an under tunic of dark purple silk, garnished with furs, over which flowed his long robe of spotless white, in ample folds. The eight-pointed cross of his order was cut on the shoulder of his mantle in black velvet. The high cap no longer invested his brows, which were only shaded by short and thick curled hair of a raven blackness, corresponding to his unusually swart complexion. Nothing could be more gracefully majestic than his step and manner, had they not been marked by a predominant air of haughtiness, easily acquired by the exercise of unresisted authority.

These two dignified persons were followed by their respective attendants, and at a more humble distance by their guide, whose figure had nothing more remarkable than it derived from the usual weeds of a pilgrim. A cloak or mantle, of coarse black serge enveloped his whole body. It was in shape something like the cloak of a modern hussar, having similar flaps for covering the arms, and was called a *Sclaveyn*,* or *Sclavonian*. Coarse sandals, bound with thongs, on his bare feet; a broad and shadowy hat, with cockle-shells* stitched on its brim, and a long staff shod with iron, to the upper end of which was attached a branch of palm, completed the palmer's attire. He followed modestly the last of the train which entered the hall, and, observing that the lower table scarce afforded room sufficient for the domestics of Cedric and the retinue of his guests, he withdrew to a settle placed beside and almost under one of the large chimneys, and seemed to employ himself in drying his garments, until the retreat of some one should make room at the board, or the hospitality of the steward should supply him with refreshments in the place he had chosen apart.

Cedric rose to receive his guests with an air of dignified hospitality, and, descending from the dais, or elevated part of his hall, made three steps towards them, and then awaited their approach.

'I grieve,' he said, 'reverend Prior, that my vow binds me to advance no farther upon this floor of my fathers, even to receive such guests as you, and this valiant Knight of the Holy Temple. But my steward has expounded to you the cause of my seeming discourtesy. Let me also pray, that you will excuse my speaking to you in my native language, and that you will reply in the same if your knowledge of it permits; if not, I sufficiently understand Norman to follow your meaning.'

'Vows,' said the Abbot, 'must be unloosed, worthy Franklin, or permit me rather to say, worthy Thane, though the title is antiquated. Vows are the knots which tie us to Heaven—they are the cords which bind the sacrifice to the horns of the altar,*— and are therefore,—as I said before,—to be unloosened and discharged, unless our holy Mother Church shall pronounce the contrary. And respecting language, I willingly hold communication in that spoken by my respected grandmother, Hilda of Middleham, who died in odour of sanctity, little short, if we may presume to say so, of her glorious namesake, the blessed Saint Hilda of Whitby,* God be gracious to her soul!'

When the Prior had ceased what he meant as a conciliatory harangue, his companion said briefly and emphatically, 'I speak ever French, the language of King Richard and his nobles; but I understand English sufficiently to communicate with the natives of the country.'

Cedric darted at the speaker one of those hasty and impatient glances, which comparisons between the two rival nations seldom failed to call forth; but, recollecting the duties of hospitality, he suppressed further show of resentment, and, motioning with his hand, caused his guests to assume two seats a little lower than his own, but placed close beside him, and gave a signal that the evening meal should be placed upon the board.

While the attendants hastened to obey Cedric's commands, his eye distinguished Gurth the swineherd, who, with his companion Wamba, had just entered the hall. 'Send these loitering knaves up hither,' said the Saxon, impatiently. And when the culprits came before the dais,—'How comes it, villains! that you have loitered abroad so late as this? Hast thou brought home thy charge, sirrah Gurth, or hast thou left them to robbers and marauders?'

'The herd is safe, so please ye,' said Gurth.

'But it does not please me, thou knave,' said Cedric, 'that I should be made to suppose otherwise for two hours, and sit here devising vengeance against my neighbours for wrongs they have not done me. I tell thee, shackles and the prison-house shall punish the next offence of this kind.'

Gurth, knowing his master's irritable temper, attempted no exculpation; but the Jester, who could presume upon Cedric's tolerance, by virtue of his privileges as a fool, replied for them both; 'In troth, uncle Cedric,* you are neither wise nor reasonable to-night.'

'How, sir?' said his master; 'you shall to the porter's lodge, and taste of the discipline there, if you give your foolery such license.'

'First let your wisdom tell me,' said Wamba, 'is it just and reasonable to punish one person for the fault of another?'

'Certainly not, fool,' answered Cedric.

'Then why should you shackle poor Gurth, uncle, for the fault of his dog Fangs? for I dare be sworn we lost not a minute by the way, when we had got our herd together, which Fangs did not manage until we heard the vesper-bell.'

'Then hang up Fangs,' said Cedric, turning hastily towards the swineherd, 'if the fault is his, and get thee another dog.'

'Under favour, uncle,' said the Jester, 'that were still somewhat on the bow-hand of fair justice;* for it was no fault of Fangs that he was lame and could not gather the herd, but the fault of those that struck off two of his fore-claws, an operation for which, if the poor fellow had been consulted, he would scarce have given his voice.'

'And who dared to lame an animal which belonged to my bondsman?' said the Saxon, kindling in wrath.

'Marry, that did old Hubert,' said Wamba, 'Sir Philip de Malvoisin's keeper of the chase. He caught Fangs strolling in the forest, and said he chased the deer contrary to his master's right, as warden of the walk.'

'The foul fiend take Malvoisin,' answered the Saxon, 'and his keeper both! I will teach them that the wood was disforested in terms of the great Forest Charter. But enough of this. Go to, knave, go to thy place—and thou, Gurth, get thee another dog, and should the keeper dare to touch it, I will mar his archery; the curse of a coward on my head, if I strike not off the forefinger of his right hand!—he shall draw bowstring no more.—I crave your pardon, my worthy guests. I am beset here with neighbours that match your infidels, Sir Knight, in Holy Land. But your homely fare is before you; feed, and let welcome make amends for hard fare.'

The feast, however, which was spread upon the board, needed no apologies from the lord of the mansion. Swine's flesh, dressed in several modes, appeared on the lower part of the board, as also that of fowls, deer, goats, and hares, and various kinds of fish, together with huge loaves and cakes of bread, and sundry confections made of fruits and honey. The smaller sorts of wild-fowl, of which there was abundance, were not served up in platters, but brought in upon small wooden spits or broaches, and offered by the pages and domestics who bore them, to each guest in succession, who cut from them such a portion as he pleased. Beside each person of rank was placed a goblet of silver; the lower board was accommodated with large drinking horns.

When the repast was about to commence, the major-domo, or steward, suddenly raising his wand, said aloud,—'Forbear!— Place for the Lady Rowena.' A side-door at the upper end of the hall now opened behind the banquet table, and Rowena, followed by four female attendants, entered the apartment. Cedric, though surprised, and perhaps not altogether agreeably so, at his ward appearing in public on this occasion, hastened to meet her, and to conduct her, with respectful ceremony, to the elevated seat at his own right hand, appropriated to the lady of the mansion. All stood up to receive her; and, replying to their courtesy by a mute gesture of salutation, she moved gracefully forward to assume her place at the board. Ere she had time to do so, the Templar whispered to the Prior, 'I shall wear no collar of gold of yours at the tournament. The Chian wine is your own.'

'Said I not so?' answered the Prior; 'but check your raptures, the Franklin observes you.'

Unheeding this remonstrance, and accustomed only to act upon the immediate impulse of his own wishes, Brian de Bois-Guilbert kept his eyes riveted on the Saxon beauty, more striking perhaps to his imagination, because differing widely from those of the Eastern sultanas.

Formed in the best proportions of her sex, Rowena was tall in stature, yet not so much so as to attract observation on account of superior height. Her complexion was exquisitely fair, but the noble cast of her head and features prevented the insipidity which sometimes attaches to fair beauties. Her clear blue eye, which sate enshrined beneath a graceful eyebrow of brown sufficiently marked to give expression to the forehead, seemed capable to kindle as well as melt, to command as well as to beseech. If mildness were the more natural expression of such a combination of features, it was plain, that in the present instance, the exercise of habitual superiority, and the reception of general homage, had given to the Saxon lady a loftier character, which mingled with and qualified that bestowed by nature. Her profuse hair, of a colour betwixt brown and flaxen, was arranged in a fanciful and graceful manner in numerous ringlets, to form which art had probably aided nature. These locks were braided with gems, and being worn at full length, intimated the noble birth and free-born condition of the maiden. A golden chain, to which was attached a small reliquary of the same metal, hung round her neck. She wore bracelets on her arms, which were bare. Her dress was an under-gown and kirtle of pale sea-green silk, over which hung a long loose robe, which reached to the ground, having very wide sleeves, which came down, however, very little below the elbow. This robe was crimson, and manufactured out of the very finest wool. A veil of silk, interwoven with gold, was attached to the upper part of it, which could be, at the wearer's pleasure, either drawn over the face and bosom after the Spanish fashion, or disposed as a sort of drapery round the shoulders.

When Rowena perceived the Knight Templar's eyes bent on her with an ardour, that, compared with the dark caverns under which they moved, gave them the effect of lighted charcoal, she drew with dignity the veil around her face, as an intimation that the determined freedom of his glance was disagreeable. Cedric saw the motion and its cause. 'Sir Templar,' said he, 'the cheeks of our Saxon maidens have seen too little of the sun to enable them to bear the fixed glance of a crusader.'

'If I have offended,' replied Sir Brian, 'I crave your pardon— that is, I crave the Lady Rowena's pardon—for my humility will carry me no lower.'

'The Lady Rowena,' said the Prior, 'has punished us all, in chastising the boldness of my friend. Let me hope she will be less cruel to the splendid train which are to meet at the tournament.'

'Our going thither,' said Cedric, 'is uncertain. I love not these vanities, which were unknown to my fathers when England was free.'

'Let us hope, nevertheless,' said the Prior, 'our company may determine you to travel thitherward; when the roads are so unsafe, the escort of Sir Brian de Bois-Guilbert is not to be despised.'

'Sir Prior,' answered the Saxon, 'wheresoever I have travelled in this land, I have hitherto found myself, with the assistance of my good sword and faithful followers, in no respect needful of other aid. At present, if we indeed journey to Ashby-de-la-Zouche, we do so with my noble neighbour and countryman, Athelstane of Coningsburgh, and with such a train as would set outlaws and feudal enemies at defiance.——I drink to you, Sir Prior, in this cup of wine, which I trust your taste will approve, and I thank you for your courtesy. Should you be so rigid in adhering to monastic rule,' he added, 'as to prefer your acid preparation of milk, I hope you will not strain courtesy to do me reason.'

'Nay,' said the Priest, laughing, 'it is only in our abbey that we confine ourselves to the *lac dulce* or the *lac acidum* either.* Conversing with the world, we use the world's fashion, and therefore I answer your pledge in this honest wine, and leave the weaker liquor to my lay-brother.'

'And I,' said the Templar, filling his goblet, 'drink wassail to the fair Rowena; for since her namesake introduced the word into England, has never been one more worthy of such a tribute. By my faith, I could pardon the unhappy Vortigern, had he half the cause that we now witness, for making shipwreck of his honour and his kingdom.'*

'I will spare your courtesy, Sir Knight,' said Rowena with dignity, and without unveiling herself; 'or rather I will tax it so far as to require of you the latest news from Palestine, a theme more agreeable to our English ears, than the compliments which your French breeding teaches.'

'I have little of importance to say, lady,' answered Sir Brian de Bois-Guilbert, 'excepting the confirmed tidings of a truce with Saladin.'*

He was interrupted by Wamba, who had taken his appropriated seat upon a chair, the back of which was decorated with two ass's ears, and which was placed about two steps behind that of his master, who, from time to time, supplied him with victuals from his own trencher; a favour, however, which the Jester shared with the favourite dogs, of whom, as we have already noticed, there were several in attendance. Here sat Wamba, with a small table before him, his heels tucked up against the bar of the chair, his cheeks sucked up so as to make his jaws resemble a pair of nut-crackers, and his eyes half-shut, yet watching with alertness every opportunity to exercise his licensed foolery.

'These truces with the infidels,' he exclaimed, without caring how suddenly he interrupted the stately Templar, 'make an old man of me!'

'Go to, knave, how so?' said Cedric, his features prepared to receive favourably the expected jest.

'Because,' answered Wamba, 'I remember three of them in my day, each of which was to endure for the course of fifty years; so that, by computation, I must be at least a hundred and fifty years old.'

'I will warrant you against dying of old age, however,' said the Templar, who now recognised his friend of the forest; 'I will assure you from all deaths but a violent one, if you give such directions to wayfarers, as you did this night to the Prior and me.'

'How, sirrah!' said Cedric, 'misdirect travellers? We must have you whipt; you are at least as much rogue as fool.'

'I pray thee, uncle,' answered the Jester, 'let my folly for once protect my roguery. I did but make a mistake between my right hand and my left; and he might have pardoned a greater, who took a fool for his counsellor and guide.'

Conversation was here interrupted by the entrance of the porter's page, who announced that there was a stranger at the gate, imploring admittance and hospitality.

'Admit him,' said Cedric, 'be he who or what he may;—a night like that which roars without, compels even wild animals to herd with tame, and to seek the protection of man, their mortal foe, rather than perish by the elements. Let his wants be ministered to with all care—look to it, Oswald.'

And the steward left the banqueting hall to see the commands of his patron obeyed.

CHAPTER V

Hath not a Jew eyes? Hath not a Jew hands, organs,
dimensions, senses, affections, passions? Fed with the
same food, hurt with the same weapons, subject to the
same diseases, healed by the same means, warmed and
cooled by the same winter and summer, as a Christian is?

*Merchant of Venice**

OSWALD, returning, whispered into the ear of his master, 'It is
a Jew, who calls himself Isaac of York;* is it fit I should marshal
him into the hall?'

'Let Gurth do thine office, Oswald,' said Wamba with his
usual effrontery; 'the swineherd will be a fit usher to the Jew.'

'St Mary,' said the Abbot, crossing himself, 'an unbelieving
Jew, and admitted into this presence!'

'A dog Jew,' echoed the Templar, 'to approach a defender of
the Holy Sepulchre?'

'By my faith,' said Wamba, 'it would seem the Templars love
the Jews' inheritance better than they do their company.'

'Peace, my worthy guests,' said Cedric; 'my hospitality must
not be bounded by your dislikes. If Heaven bore with the whole
nation of stiff-necked unbelievers for more years than a layman
can number, we may endure the presence of one Jew for a few
hours. But I constrain no man to converse or to feed with him.—
Let him have a board and a morsel apart,—unless,' he said
smiling, 'these turban'd strangers will admit his society.'

'Sir Franklin,' answered the Templar, 'my Saracen slaves are
true Moslems, and scorn as much as any Christian to hold intercourse with a Jew.'

'Now, in faith,' said Wamba, 'I cannot see that the worshippers of Mahound and Termagaunt* have so greatly the advantage over the people once chosen of Heaven.'

'He shall sit with thee, Wamba,' said Cedric; 'the fool and the
knave will be well met.'

'The fool,' answered Wamba, raising the relics of a gammon of
bacon, 'will take care to erect a bulwark against the knave.'

'Hush,' said Cedric, 'for here he comes.'

Introduced with little ceremony, and advancing with fear and hesitation, and many a bow of deep humility, a tall thin old man, who, however, had lost by the habit of stooping much of his actual height, approached the lower end of the board. His features, keen and regular, with an aquiline nose, and piercing black eyes; his high and wrinkled forehead, and long grey hair and beard, would have been considered as handsome, had they not been the marks of a physiognomy peculiar to a race, which, during those dark ages, was alike detested by the credulous and prejudiced vulgar, and persecuted by the greedy and rapacious nobility, and who, perhaps, owing to that very hatred and persecution, had adopted a national character, in which there was much, to say the least, mean and unamiable.

The Jew's dress, which appeared to have suffered considerably from the storm, was a plain russet cloak of many folds, covering a dark purple tunic. He had large boots lined with fur, and a belt around his waist, which sustained a small knife, together with a case for writing materials, but no weapon. He wore a high square yellow cap of a peculiar fashion, assigned to his nation to distinguish them from Christians, and which he doffed with great humility at the door of the hall.

The reception of this person in the hall of Cedric the Saxon, was such as might have satisfied the most prejudiced enemy of the tribes of Israel. Cedric himself coldly nodded in answer to the Jew's repeated salutations, and signed to him to take place at the lower end of the table, where, however, no one offered to make room for him. On the contrary, as he passed along the file, casting a timid supplicating glance, and turning towards each of those who occupied the lower end of the board, the Saxon domestics squared their shoulders, and continued to devour their supper with great perseverance, paying not the least attention to the wants of the new guest. The attendants of the Abbot crossed themselves, with looks of pious horror, and the very heathen Saracens, as Isaac drew near them, curled up their whiskers with indignation, and laid their hands on their poniards, as if ready to rid themselves by the most desperate means from the apprehended contamination of his nearer approach.

Probably the same motives which induced Cedric to open his hall to this son of a rejected people, would have made him insist on his attendants receiving Isaac with more courtesy. But the Abbot had, at this moment, engaged him in a most interesting discussion on the breed and character of his favourite hounds, which he would not have interrupted for matters of much greater importance than that of a Jew going to bed supperless. While Isaac thus stood an outcast in the present society, like his people among the nations, looking in vain for welcome or resting place, the pilgrim who sat by the chimney took compassion upon him, and resigned his seat, saying briefly, 'Old man, my garments are dried, my hunger is appeased, thou art both wet and fasting.' So saying, he gathered together, and brought to a flame, the decaying brands which lay scattered on the ample hearth; took from the larger board a mess of pottage and seethed kid, placed it upon the small table at which he had himself supped, and, without waiting the Jew's thanks, went to the other side of the hall;— whether from unwillingness to hold more close communication with the object of his benevolence, or from a wish to draw near to the upper end of the table, seemed uncertain.

Had there been painters in those days capable to execute such a subject, the Jew, as he bent his withered form, and expanded his chilled and trembling hands over the fire, would have formed no bad emblematical personification of the Winter season. Having dispelled the cold, he turned eagerly to the smoking mess which was placed before him, and ate with a haste and an apparent relish, that seemed to betoken long abstinence from food.

Meanwhile the Abbot and Cedric continued their discourse upon hunting; the Lady Rowena seemed engaged in conversation with one of her attendant females; and the haughty Templar, whose eye seemed to wander from the Jew to the Saxon beauty, revolved in his mind thoughts which appeared deeply to interest him.

'I marvel, worthy Cedric,' said the Abbot, as their discourse proceeded, 'that, great as your predilection is for your own manly language, you do not receive the Norman-French into your favour, so far at least as the mystery of wood-craft and hunting is concerned. Surely no tongue is so rich in the various phrases which the field-sports demand, or furnishes means to the experienced woodman so well to express his jovial art.'

'Good Father Aymer,' said the Saxon, 'be it known to you, I care not for those over-sea refinements, without which I can well enough take my pleasure in the woods. I can wind my horn, though I call not the blast either a *recheate* or a *morte*—I can cheer my dogs on the prey, and I can flay and quarter the animal when it is brought down, without using the newfangled jargon of *curee*, *arbor*, *nombles*, and all the babble of the fabulous Sir Tristrem.'[12]*

'The French,' said the Templar, raising his voice with the presumptuous and authoritative tone which he used upon all occasions, 'is not only the natural language of the chase, but that of love and of war, in which ladies should be won and enemies defied.'

'Pledge me in a cup of wine, Sir Templar,' said Cedric, 'and fill another to the Abbot, while I look back some thirty years to tell you another tale. As Cedric the Saxon then was, his plain English tale needed no garnish from French troubadours, when it was told in the ear of beauty; and the field of Northallerton, upon the day of the Holy Standard,* could tell whether the Saxon war-cry was not heard as far within the ranks of the Scottish host as the *cri de guerre* of the boldest Norman baron. To the memory of the brave who fought there!—Pledge me, my guests.' He drank deep, and went on with increasing warmth. 'Ay, that was a day of cleaving of shields, when a hundred banners were bent forward over the heads of the valiant, and blood flowed round like water, and death was held better than flight. A Saxon bard* had called it a feast of the swords—a gathering of the eagles to the prey—the clashing of bills upon shield and helmet, the shouting of battle more joyful than the clamour of a bridal. But our bards are no more,' he said; 'our deeds are lost in those of another race—our language—our very name—is hastening to decay, and none mourns for it save one solitary old man—Cupbearer! knave, fill the goblets—To the strong in arms, Sir Templar, be their race or language what it will, who now bear them best in Palestine among the champions of the Cross!'

'It becomes not one wearing this badge to answer,' said Sir

Brian de Bois-Guilbert; 'yet to whom, besides the sworn Champions of the Holy Sepulchre, can the palm be assigned among the champions of the Cross?'

'To the Knights Hospitallers,'* said the Abbot; 'I have a brother of their order.'

'I impeach not their fame,' said the Templar; 'nevertheless'——

'I think, friend Cedric,' said Wamba, interfering, 'that had Richard of the Lion's Heart been wise enough to have taken a fool's advice, he might have staid at home with his merry Englishmen, and left the recovery of Jerusalem to those same Knights who had most to do with the loss of it.'

'Were there, then, none in the English army,' said the Lady Rowena, 'whose names are worthy to be mentioned with the Knights of the Temple, and of St John?'

'Forgive me, lady,' replied De Bois-Guilbert; 'the English monarch did, indeed, bring to Palestine a host of gallant warriors, second only to those whose breasts have been the unceasing bulwark of that blessed land.'

'Second to NONE,' said the Pilgrim, who had stood near enough to hear, and had listened to this conversation with marked impatience. All turned towards the spot from whence this unexpected asseveration was heard. 'I say,' repeated the Pilgrim in a firm and strong voice, 'that the English chivalry were second to NONE who ever drew sword in defence of the Holy Land. I say besides, for I saw it, that King Richard himself, and five of his knights, held a tournament after the taking of St John-de-Acre,* as challengers against all comers. I say that, on that day, each knight ran three courses, and cast to the ground three antagonists. I add, that seven of these assailants were Knights of the Temple—and Sir Brian de Bois-Guibert well knows the truth of what I tell you.'

It is impossible for language to describe the bitter scowl of rage which rendered yet darker the swarthy countenance of the Templar. In the extremity of his resentment and confusion, his quivering fingers griped towards the handle of his sword, and perhaps only withdrew, from the consciousness that no act of violence could be safely executed in that place and presence. Cedric, whose feelings were all of a right onward and simple kind, and were seldom occupied by more than one object at once, omitted, in the joyous glee with which he heard of the glory of his countrymen, to remark the angry confusion of his guest; 'I would give thee this golden bracelet, Pilgrim,' he said, 'couldst thou tell me the names of those knights who upheld so gallantly the renown of merry England.'

'That will I do blithely,' replied the Pilgrim, 'and without guerdon;* my oath, for a time, prohibits me from touching gold.'

'I will wear the bracelet for you, if you will, friend Palmer,' said Wamba.

'The first in honour as in arms, in renown as in place,' said the Pilgrim, 'was the brave Richard, King of England.'

'I forgive him,' said Cedric; 'I forgive him his descent from the tyrant Duke William.'

'The Earl of Leicester was the second,' continued the Pilgrim; 'Sir Thomas Multon of Gilsland was the third.'

'Of Saxon descent, he at least,' said Cedric, with exultation.

'Sir Foulk Doilly the fourth,' proceeded the Pilgrim.

'Saxon also, at least by the mother's side,' continued Cedric, who listened with the utmost eagerness, and forgot, in part at least, his hatred to the Normans, in the common triumph of the King of England and his islanders. 'And who was the fifth?' he demanded.

'The fifth was Sir Edwin Turneham.'

'Genuine Saxon, by the soul of Hengist!' shouted Cedric— 'And the sixth?' he continued with eagerness—'how name you the sixth?'

'The sixth,' said the Palmer, after a pause, in which he seemed to recollect himself, 'was a young knight of lesser renown and lower rank, assumed into that honourable company, less to aid their enterprise than to make up their number—his name dwells not in my memory.'

'Sir Palmer,' said Sir Brian de Bois-Guilbert scornfully, 'this assumed forgetfulness, after so much has been remembered, comes too late to serve your purpose. I will myself tell the name of the knight before whose lance fortune and my horse's fault occasioned my falling—it was the Knight of Ivanhoe; nor was there one of the six that, for his years, had more renown in arms.—Yet this will I say, and loudly—that were he in England,

and durst repeat, in this week's tournament, the challenge of St John-de-Acre, I, mounted and armed as I now am, would give him every advantage of weapons, and abide the result.'

'Your challenge would be soon answered,' replied the Palmer, 'were your antagonist near you. As the matter is, disturb not the peaceful hall with vaunts of the issue of a conflict, which you well know cannot take place. If Ivanhoe ever returns from Palestine, I will be his surety that he meets you.'

'A goodly security!' said the Knight Templar; 'and what do you proffer as a pledge?'

'This reliquary,' said the Palmer, taking a small ivory box from his bosom, and crossing himself, 'containing a portion of the true cross, brought from the Monastery of Mount Carmel.'*

The Prior of Jorvaulx crossed himself and repeated a pater noster, in which all devoutly joined, excepting the Jew, the Mahomedans, and the Templar; the latter of whom, without vailing his bonnet, or testifying any reverence for the alleged sanctity of the relic, took from his neck a gold chain, which he flung on the board, saying—'Let Prior Aymer hold my pledge and that of this nameless vagrant, in token that when the Knight of Ivanhoe comes within the four seas of Britain, he underlies the challenge of Brian de Bois-Guilbert, which, if he answer not, I will proclaim him as a coward on the walls of every Temple Court in Europe.'

'It will not need,' said the Lady Rowena, breaking silence; 'my voice shall be heard, if no other in this hall is raised in behalf of the absent Ivanhoe. I affirm he will meet fairly every honourable challenge. Could my weak warrant add security to the inestimable pledge of this holy pilgrim, I would pledge name and fame that Ivanhoe gives this proud knight the meeting he desires.'

A crowd of conflicting emotions seemed to have occupied Cedric, and kept him silent during this discussion. Gratified pride, resentment, embarrassment, chased each other over his broad and open brow, like the shadow of clouds drifting over a harvest-field; while his attendants, on whom the name of the sixth knight seemed to produce an effect almost electrical, hung in suspense upon their master's looks. But when Rowena spoke, the sound of her voice seemed to startle him from his silence.

'Lady,' said Cedric, 'this beseems not; were further pledge necessary, I myself, offended, and justly offended, as I am, would yet gage my honour for the honour of Ivanhoe. But the wager of battle is complete, even according to the fantastic fashions of Norman chivalry—Is it not, Father Aymer?'

'It is,' replied the Prior; 'and the blessed relic and rich chain will I bestow safely in the treasury of our convent, until the decision of this warlike challenge.'

Having thus spoken, he crossed himself again and again, and after many genuflections and muttered prayers, he delivered the reliquary to Brother Ambrose, his attendant monk, while he himself swept up with less ceremony, but perhaps with no less internal satisfaction, the golden chain, and bestowed it in a pouch lined with perfumed leather, which opened under his arm. 'And now, Sir Cedric,' he said, 'my ears are chiming vespers with the strength of your good wine—permit us another pledge to the welfare of the Lady Rowena, and indulge us with liberty to pass to our repose.'

'By the rood of Bromholme,'* said the Saxon, 'you do but small credit to your fame, Sir Prior! Report speaks you a bonny monk, that would hear the matin chime ere he quitted his bowl; and, old as I am, I feared to have shame in encountering you. But, by my faith, a Saxon boy of twelve, in my time, would not so soon have relinquished his goblet.'

The Prior had his own reasons, however, for persevering in the course of temperance which he had adopted. He was not only a professional peacemaker, but from practice a hater of all feuds and brawls. It was not altogether from a love to his neighbour, or to himself, or from a mixture of both. On the present occasion, he had an instinctive apprehension of the fiery temper of the Saxon, and saw the danger that the reckless and presumptuous spirit, of which his companion had already given so many proofs, might at length produce some disagreeable explosion. He therefore gently insinuated the incapacity of the native of any other country to engage in the genial conflict of the bowl with the hardy and strong-headed Saxons; something he mentioned, but slightly, about his own holy character, and ended by pressing his proposal to depart to repose.

The grace-cup was accordingly served round, and the guests,

after making deep obeisance to their landlord and to the Lady Rowena, arose and mingled in the hall, while the heads of the family, by separate doors, retired with their attendants.

'Unbelieving dog,' said the Templar to Isaac the Jew, as he passed him in the throng, 'dost thou bend thy course to the tournament?'

'I do so propose,' replied Isaac, bowing in all humility, 'if it please your reverend valour.'

'Ay,' said the Knight, 'to gnaw the bowels of our nobles with usury, and to gull women and boys with gauds and toys—I warrant thee store of shekels in thy Jewish scrip.'

'Not a shekel, not a silver penny, not a halfling—so help me the God of Abraham!' said the Jew, clasping his hands; 'I go but to seek the assistance of some brethren of my tribe to aid me to pay the fine which the Exchequer of the Jews[13]* have imposed upon me—Father Jacob be my speed! I am an impoverished wretch—the very gaberdine* I wear is borrowed from Reuben of Tadcaster.'

The Templar smiled sourly as he replied, 'Beshrew thee for a false-hearted liar!' and passing onward, as if disdaining farther conference, he communed with his Moslem slaves in a language unknown to the bystanders. The poor Israelite seemed so staggered by the address of the military monk, that the Templar had passed on to the extremity of the hall ere he raised his head from the humble posture which he had assumed, so far as to be sensible of his departure. And when he did look around, it was with the astonished air of one at whose feet a thunderbolt has just burst, and who hears still the astounding report ringing in his ears.

The Templar and Prior were shortly after marshalled to their sleeping apartments by the steward and the cupbearer, each attended by two torchbearers and two servants carrying refreshments, while servants of inferior condition indicated to their retinue and to the other guests their respective places of repose.

CHAPTER VI

To buy his favour I extend this friendship:
If he will take it, so; if not, adieu;
And, for my love, I pray you wrong me not.

*Merchant of Venice**

As the Palmer, lighted by a domestic with a torch, past through
the intricate combination of apartments of this large and irregular mansion, the cupbearer coming behind him whispered in his
ear, that if he had no objection to a cup of good mead in his
apartment, there were many domestics in that family who would
gladly hear the news he had brought from the Holy Land, and
particularly that which concerned the Knight of Ivanhoe.
Wamba presently appeared to urge the same request, observing
that a cup after midnight was worth three after curfew. Without
disputing a maxim urged by such grave authority, the Palmer
thanked them for their courtesy, but observed that he had included in his religious vow, an obligation never to speak in
the kitchen on matters which were prohibited in the hall.
'That vow,' said Wamba to the cupbearer, 'would scarce suit a
serving-man.'

The cupbearer shrugged up his shoulders in displeasure. 'I
thought to have lodged him in the solere chamber,'* said he; 'but
since he is so unsocial to Christians, e'en let him take the next
stall to Isaac the Jew's.—Anwold,' said he to the torchbearer,
'carry the Pilgrim to the southern cell.—I give you good-night,'
he added, 'Sir Palmer, with small thanks for short courtesy.'

'Good-night, and Our Lady's benison!' said the Palmer, with
composure; and his guide moved forward.

In a small antechamber, into which several doors opened, and
which was lighted by a small iron lamp, they met a second
interruption from the waiting-maid of Rowena, who, saying in a
tone of authority, that her mistress desired to speak with the
Palmer, took the torch from the hand of Anwold, and, bidding
him await her return, made a sign to the Palmer to follow.
Apparently he did not think it proper to decline this invitation as

he had done the former; for, though his gesture indicated some surprise at the summons, he obeyed it without answer or remonstrance.

A short passage, and an ascent of seven steps, each of which was composed of a solid beam of oak, led him to the apartment of the Lady Rowena, the rude magnificence of which corresponded to the respect which was paid to her by the lord of the mansion. The walls were covered with embroidered hangings, on which different-coloured silks, interwoven with gold and silver threads, had been employed with all the art of which the age was capable, to represent the sports of hunting and hawking. The bed was adorned with the same rich tapestry, and surrounded with curtains dyed with purple. The seats had also their stained coverings, and one, which was higher than the rest, was accommodated with a footstool of ivory, curiously carved.

No fewer than four silver candelabras, holding great waxen torches, served to illuminate this apartment. Yet let not modern beauty envy the magnificence of a Saxon princess. The walls of the apartment were so ill finished and so full of crevices, that the rich hangings shook to the night blast, and, in despite of a sort of screen intended to protect them from the wind, the flame of the torches streamed sideways into the air, like the unfurled pennon of a chieftain. Magnificence there was, with some rude attempt at taste; but of comfort there was little, and, being unknown, it was unmissed.

The Lady Rowena, with three of her attendants standing at her back, and arranging her hair ere she lay down to rest, was seated in the sort of throne already mentioned, and looked as if born to exact general homage. The Pilgrim acknowledged her claim to it by a low genuflection.

'Rise, Palmer,' said she graciously. 'The defender of the absent has a right to favourable reception from all who value truth, and honour manhood.' She then said to her train, 'Retire, excepting only Elgitha; I would speak with this holy Pilgrim.'

The maidens, without leaving the apartment, retired to its further extremity, and sat down on a small bench against the wall, where they remained mute as statues, though at such a distance that their whispers could not have interrupted the conversation of their mistress.

'Pilgrim,' said the lady, after a moment's pause, during which she seemed uncertain how to address him, 'you this night mentioned a name—I mean,' she said, with a degree of effort, 'the name of Ivanhoe, in the halls where by nature and kindred it should have sounded most acceptably; and yet, such is the perverse course of fate, that of many whose hearts must have throbbed at the sound, I, only, dare ask you where, and in what condition, you left him of whom you spoke?—We heard, that, having remained in Palestine, on account of his impaired health, after the departure of the English army, he had experienced the persecution of the French faction, to whom the Templars are known to be attached.'

'I know little of the Knight of Ivanhoe,' answered the Palmer, with a troubled voice. 'I would I knew him better, since you, lady, are interested in his fate. He hath, I believe, surmounted the persecution of his enemies in Palestine, and is on the eve of returning to England, where you, lady, must know better than I, what is his chance of happiness.'

The Lady Rowena sighed deeply, and asked more particularly when the Knight of Ivanhoe might be expected in his native country, and whether he would not be exposed to great dangers by the road. On the first point, the Palmer professed ignorance; on the second, he said that the voyage might be safely made by the way of Venice and Genoa, and from thence through France to England. 'Ivanhoe,' he said, 'was so well acquainted with the language and manners of the French, that there was no fear of his incurring any hazard during that part of his travels.'

'Would to God,' said the Lady Rowena, 'he were here safely arrived, and able to bear arms in the approaching tourney, in which the chivalry of this land are expected to display their address and valour. Should Athelstane of Coningsburgh obtain the prize, Ivanhoe is like to hear evil tidings when he reaches England.—How looked he, stranger, when you last saw him? Had disease laid her hand heavy upon his strength and comeliness?'

'He was darker,' said the Palmer, 'and thinner, than when he came from Cyprus in the train of Cœur-de-Lion, and care seemed to sit heavy on his brow; but I approached not his presence, because he is unknown to me.'

'He will,' said the lady, 'I fear, find little in his native land to clear those clouds from his countenance. Thanks, good Pilgrim, for your information concerning the companion of my childhood.—Maidens,' she said, 'draw near—offer the sleeping cup to this holy man, whom I will no longer detain from repose.'

One of the maidens presented a silver cup, containing a rich mixture of wine and spice, which Rowena barely put to her lips. It was then offered to the Palmer, who, after a low obeisance, tasted a few drops.

'Accept this alms, friend,' continued the lady, offering a piece of gold, 'in acknowledgment of thy painful travail, and of the shrines thou hast visited.'

The Palmer received the boon with another low reverence, and followed Elgitha out of the apartment.

In the anteroom he found his attendant Anwold, who, taking the torch from the hand of the waiting-maid, conducted him with more haste than ceremony to an exterior and ignoble part of the building, where a number of small apartments, or rather cells, served for sleeping places to the lower order of domestics, and to strangers of mean degree.

'In which of these sleeps the Jew?' said the Pilgrim.

'The unbelieving dog,' answered Anwold, 'kennels in the cell next your holiness.—St Dunstan, how it must be scraped and cleansed ere it be again fit for a Christian!'

'And where sleeps Gurth the swineherd?' said the stranger.

'Gurth,' replied the bondsman, 'sleeps in the cell on your right, as the Jew on that to your left; you serve to keep the child of circumcision separate from the abomination of his tribe. You might have occupied a more honourable place had you accepted of Oswald's invitation.'

'It is as well as it is,' said the Palmer; 'the company, even of a Jew, can hardly spread contamination through an oaken partition.'

So saying, he entered the cabin allotted to him, and taking the torch from the domestic's hand, thanked him, and wished him good-night. Having shut the door of his cell, he placed the torch in a candlestick made of wood, and looked around his sleeping apartment, the furniture of which was of the most simple kind. It consisted of a rude wooden stool, and still ruder hutch or bed-frame, stuffed with clean straw, and accommodated with two or three sheepskins by way of bed-clothes.

The Palmer, having extinguished his torch, threw himself, without taking off any part of his clothes, on this rude couch, and slept, or at least retained his recumbent posture, till the earliest sunbeams found their way through the little grated window, which served at once to admit both air and light to his uncomfortable cell. He then started up, and after repeating his matins, and adjusting his dress, he left it, and entered that of Isaac the Jew, lifting the latch as gently as he could.

The inmate was lying in troubled slumber upon a couch similar to that on which the Palmer himself had passed the night. Such parts of his dress as the Jew had laid aside on the preceding evening, were disposed carefully around his person, as if to prevent the hazard of their being carried off during his slumbers. There was a trouble on his brow amounting almost to agony. His hands and arms moved convulsively, as if struggling with the nightmare; and besides several ejaculations in Hebrew, the following were distinctly heard in the Norman-English, or mixed language of the country: 'For the sake of the God of Abraham, spare an unhappy old man! I am poor, I am penniless—should your irons wrench my limbs asunder, I could not gratify you!'

The Palmer awaited not the end of the Jew's vision, but stirred him with his pilgrim's staff. The touch probably associated, as is usual, with some of the apprehensions excited by his dream; for the old man started up, his grey hair standing almost erect upon his head, and huddling some part of his garments about him, while he held the detached pieces with the tenacious grasp of a falcon, he fixed upon the Palmer his keen black eyes, expressive of wild surprise and of bodily apprehension.

'Fear nothing from me, Isaac,' said the Palmer, 'I come as your friend.'

'The God of Israel requite you,' said the Jew, greatly relieved; 'I dreamed—but Father Abraham be praised, it was but a dream!' Then, collecting himself, he added in his usual tone, 'And what may it be your pleasure to want at so early an hour with the poor Jew?'

'It is to tell you,' said the Palmer, 'that if you leave not this mansion instantly, and travel not with some haste, your journey may prove a dangerous one.'

'Holy father!' said the Jew, 'whom could it interest to endanger so poor a wretch as I am?'

'The purpose you can best guess,' said the Pilgrim; 'but rely on this, that when the Templar crossed the hall yesternight, he spoke to his Mussulman slaves in the Saracen language, which I well understand, and charged them this morning to watch the journey of the Jew, to seize upon him when at a convenient distance from the mansion, and to conduct him to the castle of Philip de Malvoisin, or to that of Reginald Front-de-Bœuf.'

It is impossible to describe the extremity of terror which seized upon the Jew at this information, and seemed at once to overpower his whole faculties. His arms fell down to his sides, and his head drooped on his breast, his knees bent under his weight, every nerve and muscle of his frame seemed to collapse and lose its energy, and he sunk at the foot of the Palmer, not in the fashion of one who intentionally stoops, kneels, or prostrates himself to excite compassion, but like a man borne down on all sides by the pressure of some invisible force, which crushes him to the earth without the power of resistance.

'Holy God of Abraham!' was his first exclamation, folding and elevating his wrinkled hands, but without raising his grey head from the pavement; 'Oh, holy Moses! O, blessed Aaron! the dream is not dreamed for nought,* and the vision cometh not in vain! I feel their irons already tear my sinews! I feel the rack pass over my body like the saws, and harrows, and axes of iron over the men of Rabbah, and of the cities of the children of Ammon!'*

'Stand up, Isaac, and hearken to me,' said the Palmer, who viewed the extremity of his distress with a compassion in which contempt was largely mingled; 'you have cause for your terror, considering how your brethren have been used, in order to extort from them their hoards, both by princes and nobles; but stand up, I say, and I will point out to you the means of escape. Leave this mansion instantly, while its inmates sleep sound after the last night's revel. I will guide you by the secret paths of the forest, known as well to me as to any forester that ranges it, and

I will not leave you till you are under safe conduct of some chief or baron going to the tournament, whose good-will you have probably the means of securing.'

As the ears of Isaac received the hopes of escape which this speech intimated, he began gradually, and inch by inch, as it were, to raise himself up from the ground, until he fairly rested upon his knees, throwing back his long grey hair and beard, and fixing his keen black eyes upon the Palmer's face, with a look expressive at once of hope and fear, not unmingled with suspicion. But when he heard the concluding part of the sentence, his original terror appeared to revive in full force, and he dropt once more on his face, exclaiming, '*I* possess the means of securing good-will! alas! there is but one road to the favour of a Christian, and how can the poor Jew find it, whom extortions have already reduced to the misery of Lazarus?'* Then, as if suspicion had overpowered his other feelings, he suddenly exclaimed, 'For the love of God, young man, betray me not—for the sake of the Great Father who made us all, Jew as well as Gentile, Israelite and Ishmaelite—do me no treason! I have not means to secure the good-will of a Christian beggar, were he rating it at a single penny.' As he spoke these last words, he raised himself, and grasped the Palmer's mantle with a look of the most earnest entreaty. The pilgrim extricated himself, as if there were contamination in the touch.

'Wert thou loaded with all the wealth of thy tribe,' he said, 'what interest have I to injure thee?—In this dress I am vowed to poverty, nor do I change it for aught save a horse and a coat of mail. Yet think not that I care for thy company, or propose myself advantage by it; remain here if thou wilt—Cedric the Saxon may protect thee.'

'Alas!' said the Jew, 'he will not let me travel in his train—Saxon or Norman will be equally ashamed of the poor Israelite; and to travel by myself through the domains of Philip de Malvoisin and Reginald Front-de-Bœuf—Good youth, I will go with you!—Let us haste—let us gird up our loins*—let us flee!—Here is thy staff, why wilt thou tarry?'

'I tarry not,' said the Pilgrim, giving way to the urgency of his companion; 'but I must secure the means of leaving this place—follow me.'

He led the way to the adjoining cell, which, as the reader is apprised, was occupied by Gurth the swineherd.—'Arise, Gurth,' said the Pilgrim, 'arise quickly. Undo the postern gate, and let out the Jew and me.'

Gurth, whose occupation, though now held so mean, gave him as much consequence in Saxon England as that of Eumæus in Ithaca, was offended at the familiar and commanding tone assumed by the Palmer. 'The Jew leaving Rotherwood,' said he, raising himself on his elbow, and looking superciliously at him without quitting his pallet, 'and travelling in company with the Palmer to boot'——

'I should as soon have dreamt,' said Wamba, who entered the apartment at the instant, 'of his stealing away with a gammon of bacon.'

'Nevertheless,' said Gurth, again laying down his head on the wooden log which served him for a pillow, 'both Jew and Gentile must be content to abide the opening of the great gate—we suffer no visitors to depart by stealth at these unseasonable hours.'

'Nevertheless,' said the Pilgrim, in a commanding tone, 'you will not, I think, refuse me that favour.'

So saying, he stooped over the bed of the recumbent swineherd, and whispered something in his ear in Saxon. Gurth started up as if electrified. The Pilgrim, raising his finger in an attitude as if to express caution, added, 'Gurth, beware—thou art wont to be prudent. I say, undo the postern—thou shalt know more anon.'

With hasty alacrity Gurth obeyed him, while Wamba and the Jew followed, both wondering at the sudden change in the swineherd's demeanour.

'My mule, my mule!' said the Jew, as soon as they stood without the postern.

'Fetch him his mule,' said the Pilgrim; 'and, hearest thou,— let me have another, that I may bear him company till he is beyond these parts—I will return it safely to some of Cedric's train at Ashby. And do thou'—he whispered the rest in Gurth's ear.

'Willingly, most willingly shall it be done,' said Gurth, and instantly departed to execute the commission.

'I wish I knew,' said Wamba, when his comrade's back was turned, 'what you Palmers learn in the Holy Land.'

'To say our orisons, fool,' answered the Pilgrim, 'to repent our sins, and to mortify ourselves with fastings, vigils, and long prayers.'

'Something more potent than that,' answered the Jester; 'for when would repentance or prayer make Gurth do a courtesy, or fasting or vigil persuade him to lend you a mule?—I trow you might as well have told his favourite black boar of thy vigils and penance, and wouldst have gotten as civil an answer.'

'Go to,' said the Pilgrim, 'thou art but a Saxon fool.'

'Thou sayst well,' said the Jester; 'had I been born a Norman, as I think thou art, I would have had luck on my side, and been next door to a wise man.'

At this moment Gurth appeared on the opposite side of the moat with the mules. The travellers crossed the ditch upon a drawbridge of only two planks breadth, the narrowness of which was matched with the straitness of the postern, and with a little wicket in the exterior palisade, which gave access to the forest. No sooner had they reached the mules, than the Jew, with hasty and trembling hands, secured behind the saddle a small bag of blue buckram, which he took from under his cloak, containing, as he muttered, 'a change of raiment—only a change of raiment.' Then getting upon the animal with more alacrity and haste than could have been anticipated from his years, he lost no time in so disposing of the skirts of his gaberdine as to conceal completely from observation the burden which he had thus deposited *en croupe*.*

The Pilgrim mounted with more deliberation, reaching, as he departed, his hand to Gurth, who kissed it with the utmost possible veneration. The swineherd stood gazing after the travellers until they were lost under the boughs of the forest path, when he was disturbed from his reverie by the voice of Wamba.

'Knowest thou,' said the Jester, 'my good friend Gurth, that thou art strangely courteous and most unwontedly pious on this summer morning? I would I were a black Prior or a barefoot Palmer, to avail myself of thy unwonted zeal and courtesy— certes, I would make more out of it than a kiss of the hand.'

'Thou art no fool thus far, Wamba,' answered Gurth, 'though thou arguest from appearances, and the wisest of us can do no more—But it is time to look after my charge.'

So saying, he turned back to the mansion, attended by the Jester.

Meanwhile the travellers continued to press on their journey with a dispatch which argued the extremity of the Jew's fears, since persons at his age are seldom fond of rapid motion. The Palmer, to whom every path and outlet in the wood appeared to be familiar, led the way through the most devious paths, and more than once excited anew the suspicion of the Israelite, that he intended to betray him into some ambuscade of his enemies.

His doubts might have been indeed pardoned; for, except perhaps the flying fish,* there was no race existing on the earth, in the air, or the waters, who were the object of such an unintermitting, general, and relentless persecution as the Jews of this period.* Upon the slightest and most unreasonable pretences, as well as upon accusations the most absurd and groundless, their persons and property were exposed to every turn of popular fury; for Norman, Saxon, Dane, and Briton, however adverse these races were to each other, contended which should look with greatest detestation upon a people, whom it was accounted a point of religion to hate, to revile, to despise, to plunder, and to persecute. The kings of the Norman race, and the independent nobles, who followed their example in all acts of tyranny, maintained against this devoted people a persecution of a more regular, calculated, and self-interested kind. It is a well-known story of King John, that he confined a wealthy Jew in one of the royal castles, and daily caused one of his teeth to be torn out, until, when the jaw of the unhappy Israelite was half disfurnished, he consented to pay a large sum, which it was the tyrant's object to extort from him. The little ready money which was in the country was chiefly in possession of this persecuted people, and the nobility hesitated not to follow the example of their sovereign, in wringing it from them by every species of oppression, and even personal torture. Yet the passive courage inspired by the love of gain, induced the Jews to dare the various evils to which they were subjected, in consideration of the immense profits which they were enabled to realize in a country naturally so wealthy as England. In spite of every kind of discouragement, and even of the special court of taxations already mentioned, called the Jews' Exchequer, erected for the very purpose of despoiling and distressing them, the Jews increased, multiplied, and accumulated huge sums, which they transferred from one hand to another by means of bills of exchange—an invention for which commerce is said to be indebted to them, and which enabled them to transfer their wealth from land to land, that, when threatened with oppression in one country, their treasure might be secured in another.

The obstinacy and avarice of the Jews being thus in a measure placed in opposition to the fanaticism and tyranny of those under whom they lived, seemed to increase in proportion to the persecution with which they were visited; and the immense wealth they usually acquired in commerce, while it frequently placed them in danger, was at other times used to extend their influence, and to secure to them a certain degree of protection. On these terms they lived; and their character, influenced accordingly, was watchful, suspicious, and timid—yet obstinate, uncomplying, and skilful in evading the dangers to which they were exposed.

When the travellers had pushed on at a rapid rate through many devious paths, the Palmer at length broke silence.

'That large decayed oak,' he said, 'marks the boundaries over which Front-de-Bœuf claims authority—we are long since far from those of Malvoisin. There is now no fear of pursuit.'

'May the wheels of their chariots be taken off,' said the Jew, 'like those of the host of Pharaoh,* that they may drive heavily!—But leave me not, good Pilgrim—Think but of that fierce and savage Templar, with his Saracen slaves—they will regard neither territory, nor manor, nor lordship.'

'Our road,' said the Palmer, 'should here separate; for it beseems not men of my character and thine to travel together longer than needs must be. Besides, what succour couldst thou have from me, a peaceful Pilgrim, against two armed heathens?'

'O good youth,' answered the Jew, 'thou canst defend me, and I know thou wouldst. Poor as I am, I will requite it—not with money, for money, so help me my Father Abraham, I have none—but'——

'Money and recompense,' said the Palmer, interrupting him, 'I have already said I require not of thee. Guide thee I can; and, it may be, even in some sort defend thee; since to protect a Jew against a Saracen, can scarce be accounted unworthy of a Christian. Therefore, Jew, I will see thee safe under some fitting escort. We are now not far from the town of Sheffield, where thou mayest easily find many of thy tribe with whom to take refuge.'

'The blessing of Jacob be upon thee, good youth!' said the Jew; 'in Sheffield I can harbour with my kinsman Zareth,* and find some means of travelling forth with safety.'

'Be it so,' said the Palmer; 'at Sheffield then we part, and half-an-hour's riding will bring us in sight of that town."

The half hour was spent in perfect silence on both parts; the Pilgrim perhaps disdaining to address the Jew, except in case of absolute necessity, and the Jew not presuming to force a conversation with a person whose journey to the Holy Sepulchre gave a sort of sanctity to his character. They paused on the top of a gently rising bank, and the Pilgrim, pointing to the town of Sheffield, which lay beneath them, repeated the words, 'Here, then, we part.'

'Not till you have had the poor Jew's thanks,' said Isaac; 'for I presume not to ask you to go with me to my kinsman Zareth's, who might aid me with some means of repaying your good offices.'

'I have already said,' answered the Pilgrim, 'that I desire no recompense. If, among the huge list of thy debtors, thou wilt, for my sake, spare the gyves and the dungeon to some unhappy Christian who stands in thy danger, I shall hold this morning's service to thee well bestowed.'

'Stay, stay,' said the Jew, laying hold of his garment; 'something would I do more than this, something for thyself.—God knows the Jew is poor—yes, Isaac is the beggar of his tribe—but forgive me should I guess what thou most lackest at this moment.'

'If thou wert to guess truly,' said the Palmer, 'it is what thou canst not supply, wert thou as wealthy as thou sayst thou art poor.'

'As I say?' echoed the Jew; 'O! believe it, I say but the truth;

I am a plundered, indebted, distressed man. Hard hands have wrung from me my goods, my money, my ships, and all that I possessed—Yet I can tell thee what thou lackest, and, it may be, supply it too. Thy wish even now is for a horse and armour.'

The Palmer started, and turned suddenly towards the Jew:— 'What fiend prompted that guess?' said he, hastily.

'No matter,' said the Jew, smiling, 'so that it be a true one— and, as I can guess thy want, so I can supply it.'

'But consider,' said the Palmer, 'my character, my dress, my vow.'

'I know you Christians,' replied the Jew, 'and that the noblest of you will take the staff and sandal in superstitious penance, and walk afoot to visit the graves of dead men.'

'Blaspheme not, Jew!' said the Pilgrim, sternly.

'Forgive me,' said the Jew; 'I spoke rashly. But there dropt words from you last night and this morning, that, like sparks from flint, showed the metal within; and in the bosom of that Palmer's gown, is hidden a knight's chain and spurs of gold. They glanced as you stooped over my bed in the morning.'

The Pilgrim could not forbear smiling. 'Were thy garments searched by as curious an eye, Isaac,' said he, 'what discoveries might not be made?'

'No more of that,' said the Jew, changing colour; and drawing forth his writing materials in haste, as if to stop the conversation, he began to write upon a piece of paper which he supported on the top of his yellow cap, without dismounting from his mule. When he had finished, he delivered the scroll, which was in the Hebrew character, to the Pilgrim, saying, 'In the town of Leicester all men know the rich Jew, Kirjath Jairam of Lombardy; give him this scroll—he hath on sale six Milan harnesses,* the worst would suit a crowned head—ten goodly steeds, the worst might mount a king, were he to do battle for his throne. Of these he will give thee thy choice, with every thing else that can furnish thee forth for the tournament: when it is over, thou wilt return them safely—unless thou shouldst have wherewith to pay their value to the owner.'

'But, Isaac,' said the Pilgrim, smiling, 'dost thou know that in these sports, the arms and steed of the knight who is unhorsed are forfeit to his victor? Now I may be unfortunate, and so lose what I cannot replace or repay.'

The Jew looked somewhat astounded at this possibility; but collecting his courage, he replied hastily, 'No—no—no—It is impossible—I will not think so. The blessing of Our Father will be upon thee. Thy lance will be powerful as the rod of Moses.'

So saying, he was turning his mule's head away, when the Palmer, in his turn, took hold of his gaberdine. 'Nay, but Isaac, thou knowest not all the risk. The steed may be slain, the armour injured—for I will spare neither horse nor man. Besides, those of thy tribe give nothing for nothing; something there must be paid for their use.'

The Jew twisted himself in the saddle, like a man in a fit of the colic; but his better feelings predominated over those which were most familiar to him. 'I care not,' he said, 'I care not—let me go. If there is damage, it will cost you nothing—if there is usage money, Kirjath Jairam will forgive it for the sake of his kinsman Isaac. Fare thee well!—Yet hark thee, good youth,'* said he, turning about, 'thrust thyself not too forward into this vain hurly-burly—I speak not for endangering the steed, and coat of armour, but for the sake of thine own life and limbs.'

'Gramercy for thy caution,' said the Palmer, again smiling; 'I will use thy courtesy frankly, and it will go hard with me but I will requite it.'*

They parted, and took different roads for the town of Sheffield.

CHAPTER VII

Knights, with a long retinue of their squires,
In gaudy liveries march and quaint attires;
One laced the helm, another held the lance,
A third the shining buckler did advance.
The courser paw'd the ground with restless feet,
And snorting foam'd and champ'd the golden bit.
The smiths and armourers on palfreys ride,
Files in their hands, and hammers at their side;
And nails for loosen'd spears, and thongs for shields
   provide.
The yeomen guard the streets in seemly bands;
And clowns come crowding on, with cudgels in their
   hands.

*Palamon and Arcite**

THE condition of the English nation was at this time sufficiently miserable.* King Richard was absent a prisoner, and in the power of the perfidious and cruel Duke of Austria. Even the very place of his captivity was uncertain, and his fate but very imperfectly known to the generality of his subjects, who were, in the meantime, a prey to every species of subaltern oppression.

Prince John, in league with Philip of France, Cœur-de-Lion's mortal enemy, was using every species of influence with the Duke of Austria, to prolong the captivity of his brother Richard, to whom he stood indebted for so many favours. In the meantime, he was strengthening his own faction in the kingdom, of which he proposed to dispute the succession, in case of the King's death, with the legitimate heir, Arthur Duke of Brittany, son of Geoffrey Plantagenet, the elder brother of John. This usurpation, it is well known, he afterwards effected. His own character being light, profligate, and perfidious, John easily attached to his person and faction, not only all who had reason to dread the resentment of Richard for criminal proceedings during his absence, but also the numerous class of 'lawless resolutes,'* whom the crusades had turned back on their country, accomplished in the vices of the East, impoverished in substance, and hardened in character, and who placed their hopes of harvest in civil commotion.

To these causes of public distress and apprehension, must be added, the multitude of outlaws, who, driven to despair by the oppression of the feudal nobility, and the severe exercise of the forest laws, banded together in large gangs, and, keeping possession of the forests and the wastes, set at defiance the justice and magistracy of the country. The nobles themselves, each fortified within his own castle, and playing the petty sovereign over his own dominions, were the leaders of bands scarce less lawless and oppressive than those of the avowed depredators. To maintain these retainers, and to support the extravagance and magnificence which their pride induced them to affect, the nobility borrowed sums of money from the Jews at the most usurious interest, which gnawed into their estates like consuming cankers, scarce to be cured unless when circumstances gave them an opportunity of getting free, by exercising upon their creditors some act of unprincipled violence.

Under the various burdens imposed by this unhappy state of affairs, the people of England suffered deeply for the present, and had yet more dreadful cause to fear for the future. To augment their misery, a contagious disorder of a dangerous nature spread through the land;* and, rendered more virulent by the uncleanness, the indifferent food, and the wretched lodging of the lower classes, swept off many whose fate the survivors were tempted to envy, as exempting them from the evils which were to come.

Yet amid these accumulated distresses, the poor as well as the rich, the vulgar as well as the noble, in the event of a tournament, which was the grand spectacle of that age, felt as much interested as the half-starved citizen of Madrid, who has not a real* left to buy provisions for his family, feels in the issue of a bull-feast. Neither duty nor infirmity could keep youth or age from such exhibitions. The Passage of Arms,* as it was called, which was to take place at Ashby, in the county of Leicester, as champions of the first renown were to take the field in the presence of Prince John himself, who was expected to grace the lists, had attracted universal attention, and an immense confluence of persons of all ranks hastened upon the appointed morning to the place of combat.

The scene was singularly romantic. On the verge of a wood, which approached to within a mile of the town of Ashby, was an extensive meadow, of the finest and most beautiful green turf, surrounded on one side by the forest, and fringed on the other by straggling oak-trees, some of which had grown to an immense size. The ground, as if fashioned on purpose for the martial display which was intended, sloped gradually down on all sides to a level bottom, which was enclosed for the lists with strong palisades, forming a space of a quarter of a mile in length, and about half as broad. The form of the enclosure was an oblong square, save that the corners were considerably rounded off, in order to afford more convenience for the spectators. The openings for the entry of the combatants were at the northern and southern extremities of the lists, accessible by strong wooden gates, each wide enough to admit two horsemen riding abreast. At each of these portals were stationed two heralds, attended by six trumpets, as many pursuivants, and a strong body of men-at-arms for maintaining order, and ascertaining the quality of the knights who proposed to engage in this martial game.

On a platform beyond the southern entrance, formed by a natural elevation of the ground, were pitched five magnificent pavilions, adorned with pennons of russet and black, the chosen colours of the five knights challengers. The cords of the tents were of the same colour. Before each pavilion was suspended the shield of the knight by whom it was occupied, and beside it stood his squire, quaintly disguised as a salvage or silvan man,* or in some other fantastic dress, according to the taste of his master, and the character he was pleased to assume during the game.[14] The central pavilion, as the place of honour, had been assigned to Brian de Bois-Guilbert, whose renown in all games of chivalry, no less than his connexion with the knights who had undertaken this Passage of Arms, had occasioned him to be eagerly received into the company of the challengers, and even adopted as their chief and leader, though he had so recently joined them. On one side of his tent were pitched those of Reginald Front-de-Bœuf and Richard de Malvoisin,* and on the other was the pavilion of Hugh de Grantmesnil,* a noble baron in the vicinity, whose ancestor had been Lord High Steward of England in the time of the Conqueror and his son William Rufus. Ralph de Vipont, a knight of St John of Jerusalem, who had some ancient possessions at a place called Heather, near Ashby-de-la-Zouche, occupied the fifth pavilion. From the entrance into the lists, a gently sloping passage, ten yards in breadth, led up to the platform on which the tents were pitched. It was strongly secured by a palisade on each side, as was the esplanade in front of the pavilions, and the whole was guarded by men-at-arms.

The northern access to the lists terminated in a similar entrance of thirty feet in breadth, at the extremity of which was a large enclosed space for such knights as might be disposed to enter the lists with the challengers, behind which were placed tents containing refreshments of every kind for their accommodation, with armourers, farriers, and other attendants, in readiness to give their services wherever they might be necessary.

The exterior of the lists was in part occupied by temporary galleries, spread with tapestry and carpets, and accommodated with cushions for the convenience of those ladies and nobles who were expected to attend the tournament. A narrow space, betwixt these galleries and the lists, gave accommodation for yeomanry and spectators of a better degree than the mere vulgar, and might be compared to the pit of a theatre. The promiscuous multitude arranged themselves upon large banks of turf prepared for the purpose, which, aided by the natural elevation of the ground, enabled them to overlook the galleries, and obtain a fair view into the lists. Besides the accommodation which these stations afforded, many hundreds had perched themselves on the branches of the trees which surrounded the meadow; and even the steeple of a country church, at some distance, was crowded with spectators.

It only remains to notice respecting the general arrangement, that one gallery in the very centre of the eastern side of the lists, and consequently exactly opposite to the spot where the shock of the combat was to take place, was raised higher than the others, more richly decorated, and graced by a sort of throne and canopy, on which the royal arms were emblazoned. Squires, pages, and yeomen in rich liveries, waited around this place of honour, which was designed for Prince John and his attendants. Opposite to this royal gallery was another, elevated to the same

height, on the western side of the lists; and more gaily, if less
sumptuously decorated, than that destined for the Prince himself. A train of pages and of young maidens, the most beautiful
who could be selected, gaily dressed in fancy habits of green and
pink, surrounded a throne decorated in the same colours.
Among pennons and flags bearing wounded hearts, burning
hearts, bleeding hearts, bows and quivers, and all the commonplace emblems of the triumphs of Cupid,* a blazoned inscription
informed the spectators, that this seat of honour was designed
for *La Royne de la Beaulté et des Amours*. But who was to represent the Queen of Beauty and of Love on the present occasion,
no one was prepared to guess.

Meanwhile, spectators of every description thronged forward
to occupy their respective stations, and not without many quarrels concerning those which they were entitled to hold. Some of
these were settled by the men-at-arms with brief ceremony; the
shafts of their battle-axes, and pummels of their swords, being
readily employed as arguments to convince the more refractory.
Others, which involved the rival claims of more elevated persons, were determined by the heralds, or by the two marshals of
the field, William de Wyvil, and Stephen de Martival, who,
armed at all points, rode up and down the lists to enforce and
preserve good order among the spectators.

Gradually the galleries became filled with knights and nobles,
in their robes of peace, whose long and rich-tinted mantles were
contrasted with the gayer and more splendid habits of the ladies,
who, in a greater proportion than even the men themselves,
thronged to witness a sport, which one would have thought too
bloody and dangerous to afford their sex much pleasure. The
lower and interior space was soon filled by substantial yeomen
and burghers, and such of the lesser gentry, as, from modesty,
poverty, or dubious title, durst not assume any higher place. It
was of course amongst these that the most frequent disputes for
precedence occurred.

'Dog of an unbeliever,' said an old man, whose threadbare
tunic bore witness to his poverty, as his sword, and dagger, and
golden chain intimated his pretensions to rank,—'whelp of a
she-wolf! darest thou press upon a Christian, and a Norman
gentleman of the blood of Montdidier?'

This rough expostulation was addressed to no other than our acquaintance Isaac, who, richly and even magnificently dressed in a gaberdine ornamented with lace and lined with fur, was endeavouring to make place in the foremost row beneath the gallery for his daughter, the beautiful Rebecca, who had joined him at Ashby, and who was now hanging on her father's arm, not a little terrified by the popular displeasure which seemed generally excited by her parent's presumption. But Isaac, though we have seen him sufficiently timid on other occasions, knew well that at present he had nothing to fear. It was not in places of general resort, or where their equals were assembled, that any avaricious or malevolent noble durst offer him injury. At such meetings the Jews were under the protection of the general law; and if that proved a weak assurance, it usually happened that there were among the persons assembled some barons, who, for their own interested motives, were ready to act as their protectors. On the present occasion, Isaac felt more than usually confident, being aware that Prince John was even then in the very act of negotiating a large loan from the Jews of York, to be secured upon certain jewels and lands. Isaac's own share in this transaction was considerable, and he well knew that the Prince's eager desire to bring it to a conclusion would ensure him his protection in the dilemma in which he stood.

Emboldened by these considerations, the Jew pursued his point, and jostled the Norman Christian, without respect either to his descent, quality, or religion. The complaints of the old man, however, excited the indignation of the bystanders. One of these, a stout well-set yeoman, arrayed in Lincoln-green,* having twelve arrows stuck in his belt, with a baldric and badge of silver, and a bow of six feet length in his hand, turned short round, and while his countenance, which his constant exposure to weather had rendered brown as a hazel nut, grew darker with anger, he advised the Jew to remember that all the wealth he had acquired by sucking the blood of his miserable victims had but swelled him like a bottled spider,* which might be overlooked while it kept in a corner, but would be crushed if it ventured into the light. This intimation, delivered in Norman-English with a firm voice and a stern aspect, made the Jew shrink back; and he would have probably withdrawn himself altogether from a vicin-

ity so dangerous, had not the attention of every one been called
to the sudden entrance of Prince John, who at that moment
entered the lists, attended by a numerous and gay train, consisting partly of laymen, partly of churchmen, as light in their dress,
and as gay in their demeanour, as their companions. Among the
latter was the Prior of Jorvaulx, in the most gallant trim which a
dignitary of the church could venture to exhibit. Fur and
gold were not spared in his garments; and the point of his boots,
out-heroding* the preposterous fashion of the time, turned up
so very far, as to be attached, not to his knees merely, but to his
very girdle, and effectually prevented him from putting his foot
into the stirrup. This, however, was a slight inconvenience to the
gallant Abbot, who, perhaps, even rejoicing in the opportunity to
display his accomplished horsemanship before so many spectators, especially of the fair sex, dispensed with the use of these
supports to a timid rider. The rest of Prince John's retinue
consisted of the favourite leaders of his mercenary troops, some
marauding barons and profligate attendants upon the court, with
several Knights Templars and Knights of St John.

It may be here remarked, that the knights of these two orders
were accounted hostile to King Richard, having adopted the side
of Philip of France in the long train of disputes which took place
in Palestine betwixt that monarch and the lion-hearted King of
England. It was the well-known consequence of this discord that
Richard's repeated victories had been rendered fruitless, his
romantic attempts to besiege Jerusalem disappointed, and the
fruit of all the glory which he had acquired had dwindled into an
uncertain truce with the Sultan Saladin. With the same policy
which had dictated the conduct of their brethren in the Holy
Land, the Templars and Hospitallers in England and Normandy
attached themselves to the faction of Prince John, having little
reason to desire the return of Richard to England, or the succession of Arthur, his legitimate heir. For the opposite reason,
Prince John hated and contemned the few Saxon families of
consequence which subsisted in England, and omitted no opportunity of mortifying and affronting them; being conscious that
his person and pretensions were disliked by them, as well as by
the greater part of the English commons, who feared farther
innovation upon their rights and liberties, from a sovereign of
John's licentious and tyrannical disposition.

Attended by this gallant equipage, himself well mounted, and splendidly dressed in crimson and in gold, bearing upon his hand a falcon, and having his head covered by a rich fur bonnet, adorned with a circle of precious stones, from which his long curled hair escaped and overspread his shoulders, Prince John, upon a grey and high-mettled palfrey, caracoled* within the lists at the head of his jovial party, laughing loud with his train, and eyeing with all the boldness of royal criticism the beauties who adorned the lofty galleries.

Those who remarked in the physiognomy of the Prince a dissolute audacity, mingled with extreme haughtiness and indifference to the feelings of others, could not yet deny to his countenance that sort of comeliness which belongs to an open set of features, well formed by nature, modelled by art to the usual rules of courtesy, yet so far frank and honest, that they seemed as if they disclaimed to conceal the natural workings of the soul. Such an expression is often mistaken for manly frankness, when in truth it arises from the reckless indifference of a libertine disposition, conscious of superiority of birth, of wealth, or of some other adventitious advantage, totally unconnected with personal merit. To those who did not think so deeply, and they were the greater number by a hundred to one, the splendour of Prince John's *rheno*,* (*i.e.* fur tippet,) the richness of his cloak, lined with the most costly sables, his maroquin* boots and golden spurs, together with the grace with which he managed his palfrey, were sufficient to merit clamorous applause.

In his joyous caracole round the lists, the attention of the Prince was called by the commotion, not yet subsided, which had attended the ambitious movement of Isaac towards the higher places of the assembly. The quick eye of Prince John instantly recognised the Jew, but was much more agreeably attracted by the beautiful daughter of Zion, who, terrified by the tumult, clung close to the arm of her aged father.

The figure of Rebecca* might indeed have compared with the proudest beauties of England, even though it had been judged by as shrewd a connoisseur as Prince John. Her form was exquisitely symmetrical, and was shown to advantage by a sort of Eastern dress, which she wore according to the fashion of the females of her nation. Her turban of yellow silk suited well with the darkness of her complexion. The brilliancy of her eyes, the superb arch of her eyebrows, her well-formed aquiline nose, her teeth as white as pearl, and the profusion of her sable tresses, which, each arranged in its own little spiral of twisted curls, fell down upon as much of a lovely neck and bosom as a simarre of the richest Persian silk, exhibiting flowers in their natural colours embossed upon a purple ground, permitted to be visible—all these constituted a combination of loveliness, which yielded not to the most beautiful of the maidens who surrounded her. It is true, that of the golden and pearl-studded clasps, which closed her vest from the throat to the waist, the three uppermost were left unfastened on account of the heat, which something enlarged the prospect to which we allude. A diamond necklace, with pendants of inestimable value, were by this means also made more conspicuous. The feather of an ostrich, fastened in her turban by an agraffe* set with brilliants, was another distinction of the beautiful Jewess, scoffed and sneered at by the proud dames who sat above her, but secretly envied by those who affected to deride them.

'By the bald scalp of Abraham,' said Prince John, 'yonder Jewess must be the very model of that perfection, whose charms drove frantic the wisest king that ever lived! What sayest thou, Prior Aymer?—By the Temple of that wise king, which our wiser brother Richard proved unable to recover, she is the very Bride of the Canticles!'*

'The Rose of Sharon and the Lily of the Valley,'—answered the Prior, in a sort of snuffling tone; 'but your Grace must remember she is still but a Jewess.'

'Ay!' added Prince John, without heeding him, 'and there is my Mammon of unrighteousness* too—the Marquis of Marks, the Baron of Byzants, contesting for place with penniless dogs, whose threadbare cloaks have not a single cross in their pouches to keep the devil from dancing there.* By the body of St Mark, my prince of supplies, with his lovely Jewess, shall have a place in the gallery!—What is she, Isaac? Thy wife or thy daughter, that Eastern houri that thou lockest under thy arm as thou wouldst thy treasure-casket?'

'My daughter Rebecca, so please your Grace,' answered Isaac, with a low congee,* nothing embarrassed by the Prince's salutation, in which, however, there was at least as much mockery as courtesy.

'The wiser man thou,' said John, with a peal of laughter, in which his gay followers obsequiously joined. 'But, daughter, or wife, she should be preferred according to her beauty and thy merits.—Who sits above there?' he continued, bending his eye on the gallery. 'Saxon churls, lolling at their lazy length!—out upon them!—let them sit close, and make room for my prince of usurers and his lovely daughter. I'll make the hinds know they must share the high places of the synagogue* with those whom the synagogue properly belongs to.'

Those who occupied the gallery to whom this injurious and unpolite speech was addressed, were the family of Cedric the Saxon, with that of his ally and kinsman, Athelstane* of Coningsburgh, a personage, who, on account of his descent from the last Saxon monarchs of England, was held in the highest respect by all the Saxon natives of the north of England. But with the blood of this ancient royal race, many of their infirmities had descended to Athelstane. He was comely in countenance, bulky and strong in person, and in the flower of his age—yet inanimate in expression, dull-eyed, heavy-browed, inactive and sluggish in all his motions, and so slow in resolution, that the soubriquet of one of his ancestors was conferred upon him, and he was very generally called Athelstane the Unready.* His friends, and he had many, who, as well as Cedric, were passionately attached to him, contended that this sluggish temper arose not from want of courage, but from mere want of decision; others alleged that his hereditary vice of drunkenness had obscured his faculties, never of a very acute order, and that the passive courage and meek good-nature which remained behind, were merely the dregs of a character that might have been deserving of praise, but of which all the valuable parts had flown off in the progress of a long course of brutal debauchery.

It was to this person, such as we have described him, that the Prince addressed his imperious command to make place for Isaac and Rebecca. Athelstane, utterly confounded at an order which the manners and feelings of the times rendered so injuriously insulting, unwilling to obey, yet undetermined how to resist, opposed only the *vis inertiæ** to the will of John; and, without stirring or making any motion whatever of obedience, opened his large grey eyes, and stared at the Prince with an astonishment which had in it something extremely ludicrous. But the impatient John regarded it in no such light.

'The Saxon porker,' he said, 'is either asleep or minds me not—Prick him with your lance, De Bracy,' speaking to a knight who rode near him, the leader of a band of Free Companions, or Condottieri; that is, of mercenaries belonging to no particular nation, but attached for the time to any prince by whom they were paid. There was a murmur even among the attendants of Prince John; but De Bracy, whose profession freed him from all scruples, extended his long lance over the space which separated the gallery from the lists, and would have executed the commands of the Prince before Athelstane the Unready had recovered presence of mind sufficient even to draw back his person from the weapon, had not Cedric, as prompt as his companion was tardy, unsheathed, with the speed of lightning, the short sword which he wore, and at a single blow severed the point of the lance from the handle. The blood rushed into the countenance of Prince John. He swore one of his deepest oaths, and was about to utter some threat corresponding in violence, when he was diverted from his purpose, partly by his own attendants, who gathered around him conjuring him to be patient, partly by a general exclamation of the crowd, uttered in loud applause of the spirited conduct of Cedric. The Prince rolled his eyes in indignation, as if to collect some safe and easy victim; and chancing to encounter the firm glance of the same archer whom we have already noticed, and who seemed to persist in his gesture of applause, in spite of the frowning aspect which the Prince bent upon him, he demanded his reason for clamouring thus.

'I always add my hollo,' said the yeoman, 'when I see a good shot, or a gallant blow.'

'Sayst thou?' answered the Prince; 'then thou canst hit the white thyself, I'll warrant.'

'A woodsman's mark, and at woodsman's distance, I can hit,' answered the yeoman.

'And Wat Tyrrel's mark, at a hundred yards,' said a voice from behind, but by whom uttered could not be discerned.

This allusion to the fate of William Rufus,* his grandfather, at once incensed and alarmed Prince John. He satisfied himself, however, with commanding the men-at-arms, who surrounded the lists, to keep an eye on the braggart, pointing to the yeoman.

'By St Grizzel,'* he added, 'we will try his own skill, who is so ready to give his voice to the feats of others!'

'I shall not fly the trial,' said the yeoman, with the composure which marked his whole deportment.

'Meanwhile, stand up, ye Saxon churls,' said the fiery Prince; 'for, by the light of Heaven, since I have said it, the Jew shall have his seat amongst ye!'

'By no means, an it please your Grace!—it is not fit for such as we to sit with the rulers of the land,' said the Jew; whose ambition for precedence, though it had led him to dispute place with the extenuated and impoverished descendant of the line of Montdidier, by no means stimulated him to an intrusion upon the privileges of the wealthy Saxons.

'Up, infidel dog, when I command you,' said Prince John, 'or I will have thy swarthy hide stript off, and tanned for horse-furniture!'

Thus urged, the Jew began to ascend the steep and narrow steps which led up to the gallery.

'Let me see,' said the Prince, 'who dare stop him!' fixing his eye on Cedric, whose attitude intimated his intention to hurl the Jew down headlong.

The catastrophe was prevented by the clown Wamba, who, springing betwixt his master and Isaac, and exclaiming, in answer to the Prince's defiance, 'Marry, that will I!' opposed to the beard of the Jew a shield of brawn, which he plucked from beneath his cloak, and with which, doubtless, he had furnished himself, lest the tournament should have proved longer than his appetite could endure abstinence. Finding the abomination of his tribe opposed to his very nose, while the Jester at the same time, flourished his wooden sword above his head, the Jew recoiled, missed his footing, and rolled down the steps,—an excellent jest to the spectators, who set up a loud laughter, in which Prince John and his attendants heartily joined.

'Deal me the prize, cousin Prince,' said Wamba; 'I have vanquished my foe in fair fight with sword and shield,' he added, brandishing the brawn in one hand and the wooden sword in the other.

'Who, and what art thou, noble champion?' said Prince John, still laughing.

'A fool by right of descent,' answered the Jester; 'I am Wamba, the son of Witless, who was the son of Weatherbrain, who was the son of an Alderman.'

'Make room for the Jew in front of the lower ring,' said Prince John, not unwilling perhaps to seize an apology to desist from his original purpose; 'to place the vanquished beside the victor were false heraldry.'

'Knave upon fool were worse,' answered the Jester, 'and Jew upon bacon worst of all.'

'Gramercy! good fellow,' cried Prince John, 'thou pleasest me—Here, Isaac, lend me a handful of byzants.'

As the Jew, stunned by the request, afraid to refuse, and unwilling to comply, fumbled in the furred bag which hung by his girdle, and was perhaps endeavouring to ascertain how few coins might pass for a handful, the Prince stooped from his jennet and settled Isaac's doubts by snatching the pouch itself from his side; and flinging to Wamba a couple of the gold pieces which it contained, he pursued his career round the lists, leaving the Jew to the derision of those around him, and himself receiving as much applause from the spectators as if he had done some honest and honourable action.

CHAPTER VIII

At this the challenger with fierce defy
His trumpet sounds; the challenged makes reply:
With clangour rings the field, resounds the vaulted sky.
Their visors closed, their lances in the rest,
Or at the helmet pointed or the crest,
They vanish fromt the barrier, speed the race,
And spurring see decrease the middle space.

*Palamon and Arcite**

IN the midst of Prince John's cavalcade, he suddenly stopt, and appealing to the Prior of Jorvaulx, declared the principal business of the day had been forgotten.

'By my halidom,'* said he, 'we have neglected, Sir Prior, to name the fair Sovereign of Love and of Beauty, by whose white hand the palm is to be distributed. For my part, I am liberal in my ideas, and I care not if I give my vote for the black-eyed Rebecca.'

'Holy Virgin,' answered the Prior, turning up his eyes in horror, 'a Jewess!—We should deserve to be stoned out of the lists; and I am not yet old enough to be a martyr. Besides, I swear by my patron saint, that she is far inferior to the lovely Saxon, Rowena.'

'Saxon or Jew,' answered the Prince, 'Saxon or Jew, dog or hog,* what matters it! I say, name Rebecca, were it only to mortify the Saxon churls.'

A murmur arose even among his own immediate attendants.

'This passes a jest, my lord,' said De Bracy; 'no knight here will lay lance in rest if such an insult is attempted.'

'It is the mere wantonness of insult,' said one of the oldest and most important of Prince John's followers, Waldemar Fitzurse,* 'and if your Grace attempt it, cannot but prove ruinous to your projects.'

'I entertained you, sir,' said John, reining up his palfrey haughtily, 'for my follower, but not for my counsellor.'

'Those who follow your Grace in the paths which you tread,'

said Waldemar, but speaking in a low voice, 'acquire the right of counsellors; for your interest and safety are not more deeply gaged than their own.'

From the tone in which this was spoken, John saw the necessity of acquiescence. 'I did but jest,' he said; 'and you turn upon me like so many adders! Name whom you will, in the fiend's name, and please yourselves.'

'Nay, nay,' said De Bracy, 'let the fair sovereign's throne remain unoccupied, until the conqueror shall be named, and then let him choose the lady by whom it shall be filled. It will add another grace to his triumph, and teach fair ladies to prize the love of valiant knights, who can exalt them to such distinction.'

'If Brian de Bois-Guilbert gain the prize,' said the Prior, 'I will gage my rosary that I name the Sovereign of Love and Beauty.'

'Bois-Guilbert,' answered De Bracy, 'is a good lance; but there are others around these lists, Sir Prior, who will not fear to encounter him.'

'Silence, sirs,' said Waldemar, 'and let the Prince assume his seat. The knights and spectators are alike impatient, the time advances, and highly fit it is that the sports should commence.'

Prince John, though not yet a monarch, had in Waldemar Fitzurse all the inconveniences of a favourite minister, who, in serving his sovereign, must always do so in his own way. The Prince acquiesced, however, although his disposition was precisely of that kind which is apt to be obstinate upon trifles, and, assuming his throne, and being surrounded by his followers, gave signal to the heralds to proclaim the laws of the tournament, which were briefly as follows:

First, the five challengers were to undertake all comers.

Secondly, any knight proposing to combat, might, if he pleased, select a special antagonist from among the challengers, by touching his shield. If he did so with the reverse of his lance, the trial of skill was made with what were called the arms of courtesy, that is, with lances at whose extremity a piece of round flat board was fixed, so that no danger was encountered, save from the shock of the horses and riders. But if the shield was touched with the sharp end of the lance, the combat was under-

stood to be at *outrance*,* that is, the knights were to fight with
sharp weapons, as in actual battle.

Thirdly, when the knights present had accomplished their
vow, by each of them breaking five lances, the Prince was to
declare the victor in the first day's tourney, who should receive
as prize a warhorse of exquisite beauty and matchless strength;
and in addition to this reward of valour, it was now declared, he
should have the peculiar honour of naming the Queen of Love
and Beauty, by whom the prize should be given on the ensuing
day.

Fourthly, it was announced, that, on the second day, there
should be a general tournament, in which all the knights present,
who were desirous to win praise, might take part; and being
divided into two bands, of equal numbers, might fight it out
manfully until the signal was given by Prince John to cease the
combat. The elected Queen of Love and Beauty was then to
crown the knight whom the Prince should adjudge to have borne
himself best in this second day, with a coronet composed of thin
gold plate, cut into the shape of a laurel crown. On this second
day the knightly games ceased. But on that which was to follow,
feats of archery, of bull-baiting, and other popular amusements,
were to be practised, for the more immediate amusement of the
populace. In this manner did Prince John endeavour to lay the
foundation of a popularity, which he was perpetually throwing
down by some inconsiderate act of wanton aggression upon the
feelings and prejudices of the people.

The lists now presented a most splendid spectacle. The
sloping galleries were crowded with all that was noble, great,
wealthy, and beautiful, in the northern and midland parts of
England; and the contrast of the various dresses of these dignified spectators, rendered the view as gay as it was rich, while the
interior and lower space, filled with the substantial burgesses and
yeomen of merry England, formed, in their more plain attire, a
dark fringe, or border, around this circle of brilliant embroidery,
relieving, and, at the same time, setting off its splendour.

The heralds finished their proclamation with their usual cry of
'Largesse, largesse, gallant knights!' and gold and silver pieces
were showered on them from the galleries, it being a high point
of chivalry to exhibit liberality towards those whom the age

accounted at once the secretaries and the historians of honour. The bounty of the spectators was acknowledged by the customary shouts of 'Love of Ladies—Death of Champions—Honour to the Generous—Glory to the Brave!' To which the more humble spectators added their acclamations, and a numerous band of trumpeters the flourish of their martial instruments. When these sounds had ceased, the heralds withdrew from the lists in gay and glittering procession, and none remained within them save the marshals of the field, who, armed cap-a-pie,* sat on horseback, motionless as statues, at the opposite end of the lists. Meantime, the enclosed space at the northern extremity of the lists, large as it was, was now completely crowded with knights desirous to prove their skill against the challengers, and, when viewed from the galleries, presented the appearance of a sea of waving plumage, intermixed with glistening helmets, and tall lances, to the extremities of which were, in many cases, attached small pennons of about a span's breadth, which, fluttering in the air as the breeze caught them, joined with the restless motion of the feathers to add liveliness to the scene.

At length the barriers were opened, and five knights, chosen by lot, advanced slowly into the area; a single champion riding in front, and the other four following in pairs. All were splendidly armed, and my Saxon authority (in the Wardour Manuscript) records at great length their devices, their colours, and the embroidery of their horse trappings. It is unnecessary to be particular on these subjects. To borrow lines from a contemporary poet, who has written but too little—

> 'The knights are dust,
> And their good swords are rust,
> Their souls are with the saints, we trust.'[15]

Their escutcheons have long mouldered from the walls of their castles. Their castles themselves are but green mounds and shattered ruins—the place that once knew them, knows them no more*—nay, many a race since theirs has died out and been forgotten in the very land which they occupied, with all the authority of feudal proprietors and feudal lords. What, then, would it avail the reader to know their names, or the evanescent symbols of their martial rank!

Now, however, no whit anticipating the oblivion which awaited their names and feats, the champions advanced through the lists, restraining their fiery steeds, and compelling them to move slowly, while, at the same time, they exhibited their paces, together with the grace and dexterity of the riders. As the procession entered the lists, the sound of a wild Barbaric music was heard from behind the tents of the challengers where the performers were concealed. It was of Eastern origin, having been brought from the Holy Land; and the mixture of the cymbals and bells seemed to bid welcome at once, and defiance, to the knights as they advanced. With the eyes of an immense concourse of spectators fixed upon them, the five knights advanced up the platform upon which the tents of the challengers stood, and there separating themselves, each touched slightly, and with the reverse of his lance, the shield of the antagonist to whom he wished to oppose himself. The lower order of spectators in general—nay, many of the higher class, and it is even said several of the ladies, were rather disappointed at the champions choosing the arms of courtesy. For the same sort of persons, who, in the present day, applaud most highly the deepest tragedies, were then interested in a tournament exactly in proportion to the danger incurred by the champions engaged.

Having intimated their more pacific purpose, the champions retreated to the extremity of the lists, where they remained drawn up in a line; while the challengers, sallying each from his pavilion, mounted their horses, and, headed by Brian de Bois-Guilbert, descended from the platform, and opposed themselves individually to the knights who had touched their respective shields.

At the flourish of clarions and trumpets, they started out against each other at full gallop; and such was the superior dexterity or good fortune of the challengers, that those opposed to Bois-Guilbert, Malvoisin, and Front-de-Bœuf, rolled on the ground. The antagonist of Grantmesnil, instead of bearing his lance-point fair against the crest or the shield of his enemy, swerved so much from the direct line as to break the weapon athwart the person of his opponent—a circumstance which was accounted more disgraceful than that of being actually unhorsed; because the latter might happen from accident, whereas the

former evinced awkwardness and want of management of the
weapon and of the horse. The fifth knight alone maintained
the honour of his party, and parted fairly with the Knight of St
John, both splintering their lances without advantage on either
side.

The shouts of the multitude, together with the acclamations
of the heralds, and the clangour of the trumpets, announced the
triumph of the victors and the defeat of the vanquished. The
former retreated to their pavilions, and the latter, gathering
themselves up as they could, withdrew from the lists in disgrace
and dejection, to agree with their victors concerning the redemption of their arms and their horses, which, according to the laws
of the tournament, they had forfeited. The fifth of their number
alone tarried in the lists long enough to be greeted by the
applauses of the spectators, amongst whom he retreated, to the
aggravation, doubtless, of his companions' mortification.

A second and a third party of knights took the field; and
although they had various success, yet, upon the whole, the
advantage decidedly remained with the challengers, not one of
whom lost his seat or swerved from his charge—misfortunes
which befell one or two of their antagonists in each encounter.
The spirits, therefore, of those opposed to them, seemed to be
considerably damped by their continued success. Three knights
only appeared on the fourth entry, who, avoiding the shields of
Bois-Guilbert and Front-de-Bœuf, contented themselves with
touching those of the three other knights, who had not altogether
manifested the same strength and dexterity. This politic selec-
tion did not alter the fortune of the field, the challengers were
still successful: one of their antagonists was overthrown, and
both the others failed in the *attaint*,[16] that is, in striking the
helmet and shield of their antagonist firmly and strongly, with
the lance held in a direct line, so that the weapon might break
unless the champion was overthrown.

After this fourth encounter, there was a considerable pause;
nor did it appear that any one was very desirous of renewing the
contest. The spectators murmured among themselves; for,
among the challengers, Malvoisin and Front-de-Bœuf were
unpopular from their characters, and the others, except
Grantmesnil, were disliked as strangers and foreigners.

But none shared the general feeling of dissatisfaction so keenly as Cedric the Saxon, who saw, in each advantage gained by the Norman challengers, a repeated triumph over the honour of England. His own education had taught him no skill in the games of chivalry, although, with the arms of his Saxon ancestors, he had manifested himself, on many occasions, a brave and determined soldier. He looked anxiously to Athelstane, who had learned the accomplishments of the age, as if desiring that he should make some personal effort to recover the victory which was passing into the hands of the Templar and his associates. But, though both stout of heart and strong of person, Athelstane had a disposition too inert and unambitious to make the exertions which Cedric seemed to expect from him.

'The day is against England, my lord,' said Cedric, in a marked tone; 'are you not tempted to take the lance?'

'I shall tilt to-morrow,' answered Athelstane, 'in the *mêlée*; it is not worth while for me to arm myself to-day.'

Two things displeased Cedric in this speech. It contained the Norman word *mêlée*, (to express the general conflict,) and it evinced some indifference to the honour of the country; but it was spoken by Athelstane, whom he held in such profound respect, that he would not trust himself to canvass his motives or his foibles. Moreover, he had no time to make any remark, for Wamba thrust in his word, observing, 'It was better, though scarce easier, to be the best man among a hundred, than the best man of two.'

Athelstane took the observation as a serious compliment; but Cedric, who better understood the Jester's meaning, darted at him a severe and menacing look; and lucky it was for Wamba, perhaps, that the time and place prevented his receiving, notwithstanding his place and service, more sensible marks of his master's resentment.

The pause in the tournament was still uninterrupted, excepting by the voices of the heralds exclaiming—'Love of ladies, splintering of lances! stand forth, gallant knights, fair eyes look upon your deeds!'

The music also of the challengers breathed from time to time wild bursts expressive of triumph or defiance, while the clowns grudged a holiday which seemed to pass away in inactivity; and old knights and nobles lamented in whispers the decay of martial spirit, spoke of the triumphs of their younger days, but agreed that the land did not now supply dames of such transcendent beauty as had animated the jousts of former times. Prince John began to talk to his attendants about making ready the banquet, and the necessity of adjudging the prize to Brian de Bois-Guilbert, who had, with a single spear, overthrown two knights and foiled a third.

At length, as the Saracenic music of the challengers concluded one of those long and high flourishes with which they had broken the silence of the lists, it was answered by a solitary trumpet, which breathed a note of defiance from the northern extremity. All eyes were turned to see the new champion which these sounds announced, and no sooner were the barriers opened than he paced into the lists. As far as could be judged of a man sheathed in armour, the new adventurer did not greatly exceed the middle size, and seemed to be rather slender than strongly made. His suit of armour was formed of steel, richly inlaid with gold, and the device on his shield was a young oak-tree pulled up by the roots, with the Spanish word *Desdichado*,* signifying Disinherited. He was mounted on a gallant black horse, and as he passed through the lists he gracefully saluted the Prince and the ladies by lowering his lance. The dexterity with which he managed his steed, and something of youthful grace which he displayed in his manner won him the favour of the multitude, which some of the lower classes expressed by calling out, 'Touch Ralph de Vipont's shield—touch the Hospitaller's shield; he has the least sure seat, he is your cheapest bargain.'

The champion, moving onward amid these well-meant hints, ascended the platform by the sloping alley which led to it from the lists, and, to the astonishment of all present, riding straight up to the central pavilion, struck with the sharp end of his spear the shield of Brian de Bois-Guilbert until it rang again. All stood astonished at his presumption, but none more than the redoubted Knight whom he had thus defied to mortal combat, and who, little expecting so rude a challenge, was standing carelessly at the door of the pavilion.

'Have you confessed yourself, brother,' said the Templar,

'and have you heard mass this morning, that you peril your life so frankly?'

'I am fitter to meet death than thou art,' answered the Disinherited Knight; for by this name the stranger had recorded himself in the books of the tourney.

'Then take your place in the lists,' said Bois-Guilbert, 'and look your last upon the sun; for this night thou shalt sleep in paradise.'*

'Gramercy for thy courtesy,' replied the Disinherited Knight, 'and to requite it, I advise thee to take a fresh horse and a new lance, for by my honour you will need both.'

Having expressed himself thus confidently, he reined his horse backward down the slope which he had ascended, and compelled him in the same manner to move backward through the lists, till he reached the northern extremity, where he remained stationary, in expectation of his antagonist. This feat of horsemanship again attracted the applause of the multitude.

However incensed at his adversary for the precautions which he recommended, Brian de Bois-Guilbert did not neglect his advice; for his honour was too nearly concerned, to permit his neglecting any means which might ensure victory over his presumptuous opponent. He changed his horse for a proved and fresh one of great strength and spirit. He chose a new and tough spear, lest the wood of the former might have been strained in the previous encounters he had sustained. Lastly, he laid aside his shield, which had received some little damage, and received another from his squires. His first had only borne the general device of his rider, representing two knights riding upon one horse, an emblem expressive of the original humility and poverty of the Templars, qualities which they had since exchanged for the arrogance and wealth that finally occasioned their suppression.* Bois-Guilbert's new shield bore a raven in full flight, holding in its claws a skull, and bearing the motto, *Gare le Corbeau*.*

When the two champions stood opposed to each other at the two extremities of the lists, the public expectation was strained to the highest pitch. Few augured the possibility that the encounter could terminate well for the Disinherited Knight, yet his courage and gallantry secured the general good wishes of the spectators.

The trumpets had no sooner given the signal, than the champions vanished from their posts with the speed of lightning, and closed in the centre of the lists with the shock of a thunderbolt. The lances burst into shivers up to the very grasp, and it seemed at the moment that both knights had fallen, for the shock had made each horse recoil backwards upon its haunches. The address of the riders recovered their steeds by use of the bridle and spur; and having glared on each other for an instant with eyes which seemed to flash fire through the bars of their visors, each made a demi-volte, and, retiring to the extremity of the lists, received a fresh lance from the attendants.

A loud shout from the spectators, waving of scarfs and handkerchiefs, and general acclamations, attested the interest taken by the spectators in this encounter; the most equal, as well as the best performed, which had graced the day. But no sooner had the knights resumed their station, than the clamour of applause was hushed into a silence, so deep and so dead, that it seemed the multitude were afraid even to breathe.

A few minutes' pause having been allowed, that the combatants and their horses might recover breath, Prince John with his truncheon signed to the trumpets to sound the onset. The champions a second time sprung from their stations, and closed in the centre of the lists, with the same speed, the same dexterity, the same violence, but not the same equal fortune as before.

In this second encounter, the Templar aimed at the centre of his antagonist's shield, and struck it so fair and forcibly, that his spear went to shivers, and the Disinherited Knight reeled in his saddle. On the other hand, that champion had, in the beginning of his career, directed the point of his lance towards Bois-Guilbert's shield, but, changing his aim almost in the moment of encounter, he addressed it to the helmet, a mark more difficult to hit, but which, if attained, rendered the shock more irresistible. Fair and true he hit the Norman on the visor, where his lance's point kept hold of the bars. Yet, even at this disadvantage, the Templar sustained his high reputation; and had not the girths of his saddle burst, he might not have been unhorsed. As it

chanced, however, saddle, horse, and man, rolled on the ground
under a cloud of dust.

To extricate himself from the stirrups and fallen steed, was
to the Templar scarce the work of a moment; and, stung
with madness, both at his disgrace and at the acclamations with
which it was hailed by the spectators, he drew his sword
and waved it in defiance of his conqueror. The Disinherited
Knight sprung from his steed, and also unsheathed his sword.
The marshals of the field, however, spurred their horses between
them, and reminded them, that the laws of the tournament
did not, on the present occasion, permit this species of
encounter.

'We shall meet again, I trust,' said the Templar, casting a
resentful glance at his antagonist; 'and where there are none to
separate us.'

'If we do not,' said the Disinherited Knight, 'the fault shall
not be mine. On foot or horseback, with spear, with axe, or with
sword, I am alike ready to encounter thee.'

More and angrier words would have been exchanged, but the
marshals, crossing their lances betwixt them, compelled them to
separate. The Disinherited Knight returned to his first station,
and Bois-Guilbert to his tent, where he remained for the rest of
the day in an agony of despair.

Without alighting from his horse, the conqueror called for a
bowl of wine, and opening the beaver, or lower part of his
helmet, announced that he quaffed it, 'To all true English hearts,
and to the confusion of foreign tyrants.' He then commanded his
trumpet to sound a defiance to the challengers, and desired a
herald to announce to them, that he should make no election, but
was willing to encounter them in the order in which they pleased
to advance against him.

The gigantic Front-de-Bœuf, armed in sable armour, was the
first who took the field. He bore on a white shield a black bull's
head, half defaced by the numerous encounters which he had
undergone, and bearing the arrogant motto, *Cave, Adsum.** Over
this champion the Disinherited Knight obtained a slight but
decisive advantage. Both Knights broke their lances fairly, but
Front-de-Bœuf, who lost a stirrup in the encounter, was adjudged to have the disadvantage.

In the stranger's third encounter with Sir Philip Malvoisin, he was equally successful; striking that baron so forcibly on the casque, that the laces of the helmet broke, and Malvoisin, only saved from falling by being unhelmeted, was declared vanquished like his companions.

In his fourth combat with De Grantmesnil, the Disinherited Knight showed as much courtesy as he had hitherto evinced courage and dexterity. De Grantmesnil's horse, which was young and violent, reared and plunged in the course of the career so as to disturb the rider's aim, and the stranger, declining to take the advantage which this accident afforded him, raised his lance, and passing his antagonist without touching him, wheeled his horse and rode back again to his own end of the lists, offering his antagonist, by a herald, the chance of a second encounter. This De Grantmesnil declined, avowing himself vanquished as much by the courtesy as by the address of his opponent.

Ralph de Vipont summed up the list of the stranger's triumphs, being hurled to the ground with such force, that the blood gushed from his nose and his mouth, and he was borne senseless from the lists.

The acclamations of thousands applauded the unanimous award of the Prince and marshals, announcing that day's honours to the Disinherited Knight.

CHAPTER IX

————In the midst was seen
A lady of a more majestic mien,
By stature and by beauty mark'd their sovereign Queen.

And as in beauty she surpass'd the choir,
So nobler than the rest was her attire;
A crown of ruddy gold enclosed her brow,
Plain without pomp, and rich without a show;
A branch of Agnus Castus in her hand,
She bore aloft her symbol of command.

*The Flower and the Leaf**

WILLIAM DE WYVIL and Stephen de Martival, the marshals of the field, were the first to offer their congratulations to the victor, praying him, at the same time, to suffer his helmet to be unlaced, or, at least, that he would raise his visor ere they conducted him to receive the prize of the day's tourney from the hands of Prince John. The Disinherited Knight, with all knightly courtesy, declined their request, alleging, that he could not at this time suffer his face to be seen, for reasons which he had assigned to the heralds when he entered the lists. The marshals were perfectly satisfied by this reply; for amidst the frequent and capricious vows by which knights were accustomed to bind themselves in the days of chivalry, there were none more common than those by which they engaged to remain incognito for a certain space, or until some particular adventure was achieved. The marshals, therefore, pressed no farther into the mystery of the Disinherited Knight, but, announcing to Prince John the conqueror's desire to remain unknown, they requested permission to bring him before his Grace, in order that he might receive the reward of his valour.

John's curiosity was excited by the mystery observed by the stranger; and, being already displeased with the issue of the tournament, in which the challengers whom he favoured had been successively defeated by one knight, he answered haughtily to the marshals, 'By the light of Our Lady's brow, this same knight hath been disinherited as well of his courtesy as of his lands, since he desires to appear before us without uncovering his face.—Wot ye, my lords,' he said, turning round to his train, 'who this gallant can be, that bears himself thus proudly?'

'I cannot guess,' answered De Bracy, 'nor did I think there had been within the four seas that girth Britain a champion that could bear down these five knights in one day's jousting. By my faith, I shall never forget the force with which he shocked De Vipont. The poor Hospitaller was hurled from his saddle like a stone from a sling.'

'Boast not of that,' said a Knight of St John, who was present; 'your Temple champion had no better luck. I saw your brave lance, Bois-Guilbert, roll thrice over, grasping his hands full of sand at every turn.'

De Bracy, being attached to the Templars, would have replied, but was prevented by Prince John. 'Silence, sirs!' he said; 'what unprofitable debate have we here?'

'The victor,' said De Wyvil, 'still waits the pleasure of your highness.'

'It is our pleasure,' answered John, 'that he do so wait until we learn whether there is not some one who can at least guess at his name and quality. Should he remain there till nightfall, he has had work enough to keep him warm.'

'Your Grace,' said Waldemar Fitzurse, 'will do less than due honour to the victor, if you compel him to wait till we tell your highness that which we cannot know; at least I can form no guess—unless he be one of the good lances who accompanied King Richard to Palestine, and who are now straggling homeward from the Holy Land.'

'It may be the Earl of Salisbury,'* said De Bracy; 'he is about the same pitch.'

'Sir Thomas de Multon, the Knight of Gilsland, rather,' said Fitzurse; 'Salisbury is bigger in the bones.' A whisper arose among the train, but by whom first suggested could not be ascertained. 'It might be the King—it might be Richard Cœur-de-Lion himself!'

'Over God's forbode!'* said Prince John, involuntarily turning at the same time as pale as death, and shrinking as if blighted by a flash of lightning; 'Waldemar!—De Bracy! brave knights and gentlemen, remember your promises, and stand truly by me!'

'Here is no danger impending,' said Waldemar Fitzurse; 'are you so little acquainted with the gigantic limbs of your father's son, as to think they can be held within the circumference of yonder suit of armour?—De Wyvil and Martival, you will best serve the Prince by bringing forward the victor to the throne, and ending an error that has conjured all the blood from his cheeks.—Look at him more closely,' he continued, 'your highness will see that he wants three inches of King Richard's height, and twice as much of his shoulder-breadth. The very horse he backs, could not have carried the ponderous weight of King Richard through a single course.'

While he was yet speaking, the marshals brought forward the Disinherited Knight to the foot of a wooden flight of steps, which formed the ascent from the lists to Prince John's throne. Still discomposed with the idea that his brother, so much injured, and to whom he was so much indebted, had suddenly arrived in his native kingdom, even the distinctions pointed out by Fitzurse did not altogether remove the Prince's apprehensions; and while, with a short and embarrassed eulogy upon his valour, he caused to be delivered to him the war-horse assigned as the prize, he trembled lest from the barred visor of the mailed form before him, an answer might be returned, in the deep and awful accents of Richard the Lion-hearted.

But the Disinherited Knight spoke not a word in reply to the compliment of the Prince, which he only acknowledged with a profound obeisance.

The horse was led into the lists by two grooms richly dressed, the animal itself being fully accoutred with the richest war-furniture; which, however, scarcely added to the value of the noble creature in the eyes of those who were judges. Laying one hand upon the pommel of the saddle, the Disinherited Knight vaulted at once upon the back of the steed without making use of the stirrup, and, brandishing aloft his lance, rode twice around the lists, exhibiting the points and paces of the horse with the skill of a perfect horseman.

The appearance of vanity, which might otherwise have been attributed to this display, was removed by the propriety shown in exhibiting to the best advantage the princely reward with which he had been just honoured, and the Knight was again greeted by the acclamations of all present.

In the meanwhile, the bustling Prior of Jorvaulx had reminded Prince John, in a whisper, that the victor must now display his good judgment, instead of his valour, by selecting from among the beauties who graced the galleries a lady, who should fill the throne of the Queen of Beauty and of Love, and deliver the prize of the tourney upon the ensuing day. The Prince accordingly made a sign with his truncheon, as the Knight passed him in his second career around the lists. The Knight turned towards the throne, and, sinking his lance, until the point was within a foot of the ground, remained motionless, as if expecting John's commands; while all admired the sudden dexterity with which he instantly reduced his fiery steed from a state of violent emotion and high excitation to the stillness of an equestrian statue.

'Sir Disinherited Knight,' said Prince John, 'since that is the only title by which we can address you, it is now your duty, as well as privilege, to name the fair lady, who, as Queen of Honour and of Love, is to preside over next day's festival. If, as a stranger in our land, you should require the aid of other judgment to guide your own, we can only say that Alicia, the daughter of our gallant knight Waldemar Fitzurse, has at our court been long held the first in beauty as in place. Nevertheless, it is your undoubted prerogative to confer on whom you please this crown, by the delivery of which to the lady of your choice, the election of to-morrow's Queen will be formal and complete.—Raise your lance.'

The Knight obeyed; and Prince John placed upon its point a coronet of green satin, having around its edge a circlet of gold, the upper edge of which was relieved by arrow-points and hearts placed interchangeably, like the strawberry leaves and balls upon a ducal crown.

In the broad hint which he dropped respecting the daughter of Waldemar Fitzurse, John had more than one motive, each the offspring of a mind, which was a strange mixture of carelessness and presumption with low artifice and cunning. He wished to banish from the minds of the chivalry around him his own indecent and unacceptable jest respecting the Jewess Rebecca; he was desirous of conciliating Alicia's father Waldemar, of whom he stood in awe, and who had more than once shown himself dissatisfied during the course of the day's proceedings. He had also a wish to establish himself in the good graces of the lady; for John was at least as licentious in his pleasures as profligate in his ambition. But besides all these reasons, he was desirous to raise up against the Disinherited Knight (towards whom he already entertained a strong dislike) a powerful enemy in the person of Waldemar Fitzurse, who was likely, he thought, highly to resent the injury done to his daughter, in case, as was not unlikely, the victor should make another choice.

And so indeed it proved. For the Disinherited Knight passed the gallery close to that of the Prince, in which the Lady Alicia was seated in the full pride of triumphant beauty, and, pacing forwards as slowly as he had hitherto rode swiftly around the lists, he seemed to exercise his right of examining the numerous fair faces which adorned that splendid circle.

It was worth while to see the different conduct of the beauties who underwent this examination, during the time it was proceeding. Some blushed, some assumed an air of pride and dignity, some looked straight forward, and essayed to seem utterly unconscious of what was going on, some drew back in alarm, which was perhaps affected, some endeavoured to forbear smiling, and there were two or three who laughed outright. There were also some who dropped their veils over their charms; but as the Wardour Manuscript says these were fair ones of ten years standing, it may be supposed that, having had their full share of such vanities, they were willing to withdraw their claim in order to give a fair chance to the rising beauties of the age.

At length the champion paused beneath the balcony in which the Lady Rowena was placed, and the expectation of the spectators was excited to the utmost.

It must be owned, that if an interest displayed in his success could have bribed the Disinherited Knight, the part of the lists before which he paused had merited his predilection. Cedric the Saxon, overjoyed at the discomfiture of the Templar, and still more so at the miscarriage of his two malevolent neighbours, Front-de-Bœuf and Malvoisin, had, with his body half stretched over the balcony, accompanied the victor in each course, not with his eyes only, but with his whole heart and soul. The Lady Rowena had watched the progress of the day with equal attention, though without openly betraying the same intense interest. Even the unmoved Athelstane had shown symptoms of shaking off his apathy, when, calling for a huge goblet of muscadine, he quaffed it to the health of the Disinherited Knight.

Another group, stationed under the gallery occupied by the Saxons, had shown no less interest in the fate of the day.

'Father Abraham!' said Isaac of York, when the first course was run betwixt the Templar and the Disinherited Knight, 'how fiercely that Gentile rides! Ah, the good horse that was brought all the long way from Barbary, he takes no more care of him than if he were a wild ass's colt—and the noble armour that was worth so many zecchins* to Joseph Pareira, the armourer of Milan, besides seventy in the hundred of profits, he cares for it as little as if he had found it in the highways!'

'If he risks his own person and limbs, father,' said Rebecca, 'in doing such a dreadful battle, he can scarce be expected to spare his horse and armour.'

'Child!' replied Isaac, somewhat heated, 'thou knowest not what thou speakest—His neck and limbs are his own, but his horse and armour belong to——Holy Jacob! what was I about to say!—Nevertheless, it is a good youth—See, Rebecca! see, he is again about to go up to battle against the Philistine—Pray, child—pray for the safety of the good youth,—and of the speedy horse, and the rich armour.—God of my fathers!' he again exclaimed, 'he hath conquered, and the uncircumcised Philistine hath fallen before his lance,—even as Og the King of Bashan, and Sihon, King of the Amorites,* fell before the sword of our fathers!—Surely he shall take their gold and their silver, and their war-horses, and their armour of brass and of steel, for a prey and for a spoil.'

The same anxiety did the worthy Jew display during every course that was run, seldom failing to hazard a hasty calculation concerning the value of the horse and armour which were forfeited to the champion upon each new success. There had been therefore no small interest taken in the success of the Disinherited Knight, by those who occupied the part of the lists before which he now paused.

Whether from indecision or some other motive of hesitation, the champion of the day remained stationary for more than a minute, while the eyes of the silent audience were riveted upon his motions; and then, gradually and gracefully sinking the point of his lance, he deposited the coronet which it supported at the feet of the fair Rowena. The trumpets instantly sounded, while the heralds proclaimed the Lady Rowena the Queen of Beauty and of Love for the ensuing day, menacing with suitable penalties those who should be disobedient to her authority. They then repeated their cry of Largesse, to which Cedric, in the height of his joy, replied by an ample donative, and to which Athelstane, though less promptly, added one equally large.

There was some murmuring among the damsels of Norman descent, who were as much unused to see the preference given to a Saxon beauty, as the Norman nobles were to sustain defeat in the games of chivalry which they themselves had introduced. But these sounds of disaffection were drowned by the popular shout of 'Long live the Lady Rowena, the chosen and lawful Queen of Love and of Beauty!' To which many in the lower area added, 'Long live the Saxon Princess! long live the race of the immortal Alfred!'

However unacceptable these sounds might be to Prince John, and to those around him, he saw himself nevertheless obliged to confirm the nomination of the victor, and accordingly calling to horse, he left his throne; and mounting his jennet, accompanied by his train, he again entered the lists. The Prince paused a moment beneath the gallery of the Lady Alicia, to whom he paid his compliments, observing, at the same time, to those around him—'By my halidome, sirs! if the Knight's feats in arms have shown that he hath limbs and sinews, his choice hath no less proved that his eyes are none of the clearest.'

It was on this occasion, as during his whole life, John's misfortune, not perfectly to understand the characters of those whom he wished to conciliate. Waldemar Fitzurse was rather offended than pleased at the Prince stating thus broadly an opinion, that his daughter had been slighted.

'I know no right of chivalry,' he said, 'more precious or inalienable than that of each free knight to choose his lady-love by his own judgment. My daughter courts distinction from no one;

and in her own character, and in her own sphere, will never fail to receive the full proportion of that which is her due.'

Prince John replied not; but, spurring his horse, as if to give vent to his vexation, he made the animal bound forward to the gallery where Rowena was seated, with the crown still at her feet.

'Assume,' he said, 'fair lady, the mark of your sovereignty, to which none vows homage more sincerely than ourself, John of Anjoù; and if it please you to-day, with your noble sire and friends, to grace our banquet in the Castle of Ashby, we shall learn to know the empress to whose service we devote tomorrow.'

Rowena remained silent, and Cedric answered for her in his native Saxon.

'The Lady Rowena,' he said, 'possesses not the language in which to reply to your courtesy, or to sustain her part in your festival. I also, and the noble Athelstane of Coningsburgh, speak only the language, and practise only the manners, of our fathers. We therefore decline with thanks your Highness's courteous invitation to the banquet. To-morrow, the Lady Rowena will take upon her the state to which she has been called by the free election of the victor Knight, confirmed by the acclamations of the people.'

So saying, he lifted the coronet, and placed it upon Rowena's head, in token of her acceptance of the temporary authority assigned to her.

'What says he?' said Prince John, affecting not to understand the Saxon language, in which, however, he was well skilled. The purport of Cedric's speech was repeated to him in French. 'It is well,' he said; 'to-morrow we will ourself conduct this mute sovereign to her seat of dignity.—You, at least, Sir Knight,' he added, turning to the victor, who had remained near the gallery, 'will this day share our banquet?'

The Knight, speaking for the first time, in a low and hurried voice, excused himself by pleading fatigue, and the necessity of preparing for to-morrow's encounter.

'It is well,' said Prince John, haughtily; 'although unused to such refusals, we will endeavour to digest our banquet as we may, though ungraced by the most successful in arms, and his elected Queen of Beauty.'

So saying, he prepared to leave the lists with his glittering train, and his turning his steed for that purpose, was the signal for the breaking up and dispersion of the spectators.

Yet, with the vindictive memory proper to offended pride, especially when combined with conscious want of desert, John had hardly proceeded three paces, ere again, turning around, he fixed an eye of stern resentment upon the yeoman who had displeased him in the early part of the day, and issued his commands to the men-at-arms who stood near—'On your life, suffer not that fellow to escape.'

The yeoman stood the angry glance of the Prince with the same unvaried steadiness which had marked his former deportment, saying, with a smile, 'I have no intention to leave Ashby until the day after to-morrow—I must see how Staffordshire and Leicestershire can draw their bows—the forests of Needwood and Charnwood* must rear good archers.'

'I,' said Prince John to his attendants, but not in direct reply,—'I will see how he can draw his own; and woe betide him unless his skill should prove some apology for his insolence!'

'It is full time,' said De Bracy, 'that the *outre cuidance*[17] of these peasants should be restrained by some striking example.'

Waldemar Fitzurse, who probably thought his patron was not taking the readiest road to popularity, shrugged up his shoulders and was silent. Prince John resumed his retreat from the lists, and the dispersion of the multitude became general.

In various routes, according to the different quarters from which they came, and in groups of various numbers, the spectators were seen retiring over the plain. By far the most numerous part streamed towards the town of Ashby, where many of the distinguished persons were lodged in the castle, and where others found accommodation in the town itself. Among these were most of the knights who had already appeared in the tournament, or who proposed to fight there the ensuing day, and who, as they rode slowly along, talking over the events of the day, were greeted with loud shouts by the populace. The same acclamations were bestowed upon Prince John, although he was indebted for them rather to the splendour of his appearance and train, than to the popularity of his character.

A more sincere and more general, as well as a better-merited acclamation, attended the victor of the day, until, anxious to withdraw himself from popular notice, he accepted the accommodation of one of those pavilions pitched at the extremities of the lists, the use of which was courteously tendered him by the marshals of the field. On his retiring to his tent, many who had lingered in the lists, to look upon and form conjectures concerning him, also dispersed.

The signs and sounds of a tumultuous concourse of men lately crowded together in one place, and agitated by the same passing events, were now exchanged for the distant hum* of voices of different groups retreating in all directions, and these speedily died away in silence. No other sounds were heard save the voices of the menials who stripped the galleries of their cushions and tapestry, in order to put them in safety for the night, and wrangled among themselves for the half-used bottles of wine and relics of the refreshment which had been served round to the spectators.

Beyond the precincts of the lists more than one forge was erected; and these now began to glimmer through the twilight, announcing the toil of the armourers, which was to continue through the whole night, in order to repair or alter the suits of armour to be used again on the morrow.

A strong guard of men-at-arms, renewed at intervals, from two hours to two hours, surrounded the lists, and kept watch during the night.

CHAPTER X

Thus, like the sad presaging raven, that tolls
The sick man's passport in her hollow beak,
And in the shadow of the silent night
Doth shake contagion from her sable wings;
Vex'd and tormented, runs poor Barrabas,
With fatal curses towards these Christians.

*Jew of Malta**

THE Disinherited Knight had no sooner reached his pavilion, than squires and pages in abundance tendered their services to disarm him, to bring fresh attire, and to offer him the refreshment of the bath. Their zeal on this occasion was perhaps sharpened by curiosity, since every one desired to know who the knight was that had gained so many laurels, yet had refused, even at the command of Prince John, to lift his visor or to name his name. But their officious inquisitiveness was not gratified. The Disinherited Knight refused all other assistance save that of his own squire, or rather yeoman—a clownish-looking man, who, wrapt in a cloak of dark-coloured felt, and having his head and face half-buried in a Norman bonnet made of black fur, seemed to affect the incognito as much as his master. All others being excluded from the tent, this attendant relieved his master from the more burdensome parts of his armour, and placed food and wine before him, which the exertions of the day rendered very acceptable.

The Knight had scarcely finished a hasty meal, ere his menial announced to him that five men, each leading a barbed steed,* desired to speak with him. The Disinherited Knight had exchanged his armour for the long robe usually worn by those of his condition, which, being furnished with a hood, concealed the features, when such was the pleasure of the wearer, almost as completely as the visor of the helmet itself; but the twilight, which was now fast darkening, would of itself have rendered a disguise unnecessary, unless to persons to whom the face of an individual chanced to be particularly well known.

The Disinherited Knight, therefore, stept boldly forth to the front of his tent, and found in attendance the squires of the challengers, whom he easily knew by their russet and black dresses, each of whom led his master's charger, loaded with the armour in which he had that day fought.

'According to the laws of chivalry,' said the foremost of these men, 'I, Baldwin de Oyley, squire to the redoubted Knight Brian de Bois-Guilbert, make offer to you, styling yourself, for the present, the Disinherited Knight, of the horse and armour used by the said Brian de Bois-Guilbert in this day's Passage of Arms, leaving it with your nobleness to retain or to ransom the same, according to your pleasure; for such is the law of arms.'

The other squires repeated nearly the same formula, and then stood to await the decision of the Disinherited Knight.

'To you four, sirs,' replied the Knight, addressing those who had last spoken, 'and to your honourable and valiant masters, I have one common reply. Commend me to the noble knights, your masters, and say, I should do ill to deprive them of steeds and arms which can never be used by braver cavaliers.—I would I could here end my message to these gallant knights; but being, as I term myself, in truth and earnest, the Disinherited, I must be thus far bound to your masters, that they will, of their courtesy, be pleased to ransom their steeds and armour, since that which I wear I can hardly term mine own.'

'We stand commissioned, each of us,' answered the squire of Reginald Front-de-Bœuf, 'to offer a hundred zecchins in ransom of these horses and suits of armour.'

'It is sufficient,' said the Disinherited Knight. 'Half the sum my present necessities compel me to accept; of the remaining half, distribute one moiety among yourselves, sir squires, and divide the other half betwixt the heralds and the pursuivants, and minstrels, and attendants.'

The squires, with cap in hand, and low reverences, expressed their deep sense of a courtesy and generosity not often practised, at least upon a scale so extensive. The Disinherited Knight then addressed his discourse to Baldwin, the squire of Brian de Bois-Guilbert. 'From your master,' said he, 'I will accept neither arms nor ransom. Say to him in my name, that our strife is not ended—no, not till we have fought as well with swords as with lances—as well on foot as on horseback. To this mortal quarrel he has himself defied me, and I shall not forget the challenge.—Meantime, let him be assured, that I hold him not as one of his companions, with whom I can with pleasure exchange courtesies; but rather as one with whom I stand upon terms of mortal defiance.'

'My master,' answered Baldwin, 'knows how to requite scorn with scorn, and blows with blows, as well as courtesy with courtesy. Since you disdain to accept from him any share of the ransom at which you have rated the arms of the other knights, I must leave his armour and his horse here, being well assured that he will never deign to mount the one nor wear the other.'

'You have spoken well, good squire,' said the Disinherited Knight, 'well and boldly, as it beseemeth him to speak who answers for an absent master. Leave not, however, the horse and armour here. Restore them to thy master; or, if he scorns to accept them, retain them, good friend, for thine own use. So far as they are mine, I bestow them upon you freely.'

Baldwin made a deep obeisance, and retired with his companions; and the Disinherited Knight entered the pavilion.

'Thus far, Gurth,' said he, addressing his attendant, 'the reputation of English chivalry hath not suffered in my hands.'

'And I,' said Gurth, 'for a Saxon swineherd, have not ill played the personage of a Norman squire-at-arms.'

'Yea, but,' answered the Disinherited Knight, 'thou hast ever kept me in anxiety lest thy clownish bearing should discover thee.'

'Tush!' said Gurth, 'I fear discovery from none, saving my playfellow, Wamba the Jester, of whom I could never discover whether he were most knave or fool. Yet I could scarce choose but laugh, when my old master passed so near to me, dreaming all the while that Gurth was keeping his porkers many a mile off, in the thickets and swamps of Rotherwood. If I am discovered'——

'Enough,' said the Disinherited Knight, 'thou knowest my promise.'

'Nay, for that matter,' said Gurth, 'I will never fail my friend for fear of my skin-cutting. I have a tough hide, that will bear knife or scourge as well as any boar's hide in my herd.'

'Trust me, I will requite the risk you run for my love, Gurth,' said the Knight. 'Meanwhile, I pray you to accept these ten pieces of gold.'

'I am richer,' said Gurth, putting them into his pouch, 'than ever was swineherd or bondsman.'

'Take this bag of gold to Ashby,' continued his master, 'and find out Isaac the Jew of York, and let him pay himself for the horse and arms with which his credit supplied me.'

'Nay, by St Dunstan,' replied Gurth, 'that I will not do.'

'How, knave,' replied his master, 'wilt thou not obey my commands?'

'So they be honest, reasonable, and Christian commands,' replied Gurth; 'but this is none of these. To suffer the Jew to pay himself would be dishonest, for it would be cheating my master; and unreasonable, for it were the part of a fool; and unchristian, since it would be plundering a believer to enrich an infidel.'

'See him contented, however, thou stubborn varlet,' said the Disinherited Knight.

'I will do so,' said Gurth, taking the bag under his cloak, and leaving the apartment; 'and it will go hard,' he muttered, 'but I content him with one-half of his own asking.' So saying, he departed, and left the Disinherited Knight to his own perplexed ruminations; which, upon more accounts than it is now possible to communicate to the reader, were of a nature peculiarly agitating and painful.

We must now change the scene to the village of Ashby, or rather to a country house in its vicinity belonging to a wealthy Israelite, with whom Isaac, his daughter, and retinue, had taken up their quarters; the Jews, it is well known, being as liberal in exercising the duties of hospitality and charity among their own people, as they were alleged to be reluctant and churlish in extending them to those whom they termed Gentiles, and whose treatment of them certainly merited little hospitality at their hand.

In an apartment, small indeed, but richly furnished with decorations of an Oriental taste, Rebecca was seated on a heap of embroidered cushions, which, piled along a low platform that surrounded the chamber, served, like the estrada* of the Spaniards, instead of chairs and stools. She was watching the motions of her father with a look of anxious and filial affection, while he paced the apartment with a dejected mien and disordered step; sometimes clasping his hands together—sometimes casting his eyes to the roof of the apartment, as one who laboured under great mental tribulation. 'O, Jacob!' he exclaimed—'O, all ye twelve Holy Fathers of our tribe! what a losing venture is this for one who hath duly kept every jot and tittle of the law of Moses—Fifty zecchins wrenched from me at one clutch, and by the talons of a tyrant!'

'But, father,' said Rebecca, 'you seemed to give the gold to Prince John willingly.'

'Willingly? the blotch of Egypt* upon him!—Willingly, saidst thou?—Ay, as willingly as when in the Gulf of Lyons, I flung over my merchandise to lighten the ship, while she laboured in the tempest—robed the seething billows in my choice silks*—perfumed their briny foam with myrrh and aloes—enriched their caverns with gold and silver work! And was not that an hour of unutterable misery, though my own hands made the sacrifice?'

'But it was a sacrifice which Heaven exacted to save our lives,' answered Rebecca, 'and the God of our fathers has since blessed your store and your gettings.'

'Ay,' answered Isaac, 'but if the tyrant lays hold on them as he did to-day, and compels me to smile while he is robbing me?—O, daughter, disinherited and wandering as we are, the worst evil which befalls our race is, that when we are wronged and plundered, all the world laughs around, and we are compelled to suppress our sense of injury, and to smile tamely, when we would revenge bravely.'

'Think not thus of it, my father,' said Rebecca; 'we also have advantages. These Gentiles, cruel and oppressive as they are, are in some sort dependent on the dispersed children of Zion, whom they despise and persecute. Without the aid of our wealth, they could neither furnish forth their hosts in war, nor their triumphs in peace; and the gold which we lend them returns with increase to our coffers. We are like the herb which flourisheth most when it is most trampled on.* Even this day's pageant had not proceeded without the consent of the despised Jew, who furnished the means.'

'Daughter,' said Isaac, 'thou hast harped upon* another string of sorrow. The goodly steed and the rich armour, equal to the full profit of my adventure with our Kirjath Jairam of Leicester—there is a dead loss too—ay, a loss which swallows up the gains of a week; ay, of the space between two Sabaoths*—and yet it may end better than I now think, for 'tis a good youth.'

'Assuredly,' said Rebecca, 'you shall not repent you of requiting the good deed received of the stranger knight.'

'I trust so, daughter,' said Isaac, 'and I trust too in the rebuilding of Zion; but as well do I hope with my own bodily eyes to see the walls and battlements of the new Temple, as to see a Christian, yea, the very best of Christians, repay a debt to a Jew, unless under the awe of the judge and jailor.'

So saying, he resumed his discontented walk through the apartment; and Rebecca, perceiving that her attempts at consolation only served to awaken new subjects of complaint, wisely desisted from her unavailing efforts—a prudential line of conduct, and we recommend to all who set up for comforters and advisers, to follow it in the like circumstances.

The evening was now becoming dark, when a Jewish servant entered the apartment, and placed upon the table two silver lamps, fed with perfumed oil; the richest wines, and the most delicate refreshments, were at the same time displayed by another Israelitish domestic on a small ebony table, inlaid with silver; for, in the interior of their houses, the Jews refused themselves no expensive indulgences. At the same time the servant informed Isaac, that a Nazarene (so they termed Christians, while conversing among themselves) desired to speak with him. He that would live by traffic, must hold himself at the disposal of every one claiming business with him. Isaac at once replaced on the table the untasted glass of Greek wine which he had just raised to his lips, and saying hastily to his daughter, 'Rebecca, veil thyself,' commanded the stranger to be admitted.

Just as Rebecca had dropped over her fine features a screen of silver gauze which reached to her feet, the door opened, and Gurth entered, wrapt in the ample folds of his Norman mantle. His appearance was rather suspicious than prepossessing, especially as, instead of doffing his bonnet, he pulled it still deeper over his rugged brow.

'Art thou Isaac the Jew of York?' said Gurth, in Saxon.

'I am,' replied Isaac, in the same language, (for his traffic had rendered every tongue spoken in Britain familiar to him)—'and who art thou?'

'That is not to the purpose,' answered Gurth.

'As much as my name is to thee,' replied Isaac; 'for without knowing thine, how can I hold intercourse with thee?'

'Easily,' answered Gurth; 'I, being to pay money, must know that I deliver it to the right person; thou, who art to receive it, wilt not, I think, care very greatly by whose hands it is delivered.'

'O,' said the Jew, 'you are come to pay monies?—Holy Father Abraham! that altereth our relation to each other. And from whom dost thou bring it?'

'From the Disinherited Knight,' said Gurth, 'victor in this day's tournament. It is the price of the armour supplied to him by Kirjath Jairam of Leicester, on thy recommendation. The steed is restored to thy stable. I desire to know the amount of the sum which I am to pay for the armour.'

'I said he was a good youth!' exclaimed Isaac, with joyful exultation. 'A cup of wine will do thee no harm,' he added, filling and handing to the swineherd a richer draught than Gurth had ever before tasted. 'And how much money,' continued Isaac, 'hast thou brought with thee?'

'Holy Virgin!' said Gurth, setting down the cup, 'what nectar these unbelieving dogs drink, while true Christians are fain to quaff ale as muddy and thick as the draff* we give to hogs!—What money have I brought with me?' continued the Saxon, when he had finished this uncivil ejaculation, 'even but a small sum; something in hand the whilst. What, Isaac! thou must bear a conscience, though it be a Jewish one.'

'Nay, but,' said Isaac, 'thy master has won goodly steeds and rich armours with the strength of his lance, and of his right hand—but 'tis a good youth—the Jew will take these in present payment, and render him back the surplus.'

'My master has disposed of them already,' said Gurth.

'Ah! that was wrong,' said the Jew, 'that was the part of a fool. No Christian here could buy so many horses and armour—no Jew except myself would give him half the values. But thou hast a hundred zecchins with thee in that bag,' said Isaac, prying under Gurth's cloak, 'it is a heavy one.'

'I have heads for crossbow bolts in it,' said Gurth, readily.

'Well, then'—said Isaac, panting and hesitating between habitual love of gain and a new-born desire to be liberal in the present instance, 'if I should say that I would take eighty zecchins for the good steed and the rich armour, which leaves me not a guilder's profit, have you money to pay me?'

'Barely,' said Gurth, though the sum demanded was more reasonable than he expected, 'and it will leave my master nigh penniless. Nevertheless, if such be your least offer, I must be content.'

'Fill thyself another goblet of wine,' said the Jew. 'Ah! eighty zecchins is too little. It leaveth no profit for the usages of the monies; and, besides, the good horse may have suffered wrong in this day's encounter. O, it was a hard and a dangerous meeting! man and steed rushing on each other like wild bulls of Bashan!* the horse cannot but have had wrong.'

'And I say,' replied Gurth, 'he is sound, wind and limb; and you may see him now in your stable. And I say, over and above, that seventy zecchins is enough for the armour, and I hope a Christian's word is as good as a Jew's. If you will not take seventy, I will carry this bag' (and he shook it till the contents jingled) 'back to my master.'

'Nay, nay!' said Isaac; 'lay down the talents—the shekels— the eighty zecchins, and thou shalt see I will consider thee liberally.'

Gurth at length complied; and telling out eighty zecchins upon the table, the Jew delivered out to him an acquittance for the horse and suit of armour. The Jew's hand trembled for joy as he wrapped up the first seventy pieces of gold. The last ten he told over with much deliberation, pausing, and saying something as he took each piece from the table, and dropt it into his purse. It seemed as if his avarice were struggling with his better nature, and compelling him to pouch zecchin after zecchin, while his generosity urged him to restore some part at least to his benefactor, or as a donation to his agent. His whole speech ran nearly thus:

'Seventy-one—seventy-two; thy master is a good youth—seventy-three, an excellent youth—seventy-four—that piece hath been clipt within the ring*—seventy-five—and that looketh light of weight—seventy-six—when thy master wants money, let him come to Isaac of York—seventy-seven—that is, with reasonable security.' Here he made a considerable pause, and Gurth had good hope that the last three pieces might escape the fate of their comrades; but the enumeration proceeded.—'Seventy-eight—thou art a good fellow—seventy-nine—and deservest something for thyself'——

Here the Jew paused again, and looked at the last zecchin, intending, doubtless, to bestow it upon Gurth. He weighed it upon the tip of his finger, and made it ring by dropping it upon the table. Had it rung too flat, or had it felt a hair's breadth too light, generosity had carried the day; but, unhappily for Gurth, the chime was full and true, the zecchin plump, newly coined, and a grain above weight. Isaac could not find in his heart to part with it, so dropt it into his purse as if in absence of mind, with the words, 'Eighty completes the tale, and I trust thy master will reward thee handsomely. Surely,' he added, looking earnestly at the bag, 'thou hast more coins in that pouch?'

Gurth grinned, which was his nearest approach to a laugh, as he replied, 'About the same quantity which thou hast just told over so carefully.' He then folded the quittance, and put it under his cap, adding,—'Peril of thy beard, Jew, see that this be full and ample!' He filled himself, unbidden, a third goblet of wine, and left the apartment without ceremony.

'Rebecca,' said the Jew, 'that Ishmaelite hath gone somewhat beyond me. Nevertheless his master is a good youth—ay, and I am well pleased that he hath gained shekels of gold and shekels of silver, even by the speed of his horse and by the strength of his lance, which, like that of Goliath the Philistine, might vie with a weaver's beam.'*

As he turned to receive Rebecca's answer, he observed, that during his chaffering with Gurth, she had left the apartment unperceived.

In the meanwhile, Gurth had descended the stair, and, having reached the dark antechamber or hall, was puzzling about to

discover the entrance, when a figure in white, shown by a small
silver lamp which she held in her hand, beckoned him into a side
apartment. Gurth had some reluctance to obey the summons.
Rough and impetuous as a wild boar, where only earthly force
was to be apprehended, he had all the characteristic terrors of a
Saxon respecting fauns, forest-fiends, white women, and the
whole of the superstitions which his ancestors had brought with
them from the wilds of Germany.* He remembered, moreover,
that he was in the house of a Jew, a people who, besides the other
unamiable qualities which popular report ascribed to them, were
supposed to be profound necromancers and cabalists. Nevertheless, after a moment's pause, he obeyed the beckoning summons
of the apparition, and followed her into the apartment which she
indicated, where he found to his joyful surprise that his fair
guide was the beautiful Jewess whom he had seen at the tournament, and a short time in her father's apartment.

She asked him the particulars of his transaction with Isaac,
which he detailed accurately.

'My father did but jest with thee, good fellow,' said Rebecca;
'he owes thy master deeper kindness than these arms and steed
could pay, were their value tenfold. What sum didst thou pay my
father even now?'

'Eighty zecchins,' said Gurth, surprised at the question.

'In this purse,' said Rebecca, 'thou wilt find a hundred. Restore to thy master that which is his due, and enrich thyself with
the remainder. Haste—begone—stay not to render thanks! and
beware how you pass through this crowded town, where thou
mayst easily lose both thy burden and thy life.—Reuben,' she
added, clapping her hands together, 'light forth this stranger,
and fail not to draw lock and bar behind him.'

Reuben, a dark-brow'd and black-bearded Israelite, obeyed
her summons, with a torch in his hand; undid the outward door
of the house, and conducting Gurth across a paved court, let him
out through a wicket in the entrance-gate, which he closed behind him with such bolts and chains as would well have become
that of a prison.

'By St Dunstan,' said Gurth, as he stumbled up the dark
avenue, 'this is no Jewess, but an angel from heaven! Ten
zecchins from my brave young master—twenty from this pearl

of Zion—Oh, happy day!—Such another, Gurth, will redeem
thy bondage, and make thee a brother as free of thy guild as the
best. And then do I lay down my swineherd's horn and staff, and
take the freeman's sword and buckler, and follow my young
master to the death, without hiding either my face or my name.'

CHAPTER XI

1st Outlaw. Stand, sir, and throw us that you have
about you;
If not, we'll make you sit, and rifle you.
  Speed. Sir, we are undone! these are the villains
That all the travellers do fear so much.
  Val. My friends,——
  1st Out. That's not so, sir, we are your enemies.
  2d Out. Peace! we'll hear him.
  3d Out. Ay, by my beard, will we;
For he's a proper man.

*Two Gentlemen of Verona**

THE nocturnal adventures of Gurth were not yet concluded; indeed he himself became partly of that mind, when, after passing one or two straggling houses which stood in the outskirts of the village, he found himself in a deep lane, running between two banks overgrown with hazel and holly, while here and there a dwarf oak flung its arms altogether across the path. The lane was moreover much rutted and broken up by the carriages which had recently transported articles of various kinds to the tournament; and it was dark, for the banks and bushes intercepted the light of the harvest moon.

From the village were heard the distant sounds of revelry, mixed occasionally with loud laughter, sometimes broken by screams, and sometimes by wild strains of distant music. All these sounds, intimating the disorderly state of the town, crowded with military nobles and their dissolute attendants, gave Gurth some uneasiness. 'The Jewess was right,' he said to himself. 'By heaven and St Dunstan, I would I were safe at my journey's end with all this treasure! Here are such numbers, I will not say of arrant thieves, but of errant knights and errant squires, errant monks and errant minstrels, errant jugglers and errant jesters, that a man with a single merk would be in danger, much more a poor swineherd with a whole bagful of zecchins. Would I were out of the shade of these infernal bushes, that I might at least see any of St Nicholas's clerks* before they spring on my shoulders!'

Gurth accordingly hastened his pace, in order to gain the open common to which the lane led, but was not so fortunate as to accomplish his object. Just as he had attained the upper end of the lane, where the underwood was thickest, four men sprung upon him, even as his fears anticipated, two from each side of the road, and seized him so fast, that resistance, if at first practicable, would have been now too late.—'Surrender your charge,' said one of them; 'we are the deliverers of the commonwealth, who ease every man of his burden.'

'You should not ease me of mine so lightly,' muttered Gurth, whose surly honesty could not be tamed even by the pressure of immediate violence,—'had I it but in my power to give three strokes in its defence.'

'We shall see that presently,' said the robber; and, speaking to his companions, he added, 'bring along the knave. I see he would have his head broken, as well as his purse cut, and so be let blood in two veins at once.'

Gurth was hurried along agreeably to this mandate, and having been dragged somewhat roughly over the bank, on the left-hand side of the lane, found himself in a straggling thicket, which lay betwixt it and the open common. He was compelled to follow his rough conductors into the very depth of this cover, where they stopt unexpectedly in an irregular open space, free in a great measure from trees, and on which, therefore, the beams of the moon fell without much interruption from boughs and leaves. Here his captors were joined by two other persons, apparently belonging to the gang. They had short swords by their sides, and quarter-staves in their hands, and Gurth could now observe that all six wore visors, which rendered their occupation a matter of no question, even had their former proceedings left it in doubt.

'What money hast thou, churl?' said one of the thieves.

'Thirty zecchins of my own property,' answered Gurth, doggedly.

'A forfeit—a forfeit,' shouted the robbers; 'a Saxon hath thirty zecchins, and returns sober from a village! An undeniable and unredeemable forfeit of all he hath about him.'

'I hoarded it to purchase my freedom,' said Gurth.

'Thou art an ass,' replied one of the thieves; 'three quarts of double ale had rendered thee as free as thy master, ay, and freer too, if he be a Saxon like thyself.'

'A sad truth,' replied Gurth; 'but if these same thirty zecchins will buy my freedom from you, unloose my hands, and I will pay them to you.'

'Hold,' said one who seemed to exercise some authority over the others; 'this bag which thou bearest, as I can feel through thy cloak, contains more coin than thou hast told us of.'

'It is the good knight my master's,' answered Gurth, 'of which, assuredly, I would not have spoken a word, had you been satisfied with working your will upon mine own property.'

'Thou art an honest fellow,' replied the robber, 'I warrant thee; and we worship not St Nicholas so devoutly but what thy thirty zecchins may yet escape, if thou deal uprightly with us. Meantime render up thy trust for the time.' So saying, he took from Gurth's breast the large leathern pouch, in which the purse given him by Rebecca was enclosed, as well as the rest of the zecchins, and then continued his interrogation—'Who is thy master?'

'The Disinherited Knight,' said Gurth.

'Whose good lance,' replied the robber, 'won the prize in to-day's tourney? What is his name and lineage?'

'It is his pleasure,' answered Gurth, 'that they be concealed; and from me, assuredly, you will learn nought of them.'

'What is thine own name and lineage?'

'To tell that,' said Gurth, 'might reveal my master's.'

'Thou art a saucy groom,' said the robber; 'but of that anon. How comes thy master by this gold? is it of his inheritance, or by what means hath it accrued to him?'

'By his good lance,' answered Gurth.—'These bags contain the ransom of four good horses, and four good suits of armour.'

'How much is there?' demanded the robber.

'Two hundred zecchins.'

'Only two hundred zecchins!' said the bandit; 'your master hath dealt liberally by the vanquished, and put them to a cheap ransom. Name those who paid the gold.'

Gurth did so.

'The armour and horse of the Templar Brian de Bois-Guilbert, at what ransom were they held?—Thou seest thou canst not deceive me.'

'My master,' replied Gurth, 'will take nought from the Templar save his life's-blood. They are on terms of mortal defiance, and cannot hold courteous intercourse together.'

'Indeed!'—repeated the robber, and paused after he had said the word. 'And what wert thou now doing at Ashby with such a charge in thy custody?'

'I went thither to render to Isaac the Jew of York,' replied Gurth, 'the price of a suit of armour with which he fitted my master for this tournament.'

'And how much didst thou pay to Isaac?—Methinks, to judge by weight, there is still two hundred zecchins in this pouch.'

'I paid to Isaac,' said the Saxon, 'eighty zecchins, and he restored me a hundred in lieu thereof.'

'How! what!' exclaimed all the robbers at once; 'darest thou trifle with us, that thou tellest such improbable lies?'

'What I tell you,' said Gurth, 'is as true as the moon is in heaven. You will find the just sum in a silken purse within the leathern pouch, and separate from the rest of the gold.'

'Bethink thee, man,' said the Captain, 'thou speakest of a Jew—of an Israelite,—as unapt to restore gold, as the dry sand of his deserts to return the cup of water which the pilgrim spills upon them.'

'There is no more mercy in them,' said another of the banditti, 'than in an unbribed sheriff's officer.'

'It is, however, as I say,' said Gurth.

'Strike a light instantly,' said the Captain; 'I will examine this said purse; and if it be as this fellow says, the Jew's bounty is little less miraculous than the stream which relieved his fathers in the wilderness.'*

A light was procured accordingly, and the robber proceeded to examine the purse. The others crowded around him, and even two who had hold of Gurth relaxed their grasp while they stretched their necks to see the issue of the search. Availing himself of their negligence, by a sudden exertion of strength and activity, Gurth shook himself free of their hold, and might have escaped, could he have resolved to leave his master's property behind him. But such was no part of his intention. He wrenched a quarter-staff from one of the fellows, struck down the Captain, who was altogether unaware of his purpose, and had wellnigh repossessed himself of the pouch and treasure. The thieves, however, were too nimble for him, and again secured both the bag and the trusty Gurth.

'Knave!' said the Captain, getting up, 'thou hast broken my head; and with other men of our sort thou wouldst fare the worse for thy insolence. But thou shalt know thy fate instantly. First let us speak of thy master; the knight's matters must go before the squire's, according to the due order of chivalry. Stand thou fast in the meantime—if thou stir again, thou shalt have that will make thee quiet for life—Comrades!' he then said, addressing his gang, 'this purse is embroidered with Hebrew characters, and I well believe the yeoman's tale is true. The errant knight, his master, must needs pass us toll-free. He is too like ourselves for us to make booty of him, since dogs should not worry dogs where wolves and foxes are to be found in abundance.'

'Like us?' answered one of the gang; 'I should like to hear how that is made good.'

'Why, thou fool,' answered the Captain, 'is he not poor and disinherited as we are?—Doth he not win his substance at the sword's point as we do?—Hath he not beaten Front-de-Bœuf and Malvoisin, even as we would beat them if we could? Is he not the enemy to life and death of Brian de Bois-Guilbert, whom we have so much reason to fear? And were all this otherwise, wouldst thou have us show a worse conscience than an unbeliever, a Hebrew Jew?'

'Nay, that were a shame,' muttered the other fellow; 'and yet, when I served in the band of stout old Gandelyn,* we had no such scruples of conscience. And this insolent peasant,—he too, I warrant me, is to be dismissed scatheless?'

'Not if *thou* canst scathe him,' replied the Captain.—'Here, fellow,' continued he, addressing Gurth, 'canst thou use the staff, that thou starts to it so readily?'

'I think,' said Gurth, 'thou shouldst be best able to reply to that question.'

'Nay, by my troth, thou gavest me a round knock,' replied the Captain; 'do as much for this fellow, and thou shalt pass scot-free; and if thou dost not—why, by my faith, as thou art such a sturdy knave, I think I must pay thy ransom myself.—Take thy staff, Miller,' he added, 'and keep thy head; and do you others let the fellow go, and give him a staff—there is light enough to lay on load by.'

The two champions being alike armed with quarter-staves, stepped forward into the centre of the open space, in order to have the full benefit of the moonlight; the thieves in the meantime laughing, and crying to their comrade, 'Miller! beware thy toll-dish.'* The Miller, on the other hand, holding his quarter-staff by the middle, and making it flourish round his head after the fashion which the French call *faire le moulinet*,* exclaimed boastfully, 'Come on, churl, an thou darest: thou shalt feel the strength of a miller's thumb!'

'If thou be'st a miller,' answered Gurth, undauntedly, making his weapon play around his head with equal dexterity, 'thou art doubly a thief,* and I, as a true man, bid thee defiance.'

So saying, the two champions closed together, and for a few minutes they displayed great equality in strength, courage, and skill, intercepting and returning the blows of their adversary with the most rapid dexterity, while, from the continued clatter of their weapons, a person at a distance might have supposed that there were at least six persons engaged on each side. Less obstinate, and even less dangerous combats, have been described in good heroic verse; but that of Gurth and the Miller must remain unsung, for want of a sacred poet* to do justice to its eventful progress. Yet, though quarter-staff play be out of date, what we can in prose we will do for these bold champions.

Long they fought equally, until the Miller began to lose temper at finding himself so stoutly opposed, and at hearing the laughter of his companions, who, as usual in such cases, enjoyed his vexation. This was not a state of mind favourable to the noble game of quarter-staff, in which, as in ordinary cudgel-playing, the utmost coolness is requisite; and it gave Gurth, whose temper was steady, though surly, the opportunity of acquiring a decided advantage, in availing himself of which he displayed great mastery.

The Miller pressed furiously forward, dealing blows with either end of his weapon alternately, and striving to come to half-staff distance, while Gurth defended himself against the attack, keeping his hands about a yard asunder, and covering himself by shifting his weapon with great celerity, so as to protect his head and body. Thus did he maintain the defensive, making his eye, foot, and hand keep true time, until, observing his antagonist to lose wind, he darted the staff at his face with his left hand; and, as the Miller endeavoured to parry the thrust, he slid his right hand down to his left, and with the full swing of the weapon struck his opponent on the left side of the head, who instantly measured his length upon the green sward.

'Well and yeomanly done!' shouted the robbers; 'fair play and Old England for ever! The Saxon hath saved both his purse and his hide, and the Miller has met his match.'

'Thou mayst go thy ways, my friend,' said the Captain, addressing Gurth, in special confirmation of the general voice, 'and I will cause two of my comrades to guide thee by the best way to thy master's pavilion, and to guard thee from night-walkers* that might have less tender consciences than ours; for there is many one of them upon the amble in such a night as this. Take heed, however,' he added sternly; 'remember thou hast refused to tell thy name—ask not after ours, nor endeavour to discover who or what we are; for, if thou makest such an attempt, thou wilt come by worse fortune than has yet befallen thee.'

Gurth thanked the Captain for his courtesy, and promised to attend to his recommendation. Two of the outlaws, taking up their quarter-staves, and desiring Gurth to follow close in the rear, walked roundly forward alone a by-path, which traversed the thicket and the broken ground adjacent to it. On the very verge of the thicket two men spoke to his conductors, and receiving an answer in a whisper, withdrew into the wood, and suffered them to pass unmolested. This circumstance induced Gurth to believe both that the gang was strong in numbers, and that they kept regular guards around their place of rendezvous.

When they arrived on the open heath, where Gurth might have had some trouble in finding his road, the thieves guided him straight forward to the top of a little eminence, whence he could see, spread beneath him in the moonlight, the palisades of the lists, the glimmering pavilions pitched at either end, with the pennons which adorned them fluttering in the moonbeam, and from which could be heard the hum of the song with which the sentinels were beguiling their night-watch.

Here the thieves stopt.

'We go with you no farther,' said they; 'it were not safe that we should do so.—Remember the warning you have received—keep secret what has this night befallen you, and you will have no room to repent it—neglect what is now told you, and the Tower of London shall not protect you against our revenge.'

'Good night to you, kind sirs,' said Gurth; 'I shall remember your orders, and trust that there is no offence in wishing you a safer and an honester trade.'

Thus they parted, the outlaws returning in the direction from whence they had come, and Gurth proceeding to the tent of his master, to whom, notwithstanding the injunction he had received, he communicated the whole adventures of the evening.

The Disinherited Knight was filled with astonishment, no less at the generosity of Rebecca, by which, however, he resolved he would not profit, than that of the robbers, to whose profession such a quality seemed totally foreign. His course of reflections upon these singular circumstances was, however, interrupted by the necessity for taking repose, which the fatigue of the preceding day, and the propriety of refreshing himself for the morrow's encounter, rendered alike indispensable.

The knight, therefore, stretched himself for repose upon a rich couch with which the tent was provided; and the faithful Gurth, extending his hardy limbs upon a bear-skin which formed a sort of carpet to the pavilion, laid himself across the opening of the tent, so that no one could enter without awakening him.

CHAPTER XII

The heralds left their pricking up and down,
Now ringen trumpets loud and clarion.
There is no more to say, but east and west,
In go the speares sadly in the rest,
In goth the sharp spur into the side,
There see men who can just and who can ride;
There shiver shaftes upon shieldes thick,
He feeleth through the heart-spone the prick;
Up springen speares, twenty feet in height,
Out go the swordes to the silver bright;
The helms they to-hewn and to-shred;
Out bursts the blood with stern streames red.

CHAUCER*

MORNING arose in unclouded splendour, and ere the sun was much above the horizon, the idlest or the most eager of the spectators appeared on the common, moving to the lists as to a general centre, in order to secure a favourable situation for viewing the continuation of the expected games.

The marshals and their attendants appeared next on the field, together with the heralds, for the purpose of receiving the names of the knights who intended to just, with the side which each chose to espouse. This was a necessary precaution, in order to secure equality betwixt the two bodies who should be opposed to each other.

According to due formality, the Disinherited Knight was to be considered as leader of the one body, while Brian de Bois-Guilbert, who had been rated as having done second-best in the preceding day, was named first champion of the other band. Those who had concurred in the challenge adhered to his party of course, excepting only Ralph de Vipont, whom his fall had rendered unfit so soon to put on his armour. There was no want of distinguished and noble candidates to fill up the ranks on either side.

In fact, although the general tournament, in which all knights fought at once, was more dangerous than single encounters, they were, nevertheless, more frequented and practised by the chivalry of the age. Many knights, who had not sufficient confidence in their own skill to defy a single adversary of high reputation, were, nevertheless, desirous of displaying their valour in the general combat, where they might meet others with whom they were more upon an equality. On the present occasion, about fifty knights* were inscribed as desirous of combating upon each side, when the marshals declared that no more could be admitted, to the disappointment of several who were too late in preferring their claim to be included.

About the hour of ten o'clock, the whole plain was crowded with horsemen, horsewomen, and foot-passengers, hastening to the tournament; and shortly after, a grand flourish of trumpets announced Prince John and his retinue, attended by many of those knights who meant to take share in the game, as well as others who had no such intention.

About the same time arrived Cedric the Saxon, with the Lady Rowena, unattended, however, by Athelstane. This Saxon lord had arrayed his tall and strong person in armour, in order to take his place among the combatants; and, considerably to the surprise of Cedric, had chosen to enlist himself on the part of the Knight Templar. The Saxon, indeed, had remonstrated strongly with his friend upon the injudicious choice he had made of his party; but he had only received that sort of answer usually given by those who are more obstinate in following their own course, than strong in justifying it.

His best, if not his only reason, for adhering to the party of Brian de Bois-Guilbert, Athelstane had the prudence to keep to himself. Though his apathy of disposition prevented his taking any means to recommend himself to the Lady Rowena, he was, nevertheless, by no means insensible to her charms, and considered his union with her as a matter already fixed beyond doubt, by the assent of Cedric and her other friends. It had therefore been with smothered displeasure that the proud though indolent Lord of Coningsburgh beheld the victor of the preceding day select Rowena as the object of that honour which it became his privilege to confer. In order to punish him for a preference which seemed to interfere with his own suit, Athelstane, confident of his strength, and to whom his flatterers, at least, ascribed great skill in arms, had determined not only to deprive the Disinherited Knight of his powerful succour, but, if an opportunity should occur, to make him feel the weight of his battle-axe.

De Bracy, and other knights attached to Prince John, in obedience to a hint from him, had joined the party of the challengers, John being desirous to secure, if possible, the victory to that side. On the other hand, many other knights, both English and Norman, natives and strangers, took part against the challengers, the more readily that the opposite band was to be led by so distinguished a champion as the Disinherited Knight had approved himself.

As soon as Prince John observed that the destined Queen of the day had arrived upon the field, assuming that air of courtesy which sat well upon him when he was pleased to exhibit it, he rode forward to meet her, doffed his bonnet, and, alighting from his horse, assisted the Lady Rowena from her saddle, while his followers uncovered at the same time, and one of the most distinguished dismounted to hold her palfrey.

'It is thus,' said Prince John, 'that we set the dutiful example of loyalty to the Queen of Love and Beauty, and are ourselves her guide to the throne which she must this day occupy.—Ladies,' he said, 'attend your Queen, as you wish in your turn to be distinguished by like honours.'

So saying, the Prince marshalled Rowena to the seat of honour opposite his own, while the fairest and most distinguished ladies present crowded after her to obtain places as near as possible to their temporary sovereign.

No sooner was Rowena seated than a burst of music, half-drowned by the shouts of the multitude, greeted her new dignity. Meantime, the sun shone fierce and bright upon the polished arms of the knights of either side, who crowded the opposite extremities of the lists, and held eager conference together concerning the best mode of arranging their line of battle, and supporting the conflict.

The heralds then proclaimed silence until the laws of the tourney should be rehearsed. These were calculated in some degree to abate the dangers of the day; a precaution the more necessary, as the conflict was to be maintained with sharp swords and pointed lances.

The champions were therefore prohibited to thrust with the sword, and were confined to striking. A knight, it was announced, might use a mace or battle-axe at pleasure, but the dagger was a prohibited weapon. A knight unhorsed might renew the fight on foot with any other on the opposite side in the same predicament; but mounted horsemen were in that case forbidden to assail him. When any knight could force his antagonist to the extremity of the lists, so as to touch the palisade with his person or arms, such opponent was obliged to yield himself vanquished, and his armour and horse were placed at the disposal of the conqueror. A knight thus overcome was not permitted to take farther share in the combat. If any combatant was struck down, and unable to recover his feet, his squire or page might enter the lists, and drag his master out of the press; but in that case the knight was adjudged vanquished, and his arms and horse declared forfeited. The combat was to cease as soon as Prince John should throw down his leading staff, or truncheon; another precaution usually taken to prevent the unnecessary effusion of blood by the too long endurance of a sport so desperate. Any knight breaking the rules of the tournament, or otherwise transgressing the rules of honourable chivalry, was liable to be stript of his arms, and, having his shield reversed, to be placed in that posture astride upon the bars of the palisade, and exposed to public derision, in punishment of his unknightly conduct. Having announced these precautions, the heralds concluded with an exhortation to each good knight to do his duty, and to merit favour from the Queen of Beauty and Love.

This proclamation having been made, the heralds withdrew to their stations. The knights, entering at either end of the lists in long procession, arranged themselves in a double file, precisely opposite to each other, the leader of each party being in the centre of the foremost rank, a post which he did not occupy until each had carefully arranged the ranks of his party, and stationed every one in his place.

It was a goodly, and at the same time an anxious sight, to

behold so many gallant champions, mounted bravely, and armed richly, stand ready prepared for an encounter so formidable, seated on their war-saddles like so many pillars of iron, and awaiting the signal of encounter with the same ardour as their generous steeds, which, by neighing and pawing the ground, gave signal of their impatience.

As yet the knights held their long lances upright, their bright points glancing to the sun, and the streamers with which they were decorated fluttering over the plumage of the helmets. Thus they remained while the marshals of the field surveyed their ranks with the utmost exactness, lest either party had more or fewer than the appointed number. The tale was found exactly complete. The marshals then withdrew from the lists, and William de Wyvil, with a voice of thunder, pronounced the signal words—*Laissez aller!** The trumpets sounded as he spoke—the spears of the champions were at once lowered and placed in the rests—the spurs were dashed into the flanks of the horses, and the two foremost ranks of either party rushed upon each other in full gallop, and met in the middle of the lists with a shock, the sound of which was heard at a mile's distance. The rear rank of each party advanced at a slower pace to sustain the defeated, and follow up the success of the victors, of their party.

The consequences of the encounter were not instantly seen, for the dust raised by the trampling of so many steeds darkened the air, and it was a minute ere the anxious spectators could see the fate of the encounter. When the fight became visible, half the knights on each side were dismounted, some by the dexterity of their adversary's lance,—some by the superior weight and strength of opponents, which had borne down both horse and man,—some lay stretched on earth as if never more to rise,—some had already gained their feet, and were closing hand to hand with those of their antagonists who were in the same predicament,—and several on both sides, who had received wounds by which they were disabled, were stopping their blood by their scarfs, and endeavouring to extricate themselves from the tumult. The mounted knights, whose lances had been almost all broken by the fury of the encounter, were now closely en-gaged with their swords, shouting their war-cries, and exchanging buffets, as if honour and life depended on the issue of the combat.

The tumult was presently increased by the advance of the second rank on either side, which, acting as a reserve, now rushed on to aid their companions. The followers of Brian de Bois-Guilbert shouted—'*Ha! Beau-seant! Beau-seant!*[18]*—For the Temple—For the Temple!' The opposite party shouted in answer—'*Desdichado! Desdichado!*'—which watchword they took from the motto upon their leader's shield.

The champions thus encountering each other with the utmost fury, and with alternate success, the tide of battle seemed to flow now toward the southern, now toward the northern extremity of the lists, as the one or the other party prevailed. Meantime the clang of the blows, and the shouts of the combatants, mixed fearfully with the sound of the trumpets, and drowned the groans of those who fell, and lay rolling defenceless beneath the feet of the horses. The splendid armour of the combatants was now defaced with dust and blood, and gave way at every stroke of the sword and battle-axe. The gay plumage, shorn from the crests, drifted upon the breeze like snow-flakes. All that was beautiful and graceful in the martial array had disappeared, and what was now visible was only calculated to awake terror or compassion.*

Yet such is the force of habit, that not only the vulgar spectators, who are naturally attracted by sights of horror, but even the ladies of distinction, who crowded the galleries, saw the conflict with a thrilling interest certainly, but without a wish to withdraw their eyes from a sight so terrible. Here and there, indeed, a fair cheek might turn pale, or a faint scream might be heard, as a lover, a brother, or a husband, was struck from his horse. But, in general, the ladies around encouraged the combatants, not only by clapping their hands and waving their veils and kerchiefs, but even by exclaiming, 'Brave lance! Good sword!' when any successful thrust or blow took place under their observation.

Such being the interest taken by the fair sex in this bloody game, that of the men is the more easily understood. It showed itself in loud acclamations upon every change of fortune, while all eyes were so riveted on the lists, that the spectators seemed as if they themselves had dealt and received the blows which were there so freely bestowed. And between every pause was heard the voice of the heralds, exclaiming, 'Fight on, brave knights! Man dies, but glory lives!—Fight on—death is better than defeat!—Fight on, brave knights!—for bright eyes behold your deeds!'

Amid the varied fortunes of the combat, the eyes of all endeavoured to discover the leaders of each band, who, mingling in the thick of the fight, encouraged their companions both by voice and example. Both displayed great feats of gallantry, nor did either Bois-Guilbert or the Disinherited Knight find in the ranks opposed to them a champion who could be termed their unquestioned match. They repeatedly endeavoured to single out each other, spurred by mutual animosity, and aware that the fall of either leader might be considered as decisive of victory. Such, however, was the crowd and confusion, that, during the earlier part of the conflict, their efforts to meet were unavailing, and they were repeatedly separated by the eagerness of their followers, each of whom was anxious to win honour, by measuring his strength against the leader of the opposite party.

But when the field became thin by the numbers on either side who had yielded themselves vanquished, had been compelled to the extremity of the lists, or been otherwise rendered incapable of continuing the strife, the Templar and the Disinherited Knight at length encountered hand to hand, with all the fury that mortal animosity, joined to rivalry of honour, could inspire. Such was the address of each in parrying and striking, that the spectators broke forth into a unanimous and involuntary shout, expressive of their delight and admiration.

But at this moment the party of the Disinherited Knight had the worst; the gigantic arm of Front-de-Bœuf on the one flank, and the ponderous strength of Athelstane on the other, bearing down and dispersing those immediately exposed to them. Finding themselves freed from their immediate antagonists, it seems to have occurred to both these knights at the same instant, that they would render the most decisive advantage to their party, by aiding the Templar in his contest with his rival. Turning their horses, therefore, at the same moment, the Norman spurred against the Disinherited Knight on the one side, and the Saxon on the other. It was utterly impossible that the object of this unequal and unexpected assault could have sustained it, had he not been warned by a general cry from the spectators, who could not but take interest in one exposed to such disadvantage.

'Beware! beware! Sir Disinherited!' was shouted so universally, that the knight became aware of his danger; and striking a full blow at the Templar, he reined back his steed in the same moment, so as to escape the charge of Athelstane and Front-de-Bœuf. These knights, therefore, their aim being thus eluded, rushed from opposite sides betwixt the object of their attack and the Templar, almost running their horses against each other ere they could stop their career. Recovering their horses, however, and wheeling them round, the whole three pursued their united purpose of bearing to the earth the Disinherited Knight.

Nothing could have saved him, except the remarkable strength and activity of the noble horse which he had won on the preceding day.

This stood him in the more stead, as the horse of Bois-Guilbert was wounded, and those of Front-de-Bœuf and Athelstane were both tired with the weight of their gigantic masters, clad in complete armour, and with the preceding exertions of the day. The masterly horsemanship of the Disinherited Knight, and the activity of the noble animal which he mounted, enabled him for a few minutes to keep at sword's point his three antagonists, turning and wheeling with the agility of a hawk upon the wing, keeping his enemies as far separate as he could, and rushing now against the one, now against the other, dealing sweeping blows with his sword, without waiting to receive those which were aimed at him in return.

But although the lists rang with the applauses of his dexterity, it was evident that he must at last be overpowered; and the nobles around Prince John implored him with one voice to throw down his warder,* and to save so brave a knight from the disgrace of being overcome by odds.

'Not I, by the light of Heaven!' answered Prince John; 'this same springal,* who conceals his name, and despises our proffered hospitality, hath already gained one prize, and may now afford to let others have their turn.' As he spoke thus, an unexpected incident changed the fortune of the day.

There was among the ranks of the Disinherited Knight a champion in black armour, mounted on a black horse, large of size, tall, and to all appearance powerful and strong, like the rider by whom he was mounted. This knight, who bore on his shield no device of any kind, had hitherto evinced very little interest in the event of the fight, beating off with seeming ease those combatants who attacked him, but neither pursuing his advantages, nor himself assailing any one. In short, he had hitherto acted the part rather of a spectator than of a party in the tournament, a circumstance which procured him among the spectators the name of *Le Noir Faineant*, or the Black Sluggard.*

At once this knight seemed to throw aside his apathy, when he discovered the leader of his party so hard bested; for, setting spurs to his horse, which was quite fresh, he came to his assistance like a thunderbolt, exclaiming, in a voice like a trumpet-call, '*Desdichado*, to the rescue!' It was high time; for, while the Disinherited Knight was pressing upon the Templar, Front-de-Bœuf had got nigh to him with his uplifted sword; but ere the blow could descend, the Sable Knight dealt a stroke on his head, which, glancing from the polished helmet, lighted with violence scarcely abated on the *chamfron** of the steed, and Front-de-Bœuf rolled on the ground, both horse and man equally stunned by the fury of the blow. *Le Noir Faineant* then turned his horse upon Athelstane of Coningsburgh; and his own sword having been broken in his encounter with Front-de-Bœuf, he wrenched from the hand of the bulky Saxon the battle-axe which he wielded, and, like one familiar with the use of the weapon, bestowed him such a blow upon the crest, that Athelstane also lay senseless on the field. Having achieved this double feat, for which he was the more highly applauded that it was totally unexpected from him, the knight seemed to resume the sluggishness of his character, returning calmly to the northern extremity of the lists, leaving his leader to cope as he best could with Brian de Bois-Guilbert. This was no longer matter of so much difficulty as formerly. The Templar's horse had bled much, and gave way under the shock of the Disinherited Knight's charge. Brian de Bois-Guilbert rolled on the field, encumbered with the stirrup, from which he was unable to draw his foot. His antagonist sprung from horseback, waved his fatal sword over the head of his adversary, and commanded him to yield himself; when Prince John, more moved by the Templar's dangerous situation than he had been by that of his rival, saved him the mortification of confessing himself vanquished, by casting down his warder, and putting an end to the conflict.

It was, indeed, only the relics and embers of the fight which continued to burn; for of the few knights who still continued in the lists, the greater part had, by tacit consent, forborne the conflict for some time, leaving it to be determined by the strife of the leaders.

The squires, who had found it a matter of danger and difficulty to attend their masters during the engagement, now thronged into the lists to pay their dutiful attendance to the wounded, who were removed with the utmost care and attention to the neighbouring pavilions, or to the quarters prepared for them in the adjoining village.

Thus ended the memorable field of Ashby-de-la-Zouche, one of the most gallantly contested tournaments of that age; for although only four knights, including one who was smothered by the heat of his armour, had died upon the field, yet upwards of thirty were desperately wounded, four or five of whom never recovered. Several more were disabled for life; and those who escaped best carried the marks of the conflict to the grave with them. Hence it is always mentioned in the old records, as the Gentle and Joyous Passage of Arms of Ashby.

It being now the duty of Prince John to name the knight who had done best, he determined that the honour of the day remained with the knight whom the popular voice had termed *Le Noir Faineant*. It was pointed out to the Prince, in impeachment of this decree, that the victory had been in fact won by the Disinherited Knight, who, in the course of the day, had overcome six champions with his own hand, and who had finally unhorsed and struck down the leader of the opposite party. But Prince John adhered to his own opinion, on the ground that the Disinherited Knight and his party had lost the day, but for the powerful assistance of the Knight of the Black Armour, to whom, therefore, he persisted in awarding the prize.

To the surprise of all present, however, the knight thus preferred was nowhere to be found. He had left the lists immediately when the conflict ceased, and had been observed by some
spectators to move down one of the forest glades with the
same slow pace and listless and indifferent manner which had
procured him the epithet of the Black Sluggard. After he had
been summoned twice by sound of trumpet, and proclamation
of the heralds, it became necessary to name another to receive
the honours which had been assigned to him. Prince John
had now no further excuse for resisting the claim of the
Disinherited Knight, whom, therefore, he named the champion
of the day.

Through a field slippery with blood, and encumbered with
broken armour and the bodies of slain and wounded horses, the
marshals of the lists again conducted the victor to the foot of
Prince John's throne.

'Disinherited Knight,' said Prince John, 'since by that title
only you will consent to be known to us, we a second time award
to you the honours of this tournament, and announce to you
your right to claim and receive from the hands of the Queen of
Love and Beauty, the Chaplet of Honour which your valour has
justly deserved.' The Knight bowed low and gracefully, but
returned no answer.

While the trumpets sounded, while the heralds strained their
voices in proclaiming honour to the brave and glory to the victor—while ladies waved their silken kerchiefs and embroidered
veils, and while all ranks joined in a clamorous shout of exultation, the marshals conducted the Disinherited Knight across
the lists to the foot of that throne of honour which was occupied
by the Lady Rowena.

On the lower step of this throne the champion was made to
kneel down. Indeed his whole action since the fight had ended,
seemed rather to have been upon the impulse of those around
him than from his own free will; and it was observed that he
tottered as they guided him the second time across the lists.
Rowena, descending from her station with a graceful and dignified step, was about to place the chaplet which she held in her
hand upon the helmet of the champion, when the marshals
exclaimed with one voice, 'It must not be thus—his head must

be bare.' The knight muttered faintly a few words, which were lost in the hollow of his helmet, but their purport seemed to be a desire that his casque might not be removed.

Whether 'from love of form, or from curiosity, the marshals paid no attention to his expressions of reluctance, but unhelmed him by cutting the laces of his casque, and undoing the fastening of his gorget. When the helmet was removed, the well-formed, yet sun-burnt features of a young man of twenty-five were seen, amidst a profusion of short fair hair. His countenance was as pale as death, and marked in one or two places with streaks of blood.

Rowena had no sooner beheld him than she uttered a faint shriek; but at once summoning up the energy of her disposition, and compelling herself, as it were, to proceed, while her frame yet trembled with the violence of sudden emotion, she placed upon the drooping head of the victor the splendid chaplet which was the destined reward of the day, and pronounced, in a clear and distinct tone, these words: 'I bestow on thee this chaplet, Sir Knight, as the meed of valour assigned to this day's victor:' here she paused a moment, and then firmly added, 'And upon brows more worthy could a wreath of chivalry never be placed!'

The knight stooped his head, and kissed the hand of the lovely Sovereign by whom his valour had been rewarded; and then, sinking yet farther forward, lay prostrate at her feet.

There was a general consternation. Cedric, who had been struck mute by the sudden appearance of his banished son, now rushed forward, as if to separate him from Rowena. But this had been already accomplished by the marshals of the field, who, guessing the cause of Ivanhoe's swoon, had hastened to undo his armour, and found that the head of a lance had penetrated his breastplate, and inflicted a wound in his side.

CHAPTER XIII

'Heroes, approach!' Atrides thus aloud,
'Stand forth distinguish'd from the circling crowd,
Ye who by skill or manly force may claim,
Your rivals to surpass and merit fame.
This cow, worth twenty oxen, is decreed,
For him who farthest sends the winged reed.'

*Iliad**

THE name of Ivanhoe was no sooner pronounced than it flew
from mouth to mouth, with all the celerity with which eagerness
could convey and curiosity receive it. It was not long ere it
reached the circle of the Prince, whose brow darkened as he
heard the news. Looking around him, however, with an air of
scorn, 'My lords,' said he, 'and especially you, Sir Prior, what
think ye of the doctrine the learned tell us, concerning innate
attractions and antipathies?* Methinks that I felt the presence of
my brother's minion, even when I least guessed whom yonder
suit of armour enclosed.'

'Front-de-Bœuf must prepare to restore his fief of Ivanhoe,'
said De Bracy, who, having discharged his part honourably in
the tournament, had laid his shield and helmet aside, and again
mingled with the Prince's retinue.

'Ay', answered Waldemar Fitzurse, 'this gallant is likely to
reclaim the castle and manor which Richard assigned to him, and
which your Highness's generosity has since given to Front-de-
Bœuf.'

'Front-de-Bœuf,' replied John, 'is a man more willing to swal-
low three manors such as Ivanhoe, than to disgorge one of them.
For the rest, sirs, I hope none here will deny my right to confer
the fiefs of the crown upon the faithful followers who are around
me, and ready to perform the usual military service, in the room
of those who have wandered to foreign countries, and can neither
render homage nor service when called upon.'

The audience were too much interested in the question not to
pronounce the Prince's assumed right altogether indubitable. 'A

generous Prince!—a most noble Lord, who thus takes upon himself the task of rewarding his faithful followers!'

Such were the words which burst from the train, expectants all of them of similar grants at the expense of King Richard's followers and favourites, if indeed they had not as yet received such. Prior Aymer also assented to the general proposition, observing, however, 'That the blessed Jerusalem could not indeed be termed a foreign country. She was *communis mater*—the mother of all Christians, But he saw not,' he declared, 'how the Knight of Ivanhoe could plead any advantage from this, since he' (the Prior) 'was assured that the crusaders, under Richard, had never proceeded much farther than Askalon,* which, as all the world knew, was a town of the Philistines, and entitled to none of the privileges of the Holy City.'

Waldemar, whose curiosity had led him towards the place where Ivanhoe had fallen to the ground, now returned. 'The gallant,' said he, 'is likely to give your Highness little disturbance, and to leave Front-de-Bœuf in the quiet possession of his gains—he is severely wounded.'

'Whatever becomes of him,' said Prince John, 'he is victor of the day; and were he tenfold our enemy, or the devoted friend of our brother, which is perhaps the same, his wounds must be looked to—our own physician shall attend him.'

A stern smile curled the Prince's lip as he spoke. Waldemar Fitzurse hastened to reply, that Ivanhoe was already removed from the lists, and in the custody of his friends.

'I was somewhat afflicted,' he said, 'to see the grief of the Queen of Love and Beauty, whose sovereignty of a day this event has changed into mourning. I am not a man to be moved by a woman's lament for her lover, but this same Lady Rowena suppressed her sorrow with such dignity of manner, that it could only be discovered by her folded hands, and her tearless eye, which trembled as it remained fixed on the lifeless form before her.'

'Who is this Lady Rowena,' said Prince John, 'of whom we have heard so much?'

'A Saxon heiress of large possessions,' replied the Prior Aymer; 'a rose of loveliness, and a jewel of wealth; the fairest among a thousand, a bundle of myrrh, and a cluster of camphire.'*

'We shall cheer her sorrows,' said Prince John, 'and amend her blood, by wedding her to a Norman. She seems a minor, and must therefore be at our royal disposal in marriage.——How sayst thou, De Bracy? What thinkst thou of gaining fair lands and livings, by wedding a Saxon, after the fashion of the followers of the Conqueror?'

'If the lands are to my liking, my lord,' answered De Bracy, 'it will be hard to displease me with a bride; and deeply will I hold myself bound to your highness for a good deed, which will fulfil all promises made in favour of your servant and vassal.'

'We will not forget it,' said Prince John; 'and that we may instantly go to work, command our seneschal presently to order the attendance of the Lady Rowena and her company—that is, the rude churl her guardian, and the Saxon ox whom the Black Knight struck down in the tournament, upon this evening's banquet.——De Bigot,' he added to his seneschal, 'thou wilt word this our second summons so courteously, as to gratify the pride of these Saxons, and make it impossible for them again to refuse; although, by the bones of Becket, courtesy to them is casting pearls before swine.'*

Prince John had proceeded thus far, and was about to give the signal for retiring from the lists, when a small billet was put into his hand.

'From whence?' said Prince John, looking at the person by whom it was delivered.

'From foreign parts, my lord, but from whence I know not,' replied his attendant. 'A Frenchman brought it hither, who said, he had ridden night and day to put it into the hands of your highness.'

The Prince looked narrowly at the superscription, and then at the seal, placed so as to secure the flox-silk with which the billet was surrounded, and which bore the impression of three fleurs-de-lis. John then opened the billet with apparent agitation, which visibly and greatly increased when he had perused the contents, which were expressed in these words—

heed to yourself, for the Devil is unchained!'

Prince turned as pale as death, looked first on the earth,

and then up to heaven, like a man who has received news that sentence of execution has been passed upon him. Recovering from the first effects of his surprise, he took Waldemar Fitzurse and De Bracy aside, and put the billet into their hands successively. 'It means,' he added, in a faltering voice, 'that my brother Richard has obtained his freedom.'

'This may be a false alarm, or a forged letter,' said De Bracy.

'It is France's own hand and seal,' replied Prince John.

'It is time, then,' said Fitzurse, 'to draw our party to a head, either at York, or some other centrical place. A few days later, and it will be indeed too late. Your highness must break short this present mummery.'

'The yeomen and commons,' said De Bracy, 'must not be dismissed discontented, for lack of their share in the sports.'

'The day,' said Waldemar, 'is not yet very far spent—let the archers shoot a few rounds at the target, and the prize be adjudged. This will be an abundant fulfilment of the Prince's promises, so far as this herd of Saxon serfs is concerned.'

'I thank thee, Waldemar,' said the Prince; 'thou remindest me, too, that I have a debt to pay to that insolent peasant who yesterday insulted our person. Our banquet also shall go forward to-night as we proposed. Were this my last hour of power, it should be an hour sacred to revenge and to pleasure—let new cares come with to-morrow's new day.'

The sound of the trumpets soon recalled those spectators who had already begun to leave the field; and proclamation was made that Prince John, suddenly called by high and peremptory public duties, held himself obliged to discontinue the entertainments of to-morrow's festival: nevertheless, that, unwilling so many good yeomen should depart without a trial of skill, he was pleased to appoint them, before leaving the ground, presently to execute the competition of archery intended for the morrow. To the best archer a prize was to be awarded, being a bugle-horn, mounted with silver, and a silken baldric richly ornamented with a medallion of St Hubert, the patron of silvan sport.*

More than thirty yeomen at first presented themselves as competitors, several of whom were rangers and under-keepers in the royal forests of Needwood and Charnwood. When, however, the archers understood with whom they were to be matched, upwards of twenty withdrew themselves from the contest, unwilling to encounter the dishonour of almost certain defeat. For in those days the skill of each celebrated marksman was as well known for many miles round him, as the qualities of a horse trained at Newmarket are familiar to those who frequent that well-known meeting.

The diminished list of competitors for silvan fame still amounted to eight. Prince John stepped from his royal seat to view more nearly the persons of these chosen yeomen, several of whom wore the royal livery. Having satisfied his curiosity by this investigation, he looked for the object of his resentment, whom he observed standing on the same spot, and with the same composed countenance which he had exhibited upon the preceding day.

'Fellow,' said Prince John, 'I guessed by thy insolent babble thou wert no true lover of the long-bow, and I see thou darest not adventure thy skill among such merry-men as stand yonder.'

'Under favour, sir,' replied the yeoman, 'I have another reason for refraining to shoot, besides the fearing discomfiture and disgrace.'

'And what is thy other reason?' said Prince John, who, for some cause which perhaps he could not himself have explained, felt a painful curiosity respecting this individual.

'Because,' replied the woodsman, 'I know not if these yeomen and I are used to shoot at the same marks; and because, moreover, I know not how your Grace might relish the winning of a third prize by one who has unwittingly fallen under your displeasure.'

Prince John coloured as he put the question, 'What is thy name, yeoman?'

'Locksley,' answered the yeoman.

'Then, Locksley,' said Prince John, 'thou shalt shoot in thy turn, when these yeomen have displayed their skill. If thou carriest the prize, I will add to it twenty nobles; but if thou losest it, thou shalt be stript of thy Lincoln green, and scourged out of the lists with bowstrings, for a wordy and insolent braggart.'

'And how if I refuse to shoot on such a wager?' said the yeoman.—'Your Grace's power, supported, as it is, by so many men-at-arms, may indeed easily strip and scourge me, but cannot compel me to bend or to draw my bow.'

'If thou refusest my fair proffer,' said the Prince, 'the Provost of the lists shall cut thy bowstring, break thy bow and arrows, and expel thee from the presence as a faint-hearted craven.'

'This is no fair chance you put on me, proud Prince,' said the yeoman, 'to compel me to peril myself against the best archers of Leicester and Staffordshire, under the penalty of infamy if they should overshoot me. Nevertheless, I will obey your pleasure.'

'Look to him close, men-at-arms,' said Prince John, 'his heart is sinking; I am jealous lest he attempt to escape the trial.—And do you, good fellows, shoot boldly round; a buck and a butt of wine are ready for your refreshment in yonder tent, when the prize is won.'

A target was placed at the upper end of the southern avenue which led to the lists. The contending archers took their station in turn, at the bottom of the southern access; the distance between that station and the mark allowing full distance for what was called a shot at rovers.* The archers, having previously determined by lot their order of precedence, were to shoot each three shafts in succession. The sports were regulated by an officer of inferior rank, termed the Provost of the Games; for the high rank of the marshals of the lists would have been held degraded, had they condescended to superintend the sports of the yeomanry.

One by one the archers, stepping forward, delivered their shafts yeomanlike and bravely. Of twenty-four arrows, shot in succession, ten were fixed in the target, and the others ranged so near it, that, considering the distance of the mark, it was accounted good archery. Of the ten shafts which hit the target, two within the inner ring were shot by Hubert, a forester in the service of Malvoisin, who was accordingly pronounced victorious.

'Now, Locksley,' said Prince John to the bold yeoman, with a bitter smile, 'wilt thou try conclusions with Hubert, or wilt thou yield up bow, baldric, and quiver, to the Provost of the sports?'

'Sith it be no better,' said Locksley, 'I am content to try my fortune; on condition that when I have shot two shafts at yonder mark of Hubert's, he shall be bound to shoot one at that which I shall propose.'

'That is but fair,' answered Prince John, 'and it shall not be refused thee.—If thou dost beat this braggart, Hubert, I will fill the bugle with silver-pennies for thee.'

'A man can do but his best,' answered Hubert; 'but my grandsire drew a good long bow at Hastings, and I trust not to dishonour his memory.'

The former target was now removed, and a fresh one of the same size placed in its room. Hubert, who, as victor in the first trial of skill, had the right to shoot first, took his aim with great deliberation, long measuring the distance with his eye, while he held in his hand his bended bow, with the arrow placed on the string. At length he made a step forward, and raising the bow at the full stretch of his left arm, till the centre or grasping-place was nigh level with his face, he drew his bowstring to his ear. The arrow whistled through the air, and lighted within the inner ring of the target, but not exactly in the centre.

'You have not allowed for the wind, Hubert,' said his antagonist, bending his bow, 'or that had been a better shot.'

So saying, and without showing the least anxiety to pause upon his aim, Locksley stept to the appointed station, and shot his arrow as carelessly in appearance as if he had not even looked at the mark. He was speaking almost at the instant that the shaft left the bowstring, yet it alighted in the target two inches nearer to the white spot which marked the centre than that of Hubert.

'By the light of heaven!' said Prince John to Hubert, 'an thou suffer that runagate knave to overcome thee, thou art worthy of the gallows!'

Hubert had but one set speech for all occasions. 'An your highness were to hang me,' he said, 'a man can but do his best. Nevertheless, my grandsire drew a good bow'——

'The foul fiend on thy grandsire and all his generation!' interrupted John; 'shoot, knave, and shoot thy best, or it shall be the worse for thee!'

Thus exhorted, Hubert resumed his place, and not neglecting the caution which he had received from his adversary, he made the necessary allowance for a very light air of wind, which had just arisen, and shot so successfully that his arrow alighted in the very centre of the target.

'A Hubert! a Hubert!' shouted the populace, more interested in a known person than in a stranger. 'In the clout!—in the clout!*—a Hubert for ever!'

'Thou canst not mend that shot, Locksley,' said the Prince, with an insulting smile.

'I will notch his shaft for him, however,' replied Locksley.

And letting fly his arrow with a little more precaution than before, it lighted right upon that of his competitor, which it split to shivers. The people who stood around were so astonished at his wonderful dexterity, that they could not even give vent to their surprise in their usual clamour. 'This must be the devil, and no man of flesh and blood,' whispered the yeomen to each other; 'such archery was never seen since a bow was first bent in Britain.'

'And now,' said Locksley, 'I will crave your Grace's permission to plant such a mark as is used in the North Country; and welcome every brave yeoman who shall try a shot at it to win a smile from the bonny lass he loves best.'

He then turned to leave the lists. 'Let your guards attend me,' he said, 'if you please—I go but to cut a rod from the next willow-bush.'

Prince John made a signal that some attendants should follow him in case of his escape: but the cry of 'Shame! shame!' which burst from the multitude, induced him to alter his ungenerous purpose.

Locksley returned almost instantly with a willow wand about six feet in length, perfectly straight, and rather thicker than a man's thumb. He began to peel this with great composure, observing at the same time, that to ask a good woodsman to shoot at a target to broad as had hitherto been used, was to put shame upon his skill. 'For his own part,' he said, 'and in the land where he was bred, men would as soon take for their mark King Arthur's round-table, which held sixty knights around it. A child of seven years old,' he said, 'might hit yonder target with a headless shaft; but,' added he, walking deliberately to the other end of the lists, and sticking the willow wand upright in the ground, 'he that hits that rod at five-score yards, I call him an archer fit to bear both bow and quiver before a king, an it were the stout King Richard himself.'

'My grandsire,' said Hubert, 'drew a good bow at the battle of Hastings, and never shot at such a mark in his life—and neither will I. If this yeoman can cleave that rod, I give him the buck-lers—or rather, I yield to the devil that is in his jerkin, and not to any human skill; a man can but do his best, and I will not shoot where I am sure to miss. I might as well shoot at the edge of our parson's whittle, or at a wheat straw, or at a sunbeam, as at a twinkling white streak which I can hardly see.'

'Cowardly dog!' said Prince John.—'Sirrah Locksley, do thou shoot; but, if thou hittest such a mark, I will say thou art the first man ever did so. Howe'er it be, thou shalt not crow over us with a mere show of superior skill.'

'I will do my best, as Hubert says,' answered Locksley; 'no man can do more.'

So saying, he again bent his bow, but on the present occasion looked with attention to his weapon, and changed the string, which he thought was no longer truly round, having been a little frayed by the two former shots. He then took his aim with some deliberation, and the multitude awaited the event in breathless silence. The archer vindicated their opinion of his skill: his arrow split the willow rod against which it was aimed.* A jubilee of acclamations followed; and even Prince John, in admiration of Locksley's skill, lost for an instant his dislike to his person. 'These twenty nobles,' he said, 'which, with the bugle, thou hast fairly won, are thine own; we will make them fifty, if thou wilt take livery and service with us as a yeoman of our body guard, and be near to our person. For never did so strong a hand bend a bow, or so true an eye direct a shaft.'

'Pardon me, noble Prince,' said Locksley; 'but I have vowed, that if ever I take service, it should be with your royal brother King Richard. These twenty nobles I leave to Hubert, who has this day drawn as brave a bow as his grandsire did at Hastings. Had his modesty not refused the trial, he would have hit the wand as well as I.'

Hubert shook his head as he received with reluctance the bounty of the stranger; and Locksley, anxious to escape further observation, mixed with the crowd, and was seen no more.

The victorious archer would not perhaps have escaped John's attention so easily, had not that Prince had other subjects of anxious and more important meditation pressing upon his mind at that instant. He called upon his chamberlain as he gave the signal for retiring from the lists, and commanded him instantly to gallop to Ashby, and seek out Isaac the Jew. 'Tell the dog,' he said, 'to send me, before sun-down, two thousand crowns. He knows the security; but thou mayst show him this ring for a token. The rest of the money must be paid at York within six days. If he neglects, I will have the unbelieving villain's head. Look that thou pass him not on the way; for the circumcised slave was displaying his stolen finery amongst us.'

So saying, the Prince resumed his horse, and returned to Ashby, the whole crowd breaking up and dispersing upon his retreat.

CHAPTER XIV

> In rough magnificence array'd,
> When ancient Chivalry display'd
> The pomp of her heroic games,
> And crested chiefs and tissued dames
> Assembled, at the clarion's call,
> In some proud castle's high arch'd hall.
>
> WARTON*

PRINCE JOHN held his high festival in the Castle of Ashby.*
This was not the same building of which the stately ruins still
interest the traveller, and which was erected at a later period by
the Lord Hastings, High Chamberlain of England, one of the
first victims of the tyranny of Richard the Third, and yet better
known as one of Shakspeare's characters than by his historical
fame. The castle and town of Ashby, at this time, belonged to
Roger de Quincy, Earl of Winchester, who, during the period of
our history, was absent in the Holy Land. Prince John, in the
meanwhile, occupied his castle, and disposed of his domains
without scruple; and seeking at present to dazzle men's eyes by
his hospitality and magnificence, had given orders for great
preparations, in order to render the banquet as splendid as
possible.

   The purveyors of the Prince, who exercised on this and other
occasions the full authority of royalty, had swept the country
of all that could be collected which was esteemed fit for their
master's table. Guests also were invited in great numbers; and
in the necessity in which he then found himself of courting
popularity, Prince John had extended his invitation to a few
distinguished Saxon and Danish families, as well as to the
Norman nobility and gentry of the neighbourhood. However
despised and degraded on ordinary occasions, the great numbers
of the Anglo-Saxons must necessarily render them formidable
in the civil commotions which seemed approaching, and it
was an obvious point of policy to secure popularity with their
leaders.

It was accordingly the Prince's intention, which he for some time maintained, to treat these unwonted guests with a courtesy to which they had been little accustomed. But although no man with less scruple made his ordinary habits and feelings bend to his interest, it was the misfortune of this Prince, that his levity and petulance were perpetually breaking out, and undoing all that had been gained by his previous dissimulation.

Of this fickle temper he gave a memorable example in Ireland, when sent thither by his father, Henry the Second, with the purpose of buying golden opinions* of the inhabitants of that new and important acquisition to the English crown. Upon this occasion the Irish chieftains contended which should first offer to the young Prince their loyal homage and the kiss of peace. But, instead of receiving their salutations with courtesy, John and his petulant attendants could not resist the temptation of pulling the long beards of the Irish chieftains; a conduct which, as might have been expected, was highly resented by these insulted dignitaries, and produced fatal consequences to the English domination in Ireland.* It is necessary to keep these inconsistencies of John's character in view, that the reader may understand his conduct during the present evening.

In execution of the resolution which he had formed during his cooler moments, Prince John received Cedric and Athelstane with distinguished courtesy, and expressed his disappointment, without resentment, when the indisposition of Rowena was alleged by the former as a reason for her not attending upon his gracious summons. Cedric and Athelstane were both dressed in the ancient Saxon garb, which, although not unhandsome in itself, and in the present instance composed of costly materials, was so remote in shape and appearance from that of the other guests, that Prince John took great credit to himself with Waldemar Fitzurse for refraining from laughter at a sight which the fashion of the day rendered ridiculous. Yet, in the eye of sober judgment, the short close tunic and long mantle of the Saxons was a more graceful, as well as a more convenient dress, than the garb of the Normans, whose under garment was a long doublet, so loose as to resemble a shirt or waggoner's frock, covered by a cloak of scanty dimensions, neither fit to defend the wearer from cold or from rain, and the only purpose of which appeared to be to display as much fur, embroidery, and jewellery work, as the ingenuity of the tailor could contrive to lay upon it. The Emperor Charlemagne, in whose reign they were first introduced, seems to have been very sensible of the inconveniencies arising from the fashion of this garment. 'In Heaven's name,' said he, 'to what purpose serve these abridged cloaks? If we are in bed they are no cover, on horseback they are no protection from the wind and rain, and when seated, they do not guard our legs from the damp or the frost.'*

Nevertheless, spite of this imperial objurgation, the short cloaks continued in fashion down to the time of which we treat, and particularly among the princes of the House of Anjou. They were therefore in universal use among Prince John's courtiers; and the long mantle, which formed the upper garment of the Saxons, was held in proportional derision.

The guests were seated at a table which groaned under the quantity of good cheer. The numerous cooks who attended on the Prince's progress, having exerted all their art in varying the forms in which the ordinary provisions were served up, had succeeded almost as well as the modern professors of the culinary art in rendering them perfectly unlike their natural appearance. Besides these dishes of domestic origin, there were various delicacies brought from foreign parts, and a quantity of rich pastry, as well as of the simnel-bread and wastle cakes,* which were only used at the tables of the highest nobility. The banquet was crowned with the richest wines, both foreign and domestic.

But, though luxurious, the Norman nobles were not, generally speaking, an intemperate race. While indulging themselves in the pleasures of the table, they aimed at delicacy, but avoided excess, and were apt to attribute gluttony and drunkenness to the vanquished Saxons, as vices peculiar to their inferior station. Prince John, indeed, and those who courted his pleasure by imitating his foibles, were apt to indulge to excess in the pleasures of the trencher and the goblet; and indeed it is well known that his death was occasioned by a surfeit upon peaches and new ale. His conduct, however, was an exception to the general manners of his countrymen.

With sly gravity, interrupted only by private signs to each

other, the Norman knights and nobles beheld the ruder demeanour of Athelstane and Cedric at a banquet, to the form and fashion of which they were unaccustomed. And while their manners were thus the subject of sarcastic observation, the untaught Saxons unwittingly transgressed several of the arbitrary rules established for the regulation of society. Now, it is well known, that a man may with more impunity be guilty of an actual breach either of real good breeding or of good morals, than appear ignorant of the most minute point of fashionable etiquette. Thus Cedric, who dried his hands with a towel, instead of suffering the moisture to exhale by waving them gracefully in the air,* incurred more ridicule than his companion Athelstane, when he swallowed to his own single share the whole of a large pasty composed of the most exquisite foreign delicacies, and termed at that time a *Karum-pie*. When, however, it was discovered, by a serious cross-examination, that the Thane of Coningsburgh (or Franklin, as the Normans termed him) had no idea what he had been devouring, and that he had taken the contents of the Karum-pie for larks and pigeons, whereas they were in fact beccaficoes* and nightingales, his ignorance brought him in for an ample share of the ridicule which would have been more justly bestowed on his gluttony.

The long feast had at length its end; and, while the goblet circulated freely, men talked of the feats of the preceding tournament,—of the unknown victor in the archery games, of the Black Knight, whose self-denial had induced him to withdraw from the honours he had won,—and of the gallant Ivanhoe, who had so dearly bought the honours of the day. The topics were treated with military frankness, and the jest and laugh went round the hall. The brow of Prince John alone was overclouded during these discussions; some overpowering care seemed agitating his mind, and it was only when he received occasional hints from his attendants, that he seemed to take interest in what was passing around him. On such occasions he would start up, quaff a cup of wine as if to raise his spirits, and then mingle in the conversation by some observation made abruptly or at random.

'We drink this beaker,' said he, 'to the health of Wilfred of Ivanhoe, champion of this Passage of Arms, and grieve that his wound renders him absent from our board—Let all fill to the pledge, and especially Cedric of Rotherwood, the worthy father of a son so promising.'

'No, my lord,' replied Cedric, standing up, and placing on the table his untasted cup, 'I yield not the name of son to the disobedient youth, who at once despises my commands, and relinquishes the manners and customs of his fathers.'

''Tis impossible,' cried Prince John, with well-feigned astonishment, 'that so gallant a knight should be an unworthy or disobedient son!'

'Yet, my lord,' answered Cedric, 'so it is with this Wilfred. He left my homely dwelling to mingle with the gay nobility of your brother's court, where he learned to do those tricks of horsemanship which you prize so highly. He left it contrary to my wish and command; and in the days of Alfred that would have been termed disobedience—ay, and a crime severely punishable.'

'Alas!' replied Prince John, with a deep sigh of affected sympathy, 'since your son was a follower of my unhappy brother, it need not be enquired where or from whom he learned the lesson of filial disobedience.'

Thus spake Prince John, wilfully forgetting, that of all the sons of Henry the Second, though no one was free from the charge, he himself had been most distinguished for rebellion and ingratitude to his father.

'I think,' said he, after a moment's pause, 'that my brother proposed to confer upon his favourite the rich manor of Ivanhoe.'

'He did endow him with it,' answered Cedric; 'nor is it my least quarrel with my son, that he stooped to hold, as a feudal vassal, the very domains which his fathers possessed in free and independent right.'

'We shall then have your willing sanction, good Cedric,' said Prince John, 'to confer this fief upon a person whose dignity will not be diminished by holding land of the British crown.*—Sir Reginald Front-de-Bœuf,' he said, turning towards that Baron, 'I trust you will so keep the goodly Barony of Ivanhoe, that Sir Wilfred shall not incur his father's farther displeasure by again entering upon that fief.'

'By St Anthony!' answered the black-brow'd giant, 'I will consent that your highness shall hold me a Saxon, if either

Cedric or Wilfred, or the best that ever bore English blood, shall wrench from me the gift with which your highness has graced me.'

'Whoever shall call thee Saxon, Sir Baron,' replied Cedric, offended at a mode of expression by which the Normans frequently expressed their habitual contempt of the English, 'will do thee an honour as great as it is undeserved.'

Front-de-Bœuf would have replied, but Prince John's petulance and levity got the start.

'Assuredly,' said he, 'my lords, the noble Cedric speaks truth; and his race may claim precedence over us as much in the length of their pedigrees as in the longitude of their cloaks.'

'They go before us indeed in the field—as deer before dogs,' said Malvoisin.

'And with good right may they go before us—forget not,' said the Prior Aymer, 'the superior decency and decorum of their manners.'

'Their singular abstemiousness and temperance,' said De Bracy, forgetting the plan which promised him a Saxon bride.

'Together with the courage and conduct,' said Brian de Bois-Guilbert, 'by which they distinguished themselves at Hastings and elsewhere.'

While, with smooth and smiling cheek, the courtiers, each in turn, followed their Prince's example, and aimed a shaft of ridicule at Cedric, the face of the Saxon became inflamed with passion, and he glanced his eyes fiercely from one to another, as if the quick succession of so many injuries had prevented his replying to them in turn; or, like a baited bull, who, surrounded by his tormentors, is at a loss to choose from among them the immediate object of his revenge. At length he spoke, in a voice half choked with passion; and, addressing himself to Prince John as the head and front of the offence* which he had received, 'Whatever,' he said, 'have been the follies and vices of our race, a Saxon would have been held *nidering*,'[19] (the most emphatic term for abject worthlessness,) 'who should in his own hall, and while his own wine-cup passed, have treated, or suffered to be treated, an unoffending guest as your highness has this day beheld me used; and whatever was the misfortune of our fathers on the field of Hastings, those may at least be silent,' here he looked at Front-de-Bœuf and the Templar, 'who have within these few hours once and again lost saddle and stirrup before the lance of a Saxon.'

'By my faith, a biting jest!' said Prince John. 'How like you it, sirs?—Our Saxon subjects rise in spirit and courage; become shrewd in wit, and bold in bearing, in these unsettled times—What say ye, my lords?—By this good light, I hold it best to take our galleys, and return to Normandy in time.'

'For fear of the Saxons?' said De Bracy, laughing; 'we should need no weapon but our hunting spears to bring these boars to bay.'

'A truce with your raillery, Sir Knights,' said Fitzurse;—'and it were well,' he added, addressing the Prince, 'that your highness should assure the worthy Cedric there is no insult intended him by jests, which must sound but harshly in the ear of a stranger.'

'Insult?' answered Prince John, resuming his courtesy of demeanour; 'I trust it will not be thought that I could mean, or permit any, to be offered in my presence. Here! I fill my cup to Cedric himself, since he refuses to pledge his son's health.'

The cup went round amid the well-dissembled applause of the courtiers, which, however, failed to make the impression on the mind of the Saxon that had been designed. He was not naturally acute of perception, but those too much undervalued his understanding who deemed that this flattering compliment would obliterate the sense of the prior insult. He was silent, however, when the royal pledge again passed round, 'To Sir Athelstane of Coningsburgh.'

The knight made his obeisance, and showed his sense of the honour by draining a huge goblet in answer to it.

'And now, sirs,' said Prince John, who began to be warmed with the wine which he had drank, 'having done justice to our Saxon guests, we will pray of them some requital to our courtesy.—Worthy Thane,' he continued, addressing Cedric, 'may we pray you to name to us some Norman whose mention may least sully your mouth, and to wash down with a goblet of wine all bitterness which the sound may leave behind it?'

Fitzurse arose while Prince John spoke, and gliding behind the seat of the Saxon, whispered to him not to omit the opportunity of putting an end to unkindness betwixt the two races, by naming Prince John. The Saxon replied not to this politic insinuation, but, rising up, and filling his cup to the brim, he addressed Prince John in these words: 'Your highness has required that I should name a Norman deserving to be remembered at our banquet. This, perchance, is a hard task, since it calls on the slave to sing the praises of the master—upon the vanquished, while pressed by all the evils of conquest, to sing the praises of the conqueror. Yet I *will* name a Norman—the first in arms and in place—the best and the noblest of his race. And the lips that shall refuse to pledge me to his well-earned fame, I term false and dishonoured, and will so maintain them with my life.— I quaff this goblet to the health of Richard the Lion-hearted!'

Prince John, who had expected that his own name would have closed the Saxon's speech, started when that of his injured brother was so unexpectedly introduced. He raised mechanically the wine-cup to his lips, then instantly set it down, to view the demeanour of the company at this unexpected proposal, which many of them felt it as unsafe to oppose as to comply with. Some of them, ancient and experienced courtiers, closely imitated the example of the Prince himself, raising the goblet to their lips, and again replacing it before them. There were many who, with a more generous feeling, exclaimed, 'Long live King Richard! and may he be speedily restored to us!' And some few, among whom were Front-de-Bœuf and the Templar, in sullen disdain suffered their goblets to stand untasted before them. But no man ventured directly to gainsay a pledge filled to the health of the reigning monarch.

Having enjoyed his triumph for about a minute, Cedric said to his companion, 'Up, noble Athelstane! we have remained here long enough, since we have requited the hospitable courtesy of Prince John's banquet. Those who wish to know further of our rude Saxon manners must henceforth seek us in the homes of our fathers, since we have seen enough of royal banquets, and enough of Norman courtesy.'

So saying, he arose and left the banqueting room, followed by Athelstane, and by several other guests, who, partaking of the Saxon lineage, held themselves insulted by the sarcasms of Prince John and his courtiers.

'By the bones of St Thomas,' said Prince John, as they re-treated, 'the Saxon churls have borne off the best of the day, and have retreated with triumph!'

'*Conclamatum est, poculatum est,*' said Prior Aymer; 'we have drunk and we have shouted,—it were time we left our wine flagons.'

'The monk hath some fair penitent to shrive to-night, that he is in such a hurry to depart,' said De Bracy.

'Not so, Sir Knight,' replied the Abbot; 'but I must move several miles forward this evening upon my homeward journey.'

'They are breaking up,' said the Prince in a whisper to Fitzurse; 'their fears anticipate the event, and this coward Prior is the first to shrink from me.'

'Fear not, my lord,' said Waldemar; 'I will show him such reasons as shall induce him to join us when we hold our meeting at York.—Sir Prior,' he said, 'I must speak with you in private, before you mount your palfrey.'

The other guests were now fast dispersing, with the exception of those immediately attached to Prince John's faction, and his retinue.

'This, then, is the result of your advice,' said the Prince, turning an angry countenance upon Fitzurse; 'that I should be bearded at my own board by a drunken Saxon churl, and that, on the mere sound of my brother's name, men should fall off from me as if I had the leprosy?'

'Have patience, sir,' replied his counsellor; 'I might retort your accusation, and blame the inconsiderate levity which foiled my design, and misled your own better judgment. But this is no time for recrimination. De Bracy and I will instantly go among these shuffling cowards, and convince them they have gone too far to recede.'

'It will be in vain,' said Prince John, pacing the apartment with disordered steps, and expressing himself with an agitation to which the wine he had drank partly contributed—'It will be in vain—they have seen the handwriting on the wall*—they have marked the paw of the lion in the sand—they have heard his approaching roar shake the wood—nothing will reanimate their courage.'

'Would to God,' said Fitzurse to De Bracy, 'that aught could reanimate his own! His brother's very name is an ague to him. Unhappy are the counsellors of a Prince, who wants fortitude and perseverance alike in good and in evil!'

CHAPTER XV*

And yet he thinks,—ha, ha, ha, ha,—he thinks
I am the tool and servant of his will.
Well, let it be; through all the maze of trouble
His plots and base oppression must create,
I'll shape myself a way to higher things,
And who will say 'tis wrong?

*Basil, a Tragedy**

No spider ever took more pains to repair the shattered meshes of his web, than did Waldemar Fitzurse to reunite and combine the scattered members of Prince John's cabal. Few of these were attached to him from inclination, and none from personal regard. It was therefore necessary, that Fitzurse should open to them new prospects of advantage, and remind them of those which they at present enjoyed. To the young and wild nobles, he held out the prospect of unpunished license and uncontrolled revelry; to the ambitious, that of power, and to the covetous, that of increased wealth and extended domains. The leaders of the mercenaries received a donation in gold; an argument the most persuasive to their minds, and without which all others would have proved in vain. Promises were still more liberally distributed than money by this active agent; and, in fine, nothing was left undone that could determine the wavering, or animate the disheartened. The return of King Richard he spoke of as an event altogether beyond the reach of probability; yet, when he observed, from the doubtful looks and uncertain answers which he received, that this was the apprehension by which the minds of his accomplices were most haunted, he boldly treated that event, should it really take place, as one which ought not to alter their political calculations.

'If Richard returns,' said Fitzurse, 'he returns to enrich his needy and impoverished crusaders at the expense of those who did not follow him to the Holy Land. He returns to call to a fearful reckoning, those who, during his absence, have done aught that can be construed offence or encroachment upon either the laws of the land or the privileges of the crown. He returns to avenge upon the Orders of the Temple and the Hospital, the preference which they showed to Philip of France during the wars in the Holy Land. He returns, in fine, to punish as a rebel every adherent of his brother Prince John. Are ye afraid of his power?' continued the artful confident of that Prince; 'we acknowledge him a strong and valiant knight; but these are not the days of King Arthur, when a champion could encounter an army. If Richard indeed comes back, it must be alone,—unfollowed—unfriended. The bones of his gallant army have whitened the sands of Palestine. The few of his followers who have returned have straggled hither like this Wilfred of Ivanhoe, beggared and broken men.—And what talk ye of Richard's right of birth?' he proceeded, in answer to those who objected scruples on that head. 'Is Richard's title of primogeniture more decidedly certain than that of Duke Robert of Normandy, the Conqueror's eldest son?* And yet William the Red, and Henry, his second and third brothers, were successively preferred to him by the voice of the nation. Robert had every merit which can be pleaded for Richard; he was a bold knight, a good leader, generous to his friends and to the church, and, to crown the whole, a crusader and a conqueror of the Holy Sepulchre; and yet he died a blind and miserable prisoner in the Castle of Cardiff, because he opposed himself to the will of the people, who chose that he should not rule over them. It is our right,' he said, 'to choose from the blood royal the prince who is best qualified to hold the supreme power—that is,' said he, correcting himself, 'him whose election will best promote the interests of the nobility. In personal qualifications,' he added, 'it was possible that Prince John might be inferior to his brother Richard; but when it was considered that the latter returned with the sword of vengeance in his hand, while the former held out rewards, immunities, privileges, wealth, and honours, it could not be doubted which was the king whom in wisdom the nobility were called on to support.'

These, and many more arguments, some adapted to the peculiar circumstances of those whom he addressed, had the expected weight with the nobles of Prince John's faction. Most of them consented to attend the proposed meeting at York, for the purpose of making general arrangements for placing the crown upon the head of Prince John.

It was late at night, when, worn out and exhausted with his various exertions, however gratified with the result, Fitzurse, returning to the Castle of Ashby, met with De Bracy, who had exchanged his banqueting garments for a short green kirtle,* with hose of the same cloth and colour, a leathern cap or head-piece, a short sword, a horn slung over his shoulder, a long-bow in his hand, and a bundle of arrows stuck in his belt. Had Fitzurse met this figure in an outer apartment, he would have passed him without notice, as one of the yeomen of the guard; but finding him in the inner hall, he looked at him with more attention, and recognised the Norman knight in the dress of an English yeoman.

'What mummery is this, De Bracy?' said Fitzurse, somewhat angrily; 'is this a time for Christmas gambols and quaint maskings,* when the fate of our master, Prince John, is on the very verge of decision? Why hast thou not been, like me, among these heartless cravens, whom the very name of King Richard terrifies, as it is said to do the children of the Saracens?'

'I have been attending to mine own business,' answered De Bracy calmly, 'as you, Fitzurse, have been minding yours.'

'I minding mine own business!' echoed Waldemar; 'I have been engaged in that of Prince John, our joint patron.'

'As if thou hadst any other reason for that, Waldemar,' said De Bracy, 'than the promotion of thine own individual interest? Come, Fitzurse, we know each other—ambition is thy pursuit, pleasure is mine, and they become our different ages. Of Prince John thou thinkest as I do; that he is too weak to be a determined monarch, too tyrannical to be an easy monarch, too insolent and presumptuous to be a popular monarch, and too fickle and timid to be long a monarch of any kind. But he is a monarch by whom Fitzurse and De Bracy hope to rise and thrive; and therefore you aid him with your policy, and I with the lances of my Free Companions.'

'A hopeful auxiliary,' said Fitzurse impatiently; 'playing the fool in the very moment of utter necessity.—What on earth dost thou purpose by this absurd disguise at a moment so urgent?'

'To get me a wife,' answered De Bracy coolly, 'after the manner of the tribe of Benjamin.'

'The tribe of Benjamin?' said Fitzurse; 'I comprehend thee not.'

'Wert thou not in presence yester-even,' said De Bracy, 'when we heard the Prior Aymer tell us a tale in reply to the romance which was sung by the Minstrel?—He told how, long since in Palestine, a deadly feud arose between the tribe of Benjamin and the rest of the Israelitish nation; and how they cut to pieces wellnigh all the chivalry of that tribe; and how they swore by our blessed Lady, that they would not permit those who remained to marry in their lineage; and how they became grieved for their vow, and sent to consult his holiness the Pope how they might be absolved from it; and how, by the advice of the Holy Father, the youth of the tribe of Benjamin carried off from a superb tourna-ment all the ladies who were there present, and thus won them wives without the consent either of their brides or their brides' families.'*

'I have heard the story,' said Fitzurse, 'though either the Prior or thou has made some singular alterations in date and circumstances.'

'I tell thee,' said De Bracy, 'that I mean to purvey me a wife after the fashion of the tribe of Benjamin; which is as much as to say, that in this same equipment I will fall upon that herd of Saxon bullocks, who have this night left the castle, and carry off from them the lovely Rowena.'

'Art thou mad, De Bracy?' said Fitzurse. 'Bethink thee that, though the men be Saxons, they are rich and powerful, and regarded with the more respect by their countrymen, that wealth and honour are but the lot of few of Saxon descent.'

'And should belong to none,' said De Bracy; 'the work of the Conquest should be completed.'

'This is no time for it at least,' said Fitzurse; 'the approaching crisis renders the favour of the multitude indispensable, and Prince John cannot refuse justice to any one who injures their favourites.'

'Let him grant it, if he dare,' said De Bracy; "he will soon see the difference betwixt the support of such a lusty lot of spears as mine, and that of a heartless mob of Saxon churls. Yet I mean no immediate discovery of myself. Seem I not in this garb as bold a forester as ever blew horn? The blame of the violence shall rest with the outlaws of the Yorkshire forests. I have sure spies on the Saxon's motions—To-night they sleep in the convent of Saint Wittol,* or Withold, or whatever they call that churl of a Saxon Saint at Burton-on-Trent. Next day's march brings them within our reach, and, falcon-ways, we swoop on them at once. Presently after I will appear in mine own shape, play the courteous knight, rescue the unfortunate and afflicted fair one from the hands of the rude ravishers, conduct her to Front-de-Bœuf's Castle, or to Normandy, if it should be necessary, and produce her not again to her kindred until she be the bride and dame of Maurice de Bracy.'

'A marvellously sage plan,' said Fitzurse, 'and, as I think, not entirely of thine own device.—Come, be frank, De Bracy, who aided thee in the invention? and who is to assist in the execution? for, as I think, thine own band lies as far off as York.'

'Marry, if thou must needs know,' said De Bracy, 'it was the Templar Brian de Bois-Guilbert that shaped out the enterprise, which the adventure of the men of Benjamin suggested to me. He is to aid me in the onslaught, and he and his followers will personate the outlaws, from whom my valorous arm is, after changing my garb, to rescue the lady.'

'By my halidome,' said Fitzurse, 'the plan was worthy of your united wisdom! and thy prudence, De Bracy, is most especially manifested in the project of leaving the lady in the hands of thy worthy confederate. Thou mayst, I think, succeed in taking her from her Saxon friends, but how thou wilt rescue her afterwards from the clutches of Bois-Guilbert seems considerably more doubtful—He is a falcon well accustomed to pounce on a partridge, and to hold his prey fast.'

'He is a Templar,' said De Bracy, 'and cannot therefore rival me in my plan of wedding this heiress;—and to attempt aught dishonourable against the intended bride of De Bracy—By Heaven! were he a whole Chapter of his Order in his single person, he dared not do me such an injury!'

'Then since nought that I can say,' said Fitzurse, 'will put this folly from thy imagination, (for well I know the obstinacy of thy disposition,) at least waste as little time as possible—let not thy folly be lasting as well as untimely.'

'I tell thee,' answered De Bracy, 'that it will be the work of a few hours, and I shall be at York at the head of my daring and valorous fellows, as ready to support any bold design as thy policy can be to form one.—But I hear my comrades assembling, and the steeds stamping and neighing in the outer court.—Farewell.—I go, like a true knight, to win the smiles of beauty.'

'Like a true knight?' repeated Fitzurse, looking after him; 'like a fool, I should say, or like a child, who will leave the most serious and needful occupation, to chase the down of the thistle that drives past him.—But it is with such tools that I must work;—and for whose advantage?—For that of a Prince as unwise as he is profligate, and as likely to be an ungrateful master as he has already proved a rebellious son and an unnatural brother.—But he—he, too, is but one of the tools with which I labour; and, proud as he is, should he presume to separate his interest from mine, this is a secret which he shall soon learn.'

The meditations of the statesman were here interrupted by the voice of the Prince from an interior apartment, calling out, 'Noble Waldemar Fitzurse!' and, with bonnet doffed, the future Chancellor (for to such high preferment did the wily Norman aspire) hastened to receive the orders of the future sovereign.

CHAPTER XVI

Far in a wild, unknown to public view,
From youth to age a reverend hermit grew;
The moss his bed, the cave his humble cell,
His food the fruits, his drink the crystal well;
Remote from man, with God he pass'd his days,
Prayer all his business—all his pleasure praise.

PARNELL*

THE reader cannot have forgotten that the event of the tournament was decided by the exertions of an unknown knight, whom, on account of the passive and indifferent conduct which he had manifested on the former part of the day, the spectators had entitled, *Le Noir Faineant*. This knight had left the field abruptly when the victory was achieved; and when he was called upon to receive the reward of his valour, he was nowhere to be found. In the meantime, while summoned by heralds and by trumpets, the knight was holding his course northward, avoiding all frequented paths, and taking the shortest road through the woodlands. He paused for the night at a small hostelry lying out of the ordinary route, where, however, he obtained from a wandering minstrel news of the event of the tourney.

On the next morning the knight departed early, with the intention of making a long journey; the condition of his horse, which he had carefully spared during the preceding morning, being such as enabled him to travel far without the necessity of much repose. Yet his purpose was baffled by the devious paths through which he rode, so that when evening closed upon him, he only found himself on the frontiers of the West Riding of Yorkshire. By this time both horse and man required refreshment, and it became necessary, moreover, to look out for some place in which they might spend the night, which was now fast approaching.

The place where the traveller found himself seemed unpropitious for obtaining either shelter or refreshment, and he was likely to be reduced to the usual expedient of knights-errant, who, on such occasions, turned their horses to graze, and laid themselves down to meditate on their lady-mistress, with an oak-tree for a canopy. But the Black Knight either had no mistress to meditate upon, or, being as indifferent in love as he seemed to be in war, was not sufficiently occupied by passionate reflections upon her beauty and cruelty, to be able to parry the effects of fatigue and hunger, and suffer love to act as a substitute for the solid comforts of a bed and supper. He felt dissatisfied, therefore, when, looking around, he found himself deeply involved in woods, through which indeed there were many open glades, and some paths, but such as seemed only formed by the numerous herds of cattle which grazed in the forest, or by the animals of chase, and the hunters who made prey of them.

The sun, by which the knight had chiefly directed his course, had now sunk behind the Derbyshire hills on his left, and every effort which he might make to pursue his journey was as likely to lead him out of his road as to advance him on his route. After having in vain endeavoured to select the most beaten path, in hopes it might lead to the cottage of some herdsman, or the silvan lodge of a forester, and having repeatedly found himself totally unable to determine on a choice, the knight resolved to trust to the sagacity of his horse; experience having, on former occasions, made him acquainted with the wonderful talent possessed by these animals for extricating themselves and their riders on such emergencies.

The good steed, grievously fatigued with so long a day's journey under a rider cased in mail, had no sooner found, by the slackened reins, that he was abandoned to his own guidance, than he seemed to assume new strength and spirit; and whereas formerly he had scarce replied to the spur, otherwise than by a groan, he now, as if proud of the confidence reposed in him, pricked up his ears, and assumed, of his own accord, a more lively motion. The path which the animal adopted rather turned off from the course pursued by the knight during the day; but as the horse seemed confident in his choice, the rider abandoned himself to his discretion.

He was justified by the event; for the footpath soon after appeared a little wider and more worn, and the tinkle of a small bell gave the knight to understand that he was in the vicinity of some chapel or hermitage.

Accordingly, he soon reached an open plat of turf, on the opposite side of which, a rock, rising abruptly from a gently sloping plain, offered its grey and weatherbeaten front to the traveller. Ivy mantled its sides in some places, and in others oaks and holly bushes, whose roots found nourishment in the cliffs of the crag, waved over the precipices below, like the plumage of the warrior over his steel helmet, giving grace to that whose chief expression was terror. At the bottom of the rock, and leaning, as it were, against it, was constructed a rude hut, built chiefly of the trunks of trees felled in the neighbouring forest, and secured against the weather by having its crevices stuffed with moss mingled with clay. The stem of a young fir-tree lopped of its branches, with a piece of wood tied across near the top, was planted upright by the door, as a rude emblem of the holy cross. At a little distance on the right hand, a fountain of the purest water trickled out of the rock, and was received in a hollow stone, which labour had formed into a rustic basin. Escaping from thence, the stream murmured down the descent by a channel which its course had long worn, and so wandered through the little plain to lose itself in the neighbouring wood.

Beside this fountain were the ruins of a very small chapel, of which the roof had partly fallen in. The building, when entire, had never been above sixteen feet long by twelve feet in breadth, and the roof, low in proportion, rested upon four concentric arches which sprung from the four corners of the building, each supported upon a short and heavy pillar. The ribs of two of these arches remained, though the roof had fallen down betwixt them; over the others it remained entire. The entrance to this ancient place of devotion was under a very low round arch, ornamented by several courses of that zig-zag moulding, resembling shark's teeth, which appears so often in the more ancient Saxon architecture. A belfry rose above the porch on four small pillars, within which hung the green and weatherbeaten bell, the feeble sounds of which had been some time before heard by the Black Knight.

The whole peaceful and quiet scene lay glimmering in twilight before the eyes of the traveller, giving him good assurance of lodging for the night; since it was a special duty of those hermits who dwelt in the woods, to exercise hospitality towards benighted or bewildered passengers.

Accordingly, the knight took no time to consider minutely the particulars which we have detailed, but thanking Saint Julian (the patron of travellers) who had sent him good harbourage, he leaped from his horse and assailed the door of the hermitage with the butt of his lance, in order to arouse attention and gain admittance.

It was some time before he obtained any answer, and the reply, when made, was unpropitious.

'Pass on, whosoever thou art,' was the answer given by a deep hoarse voice from within the hut, 'and disturb not the servant of God and St Dunstan in his evening devotions.'

'Worthy father,' answered the knight, 'here is a poor wanderer bewildered in these woods, who gives thee the opportunity of exercising thy charity and hospitality.'

'Good brother,' replied the inhabitant of the hermitage, 'it has pleased Our Lady and St Dunstan to destine me for the object of those virtues, instead of the exercise thereof. I have no provisions here which even a dog would share with me, and a horse of any tenderness of nurture would despise my couch—pass therefore on thy way, and God speed thee.'

'But how,' replied the knight, 'is it possible for me to find my way through such a wood as this, when darkness is coming on? I pray you, reverend father, as you are a Christian, to undo your door, and at least point out to me my road.'

'And I pray you, good Christian brother,' replied the anchorite, 'to disturb me no more. You have already interrupted one *pater*, two *aves*, and a *credo*, which I, miserable sinner that I am, should, according to my vow, have said before moonrise.'

'The road—the road!' vociferated the knight, 'give me directions for the road, if I am to expect no more from thee.'

'The road,' replied the hermit, 'is easy to hit. The path from the wood leads to a morass, and from thence to a ford, which, as the rains have abated, may now be passable. When thou hast crossed the ford, thou wilt take care of thy footing up the left bank, as it is somewhat precipitous; and the path, which hangs over the river, has lately, as I learn, (for I seldom leave the duties of my chapel,) given way in sundry places. Thou wilt then keep straight forward'——

'A broken path—a precipice—a ford, and a morass!' said the knight, interrupting him,—'Sir Hermit, if you were the holiest that ever wore beard or told bead, you shall scarce prevail on me to hold this road to-night. I tell thee, that thou, who livest by the charity of the country—ill deserved, as I doubt it is—hast no right to refuse shelter to the wayfarer when in distress. Either open the door quickly, or, by the rood, I will beat it down and make entry for myself.'

'Friend wayfarer,' replied the hermit, 'be not importunate; if thou puttest me to use the carnal weapon in mine own defence, it will be e'en the worse for you.'

At this moment a distant noise of barking and growling, which the traveller had for some time heard, became extremely loud and furious, and made the knight suppose that the hermit, alarmed by his threat of making forcible entry, had called the dogs who made this clamour to aid him in his defence, out of some inner recess in which they had been kennelled. Incensed at this preparation on the hermit's part for making good his inhospitable purpose, the knight struck the door so furiously with his foot, that posts as well as staples shook with violence.

The anchorite, not caring again to expose his door to a similar shock, now called out aloud, 'Patience, patience—spare thy strength, good traveller, and I will presently undo the door, though, it may be, my doing so will be little to thy pleasure.'

The door accordingly was opened; and the hermit, a large, strong-built man, in his sackcloth gown and hood, girt with a rope of rushes, stood before the knight. He had in one hand a lighted torch, or link, and in the other a baton of crab-tree, so thick and heavy, that it might well be termed a club. Two large shaggy dogs, half greyhound half mastiff, stood ready to rush upon the traveller as soon as the door should be opened. But when the torch glanced upon the lofty crest and golden spurs of the knight, who stood without, the hermit, altering probably his original intentions, repressed the rage of his auxiliaries, and, changing his tone to a sort of churlish courtesy, invited the knight to enter his hut, making excuse for his unwillingness to open his lodge after sunset, by alleging the multitude of robbers and outlaws who were abroad, and who gave no honour to Our Lady or St Dunstan, nor to those holy men who spent life in their service.

'The poverty of your cell, good father,' said the knight, looking around him, and seeing nothing but a bed of leaves, a crucifix rudely carved in oak, a missal, with a rough-hewn table and two stools, and one or two clumsy articles of furniture—'the poverty of your cell should seem a sufficient defence against any risk of thieves, not to mention the aid of two trusty dogs, large and strong enough, I think, to pull down a stag, and of course, to match with most men.'

'The good keeper of the forest,' said the hermit, 'hath allowed me the use of these animals, to protect my solitude until the times shall mend.'

Having said this, he fixed his torch in a twisted branch of iron which served for a candlestick; and, placing the oaken trivet before the embers of the fire, which he refreshed with some dry wood, he placed a stool upon one side of the table, and beckoned to the knight to do the same upon the other.

They sat down, and gazed with great gravity at each other, each thinking in his heart that he had seldom seen a stronger or more athletic figure than was placed opposite to him.

'Reverend hermit,' said the knight, after looking long and fixedly at his host, 'were it not to interrupt your devout meditations, I would pray to know three things of your holiness; first, where I am to put my horse?—secondly, what I can have for supper?—thirdly, where I am to take up my couch for the night?'

'I will reply to you,' said the hermit, 'with my finger, it being against my rule to speak by words where signs can answer the purpose.' So saying, he pointed successively to two corners of the hut. 'Your stable,' said he, 'is there—your bed there; and,' reaching down a platter with two handfuls of parched pease upon it from the neighbouring shelf, and placing it upon the table, he added, 'your supper is here.'

The knight shrugged his shoulders, and leaving the hut, brought in his horse, (which in the interim he had fastened to a

tree,) unsaddled him with much attention, and spread upon the
steed's weary back his own mantle.

The hermit was apparently somewhat moved to compassion
by the anxiety as well as address which the stranger displayed in
tending his horse; for, muttering something about provender left
for the keeper's palfrey, he dragged out of a recess a bundle of
forage, which he spread before the knight's charger, and immediately afterwards shook down a quantity of dried fern in the
corner which he had assigned for the rider's couch. The knight
returned him thanks for his courtesy; and, this duty done, both
resumed their seats by the table, whereon stood the trencher of
pease placed between them. The hermit, after a long grace,
which had once been Latin, but of which original language
few traces remained, excepting here and there the long rolling
termination of some word or phrase, set example to his guest, by
modestly putting into a very large mouth, furnished with teeth
which might have ranked with those of a boar both in sharpness
and whiteness, some three or four dried pease, a miserable grist
as it seemed for so large and able a mill.

The knight, in order to follow so laudable an example, laid
aside his helmet, his corslet, and the greater part of his armour,
and showed to the hermit a head thick-curled with yellow hair,
high features, blue eyes, remarkably bright and sparkling, a
mouth well formed, having an upper lip clothed with
mustachoes darker than this hair, and bearing altogether the look
of a bold, daring, and enterprising man, with which his strong
form well corresponded.

The hermit, as if wishing to answer to the confidence of his
guest, threw back his cowl, and showed a round bullet head
belonging to a man in the prime of life. His close-shaven crown,
surrounded by a circle of stiff curled black hair, had something
the appearance of a parish pinfold* begirt by its high hedge. The
features expressed nothing of monastic austerity, or of ascetic
privations; on the contrary, it was a bold bluff countenance, with
broad black eyebrows, a well-turned forehead, and cheeks as
round and vermilion as those of a trumpeter, from which descended a long and curly black beard. Such a visage, joined to the
brawny form of the holy man, spoke rather of sirloins and
haunches, than of pease and pulse. This incongruity did not

escape the guest. After he had with great difficulty accomplished the mastication of a mouthful of the dried pease, he found it absolutely necessary to request his pious entertainer to furnish him with some liquor; who replied to his request by placing before him a large can of the purest water from the fountain.

'It is from the well of St Dunstan,' said he, 'in which, betwixt sun and sun, he baptized five hundred heathen Danes and Britons—blessed be his name!' And applying his black beard to the pitcher, he took a draught much more moderate in quantity than his encomium seemed to warrant.

'It seems to me, reverend father,' said the knight, 'that the small morsels which you eat, together with this holy, but somewhat thin beverage, have thriven with you marvellously. You appear a man more fit to win the ram at a wrestling match,* or the ring at a bout at quarter-staff, or the bucklers at a sword-play, than to linger out your time in this desolate wilderness, saying masses, and living upon parched pease and cold water.'

'Sir Knight,' answered the hermit, 'your thoughts, like those of the ignorant laity, are according to the flesh. It has pleased Our Lady and my patron saint to bless the pittance to which I restrain myself, even as the pulse and water was blessed to the children Shadrach, Meshech, and Abednego,* who drank the same rather than defile themselves with the wine and meats which were appointed them by the King of the Saracens.'

'Holy father,' said the knight, 'upon whose countenance it hath pleased Heaven to work such a miracle, permit a sinful layman to crave thy name?'

'Thou mayst call me,' answered the hermit, 'the Clerk of Copmanhurst, for so I am termed in these parts—They add, it is true, the epithet holy, but I stand not upon that, as being unworthy of such addition.—And now, valiant knight, may I pray ye for the name of my honourable guest?'

'Truly,' said the knight, 'Holy Clerk of Copmanhurst, men call me in these parts the Black Knight,—many, sir, add to it the epithet of Sluggard, whereby I am no way ambitious to be distinguished.'

The hermit could scarcely forbear from smiling at his guest's reply.

'I see,' said he, 'Sir Sluggish Knight, that thou art a man of prudence and of counsel; and moreover, I see that my poor monastic fare likes thee not, accustomed, perhaps, as thou hast been, to the license of courts and of camps, and the luxuries of cities; and now I bethink me, Sir Sluggard, that when the charitable keeper of this forest-walk left these dogs for my protection, and also those bundles of forage, he left me also some food, which, being unfit for my use, the very recollection of it had escaped me amid my more weighty meditations.'

'I dare be sworn he did so,' said the knight; 'I was convinced that there was better food in the cell, Holy Clerk, since you first doffed your cowl.—Your keeper is ever a jovial fellow; and none who beheld thy grinders contending with these pease, and thy throat flooded with this ungenial element, could see thee doomed to such horse-provender and horse-beverage,' (pointing to the provisions upon the table,) 'and refrain from mending thy cheer. Let us see the keeper's bounty, therefore, without delay.'

The hermit cast a wistful look upon the knight, in which there was a sort of comic expression of hesitation, as if uncertain how far he should act prudently in trusting his guest. There was, however, as much of bold frankness in the knight's countenance as was possible to be expressed by features. His smile, too, had something in it irresistibly comic, and gave an assurance of faith and loyalty, with which his host could not refrain from sympathizing.

After exchanging a mute glance or two, the hermit went to the further side of the hut, and opened a hutch, which was concealed with great care and some ingenuity. Out of the recesses of a dark closet, into which this aperture gave admittance, he brought a large pasty, baked in a pewter platter of unusual dimensions. This mighty dish he placed before his guest, who, using his poniard to cut it open, lost no time in making himself acquainted with its contents.

'How long is it since the good keeper has been here?' said the knight to his host, after having swallowed several hasty morsels of this reinforcement to the hermit's good cheer.

'About two months,' answered the father hastily.

'By the true Lord,' answered the knight, 'every thing in your hermitage is miraculous, Holy Clerk! for I would have been sworn that the fat buck which furnished this venison had been running on foot within the week.'

The hermit was somewhat discountenanced by this observation; and, moreover, he made but a poor figure while gazing on the diminution of the pasty, on which his guest was making desperate inroads; a warfare in which his previous profession of abstinence left him no pretext for joining.

'I have been in Palestine, Sir Clerk,' said the knight, stopping short of a sudden, 'and I bethink me it is a custom there that every host who entertains a guest shall assure him of the wholesomeness of his food, by partaking of it along with him. Far be it from me to suspect so holy a man of aught inhospitable; nevertheless I will be highly bound to you would you comply with this Eastern custom.'

'To ease your unnecessary scruples, Sir Knight, I will for once depart from my rule,' replied the hermit. And as there were no forks in those days, his clutches were instantly in the bowels of the pasty.

The ice of ceremony being once broken, it seemed matter of rivalry between the guest and the entertainer which should display the best appetite; and although the former had probably fasted longest, yet the hermit fairly surpassed him.

'Holy Clerk,' said the knight, when his hunger was appeased, 'I would gage my good horse yonder against a zecchin, that that same honest keeper to whom we are obliged for the venison has left thee a stoup of wine, or a runlet of canary, or some such trifle, by way of ally to this noble pasty. This would be a circumstance, doubtless, totally unworthy to dwell in the memory of so rigid an anchorite; yet, I think, were you to search yonder crypt once more, you would find that I am right in my conjecture.'

The hermit only replied by a grin; and returning to the hutch, he produced a leathern bottle, which might contain about four quarts. He also brought forth two large drinking cups, made out of the horn of the urus,* and hooped with silver. Having made this goodly provision for washing down the supper, he seemed to think no farther ceremonious scruple necessary on his part; but filling both cups, and saying, in the Saxon fashion, '*Waes hael*, Sir Sluggish Knight!' he emptied his own at a draught.

'*Drink hael*, Holy Clerk of Copmanhurst!' answered the warrior, and did his host reason in a similar brimmer.

'Holy Clerk,' said the stranger, after the first cup was thus swallowed, 'I cannot but marvel that a man possessed of such thews and sinews as thine, and who therewithal shows the talent of so goodly a trencher-man,* should think of abiding by himself in this wilderness. In my judgment, you are fitter to keep a castle or a fort, eating of the fat and drinking of the strong, than to live here upon pulse and water, or even upon the charity of the keeper. At least, were I as thou, I should find myself both disport and plenty out of the king's deer. There is many a goodly herd in these forests, and a buck will never be missed that goes to the use of Saint Dunstan's chaplain.'

'Sir Sluggish Knight,' replied the Clerk, 'these are dangerous words, and I pray you to forbear them. I am true hermit to the king and law, and were I to spoil my liege's game, I should be sure of the prison, and, an my gown saved me not, were in some peril of hanging.'

'Nevertheless, were I as thou,' said the knight, 'I would take my walk by moonlight, when foresters and keepers were warm in bed, and ever and anon,—as I pattered my prayers,—I would let fly a shaft among the herds of dun deer that feed in the glades— Resolve me, Holy Clerk, hast thou never practised such a pastime?'

'Friend Sluggard,' answered the hermit, 'thou hast seen all that can concern thee of my house-keeping, and something more than he deserves who takes up his quarters by violence. Credit me, it is better to enjoy the good which God sends thee, than to be impertinently curious how it comes. Fill thy cup, and welcome; and do not, I pray thee, by further impertinent enquiries, put me to show that thou couldst hardly have made good thy lodging had I been earnest to oppose thee.'

'By my faith,' said the knight, 'thou makest me more curious than ever! Thou art the most mysterious hermit I ever met; and I will know more of thee ere we part. As for thy threats, know, holy man, thou speakest to one whose trade it is to find out danger wherever it is to be met with.'

'Sir Sluggish Knight, I drink to thee,' said the hermit; 'respecting thy valour much, but deeming wondrous slightly of thy discretion. If thou wilt take equal arms with me, I will give thee, in all friendship and brotherly love, such sufficing penance and complete absolution, that thou shalt not for the next twelve months sin the sin of excess of curiosity.'

The knight pledged him, and desired him to name his weapons.

'There is none,' replied the hermit, 'from the scissors of Delilah, and the tenpenny nail of Jael, to the scimitar of Goliath,* at which I am not a match for thee—But, if I am to make the election, what sayst thou, good friend, to these trinkets?'

Thus speaking, he opened another hutch, and took out from it a couple of broadswords and bucklers, such as were used by the yeomanry of the period. The knight, who watched his motions, observed that this second place of concealment was furnished with two or three good long-bows, a crossbow, a bundle of bolts for the latter, and half-a-dozen sheaves of arrows for the former. A harp, and other matters of a very uncanonical appearance, were also visible when this dark recess was opened.

'I promise thee, brother Clerk,' said he, 'I will ask thee no more offensive questions. The contents of that cupboard are an answer to all my enquiries; and I see a weapon there' (here he stooped and took out the harp) 'on which I would more gladly prove my skill with thee, than at the sword and buckler.'

'I hope, Sir Knight,' said the hermit, 'thou hast given no good reason for thy surname of the Sluggard. I do promise thee I suspect thee grievously. Nevertheless, thou art my guest, and I will not put thy manhood to the proof without thine own free will. Sit thee down, then, and fill thy cup; let us drink, sing, and be merry. If thou knowest ever a good lay, thou shalt be welcome to a nook of pasty at Copmanhurst so long as I serve the chapel of St Dunstan, which, please God, shall be till I change my grey covering for one of green turf. But come, fill a flagon, for it will crave some time to tune the harp; and nought pitches the voice and sharpens the ear like a cup of wine. For my part, I love to feel the grape at my very finger-ends before they make the harp-strings tinkle.'[20]

CHAPTER XVII

At eve, within yon studious nook,
I ope my brass-embossed book,
Portray'd with many a holy deed
Of martyrs crown'd with heavenly meed;
Then, as my taper waxes dim,
Chant, ere I sleep, my measured hymn.

. . . . .

Who but would cast his pomp away,
To take my staff and amice grey,
And to the world's tumultuous stage,
Prefer the peaceful HERMITAGE?

WARTON*

NOTWITHSTANDING the prescription of the genial hermit,
with which his guest willingly complied, he found it no easy
matter to bring the harp to harmony.

'Methinks, holy father,' said he, 'the instrument wants one
string, and the rest have been somewhat misused.'

'Ay, mark'st thou that?' replied the hermit; 'that shows thee a
master of the craft. Wine and wassail,' he added, gravely casting
up his eyes—'all the fault of wine and wassail!—I told Allan-a-
Dale, the northern minstrel,* that he would damage the harp if
he touched it after the seventh cup, but he would not be con-
trolled—Friend, I drink to thy successful performance.'

So saying, he took off his cup with much gravity, at the
same time shaking his head at the intemperance of the Scottish
harper.

The knight, in the meantime, had brought the strings into
some order, and after a short prelude, asked his host whether he
would choose a *sirvente* in the language of *oc*, or a *lai* in the
language of *oui*, or a *virelai*, or a ballad in the vulgar English.[21]

'A ballad, a ballad,' said the hermit, 'against all the *ocs* and *ouis*
of France. Downright English am I, Sir Knight, and downright
English was my patron St Dunstan, and scorned *oc* and *oui*, as he
would have scorned the parings of the devil's hoof—downright
English alone shall be sung in this cell.'

'I will assay, then,' said the knight, 'a ballad composed by a Saxon glee-man, whom I knew in Holy Land.'

It speedily appeared, that if the knight was not a complete master of the minstrel art, his taste for it had at least been cultivated under the best instructors. Art had taught him to soften the faults of a voice which had little compass, and was naturally rough rather than mellow, and, in short, had done all that culture can do in supplying natural deficiencies. His performance, therefore, might have been termed very respectable by abler judges than the hermit, especially as the knight threw into the notes now a degree of spirit, and now of plaintive enthusiasm, which gave force and energy to the verses which he sung.

THE CRUSADER'S RETURN

1.

High deeds achieved of knightly fame,
From Palestine the champion came;
The cross upon his shoulders borne,
Battle and blast had dimm'd and torn.
Each dint upon his batter'd shield
Was token of a foughten field;*
And thus, beneath his lady's bower,
He sung, as fell the twilight hour:—

2.

'Joy to the fair!—thy knight behold,
Return'd from yonder land of gold;
No wealth he brings, nor wealth can need,
Save his good arms and battle-steed;
His spurs, to dash against a foe,
His lance and sword to lay him low;
Such all the trophies of his toil,
Such—and the hope of Tekla's smile!*

3.

'Joy to the fair! whose constant knight
Her favour fired to feats of might;
Unnoted shall she not remain,
Where meet the bright and noble train;

Minstrel shall sing and herald tell—
"Mark yonder maid of beauty well,
'Tis she for whose bright eyes was won
The listed field at Askalon!

4.

'"Note well her smile!—it edged the blade
Which fifty wives to widows made,
When, vain his strength and Mahound's spell,
Iconium's turban'd Soldan* fell.
Seest thou her locks, whose sunny glow
Half shows, half shades, her neck of snow?
Twines not of them one golden thread,
But for its sake a Paynim bled."

5.

'Joy to the fair!—my name unknown,
Each deed, and all its praise thine own;
Then, oh! unbar this churlish gate,
The night dew falls, the hour is late.
Inured to Syria's glowing breath,
I feel the north breeze chill as death;
Let grateful love quell maiden shame,
And grant him bliss who brings thee fame.'

During this performance, the hermit demeaned himself much
like a first-rate critic of the present day at a new opera. He
reclined back upon his seat, with his eyes half shut; now, folding
his hands and twisting his thumbs, he seemed absorbed in attention, and anon, balancing his expanded palms, he gently
flourished them in time to the music. At one or two favourite
cadences, he threw in a little assistance of his own, where the
knight's voice seemed unable to carry the air so high as his
worshipful taste approved. When the song was ended, the
anchorite emphatically declared it a good one, and well sung.

'And yet,' said he, 'I think my Saxon countrymen had herded
long enough with the Normans, to fall into the tone of their
melancholy ditties. What took the honest knight from home?
or what could he expect but to find his mistress agreeably
engaged with a rival on his return, and his serenade, as they
call it, as little regarded as the caterwauling of a cat in the

gutter? Nevertheless, Sir Knight, I drink this cup to thee, to the success of all true lovers—I fear you are none,' he added, on observing that the knight (whose brain began to be heated with these repeated draughts) qualified his flagon from the water pitcher.

'Why,' said the knight, 'did you not tell me that this water was from the well of your blessed patron, St Dunstan?'

'Ay, truly,' said the hermit, 'and many a hundred of pagans did he baptize there, but I never heard that he drank any of it. Every thing should be put to its proper use in this world. St Dunstan knew, as well as any one, the prerogatives of a jovial friar.'

And so saying, he reached the harp, and entertained his guest with the following characteristic song, to a sort of derry-down chorus, appropriate to an old English ditty.[22]

THE BAREFOOTED FRIAR

1.

I'll give thee, good fellow, a twelvemonth or twain,
To search Europe through, from Byzantium to Spain;
But ne'er shall you find, should you search till you tire,
So happy a man as the Barefooted Friar.

2.

Your knight for his lady pricks forth in career,
And is brought home at even-song prick'd through with a spear;
I confess him in haste—for his lady desires
No comfort on earth save the Barefooted Friar's.

3.

Your monarch?—Pshaw! many a prince has been known
To barter his robes for our cowl and our gown,
But which of us e'er felt the idle desire
To exchange for a crown the grey hood of a Friar!

4.

The Friar has walk'd out, and where'er he has gone,
The land and its fatness is mark'd for his own;
He can roam where he lists, he can stop when he tires,
For every man's house is the Barefooted Friar's.

5.

He's expected at noon, and no wight till he comes
May profane the great chair, or the porridge of plums;
For the best of the cheer, and the seat by the fire,
Is the undenied right of the Barefooted Friar.

6.

He's expected at night, and the pasty's made hot,
They broach the brown ale, and they fill the black pot,
And the goodwife would wish the goodman in the mire,
Ere he lack'd a soft pillow, the Barefooted Friar.

7.

Long flourish the sandal, the cord, and the cope,
The dread of the devil and trust of the Pope;
For to gather life's roses, unscathed by the briar,
Is granted alone to the Barefooted Friar.

'By my troth,' said the knight, 'thou hast sung well and lustily,
and in high praise of thine order. And, talking of the devil, Holy
Clerk, are you not afraid that he may pay you a visit during some
of your uncanonical pastimes?'

'I uncanonical!' answered the hermit; 'I scorn the charge—I
scorn it with my heels!—I serve the duty of my chapel duly and
truly—Two masses daily, morning and evening, primes, noons,
and vespers, *aves*, *credos*, *paters*'——

'Excepting moonlight nights, when the venison is in season,'
said his guest.

'*Exceptis excipiendis*,'* replied the hermit, 'as our old abbot
taught me to say, when impertinent laymen should ask me if I
kept every punctilio of mine order.'

'True, holy father,' said the knight; 'but the devil is apt to
keep an eye on such exceptions; he goes about, thou knowest,
like a roaring lion.'

'Let him roar here if he dares,' said the friar; 'a touch of my
cord will make him roar as loud as the tongs of St Dunstan
himself did. I never feared man, and I as little fear the devil and
his imps. Saint Dunstan, Saint Dubric, Saint Winibald, Saint
Winifred, Saint Swibert, Saint Willick,* not forgetting Saint
Thomas a Kent, and my own poor merits to speed, I defy every

devil of them, come cut and long tail.*—But to let you into a secret, I never speak upon such subjects, my friend, until after morning vespers.'

He changed the conversation; fast and furious grew the mirth of the parties, and many a song was exchanged betwixt them, when their revels were interrupted by a loud knocking at the door of the hermitage.

The occasion of this interruption we can only explain by resuming the adventures of another set of our characters; for, like old Ariosto,* we do not pique ourselves upon continuing uniformly to keep company with any one personage of our drama.

CHAPTER XVIII

Away! our journey lies through dell and dingle,
Where the blithe fawn trips by its timid mother,
Where the broad oak, with intercepting boughs,
Chequers the sunbeam in the green-sward alley—
Up and away!—for lovely paths are these
To tread, when the glad Sun is on his throne;
Less pleasant, and less safe, when Cynthia's lamp
With doubtful glimmer lights the dreary forest.

*Ettrick Forest**

WHEN Cedric the Saxon saw his son drop down senseless in the lists at Ashby, his first impulse was to order him into the custody and care of his own attendants, but the words choked in his throat. He could not bring himself to acknowledge, in presence of such an assembly, the son whom he had renounced and disinherited. He ordered, however, Oswald to keep an eye upon him; and directed that officer, with two of his serfs, to convey Ivanhoe to Ashby as soon as the crowd had dispersed. Oswald, however, was anticipated in this good office. The crowd dispersed, indeed, but the knight was nowhere to be seen.

It was in vain that Cedric's cupbearer looked around for his young master—he saw the bloody spot on which he had lately sunk down, but himself he saw no longer; it seemed as if the fairies had conveyed him from the spot. Perhaps Oswald (for the Saxons were very superstitious) might have adopted some such hypothesis, to account for Ivanhoe's disappearance, had he not suddenly cast his eye upon a person attired like a squire, in whom he recognised the features of his fellow-servant Gurth. Anxious concerning his master's fate, and in despair at his sudden disappearance, the translated swineherd was searching for him everywhere, and had neglected, in doing so, the concealment on which his own safety depended. Oswald deemed it his duty to secure Gurth, as a fugitive of whose fate his master was to judge.

Renewing his enquiries concerning the fate of Ivanhoe, the only information which the cupbearer could collect from the bystanders was, that the knight had been raised with care by certain well-attired grooms, and placed in a litter belonging to a lady among the spectators, which had immediately transported him out of the press. Oswald, on receiving this intelligence, resolved to return to his master for farther instructions, carrying along with him Gurth, whom he considered in some sort as a deserter from the service of Cedric.

The Saxon had been under very intense and agonizing apprehensions concerning his son; for Nature had asserted her rights, in spite of the patriotic stoicism which laboured to disown her. But no sooner was he informed that Ivanhoe was in careful, and probably in friendly hands, than the paternal anxiety which had been excited by the dubiety of his fate, gave way anew to the feeling of injured pride and resentment, at what he termed Wilfred's filial disobedience. 'Let him wander his way,' said he—'let those leech his wounds for whose sake he encountered them. He is fitter to do the juggling tricks of the Norman chivalry than to maintain the fame and honour of his English ancestry with the glaive and brown-bill, the good old weapons of his country.'*

'If to maintain the honour of ancestry,' said Rowena, who was present, 'it is sufficient to be wise in council and brave in execution—to be boldest among the bold, and gentlest among the gentle, I know no voice, save his father's'——

'Be silent, Lady Rowena!—on this subject only I hear you not. Prepare yourself for the Prince's festival: we have been summoned thither with unwonted circumstance of honour and of courtesy, such as the haughty Normans have rarely used to our race since the fatal day of Hastings. Thither will I go, were it only to show these proud Normans how little the fate of a son, who could defeat their bravest, can affect a Saxon.'

'Thither,' said Rowena, 'do I NOT go; and I pray you to beware, lest what you mean for courage and constancy, shall be accounted hardness of heart.'

'Remain at home, then, ungrateful lady,' answered Cedric; 'thine is the hard heart, which can sacrifice the weal of an oppressed people to an idle and unauthorized attachment. I seek the noble Athelstane, and with him attend the banquet of John of Anjou.'

He went accordingly to the banquet, of which we have already mentioned the principal events. Immediately upon retiring from the castle, the Saxon thanes, with their attendants, took horse; and it was during the bustle which attended their doing so, that Cedric, for the first time, cast his eyes upon the deserter Gurth. The noble Saxon had returned from the banquet, as we have seen, in no very placid humour, and wanted but a pretext for wreaking his anger upon some one. 'The gyves!' he said, 'the gyves!—Oswald—Hundibert!—Dogs and villains!—why leave ye the knave unfettered?'

Without daring to remonstrate, the companions of Gurth bound him with a halter, as the readiest cord which occurred. He submitted to the operation without remonstrance, except that, darting a reproachful look at his master, he said, 'This comes of loving your flesh and blood better than mine own.'

'To horse, and forward!' said Cedric.

'It is indeed full time,' said the noble Athelstane; 'for, if we ride not the faster, the worthy Abbot Waltheoff's preparations for a rere-supper[23] will be altogether spoiled.'

The travellers, however, used such speed as to reach the convent of St Withold's before the apprehended evil took place. The Abbot, himself of ancient Saxon descent, received the noble Saxons with the profuse and exuberant hospitality of their nation, wherein they indulged to a late, or rather an early hour; nor did they take leave of their reverend host the next morning until they had shared with him a sumptuous refection.

As the cavalcade left the court of the monastery, an incident happened somewhat alarming to the Saxons, who, of all people of Europe, were most addicted to a superstitious observance of omens, and to whose opinions can be traced most of those notions upon such subjects, still to be found among our popular antiquities. For the Normans being a mixed race, and better informed according to the information of the times, had lost most of the superstitious prejudices which their ancestors had brought from Scandinavia, and piqued themselves upon thinking freely on such topics.

In the present instance, the apprehension of impending evil was inspired by no less respectable a prophet than a large lean black dog, which, sitting upright, howled most piteously as the foremost riders left the gate, and presently afterwards, barking wildly, and jumping to and fro, seemed bent upon attaching itself to the party.

'I like not that music, father Cedric,' said Athelstane; for by this title of respect he was accustomed to address him.

'Nor I either, uncle,' said Wamba; 'I greatly fear we shall have to pay the piper.'

'In my mind,' said Athelstane, upon whose memory the Abbot's good ale (for Burton* was already famous for that genial liquor) had made a favourable impression,—'in my mind we had better turn back, and abide with the Abbot until the afternoon. It is unlucky to travel where your path is crossed by a monk, a hare, or a howling dog, until you have eaten your next meal.'

'Away!' said Cedric, impatiently; 'the day is already too short for our journey. For the dog, I know it to be the cur of the runaway slave Gurth, a useless fugitive like its master.'

So saying, and rising at the same time in his stirrups, impatient at the interruption of his journey, he launched his javelin at poor Fangs—for Fangs it was, who, having traced his master thus far upon his stolen expedition, had here lost him, and was now, in his uncouth way, rejoicing at his reappearance. The javelin inflicted a wound upon the animal's shoulder, and narrowly missed pinning him to the earth; and Fangs fled howling from the presence of the enraged thane. Gurth's heart swelled within him; for he felt this meditated slaughter of his faithful adherent in a degree much deeper than the harsh treatment he had himself received. Having in vain attempted to raise his hand to his eyes, he said to Wamba, who, seeing his master's ill humour, had prudently retreated to the rear, 'I pray thee, do me the kindness to wipe my eyes with the skirt of thy mantle; the dust offends me, and these bonds will not let me help myself one way or another.'

Wamba did him the service he required, and they rode side by side for some time, during which Gurth maintained a moody silence. At length he could repress his feelings no longer.

'Friend Wamba,' said he, 'of all those who are fools enough to serve Cedric, thou alone hast dexterity enough to make thy folly acceptable to him. Go to him, therefore, and tell him that neither for love nor fear will Gurth serve him longer. He may strike the

head from me—he may scourge me—he may load me with
irons—but henceforth he shall never compel me either to love or
to obey him. Go to him, then, and tell him that Gurth the son of
Beowulph renounces his service.'

'Assuredly,' said Wamba, 'fool as I am, I shall not do your
fool's errand. Cedric hath another javelin stuck into his girdle,
and thou knowest he does not always miss his mark.'

'I care not,' replied Gurth, 'how soon he makes a mark of me.
Yesterday he left Wilfred, my young master, in his blood. To-
day he has striven to kill before my face the only other living
creature that ever showed me kindness. By St Edmund, St
Dunstan, St Withold, St Edward the Confessor,* and every
other Saxon saint in the calendar,' (for Cedric never swore by
any that was not of Saxon lineage, and all his household had the
same limited devotion,) 'I will never forgive him!'

'To my thinking now,' said the Jester, who was frequently
wont to act as peace-maker in the family, 'our master did not
propose to hurt Fangs, but only to affright him. For, if you
observed, he rose in his stirrups, as thereby meaning to overcast
the mark; and so he would have done, but Fangs happening to
bound up at the very moment, received a scratch, which I will be
bound to heal with a penny's breadth of tar.'

'If I thought so,' said Gurth—'if I could but think so—but
no—I saw the javelin was well aimed—I heard it whizz through
the air with all the wrathful malevolence of him who cast it, and
it quivered after it had pitched in the ground, as if with regret for
having missed its mark. By the hog dear to St Anthony,* I
renounce him!'

And the indignant swineherd resumed his sullen silence,
which no efforts of the Jester could again induce him to break.

Meanwhile Cedric and Athelstane, the leaders of the troop,
conversed together on the state of the land, on the dissensions of
the royal family, on the feuds and quarrels among the Norman
nobles, and on the chance which there was that the oppressed
Saxons might be able to free themselves from the yoke of the
Normans, or at least to elevate themselves into national consequence and independence, during the civil convulsions which
were likely to ensue. On this subject Cedric was all animation.
The restoration of the independence of his race was the idol of

his heart, to which he had willingly sacrificed domestic happiness and the interests of his own son. But, in order to achieve this great revolution in favour of the native English, it was necessary that they should be united among themselves, and act under an acknowledged head. The necessity of choosing their chief from the Saxon blood-royal was not only evident in itself, but had been made a solemn condition by those whom Cedric had intrusted with his secret plans and hopes. Athelstane had this quality at least; and though he had few mental accomplishments or talents to recommend him as a leader, he had still a goodly person, was no coward, had been accustomed to martial exercises, and seemed willing to defer to the advice of counsellors more wise than himself. Above all, he was known to be liberal and hospitable, and believed to be good-natured. But whatever pretensions Athelstane had to be considered as head of the Saxon confederacy, many of that nation were disposed to prefer to his the title of the Lady Rowena, who drew her descent from Alfred, and whose father having been a chief renowned for wisdom, courage, and generosity, his memory was highly honoured by his oppressed countrymen.

It would have been no difficult thing for Cedric, had he been so disposed, to have placed himself at the head of a third party, as formidable at least as any of the others. To counterbalance their royal descent, he had courage, activity, energy, and, above all, that devoted attachment to the cause which had procured him the epithet of THE SAXON, and his birth was inferior to none, excepting only that of Athelstane and his ward. These qualities, however, were unalloyed by the slightest shade of selfishness; and, instead of dividing yet farther his weakened nation by forming a faction of his own, it was a leading part of Cedric's plan to extinguish that which already existed, by promoting a marriage betwixt Rowena and Athelstane. An obstacle occurred to this his favourite project, in the mutual attachment of his ward and his son; and hence the original cause of the banishment of Wilfred from the house of his father.

This stern measure Cedric had adopted, in hopes that, during Wilfred's absence, Rowena might relinquish her preference, but in this hope he was disappointed; a disappointment which might be attributed in part to the mode in which his ward had been

educated. Cedric, to whom the name of Alfred was as that of a
deity, had treated the sole remaining scion of that great monarch
with a degree of observance, such as, perhaps, was in those days
scarce paid to an acknowledged princess. Rowena's will had been
in almost all cases a law to his household; and Cedric himself, as
if determined that her sovereignty should be fully acknowledged
within that little circle at least, seemed to take a pride in acting as
the first of her subjects. Thus trained in the exercise not only of
free will, but despotic authority, Rowena was, by her previous
education, disposed both to resist and to resent any attempt to
control her affections, or dispose of her hand contrary to her
inclinations, and to assert her independence in a case in which
even those females who have been trained up to obedience and
subjection, are not infrequently apt to dispute the authority of
guardians and parents. The opinions which she felt strongly, she
avowed boldly; and Cedric, who could not free himself from his
habitual deference to her opinions, felt totally at a loss how to
enforce his authority of guardian.

It was in vain that he attempted to dazzle her with the prospect of a visionary throne. Rowena, who possessed strong sense,
neither considered his plan as practicable, nor as desirable, so far
as she was concerned, could it have been achieved. Without
attempting to conceal her avowed preference of Wilfred of
Ivanhoe, she declared that, were that favoured knight out of
question, she would rather take refuge in a convent, than share a
throne with Athelstane, whom, having always despised, she now
began, on account of the trouble she received on his account,
thoroughly to detest.

Nevertheless, Cedric, whose opinion of women's constancy
was far from strong, persisted in using every means in his power
to bring about the proposed match, in which he conceived he
was rendering an important service to the Saxon cause. The
sudden and romantic appearance of his son in the lists at Ashby,
he had justly regarded as almost a death's blow to his hopes.
His paternal affection, it is true, had for an instant gained the
victory over pride and patriotism; but both had returned in
full force, and under their joint operation, he was now bent
upon making a determined effort for the union of Athelstane
and Rowena, together with expediting those other measures

which seemed necessary to forward the restoration of Saxon independence.

On this last subject, he was now labouring with Athelstane, not without having reason, every now and then, to lament, like Hotspur,* that he should have moved such a dish of skimmed milk to so honourable an action. Athelstane, it is true, was vain enough, and loved to have his ears tickled with tales of his high descent, and of his right by inheritance to homage and sovereignty. But his petty vanity was sufficiently gratified by receiving this homage at the hands of his immediate attendants, and of the Saxons who approached him. If he had the courage to encounter danger, he at least hated the trouble of going to seek it; and while he agreed in the general principles laid down by Cedric concerning the claim of the Saxons to independence, and was still more easily convinced of his own title to reign over them when that independence should be attained, yet when the means of asserting these rights came to be discussed, he was still 'Athelstane the Unready,' slow, irresolute, procrastinating, and unenterprising. The warm and impassioned exhortations of Cedric had as little effect upon his impassive temper, as red-hot balls alighting in the water, which produce a little sound and smoke, and are instantly extinguished.

If, leaving this task, which might be compared to spurring a tired jade, or to hammering upon cold iron, Cedric fell back to his ward Rowena, he received little more satisfaction from conferring with her. For, as his presence interrupted the discourse between the lady and her favourite attendant upon the gallantry and fate of Wilfred, Elgitha failed not to revenge both her mistress and herself, by recurring to the overthrow of Athelstane in the lists, the most disagreeable subject which could greet the ears of Cedric. To this sturdy Saxon, therefore, the day's journey was fraught with all manner of displeasure and discomfort; so that he more than once internally cursed the tournament, and him who had proclaimed it, together with his own folly in ever thinking of going thither.

At noon, upon the motion of Athelstane, the travellers paused in a woodland shade by a fountain, to repose their horses and partake of some provisions, with which the hospitable Abbot had loaded a sumpter mule. Their repast was a pretty long one; and

these several interruptions rendered it impossible for them to
hope to reach Rotherwood without travelling all night, a conviction which induced them to proceed on their way at a more hasty
pace than they had hitherto used.

CHAPTER XIX

A train of armed men, some noble dame
Escorting, (so their scatter'd words discover'd,
As unperceived I hung upon their rear,)
Are close at hand, and mean to pass the night
Within the castle.

Orra, a Tragedy*

THE travellers had now reached the verge of the wooded
country, and were about to plunge into its recesses, held dangerous at that time from the number of outlaws whom oppression
and poverty had driven to despair, and who occupied the forests
in such large bands as could easily bid defiance to the feeble
police of the period. From these rovers, however, notwithstanding the lateness of the hour, Cedric and Athelstane accounted
themselves secure, as they had in attendance ten servants, besides Wamba and Gurth, whose aid could not be counted upon,
the one being a jester and the other a captive. It may be added,
that in travelling thus late through the forest, Cedric and
Athelstane relied on their descent and character, as well as their
courage. The outlaws, whom the severity of the forest laws had
reduced to this roving and desperate mode of life, were chiefly
peasants and yeomen of Saxon descent, and were generally supposed to respect the persons and property of their countrymen.

As the travellers journeyed on their way, they were alarmed by
repeated cries for assistance; and when they rode up to the place
from whence they came, they were surprised to find a horse-
litter placed upon the ground, beside which sat a young woman,
richly dressed in the Jewish fashion, while an old man, whose
yellow cap proclaimed him to belong to the same nation, walked
up and down with gestures expressive of the deepest despair, and
wrung his hands, as if affected by some strange disaster.

To the enquiries of Athelstane and Cedric, the old Jew could
for some time only answer by invoking the protection of all the
patriarchs of the Old Testament successively against the sons of
Ishmael, who were coming to smite them, hip and thigh,* with

the edge of the sword. When he began to come to himself out of this agony of terror, Isaac of York (for it was our old friend) was at length able to explain, that he had hired a body-guard of six men at Ashby, together with mules for carrying the litter of a sick friend. This party had undertaken to escort him as far as Doncaster. They had come thus far in safety; but having received information from a wood-cutter that there was a strong band of outlaws lying in wait in the woods before them, Isaac's mercenaries had not only taken flight, but had carried off with them the horses which bore the litter, and left the Jew and his daughter without the means either of defence or of retreat, to be plundered, and probably murdered, by the banditti, who they expected every moment would bring down upon them. 'Would it but please your valours,' added Isaac, in a tone of deep humiliation, 'to permit the poor Jews to travel under your safeguard, I swear by the tables of our law, that never has favour been conferred upon a child of Israel since the days of our captivity, which shall be more gratefully acknowledged.'

'Dog of a Jew!' said Athelstane, whose memory was of that petty kind which stores up trifles of all kinds, but particularly trifling offences, 'dost not remember how thou didst beard us in the gallery at the tilt-yard? Fight or flee, or compound with the outlaws as thou dost list, ask neither aid nor company from us; and if they rob only such as thee, who rob all the world, I, for mine own share, shall hold them right honest folk.'

Cedric did not assent to the severe proposal of his companion. 'We shall do better,' said he, 'to leave them two of our attendants and two horses to convey them back to the next village. It will diminish our strength but little; and with your good sword, noble Athelstane, and the aid of those who remain, it will be light work for us to face twenty of those runagates.'

Rowena, somewhat alarmed by the mention of outlaws in force, and so near them, strongly seconded the proposal of her guardian. But Rebecca, suddenly quitting her dejected posture, and making her way through the attendants to the palfrey of the Saxon lady, knelt down, and, after the Oriental fashion in addressing superiors, kissed the hem of Rowena's garment. Then rising, and throwing back her veil, she implored her in the great name of the God whom they both worshipped, and by that revelation of the Law upon Mount Sinai, in which they both believed, that she would have compassion upon them, and suffer them to go forward under their safeguard. 'It is not for myself that I pray this favour,' said Rebecca; 'nor is it even for that poor old man. I know, that to wrong and to spoil our nation is a light fault, if not a merit, with the Christians; and what is it to us whether it be done in the city, in the desert, or in the field? But it is in the name of one dear to many, and dear even to you, that I beseech you to let this sick person be transported with care and tenderness under your protection. For, if evil chance him, the last moment of your life would be embittered with regret for denying that which I ask of you.'

The noble and solemn air with which Rebecca made this appeal, gave it double weight with the fair Saxon.

'The man is old and feeble,' she said to her guardian, 'the maiden young and beautiful, their friend sick and in peril of his life—Jews though they be, we cannot as Christians leave them in this extremity. Let them unload two of the sumpter-mules, and put the baggage behind two of the serfs. The mules may transport the litter, and we have led horses for the old man and his daughter.'

Cedric readily assented to what she proposed, and Athelstane only added the condition, 'that they should travel in the rear of the whole party, where Wamba,' he said, 'might attend them with his shield of boar's brawn.'

'I have left my shield in the tilt-yard,' answered the Jester, 'as has been the fate of many a better knight than myself.'

Athelstane coloured deeply, for such had been his own fate on the last day of the tournament; while Rowena, who was pleased in the same proportion, as if to make amends for the brutal jest of her unfeeling suitor, requested Rebecca to ride by her side.

'It were not fit I should do so,' answered Rebecca, with proud humility, 'where my society might be held a disgrace to my protectress.'

By this time the change of baggage was hastily achieved; for the single word 'outlaws' rendered every one sufficiently alert, and the approach of twilight made the sound yet more impressive. Amid the bustle, Gurth was taken from horseback, in the course of which removal he prevailed upon the Jester to slack the cord with which his arms were bound. It was so negligently refastened, perhaps intentionally, on the part of Wamba, that Gurth found no difficulty in freeing his arms altogether from bondage, and then, gliding into the thicket, he made his escape from the party.

The bustle had been considerable, and it was some time before Gurth was missed; for, as he was to be placed for the rest of the journey behind a servant, every one supposed that some other of his companions had him under his custody, and when it began to be whispered among them that Gurth had actually disappeared, they were under such immediate expectation of an attack from the outlaws, that it was not held convenient to pay much attention to the circumstance.

The path upon which the party travelled was now so narrow, as not to admit, with any sort of convenience, above two riders abreast, and began to descend into a dingle, traversed by a brook whose banks were broken, swampy, and overgrown with dwarf willows. Cedric and Athelstane, who were at the head of their retinue, saw the risk of being attacked at this pass; but neither of them having had much practice in war, no better mode of preventing the danger occurred to them than that they should hasten through the defile as fast as possible. Advancing, therefore, without much order, they had just crossed the brook with a part of their followers, when they were assailed in front, flank, and rear at once, with an impetuosity to which, in their confused and ill-prepared condition, it was impossible to offer effectual resistance. The shout of 'A white dragon!—a white dragon!— Saint George for merry England!'* war-cries adopted by the assailants, as belonging to their assumed character of Saxon outlaws, was heard on every side, and on every side enemies appeared with a rapidity of advance and attack which seemed to multiply their numbers.

Both the Saxon chiefs were made prisoners at the same moment, and each under circumstances expressive of his character. Cedric, the instant that an enemy appeared, launched at him his remaining javelin, which, taking better effect than that which he had hurled at Fangs, nailed the man against an oak-tree that happened to be close behind him. Thus far successful, Cedric spurred his horse against a second, drawing his sword at the same time, and striking with such inconsiderate fury, that his weapon encountered a thick branch which hung over him, and he was disarmed by the violence of his own blow. He was instantly made prisoner, and pulled from his horse by two or three of the banditti who crowded around him. Athelstane shared his captivity, his bridle having been seized, and he himself forcibly dismounted, long before he could draw his weapon, or assume any posture of effectual defence.

The attendants, embarrassed with baggage, surprised and terrified at the fate of their masters, fell an easy prey to the assailants; while the Lady Rowena, in the centre of the cavalcade, and the Jew and his daughter in the rear, experienced the same misfortune.

Of all the train none escaped except Wamba, who showed upon the occasion much more courage than those who pretended to greater sense. He possessed himself of a sword belonging to one of the domestics, who was just drawing it with a tardy and irresolute hand, laid it about him like a lion, drove back several who approached him, and made a brave though ineffectual attempt to succour his master. Finding himself overpowered, the Jester at length threw himself from his horse, plunged into the thicket, and, favoured by the general confusion, escaped from the scene of action.

Yet the valiant Jester, as soon as he found himself safe, hesitated more than once whether he should not turn back and share the captivity of a master to whom he was sincerely attached.

'I have heard men talk of the blessings of freedom,' he said to himself, 'but I wish any wise man would teach me what use to make of it now that I have it.'

As he pronounced these words aloud, a voice very near him called out in a low and cautious tone, 'Wamba!' and, at the same time, a dog, which he recognised to be Fangs, jumped up and fawned upon him. 'Gurth!' answered Wamba, with the same caution, and the swineherd immediately stood before him.

'What is the matter?' said he eagerly; 'what mean these cries, and that clashing of swords?'

'Only a trick of the times,' said Wamba; 'they are all prisoners.'

'Who are prisoners?' exclaimed Gurth, impatiently.

'My lord, and my lady, and Athelstane, and Hundibert, and Oswald.'

'In the name of God!' said Gurth, 'how came they prisoners?—and to whom?'

'Our master was too ready to fight,' said the Jester; 'and Athelstane was not ready enough, and no other person was ready at all. And they are prisoners to green cassocks, and black visors. And they lie all tumbled about on the green, like the crab-apples that you shake down to your swine. And I would laugh at it,' said the honest Jester, 'if I could for weeping.' And he shed tears of unfeigned sorrow.

Gurth's countenance kindled—'Wamba,' he said, 'thou hast a weapon, and thy heart was ever stronger than thy brain,—we are only two—but a sudden attack from men of resolution will do much—follow me!'

'Whither?—and for what purpose?' said the Jester.

'To rescue Cedric.'

'But you have renounced his service but now,' said Wamba.

'That,' said Gurth, 'was but while he was fortunate—follow me!'

As the Jester was about to obey, a third person suddenly made his appearance, and commanded them both to halt. From his dress and arms, Wamba would have conjectured him to be one of those outlaws who had just assailed his master; but, besides that he wore no mask, the glittering baldric across his shoulder, with the rich bugle-horn which it supported, as well as the calm and commanding expression of his voice and manner, made him, notwithstanding the twilight, recognise Locksley the yeoman, who had been victorious, under such disadvantageous circumstances, in the contest for the prize of archery.

'What is the meaning of all this,' said he, 'or who is it that rifle, and ransom, and make prisoners, in these forests?'

'You may look at their cassocks close by,' said Wamba, 'and see whether they be thy children's coats or no—for they are as like thine own, as one green pea-cod is to another.'

'I will learn that presently,' answered Locksley; 'and I charge ye, on peril of your lives, not to stir from the place where ye stand, until I have returned. Obey me, and it shall be the better for you and your masters.—Yet stay, I must render myself as like these men as possible.'

So saying, he unbuckled his baldric with the bugle, took a feather from his cap, and gave them to Wamba; then drew a vizard from his pouch, and, repeating his charges to them to stand fast, went to execute his purposes of reconnoitring.

'Shall we stand fast, Gurth?' said Wamba; 'or shall we e'en give him leg-bail? In my foolish mind, he had all the equipage of a thief too much in readiness, to be himself a true man.'

'Let him be the devil,' said Gurth, 'an he will. We can be no worse of waiting his return. If he belong to that party, he must already have given them the alarm, and it will avail nothing either to fight or fly. Besides, I have late experience, that arrant thieves are not the worst men in the world to have to deal with.'

The yeoman returned in the course of a few minutes.

'Friend Gurth,' he said, 'I have mingled among yon men, and have learnt to whom they belong, and whither they are bound. There is, I think, no chance that they will proceed to any actual violence against their prisoners. For three men to attempt them at this moment, were little else than madness; for they are good men of war, and have, as such, placed sentinels to give the alarm when any one approaches. But I trust soon to gather such a force, as may act in defiance of all their precautions; you are both servants, and, as I think, faithful servants, of Cedric the Saxon, the friend of the rights of Englishmen. He shall not want English hands to help him in this extremity. Come then with me, until I gather more aid.'

So saying, he walked through the wood at a great pace, followed by the jester and the swineherd. It was not consistent with Wamba's humour to travel long in silence.

'I think,' said he, looking at the baldric and bugle which he still carried, 'that I saw the arrow shot which won this gay prize, and that not so long since as Christmas.'

'And I,' said Gurth, 'could take it on my halidome, that I have heard the voice of the good yeoman who won it, by night as well as by day, and that the moon is not three days older since I did so.'

'Mine honest friends,' replied the yeoman, 'who, or what I am, is little to the present purpose; should I free your master,

you will have reason to think me the best friend you have ever
had in your lives. And whether I am known by one name or
another—or whether I can draw a bow as well or better than a
cow-keeper, or whether it is my pleasure to walk in sunshine or
by moonlight, are matters, which, as they do not concern you, so
neither need ye busy yourselves respecting them.'

'Our heads are in the lion's mouth,'* said Wamba, in a whisper to Gurth, 'get them out how we can.'

'Hush—be silent,' said Gurth. 'Offend him not by thy folly,
and I trust sincerely that all will go well.'

CHAPTER XX

When autumn nights were long and drear,
　　And forest walks were dark and dim,
How sweetly on the pilgrim's ear
　　Was wont to steal the hermit's hymn!

Devotion borrows Music's tone,
　　And Music took Devotion's wing;
And, like the bird that hails the sun,
　　They soar to heaven, and soaring sing.

*The Hermit of St Clement's Well**

It was after three hours' good walking that the servants of Cedric, with their mysterious guide, arrived at a small opening in the forest, in the centre of which grew an oak-tree of enormous magnitude, throwing its twisted branches in every direction. Beneath this tree four or five yeomen lay stretched on the ground, while another, as sentinel, walked to and fro in the moonlight shade.

Upon hearing the sound of feet approaching, the watch instantly gave the alarm, and the sleepers as suddenly started up and bent their bows. Six arrows placed on the string were pointed towards the quarter from which the travellers approached, when their guide, being recognised, was welcomed with every token of respect and attachment, and all signs and fears of a rough reception at once subsided.

'Where is the Miller?' was his first question.

'On the road towards Rotherham.'

'With how many?' demanded the leader, for such he seemed to be.

'With six men, and good hope of booty, if it please St Nicholas.'

'Devoutly spoken,' said Locksley; 'and where is Allan-a-Dale?'

'Walked up towards the Watling-street,* to watch for the Prior of Jorvaulx.'

'That is well thought on also,' replied the Captain;—'and where is the Friar?'

'In his cell.'

'Thither will I go,' said Locksley. 'Disperse and seek your companions. Collect what force you can, for there's game afoot* that must be hunted hard, and will turn to bay. Meet me here by daybreak.—And, stay,' he added, 'I have forgotten what is most necessary of the whole—Two of you take the road quickly towards Torquilstone, the Castle of Front-de-Bœuf. A set of gallants, who have been masquerading in such guise as our own, are carrying a band of prisoners thither—Watch them closely, for even if they reach the castle before we collect our force, our honour is concerned to punish them, and we will find means to do so. Keep a close watch on them therefore; and dispatch one of your comrades, the lightest of foot, to bring the news of the yeomen thereabout.'

They promised implicit obedience, and departed with alacrity on their different errands. In the meanwhile, their leader and his two companions, who now looked upon him with great respect, as well as some fear, pursued their way to the Chapel of Copmanhurst.

When they had reached the little moonlight glade, having in front the reverend, though ruinous chapel, and the rude hermitage, so well suited to ascetic devotion, Wamba whispered to Gurth, 'If this be the habitation of a thief, it makes good the old proverb, The nearer the church the farther from God.*—And by my cockscomb,' he added, 'I think it be even so—Hearken but to the black sanctus* which they are singing in the hermitage!'

In fact the anchorite and his guest were performing, at the full extent of their very powerful lungs, an old drinking song,* of which this was the burden:—

'Come, trowl the brown bowl to me,
    Bully boy, bully boy,
Come, trowl the brown bowl to me:
    Ho! jolly Jenkin, I spy a knave in drinking,
Come, trowl the brown bowl to me.'

'Now, that is not ill sung,' said Wamba, who had thrown in a few of his own flourishes to help out the chorus. 'But who, in the saint's name, ever expected to have heard such a jolly chant come from out a hermit's cell at midnight!'

'Marry, that should I,' said Gurth, 'for the jolly Clerk of Copmanhurst is a known man, and kills half the deer that are stolen in this walk. Men say that the keeper has complained to his official, and that he will be stripped of his cowl and cope altogether, if he keep not better order.'

While they were thus speaking, Locksley's loud and repeated knocks had at length disturbed the anchorite and his guest. 'By my beads,' said the hermit, stopping short in a grand flourish, 'here come more benighted guests. I would not for my cowl that they found us in this goodly exercise. All men have their en-emies, good Sir Sluggard; and there be those malignant enough to construe the hospitable refreshment which I have been offer-ing to you, a weary traveller, for the matter of three short hours, into sheer drunkenness and debauchery, vices alike alien to my profession and my disposition.'

'Base calumniators!' replied the knight; 'I would I had the chastising of them. Nevertheless, Holy Clerk, it is true that all have their enemies; and there be those in this very land whom I would rather speak to through the bars of my helmet than bare-faced.'

'Get thine iron pot on thy head then, friend Sluggard, as quickly as thy nature will permit,' said the hermit, 'while I remove these pewter flagons, whose late contents run strangely in mine own pate; and to drown the clatter—for, in faith, I feel somewhat unsteady—strike into the tune which thou hearest me sing; it is no matter for the words—I scarce know them myself.'

So saying, he struck up a thundering *De profundis clamavi*,* under cover of which he removed the apparatus of their banquet; while the knight, laughing heartily, and arming himself all the while, assisted his host with his voice from time to time as his mirth permitted.

'What devil's matins are you after at this hour?' said a voice from without.

'Heaven forgive you, Sir Traveller!' said the hermit, whose own noise, and perhaps his nocturnal potations, prevented from

recognising accents which were tolerably familiar to him—
'Wend on your way, in the name of God and Saint Dunstan, and
disturb not the devotions of me and my holy brother.'

'Mad priest,' answered the voice from without, 'open to
Locksley!'

'All's safe—all's right,' said the hermit to his companion.

'But who is he?' said the Black Knight; 'it imports me much to
know.'

'Who is he?' answered the hermit; 'I tell thee he is a friend.'

'But what friend?' answered the knight; 'for he may be friend
to thee and none of mine?'

'What friend?' replied the hermit; 'that, now, is one of the
questions that is more easily asked than answered. What
friend?—why, he is, now that I bethink me a little, the very same
honest keeper I told thee of a while since.'

'Ay, as honest a keeper as thou art a pious hermit,' replied the
knight, 'I doubt it not. But undo the door to him before he beat
it from its hinges.'

The dogs, in the meantime, which had made a dreadful baying
at the commencement of the disturbance, seemed now to recognise the voice of him who stood without; for, totally changing
their manner, they scratched and whined at the door, as if
interceding for his admission. The hermit speedily unbolted his
portal, and admitted Locksley, with his two companions.

'Why, hermit,' was the yeoman's first question as soon as he
beheld the knight, 'what boon companion hast thou here?'

'A brother of our order,' replied the friar, shaking his head;
'we have been at our orisons all night.'

'He is a monk of the church militant,* I think,' answered
Locksley; 'and there be more of them abroad. I tell thee, friar,
thou must lay down the rosary and take up the quarter-staff; we
shall need every one of our merry men, whether clerk or layman.—But,' he added, taking him a step aside, 'art thou mad? to
give admittance to a knight thou dost not know? Hast thou forgot
our articles?'

'Not know him!' replied the friar, boldly, 'I know him as well
as the beggar knows his dish.'

'And what is his name, then?' demanded Locksley.

'His name,' said the hermit—'his name is Sir Anthony of

Scrabelstone—as if I would drink with a man, and did not know his name!'

'Thou hast been drinking more than enough, friar,' said the woodsman, 'and, I fear, prating more than enough too.'

'Good yeoman,' said the knight, coming forward, 'be not wroth with my merry host. He did but afford me the hospitality which I would have compelled from him if he had refused it.'

'Thou compel!' said the friar; 'wait but till I have changed this grey gown for a green cassock, and if I make not a quarter-staff ring twelve upon thy pate, I am neither true clerk nor good woodsman.'

While he spoke thus, he stript off his gown, and appeared in a close black buckram doublet and drawers, over which he speedily did on a cassock of green, and hose of the same colour. 'I pray thee truss my points,' said he to Wamba, 'and thou shalt have a cup of sack for thy labour.'

'Gramercy for thy sack,' said Wamba; 'but think'st thou it is lawful for me to aid you to transmew* thyself from a holy hermit into a sinful forester?'

'Never fear,' said the hermit; 'I will but confess the sins of my green cloak to my greyfriar's frock, and all shall be well again.'

'Amen!' answered the Jester; 'a broadcloth penitent should have a sackcloth confessor, and your frock may absolve my motley doublet into the bargain.'

So saying, he accommodated the friar with his assistance in tying the endless number of points, as the laces which attached the hose to the doublet were then termed.

While they were thus employed, Locksley led the knight a little apart, and addressed him thus:—'Deny it not, Sir Knight—you are he who decided the victory to the advantage of the English against the strangers on the second day of the tournament at Ashby.'

'And what follows if you guess truly, good yeoman?' replied the knight.

'I should in that case hold you,' replied the yeoman, 'a friend to the weaker party.'

'Such is the duty of a true knight at least,' replied the Black Champion; 'and I would not willingly that there were reason to think otherwise of me.'

'But for my purpose,' said the yeoman, 'thou shouldst be as well a good Englishman as a good knight; for that, which I have to speak of, concerns, indeed, the duty of every honest man, but is more especially that of a true-born native of England.'

'You can speak to no one,' replied the knight, 'to whom England, and the life of every Englishman, can be dearer than to me.'

'I would willingly believe so,' said the woodsman, 'for never had this country such need to be supported by those who love her. Hear me, and I will tell thee of an enterprise, in which, if thou be'st really that which thou seemest, thou mayst take an honourable part. A band of villains, in the disguise of better men than themselves, have made themselves master of the person of a noble Englishman, called Cedric the Saxon, together with his ward, and his friend Athelstane of Coningsburgh, and have transported them to a castle in this forest, called Torquilstone. I ask of thee, as a good knight and a good Englishman, wilt thou aid in their rescue?'

'I am bound by my vow to do so,' replied the knight; 'but I would willingly know who you are, who request my assistance in their behalf?'

'I am,' said the forester, 'a nameless man; but I am the friend of my country, and of my country's friends—With this account of me you must for the present remain satisfied, the more especially since you yourself desire to continue unknown. Believe, however, that my word, when pledged, is as inviolate as if I wore golden spurs.'

'I willingly believe it,' said the knight; 'I have been accustomed to study men's countenances, and I can read in thine honesty and resolution. I will, therefore, ask thee no further questions, but aid thee in setting at freedom these oppressed captives; which done, I trust we shall part better acquainted, and well satisfied with each other.'

'So,' said Wamba to Gurth,—for the friar being now fully equipped, the Jester, having approached to the other side of the hut, had heard the conclusion of the conversation,—'So we have got a new ally?—I trust the valour of the knight will be truer metal than the religion of the hermit, or the honesty of the yeoman; for this Locksley looks like a born deer-stealer, and the priest like a lusty hypocrite.'

'Hold thy peace, Wamba,' said Gurth; 'it may all be as thou dost guess; but were the horned devil to rise and proffer me his assistance to set at liberty Cedric and the Lady Rowena, I fear I should hardly have religion enough to refuse the foul fiend's offer, and bid him get behind me.'*

The friar was now completely accoutred as a yeoman, with sword and buckler, bow, and quiver, and a strong partisan over his shoulder. He left his cell at the head of the party, and, having carefully locked the door, deposited the key under the threshold.

'Art thou in condition to do good service, friar,' said Locksley, 'or does the brown bowl still run in thy head?'

'Not more than a draught of St Dunstan's fountain will allay,' answered the priest; 'something there is of a whizzing in my brain, and of instability in my legs, but you shall presently see both pass away.'

So saying, he stepped to the stone basin, in which the waters of the fountain as they fell formed bubbles which danced in the white moonlight, and took so long a draught as if he had meant to exhaust the spring.

'When didst thou drink as deep a draught of water before, Holy Clerk of Copmanhurst?' said the Black Knight.

'Never since my wine-butt leaked, and let out its liquor by an illegal vent,' replied the friar, 'and so left me nothing to drink but my patron's bounty here.'

Then plunging his hands and head into the fountain, he washed from them all marks of the midnight revel.

Thus refreshed and sobered, the jolly priest twirled his heavy partisan round his head with three fingers, as if he had been balancing a reed, exclaiming at the same time, 'Where be those false ravishers, who carry off wenches against their will? May the foul fiend fly off with me, if I am not man enough for a dozen of them.'

'Swearest thou, Holy Clerk?' said the Black Knight.

'Clerk me no Clerks,'* replied the transformed priest; 'by Saint George and the Dragon, I am no longer a shaveling than while my frock is on my back—When I am cased in my green cassock, I will drink, swear, and woo a lass, with any blithe forester in the West Riding.'

'Come on, Jack Priest,' said Locksley, 'and be silent; thou art as noisy as a whole convent on a holy eve, when the Father Abbot has gone to bed.—Come on you, too, my masters, tarry not to talk of it—I say, come on, we must collect all our forces, and few enough we shall have, if we are to storm the Castle of Reginald Front-de-Bœuf.'

'What! is it Front-de-Bœuf,' said the Black Knight, 'who has stopt on the king's highway the king's liege subjects?—Is he turned thief and oppressor?'

'Oppressor he ever was,' said Locksley.

'And for thief,' said the priest, 'I doubt if ever he were even half so honest a man as many a thief of my acquaintance.'

'Move on, priest, and be silent,' said the yeoman; 'it were better you led the way to the place of rendezvous, than say what should be left unsaid, both in decency and prudence.'

CHAPTER XXI

Alas, how many hours and years have past,
Since human forms have round this table sate,
Or lamp, or taper, on its surface gleam'd!
Methinks, I hear the sound of time long pass'd
Still murmuring o'er us, in the lofty void
Of these dark arches, like the ling'ring voices
Of those who long within their graves have slept.

*Orra, a Tragedy**

WHILE these measures were taking in behalf of Cedric and his companions, the armed men by whom the latter had been seized, hurried their captives along towards the place of security, where they intended to imprison them. But darkness came on fast, and the paths of the wood seemed but imperfectly known to the marauders. They were compelled to make several long halts, and once or twice to return on their road to resume the direction which they wished to pursue. The summer morn had dawned upon them ere they could travel in full assurance that they held the right path. But confidence returned with light, and the cavalcade now moved rapidly forward. Meanwhile, the following dialogue took place between the two leaders of the banditti.

'It is time thou shouldst leave us, Sir Maurice,' said the Templar to De Bracy, 'in order to prepare the second part of thy mystery. Thou art next, thou knowest, to act the Knight Deliverer.'

'I have thought better of it,' said De Bracy; 'I will not leave thee till the prize is fairly deposited in Front-de-Bœuf's castle. There will I appear before the Lady Rowena in mine own shape, and trust that she will set down to the vehemence of my passion the violence of which I have been guilty.'

'And what has made thee change thy plan, De Bracy?' replied the Knight Templar.

'That concerns thee nothing,' answered his companion.

'I would hope, however, Sir Knight,' said the Templar, 'that this alteration of measures arises from no suspicion of my honourable meaning, such as Fitzurse endeavoured to instil into thee?'

'My thoughts are my own,' answered De Bracy; 'the fiend laughs, they say, when one thief robs another; and we know, that were he to spit fire and brimstone instead, it would never prevent a Templar from following his bent.'

'Or the leader of a Free Company,' answered the Templar, 'from dreading at the hands of a comrade and friend, the injustice he does to all mankind.'

'This is unprofitable and perilous recrimination,' answered De Bracy: 'suffice it to say, I know the morals of the Temple-Order, and I will not give thee the power of cheating me out of the fair prey for which I have run such risks.'

'Psha,' replied the Templar, 'what hast thou to fear?—Thou knowest the vows of our order.'

'Right well,' said De Bracy, 'and also how they are kept. Come, Sir Templar, the laws of gallantry have a liberal interpretation in Palestine, and this is a case in which I will trust nothing to your conscience.'

'Hear the truth, then,' said the Templar; 'I care not for your blue-eyed beauty. There is in that train one who will make me a better mate.'

'What! wouldst thou stoop to the waiting damsel?' said De Bracy.

'No, Sir Knight,' said the Templar, haughtily. 'To the waiting-woman will I not stoop. I have a prize among the captives as lovely as thine own.'

'By the mass, thou meanest the fair Jewess!' said De Bracy.

'And if I do,' said Bois-Guilbert, 'who shall gainsay me?'

'No one that I know,' said De Bracy, 'unless it be your vow of celibacy, or a check of conscience for an intrigue with a Jewess.'

'For my vow,' said the Templar, 'our Grand Master hath granted me a dispensation. And for my conscience, a man that has slain three hundred Saracens, need not reckon up every little failing, like a village girl at her first confession upon Good Friday eve.'

'Thou knowest best thine own privileges,' said De Bracy.

'Yet, I would have sworn thy thought had been more on the old usurer's money bags, than on the black eyes of the daughter.'

'I can admire both,' answered the Templar; 'besides, the old Jew is but half-prize. I must share his spoils with Front-de-Bœuf, who will not lend us the use of his castle for nothing. I must have something that I can term exclusively my own by this foray of ours, and I have fixed on the lovely Jewess as my peculiar prize. But, now thou knowest my drift, thou wilt resume thine own original plan, wilt thou not?—Thou hast nothing, thou seest, to fear from my interference.'

'No,' replied De Bracy, 'I will remain beside my prize. What thou sayst is passing true, but I like not the privileges acquired by the dispensation of the Grand Master, and the merit acquired by the slaughter of three hundred Saracens. You have too good a right to a free pardon, to render you very scrupulous about peccadilloes.'

While this dialogue was proceeding, Cedric was endeavouring to wring out of those who guarded him an avowal of their character and purpose. 'You should be Englishmen,' said he; 'and yet, sacred Heaven! you prey upon your countrymen as if you were very Normans. You should be my neighbours, and, if so, my friends; for which of my English neighbours have reason to be otherwise? I tell ye, yeomen, that even those among ye who have been branded with outlawry have had from me protection; for I have pitied their miseries, and curst the oppression of their tyrannic nobles. What, then, would you have of me? or in what can this violence serve ye?—Ye are worse than brute beasts in your actions, and will you imitate them in their very dumbness?'

It was in vain that Cedric expostulated with his guards, who had too many good reasons for their silence to be induced to break it either by his wrath or his expostulations. They continued to hurry him along, travelling at a very rapid rate, until, at the end of an avenue of huge trees, arose Torquilstone, now the hoary and ancient castle of Reginald Front-de-Bœuf. It was a fortress of no great size, consisting of a donjon, or large and high square tower, surrounded by buildings of inferior height, which were encircled by an inner court-yard. Around the exterior wall was a deep moat, supplied with water from a neighbouring rivulet. Front-de-Bœuf, whose character placed him often at feud with his enemies, had made considerable additions to the strength of his castle, by building towers upon the outward wall, so as to flank it at every angle. The access, as usual in castles of the period, lay through an arched barbican, or outwork, which was terminated and defended by a small turret at each corner.

Cedric no sooner saw the turrets of Front-de-Bœuf's castle raise their grey and moss-grown battlements, glimmering in the morning sun above the wood by which they were surrounded, than he instantly augured more truly concerning the cause of his misfortune.

'I did injustice,' he said, 'to the thieves and outlaws of these woods, when I supposed such banditti to belong to their bands; I might as justly have confounded the foxes of these brakes with the ravening wolves of France. Tell me, dogs—is it my life or my wealth that your master aims at? Is it too much that two Saxons, myself and the noble Athelstane, should hold land in the country which was once the patrimony of our race?—Put us then to death, and complete your tyranny by taking our lives, as you began with our liberties. If the Saxon Cedric cannot rescue England, he is willing to die for her. Tell your tyrannical master, I do only beseech him to dismiss the Lady Rowena in honour and safety. She is a woman, and he need not dread her; and with us will die all who dare fight in her cause.'

The attendants remained as mute to this address as to the former, and they now stood before the gate of the castle. De Bracy winded his horn three times, and the archers and crossbow men, who had manned the wall upon seeing their approach, hastened to lower the drawbridge, and admit them. The prisoners were compelled by their guards to alight, and were conducted to an apartment where a hasty repast was offered them, of which none but Athelstane felt any inclination to partake. Neither had the descendant of the Confessor much time to do justice to the good cheer placed before them, for their guards gave him and Cedric to understand that they were to be imprisoned in a chamber apart from Rowena. Resistance was vain; and they were compelled to follow to a large room, which, rising on clumsy Saxon pillars, resembled those refectories and chapter-houses which may be still seen in the most ancient parts of our most ancient monasteries.

The Lady Rowena was next separated from her train, and conducted, with courtesy, indeed, but still without consulting her inclination, to a distant apartment. The same alarming distinction was conferred on Rebecca, in spite of her father's entreaties, who offered even money, in this extremity of distress, that she might be permitted to abide with him. 'Base unbeliever,' answered one of his guards, 'when thou hast seen thy lair, thou wilt not wish thy daughter to partake it.' And, without farther discussion, the old Jew was forcibly dragged off in a different direction from the other prisoners. The domestics, after being carefully searched and disarmed, were confined in another part of the castle; and Rowena was refused even the comfort she might have derived from the attendance of her handmaiden Elgitha.

The apartment in which the Saxon chiefs were confined, for to them we turn our first attention, although at present used as a sort of guard-room, had formerly been the great hall of the castle. It was now abandoned to meaner purposes, because the present lord, among other additions to the convenience, security, and beauty of his baronial residence, had erected a new and noble hall, whose vaulted roof was supported by lighter and more elegant pillars, and fitted up with that higher degree of ornament, which the Normans had already introduced into architecture.

Cedric paced the apartment, filled with indignant reflections on the past and on the present, while the apathy of his companion served, instead of patience and philosophy, to defend him against every thing save the inconvenience of the present moment; and so little did he feel even this last, that he was only from time to time roused to a reply by Cedric's animated and impassioned appeal to him.

'Yes,' said Cedric, half speaking to himself, and half addressing himself to Athelstane, 'it was in this very hall that my father feasted with Torquil Wolfganger, when he entertained the valiant and unfortunate Harold, then advancing against the Norwegians, who had united themselves to the rebel Tosti. It was in this hall that Harold returned the magnanimous answer to the ambassador of his rebel brother. Oft have I heard my father kindle as he told the tale.* The envoy of Tosti was admitted, when this ample room could scarce contain the crowd of noble Saxon leaders, who were quaffing the blood-red wine* around their monarch.'

'I hope,' said Athelstane, somewhat moved by this part of his friend's discourse, 'they will not forget to send us some wine and refections at noon—we had scarce a breathing-space allowed to break our fast, and I never have the benefit of my food when I eat immediately after dismounting from horseback, though the leeches recommend that practice.'

Cedric went on with his story without noticing this interjectional observation of his friend.

'The envoy of Tosti,' he said, 'moved up the hall, undismayed by the frowning countenances of all around him, until he made his obeisance before the throne of King Harold.

"What terms," he said, "Lord King, hath thy brother Tosti to hope, if he should lay down his arms, and crave peace at thy hands?"

"A brother's love," cried the generous Harold, "and the fair earldom of Northumberland."

"But should Tosti accept these terms," continued the envoy, "what lands shall be assigned to his faithful ally, Hardrada, King of Norway?"

"Seven feet of English ground," answered Harold, fiercely, "or, as Hardrada is said to be a giant, perhaps we may allow him twelve inches more."

'The hall rung with acclamations, and cup and horn was filled to the Norwegian, who should be speedily in possession of his English territory.'

'I could have pledged him with all my soul,' said Athelstane, 'for my tongue cleaves to my palate.'

'The baffled envoy,' continued Cedric, pursuing with animation his tale, though it interested not the listener, 'retreated, to carry to Tosti and his ally the ominous answer of his injured brother. It was then that the distant towers of York, and the bloody streams of the Derwent,[24] beheld that direful conflict, in which, after displaying the most undaunted valour, the King of Norway, and Tosti, both fell, with ten thousand of their bravest followers. Who would have thought that upon the proud day when this battle was won, the very gale which waved the Saxon banners in triumph, was filling the Norman sails, and impelling them to the fatal shores of Sussex?—Who would have thought that Harold, within a few brief days, would himself possess no more of his kingdom, than the share which he allotted in his wrath to the Norwegian invader?—Who would have thought that you, noble Athelstane—that you, descended of Harold's blood,* and that I, whose father was not the worst defender of the Saxon crown, should be prisoners to a vile Norman, in the very hall in which our ancestors held such high festival?'

'It is sad enough,' replied Athelstane; 'but I trust they will hold us to a moderate ransom—At any rate it cannot be their purpose to starve us outright; and yet, although it is high noon, I see no preparations for serving dinner. Look up at the window, noble Cedric, and judge by the sunbeams if it is not on the verge of noon.'

'It may be so,' answered Cedric; 'but I cannot look on that stained lattice without its awakening other reflections than those which concern the passing moment, or its privations. When that window was wrought, my noble friend, our hardy fathers knew not the art of making glass, or of staining it*—The pride of Wolfganger's father brought an artist from Normandy to adorn his hall with this new species of emblazonment, that breaks the golden light of God's blessed day into so many fantastic hues. The foreigner came here poor, beggarly, cringing, and subservient, ready to doff his cap to the meanest native of the household. He returned pampered and proud, to tell his rapacious countrymen of the wealth and the simplicity of the Saxon nobles—a folly, oh, Athelstane, foreboded of old, as well as foreseen, by those descendants of Hengist and his hardy tribes, who retained the simplicity of their manners. We made these strangers our bosom friends, our confidential servants; we borrowed their artists and their arts, and despised the honest simplicity and hardihood with which our brave ancestors supported themselves, and we became enervated by Norman arts long ere we fell under Norman arms. Far better was our homely diet, eaten in peace and liberty, than the luxurious dainties, the love of which hath delivered us as bondsmen to the foreign conqueror!'

'I should,' replied Athelstane, 'hold very humble diet a luxury at present; and it astonishes me, noble Cedric, that you can bear so truly in mind the memory of past deeds, when it appeareth you forget the very hour of dinner.'

'It is time lost,' muttered Cedric apart and impatiently, 'to speak to him of aught else but that which concerns his appetite! The soul of Hardicanute ᵏ hath taken possession of him, and he hath no pleasure save to fill, to swill, and to call for more.—Alas!' said he, looking at Athelstane with compassion, 'that so dull a spirit should be lodged in so goodly a form! Alas! that such an enterprise as the regeneration of England should turn on a hinge so imperfect! Wedded to Rowena, indeed, her nobler and more generous soul may yet awake the better nature which is torpid within him. Yet how should this be, while Rowena, Athelstane, and I myself, remain the prisoners of this brutal marauder, and have been made so perhaps from a sense of the dangers which our liberty might bring to the usurped power of his nation?'

While the Saxon was plunged in these painful reflections, the door of their prison opened, and gave entrance to a sewer,* holding his white rod of office. This important person advanced into the chamber with a grave pace, followed by four attendants, bearing in a table covered with dishes, the sight and smell of which seemed to be an instant compensation to Athelstane for all the inconvenience he had undergone. The persons who attended on the feast were masked and cloaked.

'What mummery is this?' said Cedric; 'think you that we are ignorant whose prisoners we are, when we are in the castle of your master? Tell him,' he continued, willing to use this opportunity to open a negotiation for his freedom,—'Tell your master, Reginald Front-de-Bœuf, that we know no reason he can have for withholding our liberty, excepting his unlawful desire to enrich himself at our expense. Tell him that we yield to his rapacity, as in similar circumstances we should do to that of a literal robber. Let him name the ransom at which he rates our liberty, and it shall be paid, providing the exaction is suited to our means.'

The sewer made no answer, but bowed his head.

'And tell Sir Reginald Front-de-Bœuf,' said Athelstane, 'that

I send him my mortal defiance, and challenge him to combat with me, on foot or horseback, at any secure place, within eight days after our liberation; which, if he be a true knight, he will not, under these circumstances, venture to refuse or to delay.'

'I shall deliver to the knight your defiance,' answered the sewer; 'meanwhile I leave you to your food.'

The challenge of Athelstane was delivered with no good grace; for a large mouthful, which required the exercise of both jaws at once, added to a natural hesitation, considerably damped the effect of the bold defiance it contained. Still, however, his speech was hailed by Cedric as an incontestible token of reviving spirit in his companion, whose previous indifference had begun, notwithstanding his respect for Athelstane's descent, to wear out his patience. But he now cordially shook hands with him in token of his approbation, and was somewhat grieved when Athelstane observed, 'that he would fight a dozen such men as Front-de-Bœuf, if, by so doing, he could hasten his departure from a dungeon where they put so much garlic into their pottage.' Notwithstanding this intimation of a relapse into the apathy of sensuality, Cedric placed himself opposite to Athelstane, and soon showed, that if the distresses of his country could banish the recollection of food while the table was uncovered, yet no sooner were the victuals put there, than he proved that the appetite of his Saxon ancestors had descended to him along with their other qualities.

The captives had not long enjoyed their refreshment, however, ere their attention was disturbed even from this most serious occupation by the blast of a horn winded before the gate. It was repeated three times, with as much violence as if it had been blown before an enchanted castle by the destined knight,* at whose summons halls and towers, barbican and battlement, were to roll off like a morning vapour. The Saxons started from the table, and hastened to the window. But their curiosity was disappointed; for these outlets only looked upon the court of the castle, and the sound came from beyond its precincts. The summons, however, seemed of importance, for a considerable degree of bustle instantly took place in the castle.

CHAPTER XXII

My daughter—O my ducats—O my daughter!
————O my Christian ducats!
Justice—the Law—my ducats, and my daughter!

*Merchant of Venice**

LEAVING the Saxon chiefs to return to their banquet as soon as their ungratified curiosity should permit them to attend to the calls of their half-satiated appetite, we have to look in upon the yet more severe imprisonment of Isaac of York. The poor Jew had been hastily thrust into a dungeon-vault of the castle, the floor of which was deep beneath the level of the ground, and very damp, being lower than even the moat itself. The only light was received through one or two loop-holes far above the reach of the captive's hand. These apertures admitted, even at mid-day, only a dim and uncertain light, which was changed for utter darkness long before the rest of the castle had lost the blessing of day. Chains and shackles, which had been the portion of former captives, from whom active exertions to escape had been apprehended, hung rusted and empty on the walls of the prison, and in the rings of one of those sets of fetters there remained two mouldering bones, which seemed to have been once those of the human leg, as if some prisoner had been left not only to perish there, but to be consumed to a skeleton.

At one end of this ghastly apartment was a large fire-grate, over the top of which were stretched some transverse iron bars, half devoured with rust.

The whole appearance of the dungeon might have appalled a stouter heart than that of Isaac, who, nevertheless, was more composed under the imminent pressure of danger, than he had seemed to be while affected by terrors, of which the cause was as yet remote and contingent. The lovers of the chase say that the hare feels more agony during the pursuit of the greyhounds, than when she is struggling in their fangs.[25] And thus it is probable, that the Jews, by the very frequency of their fear on all occasions, had their minds in some degree prepared for every effort of tyranny which could be practised upon them; so that no aggression, when it had taken place, could bring with it that surprise which is the most disabling quality of terror. Neither was it the first time that Isaac had been placed in circumstances so dangerous. He had therefore experience to guide him, as well as hope, that he might again, as formerly, be delivered as a prey from the fowler.* Above all, he had upon his side the unyielding obstinacy of his nation, and that unbending resolution, with which Israelites have been frequently known to submit to the uttermost evils which power and violence can inflict upon them, rather than gratify their oppressors by granting their demands.

In this humour of passive resistance, and with his garment collected beneath him to keep his limbs from the wet pavement, Isaac sat in a corner of his dungeon, where his folded hands, his dishevelled hair and beard, his furred cloak and high cap, seen by the wiry and broken light, would have afforded a study for Rembrandt, had that celebrated painter existed at the period.* The Jew remained, without altering his position, for nearly three hours, at the expiry of which steps were heard on the dungeon stair. The bolts screamed as they were withdrawn—the hinges creaked as the wicket opened, and Reginald Front-de-Bœuf, followed by the two Saracen slaves of the Templar, entered the prison.

Front-de-Bœuf, a tall and strong man, whose life had been spent in public war or in private feuds and broils, and who had hesitated at no means of extending his feudal power, had features corresponding to his character, and which strongly expressed the fiercer and more malignant passions of the mind. The scars with which his visage was seamed, would, on features of a different cast, have excited the sympathy and veneration due to the marks of honourable valour; but, in the peculiar case of Front-de-Bœuf, they only added to the ferocity of his countenance, and to the dread which his presence inspired. This formidable baron was clad in a leathern doublet, fitted close to his body, which was frayed and soiled with the stains of his armour.* He had no weapon, excepting a poniard at his belt, which served to counterbalance the weight of the bunch of rusty keys that hung at his right side.

The black slaves who attended Front-de-Bœuf were stripped

of their gorgeous apparel, and attired in jerkins and trowsers of coarse linen, their sleeves being tucked up above the elbow, like those of butchers when about to exercise their function in the slaughter-house. Each had in his hand a small pannier; and, when they entered the dungeon, they stopt at the door until Front-de-Bœuf himself carefully locked and double-locked it. Having taken this precaution, he advanced slowly up the apartment towards the Jew, upon whom he kept his eye fixed, as if he wished to paralyze him with his glance, as some animals are said to fascinate their prey. It seemed indeed as if the sullen and malignant eye of Front-de-Bœuf possessed some portion of that supposed power over his unfortunate prisoner. The Jew sate with his mouth a-gape, and his eyes fixed on the savage baron with such earnestness of terror, that his frame seemed literally to shrink together, and to diminish in size while encountering the fierce Norman's fixed and baleful gaze. The unhappy Isaac was deprived not only of the power of rising to make the obeisance which his terror dictated, but he could not even doff his cap, or utter any word of supplication; so strongly was he agitated by the conviction that tortures and death were impending over him.

On the other hand, the stately form of the Norman appeared to dilate in magnitude, like that of the eagle, which ruffles up its plumage when about to pounce on its defenceless prey. He paused within three steps of the corner in which the unfortunate Jew had now, as it were, coiled himself up into the smallest possible space, and made a sign for one of the slaves to approach. The black satellite came forward accordingly, and, producing from his basket a large pair of scales and several weights, he laid them at the feet of Front-de-Bœuf, and again retired to the respectful distance, at which his companion had already taken his station.

The motions of these men were slow and solemn, as if there impended over their souls some preconception of horror and of cruelty. Front-de-Bœuf himself opened the scene by thus addressing his ill-fated captive.

'Most accursed dog of an accursed race,' he said, awaking with his deep and sullen voice the sullen echoes of his dungeon vault, 'seest thou these scales?'

The unhappy Jew returned a feeble affirmative.

'In these very scales shalt thou weigh me out,' said the relentless Baron, 'a thousand silver pounds, after the just measure and weight of the Tower of London.'*

'Holy Abraham!' returned the Jew, finding voice through the very extremity of his danger, 'heard man ever such a demand?—Who ever heard, even in a minstrel's tale, of such a sum as a thousand pounds of silver?—What human sight was ever blessed with the vision of such a mass of treasure?—Not within the walls of York, ransack my house and that of all my tribe, wilt thou find the tithe of that huge sum of silver that thou speakest of.'

'I am reasonable,' answered Front-de-Bœuf, 'and if silver be scant, I refuse not gold. At the rate of a mark of gold for each six pounds of silver, thou shalt free thy unbelieving carcass from such punishment as thy heart has never even conceived.'

'Have mercy on me, noble knight!' exclaimed Isaac; 'I am old, and poor, and helpless. It were unworthy to triumph over me—It is a poor deed to crush a worm.'

'Old thou mayst be,' replied the knight; 'more shame to their folly who have suffered thee to grow grey in usury and knavery—Feeble thou mayst be, for when had a Jew either heart or hand—But rich it is well known thou art.'

'I swear to you, noble knight,' said the Jew, 'by all which I believe, and by all which we believe in common'——

'Perjure not thyself,' said the Norman, interrupting him, 'and let not thine obstinacy seal thy doom, until thou hast seen and well considered the fate that awaits thee. Think not I speak to thee only to excite thy terror, and practise on the base cowardice thou hast derived from thy tribe. I swear to thee by that which thou dost NOT believe, by the gospel which our church teaches, and by the keys which are given her to bind and to loose,* that my purpose is deep and peremptory. This dungeon is no place for trifling. Prisoners ten thousand times more distinguished than thou have died within these walls, and their fate hath never been known! But for thee is reserved a long and lingering death, to which theirs were luxury.'

He again made a signal for the slaves to approach, and spoke to them apart, in their own language; for he also had been in Palestine, where, perhaps, he had learnt his lesson of cruelty.

The Saracens produced from their baskets a quantity of charcoal, a pair of bellows, and a flask of oil. While the one struck a light with a flint and steel, the other disposed the charcoal in the large rusty grate which we have already mentioned, and exercised the bellows until the fuel came to a red glow.

'Seest thou, Isaac,' said Front-de-Bœuf, 'the range of iron bars above that glowing charcoal?[26]—on that warm couch thou shalt lie, stripped of thy clothes as if thou wert to rest on a bed of down. One of these slaves shall maintain the fire beneath thee, while the other shall anoint thy wretched limbs with oil, lest the roast should burn.—Now, choose betwixt such a scorching bed and the payment of a thousand pounds of silver; for, by the head of my father, thou hast no other option.'

'It is impossible,' exclaimed the miserable Jew—'it is impossible that your purpose can be real! The good God of nature never made a heart capable of exercising such cruelty!'

'Trust not to that, Isaac,' said Front-de-Bœuf, 'it were a fatal error. Dost thou think that I, who have seen a town sacked, in which thousands of my Christian countrymen perished by sword, by flood, and by fire, will blench from my purpose for the outcries or screams of one single wretched Jew?—or thinkest thou that these swarthy slaves, who have neither law, country, nor conscience, but their master's will—who use the poison, or the stake, or the poniard, or the cord, at his slightest wink— thinkest thou that *they* will have mercy, who do not even understand the language in which it is asked?—Be wise, old man; discharge thyself of a portion of thy superfluous wealth; repay to the hands of a Christian a part of what thou hast acquired by the usury thou hast practised on those of his religion. Thy cunning may soon swell out once more thy shrivelled purse, but neither leech nor medicine can restore thy scorched hide and flesh wert thou once stretched on these bars. Tell down thy ransom, I say, and rejoice that at such rate thou canst redeem thee from a dungeon, the secrets of which few have returned to tell. I waste no more words with thee—choose between thy dross and thy flesh and blood, and as thou choosest, so shall it be.'

'So may Abraham, Jacob, and all the fathers of our people assist me,' said Isaac, 'I cannot make the choice, because I have not the means of satisfying your exorbitant demand!'

'Seize him and strip him, slaves,' said the knight, 'and let the fathers of his race assist him if they can.'

The assistants, taking their directions more from the Baron's eye and his hand than his tongue, once more stepped forward, laid hands on the unfortunate Isaac, plucked him up from the ground, and, holding him between them, waited the hard-hearted Baron's farther signal. The unhappy Jew eyed their countenances and that of Front-de-Bœuf, in hope of discovering some symptoms of relenting; but that of the Baron exhibited the same cold, half-sullen, half-sarcastic smile which had been the prelude to his cruelty; and the savage eyes of the Saracens, rolling gloomily under their dark brows, acquiring a yet more sinister expression by the whiteness of the circle which surrounds the pupil, evinced rather the secret pleasure which they expected from the approaching scene, than any reluctance to be its directors or agents. The Jew then looked at the glowing furnace, over which he was presently to be stretched, and seeing no chance of his tormentor's relenting, his resolution gave way.

'I will pay,' he said, 'the thousand pounds of silver—That is,' he added, after a moment's pause, 'I will pay it with the help of my brethren; for I must beg as a mendicant at the door of our synagogue ere I make up so unheard-of a sum.—When and where must it be delivered?'

'Here,' replied Front-de-Bœuf, 'here it must be delivered—weighed it must be—weighed and told down on this very dungeon floor.—Thinkest thou I will part with thee until thy ransom is secure?'

'And what is to be my surety,' said the Jew, 'that I shall be at liberty after this ransom is paid?'

'The word of a Norman noble, thou pawn-broking slave,' answered Front-de-Bœuf; 'the faith of a Norman nobleman, more pure than the gold and silver of thee and all thy tribe.'

'I crave pardon, noble lord,' said Isaac timidly, 'but wherefore should I rely wholly on the word of one who will trust nothing to mine?'

'Because thou canst not help it, Jew,' said the knight, sternly. 'Wert thou now in thy treasure-chamber at York, and were I craving a loan of thy shekels, it would be thine to dictate the time of payment, and the pledge of security. This is *my* treasure-chamber. Here I have thee at advantage, nor will I again deign to repeat the terms on which I grant thee liberty.'

The Jew groaned deeply.—'Grant me,' he said, 'at least with my own liberty, that of the companions with whom I travel. They scorned me as a Jew, yet they pitied my desolation, and because they tarried to aid me by the way, a share of my evil hath come upon them; moreover, they may contribute in some sort to my ransom.'

'If thou meanest yonder Saxon churls,' said Front-de-Bœuf, 'their ransom will depend upon other terms than thine. Mind thine own concerns, Jew, I warn thee, and meddle not with those of others.'

'I am, then,' said Isaac, 'only to be set at liberty, together with mine wounded friend?'

'Shall I twice recommend it,' said Front-de-Bœuf, 'to a son of Israel, to meddle with his own concerns, and leave those of others alone?—Since thou hast made thy choice, it remains but that thou payest down thy ransom, and that at a short day.'

'Yet hear me,' said the Jew—'for the sake of that very wealth which thou wouldst obtain at the expense of thy'——Here he stopt short, afraid of irritating the savage Norman. But Front-de-Bœuf only laughed, and himself filled up the blank at which the Jew had hesitated. 'At the expense of my conscience, thou wouldst say, Isaac; speak it out—I tell thee, I am reasonable. I can bear the reproaches of a loser, even when that loser is a Jew. Thou wert not so patient, Isaac, when thou didst invoke justice against Jacques Fitzdotterel,* for calling thee a usurious blood-sucker, when thy exactions had devoured his patrimony.'

'I swear by the Talmud,' said the Jew, 'that your valour has been misled in that matter. Fitzdotterel drew his poniard upon me in mine own chamber, because I craved him for mine own silver. The term of payment was due at the Passover.'

'I care not what he did,' said Front-de-Bœuf; 'the question is, when shall I have mine own?—when shall I have the shekels, Isaac?'

'Let my daughter Rebecca go forth to York,' answered Isaac, 'with your safe conduct, noble knight, and so soon as man and horse can return, the treasure'——Here he groaned deeply, but added, after the pause of a few seconds,—'The treasure shall be told down on this very floor.'

'Thy daughter!' said Front-de-Bœuf, as if surprised,—'By heavens, Isaac, I would I had known of this. I deemed that yonder black-browed girl had been thy concubine, and I gave her to be a handmaiden to Sir Brian de Bois-Guilbert, after the fashion of patriarchs and heroes of the days of old, who set us in these matters a wholesome example.'

The yell which Isaac raised at this unfeeling communication made the very vault to ring, and astounded the two Saracens so much that they let go their hold of the Jew. He availed himself of his enlargement to throw himself on the pavement, and clasp the knees of Front-de-Bœuf.

'Take all that you have asked,' said he, 'Sir Knight—take ten times more—reduce me to ruin and to beggary, if thou wilt,—nay, pierce me with thy poniard, broil me on that furnace, but spare my daughter, deliver her in safety and honour!—As thou art born of woman, spare the honour of a helpless maiden—She is the image of my deceased Rachael, she is the last of six pledges of her love—Will you deprive a widowed husband of his sole remaining comfort?—Will you reduce a father to wish that his only living child were laid beside her dead mother, in the tomb of our fathers?'

'I would,' said the Norman, somewhat relenting, 'that I had known of this before. I thought your race had loved nothing save their money-bags.'

'Think not so vilely of us, Jews though we be,' said Isaac, eager to improve the moment of apparent sympathy; 'the hunted fox, the tortured wildcat, loves its young—the despised and persecuted race of Abraham love their children!'

'Be it so,' said Front-de-Bœuf; 'I will believe it in future, Isaac, for thy very sake—but it aids us not now, I cannot help what has happened, or what is to follow; my word is passed to my comrade in arms, nor would I break it for ten Jews and Jewesses to boot. Besides, why shouldst thou think evil is to come to the girl, even if she became Bois-Guilbert's booty?'

'There will, there must!' exclaimed Isaac, wringing his hands in agony; 'when did Templars breathe aught but cruelty to men, and dishonour to women!'

'Dog of an infidel,' said Front-de-Bœuf, with sparkling eyes, and not sorry, perhaps, to seize a pretext for working himself into a passion, 'blaspheme not the Holy Order of the Temple of Zion, but take thought instead to pay me the ransom thou hast promised, or woe betide thy Jewish throat!'

'Robber and villain!' said the Jew, retorting the insults of his oppressor with passion, which, however impotent, he now found it impossible to bridle, 'I will pay thee nothing—not one silver penny will I pay thee, unless my daughter is delivered to me in safety and honour!'

'Art thou in thy senses, Israelite?' said the Norman, sternly—'has thy flesh and blood a charm against heated iron and scalding oil?'

'I care not!' said the Jew, rendered desperate by paternal affection; 'do thy worst. My daughter is my flesh and blood, dearer to me a thousand times than those limbs which thy cruelty threatens. No silver will I give thee, unless I were to pour it molten down thy avaricious throat—no, not a silver penny will I give thee, Nazarene, were it to save thee from the deep damnation* thy whole life has merited! Take my life if thou wilt, and say, the Jew, amidst his tortures, knew how to disappoint the Christian.'

'We shall see that,' said Front-de-Bœuf; 'for by the blessed rood, which is the abomination of thy accursed tribe, thou shalt feel the extremities of fire and steel!—Strip him, slaves, and chain him down upon the bars.'

In spite of the feeble struggles of the old man, the Saracens had already torn from him his upper garment, and were proceeding totally to disrobe him, when the sound of a bugle, twice winded without the castle, penetrated even to the recesses of the dungeon, and immediately after loud voices were heard calling for Sir Reginald Front-de-Bœuf. Unwilling to be found engaged in his hellish occupation, the savage Baron gave the slaves a signal to restore Isaac's garment, and, quitting the dungeon with his attendants, he left the Jew to thank God for his own deliverance, or to lament over his daughter's captivity, and probable fate, as his personal or parental feelings might prove strongest.

CHAPTER XXIII

Nay, if the gentle spirit of moving words
Can no way change you to a milder form,
I'll woo you, like a soldier, at arms' end,
And love you 'gainst the nature of love, force you.

*Two Gentlemen of Verona**

THE apartment to which the Lady Rowena had been introduced was fitted up with some rude attempts at ornament and magnificence, and her being placed there might be considered as a peculiar mark of respect not offered to the other prisoners. But the wife of Front-de-Bœuf, for whom it had been originally furnished, was long dead, and decay and neglect had impaired the few ornaments with which her taste had adorned it. The tapestry hung down from the walls in many places, and in others was tarnished and faded under the effects of the sun, or tattered and decayed by age. Desolate, however, as it was, this was the apartment of the castle which had been judged most fitting for the accommodation of the Saxon heiress; and here she was left to meditate upon her fate, until the actors in this nefarious drama had arranged the several parts which each of them was to perform. This had been settled in a council held by Front-de-Bœuf, De Bracy, and the Templar, in which, after a long and warm debate concerning the several advantages which each insisted upon deriving from his peculiar share in this audacious enterprise, they had at length determined the fate of their unhappy prisoners.

It was about the hour of noon, therefore, when De Bracy, for whose advantage the expedition had been first planned, appeared to prosecute his views upon the hand and possessions of the Lady Rowena.

The interval had not entirely been bestowed in holding council with his confederates, for De Bracy had found leisure to decorate his person with all the foppery of the times. His green cassock and vizard were now flung aside. His long luxuriant hair was trained to flow in quaint tresses down his richly furred cloak.

His beard was closely shaved, his doublet reached to the middle of his leg, and the girdle which secured it, and at the same time supported his ponderous sword, was embroidered and embossed with gold work. We have already noticed the extravagant fashion of the shoes at this period, and the points of Maurice de Bracy's might have challenged the prize of extravagance with the gayest, being turned up and twisted like the horns of a ram. Such was the dress of a gallant of the period;* and, in the present instance, that effect was aided by the handsome person and good demeanour of the wearer, whose manners partook alike of the grace of a courtier, and the frankness of a soldier.

He saluted Rowena by doffing his velvet bonnet, garnished with a golden brooch, representing St Michael trampling down the Prince of Evil. With this, he gently motioned the lady to a seat; and, as she still retained her standing posture, the knight ungloved his right hand, and motioned to conduct her thither. But Rowena declined, by her gesture, the proffered compliment, and replied, 'If I be in the presence of my jailor, Sir Knight—nor will circumstances allow me to think otherwise—it best becomes his prisoner to remain standing till she learns her doom.'

'Alas! fair Rowena,' returned De Bracy, 'you are in presence of your captive, not your jailor; and it is from your fair eyes that De Bracy must receive that doom which you fondly expect from him.'

'I know you not, sir,' said the lady, drawing herself up with all the pride of offended rank and beauty; 'I know you not—and the insolent familiarity with which you apply to me the jargon of a troubadour, forms no apology for the violence of a robber.'

'To thyself, fair maid,' answered De Bracy, in his former tone—'to thine own charms be ascribed whate'er I have done which passed the respect due to her, whom I have chosen queen of my heart, and loadstar of my eyes.'

'I repeat to you, Sir Knight, that I know you not, and that no man wearing chain and spurs ought thus to intrude himself upon the presence of an unprotected lady.'

'That I am unknown to you,' said De Bracy, 'is indeed my misfortune; yet let me hope that De Bracy's name has not been always unspoken, when minstrels or heralds have praised deeds of chivalry, whether in the lists or in the battle-field.'

'To heralds and to minstrels, then, leave thy praise, Sir Knight,' replied Rowena, 'more suiting for their mouths than for thine own; and tell me which of them shall record in song, or in book of tourney, the memorable conquest of this night, a conquest obtained over an old man, followed by a few timid hinds; and its booty, an unfortunate maiden, transported against her will to the castle of a robber?'

'You are unjust, Lady Rowena,' said the knight, biting his lips in some confusion, and speaking in a tone more natural to him than that of affected gallantry, which he had at first adopted; 'yourself free from passion, you can allow no excuse for the frenzy of another, although caused by your own beauty.'

'I pray you, Sir Knight,' said Rowena, 'to cease a language so commonly used by strolling minstrels, that it becomes not the mouth of knights or nobles. Certes, you constrain me to sit down, since you enter upon such commonplace terms, of which each vile crowder* hath a stock that might last from hence to Christmas.'

'Proud damsel,' said De Bracy, incensed at finding his gallant style procured him nothing but contempt—'proud damsel, thou shalt be as proudly encountered. Know then, that I have supported my pretensions to your hand in the way that best suited thy character. It is meeter for thy humour to be wooed with bow and bill, than in set terms, and in courtly language.'*

'Courtesy of tongue,' said Rowena, 'when it is used to veil churlishness of deed, is but a knight's girdle around the breast of a base clown. I wonder not that the restraint appears to gall you—more it were for your honour to have retained the dress and language of an outlaw, than to veil the deeds of one under an affectation of gentle language and demeanour.'

'You counsel well, lady,' said the Norman; 'and in the bold language which best justifies bold action, I tell thee, thou shalt never leave this castle, or thou shalt leave it as Maurice de Bracy's wife. I am not wont to be baffled in my enterprises, nor needs a Norman noble scrupulously to vindicate his conduct to the Saxon maiden whom he distinguishes by the offer of his hand. Thou art proud, Rowena, and thou art the fitter to be my wife. By what other means couldst thou be raised to high honour and to princely place, saving by my alliance? How else wouldst thou escape from the mean precincts of a country grange, where Saxons herd with the swine which form their wealth, to take thy seat, honoured as thou shouldst be, and shalt be, amid all in England that is distinguished by beauty, or dignified by power?'

'Sir Knight,' replied Rowena, 'the grange which you contemn hath been my shelter from infancy; and, trust me, when I leave it—should that day ever arrive—it shall be with one who has not learnt to despise the dwelling and manners in which I have been brought up.'

'I guess your meaning, lady,' said De Bracy, 'though you may think it lies too obscure for my apprehension. But dream not, that Richard Cœur de Lion will ever resume his throne, far less that Wilfred of Ivanhoe, his minion, will ever lead thee to his footstool, to be there welcomed as the bride of a favourite. Another suitor might feel jealousy while he touched this string; but my firm purpose cannot be changed by a passion so childish and so hopeless. Know, lady, that this rival is in my power, and that it rests but with me to betray the secret of his being within the castle to Front-de-Bœuf, whose jealousy will be more fatal than mine.'

'Wilfred here?' said Rowena, in disdain; 'that is as true as that Front-de-Bœuf is his rival.'

De Bracy looked at her steadily for an instant. 'Wert thou really ignorant of this?' said he; 'didst thou not know that Wilfred of Ivanhoe travelled in the litter of the Jew?—a meet conveyance for the crusader, whose doughty arm was to reconquer the Holy Sepulchre!' And he laughed scornfully.

'And if he is here,' said Rowena, compelling herself to a tone of indifference, though trembling with an agony of apprehension which she could not suppress, 'in what is he the rival of Front-de-Bœuf? or what has he to fear beyond a short imprisonment, and an honourable ransom, according to the use of chivalry?'

'Rowena,' said De Bracy, 'art thou, too, deceived by the common error of thy sex, who think there can be no rivalry but that respecting their own charms? Knowest thou not there is a jealousy of ambition and of wealth, as well as of love; and that this our host, Front-de-Bœuf, will push from his road him who opposes his claim to the fair barony of Ivanhoe, as readily, eagerly, and unscrupulously, as if he were preferred to him by some blue-eyed damsel? But smile on my suit, lady, and the wounded champion shall have nothing to fear from Front-de-Bœuf, whom else thou mayst mourn for, as in the hands of one who has never shown compassion.'

'Save him, for the love of Heaven!' said Rowena, her firmness giving way under terror for her lover's impending fate.

'I can—I will—it is my purpose,' said De Bracy; 'for, when Rowena consents to be the bride of De Bracy, who is it shall dare to put forth a violent hand upon her kinsman—the son of her guardian—the companion of her youth? But it is thy love must buy his protection. I am not romantic fool enough to further the fortune, or avert the fate, of one who is likely to be a successful obstacle between me and my wishes. Use thine influence with me in his behalf, and he is safe,—refuse to employ it, Wilfred dies, and thou thyself art not the nearer to freedom.'

'Thy language,' answered Rowena, 'hath in its indifferent bluntness something which cannot be reconciled with the horrors it seems to express. I believe not that thy purpose is so wicked, or thy power so great.'

'Flatter thyself, then, with that belief,' said De Bracy, 'until time shall prove it false. Thy lover lies wounded in this castle—thy preferred lover. He is a bar betwixt Front-de-Bœuf and that which Front-de-Bœuf loves better than either ambition or beauty. What will it cost beyond the blow of a poniard, or the thrust of a javelin, to silence his opposition for ever? Nay, were Front-de-Bœuf afraid to justify a deed so open, let the leech but give his patient a wrong draught—let the chamberlain, or the nurse who tends him, but pluck the pillow from his head, and Wilfred, in his present condition, is sped without the effusion of blood. Cedric also'——

'And Cedric also,' said Rowena, repeating his words; 'my noble—my generous guardian! I deserved the evil I have encountered, for forgetting his fate even in that of his son!'

'Cedric's fate also depends upon thy determination,' said De Bracy; 'and I leave thee to form it.'

Hitherto, Rowena had sustained her part in this trying scene with undismayed courage, but it was because she had not considered the danger as serious and imminent. Her disposition was naturally that which physiognomists consider as proper to fair complexions, mild, timid, and gentle; but it had been tempered, and, as it were, hardened, by the circumstances of her education. Accustomed to see the will of all, even of Cedric himself, (sufficiently arbitrary with others,) give way before her wishes, she had acquired that sort of courage and self-confidence which arises from the habitual and constant deference of the circle in which we move. She could scarce conceive the possibility of her will being opposed, far less that of its being treated with total disregard.

Her haughtiness and habit of domination was, therefore, a fictitious character, induced over that which was natural to her, and it deserted her when her eyes were opened to the extent of her own danger, as well as that of her lover and her guardian; and when she found her will, the slightest expression of which was wont to command respect and attention, now placed in opposition to that of a man of a strong, fierce, and determined mind, who possessed the advantage over her, and was resolved to use it, she quailed before him.

After casting her eyes around, as if to look for the aid which was nowhere to be found, and after a few broken interjections, she raised her hands to heaven, and burst into a passion of uncontrolled vexation and sorrow. It was impossible to see so beautiful a creature in such extremity without feeling for her, and De Bracy was not unmoved, though he was yet more embarrassed than touched. He had, in truth, gone too far to recede; and yet, in Rowena's present condition, she could not be acted on either by argument or threats. He paced the apartment to and fro, now vainly exhorting the terrified maiden to compose herself, now hesitating concerning his own line of conduct.

If, thought he, I should be moved by the tears and sorrow of this disconsolate damsel, what should I reap but the loss of those fair hopes for which I have encountered so much risk, and the ridicule of Prince John and his jovial comrades? 'And yet,' he said to himself, 'I feel myself ill framed for the part which I am playing. I cannot look on so fair a face while it is disturbed with agony, or on those eyes when they are drowned in tears. I would she had retained her original haughtiness of disposition, or that

I had a larger share of Front-de-Bœuf's thrice-tempered hardness of heart!'

Agitated by these thoughts, he could only bid the unfortunate
Rowena be comforted, and assure her, that as yet she had no
reason for the excess of despair to which she was now giving way.
But in this task of consolation De Bracy was interrupted by the
horn, 'hoarse-winded blowing far and keen,'* which had at
the same time alarmed the other inmates of the castle, and
interrupted their several plans of avarice and of license. Of them
all, perhaps, De Bracy least regretted the interruption; for his
conference with the Lady Rowena had arrived at a point,
where he found it equally difficult to prosecute or to resign his
enterprise.

And here we cannot but think it necessary to offer some better
proof than the incidents of an idle tale, to vindicate the melancholy representation of manners which has been just laid before
the reader. It is grievous to think that those valiant barons, to
whose stand against the crown the liberties of England were
indebted for their existence, should themselves have been such
dreadful oppressors, and capable of excesses contrary not only to
the laws of England, but to those of nature and humanity. But,
alas! we have only to extract from the industrious Henry* one of
those numerous passages which he has collected from contemporary historians, to prove that fiction itself can hardly reach the
dark reality of the horrors of the period.

The description given by the author of the Saxon Chronicle of
the cruelties exercised in the reign of King Stephen by the great
barons and lords of castles, who were all Normans, affords a
strong proof of the excesses of which they were capable when
their passions were inflamed. 'They grievously oppressed the
poor people by building castles; and when they were built, they
filled them with wicked men, or rather devils, who seized both
men and women who they imagined had any money, threw them
into prison, and put them to more cruel tortures than the martyrs ever endured. They suffocated some in mud, and suspended
others by the feet, or the head, or the thumbs, kindling fires
below them. They squeezed the heads of some with knotted
cords till they pierced their brains, while they threw others into
dungeons swarming with serpents, snakes, and toads.' But it

would be cruel to put the reader to the pain of perusing the remainder of this description.[27]

As another instance of these bitter fruits of conquest, and perhaps the strongest that can be quoted, we may mention, that the Empress Matilda,* though a daughter of the King of Scotland, and afterwards both Queen of England and Empress of Germany, the daughter, the wife, and the mother of monarchs, was obliged, during her early residence for education in England, to assume the veil of a nun, as the only means of escaping the licentious pursuit of the Norman nobles. This excuse she stated before a great council of the clergy of England, as the sole reason for her having taken the religious habit. The assembled clergy admitted the validity of the plea, and the notoriety of the circumstances upon which it was founded; giving thus an indubitable and most remarkable testimony to the existence of that disgraceful license by which that age was stained. It was a matter of public knowledge, they said, that after the conquest of King William, his Norman followers, elated by so great a victory, acknowledged no law but their own wicked pleasure, and not only despoiled the conquered Saxons of their lands and their goods, but invaded the honour of their wives and of their daughters with the most unbridled license; and hence it was then common for matrons and maidens of noble families to assume the veil, and take shelter in convents, not as called thither by the vocation of God, but solely to preserve their honour from the unbridled wickedness of man.

Such and so licentious were the times, as announced by the public declaration of the assembled clergy, recorded by Eadmer; and we need add nothing more to vindicate the probability of the scenes which we have detailed, and are about to detail, upon the more apocryphal authority of the Wardour MS.

CHAPTER XXIV

I'll woo her as the lion woos his bride.

*Douglas**

WHILE the scenes we have described were passing in other parts
of the castle, the Jewess Rebecca awaited her fate in a distant and
sequestered turret. Hither she had been led by two of her disguised ravishers, and on being thrust into the little cell, she
found herself in the presence of an old sibyl, who kept murmuring to herself a Saxon rhyme, as if to beat time to the revolving
dance which her spindle was performing upon the floor. The hag
raised her head as Rebecca entered, and scowled at the fair
Jewess with the malignant envy with which old age and ugliness,
when united with evil conditions, are apt to look upon youth and
beauty.

'Thou must up and away, old house-cricket,' said one of the
men; 'our noble master commands it—Thou must e'en leave this
chamber to a fairer guest.'

'Ay,' grumbled the hag, 'even thus is service requited. I have
known when my bare word would have cast the best man-at-
arms among ye out of saddle and out of service; and now must I
up and away at the command of every groom such as thou.'

'Good Dame Urfried,' said the other man, 'stand not to reason
on it, but up and away. Lords' hests must be listened to with a
quick ear. Thou hast had thy day, old dame, but thy sun has long
been set. Thou art now the very emblem of an old war-horse
turned out on the barren heath—thou hast had thy paces in thy
time, but now a broken amble is the best of them—Come, amble
off with thee.'

'Ill omens dog ye both!' said the old woman; 'and a kennel be
your burying-place! May the evil demon Zernebock* tear me
limb from limb, if I leave my own cell ere I have spun out the
hemp on my distaff!'

'Answer it to our lord, then, old housefiend,' said the man,
and retired; leaving Rebecca in company with the old woman,
upon whose presence she had been thus unwillingly forced.

'What devil's deed have they now in the wind?' said the old hag, murmuring to herself, yet from time to time casting a sidelong and malignant glance at Rebecca; 'but it is easy to guess—Bright eyes, black locks, and a skin like paper, ere the priest stains it with his black unguent—Ay, it is easy to guess why they send her to this lone turret, whence a shriek could no more be heard than at the depth of five hundred fathoms beneath the earth.—Thou wilt have owls for thy neighbours, fair one; and their screams will be heard as far, and as much regarded, as thine own. Outlandish, too,' she said, marking the dress and turban of Rebecca—'What country art thou of?—a Saracen? or an Egyptian?*—Why dost not answer?—thou canst weep, canst thou not speak?'

'Be not angry, good mother,' said Rebecca.

'Thou needst say no more,' replied Urfried; 'men know a fox by the train,* and a Jewess by her tongue.'

'For the sake of mercy,' said Rebecca, 'tell me what I am to expect as the conclusion of the violence which hath dragged me hither! Is it my life they seek, to atone for my religion? I will lay it down cheerfully.'

'Thy life, minion?' answered the sibyl; 'what would taking thy life pleasure them?—Trust me, thy life is in no peril. Such usage shalt thou have as was once thought good enough for a noble Saxon maiden. And shall a Jewess, like thee, repine because she hath no better? Look at me—I was as young and twice as fair as thou, when Front-de-Bœuf, father of this Reginald, and his Normans, stormed this castle. My father and his seven sons defended their inheritance from story to story, from chamber to chamber—There was not a room, not a step of the stair, that was not slippery with their blood. They died—they died every man; and ere their bodies were cold, and ere their blood was dried, I had become the prey and the scorn of the conqueror!'

'Is there no help?—Are there no means of escape?' said Rebecca—'Richly, richly would I requite thine aid.'

'Think not of it,' said the hag; 'from hence there is no escape but through the gates of death; and it is late, late,' she added, shaking her grey head, 'ere these open to us—Yet it is comfort to think that we leave behind us on earth those who shall be wretched as ourselves. Fare thee well, Jewess!—Jew or Gentile, thy fate would be the same; for thou hast to do with them that have neither scruple nor pity. Fare thee well, I say. My thread is spun out*—thy task is yet to begin.'

'Stay! stay! for Heaven's sake!' said Rebecca; 'stay, though it be to curse and to revile me—thy presence is yet some protection.'

'The presence of the mother of God were no protection,' answered the old woman. 'There she stands,' pointing to a rude image of the Virgin Mary, 'see if she can avert the fate that awaits thee.'

She left the room as she spoke, her features writhed into a sort of sneering laugh, which made them seem even more hideous than their habitual frown. She locked the door behind her, and Rebecca might hear her curse every step for its steepness, as slowly and with difficulty she descended the turret-stair.

Rebecca was now to expect a fate even more dreadful than that of Rowena; for what probability was there that either softness or ceremony would be used towards one of her oppressed race, whatever shadow of these might be preserved towards a Saxon heiress? Yet had the Jewess this advantage, that she was better prepared by habits of thought, and by natural strength of mind, to encounter the dangers to which she was exposed. Of a strong and observing character, even from her earliest years, the pomp and wealth which her father displayed within his walls, or which she witnessed in the houses of other wealthy Hebrews, had not been able to blind her to the precarious circumstances under which they were enjoyed. Like Damocles at his celebrated banquet, Rebecca perpetually beheld, amid that gorgeous display, the sword which was suspended over the heads of her people by a single hair.* These reflections had tamed and brought down to a pitch of sounder judgment a temper, which, under other circumstances, might have waxed haughty, supercilious, and obstinate.

From her father's example and injunctions, Rebecca had learnt to bear herself courteously towards all who approached her. She could not indeed imitate his excess of subservience, because she was a stranger to the meanness of mind, and to the constant state of timid apprehension, by which it was dictated; but she bore herself with a proud humility, as if submitting to the

evil circumstances in which she was placed as the daughter of a
despised race, while she felt in her mind the consciousness that
she was entitled to hold a higher rank from her merit, than the
arbitrary despotism of religious prejudice permitted her to aspire
to.

Thus prepared to expect adverse circumstances, she had
acquired the firmness necessary for acting under them. Her
present situation required all her presence of mind, and she
summoned it up accordingly.

Her first care was to inspect the apartment; but it afforded few
hopes either of escape or protection. It contained neither secret
passage nor trap-door, and unless where the door by which she
had entered joined the main building, seemed to be circumscribed by the round exterior wall of the turret. The door had no
inside bolt or bar. The single window opened upon an embattled
space* surmounting the turret, which gave Rebecca, at first
sight, some hopes of escaping; but she soon found it had no
communication with any other part of the battlements, being an
isolated bartisan,* or balcony, secured, as usual, by a parapet,
with embrasures, at which a few archers might be stationed for
defending the turret, and flanking with their shot the wall of the
castle on that side.

There was therefore no hope but in passive fortitude, and in
that strong reliance on Heaven natural to great and generous
characters. Rebecca, however erroneously taught to interpret the
promises of Scripture to the chosen people of Heaven, did not
err in supposing the present to be their hour of trial, or in
trusting that the children of Zion would be one day called in with
the fulness of the Gentiles.* In the meanwhile, all around her
showed that their present state was that of punishment and
probation, and that it was their especial duty to suffer without
sinning. Thus prepared to consider herself as the victim of misfortune, Rebecca had early reflected upon her own state, and
schooled her mind to meet the dangers which she had probably
to encounter.

The prisoner trembled, however, and changed colour, when a
step was heard on the stair, and the door of the turret-chamber
slowly opened, and a tall man, dressed as one of those banditti to
whom they owed their misfortune, slowly entered, and shut the

door behind him; his cap, pulled down upon his brows, concealed the upper part of his face, and he held his mantle in such a manner as to muffle the rest. In this guise, as if prepared for the execution of some deed, at the thought of which he was himself ashamed, he stood before the affrighted prisoner; yet, ruffian as his dress bespoke him, he seemed at a loss to express what purpose had brought him thither, so that Rebecca, making an effort upon herself, had time to anticipate his explanation. She had already unclasped two costly bracelets and a collar, which she hastened to proffer to the supposed outlaw, concluding naturally that to gratify his avarice was to bespeak his favour.

'Take these,' she said, 'good friend, and for God's sake be merciful to me and my aged father! These ornaments are of value, yet are they trifling to what he would bestow to obtain our dismissal from this castle, free and uninjured.'

'Fair flower of Palestine,' replied the outlaw, 'these pearls are orient, but they yield in whiteness to your teeth; the diamonds are brilliant, but they cannot match your eyes; and ever since I have taken up this wild trade, I have made a vow to prefer beauty to wealth.'

'Do not do yourself such wrong,' said Rebecca; 'take ransom, and have mercy!—Gold will purchase you pleasure,—to misuse us, could only bring thee remorse. My father will willingly satiate thy utmost wishes; and if thou wilt act wisely, thou mayst purchase with our spoils thy restoration to civil society—mayst obtain pardon for past errors, and be placed beyond the necessity of committing more.'

'It is well spoken,' replied the outlaw in French, finding it difficult probably to sustain, in Saxon, a conversation which Rebecca had opened in that language; 'but know, bright lily of the vale of Baca!* that thy father is already in the hands of a powerful alchemist, who knows how to convert into gold and silver even the rusty bars of a dungeon grate. The venerable Isaac is subjected to an alembic,* which will distil from him all he holds dear, without any assistance from my requests or thy entreaty. Thy ransom must be paid by love and beauty, and in no other coin will I accept it.'

'Thou art no outlaw,' said Rebecca, in the same language in

which he addressed her; 'no outlaw had refused such offers. No outlaw in this land uses the dialect in which thou hast spoken. Thou art no outlaw, but a Norman—a Norman, noble perhaps in birth—O, be so in thy actions, and cast off this fearful mask of outrage and violence!'

'And thou, who canst guess so truly,' said Brian de Bois-Guilbert, dropping the mantle from his face, 'art no true daughter of Israel, but in all, save youth and beauty, a very witch of Endor.* I am not an outlaw, then, fair rose of Sharon. And I am one who will be more prompt to hang thy neck and arms with pearls and diamonds, which so well become them, than to deprive thee of these ornaments.'

'What wouldst thou have of me,' said Rebecca, 'if not my wealth?—We can have nought in common between us—you are a Christian—I am a Jewess.—Our union were contrary to the laws, alike of the church and the synagogue.'

'It were so, indeed,' replied the Templar, laughing; 'wed with a Jewess? *Despardieux!**—Not if she were the Queen of Sheba! And know, besides, sweet daughter of Zion, that were the most Christian king to offer me his most Christian daughter, with Languedoc for a dowery, I could not wed her. It is against my vow to love any maiden, otherwise than *par amours,** as I will love thee. I am a Templar. Behold the cross of my Holy Order.'

'Darest thou appeal to it,' said Rebecca, 'on an occasion like the present?'

'And if I do so,' said the Templar, 'it concerns not thee, who art no believer in the blessed sign of our salvation.'

'I believe as my fathers taught,' said Rebecca; 'and may God forgive my belief if erroneous! But you, Sir Knight, what is *yours*, when you appeal without scruple to that which you deem most holy, even while you are about to transgress the most solemn of your vows as a knight, and as a man of religion?'

'It is gravely and well preached, O daughter of Sirach!' answered the Templar; 'but, gentle Ecclesiastica,* thy narrow Jewish prejudices make thee blind to our high privilege. Marriage were an enduring crime on the part of a Templar; but what lesser folly I may practise, I shall speedily be absolved from at the next Preceptory of our Order. Not the wisest of monarchs, not his father, whose examples you must needs allow are weighty, claimed wider privileges than we poor soldiers of the Temple of Zion have won by our zeal in its defence. The protectors of Solomon's Temple may claim license by the example of Solomon.'

'If thou readest the Scripture,' said the Jewess, 'and the lives of the saints, only to justify thine own license and profligacy, thy crime is like that of him who extracts poison from the most healthful and necessary herbs.'

The eyes of the Templar flashed fire at this reproof—'Hearken,' he said, 'Rebecca; I have hitherto spoken mildly to thee, but now my language shall be that of a conqueror. Thou art the captive of my bow and spear—subject to my will by the laws of all nations; nor will I abate an inch of my right, or abstain from taking by violence what thou refusest to entreaty or necessity.'

'Stand back,' said Rebecca—'stand back, and hear me ere thou offerest to commit a sin so deadly! My strength thou mayst indeed overpower, for God made women weak, and trusted their defence to man's generosity. But I will proclaim thy villainy, Templar, from one end of Europe to the other. I will owe to the superstition of thy brethren what their compassion might refuse me. Each Preceptory—each Chapter of thy Order, shall learn, that, like a heretic, thou hast sinned with a Jewess. Those who tremble not at thy crime, will hold thee accursed for having so far dishonoured the cross thou wearest, as to follow a daughter of my people.'

'Thou art keen-witted, Jewess,' replied the Templar, well aware of the truth of what she spoke, and that the rules of his Order condemned in the most positive manner, and under high penalties, such intrigues as he now prosecuted, and that, in some instances, even degradation had followed upon it—'thou art sharp-witted,' he said; 'but loud must be thy voice of complaint, if it is heard beyond the iron walls of this castle; within these, murmurs, laments, appeals to justice, and screams for help, die alike silent away. One thing only can save thee, Rebecca. Submit to thy fate—embrace our religion, and thou shalt go forth in such state, that many a Norman lady shall yield as well in pomp as in beauty to the favourite of the best lance among the defenders of the Temple.'

'Submit to my fate!' said Rebecca—'and, sacred Heaven! to what fate?—embrace thy religion! and what religion can it be that harbours such a villain?—*thou* the best lance of the Templars!—Craven knight!—forsworn priest! I spit at thee, and I defy thee.—The God of Abraham's promise hath opened an escape to his daughter—even from this abyss of infamy!'

As she spoke, she threw open the latticed window which led to the bartisan, and in an instant after, stood on the very verge of the parapet, with not the slightest screen between her and the tremendous depth below. Unprepared for such a desperate effort, for she had hitherto stood perfectly motionless, Bois-Guilbert had neither time to intercept nor to stop her. As he offered to advance, she exclaimed, 'Remain where thou art, proud Templar, or at thy choice advance!—one foot nearer, and I plunge myself from the precipice; my body shall be crushed out of the very form of humanity upon the stones of that court-yard, ere it become the victim of thy brutality!'

As she spoke this, she clasped her hands and extended them towards heaven, as if imploring mercy on her soul before she made the final plunge.* The Templar hesitated, and a resolution which had never yielded to pity or distress, gave way to his admiration of her fortitude. 'Come down,' he said, 'rash girl!—I swear by earth, and sea, and sky, I will offer thee no offence.'

'I will not trust thee, Templar,' said Rebecca; 'thou hast taught me better how to estimate the virtues of thine Order. The next Preceptory would grant thee absolution for an oath, the keeping of which concerned nought but the honour or the dishonour of a miserable Jewish maiden.'

'You do me injustice,' exclaimed the Templar fervently; 'I swear to you by the name which I bear—by the cross on my bosom—by the sword on my side—by the ancient crest of my fathers do I swear, I will do thee no injury whatsoever! If not for thyself, yet for thy father's sake forbear! I will be his friend, and in this castle he will need a powerful one.'

'Alas!' said Rebecca, 'I know it but too well—dare I trust thee?'

'May my arms be reversed, and my name dishonoured,' said Brian de Bois-Guilbert, 'if thou shalt have reason to complain of me! Many a law, many a commandment have I broken, but my word never.'

'I will then trust thee,' said Rebecca, 'thus far;' and she descended from the verge of the battlement, but remained standing close by one of the embrasures, or *machicolles*, as they were then called.—'Here,' she said, 'I take my stand. Remain where thou art, and if thou shalt attempt to diminish by one step the distance now between us, thou shalt see that the Jewish maiden will rather trust her soul with God, than her honour to the Templar!'

While Rebecca spoke thus, her high and firm resolve, which corresponded so well with the expressive beauty of her countenance, gave to her looks, air, and manner, a dignity that seemed more than mortal. Her glance quailed not, her cheek blanched not, for the fear of a fate so instant and so horrible; on the contrary, the thought that she had her fate at her command, and could escape at will from infamy to death, gave a yet deeper colour of carnation to her complexion, and a yet more brilliant fire to her eye. Bois-Guilbert, proud himself and high-spirited, thought he had never beheld beauty so animated and so commanding.

'Let there be peace between us, Rebecca,' he said.

'Peace, if thou wilt,' answered Rebecca—'Peace—but with this space between.'

'Thou needst no longer fear me,' said Bois-Guilbert.

'I fear thee not,' replied she; 'thanks to him that reared this dizzy tower so high, that nought could fall from it and live— thanks to him, and to the God of Israel!—I fear thee not.'

'Thou dost me injustice,' said the Templar; 'by earth, sea, and sky, thou dost me injustice! I am not naturally that which you have seen me, hard, selfish, and relentless. It was woman that taught me cruelty,* and on woman therefore I have exercised it; but not upon such as thou. Hear me, Rebecca—Never did knight take lance in his hand with a heart more devoted to the lady of his love than Brian de Bois-Guilbert. She, the daughter of a petty baron, who boasted for all his domains but a ruinous tower, and an unproductive vineyard, and some few leagues of the barren Landes of Bourdeaux, her name was known wherever deeds of arms were done, known wider than that of many a lady's that had a county for a dowery.—Yes,' he continued, pacing up and down the little platform, with an animation in which he seemed to lose all consciousness of Rebecca's presence—'Yes, my deeds, my danger, my blood, made the name of Adelaide de Montemare known from the court of Castile to that of Byzantium. And how was I requited?—When I returned with my dear-bought honours, purchased by toil and blood, I found her wedded to a Gascon squire, whose name was never heard beyond the limits of his own paltry domain! Truly did I love her, and bitterly did I revenge me of her broken faith! But my vengeance has recoiled on myself. Since that day I have separated myself from life and its ties—My manhood must know no domestic home—must be soothed by no affectionate wife—My age must know no kindly hearth—My grave must be solitary, and no offspring must outlive me, to bear the ancient name of Bois-Guilbert. At the feet of my Superior I have laid down the right of self-action—the privilege of independence. The Templar, a serf in all but the name, can possess neither lands nor goods, and lives, moves, and breathes, but at the will and pleasure of another.'

'Alas!' said Rebecca, 'what advantages could compensate for such an absolute sacrifice?'

'The power of vengeance, Rebecca,' replied the Templar, 'and the prospects of ambition.'

'An evil recompense,' said Rebecca, 'for the surrender of the rights which are dearest to humanity.'

'Say not so, maiden,' answered the Templar; 'revenge is a feast for the gods! And if they have reserved it, as priests tell us, to themselves, it is because they hold it an enjoyment too precious for the possession of mere mortals.—And ambition? it is a temptation which could disturb even the bliss of heaven itself.'—He paused a moment, and then added, 'Rebecca! she who could prefer death to dishonour, must have a proud and a powerful soul. Mine thou must be!—Nay, start not,' he added, 'it must be with thine own consent, and on thine own terms. Thou must consent to share with me hopes more extended than can be viewed from the throne of a monarch!—Hear me ere you answer, and judge ere you refuse.—The Templar loses, as thou hast said, his social rights, his power of free agency, but he becomes a member and a limb of a mighty body, before which thrones already tremble,—even as the single drop of rain which mixes with the sea becomes an individual part of that resistless ocean, which undermines rocks and ingulfs royal armadas. Such a swelling flood is that powerful league. Of this mighty Order I am no mean member, but already one of the Chief Commanders, and may well aspire one day to hold the batoon of Grand Master. The poor soldiers of the Temple will not alone place their foot upon the necks of kings—a hemp-sandall'd monk can do that. Our mailed step shall ascend their throne—our gauntlet shall wrench the sceptre from their gripe.* Not the reign of your vainly-expected Messiah offers such power to your dispersed tribes as my ambition may aim at. I have sought but a kindred spirit to share it, and I have found such in thee.'

'Sayest thou this to one of my people?' answered Rebecca. 'Bethink thee'——

'Answer me not,' said the Templar, 'by urging the difference of our creeds; within our secret conclaves we hold these nursery tales in derision. Think not we long remained blind to the idiotical folly of our founders, who forswore every delight of life for the pleasure of dying martyrs by hunger, by thirst, and by pestilence, and by the swords of savages, while they vainly strove to defend a barren desert, valuable only in the eyes of superstition. Our Order soon adopted bolder and wider views, and found out a better indemnification for our sacrifices. Our immense possessions in every kingdom of Europe, our high military fame, which brings within our circle the flower of chivalry from every Christian clime—these are dedicated to ends of which our pious founders little dreamed, and which are equally concealed from such weak spirits as embrace our Order on the ancient principles, and whose superstition makes them our passive tools. But I will not further withdraw the veil of our mysteries. That bugle-sound announces something which may require my presence. Think on what I have said.—Farewell!—I do not say forgive me the violence I have threatened, for it was necessary to the display of thy character. Gold can be only known by the application of the touchstone. I will soon return, and hold further conference with thee.'

He re-entered the turret-chamber, and descended the stair, leaving Rebecca scarcely more terrified at the prospect of the death to which she had been so lately exposed, than at the furious ambition of the bold bad man in whose power she found herself so unhappily placed. When she entered the turret-chamber, her first duty was to return thanks to the God of Jacob for the protection which he had afforded her, and to implore its continuance for her and for her father. Another name glided into her petition—it was that of the wounded Christian, whom fate had placed in the hands of bloodthirsty men, his avowed enemies. Her heart indeed checked her, as if, even in communing with the Deity in prayer, she mingled in her devotions the recollection of one with whose fate hers could have no alliance—a Nazarene, and an enemy to her faith. But the petition was already breathed, nor could all the narrow prejudices of her sect induce Rebecca to wish it recalled.

CHAPTER XXV

A damn'd cramp piece of penmanship as ever I saw in
my life!

*She Stoops to Conquer**

WHEN the Templar reached the hall of the castle, he found De
Bracy already there. 'Your love-suit,' said De Bracy, 'hath, I
suppose, been disturbed, like mine, by this obstreperous summons. But you have come later and more reluctantly, and therefore I presume your interview has proved more agreeable than
mine.'

'Has your suit, then, been unsuccessfully paid to the Saxon
heiress?' said the Templar.

'By the bones of Thomas a Becket,' answered De Bracy, 'the
Lady Rowena must have heard that I cannot endure the sight of
women's tears.'

'Away!' said the Templar; 'thou a leader of a Free Company,
and regard a woman's tears! A few drops sprinkled on the torch
of love, make the flame blaze the brighter.'

'Gramercy for the few drops of thy sprinkling,' replied De
Bracy; 'but this damsel hath wept enough to extinguish a
beacon-light. Never was such wringing of hands and such over-
flowing of eyes, since the days of St Niobe,* of whom Prior
Aymer told us.[28] A water-fiend hath possessed the fair Saxon.'

'A legion of fiends have occupied the bosom of the Jewess,'
replied the Templar; 'for, I think no single one, not even
Apollyon* himself, could have inspired such indomitable pride
and resolution.—But where is Front-de-Bœuf? That horn is
sounded more and more clamorously.'

'He is negotiating with the Jew, I suppose,' replied De Bracy,
coolly; 'probably the howls of Isaac have drowned the blast of the
bugle. Thou mayst know, by experience, Sir Brian, that a Jew
parting with his treasures on such terms as our friend Front-de-
Bœuf is like to offer, will raise a clamour loud enough to be heard
over twenty horns and trumpets to boot. But we will make the
vassals call him.'

They were soon after joined by Front-de-Bœuf, who had been disturbed in his tyrannic cruelty in the manner with which the reader is acquainted, and had only tarried to give some necessary directions.

'Let us see the cause of this cursed clamour,' said Front-de-Bœuf—'here is a letter, and, if I mistake not, it is in Saxon.'

He looked at it, turning it round and round as if he had had really some hopes of coming at the meaning by inverting the position of the paper, and then handed it to De Bracy.

'It may be magic spells for aught I know,' said De Bracy, who possessed his full proportion of the ignorance which characterised the chivalry of the period. 'Our chaplain attempted to teach me to write,' he said, 'but all my letters were formed like spearheads and sword-blades, and so the old shaveling gave up the task.'

'Give it me,' said the Templar. 'We have that of the priestly character, that we have some knowledge to enlighten our valour.'

'Let us profit by your most reverend knowledge, then,' said De Bracy; 'what says the scroll?'

'It is a formal letter of defiance,' answered the Templar; 'but, by our Lady of Bethlehem, if it be not a foolish jest, it is the most extraordinary cartel that ever was sent across the drawbridge of a baronial castle.'

'Jest!' said Front-de-Bœuf, 'I would gladly know who dares jest with me in such a matter!—Read it, Sir Brian.'

The Templar accordingly read it as follows:—

'I, Wamba, the son of Witless, Jester to a noble and free-born man, Cedric of Rotherwood, called the Saxon,—And I, Gurth, the son of Beowulph, the swineherd'——

'Thou art mad,' said Front-de-Bœuf, interrupting the reader.

'By St Luke, it is so set down,' answered the Templar. Then resuming his task, he went on,—'I, Gurth, the son of Beowulph, swineherd unto the said Cedric, with the assistance of our allies and confederates, who make common cause with us in this our feud, namely, the good knight, called for the present *Le Noir Faineant*, and the stout yeoman, Robert Locksley, called Cleave-the-wand, Do you, Reginald Front-de-Bœuf, and your allies and accomplices whomsoever, to wit, that whereas you have, without cause given or feud declared, wrongfully and by mastery seized upon the person of our lord and master the said Cedric; also upon the person of a noble and freeborn damsel, the Lady Rowena of Hargottstanstede; also upon the person of a noble and freeborn man, Athelstane of Coningsburgh; also upon the persons of certain freeborn men, their *cnichts*; also upon certain serfs, their born bondsmen; also upon a certain Jew, named Isaac of York, together with his daughter, a Jewess, and certain horses and mules: which noble persons, with their *cnichts* and slaves, and also with the horses and mules, Jew and Jewess beforesaid, were all in peace with his majesty, and travelling as liege subjects upon the king's highway; therefore we require and demand that the said noble persons, namely, Cedric of Rotherwood, Rowena of Hargottstandstede, Athelstane of Coningsburgh, with their servants, *cnichts*, and followers, also the horses and mules, Jew and Jewess aforesaid, together with all goods and chattels to them pertaining, be, within an hour after the delivery hereof, delivered to us, or to those whom we shall appoint to receive the same, and that untouched and unharmed in body and goods. Failing of which, we do pronounce to you, that we hold ye as robbers and traitors, and will wager our bodies against ye in battle, siege, or otherwise, and do our utmost to your annoyance and destruction. Wherefore may God have you in his keeping.—Signed by us upon the eve of St Withold's day, under the great trysting oak in the Hart-hill Walk, the above being written by a holy man, Clerk to God, our Lady, and St Dunstan, in the Chapel of Copmanhurst.'

At the bottom of this document was scrawled, in the first place, a rude sketch of a cock's head and comb, with a legend expressing this hieroglyphic to be the sign-manual* of Wamba, son of Witless. Under this respectable emblem stood a cross, stated to be the mark of Gurth, the son of Beowulph. Then was written, in rough bold characters, the words, *Le Noir Faineant*. And, to conclude the whole, an arrow, neatly enough drawn, was described as the mark of the yeoman Locksley.

The knights heard this uncommon document read from end to end, and then gazed upon each other in silent amazement, as being utterly at a loss to know what it could portend. De Bracy was the first to break silence by an uncontrollable fit of laughter, wherein he was joined, though with more moderation, by the Templar. Front-de-Bœuf, on the contrary, seemed impatient of their ill-timed jocularity.

'I give you plain warning,' he said, 'fair sirs, that you had better consult how to bear yourselves under these circumstances, than give way to such misplaced merriment.'

'Front-de-Bœuf has not recovered his temper since his late overthrow,' said De Bracy to the Templar; 'he is cowed at the very idea of a cartel, though it come but from a fool and a swineherd.'

'By St Michael,' answered Front-de-Bœuf, 'I would thou couldst stand the whole brunt of this adventure thyself, De Bracy. These fellows dared not have acted with such inconceivable impudence, had they not been supported by some strong bands. There are enough of outlaws in this forest to resent my protecting the deer. I did but tie one fellow, who was taken redhanded and in the fact, to the horns of a wild stag, which gored him to death in five minutes, and I had as many arrows shot at me as there were launched against yonder target at Ashby.—Here, fellow,' he added, to one of his attendants, 'hast thou sent out to see by what force this precious challenge is to be supported?'

'There are at least two hundred men assembled in the woods,' answered a squire who was in attendance.

'Here is a proper matter!' said Front-de-Bœuf; 'this comes of lending you the use of my castle, that cannot manage your undertaking quietly, but you must bring this nest of hornets about my ears!'

'Of hornets?' said De Bracy; 'of stingless drones rather; a band of lazy knaves, who take to the wood, and destroy the venison rather than labour for their maintenance.'

'Stingless!' replied Front-de-Bœuf; 'fork-headed shafts of a cloth-yard in length,* and these shot within the breadth of a French crown, are sting enough.'

'For shame, Sir Knight!' said the Templar. 'Let us summon our people, and sally forth upon them. One knight—ay, one man-at-arms, were enough for twenty such peasants.'

'Enough, and too much,' said De Bracy; 'I should only be ashamed to couch lance against them.'

'True,' answered Front-de-Bœuf; 'were they black Turks or Moors, Sir Templar, or the craven peasants of France, most valiant De Bracy; but these are English yeomen, over whom we shall have no advantage, save what we may derive from our arms and horses, which will avail us little in the glades of the forest. Sally, saidst thou? we have scarce men enough to defend the castle. The best of mine are at York; so is all your band, De Bracy; and we have scarcely twenty, besides the handful that were engaged in this mad business.'

'Thou dost not fear,' said the Templar, 'that they can assemble in force sufficient to attempt the castle?'

'Not so, Sir Brian,' answered Front-de-Bœuf. 'These outlaws have indeed a daring captain; but without machines, scaling ladders, and experienced leaders, my castle may defy them.'

'Send to thy neighbours,' said the Templar; 'let them assemble their people, and come to the rescue of three knights, besieged by a jester and a swineherd in the baronial castle of Reginald Front-de-Bœuf!'

'You jest, Sir Knight,' answered the baron; 'but to whom should I send?—Malvoisin is by this time at York with his retainers, and so are my other allies; and so should I have been, but for this infernal enterprise.'

'Then send to York, and recall our people,' said De Bracy. 'If they abide the shaking of my standard, or the sight of my Free Companions, I will give them credit for the boldest outlaws ever bent bow in green-wood.'

'And who shall bear such a message?' said Front-de-Bœuf; 'they will beset every path, and rip the errand out of his bosom.—I have it,' he added, after pausing for a moment— 'Sir Templar, thou canst write as well as read, and if we can but find the writing materials of my chaplain, who died a twelvemonth since in the midst of his Christmas carousals'——

'So please ye,' said the squire, who was still in attendance, 'I think old Urfried has them somewhere in keeping, for love of the confessor. He was the last man, I have heard her tell, who ever said aught to her, which man ought in courtesy to address to maid or matron.'

'Go, search them out, Engelred,' said Front-de-Bœuf; 'and

then, Sir Templar, thou shalt return an answer to this bold challenge.'

'I would rather do it at the sword's point than at that of the pen,' said Bois-Guilbert; 'but be it as you will.'

He sat down accordingly, and indited, in the French language, an epistle of the following tenor:—

'Sir Reginald Front-de-Bœuf, with his noble and knightly allies and confederates, receive no defiances at the hands of slaves, bondsmen, or fugitives. If the person calling himself the Black Knight have indeed a claim to the honours of chivalry, he ought to know that he stands degraded by his present association, and has no right to ask reckoning at the hands of good men of noble blood. Touching the prisoners we have made, we do in Christian charity require you to send a man of religion, to receive their confession, and reconcile them with God; since it is our fixed intention to execute them this morning before noon, so that their heads being placed on the battlements, shall show to all men how lightly we esteem those who have bestirred themselves in their rescue. Wherefore, as above, we require you to send a priest to reconcile them to God, in doing which you shall render them the last earthly service.'

This letter being folded, was delivered to the squire, and by him to the messenger who waited without, as the answer to that which he had brought.

The yeoman having thus accomplished his mission, returned to the head-quarters of the allies, which were for the present established under a venerable oak-tree, about three arrow-flights distant from the castle. Here Wamba and Gurth, with their allies the Black Knight and Locksley, and the jovial hermit, awaited with impatience an answer to their summons. Around, and at a distance from them, were seen many a bold yeoman, whose silvan dress and weatherbeaten countenances showed the ordinary nature of their occupation. More than two hundred had already assembled, and others were fast coming in. Those whom they obeyed as leaders were only distinguished from the others by a feather in the cap, their dress, arms, and equipments being in all other respects the same.

Besides these bands, a less orderly and a worse armed force, consisting of the Saxon inhabitants of the neighbouring township, as well as many bondsmen and servants from Cedric's extensive estate, had already arrived, for the purpose of assisting in his rescue. Few of these were armed otherwise than with such rustic weapons as necessity sometimes converts to military purposes. Boar-spears, scythes, flails, and the like, were their chief arms; for the Normans, with the usual policy of conquerors, were jealous of permitting to the vanquished Saxons the possession or the use of swords and spears. These circumstances rendered the assistance of the Saxons far from being so formidable to the besieged, as the strength of the men themselves, their superior numbers, and the animation inspired by a just cause, might otherwise well have made them. It was to the leaders of this motley army that the letter of the Templar was now delivered.

Reference was at first made to the chaplain for an exposition of its contents.

'By the crook of St Dunstan,' said that worthy ecclesiastic, 'which hath brought more sheep within the sheepfold than the crook of e'er another saint in Paradise, I swear that I cannot expound unto you this jargon, which, whether it be French or Arabic, is beyond my guess.'

He then gave the letter to Gurth, who shook his head gruffly, and passed it to Wamba. The Jester looked at each of the four corners of the paper with such a grin of affected intelligence as a monkey is apt to assume upon similar occasions, then cut a caper, and gave the letter to Locksley.

'If the long letters were bows, and the short letters broad arrows, I might know something of the matter,' said the brave yeoman; 'but as the matter stands, the meaning is as safe, for me, as the stag that's at twelve miles distance.'

'I must be clerk, then,' said the Black Knight; and taking the letter from Locksley, he first read it over to himself, and then explained the meaning in Saxon to his confederates.

'Execute the noble Cedric!' exclaimed Wamba; 'by the rood, thou must be mistaken, Sir Knight.'

'Not I, my worthy friend,' replied the knight, 'I have explained the words as they are here set down.'

'Then, by St Thomas of Canterbury,' replied Gurth, 'we will have the castle, should we tear it down with our hands!'

'We have nothing else to tear it with,' replied Wamba; 'but mine are scarce fit to make mammocks* of freestone and mortar.'

''Tis but a contrivance to gain time,' said Locksley; 'they dare not do a deed for which I could exact a fearful penalty.'

'I would,' said the Black Knight, 'there were some one among us who could obtain admission into the castle, and discover how the case stands with the besieged. Methinks, as they require a confessor to be sent, this holy hermit might at once exercise his pious vocation, and procure us the information we desire.'

'A plague on thee, and thy advice!' said the pious hermit; 'I tell thee, Sir Slothful Knight, that when I doff my friar's frock, my priesthood, my sanctity, my very Latin, are put off along with it; and when in my green jerkin, I can better kill twenty deer than confess one Christian.'

'I fear,' said the Black Knight, 'I fear greatly, there is no one here that is qualified to take upon him, for the nonce, this same character of father confessor?'

All looked on each other, and were silent.

'I see,' said Wamba, after a short pause, 'that the fool must be still the fool, and put his neck in the venture which wise men shrink from. You must know, my dear cousins and countrymen, that I wore russet before I wore motley, and was bred to be a friar, until a brain-fever came upon me and left me just wit enough to be a fool. I trust, with the assistance of the good hermit's frock, together with the priesthood, sanctity, and learning which are stitched into the cowl of it, I shall be found qualified to administer both worldly and ghostly comfort to our worthy master Cedric, and his companions in adversity.'

'Hath he sense enough, thinkst thou?' said the Black Knight, addressing Gurth.

'I know not,' said Gurth; 'but if he hath not, it will be the first time he hath wanted wit to turn his folly to account.'

'On with the frock, then, good fellow,' quoth the Knight, 'and let thy master send us an account of their situation within the castle. Their numbers must be few, and it is five to one they may be accessible by a sudden and bold attack. Time wears—away with thee.'

'And, in the meantime,' said Locksley, 'we will beset the place so closely, that not so much as a fly shall carry news from thence.

So that, my good friend,' he continued, addressing Wamba, 'thou mayst assure these tyrants, that whatever violence they exercise on the persons of their prisoners, shall be most severely repaid upon their own.'

'*Pax vobiscum*,'* said Wamba, who was now muffled in his religious disguise.

And so saying, he imitated the solemn and stately deportment of a friar, and departed to execute his mission.

CHAPTER XXVI

The hottest horse will oft be cool,
    The dullest will show fire;
The friar will often play the fool,
    The fool will play the friar.

*Old Song**

WHEN the Jester, arrayed in the cowl and frock of the hermit, and having his knotted cord twisted round his middle, stood before the portal of the castle of Front-de-Bœuf, the warder demanded of him his name and errand.

'*Pax vobiscum*,' answered the Jester, 'I am a poor brother of the Order of St Francis,* who come hither to do my office to certain unhappy prisoners now secured within this castle.'

'Thou art a bold friar,' said the warder, 'to come hither, where, saving our own drunken confessor, a cock of thy feather hath not crowed these twenty years.'

'Yet I pray thee, do mine errand to the lord of the castle,' answered the pretended friar; 'trust me it will find good acceptance with him, and the cock shall crow, that the whole castle shall hear him.'

'Gramercy,' said the warder; 'but if I come to shame for leaving my post upon thine errand, I will try whether a friar's grey gown be proof against a grey-goose shaft.'*

With this threat he left his turret, and carried to the hall of the castle his unwonted intelligence, that a holy friar stood before the gate and demanded instant admission. With no small wonder he received his master's commands to admit the holy man immediately; and, having previously manned the entrance to guard against surprise, he obeyed, without further scruple, the commands which he had received. The harebrained self-conceit which had emboldened Wamba to undertake this dangerous office, was scarce sufficient to support him when he found himself in the presence of a man so dreadful, and so much dreaded, as Reginald Front-de-Bœuf, and he brought out his *pax vobiscum*, to which he, in a good measure, trusted for supporting his character, with more anxiety and hesitation than had hitherto accompanied it. But Front-de-Bœuf was accustomed to see men of all ranks tremble in his presence, so that the timidity of the supposed father did not give him any cause of suspicion. 'Who and whence art thou, priest?' said he.

'*Pax vobiscum*,' reiterated the Jester, 'I am a poor servant of St Francis, who, travelling through this wilderness, have fallen among thieves, (as Scripture hath it,) *quidam viator incidit in latrones*,* which thieves have sent me unto this castle in order to do my ghostly office on two persons condemned by your honourable justice.'

'Ay, right,' answered Front-de-Bœuf; 'and canst thou tell me, holy father, the number of those banditti?'

'Gallant sir,' answered the Jester, '*nomen illis legio*,* their name is legion.'

'Tell me in plain terms what numbers there are, or, priest, thy cloak and cord will ill protect thee.'

'Alas!' said the supposed friar, '*cor meum eructavit*,* that is to say, I was like to burst with fear! but I conceive they may be— what of yeomen—what of commons, at least five hundred men.'

'What!' said the Templar, who came into the hall that moment, 'muster the wasps so thick here? it is time to stifle such a mischievous brood.' Then taking Front-de-Bœuf aside, 'Knowest thou the priest?'

'He is a stranger from a distant convent,' said Front-de-Bœuf; 'I know him not.'

'Then trust him not with thy purpose in words,' answered the Templar. 'Let him carry a written order to De Bracy's company of Free Companions, to repair instantly to their master's aid. In the meantime, and that the shaveling may suspect nothing, permit him to go freely about his task of preparing these Saxon hogs for the slaughter-house.'

'It shall be so,' said Front-de-Bœuf. And he forthwith appointed a domestic to conduct Wamba to the apartment where Cedric and Athelstane were confined.

The impatience of Cedric had been rather enhanced than diminished by his confinement. He walked from one end of the hall to the other, with the attitude of one who advances to charge an enemy, or to storm the breach of a beleaguered place, sometimes ejaculating to himself, sometimes addressing Athelstane, who stoutly and stoically awaited the issue of the adventure, digesting, in the meantime, with great composure, the liberal meal which he had made at noon, and not greatly interesting himself about the duration of his captivity, which he concluded, would, like all earthly evils, find an end in Heaven's good time.

'*Pax vobiscum*,' said the Jester, entering the apartment; 'the blessing of St Dunstan, St Dennis, St Duthoc, and all other saints whatsoever, be upon ye and about ye.'

'Enter freely,' answered Cedric to the supposed friar; 'with what intent art thou come hither?'

'To bid you prepare yourselves for death,' answered the Jester.

'It is impossible!' replied Cedric, starting. 'Fearless and wicked as they are, they dare not attempt such open and gratu-itous cruelty!'

'Alas!' said the Jester, 'to restrain them by their sense of humanity, is the same as to stop a runaway horse with a bridle of silk thread. Bethink thee, therefore, noble Cedric, and you also, gallant Athelstane, what crimes you have committed in the flesh; for this very day will ye be called to answer at a higher tribunal.'*

'Hearest thou this, Athelstane?' said Cedric; 'we must rouse up our hearts to this last action, since better it is we should die like men, than live like slaves.'

'I am ready,' answered Athelstane, 'to stand the worst of their malice, and shall walk to my death with as much composure as ever I did to my dinner.'

'Let us then unto our holy gear, father,' said Cedric.

'Wait yet a moment, good uncle,' said the Jester, in his natural tone; 'better look long before you leap in the dark.'*

'By my faith,' said Cedric, 'I should know that voice!'

'It is that of your trusty slave and jester,' answered Wamba, throwing back his cowl. 'Had you taken a fool's advice formerly, you would not have been here at all. Take a fool's advice now, and you will not be here long.'

'How mean'st thou, knave?' answered the Saxon.

'Even thus,' replied Wamba; 'take thou this frock and cord, which are all the orders I ever had, and march quietly out of the castle, leaving me your cloak and girdle to take the long leap in thy stead.'

'Leave thee in my stead!' said Cedric, astonished at the proposal; 'why, they would hang thee, my poor knave.'

'E'en let them do as they are permitted,' said Wamba; 'I trust—no disparagement to your birth—that the son of Witless may hang in a chain with as much gravity as the chain hung upon his ancestor the alderman.'

'Well, Wamba,' answered Cedric, 'for one thing will I grant thy request. And that is, if thou wilt make the exchange of garments with Lord Athelstane instead of me.'

'No, by St Dunstan,' answered Wamba; 'there were little reason in that. Good right there is, that the son of Witless should suffer to save the son of Hereward; but little wisdom there were in his dying for the benefit of one whose fathers were strangers to his.'

'Villain,' said Cedric, 'the fathers of Athelstane were monarchs of England!'

'They might be whomsoever they pleased,' replied Wamba; 'but my neck stands too straight upon my shoulders to have it twisted for their sake. Wherefore, good my master, either take my proffer yourself, or suffer me to leave this dungeon as free as I entered.'

'Let the old tree wither,' continued Cedric, 'so the stately hope of the forest be preserved. Save the noble Athelstane, my trusty Wamba! it is the duty of each who has Saxon blood in his veins. Thou and I will abide together the utmost rage of our injurious oppressors, while he, free and safe, shall arouse the awakened spirits of our countrymen to avenge us.'

'Not so, father Cedric,' said Athelstane, grasping his hand, — for, when roused to think or act, his deeds and sentiments were not unbecoming his high race—'Not so,' he continued; 'I would rather remain in this hall a week without food save the prisoner's stinted loaf, or drink save the prisoner's measure of water, than embrace the opportunity to escape which the slave's untaught kindness has purveyed for his master.'

'You are called wise men, sirs,' said the Jester, 'and I a crazed fool; but, uncle Cedric, and cousin Athelstane, the fool shall decide this controversy for ye, and save ye the trouble of strain-

ing courtesies any farther. I am like John-a-Duck's mare, that
will let no man mount her but John-a-Duck.* I came to save my
master, and if he will not consent—basta*—I can but go away
home again. Kind service cannot be chucked from hand to hand
like a shuttlecock or stool-ball.* I'll hang for no man but my own
born master.'

'Go, then, noble Cedric,' said Athelstane, 'neglect not this
opportunity. Your presence without may encourage friends to
our rescue—your remaining here would ruin us all.'

'And is there any prospect, then, of rescue from without?' said
Cedric, looking to the Jester.

'Prospect, indeed!' echoed Wamba; 'let me tell you, when
you fill my cloak, you are wrapped in a general's cassock. Five
hundred men are there without, and I was this morning one
of their chief leaders. My fool's cap was a casque, and my
bauble a truncheon. Well, we shall see what good they will
make by exchanging a fool for a wise man. Truly, I fear they
will lose in valour what they may gain in discretion. And so
farewell, master, and be kind to poor Gurth and his dog Fangs;
and let my cockscomb hang in the hall at Rotherwood,
in memory that I flung away my life for my master, like a
faithful————fool.'

The last word came out with a sort of double expression,
betwixt jest and earnest. The tears stood in Cedric's eyes.

'Thy memory shall be preserved,' he said, 'while fidelity and
affection have honour upon earth! But that I trust I shall find the
means of saving Rowena, and thee, Athelstane, and thee also, my
poor Wamba, thou shouldst not overbear me in this matter.'

The exchange of dress was now accomplished, when a sudden
doubt struck Cedric.

'I know no language,' he said, 'but my own, and a few words
of their mincing Norman. How shall I bear myself like a reverend brother?'

'The spell lies in two words,' replied Wamba—'*Pax vobiscum*
will answer all queries. If you go or come, eat or drink, bless or
ban, *Pax vobiscum* carries you through it all. It is as useful to a
friar as a broomstick to a witch, or a wand to a conjurer. Speak it
but thus, in a deep grave tone,—*Pax vobiscum!*—it is irresistible—Watch and ward,* knight and squire, foot and horse, it

acts as a charm upon them all. I think, if they bring me out to be hanged to-morrow, as is much to be doubted they may, I will try its weight upon the finisher of the sentence.'

'If such prove the case,' said his master, 'my religious orders are soon taken—*Pax vobiscum*. I trust I shall remember the password.—Noble Athelstane, farewell; and farewell, my poor boy, whose heart might make amends for a weaker head—I will save you, or return and die with you. The royal blood of our Saxon kings shall not be spilt while mine beats in my veins; nor shall one hair fall from the head of the kind knave who risked himself for his master, if Cedric's peril can prevent it.—Farewell.'

'Farewell, noble Cedric,' said Athelstane; 'remember it is the true part of a friar to accept refreshment, if you are offered any.'

'Farewell, uncle,' added Wamba; 'and remember *Pax vobiscum*.'

Thus exhorted, Cedric sallied forth upon his expedition; and it was not long ere he had occasion to try the force of that spell which his Jester had recommended as omnipotent. In a low-arched and dusky passage, by which he endeavoured to work his way to the hall of the castle, he was interrupted by a female form.

'*Pax vobiscum!*' said the pseudo friar, and was endeavouring to hurry past, when a soft voice replied, '*Et vobis—quæso, domine reverendissime, pro misericordia vestra.*'*

'I am somewhat deaf,' replied Cedric, in good Saxon, and at the same time muttered to himself, 'A curse on the fool and his *Pax vobiscum!* I have lost my javelin at the first cast.'

It was, however, no unusual thing for a priest of those days to be deaf of his Latin ear, and this the person who now addressed Cedric knew full well.

'I pray you of dear love, reverend father,' she replied in his own language, 'that you will deign to visit with your ghostly comfort a wounded prisoner of this castle, and have such compassion upon him and us as thy holy office teaches—Never shall good deed so highly advantage thy convent.'

'Daughter,' answered Cedric, much embarrassed, 'my time in this castle will not permit me to exercise the duties of mine office—I must presently forth—there is life and death upon my speed.'

'Yet, father, let me entreat you by the vow you have taken on you,' replied the suppliant, 'not to leave the oppressed and endangered without counsel or succour.'

'May the fiend fly away with me, and leave me in Ifrin* with the souls of Odin and of Thor!' answered Cedric impatiently, and would probably have proceeded in the same tone of total departure from his spiritual character, when the colloquy was interrupted by the harsh voice of Urfried, the old crone of the turret.

'How, minion,' said she to the female speaker, 'is this the manner in which you requite the kindness which permitted thee to leave thy prison-cell yonder?—Puttest thou the reverend man to use ungracious language to free himself from the importunities of a Jewess?'

'A Jewess!' said Cedric, availing himself of the information to get clear of their interruption,—'Let me pass, woman! stop me not at your peril. I am fresh from my holy office, and would avoid pollution.'

'Come this way, father,' said the old hag, 'thou art a stranger in this castle, and canst not leave it without a guide. Come hither, for I would speak with thee.—And you, daughter of an accursed race, go to the sick man's chamber, and tend him until my return; and woe betide you if you again quit it without my permission!'

Rebecca retreated. Her importunities had prevailed upon Urfried to suffer her to quit the turret, and Urfried had employed her services where she herself would most gladly have paid them, by the bedside of the wounded Ivanhoe. With an understanding awake to their dangerous situation, and prompt to avail herself of each means of safety which occurred, Rebecca had hoped something from the presence of a man of religion, who, she learned from Urfried, had penetrated into this godless castle. She watched the return of the supposed ecclesiastic, with the purpose of addressing him, and interesting him in favour of the prisoners; with what imperfect success the reader has been just acquainted.

CHAPTER XXVII

Fond wretch! and what canst thou relate,
   But deeds of sorrow, shame, and sin?
Thy deeds are proved—thou know'st thy fate;
   But come, thy tale—begin—begin.
    .   /   .   .

But I have griefs of other kind,
   Troubles and sorrows more severe;
Give me to ease my tortured mind,
   Lend to my woes a patient ear;
And let me, if I may not find
   A friend to help—find one to hear.

*Crabbe's Hall of Justice**

WHEN Urfried had with clamours and menaces driven Rebecca back to the apartment from which she had sallied, she proceeded to conduct the unwilling Cedric into a small apartment, the door of which she heedfully secured. Then fetching from a cupboard a stoup of wine and two flagons, she placed them on the table, and said in a tone rather asserting a fact than asking a question, 'Thou art Saxon, father—Deny it not,' she continued, observing that Cedric hastened not to reply; 'the sounds of my native language are sweet to mine ears, though seldom heard save from the tongues of the wretched and degraded serfs on whom the proud Normans impose the meanest drudgery of this dwelling. Thou art a Saxon, father—a Saxon, and, save as thou art a servant of God, a freeman.—Thine accents are sweet in mine ear.'

'Do not Saxon priests visit this castle, then?' replied Cedric; 'it were, methinks, their duty to comfort the outcast and oppressed children of the soil.'

'They come not—or if they come, they better love to revel at the boards of their conquerors,' answered Urfried, 'than to hear the groans of their countryment—so, at least, report speaks of them—of myself I can say little. This castle, for ten years, has opened to no priest save the debauched Norman chaplain who partook the nightly revels of Front-de-Bœuf, and he has been

long gone to render an account of his stewardship.*—But thou
art a Saxon—a Saxon priest, and I have one question to ask of
thee.'

'I am a Saxon,' answered Cedric, 'but unworthy, surely, of
the name of priest. Let me begone on my way—I swear I will
return, or send one of our fathers more worthy to hear your
confession.'

'Stay yet a while,' said Urfried; 'the accents of the voice which
thou hearest now will soon be choked with the cold earth, and I
would not descend to it like the beast I have lived. But wine must
give me strength to tell the horrors of my tale.' She poured out
a cup, and drank it with a frightful avidity, which seemed desirous of draining the last drop in the goblet. 'It stupifies,' she said,
looking upwards as she finished her draught, 'but it cannot
cheer—Partake it, father, if you would hear my tale without
sinking down upon the pavement.' Cedric would have avoided
pledging her in this ominous conviviality, but the sign which she
made to him expressed impatience and despair. He complied
with her request, and answered her challenge in a large wine-
cup; she then proceeded with her story, as if appeased by his
complaisance.

'I was not born,' she said, 'father, the wretch that thou now
seest me. I was free, was happy, was honoured, loved, and was
beloved. I am now a slave, miserable and degraded—the sport of
my masters' passions while I had yet beauty—the object of their
contempt, scorn, and hatred, since it has passed away. Dost thou
wonder, father, that I should hate mankind, and, above all, the
race that has wrought this change in me? Can the wrinkled
decrepit hag before thee, whose wrath must vent itself in impotent curses, forget she was once the daughter of the noble Thane
of Torquilstone, before whose frown a thousand vassals
trembled?'

'Thou the daughter of Torquil Wolfganger!' said Cedric, re-
coiling as he spoke; 'thou—thou—the daughter of that noble
Saxon, my father's friend and companion in arms!'

'Thy father's friend!' echoed Urfried; 'then Cedric called the
Saxon stands before me, for the noble Hereward of Rotherwood
had but one son, whose name is well known among his countrymen. But if thou art Cedric of Rotherwood, why this religious

dress?—hast thou too despaired of saving thy country, and sought refuge from oppression in the shade of the convent?'

'It matters not who I am,' said Cedric; 'proceed, unhappy woman, with thy tale of horror and guilt!—Guilt there must be—there is guilt even in thy living to tell it.'

'There is—there is,' answered the wretched woman, 'deep, black, damning guilt—guilt, that lies like a load at my breast—guilt, that all the penitential fires of hereafter cannot cleanse.—Yes, in these halls, stained with the noble and pure blood of my father and my brethren—in these very halls, to have lived the paramour of their murderer, the slave at once and the partaker of his pleasures, was to render every breath which I drew of vital air, a crime and a curse.'

'Wretched woman!' exclaimed Cedric. 'And while the friends of thy father—while each true Saxon heart, as it breathed a requiem for his soul, and those of his valiant sons, forgot not in their prayers the murdered Ulrica—while all mourned and honoured the dead, thou hast lived to merit our hate and execration—lived to unite thyself with the vile tyrant who murdered thy nearest and dearest—who shed the blood of infancy, rather than a male of the noble house of Torquil Wolfganger should survive—with him hast thou lived to unite thyself, and in the bands of lawless love!'

'In lawless bands, indeed, but not in those of love!' answered the hag; 'love will sooner visit the regions of eternal doom, than those unhallowed vaults.—No, with that at least I cannot reproach myself—hatred to Front-de-Bœuf and his race governed my soul most deeply, even in the hour of his guilty endearments.'

'You hated him, and yet you lived,' replied Cedric; 'wretch! was there no poniard—no knife—no bodkin!*—Well was it for thee, since thou didst prize such an existence, that the secrets of a Norman castle are like those of the grave. For had I but dreamed of the daughter of Torquil living in foul communion with the murderer of her father, the sword of a true Saxon had found thee out even in the arms of thy paramour!'

'Wouldst thou indeed have done this justice to the name of Torquil?' said Ulrica, for we may now lay aside her assumed name of Urfried; 'thou art then the true Saxon report speaks thee! for even within these accursed walls, where, as thou well sayest, guilt shrouds itself in inscrutable mystery, even there has the name of Cedric been sounded—and I, wretched and degraded, have rejoiced to think that there yet breathed an avenger of our unhappy nation.—I also have had my hours of vengeance—I have fomented the quarrels of our foes, and heated drunken revelry into murderous broil—I have seen their blood flow—I have heard their dying groans!—Look on me, Cedric—are there not still left on this foul and faded face some traces of the features of Torquil?'

'Ask me not of them, Ulrica,' replied Cedric, in a tone of grief mixed with abhorrence; 'these traces form such a resemblance as arises from the grave of the dead, when a fiend has animated the lifeless corpse.'

'Be it so,' answered Ulrica; 'yet wore these fiendish features the mask of a spirit of light when they were able to set at variance the elder Front-de-Bœuf and his son Reginald! The darkness of hell should hide what followed, but revenge must lift the veil, and darkly intimate what it would raise the dead to speak aloud. Long had the smouldering fire of discord glowed between the tyrant father and his savage son—long had I nursed, in secret, the unnatural hatred—it blazed forth in an hour of drunken wassail, and at his own board fell my oppressor by the hand of his own son—such are the secrets these vaults conceal!—Rend asunder, ye accursed arches,' she added, looking up towards the roof, 'and bury in your fall all who are conscious of the hideous mystery!'

'And thou, creature of guilt and misery,' said Cedric, 'what became thy lot on the death of thy ravisher?'

'Guess it, but ask it not.—Here—here I dwelt, till age, premature age, has stamped its ghastly features on my countenance—scorned and insulted where I was once obeyed, and compelled to bound the revenge which had once such ample scope, to the efforts of petty malice of a discontented menial, or the vain or unheeded curses of an impotent hag—condemned to hear from my lonely turret the sounds of revelry in which I once partook, or the shrieks and groans of new victims of oppression.'

'Ulrica,' said Cedric, 'with a heart which still, I fear, regrets the lost reward of thy crimes, as much as the deeds by which thou didst acquire that meed, how didst thou dare to address thee to one who wears this robe? Consider, unhappy woman, what could the sainted Edward himself do for thee, were he here in bodily presence? The royal Confessor was endowed by Heaven with power to cleanse the ulcers of the body,* but only God himself can cure the leprosy of the soul.'

'Yet, turn not from me, stern prophet of wrath,' she exclaimed, 'but tell me, if thou canst, in what shall terminate these new and awful feelings that burst on my solitude—Why do deeds, long since done, rise before me in new and irresistible horrors? What fate is prepared beyond the grave for her, to whom God has assigned on earth a lot of such unspeakable wretchedness? Better had I turn to Woden, Hertha, and Zernebock—to Mista, and to Skogula, the Gods of our yet unbaptized ancestors,* than endure the dreadful anticipations which have of late haunted my waking and my sleeping hours!'

'I am no priest,' said Cedric, turning with disgust from this miserable picture of guilt, wretchedness, and despair; 'I am no priest, though I wear a priest's garment.'

'Priest or layman,' answered Ulrica, 'thou art the first I have seen for twenty years, by whom God was feared or man regarded; and dost thou bid me despair?'

'I bid thee repent,' said Cedric. 'Seek to prayer and penance, and mayest thou find acceptance! But I cannot, I will not, longer abide with thee.'

'Stay yet a moment!' said Ulrica; 'leave me not now, son of my father's friend, lest the demon who has governed my life should tempt me to avenge myself of thy hard-hearted scorn—Thinkest thou, if Front-de-Bœuf found Cedric the Saxon in his castle, in such a disguise, that thy life would be a long one?—Already his eye has been upon thee like a falcon on his prey.'

'And be it so,' said Cedric; 'and let him tear me with beak and talons, ere my tongue say one word which my heart doth not warrant. I will die a Saxon—true in word, open in deed—I bid thee avaunt!*—touch me not, stay me not!—The sight of Front-de-Bœuf himself is less odious to me than thou, degraded and degenerate as thou art.'

'Be it so,' said Ulrica, no longer interrupting him; 'go thy way, and forget, in the insolence of thy superiority, that the wretch before thee is the daughter of thy father's friend.—Go thy way—if I am separated from mankind by my sufferings—separated from those whose aid I might most justly expect—not less will I be separated from them in my revenge!—No man shall aid me, but the ears of all men shall tingle to hear of the deed which I shall dare to do!—Farewell!—thy scorn has burst the last tie which seemed yet to unite me to my kind—a thought that my woes might claim the compassion of my people.'

'Ulrica,' said Cedric, softened by this appeal, 'hast thou borne up and endured to live through so much guilt and so much misery, and wilt thou now yield to despair when thine eyes are opened to thy crimes, and when repentance were thy fitter occupation?'

'Cedric,' answered Ulrica, 'thou little knowest the human heart. To act as I have acted, to think as I have thought, requires the maddening love of pleasure, mingled with the keen appetite of revenge, the proud consciousness of power; draughts too intoxicating for the human heart to bear, and yet retain the power to prevent. Their force has long passed away—Age has no pleasures, wrinkles have no influence, revenge itself dies away in impotent curses. Then comes remorse, with all its vipers, mixed with vain regrets for the past, and despair for the furture!—Then, when all other strong impulses have ceased, we become like the fiends in hell, who may feel remorse, but never repentance.—But thy words have awakened a new soul within me—Well hast thou said, all is possible for those who dare to die!—Thou hast shown me the means of revenge, and be assured I will embrace them. It has hitherto shared this wasted bosom with other and with rival passions—henceforward it shall possess me wholly, and thou thyself shalt say, that, whatever was the life of Ulrica, her death well became the daughter of the noble Torquil. There is a force without beleaguering this accursed castle—hasten to lead them to the attack, and when thou shalt see a red flag wave from the turret on the eastern angle of the donjon,* press the Normans hard—they will then have enough to do within, and you may win the wall in spite both of bow and mangonel.*—Begone, I pray thee—follow thine own fate, and leave me to mine.'

Cedric would have enquired farther into the purpose which

she thus darkly announced, but the stern voice of Front-de-Bœuf was heard, exclaiming, 'Where tarries this loitering priest? By the scallop-shell of Compostella, I will make a martyr of him, if he loiters here to hatch treason among my domestics!'

'What a true prophet,' said Ulrica, 'is an evil conscience! But heed him not—out and to thy people—Cry your Saxon onslaught, and let them sing their war-song of Rollo,* if they will; vengeance shall bear a burden* to it.'

As she thus spoke, she vanished through a private door, and Reginald Front-de-Bœuf entered the apartment. Cedric, with some difficulty, compelled himself to make obeisance to the haughty Baron, who returned his courtesy with a slight inclination of the head.

'Thy penitents, father, have made a long shrift—it is the better for them, since it is the last they shall ever make. Hast thou prepared them for death?'

'I found them,' said Cedric, in such French as he could command, 'expecting the worst, from the moment they knew into whose power they had fallen.'

'How now, Sir Friar,' replied Front-de-Bœuf, 'thy speech, methinks, smacks of a Saxon tongue?'

'I was bred in the convent of St Withold of Burton,' answered Cedric.

'Ay?' said the Baron; 'it had been better for thee to have been a Norman, and better for my purpose too; but need has no choice of messengers. That St Withold's of Burton is a howlet's nest worth the harrying. The day will soon come that the frock shall protect the Saxon as little as the mail-coat.'

'God's will be done,' said Cedric, in a voice tremulous with passion, which Front-de-Bœuf imputed to fear.

'I see,' said he, 'thou dreamest already that our men-at-arms are in thy refectory and thy ale-vaults. But do me one cast of thy holy office, and, come what list of others, thou shalt sleep as safe in thy cell as a snail within his shell of proof.'

'Speak your commands,' said Cedric, with suppressed emotion.

'Follow me through this passage, then, that I may dismiss thee by the postern.'

And as he strode on his way before the supposed friar, Front-de-Bœuf thus schooled him in the part which he desired he should act.

'Thou seest, Sir Friar, yon herd of Saxon swine, who have dared to environ this castle of Torquilstone—Tell them whatever thou hast a mind of the weakness of this fortalice, or aught else that can detain them before it for twenty-four hours. Meantime bear thou this scroll—But soft—canst read, Sir Priest?'

'Not a jot I,' answered Cedric, 'save on my breviary; and then I know the characters, because I have the holy service by heart, praised be Our Lady and St Withold!'

'The fitter messenger for my purpose.—Carry thou this scroll to the castle of Philip de Malvoisin; say it cometh from me, and is written by the Templar Brian de Bois-Guilbert, and that I pray him to send it to York with all the speed man and horse can make. Meanwhile, tell him to doubt nothing, he shall find us whole and sound behind our battlement—Shame on it, that we should be compelled to hide thus by a pack of runagates, who are wont to fly even at the flash of our pennons and the tramp of our horses! I say to thee, priest, contrive some cast of thine art to keep the knaves where they are, until our friends bring up their lances. My vengeance is awake, and she is a falcon that slumbers not till she has been gorged.'

'By my patron saint,' said Cedric, with deeper energy than became his character, 'and by every saint who has lived and died in England, your commands shall be obeyed! Not a Saxon shall stir from before these walls, if I have art and influence to detain them there.'

'Ha!' said Front-de-Bœuf, 'thou changest thy tone, Sir Priest, and speakest brief and bold, as if thy heart were in the slaughter of the Saxon herd; and yet thou art thyself of kindred to the swine?'

Cedric was no ready practiser of the art of dissimulation, and would at this moment have been much the better of a hint from Wamba's more fertile brain. But necessity, according to the ancient proverb, sharpens invention, and he muttered something under his cowl concerning the men in question being excommunicated outlaws both to church and to kingdom.

'*Despardieux*,' answered Front-de-Bœuf, 'thou hast spoken

the very truth—I forgot that the knaves can strip a fat abbot, as well as if they had been born south of yonder salt channel. Was it not he of St Ives whom they tied to an oak-tree, and compelled to sing a mass while they were rifling his mails and his wallets?*—No, by our Lady—that jest was played by Gualtier of Middleton, one of our own companions-at-arms. But they were Saxons who robbed the chapel at St Bees of cup, candlestick, and chalice, were they not?'

'They were godless men,' answered Cedric.

'Ay, and they drank out all the good wine and ale that lay in store for many a secret carousal, when ye pretend ye are but busied with vigils and primes!—Priest, thou art bound to revenge such sacrilege.'

'I am indeed bound to vengeance,' murmured Cedric; 'Saint Withold knows my heart.'

Front-de-Bœuf, in the meanwhile, led the way to a postern, where, passing the moat on a single plank, they reached a small barbican, or exterior defence, which communicated with the open field by a well-fortified sallyport.

'Begone, then; and if thou wilt do mine errand, and if thou return hither when it is done, thou shalt see Saxon flesh cheap as ever was hog's in the shambles of Sheffield. And, hark thee, thou seemest to be a jolly confessor—come hither after the onslaught, and thou shalt have as much Malvoisie as would drench thy whole convent.'

'Assuredly we shall meet again,' answered Cedric.

'Something in hand the whilst,' continued the Norman; and, as they parted at the postern door, he thrust into Cedric's reluctant hand a gold byzant, adding, 'Remember, I will flay off both cowl and skin, if thou failest in thy purpose.'

'And full leave will I give thee to do both,' answered Cedric, leaving the postern, and striding forth over the free field with a joyful step, 'if, when we meet next, I deserve not better at thine hand.'—Turning then back towards the castle, he threw the piece of gold towards the donor, exclaiming at the same time, 'False Norman, thy money perish with thee!'

Front-de-Bœuf heard the words imperfectly, but the action was suspicious—'Archers,' he called to the warders on the outward battlements, 'send me an arrow through yon monk's frock!—yet stay,' he said, as his retainers were bending their bows, 'it avails not—we must thus far trust him since we have no better shift. I think he dares not betray me—at the worst I can but treat with these Saxon dogs whom I have safe in kennel.—Ho! Giles jailor, let them bring Cedric of Rotherwood before me, and the other churl, his companion—him I mean of Coningsburgh—Athelstane there, or what call they him? Their very names are an encumbrance to a Norman knight's mouth, and have, as it were, a flavour of bacon—Give me a stoup of wine, as jolly Prince John said, that I may wash away the relish—place it in the armoury, and thither lead the prisoners.'

His commands were obeyed; and, upon entering that Gothic apartment, hung with many spoils won by his own valour and that of his father, he found a flagon of wine on the massive oaken table, and the two Saxon captives under the guard of four of his dependants. Front-de-Bœuf took a long draught of wine, and then addressed his prisoners;—for the manner in which Wamba drew the cap over his face, the change of dress, the gloomy and broken light, and the Baron's imperfect acquaintance with the features of Cedric, (who avoided his Norman neighbours, and seldom stirred beyond his own domains,) prevented him from discovering that the most important of his captives had made his escape.

'Gallants of England,' said Front-de-Bœuf, 'how relish ye your entertainment at Torquilstone?—Are ye yet aware what your *surquedy* and *outrecuidance*[29] merit, for scoffing at the entertainment of a prince of the House of Anjou?—Have ye forgotten how ye requited the unmerited hospitality of the royal John? By God and St Dennis,* an ye pay not the richer ransom, I will hang ye up by the feet from the iron bars of these windows, till the kites and hooded crows have made skeletons of you!—Speak out, ye Saxon dogs—what bid ye for your worthless lives?—How say you, you of Rotherwood?'

'Not a doit* I,' answered poor Wamba—'and for hanging up by the feet, my brain has been topsy-turvy, they say, ever since the biggin was bound first round my head;* so turning me upside down may peradventure restore it again.'

'Saint Genevieve!'* said Front-de-Bœuf, 'what have we got here?'

And with the back of his hand he struck Cedric's cap from the head of the Jester, and throwing open his collar, discovered the fatal badge of servitude, the silver collar round his neck.

'Giles—Clement—dogs and varlets!' exclaimed the furious Norman, 'what have you brought me here?'

'I think I can tell you,' said De Bracy, who just entered the apartment. 'This is Cedric's clown, who fought so manful a skirmish with Isaac of York about a question of precedence.'

'I shall settle it for them both,' replied Front-de-Bœuf; 'they shall hang on the same gallows, unless his master and this boar of Coningsburgh will pay well for their lives. Their wealth is the least they can surrender; they must also carry off with them the swarms that are besetting the castle, subscribe a surrender of their pretended immunities, and live under us as serfs and vassals; too happy if, in the new world that is about to begin, we leave them the breath of their nostrils.—Go,' said he to two of his attendants, 'fetch me the right Cedric hither, and I pardon your error for once; the rather that you but mistook a fool for a Saxon franklin.'

'Ay, but,' said Wamba, 'your chivalrous excellency will find there are more fools than franklins among us.'

'What means the knave?' said Front-de-Bœuf, looking towards his followers, who, lingering and loath, faltered forth their belief, that if this were not Cedric who was there in presence, they knew not what was become of him.

'Saints of Heaven!' exclaimed De Bracy, 'he must have escaped in the monk's garments!'

'Fiends of hell!' echoed Front-de-Bœuf, 'it was then the boar of Rotherwood whom I ushered to the postern, and dismissed with my own hands!—And thou,' he said to Wamba, 'whose folly could overreach the wisdom of idiots yet more gross than thyself—I will give thee holy orders—I will shave thy crown for thee!—Here, let them tear the scalp from his head, and then pitch him headlong from the battlements—Thy trade is to jest, canst thou jest now?'

'You deal with me better than your word, noble knight,' whimpered forth poor Wamba, whose habits of buffoonery were not to be overcome even by the immediate prospect of death; 'if you give me the red cap you propose, out of a simple monk you will make a cardinal.'*

'The poor wretch,' said De Bracy, 'is resolved to die in his vocation.—Front-de-Bœuf, you shall not slay him. Give him to me to make sport for my Free Companions.—How sayst thou, knave? Wilt thou take heart of grace, and go to the wars with me?'

'Ay, with my master's leave,' said Wamba; 'for, look you, I must not slip collar' (and he touched that which he wore) 'without his permission.'

'Oh, a Norman saw will soon cut a Saxon collar,' said De Bracy.

'Ay, noble sir,' said Wamba, 'and thence goes the proverb—

> "Norman saw on English oak,
> On English neck a Norman yoke;*
> Norman spoon in English dish,
> And England ruled as Normans wish;
> Blithe world in England never will be more,
> Till England's rid of all the four."'

'Thou dost well, De Bracy,' said Front-de-Bœuf, 'to stand there listening to a fool's jargon, when destruction is gaping for us! Seest thou not we are overreached, and that our proposed mode of communicating with our friends without has been disconcerted by this same motley gentleman thou art so fond to brother? What views have we to expect but instant storm?'

'To the battlements then,' said De Bracy; 'when didst thou ever see me the graver for the thoughts of battle? Call the Templar yonder, and let him fight but half so well for his life as he has done for his Order—Make thou to the walls thyself with thy huge body—Let me do my poor endeavour in my own way, and I tell thee the Saxon outlaws may as well attempt to scale the clouds, as the castle of Torquilstone; or, if you will treat with the banditti, why not employ the mediation of this worthy franklin, who seems in such deep contemplation of the wine-flagon?—Here, Saxon,' he continued, addressing Athelstane, and handing the cup to him, 'rinse thy throat with that noble liquor, and rouse up thy soul to say what thou wilt do for thy liberty.'

'What a man of mould* may,' answered Athelstane, 'providing it be what a man of manhood ought.—Dismiss me free, with my companions, and I will pay a ransom of a thousand marks.'

'And wilt moreover assure us the retreat of that scum of mankind who are swarming around the castle, contrary to God's peace and the king's?' said Front-de-Bœuf.

'In so far as I can,' answered Athelstane, 'I will withdraw them; and I fear not but that my father Cedric will do his best to assist me.'

'We are agreed then,' said Front-de-Bœuf—'thou and they are to be set at freedom, and peace is to be on both sides, for payment of a thousand marks. It is a trifling ransom, Saxon, and thou wilt owe gratitude to the moderation which accepts of it in exchange of your persons. But mark, this extends not to the Jew Isaac.'

'Nor to the Jew Isaac's daughter,' said the Templar, who had now joined them.

'Neither,' said Front-de-Bœuf, 'belong to this Saxon's company.'

'I were unworthy to be called Christian, if they did,' replied Athelstance: 'deal with the unbelievers as ye list.'

'Neither does the ransom include the Lady Rowena,' said De Bracy. 'It shall never be said I was scared out of a fair prize without striking a blow for it.'

'Neither,' said Front-de-Bœuf, 'does our treaty refer to this wretched Jester, whom I retain, that I may make him an example to every knave who turns jest into earnest.'

'The Lady Rowena,' answered Athelstane, with the most steady countenance, 'is my affianced bride. I will be drawn by wild horses before I consent to part with her. The slave Wamba has this day saved the life of my father Cedric—I will lose mine ere a hair of his head be injured.'

'Thy affianced bride?—The Lady Rowena the affianced bride of a vassal like thee?' said De Bracy; 'Saxon, thou dreamest that the days of thy seven kingdoms are returned again. I tell thee, the Princes of the House of Anjou confer not their wards on men of such lineage as thine.'

'My lineage, proud Norman,' replied Athelstane, 'is drawn

from a source more pure and ancient than that of a beggarly Frenchman, whose living is won by selling the blood of the thieves whom he assembles under his paltry standard. Kings were my ancestors, strong in war and wise in council, who every day feasted in their hall more hundreds than thou canst number individual followers; whose names have been sung by minstrels, and their laws recorded by Wittenagemotes; whose bones were interred amid the prayers of saints, and over whose tombs minsters have been builded.'

'Thou hast it, De Bracy,' said Front-de-Bœuf, well pleased with the rebuff which his companion had received; 'the Saxon hath hit thee fairly.'

'As fairly as a captive can strike,' said De Bracy, with apparent carelessness; 'for he whose hands are tied should have his tongue at freedom.—But thy glibness of reply, comrade,' rejoined he, speaking to Athelstane, 'will not win the freedom of the Lady Rowena.'

To this Athelstane, who had already made a longer speech than was his custom to do on any topic, however interesting, returned no answer. The conversation was interrupted by the arrival of a menial, who announced that a monk demanded admittance at the postern gate.

'In the name of Saint Bennet, the prince of these bull-beggars,'* said Front-de-Bœuf, 'have we a real monk this time, or another impostor? Search him, slaves—for an ye suffer a second impostor to be palmed upon you, I will have your eyes torn out, and hot coals put into the sockets.'

'Let me endure the extremity of your anger, my lord,' said Giles, 'if this be not a real shaveling. Your squire Jocelyn knows him well, and will vouch him to be brother Ambrose, a monk in attendance upon the Prior of Jorvaulx.'

'Admit him,' said Front-de-Bœuf; 'most likely he brings us news from his jovial master. Surely the devil keeps holiday, and the priests are relieved from duty, that they are strolling thus wildly through the country. Remove these prisoners; and, Saxon, think on what thou hast heard.'

'I claim,' said Athelstane, 'an honourable imprisonment, with due care of my board and of my couch, as becomes my rank, and as is due to one who is in treaty for ransom. Moreover, I hold him that deems himself the best of you, bound to answer to me with his body for this aggression on my freedom. This defiance hath already been sent to thee by thy sewer; thou underliest it, and art bound to answer me—There lies my glove.'

'I answer not the challenge of my prisoner,' said Front-de-Bœuf; 'nor shalt thou, Maurice de Bracy.—Giles,' he continued, 'hang the franklin's glove upon the tine of yonder branched antlers: there shall it remain until he is a free man. Should he then presume to demand it, or to affirm he was unlawfully made my prisoner, by the belt of Saint Christopher, he will speak to one who hath never refused to meet a foe on foot or on horseback, alone or with his vassals at his back!'

The Saxon prisoners were accordingly removed, just as they introduced the monk Ambrose, who appeared to be in great perturbation.

'This is the real *Deus vobiscum*,' said Wamba, as he passed the reverend brother; 'the others were but counterfeits.'

'Holy Mother!' said the monk, as he addressed the assembled knights, 'I am at last safe and in Christian keeping!'

'Safe thou art,' replied De Bracy; 'and for Christianity, here is the stout Baron Reginald Front-de-Bœuf, whose utter abomination is a Jew; and the good Knight Templar, Brian de Bois-Guilbert, whose trade is to slay Saracens—If these are not good marks of Christianity, I know no other which they bear about them.'

'Ye are friends and allies of our reverend father in God, Aymer, Prior of Jorvaulx,' said the monk, without noticing the tone of De Bracy's reply; 'ye owe him aid both by knightly faith and holy charity; for what saith the blessed Saint Augustin, in his treatise *De Civitate Dei*'*——

'What saith the devil!' interrupted Front-de-Bœuf; 'or rather what dost *thou* say, Sir Priest? We have little time to hear texts from the holy fathers.'

'*Sancta Maria!*' ejaculated Father Ambrose, 'how prompt to ire are these unhallowed laymen!—But be it known to you, brave knights, that certain murderous caitiffs, casting behind them fear of God, and reverence of his church, and not regarding the bull of the holy see, *Si quis, suadente Diabolo*'*——

'Brother priest,' said the Templar, 'all this we know or guess at—tell us plainly, is thy master, the Prior, made prisoner, and to whom?'

'Surely,' said Ambrose, 'he is in the hands of the men of Belial,* infesters of these woods, and contemners of the holy text, "Touch not mine anointed, and do my prophets nought of evil." '*

'Here is a new argument for our swords, sirs,' said Front-de-Bœuf, turning to his companions; 'and so, instead of reaching us any assistance, the Prior of Jorvaulx requests aid at our hands? a man is well helped of these lazy churchmen when he hath most to do!—But speak out, priest, and say at once, what doth thy master expect from us?'

'So please you,' said Ambrose, 'violent hands having been imposed on my reverend superior, contrary to the holy ordinance which I did already quote, and the men of Belial having rifled his mails and budgets, and stripped him of two hundred marks of pure refined gold, they do yet demand of him a large sum beside, ere they will suffer him to depart from their uncircumcised hands. Wherefore the reverend father in God prays you, as his dear friends, to rescue him, either by paying down the ransom at which they hold him, or by force of arms, at your best discretion.'

'The foul fiend quell the Prior!' said Front-de-Bœuf; 'his morning's draught has been a deep one. When did thy master hear of a Norman baron unbuckling his purse to relieve a churchman, whose bags are ten times as weighty as ours?—And how can we do aught by valour to free him, that are cooped up here by ten times our number, and expect an assault every moment?'

'And that was what I was about to tell you,' said the monk, 'had your hastiness allowed me time. But, God help me, I am old, and these foul onslaughts distract an aged man's brain. Nevertheless, it is of verity that they assemble a camp, and raise a bank against the walls of this castle.'

'To the battlements!' cried De Bracy, 'and let us mark what these knaves do without;' and so saying, he opened a latticed window which led to a sort of bartisan or projecting balcony, and immediately called from thence to those in the apartment—'Saint Dennis, but the old monk hath brought true tidings!—

They bring forward mantelets and pavisses,[30] and the archers muster on the skirts of the wood like a dark cloud before a hailstorm.'

Reginald Front-de-Bœuf also looked out upon the field, and immediately snatched his bugle; and, after winding a long and loud blast, commanded his men to their posts on the walls.

'De Bracy, look to the eastern side, where the walls are lowest—Noble Bois-Guilbert, thy trade hath well taught thee how to attack and defend, look thou to the western side—I myself will take post at the barbican. Yet, do not confine your exertions to any one spot, noble friends!—we must this day be everywhere, and multiply ourselves, were it possible, so as to carry by our presence succour and relief wherever the attack is hottest. Our numbers are few, but activity and courage may supply that defect, since we have only to do with rascal clowns.'

'But, noble knights,' exclaimed Father Ambrose, amidst the bustle and confusion occasioned by the preparations for defence, 'will none of ye hear the message of the reverend father in God, Aymer, Prior of Jorvaulx?—I beseech thee to hear me, noble Sir Reginald!'

'Go patter thy petitions to heaven,' said the fierce Norman, 'for we on earth have no time to listen to them.—Ho! there, Anselm! see that seething pitch and oil are ready to pour on the heads of these audacious traitors—Look that the crossbowmen lack not bolts.[31]—Fling abroad my banner with the old bull's head—the knaves shall soon find with whom they have to do this day!'

'But, noble sir,' continued the monk, persevering in his endeavours to draw attention, 'consider my vow of obedience, and let me discharge myself of my Superior's errand.'

'Away with this prating dotard,' said Front-de-Bœuf, 'lock him up in the chapel, to tell his beads till the broil be over. It will be a new thing to the saints in Torquilstone to hear aves and paters; they have not been so honoured, I trow, since they were cut out of stone.'

'Blaspheme not the holy saints, Sir Reginald,' said De Bracy, 'we shall have need of their aid to-day before yon rascal rout disband.'

'I expect little aid from their hand,' said Front-de-Bœuf, 'unless we were to hurl them from the battlements on the heads of the villains. There is a huge lumbering Saint Christopher yonder, sufficient to bear a whole company to the earth.'

The Templar had in the meantime been looking out on the proceedings of the besiegers, with rather more attention than the brutal Front-de-Bœuf or his giddy companion.

'By the faith of mine order,' he said, 'these men approach with more touch of discipline than could have been judged, however they come by it. See ye how dexterously they avail themselves of every cover which a tree or bush affords, and shun exposing themselves to the shot of our crossbows? I spy neither banner nor pennon among them, and yet will I gage my golden chain, that they are led on by some noble knight or gentleman, skilful in the practice of wars.'

'I espy him,' said De Bracy; 'I see the waving of a knight's crest, and the gleam of his armour. See yon tall man in the black mail, who is busied marshalling the farther troop of the rascaille yeomen—by Saint Dennis, I hold him to be the same whom we called *Le Noir Faineant*, who overthrew thee, Front-de-Bœuf, in the lists at Ashby.'

'So much the better,' said Front-de-Bœuf, 'that he comes here to give me my revenge. Some hilding fellow he must be,* who dared not stay to assert his claim to the tourney prize which chance had assigned him. I should in vain have sought for him where knights and nobles seek their foes, and right glad am I he hath here shown himself among yon villain yeomanry.'

The demonstrations of the enemy's immediate approach cut off all farther discourse. Each knight repaired to his post, and at the head of the few followers whom they were able to muster, and who were in numbers inadequate to defend the whole extent of the walls, they awaited with calm determination the threatened assault.

CHAPTER XXVIII*

This wandering race, sever'd from other men,
Boast yet their intercourse with human arts;
The seas, the woods, the deserts, which they haunt,
Find them acquainted with their secret treasures:
And unregarded herbs, and flowers, and blossoms,
Display undreamt-of powers when gather'd by them.

*The Jew**

OUR history must needs retrograde for the space of a few pages, to inform the reader of certain passages material to his understanding the rest of this important narrative. His own intelligence may indeed have easily anticipated that, when Ivanhoe sunk down, and seemed abandoned by all the world, it was the importunity of Rebecca which prevailed on her father to have the gallant young warrior transported from the lists to the house which for the time the Jews inhabited in the suburbs of Ashby.

It would not have been difficult to have persuaded Isaac to this step in any other circumstances, for his disposition was kind and grateful. But he had also the prejudices and scrupulous timidity of his persecuted people, and those were to be conquered.

'Holy Abraham!' he exclaimed, 'he is a good youth, and my heart bleeds to see the gore trickle down his rich embroidered hacqueton,* and his corslet of goodly price—but to carry him to our house!—damsel, hast thou well considered?—he is a Christian, and by our law we may not deal with the stranger and Gentile, save for the advantage of our commerce.'

'Speak not so, my dear father,' replied Rebecca; 'we may not indeed mix with them in banquet and in jollity; but in wounds and in misery, the Gentile becometh the Jew's brother.'

'I would I knew what the Rabbi Jacob Ben Tudela* would opine on it,' replied Isaac;—'nevertheless, the good youth must not bleed to death. Let Seth and Reuben bear him to Ashby.'

'Nay, let them place him in my litter,' said Rebecca; 'I will mount one of the palfreys.'

'That were to expose thee to the gaze of those dogs of Ishmael and of Edom,'* whispered Isaac, with a suspicious glance towards the crowd of knights and squires. But Rebecca was already busied in carrying her charitable purpose into effect, and listed not what he said, until Isaac, seizing the sleeve of her mantle, again exclaimed, in a hurried voice—'Beard of Aaron!*—what if the youth perish!—if he die in our custody, shall we not be held guilty of his blood, and be torn to pieces by the multitude?'

'He will not die, my father,' said Rebecca, gently extricating herself from the grasp of Isaac—'he will not die unless we abandon him; and if so, we are indeed answerable for his blood to God and to man.'

'Nay,' said Isaac, releasing his hold, 'it grieveth me as much to see the drops of his blood, as if they were so many golden byzants from mine own purse; and I well know, that the lessons of Miriam, daughter of the Rabbi Manasses of Byzantium,* whose soul is in Paradise, have made thee skilful in the art of healing, and that thou knowest the craft of herbs, and the force of elixirs. Therefore, do as thy mind giveth thee—thou art a good damsel, a blessing, and a crown, and a song of rejoicing unto me and unto my house, and unto the people of my fathers.'

The apprehensions of Isaac, however, were not ill founded; and the generous and grateful benevolence of his daughter exposed her, on her return to Ashby, to the unhallowed gaze of Brian de Bois-Guilbert. The Templar twice passed and repassed them on the road, fixing his bold and ardent look on the beautiful Jewess; and we have already seen the consequences of the admiration which her charms excited, when accident threw her into the power of that unprincipled voluptuary.

Rebecca lost no time in causing the patient to be transported to their temporary dwelling, and proceeded with her own hands to examine and to bind up his wounds. The youngest reader of romances and romantic ballads, must recollect how often the females, during the dark ages, as they are called, were initiated into the mysteries of surgery, and how frequently the gallant knight submitted the wounds of his person to her cure, whose eyes had yet more deeply penetrated his heart.*

But the Jews, both male and female, possessed and practised

the medical science in all its branches, and the monarchs and powerful barons of the time frequently committed themselves to the charge of some experienced sage among this despised people, when wounded or in sickness. The aid of the Jewish physicians was not the less eagerly sought after, though a general belief prevailed among the Christians, that the Jewish Rabbins were deeply acquainted with the occult sciences, and particularly with the cabalistical art, which had its name and origin in the studies of the sages of Israel. Neither did the Rabbins disown such acquaintance with supernatural arts, which added nothing (for what could add aught?) to the hatred with which their nation was regarded, while it diminished the contempt with which that malevolence was mingled. A Jewish magician might be the subject of equal abhorrence with a Jewish usurer, but he could not be equally despised. It is besides probable, considering the wonderful cures they are said to have performed, that the Jews possessed some secrets of the healing art peculiar to themselves, and which, with the exclusive spirit arising out of their condition, they took great care to conceal from the Christians amongst whom they dwelt.

The beautiful Rebecca had been heedfully brought up in all the knowledge proper to her nation, which her apt and powerful mind had retained, arranged, and enlarged, in the course of a progress beyond her years, her sex, and even the age in which she lived. Her knowledge of medicine and of the healing art had been acquired under an aged Jewess, the daughter of one of their most celebrated doctors, who loved Rebecca as her own child, and was believed to have communicated to her secrets, which had been left to herself by her sage father at the same time, and under the same circumstances. The fate of Miriam had indeed been to fall a sacrifice to the fanaticism of the times; but her secrets had survived in her apt pupil.

Rebecca, thus endowed with knowledge as with beauty, was universally revered and admired by her own tribe, who almost regarded her as one of those gifted women mentioned in the sacred history. Her father himself, out of reverence for her talents, which involuntarily mingled itself with his unbounded affection, permitted the maiden a greater liberty than was usually indulged to those of her sex by the habits of her people, and was, as we have just seen, frequently guided by her opinion, even in preference to his own.

When Ivanhoe reached the habitation of Isaac, he was still in a state of unconsciousness, owing to the profuse loss of blood which had taken place during his exertions in the lists. Rebecca examined the wound, and having applied to it such vulnerary remedies as her art prescribed, informed her father that if fever could be averted, of which the great bleeding rendered her little apprehensive, and if the healing balsam of Miriam retained its virtue, there was nothing to fear for his guest's life, and that he might with safety travel to York with them on the ensuing day. Isaac looked a little blank at this annunciation. His charity would willingly have stopped short at Ashby, or at most would have left the wounded Christian to be tended in the house where he was residing at present, with an assurance to the Hebrew to whom it belonged, that all expenses should be duly discharged. To this, however, Rebecca opposed many reasons, of which we shall only mention two that had peculiar weight with Isaac. The one was, that she would on no account put the phial of precious balsam into the hands of another physician even of her own tribe, lest that valuable mystery should be discovered; the other, that this wounded knight, Wilfred of Ivanhoe, was an intimate favourite of Richard Cœur-de-Lion, and that, in case the monarch should return, Isaac, who had supplied his brother John with treasure to prosecute his rebellious purposes, would stand in no small need of a powerful protector who enjoyed Richard's favour.

'Thou art speaking but sooth, Rebecca,' said Isaac, giving way to these weighty arguments—'it were an offending of Heaven to betray the secrets of the blessed Miriam; for the good which Heaven giveth, is not rashly to be squandered upon others, whether it be talents of gold and shekels of silver, or whether it be the secret mysteries of a wise physician—assuredly they should be preserved to those to whom Providence hath vouchsafed them. And him whom the Nazarenes of England call the Lion's Heart, assuredly it were better for me to fall into the hands of a strong lion of Idumea than into his, if he shall have got assurance of my dealing with his brother. Wherefore I will lend ear to thy counsel, and this youth shall journey with us unto York, and our house shall be as a home to him until his wounds shall be healed. And if he of the Lion Heart shall return to the land, as is now noised abroad, then shall this Wilfred of Ivanhoe be unto me as a wall of defence, when the king's displeasure shall burn high against thy father. And if he doth not return, this Wilfred may natheless repay us our charges when he shall gain treasure by the strength of his spear and of his sword, even as he did yesterday and this day also. For the youth is a good youth, and keepeth the day which he appointeth,* and restoreth that which he borroweth, and succoureth the Israelite, even the child of my father's house, when he is encompassed by strong thieves and sons of Belial.'

It was not until evening was nearly closed that Ivanhoe was restored to consciousness of his situation. He awoke from a broken slumber, under the confused impressions which are naturally attendant on the recovery from a state of insensibility. He was unable for some time to recall exactly to memory the circumstances which had preceded his fall in the lists, or to make out any connected chain of the events in which he had been engaged upon the yesterday. A sense of wounds and injury, joined to great weakness and exhaustion, was mingled with the recollection of blows dealt and received, of steeds rushing upon each other, overthrowing and overthrown—of shouts and clashing of arms, and all the heady tumult of a confused fight. An effort to draw aside the curtain of his couch was in some degree successful, although rendered difficult by the pain of his wound.

To his great surprise he found himself in a room magnificently furnished, but having cushions instead of chairs to rest upon, and in other respects partaking so much of Oriental costume, that he began to doubt whether he had not, during his sleep, been transported back again to the land of Palestine. The impression was increased, when, the tapestry being drawn aside, a female form, dressed in a rich habit, which partook more of the Eastern taste than that of Europe, glided through the door which it concealed, and was followed by a swarthy domestic.

As the wounded knight was about to address this fair apparition, she imposed silence by placing her slender finger upon her ruby lips, while the attendant, approaching him, proceeded to uncover Ivanhoe's side, and the lovely Jewess satisfied herself that the bandage was in its place, and the wound doing well. She performed her task with a graceful and dignified simplicity and modesty, which might, even in more civilized days, have served to redeem it from whatever might seem repugnant to female delicacy. The idea of so young and beautiful a person engaged in attendance on a sick-bed, or in dressing the wound of one of a different sex, was melted away and lost in that of a beneficent being contributing her effectual aid to relieve pain, and to avert the stroke of death. Rebecca's few and brief directions were given in the Hebrew language to the old domestic; and he, who had been frequently her assistant in similar cases, obeyed them without reply.

The accents of an unknown tongue, however harsh they might have sounded when uttered by another, had, coming from the beautiful Rebecca, the romantic and pleasing effect which fancy ascribes to the charms pronounced by some beneficent fairy, unintelligible, indeed, to the ear, but, from the sweetness of utterance, and benignity of aspect, which accompanied them, touching and affecting to the heart. Without making an attempt at further question, Ivanhoe suffered them in silence to take the measures they thought most proper for his recovery; and it was not until those were completed, and this kind physician about to retire, that his curiosity could no longer be suppressed.— 'Gentle maiden,' he began in the Arabian tongue, with which his Eastern travels had rendered him familiar, and which he thought most likely to be understood by the turban'd and caftan'd damsel who stood before him—'I pray you, gentle maiden, of your courtesy'——

But here he was interrupted by his fair physician, a smile which she could scarce suppress dimpling for an instant a face, whose general expression was that of contemplative melancholy. 'I am of England, Sir Knight, and speak the English tongue, although my dress and my lineage belong to another climate.'

'Noble damsel,'—again the Knight of Ivanhoe began; and again Rebecca hastened to interrupt him.

'Bestow not on me, Sir Knight,' she said, 'the epithet of noble. It is well you should speedily know that your handmaiden is a poor Jewess, the daughter of that Isaac of York, to whom you were so lately a good and kind lord. It well becomes him, and those of his household, to render to you such careful tendance as your present state necessarily demands.'

I know not whether the fair Rowena would have been altogether satisfied with the species of emotion with which her devoted knight had hitherto gazed on the beautiful features, and fair form, and lustrous eyes, of the lovely Rebecca; eyes whose brilliancy was shaded, and, as it were, mellowed, by the fringe of her long silken eyelashes, and which a minstrel would have compared to the evening star darting its rays through a bower of jessamine. But Ivanhoe was too good a Catholic to retain the same class of feelings towards a Jewess. This Rebecca had foreseen, and for this very purpose she had hastened to mention her father's name and lineage; yet—for the fair and wise daughter of Isaac was not without a touch of female weakness—she could not but sigh internally when the glance of respectful admiration, not altogether unmixed with tenderness, with which Ivanhoe had hitherto regarded his unknown benefactress, was exchanged at once for a manner cold, composed, and collected, and fraught with no deeper feeling than that which expressed a grateful sense of courtesy received from an unexpected quarter, and from one of an inferior race. It was not that Ivanhoe's former carriage expressed more than that general devotional homage which youth always pays to beauty; yet it was mortifying that one word should operate as a spell to remove poor Rebecca, who could not be supposed altogether ignorant of her title to such homage, into a degraded class, to whom it could not be honourably rendered.

But the gentleness and candour of Rebecca's nature imputed no fault to Ivanhoe for sharing in the universal prejudices of his age and religion. On the contrary, the fair Jewess, though sensible her patient now regarded her as one of a race of reprobation, with whom it was disgraceful to hold any beyond the most necessary intercourse, ceased not to pay the same patient and devoted attention to his safety and convalescence. She informed him of the necessity they were under of removing to York, and of her father's resolution to transport him thither, and tend him in his own house until his health should be restored. Ivanhoe expressed great repugnance to this plan, which he grounded on unwillingness to give farther trouble to his benefactors.

'Was there not,' he said, 'in Ashby, or near it, some Saxon franklin, or even some wealthy peasant, who would endure the burden of a wounded countryman's residence with him until he should be again able to bear his armour?—Was there no convent of Saxon endowment, where he could be received?—Or could he not be transported as far as Burton, where he was sure to find hospitality with Waltheoff, the Abbot of St Withold's, to whom he was related?'

'Any, the worst of these harbourages,' said Rebecca, with a melancholy smile, 'would unquestionably be more fitting for your residence than the abode of a despised Jew; yet, Sir Knight, unless you would dismiss your physician, you cannot change your lodging. Our nation, as you well know, can cure wounds, though we deal not in inflicting them; and in our own family, in particular, are secrets which have been handed down since the days of Solomon, and of which you have already experienced the advantages. No Nazarene—I crave your forgiveness, Sir Knight—no Christian leech, within the four seas of Britain, could enable you to bear your corslet within a month.'

'And how soon wilt *thou* enable me to brook it?' said Ivanhoe, impatiently.

'Within eight days, if thou wilt be patient and conformable to my directions,' replied Rebecca.

'By Our Blessed Lady,' said Wilfred, 'if it be not a sin to name her here, it is no time for me or any true knight to be bedridden; and if thou accomplish thy promise, maiden, I will pay thee with my casque full of crowns, come by them as I may.'

'I will accomplish my promise,' said Rebecca, 'and thou shalt bear thine armour on the eighth day from hence, if thou wilt grant me but one boon in the stead of the silver thou dost promise me.'

'If it be within my power, and such as a true Christian knight may yield to one of thy people,' replied Ivanhoe, 'I will grant thy boon blithely and thankfully.'

'Nay,' answered Rebecca, 'I will but pray of thee to believe henceforward that a Jew may do good service to a Christian, without desiring other guerdon than the blessing of the Great Father who made both Jew and Gentile.'

'It were sin to doubt it, maiden,' replied Ivanhoe; 'and I repose myself on thy skill without further scruple or question, well trusting you will enable me to bear my corslet on the eighth day. And now, my kind leech, let me enquire of the news abroad. What of the noble Saxon Cedric and his household?—what of the lovely Lady'—He stopt, as if unwilling to speak Rowena's name in the house of a Jew—'Of her, I mean, who was named Queen of the tournament?'

'And who was selected by you, Sir Knight, to hold that dignity, with judgment which was admired as much as your valour,' replied Rebecca.

The blood which Ivanhoe had lost did not prevent a flush from crossing his cheek, feeling that he had incautiously betrayed his deep interest in Rowena by the awkward attempt he had made to conceal it.

'It was less of her I would speak,' said he, 'than of Prince John; and I would fain know somewhat of a faithful squire, and why he now attends me not?'

'Let me use my authority as a leech,' answered Rebecca, 'and enjoin you to keep silence, and avoid agitating reflections, whilst I apprize you of what you desire to know. Prince John hath broken off the tournament, and set forward in all haste towards York, with the nobles, knights, and churchmen of his party, after collecting such sums as they could wring, by fair means or foul, from those who are esteemed the wealthy of the land. It is said he designs to assume his brother's crown.'

'Not without a blow struck in its defence,' said Ivanhoe, raising himself upon the couch, 'if there were but one true subject in England. I will fight for Richard's title with the best of them— ay, one to two, in his just quarrel!'

'But that you may be able to do so,' said Rebecca, touching his shoulder with her hand, 'you must now observe my directions, and remain quiet.'

'True, maiden,' said Ivanhoe, 'as quiet as these disquieted times will permit—And of Cedric and his household?'

'His steward came but brief while since,' said the Jewess, 'panting with haste, to ask my father for certain monies, the price of wool the growth of Cedric's flocks, and from him I learned that Cedric and Athelstane of Coningsburgh had left Prince

John's lodging in high displeasure, and were about to set forth on their return homeward.'

'Went any lady with them to the banquet?' said Wilfred.

'The Lady Rowena,' said Rebecca, answering the question with more precision that it had been asked—'The Lady Rowena went not to the Prince's feast, and, as the steward reported to us, she is now on her journey back to Rotherwood, with her guardian Cedric. And touching your faithful squire Gurth'——

'Ha!' exclaimed the knight, 'knowest thou his name?—But thou dost,' he immediately added, 'and well thou mayst, for it was from thy hand, and, as I am now convinced, from thine own generosity of spirit, that he received but yesterday a hundred zecchins.'

'Speak not of that,' said Rebecca, blushing deeply; 'I see how easy it is for the tongue to betray what the heart would gladly conceal.'

'But this sum of gold,' said Ivanhoe, gravely, 'my honour is concerned in repaying it to your father.'

'Let it be as thou wilt,' said Rebecca, 'when eight days have passed away; but think not, and speak not now, of aught that may retard thy recovery.'

'Be it so, kind maiden,' said Ivanhoe; 'I were most ungrateful to dispute thy commands. But one word of the fate of poor Gurth, and I have done with questioning thee.'

'I grieve to tell thee, Sir Knight,' answered the Jewess, 'that he is in custody by the order of Cedric.'—And then observing the distress which her communication gave to Wilfred, she instantly added, 'But the steward Oswald said, that if nothing occurred to renew his master's displeasure against him, he was sure that Cedric would pardon Gurth, a faithful serf, and one who stood high in favour, and who had but committed this error out of the love which he bore to Cedric's son. And he said, moreover, that he and his comrades, and especially Wamba the Jester, were resolved to warn Gurth to make his escape by the way, in case Cedric's ire against him could not be mitigated.'

'Would to God they may keep their purpose!' said Ivanhoe; 'but it seems as if I were destined to bring ruin on whomsoever hath shown kindness to me. My king, by whom I was honoured and distinguished, thou seest that the brother most indebted to him is raising his arms to grasp his crown;—my regard hath brought restraint and trouble on the fairest of her sex;—and now my father in his mood may slay this poor bondsman, but for his love and loyal service to me!—Thou seest, maiden, what an ill-fated wretch thou dost labour to assist; be wise, and let me go, ere the misfortunes which track my footsteps like slot-hounds, shall involve thee also in their pursuit.'

'Nay,' said Rebecca, 'thy weakness and thy grief, Sir Knight, make thee miscalculate the purposes of Heaven. Thou hast been restored to thy country when it most needed the assistance of a strong hand and a true heart, and thou hast humbled the pride of thine enemies and those of thy king, when their horn was most highly exalted;* and for the evil which thou hast sustained, seest thou not that Heaven has raised thee a helper and a physician, even among the most despised of the land?—Therefore, be of good courage, and trust that thou art preserved for some marvel which thine arm shall work before this people. Adieu—and having taken the medicine which I shall send thee by the hand of Reuben, compose thyself again to rest, that thou mayst be the more able to endure the journey on the succeeding day.'

Ivanhoe was convinced by the reasoning, and obeyed the directions, of Rebecca. The draught which Reuben administered was of a sedative and narcotic quality, and secured the patient sound and undisturbed slumbers. In the morning his kind physician found him entirely free from feverish symptoms, and fit to undergo the fatigue of a journey.

He was deposited in the horse-litter which had brought him from the lists, and every precaution taken for his travelling with ease. In one circumstance only even the entreaties of Rebecca were unable to secure sufficient attention to the accommodation of the wounded knight. Isaac, like the enriched traveller of Juvenal's tenth satire,* had ever the fear of robbery before his eyes, conscious that he would be alike accounted fair game by the marauding Norman noble, and by the Saxon outlaw. He therefore journeyed at a great rate, and made short halts, and shorter repasts, so that he passed by Cedric and Athelstane who had several hours the start of him, but who had been delayed by their protracted feasting at the convent of Saint Withold's. Yet such was the virtue of Miriam's balsam, or such the strength of

Ivanhoe's constitution, that he did not sustain from the hurried journey that inconvenience which his kind physician had apprehended.

In another point of view, however, the Jew's haste proved somewhat more than good speed. The rapidity with which he insisted on travelling, bred several disputes between him and the party whom he had hired to attend him as a guard. These men were Saxons, and not free by any means from the national love of ease and good living which the Normans stigmatized as laziness and gluttony. Reversing Shylock's position, they had accepted the employment in hopes of feeding upon the wealthy Jew,* and were very much displeased when they found themselves disappointed, by the rapidity with which he insisted on their proceeding. They remonstrated also upon the risk of damage to their horses by these forced marches. Finally, there arose betwixt Isaac and his satellites a deadly feud, concerning the quantity of wine and ale to be allowed for consumption at each meal. And thus it happened, that when the alarm of danger approached, and that which Isaac feared was likely to come upon him, he was deserted by the discontented mercenaries on whose protection he had relied, without using the means necessary to secure their attachment.

In this deplorable condition the Jew, with his daughter and her wounded patient, were found by Cedric, as has already been noticed, and soon afterwards fell into the power of De Bracy and his confederates. Little notice was at first taken of the horse-litter, and it might have remained behind but for the curiosity of De Bracy, who looked into it under the impression that it might contain the object of his enterprise, for Rowena had not unveiled herself. But De Bracy's astonishment was considerable, when he discovered that the litter contained a wounded man, who, conceiving himself to have fallen into the power of Saxon outlaws, with whom his name might be a protection for himself and his friends, frankly avowed himself to be Wilfred of Ivanhoe.

The ideas of chivalrous honour, which, amidst his wildness and levity, never utterly abandoned De Bracy, prohibited him from doing the knight any injury in his defenceless condition, and equally interdicted his betraying him to Front-de-Bœuf, who would have had no scruples to put to death, under any circumstances, the rival claimant of the fief of Ivanhoe. On the other hand, to liberate a suitor preferred by the Lady Rowena, as the events of the tournament, and indeed Wilfred's previous banishment from his father's house, had made matter of notoriety, was a pitch far above the flight of De Bracy's generosity. A middle course betwixt good and evil was all which he found himself capable of adopting, and he commanded two of his own squires to keep close by the litter, and to suffer no one to approach it. If questioned, they were directed by their master to say, that the empty litter of the Lady Rowena was employed to transport one of their comrades who had been wounded in the scuffle. On arriving at Torquilstone, while the Knight Templar and the lord of that castle were each intent upon their own schemes, the one on the Jew's treasure, and the other on his daughter, De Bracy's squires conveyed Ivanhoe, still under the name of a wounded comrade, to a distant apartment. This explanation was accordingly returned by these men to Front-de-Bœuf, when he questioned them why they did not make for the battlements upon the alarm.

'A wounded companion!' he replied in great wrath and astonishment. 'No wonder that churls and yeomen wax so presumptuous as even to lay leaguer before castles, and that clowns and swineherds send defiances to nobles, since men-at-arms have turned sick men's nurses, and Free Companions are grown keepers of dying folk's curtains, when the castle is about to be assailed.—To the battlements, ye loitering villains!' he exclaimed, raising his stentorian voice till the arches around rung again, 'to the battlements, or I will splinter your bones with this truncheon!'

The men sulkily replied, 'that they desired nothing better than to go to the battlements, providing Front-de-Bœuf would bear them out with their master, who had commanded them to tend the dying man.'

'The dying man, knaves!' rejoined the Baron; 'I promise thee we shall all be dying men an we stand not to it the more stoutly. But I will relieve the guard upon this caitiff companion of yours.—Here, Urfried—hag—fiend of a Saxon witch—hearest me not?—tend me this bedridden fellow, since he must needs be tended, whilst these knaves use their weapons.—Here be two arblasts, comrades, with windlaces and quarrells[32]—to the barbican with you, and see you drive each bolt through a Saxon brain.'

The men, who, like most of their description, were fond of enterprise and detested inaction, went joyfully to the scene of danger as they were commanded, and thus the charge of Ivanhoe was transferred to Urfried, or Ulrica. But she, whose brain was burning with remembrance of injuries and with hopes of vengeance, was readily induced to devolve upon Rebecca the care of her patient.

CHAPTER XXIX

Ascend the watch-tower yonder, valiant soldier,
Look on the field, and say how goes the battle.

SCHILLER'S *Maid of Orleans**

A MOMENT of peril is often also a moment of open-hearted kindness and affection. We are thrown off our guard by the general agitation of our feelings, and betray the intensity of those, which, at more tranquil periods, our prudence at least conceals, if it cannot altogether suppress them. In finding herself once more by the side of Ivanhoe, Rebecca was astonished at the keen sensation of pleasure which she experienced, even at a time when all around them both was danger, if not despair. As she felt his pulse, and enquired after his health, there was a softness in her touch and in her accents, implying a kinder interest than she would herself have been pleased to have voluntarily expressed. Her voice faltered and her hand trembled, and it was only the cold question of Ivanhoe, 'Is it you, gentle maiden?' which recalled her to herself, and reminded her the sensations which she felt were not and could not be mutual. A sigh escaped, but it was scarce audible; and the questions which she asked the knight concerning his state of health were put in the tone of calm friendship. Ivanhoe answered her hastily that he was, in point of health, as well, and better than he could have expected—'Thanks,' he said, 'dear Rebecca, to thy helpful skill.'

'He calls me *dear* Rebecca,' said the maiden to herself, 'but it is in the cold and careless tone which ill suits the word. His war-horse—his hunting hound, are dearer to him than the despised Jewess!'

'My mind, gentle maiden,' continued Ivanhoe, 'is more disturbed by anxiety, than my body with pain. From the speeches of these men who were my warders just now, I learn that I am a prisoner, and, if I judge aright of the loud hoarse voice which even now dispatched them hence on some military duty, I am in the castle of Front-de-Bœuf—If so, how will this end, or how can I protect Rowena and my father?'

'He names not the Jew or Jewess,' said Rebecca, internally; 'yet what is our portion in him, and how justly am I punished by Heaven for letting my thoughts dwell upon him!' She hastened after this brief self-accusation to give Ivanhoe what information she could; but it amounted only to this, that the Templar Bois-Guilbert, and the Baron Front-de-Bœuf, were commanders within the castle; that it was beleaguered from without, but by whom she knew not. She added, that there was a Christian priest within the castle who might be possessed of more information.

'A Christian priest!' said the knight, joyfully; 'fetch him hither, Rebecca, if thou canst—say a sick man desires his ghostly counsel—say what thou wilt, but bring him—something I must do or attempt, but how can I determine until I know how matters stand without?'

Rebecca, in compliance with the wishes of Ivanhoe, made that attempt to bring Cedric into the wounded Knight's chamber, which was defeated as we have already seen by the interference of Urfried, who had been also on the watch to intercept the supposed monk. Rebecca retired to communicate to Ivanhoe the result of her errand.

They had not much leisure to regret the failure of this source of intelligence, or to contrive by what means it might be supplied; for the noise within the castle, occasioned by the defensive preparations which had been considerable for some time, now increased into tenfold bustle and clamour. The heavy, yet hasty step of the men-at-arms, traversed the battlements, or resounded on the narrow and winding passages and stairs which led to the various bartisans and points of defence. The voices of the knights were heard, animating their followers, or directing means of defence, while their commands were often drowned in the clashing of armour, or the clamorous shouts of those whom they addressed. Tremendous as these sounds were, and yet more terrible from the awful event which they presaged, there was a sublimity mixed with them, which Rebecca's high-toned mind could feel even in that moment of terror. Her eye kindled, although the blood fled from her cheeks; and there was a strong mixture of fear, and of a thrilling sense of the sublime, as she repeated, half whispering to herself, half speaking to her companion, the sacred text,—'The quiver rattleth—the glittering spear and the shield—the noise of the captains and the shouting!'*

But Ivanhoe was like the war-horse of that sublime passage, glowing with impatience at his inactivity, and with his ardent desire to mingle in the affray of which these sounds were the introduction. 'If I could but drag myself,' he said, 'to yonder window, that I might see how this brave game is like to go—If I had but bow to shoot a shaft, or battle-axe to strike were it but a single blow for our deliverance!—It is in vain—it is in vain—I am alike nerveless and weaponless!'

'Fret not thyself, noble knight,' answered Rebecca, 'the sounds have ceased of a sudden—it may be they join not battle.'

'Thou knowest nought of it,' said Wilfred, impatiently; 'this dead pause only shows that the men are at their posts on the walls, and expecting an instant attack; what we have heard was but the instant muttering of the storm—it will burst anon in all its fury.—Could I but reach yonder window!'

'Thou wilt but injure thyself by the attempt, noble knight,' replied his attendant. Observing his extreme solicitude, she firmly added, 'I myself will stand at the lattice, and describe to you as I can what passes without.'

'You must not—you shall not!' exclaimed Ivanhoe; 'each lattice, each aperture, will be soon a mark for the archers; some random shaft'—

'It shall be welcome!' murmured Rebecca, as with firm pace she ascended two or three steps, which led to the window of which they spoke.

'Rebecca, dear Rebecca!' exclaimed Ivanhoe, 'this is no maiden's pastime—do not expose thyself to wounds and death, and render me for ever miserable for having given the occasion; at least, cover thyself with yonder ancient buckler, and show as little of your person at the lattice as may be.'

Following with wonderful promptitude the directions of Ivanhoe, and availing herself of the protection of the large ancient shield, which she placed against the lower part of the window, Rebecca, with tolerable security to herself, could witness part of what was passing without the castle, and report to

Ivanhoe the preparations which the assailants were making for the storm. Indeed the situation which she thus obtained was peculiarly favourable for this purpose, because, being placed on an angle of the main building, Rebecca could not only see what passed beyond the precincts of the castle, but also commanded a view of the outwork likely to be the first object of the meditated assault. It was an exterior fortification of no great height or strength, intended to protect the postern-gate, through which Cedric had been recently dismissed by Front-de-Bœuf. The castle moat divided this species of barbican from the rest of the fortress, so that, in case of its being taken, it was easy to cut off the communication with the main building, by withdrawing the temporary bridge. In the outwork was a sallyport corresponding to the postern of the castle, and the whole was surrounded by a strong palisade. Rebecca could observe, from the number of men placed for the defence of this post, that the besieged entertained apprehensions for its safety; and from the mustering of the assailants in a direction nearly opposite to the outwork, it seemed no less plain that it had been selected as a vulnerable point of attack.

These appearances she hastily communicated to Ivanhoe, and added, 'The skirts of the wood seem lined with archers, although only a few are advanced from its dark shadow.'

'Under what banner? asked Ivanhoe.

'Under no ensign of war which I can observe,' answered Rebecca.

'A singular novelty,'* muttered the knight, 'to advance to storm such a castle without pennon or banner displayed!—Seest thou who they be that act as leaders?'

'A knight, clad in sable armour, is the most conspicuous,' said the Jewess; 'he alone is armed from head to heel, and seems to assume the direction of all around him.'

'What device does he bear on his shield?' replied Ivanhoe.

'Something resembling a bar of iron, and a padlock painted blue on the black shield.'[33]

'A fetterlock and shacklebolt azure,' said Ivanhoe; 'I know not who may bear the device, but well I ween it might now be mine own. Canst thou not see the motto?'

'Scarce the device itself at this distance,' replied Rebecca;

'but when the sun glances fair upon his shield, it shows as I tell you.'

'Seem there no other leaders?' exclaimed the anxious enquirer.

'None of mark and distinction that I can behold from this station,' said Rebecca; 'but, doubtless, the other side of the castle is also assailed. They appear even now preparing to advance— God of Zion, protect us!—What a dreadful sight!—Those who advance first bear huge shields and defences made of plank; the others follow, bending their bows as they come on.—They raise their bows!—God of Moses, forgive the creatures thou hast made!'

Her description was here suddenly interrupted by the signal for assault, which was given by the blast of a shrill bugle, and at once answered by a flourish of the Norman trumpets from the battlements, which, mingled with the deep and hollow clang of the nakers,* (a species of kettle-drum,) retorted in notes of defiance the challenge of the enemy. The shouts of both parties augmented the fearful din, the assailants crying, 'Saint George for merry England!' and the Normans answering them with loud cries of *'En avant De Bracy!—Beauseant! Beau-seant!—Front-de-Bœuf à la rescousse!'* according to the war-cries of their different commanders.

It was not, however, by clamour that the contest was to be decided, and the desperate efforts of the assailants were met by an equally vigorous defence on the part of the besieged. The archers, trained by their woodland pastimes to the most effective use of the long-bow, shot, to use the appropriate phrase of the time, so 'wholly together,'* that no point at which a defender could show the least part of his person, escaped their cloth-yard shafts. By this heavy discharge, which continued as thick and sharp as hail, while, notwithstanding, every arrow had its individual aim, and flew by scores together against each embrasure and opening in the parapets, as well as at every window where a defender either occasionally had post, or might be suspected to be stationed,—by this sustained discharge, two or three of the garrison were slain, and several others wounded. But, confident in their armour of proof, and in the cover which their situation afforded, the followers of Front-de-Bœuf, and his allies, showed an obstinacy in defence proportioned to the fury of the attack, and replied with the discharge of their large crossbows, as well as with their long-bows, slings, and other missile weapons, to the close and continued shower of arrows; and, as the assailants were necessarily but indifferently protected, did considerably more damage than they received at their hand. The whizzing of shafts and of missiles, on both sides, was only interrupted by the shouts which arose when either side inflicted or sustained some notable loss.

'And I must lie here like a bedridden monk,' exclaimed Ivanhoe, 'while the game that gives me freedom or death is played out by the hand of others!—Look from the window once again, kind maiden, but beware that you are not marked by the archers beneath—Look out once more, and tell me if they yet advance to the storm.'

With patient courage, strengthened by the interval which she had employed in mental devotion, Rebecca again took post at the lattice, sheltering herself, however, so as not to be visible from beneath.

'What dost thou see, Rebecca?' again demanded the wounded knight.

'Nothing but the cloud of arrows flying so thick as to dazzle mine eyes, and to hide the bowmen who shoot them.'

'That cannot endure,' said Ivanhoe; 'if they press not right on to carry the castle by pure force of arms, the archery may avail but little against stone walls and bulwarks. Look for the Knight of the Fetterlock, fair Rebecca, and see how he bears himself; for as the leader is, so will his followers be.'

'I see him not,' said Rebecca.

'Foul craven!' exclaimed Ivanhoe; 'does he blench from the helm when the wind blows highest?'

'He blenches not! he blenches not!' said Rebecca, 'I see him now; he leads a body of men close under the outer barrier of the barbican.[34] They pull down the piles and palisades; they hew down the barriers with axes.—His high black plume floats abroad over the throng, like a raven over the field of the slain.— They have made a breach in the barriers—they rush in—they are thrust back!—Front-de-Bœuf heads the defenders; I see his gigantic form above the press. They throng again to the breach, and the pass is disputed hand to hand, and man to man. God of Jacob! it is the meeting of two fierce tides—the conflict of two oceans moved by adverse winds!'

She turned her head from the lattice, as if unable longer to endure a sight so terrible.

'Look forth again, Rebecca,' said Ivanhoe, mistaking the cause of her retiring; 'the archery must in some degree have ceased, since they are now fighting hand to hand.—Look again, there is now less danger.'

Rebecca again looked forth, and almost immediately exclaimed, 'Holy prophets of the law! Front-de-Bœuf and the Black Knight fight hand to hand on the breach, amid the roar of their followers, who watch the progress of the strife—Heaven strike with the cause of the oppressed and of the captive!' She then uttered a loud shriek, and exclaimed, 'He is down!—he is down!'

'Who is down?' cried Ivanhoe; 'for our dear Lady's sake, tell me which has fallen?'

'The Black Knight,' answered Rebecca, faintly; then instantly again shouted with joyful eagerness—'But no—but no!—the name of the Lord of Hosts be blessed!—he is on foot again, and fights as if there were twenty men's strength in his single arm—His sword is broken—he snatches an axe from a yeoman—he presses Front-de-Bœuf with blow on blow—The giant stoops and totters like an oak under the steel of the woodman—he falls—he falls!'

'Front-de-Bœuf?' exclaimed Ivanhoe.

'Front-de-Bœuf!' answered the Jewess; 'his men rush to the rescue, headed by the haughty Templar—their united force compels the champion to pause—They drag Front-de-Bœuf within the walls.'

'The assailants have won the barriers, have they not?' said Ivanhoe.

'They have—they have!' exclaimed Rebecca—'and they press the besieged hard upon the outer wall; some plant ladders, some swarm like bees, and endeavour to ascend upon the shoulders of each other—down go stones, beams, and trunks of trees upon their heads, and as fast as they bear the wounded to the rear, fresh men supply their places in the assault—Great God! hast thou given men thine own image, that it should be thus cruelly defaced by the hands of their brethren!'

'Think not of that,' said Ivanhoe; 'this is no time for such thoughts—Who yield?—who push their way?'

'The ladders are thrown down,' replied Rebecca, shuddering; 'the soldiers lie grovelling under them like crushed reptiles—The besieged have the better.'

'Saint George strike for us!' exclaimed the knight; 'do the false yeomen give way?'

'No!' exclaimed Rebecca, 'they bear themselves right yeomanly—the Black Knight approaches the postern with his huge axe—the thundering blows which he deals, you may hear them above all the din and shouts of the battle—Stones and beams are hailed down on the bold champion—he regards them no more than if they were thistledown or feathers!'

'By Saint John of Acre,' said Ivanhoe, raising himself joyfully on his couch, 'methought there was but one man in England that might do such a deed!'

'The postern gate shakes,' continued Rebecca; 'it crashes—it is splintered by his blows—they rush in—the outwork is won—Oh, God!—they hurl the defenders from the battlements—they throw them into the moat—O men, if ye be indeed men, spare them that can resist no longer!'

'The bridge—the bridge which communicates with the castle—have they won that pass?' exclaimed Ivanhoe.

'No,' replied Rebecca, 'The Templar has destroyed the plank on which they crossed—few of the defenders escaped with him into the castle—the shrieks and cries which you hear tell the fate of the others—Alas!—I see it is still more difficult to look upon victory than upon battle.'

'What do they now, maiden?' said Ivanhoe; 'look forth yet again—this is no time to faint at bloodshed.'

'It is over for the time,' answered Rebecca; 'our friends strengthen themselves within the outwork which they have mastered, and it affords them so good a shelter from the foemen's shot, that the garrison only bestow a few bolts on it from interval to interval, as if rather to disquiet than effectually to injure them.'

'Our friends,' said Wilfred, 'will surely not abandon an enterprise so gloriously begun and so happily attained.—O no! I will put my faith in the good knight whose axe hath rent heart-of-oak and bars of iron.—Singular,' he again muttered to himself, 'if there be two who can do a deed of such *derring-do!**—a fetterlock, and a shacklebolt on a field sable—what may that mean?—seest thou nought else, Rebecca, by which the Black Knight may be distinguished?'

'Nothing,' said the Jewess; 'all about him is black as the wing of the night raven. Nothing can I spy that can mark him further—but having once seen him put forth his strength in battle, methinks I could know him again among a thousand warriors. He rushes to the fray as if he were summoned to a banquet. There is more than mere strength, there seems as if the whole soul and spirit of the champion were given to every blow which he deals upon his enemies. God assoilzie him* of the sin of bloodshed!—it is fearful, yet magnificent, to behold how the arm and heart of one man can triumph over hundreds.'

'Rebecca,' said Ivanhoe, 'thou hast painted a hero; surely they rest but to refresh their force, or to provide the means of crossing the moat—Under such a leader as thou hast spoken this knight to be, there are no craven fears, no cold-blooded delays, no yielding up a gallant emprize; since the difficulties which render it arduous render it also glorious. I swear by the honour of my house—I vow by the name of my bright lady-love, I would endure ten years' captivity to fight one day by that good knight's side in such a quarrel as this!'

'Alas,' said Rebecca, leaving her station at the window, and approaching the couch of the wounded knight, 'this impatient yearning after action—this struggling with and repining at your present weakness, will not fail to injure your returning health—How couldst thou hope to inflict wounds on others, ere that be healed which thou thyself hast received?'

'Rebecca,' he replied, 'thou knowest not how impossible it is for one trained to actions of chivalry to remain passive as a priest, or a woman, when they are acting deeds of honour around him. The love of battle is the food upon which we live—the dust of the *mêlée* is the breath of our nostrils! We live not—we wish not to live—longer than while we are victorious and renowned—

Such, maiden, are the laws of chivalry to which we are sworn, and to which we offer all that we hold dear.'

'Alas!' said the fair Jewess, 'and what is it, valiant knight, save an offering of sacrifice to a demon of vain glory, and a passing through the fire to Moloch?*—What remains to you as the prize of all the blood you have spilled—of all the travail and pain you have endured—of all the tears which your deeds have caused, when death hath broken the strong man's spear, and overtaken the speed of his war-horse?'

'What remains?' cried Ivanhoe; 'Glory, maiden, glory! which gilds our sepulchre and embalms our name.'

'Glory?' continued Rebecca; 'alas, is the rusted mail which hangs as a hatchment* over the champion's dim and mouldering tomb—is the defaced sculpture of the inscription which the ignorant monk can hardly read to the enquiring pilgrim—are these sufficient rewards for the sacrifice of every kindly affection, for a life spent miserably that ye may make others miserable? Or is there such virtue in the rude rhymes of a wandering bard, that domestic love, kindly affection, peace and happiness, are so wildly bartered, to become the hero of those ballads which vagabond minstrels sing to drunken churls over their evening ale?'

'By the soul of Hereward!' replied the knight impatiently, 'thou speakest, maiden, of thou knowest not what. Thou wouldst quench the pure light of chivalry, which alone distinguishes the noble from the base, the gentle knight from the churl and the savage; which rates our life far, far beneath the pitch of our honour; raises us victorious over pain, toil, and suffering, and teaches us to fear no evil but disgrace. Thou art no Christian, Rebecca; and to thee are unknown those high feelings which swell the bosom of a noble maiden when her lover hath done some deed of emprize which sanctions his flame. Chivalry!— why, maiden, she is the nurse of pure and high affection—the stay of the oppressed, the redresser of grievances, the curb of the power of the tyrant—Nobility were but an empty name without her, and liberty finds the best protection in her lance and her sword.'

'I am, indeed,' said Rebecca, 'sprung from a race whose courage was distinguished in the defence of their own land, but who warred not, even while yet a nation, save at the command of the Deity, or in defending their country from oppression. The sound of the trumpet wakes Judah no longer, and her despised children are now but the unresisting victims of hostile and military oppression. Well hast thou spoken, Sir Knight,—until the God of Jacob shall raise up for his chosen people a second Gideon, or a new Maccabeus,* it ill beseemeth the Jewish damsel to speak of battle or of war.'

The high-minded maiden concluded the argument in a tone of sorrow, which deeply expressed her sense of the degradation of her people, embittered perhaps by the idea that Ivanhoe considered her as one not entitled to interfere in a case of honour, and incapable of entertaining or expressing sentiments of honour and generosity.

'How little he knows this bosom,' she said, 'to imagine that cowardice or meanness of soul must needs be its guests, because I have censured the fantastic chivalry of the Nazarenes! Would to heaven that the shedding of mine own blood, drop by drop, could redeem the captivity of Judah! Nay, would to God it could avail to set free my father, and this his benefactor, from the chains of the oppressor! The proud Christian should then see whether the daughter of God's chosen people dared not to die as bravely as the vainest Nazarene maiden, that boasts her descent from some petty chieftain of the rude and frozen north!'

She then looked towards the couch of the wounded knight.

'He sleeps,' she said; 'nature exhausted by sufferance and the waste of spirits, his wearied frame embraces the first moment of temporary relaxation to sink into slumber. Alas! is it a crime that I should look upon him, when it may be for the last time?— When yet but a short space, and those fair features will be no longer animated by the bold and buoyant spirit which forsakes them not even in sleep!—When the nostril shall be distended, the mouth agape, the eyes fixed and bloodshot; and when the proud and noble knight may be trodden on by the lowest caitiff of this accursed castle, yet stir not when the heel is lifted up against him!—And my father!—oh, my father! evil is it with his daughter, when his grey hairs are not remembered because of the golden locks of youth!—What know I but that these evils are the messengers of Jehovah's wrath to the unnatural child, who

thinks of a stranger's captivity before a parent's? who forgets the
desolation of Judah, and looks upon the comeliness of a Gentile
and a stranger?—But I will tear this folly from my heart,*
though every fibre bleed as I rend it away!'

She wrapped herself closely in her veil, and sat down at a
distance from the couch of the wounded knight, with her back
turned towards it, fortifying, or endeavouring to fortify her
mind, not only against the impending evils from without, but
also against those treacherous feelings which assailed her from
within.

CHAPTER XXX

Approach the chamber, look upon his bed.
His is the passing of no peaceful ghost,
Which, as the lark arises to the sky,
'Mid morning's sweetest breeze and softest dew,
Is wing'd to heaven by good men's sighs and tears!—
Anselm parts otherwise.

*Old Play**

DURING the interval of quiet which followed the first success of the besiegers, while the one party was preparing to pursue their advantage, and the other to strengthen their means of defence, the Templar and De Bracy held brief council together in the hall of the castle.

'Where is Front-de-Bœuf?' said the latter, who had superintended the defence of the fortress on the other side; 'men say he hath been slain.'

'He lives,' said the Templar, coolly, 'lives as yet; but had he worn the bull's head of which he bears the name, and ten plates of iron to fence it withal, he must have gone down before yonder fatal axe. Yet a few hours, and Front-de-Bœuf is with his fathers—a powerful limb lopped off Prince John's enterprise.'

'And a brave addition to the kingdom of Satan,' said De Bracy; 'this comes of reviling saints and angels, and ordering images of holy things and holy men to be flung down on the heads of these rascaille yeomen.'

'Go to—thou art a fool,' said the Templar; 'thy superstition is upon a level with Front-de-Bœuf's want of faith; neither of you can render a reason for your belief or unbelief.'

'Benedicite, Sir Templar,' replied De Bracy, 'I pray you to keep better rule with your tongue when I am the theme of it. By the Mother of Heaven, I am a better Christian man than thou and thy fellowship; for the *bruit* goeth shrewdly out, that the most holy Order of the Temple of Zion nurseth not a few heretics within its bosom, and that Sir Brian de Bois-Guilbert is of the number.'

'Care not thou for such reports,' said the Templar; 'but let us think of making good the castle.—How fought these villain yeomen on thy side?'

'Like fiends incarnate,' said De Bracy. 'They swarmed close up to the walls, headed, as I think, by the knave who won the prize at the archery, for I knew his horn and baldric. And this is old Fitzurse's boasted policy, encouraging these malapert knaves to rebel against us! Had I not been armed in proof, the villain had marked me down seven times with as little remorse as if I had been a buck in season. He told every rivet on my armour with a cloth-yard shaft, that rapped against my ribs with as little compunction as if my bones had been of iron—But that I wore a shirt of Spanish mail under my plate-coat, I had been fairly sped.'

'But you maintained your post?' said the Templar. 'We lost the outwork on our part.'

'That is a shrewd loss,' said De Bracy; 'the knaves will find cover there to assault the castle more closely, and may, if not well watched, gain some unguarded corner of a tower, or some forgotten window, and so break in upon us. Our numbers are too few for the defence of every point, and the men complain that they can nowhere show themselves, but they are the mark for as many arrows as a parish-butt on a holyday even.* Front-de-Bœuf is dying too, so we shall receive no more aid from his bull's head and brutal strength. How think you, Sir Brian, were we not better make a virtue of necessity, and compound with the rogues by delivering up our prisoners?'

'How?' exclaimed the Templar; 'deliver up our prisoners, and stand an object alike of ridicule and execration, as the doughty warriors who dared by a night-attack to possess themselves of the persons of a party of defenceless travellers, yet could not make good a strong castle against a vagabond troop of outlaws, led by swineherds, jesters, and the very refuse of mankind?—Shame on thy counsel, Maurice de Bracy!—The ruins of this castle shall bury both my body and my shame, ere I consent to such base and dishonourable composition.'

'Let us to the walls, then,' said De Bracy, carelessly; 'that man never breathed, be he Turk or Templar, who held life at lighter rate than I do. But I trust there is no dishonour in wishing I had here some two scores of my gallant troop of Free Companions?—Oh, my brave lances! if ye knew but how hard your captain were this day bested, how soon should I see my banner at the head of your clump of spears! And how short while would these rabble villains stand to endure your encounter!'

'Wish for whom thou wilt,' said the Templar, 'but let us make what defence we can with the soldiers who remain—They are chiefly Front-de-Bœuf's followers, hated by the English for a thousand acts of insolence and oppression.'

'The better,' said De Bracy; 'the rugged slaves will defend themselves to the last drop of their blood, ere they encounter the revenge of the peasants without. Let us up and be doing, then, Brian de Bois-Guilbert; and, live or die, thou shalt see Maurice de Bracy bear himself this day as a gentleman of blood and lineage.'

'To the walls!' answered the Templar; and they both ascended the battlements to do all that skill could dictate, and manhood accomplish, in defence of the place. They readily agreed that the point of greatest danger was that opposite to the outwork of which the assailants had possessed themselves. The castle, indeed, was divided from that barbican by the moat, and it was impossible that the besiegers could assail the postern-door, with which the outwork corresponded, without surmounting that obstacle; but it was the opinion both of the Templar and De Bracy, that the besiegers, if governed by the same policy their leader had already displayed, would endeavour, by a formidable assault, to draw the chief part of the defenders' observation to this point, and take measures to avail themselves of every negligence which might take place in the defence elsewhere. To guard against such an evil, their numbers only permitted the knights to place sentinels from space to space along the walls in communication with each other, who might give the alarm whenever danger was threatened. Meanwhile, they agreed that De Bracy should command the defence at the postern, and the Templar should keep with him a score of men or thereabouts as a body of reserve, ready to hasten to any other point which might be suddenly threatened. The loss of the barbican had also this unfortunate effect, that, notwithstanding the superior height of the castle walls, the besieged could not see from them, with the

same precision as before, the operations of the enemy; for some
straggling underwood approached so near the sallyport of the
outwork, that the assailants might introduce into it whatever
force they thought proper, not only under cover, but even without the knowledge of the defenders. Utterly uncertain, therefore,
upon what point the storm was to burst, De Bracy and his
companion were under the necessity of providing against every
possible contingency, and their followers, however brave, experienced the anxious dejection of mind incident to men enclosed by enemies, who possessed the power of choosing their
time and mode of attack.

Meanwhile, the lord of the beleaguered and endangered castle
lay upon a bed of bodily pain and mental agony. He had not the
usual resource of bigots in that superstitious period, most of
whom were wont to atone for the crimes they were guilty of by
liberality to the church, stupifying by this means their terrors by
the idea of atonement and forgiveness; and although the refuge
which success thus purchased, was no more like to the peace of
mind which follows on sincere repentance, than the turbid stu-
pefaction procured by opium resembles healthy and natural
slumbers, it was still a state of mind preferable to the agonies of
awakened remorse. But among the vices of Front-de-Bœuf, a
hard and griping man, avarice was predominant; and he preferred setting church and churchmen at defiance, to purchasing
from them pardon and absolution at the price of treasure and of
manors. Nor did the Templar, an infidel of another stamp, justly
characterise his associate, when he said Front-de-Bœuf could
assign no cause for his unbelief and contempt for the established
faith; for the Baron would have alleged that the Church sold her
wares too dear, that the spiritual freedom which she put up to
sale was only to be bought like that of the chief captain of
Jerusalem, 'with a great sum,'* and Front-de-Bœuf preferred
denying the virtue of the medicine, to paying the expense of the
physician.

But the moment had now arrived when earth and all his
treasures were gliding from before his eyes, and when the savage
Baron's heart, though hard as a nether millstone,* became appalled as he gazed forward into the waste darkness of futurity.
The fever of his body aided the impatience and agony of his

mind, and his death-bed exhibited a mixture of the newly awakened feelings of horror, combating with the fixed and inveterate obstinacy of his disposition;—a fearful state of mind, only to be equalled in those tremendous regions, where there are complaints without hope, remorse without repentance, a dreadful sense of present agony, and a presentiment that it cannot cease or be diminished!

'Where be these dog-priests now,' growled the Baron, 'who set such price on their ghostly mummery?—where be all those unshod Carmelites, for whom old Front-de-Bœuf founded the convent of St Anne, robbing his heir of many a fair rood of meadow, and many a fat field and close—where be the greedy hounds now?—Swilling, I warrant me, at the ale, or playing their juggling tricks at the bedside of some miserly churl.—Me, the heir of their founder—me, whom their foundation binds them to pray for—me—ungrateful villains as they are!—they suffer to die like the houseless dog on yonder common, unshriven and unhouseled!*—Tell the Templar to come hither—he is a priest, and may do something—But no!—as well confess myself to the devil as to Brian de Bois-Guilbert, who recks neither of heaven nor of hell.—I have heard old men talk of prayer—prayer by their own voice—such need not to court or to bribe the false priest—But I—I dare not!'

'Lives Reginald Front-de-Bœuf,' said a broken and shrill voice close by his bedside, 'to say there is that which he dares not!'

The evil conscience and the shaken nerves of Front-de-Bœuf heard, in this strange interruption to his soliloquy, the voice of one of those demons, who, as the superstition of the times believed, beset the beds of dying men, to distract their thoughts, and turn them from the meditations which concerned their eternal welfare. He shuddered and drew himself together; but, instantly summoning up his wonted resolution, he exclaimed, 'Who is there?—what art thou, that darest to echo my words in a tone like that of the night-raven?—Come before my couch that I may see thee.'

'I am thine evil angel, Reginald Front-de-Bœuf,' replied the voice.

'Let me behold thee then in thy bodily shape, if thou be'st

indeed a fiend,' replied the dying knight; 'think not that I will blench from thee.—By the eternal dungeon, could I but grapple with these horrors that hover round me, as I have done with mortal dangers, heaven or hell should never say that I shrunk from the conflict!'

'Think on thy sins, Reginald Front-de-Bœuf,' said the almost unearthly voice, 'on rebellion, on rapine, on murder!—Who stirred up the licentious John to war against his grey-headed father—against his generous brother?'

'Be thou fiend, priest, or devil,' replied Front-de-Bœuf, 'thou liest in thy throat!—Not I stirred John to rebellion—not I alone—there were fifty knights and barons, the flower of the midland counties—better men never laid lance in rest—And must I answer for the fault done by fifty?—False fiend, I defy thee! Depart, and haunt my couch no more—let me die in peace if thou be mortal—if thou be a demon, thy time is not yet come.'

'In peace thou shalt NOT die,' repeated the voice; 'even in death shalt thou think on thy murders—on the groans which this castle has echoed—on the blood that is engrained in its floors!'

'Thou canst not shake me by thy petty malice,' answered Front-de-Bœuf, with a ghastly and constrained laugh. 'The infidel Jew—it was merit with heaven to deal with him as I did, else wherefore are men canonized who dip their hands in the blood of Saracens?—The Saxon porkers, whom I have slain, they were the foes of my country, and of my lineage, and of my liege lord.—Ho! ho! thou seest there is no crevice in my coat of plate—Art thou fled?—art thou silenced?'

'No, foul parricide!' replied the voice; 'think of thy father!— think of his death!—think of his banquet-room flooded with his gore, and that poured forth by the hand of a son!'

'Ha!' answered the Baron, after a long pause, 'an thou knowest that, thou art indeed the author of evil, and as omniscient as the monks call thee!—That secret I deemed locked in my own breast, and in that of one besides—the temptress, the partaker of my guilt.—Go, leave me, fiend! and seek the Saxon witch Ulrica, who alone could tell thee what she and I alone witnessed.—Go, I say, to her, who washed the wounds, and straighted the corpse, and gave to the slain man the outward show of one parted in time and in the course of nature—Go to her, she was my temptress, the foul provoker, the more foul rewarder, of the deed—let her, as well as I, taste of the tortures which anticipate hell!'

'She already tastes them,' said Ulrica, stepping before the couch of Front-de-Bœuf; 'she hath long drunken of this cup, and its bitterness is now sweetened to see that thou dost partake it.—Grind not thy teeth, Front-de-Bœuf—roll not thine eyes—clench not thy hand, nor shake it at me with that gesture of menace!—The hand which, like that of thy renowned ancestor who gained thy name, could have broken with one stroke the skull of a mountain-bull, is now unnerved and powerless as mine own!'

'Vile murderous hag!' replied Front-de-Bœuf; 'detestable screech-owl! it is then thou who art come to exult over the ruins thou hast assisted to lay low?'

'Ay, Reginald Front-de-Bœuf,' answered she, 'it is Ulrica!—it is the daughter of the murdered Torquil Wolfganger!—it is the sister of his slaughtered sons!—it is she who demands of thee, and of thy father's house, father and kindred, name and fame—all that she has lost by the name of Front-de-Bœuf!—Think of my wrongs, Front-de-Bœuf, and answer me if I speak not truth. Thou hast been my evil angel, and I will be thine—I will dog thee till the very instant of dissolution!'

'Detestable fury!' exclaimed Front-de-Bœuf, 'that moment shalt thou never witness—Ho! Giles, Clement, and Eustace! Saint Maur, and Stephen! seize this damned witch, and hurl her from the battlements headlong—she has betrayed us to the Saxon!—Ho! Saint Maur! Clement! false-hearted knaves, where tarry ye?'

'Call on them again, valiant Baron,' said the hag, with a smile of grisly mockery; 'summon thy vassals around thee, doom them that loiter to the scourge and the dungeon—But know, mighty chief,' she continued, suddenly changing her tone, 'thou shalt have neither answer, nor aid, nor obedience at their hands.—Listen to these horrid sounds,' for the din of the recommenced assault and defence now rung fearfully loud from the battlements of the castle; 'in that war-cry is the downfall of thy house—The blood-cemented fabric of Front-de-Bœuf's power totters to the foundation, and before the foes he most despised!—The Saxon, Reginald!—the scorned Saxon assails thy walls!—Why liest thou here, like a worn-out hind, when the Saxon storms thy place of strength?'

'Gods and fiends!' exclaimed the wounded knight; 'O, for one moment's strength, to drag myself to the *mêlée*, and perish as becomes my name!'

'Think not of it, valiant warrior!' replied she; 'thou shalt die no soldier's death, but perish like the fox in his den, when the peasants have set fire to the cover around it.'

'Hateful hag! thou liest!'* exclaimed Front-de-Bœuf; 'my followers bear them bravely—my walls are strong and high—my comrades in arms fear not a whole host of Saxons, were they headed by Hengist and Horsa!—The war-cry of the Templar and of the Free Companions rises high over the conflict! And by mine honour, when we kindle the blazing beacon, for joy of our defence, it shall consume thee, body and bones; and I shall live to hear thou art gone from earthly fires to those of that hell, which never sent forth an incarnate fiend more utterly diabolical!'

'Hold thy belief,' replied Ulrica, 'till the proof reach thee—But, no!' she said, interrupting herself, 'thou shalt know, even now, the doom, which all thy power, strength, and courage, is unable to avoid, though it is prepared for thee by this feeble hand. Markest thou the smouldering and suffocating vapour which already eddies in sable folds through the chamber?—Didst thou think it was but the darkening of thy bursting eyes—the difficulty of thy cumbered breathing?—No! Front-de-Bœuf, there is another cause—Rememberest thou the magazine of fuel that is stored beneath these apartments?'

'Woman!' he exclaimed with fury, 'thou hast not set fire to it?—By heaven, thou hast, and the castle is in flames!'

'They are fast rising at least,' said Ulrica, with frightful composure; 'and a signal shall soon wave to warn the besiegers to press hard upon those who would extinguish them.—Farewell, Front-de-Bœuf!—May Mista, Skogula, and Zernebock, gods of the ancient Saxons—fiends, as the priests now call them—supply the place of comforters at your dying bed, which Ulrica now relinquishes!—But know, if it will give thee comfort to know it, that Ulrica is bound to the same dark coast with thyself, the

companion of thy punishment as the companion of thy guilt.—
And now, parricide, farewell for ever!—May each stone of this
vaulted roof find a tongue* to echo that title into thine ear!'

So saying, she left the apartment; and Front-de-Bœuf could
hear the crash of the ponderous key, as she locked and double-
locked the door behind her, thus cutting off the most slender
chance of escape. In the extremity of agony he shouted upon his
servants and allies—'Stephen and Saint Maur!—Clement and
Giles!—I burn here unaided!—To the rescue—to the rescue,
brave Bois-Guilbert, valiant De Bracy!—It is Front-de-Bœuf
who calls!—It is your master, ye traitor squires!—Your ally—
your brother in arms, ye perjured and faithless knights!—all the
curses due to traitors upon your recreant heads, do you abandon
me to perish thus miserably!—They hear me not—they cannot
hear me—my voice is lost in the din of battle.—The smoke rolls
thicker and thicker—the fire has caught upon the floor below—
O, for one draught of the air of heaven, were it to be purchased
by instant annihilation!' And in the mad frenzy of despair, the
wretch now shouted with the shouts of the fighters, now muttered curses on himself, on mankind, and on Heaven itself.—
'The red fire flashes through the thick smoke!' he exclaimed; 'the
demon marches against me under the banner of his own element—Foul spirit, avoid!*—I go not with thee without my
comrades—all, all are thine, that garrison these walls—Thinkest
thou Front-de-Bœuf will be singled out to go alone?—No—the
infidel Templar—the licentious De Bracy—Ulrica, the foul
murdering strumpet—the men who aided my enterprises—the
dog Saxons and accursed Jews, who are my prisoners—all, all
shall attend me—a goodly fellowship as ever took the downward
road—Ha, ha, ha!' and he laughed in his frenzy till the vaulted
roof rang again. 'Who laughed there?' exclaimed Front-de-
Bœuf, in altered mood, for the noise of the conflict did not
prevent the echoes of his own mad laughter from returning upon
his ear—'who laughed there?—Ulrica, was it thou?—Speak,
witch, and I forgive thee—for, only thou or the fiend of hell
himself could have laughed at such a moment. Avaunt—
avaunt!'——

But it were impious to trace any farther the picture of the
blasphemer and parricide's death-bed.

CHAPTER XXXI*

Once more unto the breach, dear friends, once more,
Or close the wall up with our English dead.
————And you, good yeomen,
Whose limbs were made in England, show us here
The mettle of your pasture—let us swear
That you are worth your breeding.

King Henry V

CEDRIC, although not greatly confident in Ulrica's message, omitted not to communicate her promise to the Black Knight and Locksley. They were well pleased to find they had a friend within the place, who might, in the moment of need, be able to facilitate their entrance, and readily agreed with the Saxon that a storm, under whatever disadvantages, ought to be attempted, as the only means of liberating the prisoners now in the hands of the cruel Front-de-Bœuf.

'The royal blood of Alfred is endangered,' said Cedric.

'The honour of a noble lady is in peril,' said the Black Knight.

'And, by the Saint Christopher at my baldric,'* said the good yeoman, 'were there no other cause than the safety of that poor faithful knave, Wamba, I would jeopard* a joint ere a hair of his head were hurt.'

'And so would I,' said the Friar; 'what, sirs! I trust well that a fool—I mean, d'ye see me, sirs, a fool that is free of his guild and master of his craft, and can give as much relish and flavour to a cup of wine as ever a flitch of bacon can—I say, brethren, such a fool shall never want a wise clerk to pray for or fight for him at a strait, while I can say a mass or flourish a partisan.'

And with that he made his heavy halberd to play around his head as a shepherd boy flourishes his light crook.

'True, Holy Clerk,' said the Black Knight, 'true as if Saint Dunstan himself had said it.—And now, good Locksley, were it not well that noble Cedric should assume the direction of this assault?'

'Not a jot I,' returned Cedric; 'I have never been wont to study either how to take or how to hold out those abodes of tyrannic power, which the Normans have erected in this groaning land. I will fight among the foremost; but my honest neighbours well know I am not a trained soldier in the discipline of wars, or the attack of strongholds.'

'Since it stands thus with noble Cedric,' said Locksley, 'I am most willing to take on me the direction of the archery; and ye shall hang me up on my own trysting-tree,* an the defenders be permitted to show themselves over the walls without being stuck with as many shafts as there are cloves in a gammon of bacon at Christmas.'

'Well said, stout yeoman,' answered the Black Knight; 'and if I be thought worthy to have a charge in these matters, and can find among these brave men as many as are willing to follow a true English knight, for so I may surely call myself, I am ready, with such skill as my experience has taught me, to lead them to the attack of these walls.'

The parts being thus distributed to the leaders, they commenced the first assault, of which the reader has already heard the issue.

When the barbican was carried, the Sable Knight sent notice of the happy event to Locksley, requesting him at the same time, to keep such a strict observation on the castle as might prevent the defenders from combining their force for a sudden sally, and recovering the outwork which they had lost. This the knight was chiefly desirous of avoiding, conscious that the men whom he led, being hasty and untrained volunteers, imperfectly armed and unaccustomed to discipline, must, upon any sudden attack, fight at great disadvantage with the veteran soldiers of the Norman knights, who were well provided with arms both defensive and offensive; and who, to match the zeal and high spirit of the besiegers, had all the confidence which arises from perfect discipline and the habitual use of weapons.

The knight employed the interval in causing to be constructed a sort of floating bridge, or long raft, by means of which he hoped to cross the moat in despite of the resistance of the enemy. This was a work of some time, which the leaders the less regretted, as it gave Ulrica leisure to execute her plan of diversion in their favour, whatever that might be.

When the raft was completed, the Black Knight addressed the besiegers:—'It avails not waiting here longer, my friends; the sun is descending to the west—and I have that upon my hands which will not permit me to tarry with you another day. Besides, it will be a marvel if the horsemen come not upon us from York, unless we speedily accomplish our purpose. Wherefore, one of ye go to Locksley, and bid him commence a discharge of arrows on the opposite side of the castle, and move forward as if about to assault it; and you, true English hearts, stand by me, and be ready to thrust the raft endlong over the moat whenever the postern on our side is thrown open. Follow me boldly across, and aid me to burst yon sallyport in the main wall of the castle. As many of you as like not this service, or are but ill armed to meet it, do you man the top of the outwork, draw your bowstrings to your ears, and mind you quell with your shot whatever shall appear to man the rampart—Noble Cedric, wilt thou take the direction of those which remain?'

'Not so, by the soul of Hereward!' said the Saxon; 'lead I cannot; but may posterity curse me in my grave, if I follow not with the foremost wherever thou shalt point the way—The quarrel is mine, and well it becomes me to be in the van of the battle.'

'Yet, bethink thee, noble Saxon,' said the knight, 'thou hast neither hauberk, nor corslet, nor aught but that light helmet, target, and sword.'

'The better!' answered Cedric; 'I shall be the lighter to climb these walls. And,—forgive the boast, Sir Knight,—thou shalt this day see the naked breast of a Saxon as boldly presented to the battle as ever ye beheld the steel corslet of a Norman.'

'In the name of God, then,' said the knight, 'fling open the door, and launch the floating bridge.'

The portal, which led from the inner-wall of the barbican to the moat, and which corresponded with a sallyport in the main wall of the castle, was now suddenly opened; the temporary bridge was then thrust forward, and soon flashed in the waters, extending its length between the castle and outwork, and forming a slippery and precarious passage for two men abreast to cross the moat. Well aware of the importance of taking the foe by surprise, the Black Knight, closely followed by Cedric, threw himself upon the bridge, and reached the opposite side. Here he began to thunder with his axe upon the gate of the castle, protected in part from the shot and stones cast by the defenders by the ruins of the former drawbridge, which the Templar had demolished in his retreat from the barbican, leaving the counterpoise still attached to the upper part of the portal. The followers of the knight had no such shelter; two were instantly shot with crossbow bolts, and two more fell into the moat; the others retreated back into the barbican.

The situation of Cedric and of the Black Knight was now truly dangerous, and would have been still more so, but for the constancy of the archers in the barbican, who ceased not to shower their arrows upon the battlements, distracting the attention of those by whom they were manned, and thus affording a respite to their two chiefs from the storm of missiles which must otherwise have overwhelmed them. But their situation was eminently perilous, and was becoming more so with every moment.

'Shame on ye all!' cried De Bracy to the soldiers around him; 'do ye call yourselves crossbowmen, and let these two dogs keep their station under the walls of the castle?——Heave over the coping stones from the battlement, an better may not be——Get pick-axe and levers, and down with that huge pinnacle!' pointing to a heavy piece of stone carved-work that projected from the parapet.

At this moment the besiegers caught sight of the red flag upon the angle of the tower which Ulrica had described to Cedric. The stout yeoman Locksley was the first who was aware of it, as he was hasting to the outwork, impatient to see the progress of the assault.

'Saint George!' he cried, 'Merry Saint George for England!—— To the charge, bold yeomen!——why leave ye the good knight and noble Cedric to storm the pass alone?——make in, mad priest, show thou canst fight for thy rosary,——make in, brave yeomen!—— the castle is ours, we have friends within——See yonder flag, it is the appointed signal——Torquilstone is ours!——Think of honour, think of spoil——One effort, and the place is ours!'

With that he bent his good bow, and sent a shaft right through the breast of one of the men-at-arms, who, under De Bracy's direction, was loosening a fragment from one of the battlements to precipitate on the heads of Cedric and the Black Knight. A second soldier caught from the hands of the dying man the iron crow, with which he heaved at and had loosened the stone pinnacle, when, receiving an arrow through his head-piece, he dropped from the battlements into the moat a dead man. The men-at-arms were daunted, for no armour seemed proof against the shot of this tremendous archer.

'Do you give ground, base knaves!' said De Bracy; '*Mount joye Saint Dennis!**—Give me the lever!'

And, snatching it up, he again assailed the loosened pinnacle, which was of weight enough, if thrown down, not only to have destroyed the remnant of the drawbridge, which sheltered the two foremost assailants, but also to have sunk the rude float of planks over which they had crossed. All saw the danger, and the boldest, even the stout Friar himself, avoided setting foot on the raft. Thrice did Locksley bend his shaft against De Bracy, and thrice did his arrow bound back from the knight's armour of proof.

'Curse on thy Spanish steel-coat!' said Locksley, 'had English smith forged it, these arrows had gone through, an as if it had been silk or sendal.'* He then began to call out, 'Comrades! friends! noble Cedric! bear back, and let the ruin fall.'

His warning voice was unheard, for the din which the knight himself occasioned by his strokes upon the postern would have drowned twenty war-trumpets. The faithful Gurth indeed sprung forward on the planked bridge, to warn Cedric of his impending fate, or to share it with him. But his warning would have come too late; the massive pinnacle already tottered, and De Bracy, who still heaved at his task, would have accomplished it, had not the voice of the Templar sounded close in his ears:—

'All is lost, De Bracy, the castle burns.'

'Thou art mad to say so!' replied the knight.

'It is all in a light flame on the western side. I have striven in vain to extinguish it.'

With the stern coolness which formed the basis of his character, Brian de Bois-Guilbert communicated this hideous intelligence, which was not so calmly received by his astonished comrade.

'Saints of Paradise!' said De Bracy; 'what is to be done? I vow to Saint Nicholas of Limoges* a candlestick of pure gold'——

'Spare thy vow,' said the Templar, 'and mark me. Lead thy men down, as if to a sally; throw the postern-gate open—There are but two men who occupy the float, fling them into the moat, and push across for the barbican. I will charge from the main-gate, and attack the barbican on the outside; and if we can regain that post, be assured we shall defend ourselves until we are relieved, or at least till they grant us fair quarter.'

'It is well thought upon,' said De Bracy; 'I will play my part—Templar, thou wilt not fail me?'

'Hand and glove, I will not!' said Bois-Guilbert. 'But haste thee, in the name of God!'

De Bracy hastily drew his men together, and rushed down to the postern-gate, which he caused instantly to be thrown open. But scarce was this done ere the portentous strength of the Black Knight forced his way inward in despite of De Bracy and his followers. Two of the foremost instantly fell, and the rest gave way notwithstanding all their leader's efforts to stop them.

'Dogs!' said De Bracy, 'will ye let *two* men win our only pass for safety?'

'He is the devil!' said a veteran man-at-arms, bearing back from the blows of their sable antagonist.

'And if he be the devil,' replied De Bracy, 'would you fly from him into the mouth of hell?—the castle burns behind us, villains!—let despair give you courage, or let me forward! I will cope with this champion myself.'

And well and chivalrously did De Bracy that day maintain the fame he had acquired in the civil wars of that dreadful period. The vaulted passage to which the postern gave entrance, and in which these two redoubted champions were now fighting hand to hand, rung with the furious blows which they dealt each other, De Bracy with his sword, the Black Knight with his ponderous axe. At length the Norman received a blow, which, though its force was partly parried by his shield, for otherwise never more would De Bracy have again moved limb, descended yet with such violence on his crest, that he measured his length on the paved floor.

'Yield thee, De Bracy,' said the Black Champion, stooping

over him, and holding against the bars of his helmet the fatal poniard with which the knights dispatched their enemies, (and which was called the dagger of mercy,)*—'yield thee, Maurice de Bracy, rescue or no rescue, or thou art but a dead man.'

'I will not yield,' replied De Bracy faintly, 'to an unknown conqueror. Tell me thy name, or work thy pleasure on me—it shall never be said that Maurice de Bracy was prisoner to a nameless churl.'

The Black Knight whispered something into the ear of the vanquished.

'I yield me to be true prisoner, rescue or no rescue,' answered the Norman, exchanging his tone of stern and determined obstinacy for one of deep though sullen submission.

'Go to the barbican,' said the victor, in a tone of authority, 'and there wait my further orders.'

'Yet first, let me say,' said De Bracy, 'what it imports thee to know. Wilfred of Ivanhoe is wounded and a prisoner, and will perish in the burning castle without present help.'

'Wilfred of Ivanhoe!' exclaimed the Black Knight—'prisoner, and perish!—The life of every man in the castle shall answer it if a hair of his head be singed—Show me his chamber!'

'Ascend yonder winding stair,' said De Bracy; 'it leads to his apartment—Wilt thou not accept my guidance?' he added, in a submissive voice.

'No. To the barbican, and there wait my orders. I trust thee not, De Bracy.'

During this combat and the brief conversation which ensued, Cedric, at the head of a body of men, among whom the Friar was conspicuous, had pushed across the bridge as soon as they saw the postern open, and drove back the dispirited and despairing followers of De Bracy, of whom some asked quarter, some offered vain resistance, and the greater part fled towards the courtyard. De Bracy himself arose from the ground, and cast a sorrowful glance after his conqueror. 'He trusts me not!' he repeated; 'but have I deserved his trust?' He then lifted his sword from the floor, took off his helmet in token of submission, and, going to the barbican, gave up his sword to Locksley, whom he met by the way.

As the fire augmented, symptoms of it became soon apparent in the chamber, where Ivanhoe was watched and tended by the Jewess Rebecca. He had been awakened from his brief slumber by the noise of the battle; and his attendant, who had, at his anxious desire, again placed herself at the window to watch and report to him the fate of the attack, was for some time prevented from observing either, by the increase of the smouldering and stifling vapour. At length the volumes of smoke which rolled into the apartment—the cries for water, which were heard even above the din of the battle made them sensible of the progress of this new danger.

'The castle burns,' said Rebecca; 'it burns!—What can we do to save ourselves?'

'Fly, Rebecca, and save thine own life,' said Ivanhoe, 'for no human aid can avail me.'

'I will not fly,' answered Rebecca; 'we will be saved or perish together—And yet, great God!—my father, my father—what will be his fate!'

At this moment the door of the apartment flew open, and the Templar presented himself,—a ghastly figure, for his gilded armour was broken and bloody, and the plume was partly shorn away, partly burnt from his casque. 'I have found thee,' said he to Rebecca; 'thou shalt prove I will keep my word to share weal and woe with thee—There is but one path to safety, I have cut my way through fifty dangers to point it to thee—up, and instantly follow me!'[35]

'Alone,' answered Rebecca, 'I will not follow thee. If thou wert born of woman—if thou hast but a touch of human charity in thee—if thy heart be not hard as thy breastplate—save my aged father—save this wounded knight!'

'A knight,' answered the Templar, with his characteristic calmness, 'a knight, Rebecca, must encounter his fate, whether it meet him in the shape of sword or flame—and who recks how or where a Jew meets with his?'

'Savage warrior,' said Rebecca, 'rather will I perish in the flames than accept safety from thee!'

'Thou shalt not choose, Rebecca—once didst thou foil me, but never mortal did so twice.'

So saying, he seized on the terrified maiden, who filled the air with her shrieks, and bore her out of the room in his arms in spite of her cries, and without regarding the menaces and defiance which Ivanhoe thundered against him. 'Hound of the Temple—stain to thine Order—set free the damsel! Traitor of Bois-Guilbert, it is Ivanhoe commands thee!—Villain, I will have thy heart's blood!'

'I had not found thee, Wilfred,' said the Black Knight, who at that instant entered the apartment, 'but for thy shouts.'

'If thou be'st true knight,' said Wilfred, 'think not of me—pursue yon ravisher—save the Lady Rowena—look to the noble Cedric!'

'In their turn,' answered he of the fetterlock, 'but thine is first.'

And seizing upon Ivanhoe, he bore him off with as much ease as the Templar had carried off Rebecca, rushed with him to the postern, and having there delivered his burden to the care of two yeomen, he again entered the castle to assist in the rescue of the other prisoners.

One turret was now in bright flames, which flashed out furiously from window and shot-hole. But in other parts, the great thickness of the walls and the vaulted roofs of the apartments, resisted the progress of the flames, and there the rage of man still triumphed, as the scarce more dreadful element held mastery elsewhere; for the besiegers pursued the defenders of the castle from chamber to chamber, and satiated in their blood the vengeance which had long animated them against the soldiers of the tyrant Front-de-Bœuf. Most of the garrison resisted to the uttermost—few of them asked quarter—none received it. The air was filled with groans and clashing of arms—the floors were slippery with the blood of despairing and expiring wretches.

Through this scene of confusion, Cedric rushed in quest of Rowena, while the faithful Gurth, following him closely through the *mêlée*, neglected his own safety while he strove to avert the blows that were aimed at his master. The noble Saxon was so fortunate as to reach his ward's apartment just as she had abandoned all hope of safety, and, with a crucifix clasped in agony to her bosom, sat in expectation of instant death. He committed her to the charge of Gurth, to be conducted in safety to the barbican, the road to which was now cleared of the enemy, and not yet interrupted by the flames. This accomplished, the loyal Cedric hastened in quest of his friend Athelstane, determined, at every risk to himself, to save that last scion of Saxon royalty. But ere Cedric penetrated as far as the old hall in which he had himself been a prisoner, the inventive genius of Wamba had procured liberation for himself and his companion in adversity.

When the noise of the conflict announced that it was at the hottest, the Jester began to shout, with the utmost power of his lungs, 'Saint George and the dragon!—Bonny Saint George for merry England!—The castle is won!' And these sounds he rendered yet more fearful, by banging against each other two or three pieces of rusty armour which lay scattered around the hall.

A guard, which had been stationed in the outer, or anteroom, and whose spirits were already in a state of alarm, took fright at Wamba's clamour, and, leaving the door open behind them, ran to tell the Templar that foemen had entered the old hall. Meantime the prisoners found no difficulty in making their escape into the anteroom, and from thence into the court of the castle, which was now the last scene of contest. Here sat the fierce Templar, mounted on horseback, surrounded by several of the garrison both on horse and foot, who had united their strength to that of this renowned leader, in order to secure the last chance of safety and retreat which remained to them. The drawbridge had been lowered by his orders, but the passage was beset; for the archers, who had hitherto only annoyed the castle on that side by their missiles, no sooner saw the flames breaking out, and the bridge lowered, than they thronged to the entrance, as well to prevent the escape of the garrison, as to secure their own share of booty ere the castle should be burnt down. On the other hand, a party of the besiegers who had entered by the postern were now issuing out into the court-yard, and attacking with fury the remnant of the defenders who were thus assaulted on both sides at once.

Animated, however, by despair, and supported by the example of their indomitable leader, the remaining soldiers of the castle fought with the utmost valour; and, being well armed, succeeded more than once in driving back the assailants, though much inferior in numbers. Rebecca, placed on horseback before one of the Templar's Saracen slaves, was in the midst of the little party; and Bois-Guilbert, notwithstanding the confusion of the bloody fray, showed every attention to her safety. Repeatedly he was by her side, and, neglecting his own defence, held before her the fence of his triangular steel-plated shield; and anon starting from his position by her, he cried his war-cry, dashed forward, struck to earth the most forward of the assailants, and was on the same instant once more at her bridle rein.

Athelstane, who, as the reader knows, was slothful, but not cowardly, beheld the female form whom the Templar protected thus sedulously, and doubted not that it was Rowena whom the knight was carrying off, in despite of all resistance which could be offered.

'By the soul of Saint Edward,' he said, 'I will rescue her from yonder over-proud knight, and he shall die by my hand!'

'Think what you do!' cried Wamba; 'hasty hand catches frog for fish*—by my bauble, yonder is none of my Lady Rowena— see but her long dark locks!—Nay, an ye will not know black from white, ye may be leader, but I will be no follower—no bones of mine shall be broken unless I know for whom.—And you without armour too!—Bethink you, silk bonnet never kept out steel blade.—Nay, then, if wilful will to water, wilful must drench.—*Deus vobiscum*, most doughty Athelstane!'—he concluded, loosening the hold which he had hitherto kept upon the Saxon's tunic.

To snatch a mace from the pavement, on which it lay beside one whose dying grasp had just relinquished it—to rush on the Templar's band, and to strike in quick succession to the right and left, levelling a warrior at each blow, was, for Athelstane's great strength, now animated with unusual fury, but the work of a single moment; he was soon within two yards of Bois-Guilbert, whom he defied in his loudest tone.

'Turn, false-hearted Templar! let go her whom thou art unworthy to touch—turn, limb of a band of murdering and hypocritical robbers!'

'Dog!' said the Templar, grinding his teeth, 'I will teach thee to blaspheme the holy Order of the Temple of Zion;' and with these words, half-wheeling his steed, he made a demi-courbette* towards the Saxon, and rising in the stirrups, so as to take full advantage of the descent of the horse, he discharged a fearful blow upon the head of Athelstane.

Well said Wamba, that silken bonnet keeps out no steel blade. So trenchant was the Templar's weapon, that it shore asunder, as it had been a willow twig, the tough and plaited handle of the mace, which the ill-fated Saxon reared to parry the blow, and, descending on his head, levelled him with the earth.*

'*Ha! Beau-seant!*' exclaimed Bois-Guilbert, 'thus be it to the maligners of the Temple-knights!' Taking advantage of the dismay which was spread by the fall of Athelstane, and calling aloud, 'Those who would save themselves, follow me!' he pushed across the drawbridge, dispersing the archers who would have intercepted them. He was followed by his Saracens, and some five or six men-at-arms, who had mounted their horses. The Templar's retreat was rendered perilous by the numbers of arrows shot off at him and his party; but this did not prevent him from galloping round to the barbican, of which, according to his previous plan, he supposed it possible De Bracy might have been in possession.

'De Bracy! De Bracy!' he shouted, 'art thou there?'

'I am here,' replied De Bracy, 'but I am a prisoner.'

'Can I rescue thee?' cried Bois-Guilbert.

'No,' replied De Bracy; 'I have rendered me, rescue or no rescue. I will be true prisoner. Save thyself—there are hawks abroad—put the seas betwixt you and England—I dare not say more.'

'Well,' answered the Templar, 'an thou wilt tarry there, remember I have redeemed word and glove. Be the hawks where they will, methinks the walls of the Preceptory of Templestowe will be cover sufficient, and thither will I, like heron to her haunt.'

Having thus spoken, he galloped off with his followers.

Those of the castle who had not gotten to horse, still continued to fight desperately with the besiegers, after the departure of the Templar, but rather in despair of quarter than that they entertained any hope of escape. The fire was spreading rapidly through all parts of the castle, when Ulrica, who had first kindled it, appeared on a turret, in the guise of one of the ancient furies, yelling forth a war-song, such as was of yore raised on the field of

battle by the scalds of the yet heathen Saxons. Her long dishevelled grey hair flew back from her uncovered head; the inebriat-
ing delight of gratified vengeance contended in her eyes with the
fire of insanity; and she brandished the distaff which she held in
her hand, as if she had been one of the Fatal Sisters,* who spin
and abridge the thread of human life. Tradition has preserved
some wild strophes of the barbarous hymn which she chanted
wildly amid that scene of fire and of slaughter:—

1.

Whet the bright steel,
Sons of the White Dragon!
Kindle the torch,
Daughter of Hengist!
The steel glimmers not for the carving of the banquet,
It is hard, broad, and sharply pointed;
The torch goeth not to the bridal chamber,
It steams and glitters blue with sulphur.
Whet the steel, the raven croaks!
Light the torch, Zernebock is yelling!
Whet the steel, sons of the Dragon!
Kindle the torch, daughter of Hengist!

2.

The black cloud is low over the thane's castle;
The eagle screams—he rides on its bosom.
Scream not, grey rider of the sable cloud,
Thy banquet is prepared!
The maidens of Valhalla look forth,
The race of Hengist will send them guests.
Shake your black tresses, maidens of Valhalla!
And strike your loud timbrels for joy!
Many a haughty step bends to your halls,
Many a helmed head.

3.

Dark sits the evening upon the thane's castle,
The black clouds gather round;
Soon shall they be red as the blood of the valiant!
The destroyer of forests shall shake his red crest
    against them.
He, the bright consumer of palaces,

Broad waves he his blazing banner,
Red, wide and dusky,
Over the strife of the valiant:
His joy is in the clashing swords and broken bucklers;
He loves to lick the hissing blood as it bursts warm
   from the wound!

4.

All must perish!
The sword cleaveth the helmet;
The strong armour is pierced by the lance;
Fire devoureth the dwelling of princes,
Engines break down the fences of the battle.
All must perish!
The race of Hengist is gone——
The name of Horsa is no more!
Shrink not then from your doom, sons of the sword!
Let your blades drink blood like wine;
Feast ye in the banquet of slaughter,
By the light of the blazing halls!
Strong be your swords while your blood is warm,
And spare neither for pity nor fear,
For vengeance hath but an hour;
Strong hate itself shall expire!
I also must perish![36]

    The towering flames had now surmounted every obstruction, and rose to the evening skies one huge and burning beacon, seen far and wide through the adjacent country. Tower after tower crashed down, with blazing roof and rafter; and the combatants were driven from the court-yard. The vanquished, of whom very few remained, scattered and escaped into the neighbouring wood. The victors, assembling in large bands, gazed with wonder, not unmixed with fear, upon the flames, in which their own ranks and arms glanced dusky red. The maniac figure of the Saxon Ulrica was for a long time visible on the lofty stand she had chosen, tossing her arms abroad with wild exultation, as if she reigned empress of the conflagration which she had raised. At length, with a terrific crash, the whole turret gave way, and she perished in the flames which had consumed her tyrant. An awful pause of horror silenced each murmur of the armed spectators, who, for the space of several minutes, stirred not a finger, save to sign the cross. The voice of Locksley was then heard, 'Shout, yeomen!—the den of tyrants is no more! Let each bring his spoil to our chosen place of rendezvous at the Trysting-tree in the Harthill-walk; for there at break of day will we make just partition among our own bands, together with our worthy allies in this great deed of vengeance.'

CHAPTER XXXII

Trust me each state must have its policies:
Kingdoms have edicts, cities have their charters;
Even the wild outlaw, in his forest-walk,
Keeps yet some touch of civil discipline;
For not since Adam wore his verdant apron,
Hath man with man in social union dwelt,
But laws were made to draw that union closer.

Old Play*

THE daylight had dawned upon the glades of the oak forest. The green boughs glittered with all their pearls of dew. The hind led her fawn from the covert of high fern to the more open walks of the greenwood, and no huntsman was there to watch or intercept the stately hart, as he paced at the head of the antler'd herd.

The outlaws were all assembled around the Trysting-tree in the Harthill-walk, where they had spent the night in refreshing themselves after the fatigues of the siege, some with wine, some with slumber, many with hearing and recounting the events of the day, and computing the heaps of plunder which their success had placed at the disposal of their Chief.

The spoils were indeed very large; for, notwithstanding that much was consumed, a great deal of plate, rich armour, and splendid clothing, had been secured by the exertions of the dauntless outlaws, who could be appalled by no danger when such rewards were in view. Yet so strict were the laws of their society, that no one ventured to appropriate any part of the booty, which was brought into one common mass, to be at the disposal of their leader.

The place of rendezvous was an aged oak; not however the same to which Locksley had conducted Gurth and Wamba in the earlier part of the story, but one which was the centre of a silvan amphitheatre, within half a mile of the demolished castle of Torquilstone. Here Locksley assumed his seat—a throne of turf erected under the twisted branches of the huge oak, and his silvan followers were gathered around him. He assigned to the

Black Knight a seat at his right hand, and to Cedric a place upon his left.

'Pardon my freedom, noble sirs,' he said, 'but in these glades I am monarch—they are my kingdom; and these my wild subjects would reck but little of my power, were I, within my own dominions, to yield place to mortal man.—Now, sirs, who hath seen our chaplain? where is our curtal Friar? A mass amongst Christian men best begins a busy morning.'—No one had seen the Clerk of Copmanhurst. 'Over gods forbode!' said the outlaw chief, 'I trust the jolly priest hath but abidden* by the wine-pot a thought too late. Who saw him since the castle was ta'en?'

'I,' quoth the Miller, 'marked him busy about the door of a cellar, swearing by each saint in the calendar he would taste the smack of Front-de-Bœuf's Gascoigne wine.'

'Now, the saints, as many as there be of them,' said the Captain, 'forefend, lest he has drunk too deep of the wine-butts, and perished by the fall of the castle!—Away, Miller!—take with you enow of men, seek the place where you last saw him—throw water from the moat on the scorching ruins—I will have them removed stone by stone ere I lose my curtal Friar.'

The numbers who hastened to execute this duty, considering that an interesting division of spoil was about to take place, showed how much the troop had at heart the safety of their spiritual father.

'Meanwhile, let us proceed,' said Locksley; 'for when this bold deed shall be sounded abroad, the bands of De Bracy, of Malvoisin, and other allies of Front-de-Bœuf, will be in motion against us, and it were well for our safety that we retreat from the vicinity.—Noble Cedric,' he said, turning to the Saxon, 'that spoil is divided into two portions; do thou make choice of that which best suits thee, to recompense thy people who were partakers with us in this adventure.'

'Good yeoman,' said Cedric, 'my heart is oppressed with sadness. The noble Athelstane of Coningsburgh is no more—the last sprout of the sainted Confessor! Hopes have perished with him which can never return!—A sparkle hath been quenched by his blood, which no human breath can again rekindle! My people, save the few who are now with me, do but tarry my presence to transport his honoured remains to their last mansion. The Lady Rowena is desirous to return to Rotherwood, and must be escorted by a sufficient force. I should, therefore, ere now, have left this place; and I waited—not to share the booty, for, so help me God and Saint Withold! as neither I nor any of mine will touch the value of a liard,*—I waited but to render my thanks to thee and to thy bold yeomen, for the life and honour ye have saved.'

'Nay, but,' said the chief Outlaw, 'we did but half the work at most—take of the spoil what may reward your own neighbours and followers.'

'I am rich enough to reward them from mine own wealth,' answered Cedric.

'And some,' said Wamba, 'have been wise enough to reward themselves; they do not march off empty-handed altogether. We do not all wear motley.'

'They are welcome,' said Locksley; 'our laws bind none but ourselves.'

'But, thou, my poor knave,' said Cedric, turning about and embracing his Jester, 'how shall I reward thee, who feared not to give thy body to chains and death instead of mine!—All forsook me, when the poor fool was faithful!'

A tear stood in the eye of the rough Thane as he spoke—a mark of feeling which even the death of Athelstane had not extracted; but there was something in the half-instinctive attachment of his clown, that waked his nature more keenly than even grief itself.

'Nay,' said the Jester, extricating himself from his master's caress, 'if you pay my service with the water of your eye, the Jester must weep for company, and then what becomes of his vocation?—But, uncle, if you would indeed pleasure me, I pray you to pardon my playfellow Gurth, who stole a week from your service to bestow it on your son.'

'Pardon him!' exclaimed Cedric; 'I will both pardon and reward him.—Kneel down, Gurth.'—The swineherd was in an instant at his master's feet—'THEOW and ESNE art thou no longer,' said Cedric, touching him with a wand; 'FOLK-FREE and SACLESS* art thou in town and from town, in the forest as in the field. A hide of land I give to thee in my steads of Walbrugham, from me and mine to thee and thine aye and for ever; and God's malison on his head who this gainsays!'

No longer a serf, but a freeman and a landholder, Gurth sprung upon his feet, and twice bounded aloft to almost his own height from the ground.

'A smith and a file,' he cried, 'to do away the collar from the neck of a freeman!—Noble master! doubled is my strength by your gift, and doubly will I fight for you!—There is a free spirit in my breast—I am a man changed to myself and all around.—Ha, Fangs!' he continued,—for that faithful cur, seeing his master thus transported, began to jump upon him, to express his sympathy,—'knowest thou thy master still?'

'Ay,' said Wamba, 'Fangs and I still know thee, Gurth, though we must needs abide by the collar; it is only thou art likely to forget both us and thyself.'

'I shall forget myself indeed ere I forget thee, true comrade,' said Gurth; 'and were freedom fit for thee, Wamba, the master would not let thee want it.'

'Nay,' said Wamba, 'never think I envy thee, brother Gurth; the serf sits by the hall-fire when the freeman must forth to the field of battle—And what saith Oldhelm of Malmsbury*—Better a fool at a feast than a wise man at a fray.'

The tramp of horses was now heard, and the Lady Rowena appeared, surrounded by several riders, and a much stronger party of footmen, who joyfully shook their pikes and clashed their brown-bills for joy of her freedom. She herself, richly attired, and mounted on a dark chestnut palfrey, had recovered all the dignity of her manner, and only an unwonted degree of paleness showed the sufferings she had undergone. Her lovely brow, though sorrowful, bore on it a cast of reviving hope for the future, as well as of grateful thankfulness for the past deliverance—She knew that Ivanhoe was safe, and she knew that Athelstane was dead. The former assurance filled her with the most sincere delight; and if she did not absolutely rejoice at the latter, she might be pardoned for feeling the full advantage of being freed from further persecution on the only subject in which she had ever been contradicted by her guardian Cedric.

As Rowena bent her steed towards Locksley's seat, that bold

yeoman, with all his followers, rose to receive her, as if by a
general instinct of courtesy. The blood rose to her cheeks, as,
courteously waving her hand, and bending so low that her
beautiful and loose tresses were for an instant mixed with the
flowing mane of her palfrey, she expressed in few but apt words
her obligations and her gratitude to Locksley and her other
deliverers.—'God bless you, brave men,' she concluded, 'God
and Our Lady bless you and requite you for gallantly perilling
yourselves in the cause of the oppressed!—If any of you should
hunger, remember Rowena has food—if you should thirst, she
has many a butt of wine and brown ale—and if the Normans
drive ye from these walks, Rowena has forests of her own, where
her gallant deliverers may range at full freedom, and never
ranger ask whose arrow hath struck down the deer.'

'Thanks, gentle lady,' said Locksley; 'thanks from my company and myself. But, to have saved you requites itself. We who
walk the greenwood do many a wild deed, and the Lady
Rowena's deliverance may be received as an atonement.'

Again bowing from her palfrey, Rowena turned to depart; but
pausing a moment, while Cedric, who was to attend her, was also
taking his leave, she found herself unexpectedly close by the
prisoner De Bracy. He stood under a tree in deep meditation, his
arms crossed upon his breast, and Rowena was in hopes she
might pass him unobserved. He looked up, however, and, when
aware of her presence, a deep flush of shame suffused his handsome countenance. He stood a moment most irresolute; then,
stepping forward, took her palfrey by the rein, and bent his knee
before her.

'Will the Lady Rowena deign to cast an eye on a captive
knight—on a dishonoured soldier?'

'Sir Knight,' answered Rowena, 'in enterprises such as yours,
the real dishonour lies not in failure, but in success.'

'Conquest, lady, should soften the heart,' answered De Bracy;
'let me but know that the Lady Rowena forgives the violence
occasioned by an ill-fated passion, and she shall soon learn that
De Bracy knows how to serve her in nobler ways.'

'I forgive you, Sir Knight,' said Rowena, 'as a Christian.'

'That means,' said Wamba, 'that she does not forgive him at
all.'

'But I can never forgive the misery and desolation your madness has occasioned,' continued Rowena.

'Unloose your hold on the lady's rein,' said Cedric, coming up. 'By the bright sun above us, but it were shame, I would pin thee to the earth with my javelin—but be well assured, thou shalt smart, Maurice de Bracy, for thy share in this foul deed.'

'He threatens safely who threatens a prisoner,' said De Bracy; 'but when had a Saxon any touch of courtesy?'

Then retiring two steps backward, he permitted the lady to move on.

Cedric, ere they departed, expressed his peculiar gratitude to the Black Champion, and earnestly entreated him to accompany him to Rotherwood.

'I know,' he said, 'that ye errant knights desire to carry your fortunes on the point of your lance, and reck not of land or goods; but war is a changeful mistress, and a home is sometimes desirable even to the champion whose trade is wandering. Thou hast earned one in the halls of Rotherwood, noble knight. Cedric has wealth enough to repair the injuries of fortune, and all he has is his deliverer's—Come, therefore, to Rotherwood, not as a guest, but as a son or brother.'

'Cedric has already made me rich,' said the Knight,—'he has taught me the value of Saxon virtue. To Rotherwood will I come, brave Saxon, and that speedily; but, as now, pressing matters of moment detain me from your halls. Peradventure when I come hither, I will ask such a boon as will put even thy generosity to the test.'

'It is granted ere spoken out,' said Cedric, striking his ready hand into the gauntleted palm of the Black Knight,—'it is granted already, were it to affect half my fortune.'

'Gage not thy promise so lightly,' said the Knight of the Fetterlock; 'yet well I hope to gain the boon I shall ask. Meanwhile, adieu.'

'I have but to say,' added the Saxon, 'that, during the funeral rites of the noble Athelstane, I shall be an inhabitant of the halls of his castle of Coningsburgh—They will be open to all who choose to partake of the funeral banqueting; and, I speak in name of the noble Edith, mother of the fallen prince, they will never be shut against him who laboured so bravely, though unsuccessfully, to save Athelstane from Norman chains and Norman steel.'

'Ay, ay,' said Wamba, who had resumed his attendance on his master, 'rare feeding there will be—pity that the noble Athelstane cannot banquet at his own funeral.—But he,' continued the Jester, lifting up his eyes gravely, 'is supping in Paradise, and doubtless does honour to the cheer.'

'Peace, and move on,' said Cedric, his anger at this untimely jest being checked by the recollection of Wamba's recent services. Rowena waved a graceful adieu to him of the Fetterlock— the Saxon bade God speed him, and on they moved through a wide glade of the forest.

They had scarce departed, ere a sudden procession moved from under the greenwood branches, swept slowly round the silvan amphitheatre, and took the same direction with Rowena and her followers. The priests of a neighbouring convent, in expectation of the ample donation, or soul-scat,* which Cedric had propined, attended upon the car in which the body of Athelstane was laid, and sang hymns as it was sadly and slowly borne on the shoulders of his vassals to his castle of Coningsburgh, to be there deposited in the grave of Hengist, from whom the deceased derived his long descent. Many of his vassals had assembled at the news of his death, and followed the bier with all the external marks, at least, of dejection and sorrow. Again the outlaws arose, and paid the same rude and spontaneous homage to death, which they had so lately rendered to beauty—the slow chant and mournful step of the priests brought back to their remembrance such of their comrades as had fallen in the yesterday's affray. But such recollections dwell not long with those who lead a life of danger and enterprise, and ere the sound of the death-hymn had died on the wind, the outlaws were again busied in the distribution of their spoil.

'Valiant knight,' said Locksley to the Black Champion, 'without whose good heart and mighty arm our enterprise must altogether have failed, will it please you to take from that mass of spoil whatever may best serve to pleasure you, and to remind you of this my Trysting-tree?'

'I accept the offer,' said the Knight, 'as frankly as it is given;

and I ask permission to dispose of Sir Maurice de Bracy at my own pleasure.'

'He is thine already,' said Locksley, 'and well for him! else the tyrant had graced the highest bough of this oak, with as many of his Free Companions as we could gather, hanging thick as acorns around him.—But he is thy prisoner, and he is safe, though he had slain my father.'

'De Bracy,' said the Knight, 'thou art free—depart. He whose prisoner thou art scorns to take mean revenge for what is past. But beware of the future, lest a worse thing befall thee.— Maurice de Bracy, I say BEWARE!'

De Bracy bowed low and in silence, and was about to withdraw, when the yeomen burst at once into a shout of execration and derision. The proud knight instantly stopped, turned back, folded his arms, drew up his form to its full height, and exclaimed, 'Peace, ye yelping curs! who open upon a cry which ye followed not when the stag was at bay—De Bracy scorns your censure as he would disdain your applause. To your brakes and caves, ye outlawed thieves! and be silent when aught knightly or noble is but spoken within a league of your fox-earths.'

This ill-timed defiance might have procured for De Bracy a volley of arrows, but for the hasty and imperative interference of the outlaw Chief. Meanwhile the knight caught a horse by the rein, for several which had been taken in the stables of Front-de-Bœuf stood accoutred around, and were a valuable part of the booty. He threw himself upon the saddle, and galloped off through the wood.

When the bustle occasioned by this incident was somewhat composed, the chief Outlaw took from his neck the rich horn and baldric which he had recently gained at the strife of archery near Ashby.

'Noble knight,' he said to him of the Fetterlock, 'if you disdain not to grace by your acceptance a bugle which an English yeoman has once worn, this I will pray you to keep as a memorial of your gallant bearing—and if ye have aught to do, and, as happeneth oft to a gallant knight, ye chance to be hard bested[37] in any forest between Trent and Tees, wind three mots[37] upon the horn thus, *Wa-sa-hoa!* and it may well chance ye shall find helpers and rescue.'*

He then gave breath to the bugle, and winded once and again the call which he described, until the knight had caught the notes.

'Gramercy for the gift, bold yeoman,' said the Knight; 'and better help than thine and thy rangers would I never seek, were it at my utmost need.' And then in his turn he winded the call till all the greenwood rang.

'Well blown and clearly,' said the yeoman; 'beshrew me an thou knowest not as much of woodcraft as of war!—thou hast been a striker of deer in thy day, I warrant.—Comrades, mark these three mots—it is the call of the Knight of the Fetterlock; and he who hears it, and hastens not to serve him at his need, I will have him scourged out of our band with his own bowstring.'

'Long live our leader!' shouted the yeomen, 'and long live the Black Knight of the Fetterlock!—May he soon use our service, to prove how readily it will be paid.'

Locksley now proceeded to the distribution of the spoil, which he performed with the most laudable impartiality. A tenth part of the whole was set apart for the church, and for pious uses; a portion was next allotted to a sort of public treasury; a part was assigned to the widows and children of those who had fallen, or to be expended in masses for the souls of such as had left no surviving family. The rest was divided amongst the outlaws, according to their rank and merit; and the judgment of the Chief, on all such doubtful questions as occurred, was delivered with great shrewdness, and received with absolute submission. The Black Knight was not a little surprised to find that men, in a state so lawless, were nevertheless among themselves so regularly and equitably governed, and all that he observed added to his opinion of the justice and judgment of their leader.

When each had taken his own proportion of the booty, and while the treasurer, accompanied by four tall yeomen, was transporting that belonging to the state to some place of concealment or of security, the portion devoted to the church still remained unappropriated.

'I would,' said the leader, 'we could hear tidings of our joyous chaplain—he was never wont to be absent when meat was to be blessed, or spoil to be parted; and it is his duty to take care of these the tithes of our successful enterprise. It may be the office has helped to cover some of his canonical irregularities. Also, I have a holy brother of his a prisoner at no great distance, and I would fain have the Friar to help me to deal with him in due sort—I greatly misdoubt the safety of the bluff priest.'

'I were right sorry for that,' said the Knight of the Fetterlock, 'for I stand indebted to him for the joyous hospitality of a merry night in his cell. Let us to the ruins of the castle; it may be we shall there learn some tidings of him.'

While they thus spoke, a loud shout among the yeomen announced the arrival of him for whom they feared, as they learned from the stentorian voice of the Friar himself, long before they saw his burly person.

'Make room, my merry-men!' he exclaimed; 'room for your godly father and his prisoner—Cry welcome once more.—I come, noble leader, like an eagle with my prey in my clutch.'— And making his way through the ring, amidst the laughter of all around, he appeared in majestic triumph, his huge partisan in one hand, and in the other a halter, one end of which was fastened to the neck of the unfortunate Isaac of York, who, bent down by sorrow and terror, was dragged on by the victorious priest, who shouted aloud, 'Where is Allan-a-Dale, to chronicle me in a ballad, or if it were but a lay?—By Saint Hermangild,* the jingling crowder is ever out of the way where there is an apt theme for exalting valour!'

'Curtal Priest,' said the Captain, 'thou hast been at a wet mass this morning, as early as it is. In the name of Saint Nicholas, whom hast thou got here?'

'A captive to my sword and to my lance, noble Captain,' replied the Clerk of Copmanhurst; 'to my bow and to my halberd, I should rather say; and yet I have redeemed him by my divinity from a worse captivity. Speak, Jew—have I not ransomed thee from Sathanas?—have I not taught thee thy *credo*, thy *pater*, and thine *Ave Maria?*—Did I not spend the whole night in drinking to thee, and in expounding of mysteries?'

'For the love of God!' ejaculated the poor Jew, 'will no one take me out of the keeping of this mad—I mean this holy man?'

'How's this, Jew?' said the Friar, with a menacing aspect; 'dost thou recant, Jew?—Bethink thee, if thou dost relapse into thine infidelity, though thou art not so tender as a suckling pig—I would I had one to break my fast upon—thou art not too tough to be roasted! Be conformable, Isaac, and repeat the words after me. *Ave Maria!*——

'Nay, we will have no profanation, mad Priest,' said Locksley; 'let us rather hear where you found this prisoner of thine.'

'By Saint Dunstan,' said the Friar, 'I found him where I sought for better ware! I did step into the cellarage to see what might be rescued there; for though a cup of burnt wine, with spice, be an evening's draught for an emperor, it were waste, methought, to let so much good liquor be mulled at once; and I had caught up one runlet of sack, and was coming to call more aid among these lazy knaves, who are ever to seek when a good deed is to be done, when I was avised of a strong door—Aha! thought I, here is the choicest juice of all in this secret crypt; and the knave butler, being disturbed in his vocation, hath left the key in the door—In therefore I went, and found just nought besides a commodity of rusted chains and this dog of a Jew, who presently rendered himself my prisoner, rescue or no rescue. I did but refresh myself after the fatigue of the action, with the unbeliever, with one humming cup of sack, and was proceeding to lead forth my captive, when, crash after crash, as with wild thunder-dint and levin-fire,* down toppled the masonry of an outer tower, (marry beshrew their hands that built it not the firmer!) and blocked up the passage. The roar of one falling tower followed another—I gave up thought of life; and deeming it a dishonour to one of my profession to pass out of this world in company with a Jew, I heaved up my halberd to beat his brains out; but I took pity on his grey hairs, and judged it better to lay down the partisan, and take up my spiritual weapon for his conversion. And truly, by the blessing of Saint Dunstan, the seed has been sown in good soil;* only that, with speaking to him of mysteries through the whole night, and being in a manner fasting, (for the few draughts of sack which I sharpened my wits with were not worth marking,) my head is wellnigh dizzied, I trow.—But I was clean exhausted.—Gilbert and Wibbald know in what state they found me—quite and clean exhausted.'

'We can bear witness,' said Gilbert; 'for when we had cleared away the ruin, and by Saint Dunstan's help lighted upon the dungeon stair, we found the runlet of sack half empty, the Jew half dead, and the Friar more than half—exhausted, as he calls it.'

'Ye be knaves! ye lie!' retorted the offended Friar; 'it was you and your gormandizing companions that drank up the sack, and called it your morning draught—I am a pagan, an I kept it not for the Captain's own throat. But what recks it? The Jew is converted, and understands all I have told him, very nearly, if not altogether, as well as myself.'

'Jew,' said the Captain, 'is this true? hast thou renounced thine unbelief?'

'May I so find mercy in your eyes,' said the Jew, 'as I know not one word which the reverend prelate spake to me all this fearful night. Alas! I was so distraught with agony, and fear, and grief, that had our holy father Abraham come to preach to me, he had found but a deaf listener.'

'Thou liest, Jew, and thou knowest thou dost,' said the Friar; 'I will remind thee but of one word of our conference—thou didst promise to give all thy substance to our holy Order.'

'So help me the Promise,* fair sirs,' said Isaac, even more alarmed than before, 'as no such sounds ever crossed my lips! Alas! I am an aged beggar'd man—I fear me a childless—have ruth on me, and let me go!'

'Nay,' said the Friar, 'if thou dost retract vows made in favour of holy Church, thou must do penance.'

Accordingly, he raised his halberd, and would have laid the staff of it lustily on the Jew's shoulders, had not the Black Knight stopped the blow, and thereby transferred the Holy Clerk's resentment to himself.

'By Saint Thomas of Kent,' said he, 'an I buckle to my gear, I will teach thee, Sir Lazy Loon, to mell with thine own matters, maugre thine iron case there!'

'Nay, be not wroth with me,' said the Knight; 'thou knowest I am thy sworn friend and comrade.'

'I know no such thing,' answered the Friar; 'and defy thee for a meddling coxcomb!'

'Nay, but,' said the Knight, who seemed to take a pleasure in provoking his quondam host, 'hast thou forgotten how, that for my sake (for I say nothing of the temptation of the flagon and the pasty) thou didst break thy vow of fast and vigil?'

'Truly, friend,' said the Friar, clenching his huge fist, 'I will bestow a buffet on thee.'

'I accept of no such presents,' said the Knight; 'I am content to take thy cuff[38] as a loan, but I will repay thee with usury as deep as ever thy prisoner there exacted in his traffic.'

'I will prove that presently,' said the Friar.

'Hola!' cried the Captain, 'what art thou after, mad Friar? brawling beneath our Trysting-tree?'

'No brawling,' said the Knight, 'it is but a friendly interchange of courtesy.—Friar, strike an thou darest—I will stand thy blow, if thou wilt stand mine.'

'Thou hast the advantage with that iron pot on thy head,' said the churchman; 'but have at thee—Down thou goest, an thou wert Goliath of Gath in his brazen helmet.'*

The Friar bared his brawny arm up to the elbow, and putting his full strength to the blow, gave the Knight a buffet that might have felled an ox. But his adversary stood firm as a rock. A loud shout was uttered by all the yeomen around; for the Clerk's cuff was proverbial amongst them, and there were few who, in jest or earnest, had not had occasion to know its vigour.

'Now, Priest,' said the Knight, pulling off his gauntlet, 'if I had vantage on my head, I will have none on my hand—stand fast as a true man.'

'*Genam meam dedi vapulatori**—I have given my cheek to the smiter,' said the Priest; 'an thou canst stir me from the spot, fellow, I will freely bestow on thee the Jew's ransom.'

So spoke the burly Priest, assuming, on his part, high defiance. But who may resist his fate? The buffet of the Knight was given with such strength and good-will, that the Friar rolled head over heels upon the plain, to the great amazement of all the spectators. But he arose neither angry nor crest-fallen.

'Brother,' said he to the Knight, 'thou shouldst have used thy strength with more discretion. I had mumbled but a lame mass an thou hadst broken my jaw, for the piper plays ill that wants the nether chops.* Nevertheless, there is my hand, in friendly witness, that I will exchange no more cuffs with thee, having been a loser by the barter. End now all unkindness. Let us put the Jew to ransom, since the leopard will not change his spots,* and a Jew he will continue to be.'

'The Priest,' said Clement,* 'is not half so confident of the Jew's conversion, since he received that buffet on the ear.'

'Go to, knave, what pratest thou of conversions?—what, is there no respect?—all masters and no men?—I tell thee, fellow, I was somewhat totty* when I received the good knight's blow, or I had kept my ground under it. But an thou gibest more of it, thou shalt learn I can give as well as take.'

'Peace all!' said the Captain. 'And thou, Jew, think of thy ransom; thou needest not to be told that thy race are held to be accursed in all Christian communities, and trust me that we cannot endure thy presence among us. Think, therefore, of an offer, while I examine a prisoner of another cast.'

'Were many of Front-de-Bœuf's men taken?' demanded the Black Knight.

'None of note enough to be put to ransom,' answered the Captain; 'a set of hilding fellows there were, whom we dismissed to find them a new master—enough had been done for revenge and profit; the bunch of them were not worth a cardecu.* The prisoner I speak of is better booty—a jolly monk riding to visit his leman, an I may judge by his horse-gear and wearing apparel.—Here cometh the worthy prelate, as pert as a pyet.'* And, between two yeomen, was brought before the silvan throne of the outlaw Chief, our old friend, Prior Aymer of Jorvaulx.

CHAPTER XXXIII

——Flower of warriors,
How is't with Titus Lartius?
  Marcius. As with a man busied about decrees,
Condemning some to death and some to exile,
Ransoming him or pitying, threatening the other.

*Coriolanus**

THE captive Abbot's features and manners exhibited a whimsi-cal mixture of offended pride, and deranged foppery and bodily terror.

'Why, how now, my masters?' said he, with a voice in which all three emotions were blended. 'What order is this among ye? Be ye Turks or Christians, that handle a churchman?—Know ye what it is, *manus imponere in servos Domini*?* Ye have plundered my mails—torn my cope of curious cut lace, which might have served a cardinal!—Another in my place would have been at his *excommunicabo vos*;* but I am placable, and if ye order forth my palfreys, release my brethren, and restore my mails, tell down with all speed an hundred crowns to be expended in masses at the high altar of Jorvaulx Abbey, and make your vow to eat no venison until next Pentecost, it may be you shall hear little more of this mad frolic.'

'Holy Father,' said the chief Outlaw, 'it grieves me to think that you have met with such usage from any of my followers, as calls for your fatherly reprehension.'

'Usage!' echoed the priest, encouraged by the mild tone of the silvan leader; 'it were usage fit for no hound of good race—much less for a Christian—far less for a priest—and least of all for the Prior of the holy community of Jorvaulx. Here is a profane and drunken minstrel, called Allan-a-Dale—*nebulo quidam**—who has menaced me with corporal punishment—nay, with death itself, an I pay not down four hundred crowns of ransom, to the boot of all the treasure he hath already robbed me of—gold chains and gymmal rings to an unknown value; besides what is broken and spoiled among their rude hands, such as my pouncet-box and silver crisping-tongs.'*

'It is impossible that Allan-a-dale can have thus treated a man of your reverend bearing,' replied the Captain.

'It is true as the gospel of Saint Nicodemus,'* said the Prior; 'he swore, with many a cruel north-country oath, that he would hang me up on the highest tree in the greenwood.'

'Did he so in very deed? Nay, then, reverend father, I think you had better comply with his demands—for Allan-a-Dale is the very man to abide by his word when he has so pledged it.'[39]

'You do but jest with me,' said the astounded Prior, with a forced laugh; 'and I love a good jest with all my heart. But, ha! ha! ha! when the mirth has lasted the livelong night, it is time to be grave in the morning.'

'And I am as grave as a father confessor,' replied the Outlaw; 'you must pay a round ransom, Sir Prior, or your convent is likely to be called to a new election; for your place will know you no more.'

'Are ye Christians,' said the Prior, 'and hold this language to a churchman?'

'Christians! ay, marry are we, and have divinity among us to boot,' answered the Outlaw. 'Let our buxom chaplain stand forth, and expound to this reverend father the texts which concern this matter.'

The Friar, half-drunk, half-sober, had huddled a friar's frock over his green cassock, and now summoning together whatever scraps of learning he had acquired by rote in former days, 'Holy father,' said he, '*Deus faciat salvam benignitatem vestram**—You are welcome to the greenwood.'

'What profane mummery is this?' said the Prior. 'Friend, if thou be'st indeed of the church, it were a better deed to show me how I may escape from these men's hands, than to stand ducking and grinning here like a morris-dancer.'*

'Truly, reverend father,' said the Friar, 'I know but one mode in which thou mayst escape. This is Saint Andrew's day with us, we are taking our tithes.'*

'But not of the church, then, I trust, my good brother?' said the Prior.

'Of church and lay,' said the Friar; 'and therefore, Sir Prior, *facite vobis amicos de Mammone iniquitatis**—make yourselves friends of the Mammon of unrighteousness, for no other friendship is like to serve your turn.'

'I love a jolly woodsman at heart,' said the Prior, softening his tone; 'come, ye must not deal too hard with me—I can well of woodcraft, and can wind a horn clear and lustily, and hollo till every oak rings again—Come, ye must not deal too hard with me.'

'Give him a horn,' said the Outlaw; 'we will prove the skill he boasts of.'

The Prior Aymer winded a blast accordingly. The Captain shook his head.

'Sir Prior,' he said, 'thou blowest a merry note, but it may not ransom thee—we cannot afford, as the legend on a good knight's shield hath it, to set thee free for a blast.* Moreover, I have found thee—thou art one of those, who, with new French graces and Tra-li-ras, disturb the ancient English bugle notes.——Prior, that last flourish on the recheat hath added fifty crowns to thy ransom, for corrupting the true old manly blasts of venerie.'

'Well, friend,' said the Abbot, peevishly, 'thou art ill to please with thy woodcraft. I pray thee be more conformable in this matter of my ransom. At a word—since I must needs, for once, hold a candle to the devil*—what ransom am I to pay for walking on Watling-street, without having fifty men at my back?'

'Were it not well,' said the Lieutenant of the gang apart to the Captain, 'that the Prior should name the Jew's ransom, and the Jew name the Prior's?'

'Thou art a mad knave,' said the Captain, 'but thy plan transcends!—Here, Jew, step forth—Look at that holy Father Aymer, Prior of the rich Abbey of Jorvaulx, and tell us at what ransom we should hold him?—Thou knowest the income of his convent, I warrant thee.'

'O, assuredly,' said Isaac. 'I have trafficked with the good fathers, and bought wheat and barley, and fruits of the earth, and also much wool. O, it is a rich abbey-stede, and they do live upon the fat, and drink the sweet wines upon the lees,* these good fathers of Jorvaulx. Ah, if an outcast like me had such a home to go to, and such incomings by the year and by the month, I would pay much gold and silver to redeem my captivity.'

'Hound of a Jew!' exclaimed the Prior, 'no one knows better than thy own cursed self, that our holy house of God is indebted for the finishing of our chancel'——

'And for the storing of your cellars in the last season with the due allowance of Gascon wine,' interrupted the Jew; 'but that—that is small matters.'

'Hear the infidel dog!' said the churchman; 'he jangles as if our holy community did come under debts for the wines we have a license to drink, *propter necessitatem, et ad frigus depellendum.** The circumcised villain blasphemeth the holy church, and Christian men listen and rebuke him not!'

'All this helps nothing,' said the leader.—'Isaac, pronounce what he may pay, without flaying both hide and hair.'

'An six hundred crowns,' said Isaac, 'the good Prior might well pay to your honoured valours, and never sit less soft in his stall.'

'Six hundred crowns,' said the leader, gravely; 'I am contented—thou hast well spoken, Isaac—six hundred crowns.—It is a sentence, Sir Prior.'

'A sentence!—a sentence!'* exclaimed the band; 'Solomon had not done it better.'

'Thou hearest thy doom, Prior,' said the leader.

'Ye are mad, my masters,' said the Prior; 'where am I to find such a sum? If I sell the very pyx and candlesticks on the altar at Jorvaulx, I shall scarce raise the half; and it will be necessary for that purpose that I go to Jorvaulx myself; ye may retain as borrows[40] my two priests.'

'That will be but blind trust,' said the Outlaw; 'we will retain thee, Prior, and send them to fetch thy ransom. Thou shalt not want a cup of wine and a collop of venison the while; and if thou lovest woodcraft, thou shalt see such as your north country never witnessed.'

'Or, if so please you,' said Isaac, willing to curry favour with the outlaws, 'I can send to York for the six hundred crowns, out of certain monies in my hands, if so be that the most reverend Prior present will grant me a quittance.'

'He shall grant thee whatever thou dost list, Isaac,' said the Captain; 'and thou shalt lay down the redemption money for Prior Aymer as well as for thyself.'

'For myself! ah, courageous sirs,' said the Jew, 'I am a broken and impoverished man; a beggar's staff must be my portion through life, supposing I were to pay you fifty crowns.'

'The Prior shall judge of that matter,' replied the Captain. —'How say you, Father Aymer? Can the Jew afford a good ransom?'

'*Can* he afford a ransom?' answered the Prior—'Is he not Isaac of York, rich enough to redeem the captivity of the ten tribes of Israel, who were led into Assyrian bondage?—I have seen but little of him myself, but our cellarer and treasurer have dealt largely with him, and report says that his house at York is so full of gold and silver as is a shame in any Christian land. Marvel it is to all living Christian hearts that such gnawing adders should be suffered to eat into the bowels of the state, and even of the holy church herself, with foul usuries and extortions.'

'Hold, father,' said the Jew, 'mitigate and assuage your choler.* I pray of your reverence to remember that I force my monies upon no one. But when churchman and layman, prince and prior, knight and priest, come knocking to Isaac's door, they borrow not his shekels with these uncivil terms. It is then, Friend Isaac, will you pleasure us in this matter, and our day shall be truly kept, so God sa' me?—and Kind Isaac, if ever you served man, show yourself a friend in this need! And when the day comes, and I ask my own, then what hear I but Damned Jew, and The curse of Egypt* on your tribe, and all that may stir up the rude and uncivil populace against poor strangers!'

'Prior,' said the Captain, 'Jew though he be, he hath in this spoken well. Do thou, therefore, name his ransom, as he named thine, without farther rude terms.'

'None but *latro famosus**—the interpretation whereof,' said the Prior, 'will I give at some other time and tide—would place a Christian prelate and an unbaptized Jew upon the same bench. But since ye require me to put a price upon this caitiff, I tell you openly that ye will wrong yourselves if you take from him a penny under a thousand crowns.'

'A sentence!—a sentence!' exclaimed the chief Outlaw.

'A sentence!—a sentence!' shouted his assessors; 'the Christian has shown his good nurture, and dealt with us more generously than the Jew.'

'The God of my fathers help me!' said the Jew; 'will ye bear to the ground an impoverished creature?—I am this day childless, and will ye deprive me of the means of livelihood?'

'Thou wilt have the less to provide for, Jew, if thou art child-less,' said Aymer.

'Alas! my lord,' said Isaac, 'your law permits you not to know how the child of our bosom is entwined with the strings of our heart—O Rebecca! daughter of my beloved Rachel! were each leaf on that tree a zecchin, and each zecchin mine own, all that mass of wealth would I give to know whether thou art alive, and escaped the hands of the Nazarene!'

'Was not thy daughter dark-haired?' said one of the outlaws; 'and wore she not a veil of twisted sendal, broidered with silver?'

'She did!—she did!' said the old man, trembling with eager-ness, as formerly with fear. 'The blessing of Jacob be upon thee! canst thou tell me aught of her safety?'

'It was she, then,' said the yeoman, 'who was carried off by the proud Templar, when he broke through our ranks on yester-even. I had drawn my bow to send a shaft after him, but spared him even for the sake of the damsel, who I feared might take harm from the arrow.'

'Oh!' answered the Jew, 'I would to God thou hadst shot, though the arrow had pierced her bosom!—Better the tomb of her fathers than the dishonourable couch of the licentious and savage Templar. Ichabod! Ichabod! the glory hath departed from my house!'*

'Friends,' said the Chief, looking round, 'the old man is but a Jew, natheless his grief touches me.—Deal uprightly with us, Isaac—will paying this ransom of a thousand crowns leave thee altogether penniless?'

Isaac, recalled to think of his worldly goods, the love of which, by dint of inveterate habit, contended even with his parental affection, grew pale, stammered, and could not deny there might be some small surplus.

'Well—go to—what though there be,' said the Outlaw, 'we will not reckon with thee too closely. Without treasure thou mayst as well hope to redeem thy child from the clutches of Sir Brian de Bois-Guilbert, as to shoot a stag-royal with a headless shaft.—We will take thee at the same ransom with

Prior Aymer, or rather at one hundred crowns lower, which hundred crowns shall be mine own peculiar loss, and not light upon this worshipful community; and so we shall avoid the heinous offence of rating a Jew merchant as high as a Christian prelate, and thou wilt have six hundred crowns remaining to treat for thy daughter's ransom. Templars love the glitter of silver shekels as well as the sparkle of black eyes.—Hasten to make thy crowns chink in the ear of De Bois-Guilbert, ere worse comes of it. Thou wilt find him, as our scouts have brought notice, at the next Preceptory house of his Order.—Said I well, my merry mates?'

The yeomen expressed their wonted acquiescence in their leader's opinion; and Isaac, relieved of one half of his apprehensions, by learning that his daughter lived, and might possibly be ransomed, threw himself at the feet of the generous Outlaw, and, rubbing his beard against his buskins, sought to kiss the hem of his green cassock. The Captain drew himself back, and extricated himself from the Jew's grasp, not without some marks of contempt.

'Nay, beshrew thee, man, up with thee! I am English born, and love no such Eastern prostrations—Kneel to God, and not to a poor sinner, like me.'

'Ay, Jew,' said Prior Aymer, 'Kneel to God, as represented in the servant of his altar, and who knows, with thy sincere repentance and due gifts to the shrine of Saint Robert, what grace thou mayst acquire for thyself and thy daughter Rebecca? I grieve for the maiden, for she is of fair and comely countenance,—I beheld her in the lists of Ashby. Also Brian de Bois-Guilbert is one with whom I may do much—bethink thee how thou mayst deserve my good word with him.'

'Alas! alas!' said the Jew, 'on every hand the spoilers arise against me—I am given as a prey unto the Assyrian, and a prey unto him of Egypt.'

'And what else should be the lot of thy accursed race?' answered the Prior; 'for what saith holy writ, *verbum Domini projecerunt, et sapientia est nulla in eis*—they have cast forth the word of the Lord, and there is no wisdom in them; *propterea dabo mulieres eorum exteris*—I will give their women to strangers, that is to the Templar, as in the present matter; *et thesauros eorum* *hæredibus alienis*, and their treasures to others*—as in the present case to these honest gentlemen.'

Isaac groaned deeply, and began to wring his hands, and to relapse into his state of desolation and despair. But the leader of the yeomen led him aside.

'Advise thee well, Isaac,' said Locksley gravely, 'what thou wilt do in this matter; my counsel to thee is to make a friend of this churchman. He is vain, Isaac, and he is covetous; at least he needs money to supply his perfusion. Thou canst easily gratify his greed; for think not that I am blinded by thy pretexts of poverty. I am intimately acquainted, Isaac, with the very iron chest in which thou dost keep thy money-bags—What! know I not the great stone beneath the apple-tree, that leads into the vaulted chamber under thy garden at York?' The Jew grew as pale as death—'But fear nothing from me,' continued the yeoman, 'for we are of old acquainted. Dost thou not remember the sick yeoman whom thy fair daughter Rebecca redeemed from the gyves at York, and kept him in thy house till his health was restored, when thou didst dismiss him recovered, and with a piece of money?—Usurer as thou art, thou didst never place coin at better interest than that poor silver mark, for it has this day saved thee five hundred crowns.'

'And thou art he whom we called Diccon Bend-the-Bow?' said Isaac; 'I thought ever I knew the accent of thy voice.'

'I am Bend-the-Bow,' said the Captain, 'and Locksley, and have a good name besides all these.'

'But thou art mistaken, good Bend-the-Bow, concerning that same vaulted apartment. So help me Heaven, as there is nought in it but some merchandises which I will gladly part with to you—one hundred yards of Lincoln green to make doublets to thy men, and a hundred staves of Spanish yew to make bows, and one hundred silken bowstrings, tough, round, and sound—these will I send thee for thy good-will, honest Diccon, an thou wilt keep silence about the vault, my good Diccon.'

'Silent as a dormouse,' said the Outlaw; 'and never trust me but I am grieved for thy daughter. But I may not help it—The Templar's lances are too strong for my archery in the open field—they would scatter us like dust. Had I but known it was Rebecca when she was borne off, something might have been done; but now thou must needs proceed by policy. Come, shall I treat for thee with the Prior?'

'In God's name, Diccon, an thou canst, aid me to recover the child of my bosom!'

'Do not thou interrupt me with thine ill-timed avarice,' said the Outlaw, 'and I will deal with him in thy behalf.'

He then turned from the Jew, who followed him, however, as closely as his shadow.

'Prior Aymer,' said the Captain, 'come apart with me under this tree. Men say thou dost love wine, and a lady's smile, better than beseems thy Order, Sir Priest; but with that I have nought to do. I have heard, too, thou dost love a brace of good dogs and a fleet horse, and it may well be that, loving things which are costly to come by, thou hatest not a purse of gold. But I have never heard that thou didst love oppression or cruelty.—Now, here is Isaac willing to give thee the means of pleasure and pastime in a bag containing one hundred marks of silver, if thy intercession with thine ally the Templar shall avail to procure the freedom of his daughter.'

'In safety and honour, as when taken from me,' said the Jew, 'otherwise it is no bargain.'

'Peace, Isaac,' said the Outlaw, 'or I give up thine interest.— What say you to this my purpose, Prior Aymer?'

'The matter,' quoth the Prior, 'is of a mixed condition; for, if I do a good deed on the one hand, yet, on the other, it goeth to the vantage of a Jew, and in so much is against my conscience. Yet, if the Israelite will advantage the Church by giving me somewhat over to the building of our dortour,[41] I will take it on my conscience to aid him in the matter of his daughter.'

'For a score of marks to the dortour,' said the Outlaw,—'Be still, I say, Isaac!—or for a brace of silver candlesticks to the altar, we will not stand with you.'

'Nay, but, good Diccon Bend-the-Bow'—said Isaac, endeavouring to interpose.

'Good Jew—good beast—good earthworm!' said the yeoman, losing patience; 'an thou dost go on to put thy filthy lucre in the balance with thy daughter's life and honour, by Heaven, I will strip thee of every maravedi* thou hast in the world, before three days are out!'

Isaac shrunk together, and was silent.

'And what pledge am I to have for all this?' said the Prior.

'When Isaac returns successful through your mediation,' said the Outlaw, 'I swear by Saint Hubert, I will see that he pays thee the money in good silver, or I will reckon with him for it in such sort, he had better have paid twenty such sums.'

'Well then, Jew,' said Aymer, 'since I must needs meddle in this matter, let me have the use of thy writing-tablets—though, hold—rather than use thy pen, I would fast for twenty-four hours, and where shall I find one?'

'If your holy scruples can dispense with using the Jew's tablets, for the pen I can find a remedy,' said the yeoman; and, bending his bow, he aimed his shaft at a wild-goose which was soaring over their heads, the advanced-guard of a phalanx of his tribe, which were winging their way to the distant and solitary fens of Holderness. The bird came fluttering down, transfixed with the arrow.

'There, Prior,' said the Captain, 'are quills enow to supply all the monks of Jorvaulx for the next hundred years, an they take not to writing chronicles.'

The Prior sat down, and at great leisure indited an epistle to Brian de Bois-Guilbert, and having carefully sealed up the tablets, delivered them to the Jew, saying, 'This will be thy safe-conduct to the Preceptory of Templestowe, and, as I think, is most likely to accomplish the delivery of thy daughter, if it be well backed with proffers of advantage and commodity at thine own hand; for, trust me well, the good Knight Bois-Guilbert is of their confraternity that do nought for nought.'

'Well, Prior,' said the Outlaw, 'I will detain thee no longer here than to give the Jew a quittance for the six hundred crowns at which thy ransom is fixed—I accept of him for my pay-master; and if I hear that ye boggle at allowing him in his accompts the sum so paid by him, Saint Mary refuse me, an I burn not the abbey over thine head, though I hang ten years the sooner!'

With a much worse grace than that wherewith he had penned the letter to Bois-Guilbert, the Prior wrote an acquittance, discharging Isaac of York of six hundred crowns, advanced to him in his need for acquittal of his ransom, and faithfully promising to hold true compt with him for that sum.

'And now,' said Prior Aymer, 'I will pray you of restitution of my mules and palfreys, and the freedom of the reverend brethren attending upon me, and also of the gymmal rings, jewels, and fair vestures, of which I have been despoiled, having now satisfied you for my ransom as a true prisoner.'

'Touching your brethren, Sir Prior,' said Locksley, 'they shall have present freedom, it were unjust to detain them; touching your horses and mules, they shall also be restored, with such spending-money as may enable you to reach York, for it were cruel to deprive you of the means of journeying.—But as concerning rings, jewels, chains, and what else, you must understand that we are men of tender consciences, and will not yield to a venerable man like yourself, who should be dead to the vanities of this life, the strong temptation to break the rule of his foundation, by wearing rings, chains, or other vain gauds.'

'Think what you do, my masters,' said the Prior, 'ere you put your hand on the Church's patrimony—These things are *inter res sacras*,* and I wot not what judgment might ensue were they to be handled by laical hands.'

'I will take care of that, reverend Prior,' said the Hermit of Copmanhurst; 'for I will wear them myself.'

'Friend, or brother,' said the Prior, in answer to this solution of his doubts, 'if thou hast really taken religious orders, I pray thee to look how thou wilt answer to thine official for the share thou hast taken in this day's work.'

'Friend Prior,' returned the Hermit, 'you are to know that I belong to a little diocese, where I am my own diocesan, and care as little for the Bishop of York as I do for the Abbot of Jorvaulx, the Prior, and all the convent.'

'Thou art utterly irregular,' said the Prior; 'one of those disorderly men, who, taking on them the sacred character without due cause, profane the holy rites, and endanger the souls of those who take counsel at their hands; *lapides pro pane condonantes iis*,* giving them stones instead of bread, as the Vulgate hath it.'

'Nay,' said the Friar, 'an my brain-pan could have been broken by Latin, it had not held so long together.—I say, that easing a world of such misproud priests as thou art of their jewels and their gimcracks, is a lawful spoiling of the Egyptians.'*

'Thou be'st a hedge-priest,'[42] said the Prior, in great wrath, '*excommunicabo vos.*'

'Thou be'st thyself more like a thief and a heretic,' said the Friar, equally indignant; 'I will pouch up no such affront before my parishioners, as thou thinkest it not shame to put upon me, although I be a reverend brother to thee. *Ossa ejus perfringam,** I will break your bones, as the Vulgate hath it.'

'Hola!' cried the Captain, 'come the reverend brethren to such terms?—Keep thine assurance of peace, Friar.—Prior, an thou hast not made thy peace perfect with God, provoke the Friar no further.—Hermit, let the reverend father depart in peace, as a ransomed man.'

The yeomen separated the incensed priests, who continued to raise their voices, vituperating each other in bad Latin, which the Prior delivered the more fluently, and the Hermit with the greater vehemence. The Prior at length recollected himself sufficiently to be aware that he was compromising his dignity, by squabbling with such a hedge-priest as the Outlaw's chaplain, and being joined by his attendants, rode off with considerably less pomp, and in a much more apostolical condition, so far as worldly matters were concerned, than he had exhibited before this rencounter.

It remained that the Jew should produce some security for the ransom which he was to pay on the Prior's account, as well as upon his own. He gave, accordingly, an order sealed with his signet, to a brother of his tribe at York, requiring him to pay to the bearer the sum of a thousand crowns, and to deliver certain merchandises specified in the note.

'My brother Sheva,' he said, groaning deeply, 'hath the key of my warehouses.'

'And of the vaulted chamber,' whispered Locksley.

'No, no—may Heaven forefend!' said Isaac; 'evil is the hour that let any one whomsoever into that secret!'

'It is safe with me,' said the Outlaw, 'so be that this thy scroll produce the sum therein nominated and set down.—But what now, Isaac? art dead? art stupified? hath the payment of a thousand crowns put thy daughter's peril out of thy mind?'

The Jew started to his feet—'No, Diccon, no—I will presently set forth.—Farewell, thou whom I may not call good, and dare not and will not call evil.'

Yet ere Isaac departed, the Outlaw Chief bestowed on him this parting advice:—'Be liberal of thine offers, Isaac, and spare not thy purse for thy daughter's safety. Credit me, that the gold thou shalt spare in her cause, will hereafter give thee as much agony as if it were poured molten down thy throat.'

Isaac acquiesced with a deep groan, and set forth on his journey, accompanied by two tall foresters, who were to be his guides, and at the same time his guards, through the wood.

The Black Knight, who had seen with no small interest these various proceedings, now took his leave of the Outlaw in turn; nor could he avoid expressing his surprise at having witnessed so much of civil policy amongst persons cast out from all the ordinary protection and influence of the laws.

'Good fruit, Sir Knight,' said the yeoman, 'will sometimes grow on a sorry tree; and evil times are not always productive of evil alone and unmixed. Amongst those who are drawn into this lawless state, there are, doubtless, numbers who wish to exercise its license with some moderation, and some who regret, it may be, that they are obliged to follow such a trade at all.'

'And to one of those,' said the Knight, 'I am now, I presume, speaking?'

'Sir Knight,' said the Outlaw, 'we have each our secret. You are welcome to form your judgment of me, and I may use my conjectures touching you, though neither of our shafts may hit the mark they are shot at. But as I do not pray to be admitted into your mystery, be not offended that I preserve my own.'

'I crave pardon, brave Outlaw,' said the Knight, 'your reproof is just. But it may be we shall meet hereafter with less of concealment on either side.—Meanwhile we part friends, do we not?'

'There is my hand upon it,' said Locksley; 'and I will call it the hand of a true Englishman, though an outlaw for the present.'

'And there is mine in return,' said the Knight, 'and I hold it honoured by being clasped with yours. For he that does good, having the unlimited power to do evil, deserves praise not only for the good which he performs, but for the evil which he forbears. Fare thee well, gallant Outlaw!'

Thus parted that fair fellowship;* and He of the Fetterlock, mounting upon his strong war-horse, rode off through the forest.

CHAPTER XXXIV

King John. I'll tell thee what, my friend,
He is a very serpent in my way;
And wheresoe'er this foot of mine doth tread,
He lies before me.—Dost thou understand me?

King John*

THERE was brave feasting in the Castle of York, to which Prince John had invited those nobles, prelates, and leaders, by whose assistance he hoped to carry through his ambitious projects upon his brother's throne. Waldemar Fitzurse, his able and politic agent, was at secret work among them, tempering all to that pitch of courage which was necessary in making an open declaration of their purpose. But their enterprise was delayed by the absence of more than one main limb of the confederacy. The stubborn and daring, though brutal courage of Front-de-Bœuf; the buoyant spirits and bold bearing of De Bracy; the sagacity, martial experience, and renowned valour of Brian de Bois-Guilbert, were important to the success of their conspiracy; and, while cursing in secret their unnecessary and unmeaning absence, neither John nor his adviser dared to proceed without them. Isaac the Jew also seemed to have vanished, and with him the hope of certain sums of money, making up the subsidy for which Prince John had contracted with that Israelite and his brethren. This deficiency was likely to prove perilous in an emergency so critical.

It was on the morning after the fall of Torquilstone, that a confused report began to spread abroad in the city of York, that De Bracy and Bois-Guilbert, with their confederate Front-de-Bœuf, had been taken or slain. Waldemar brought the rumour to Prince John, announcing, that he feared its truth the more that they had set out with a small attendance, for the purpose of committing an assault on the Saxon Cedric and his attendants. At another time the Prince would have treated this deed of violence as a good jest; but now, that it interfered with and impeded his own plans, he exclaimed against the perpetrators, and spoke of the broken laws, and the infringement of public order and of private property, in a tone which might have become King Alfred.

'The unprincipled marauders!' he said—'were I ever to become monarch of England, I would hang such transgressors over the drawbridges of their own castles.'

'But to become monarch of England,' said his Ahithophel* coolly, 'it is necessary not only that your Grace should endure the transgressions of these unprincipled marauders, but that you should afford them your protection, notwithstanding your landable zeal for the laws they are in the habit of infringing. We shall be finely helped, if the churl Saxons should have realized your Grace's vision, of converting feudal drawbridges into gibbets; and yonder bold-spirited Cedric seemeth one to whom such an imagination might occur. Your Grace is well aware, it will be dangerous to stir without Front-de-Bœuf, De Bracy, and the Templar; and yet we have gone too far to recede with safety.'

Prince John struck his forehead with impatience, and then began to stride up and down the apartment.

'The villains,' he said, 'the base treacherous villains, to desert me at this pinch!'

'Nay, say rather the feather-pated giddy madmen,' said Waldemar, 'who must be toying with follies when such business was in hand.'

'What is to be done?' said the Prince, stopping short before Waldemar.

'I know nothing which can be done,' answered his counsellor, 'save that which I have already taken order for.—I came not to bewail this evil chance with your Grace, until I had done my best to remedy it.'

'Thou art ever my better angel, Waldemar,' said the Prince; 'and when I have such a chancellor to advise withal, the reign of John will be renowned in our annals.—What hast thou commanded?'

'I have ordered Louis Winkelbrand, De Bracy's lieutenant, to cause his trumpet sound to horse, and to display his banner, and to set presently forth towards the castle of Front-de-Bœuf, to do what yet may be done for the succour of our friends.'

Prince John's face flushed with the pride of a spoilt child, who has undergone what it conceives to be an insult.

'By the face of God!' he said, 'Waldemar Fitzurse, much hast thou taken upon thee! and over malapert thou wert to cause trumpet to blow, or banner to be raised, in a town where ourselves were in presence, without our express command.'

'I crave your Grace's pardon,' said Fitzurse, internally cursing the idle vanity of his patron; 'but when time pressed, and even the loss of minutes might be fatal, I judged it best to take this much burden upon me, in a matter of such importance to your Grace's interest.'

'Thou art pardoned, Fitzurse,' said the Prince, gravely; 'thy purpose hath atoned for thy hasty rashness.—But whom have we here?—De Bracy himself, by the rood!—and in strange guise doth he come before us.'

It was indeed De Bracy—'bloody with spurring, fiery red with speed.'* His armour bore all the marks of the late obstinate fray, being broken, defaced, and stained with blood in many places, and covered with clay and dust from the crest to the spur. Undoing his helmet, he placed it on the table, and stood a moment as if to collect himself before he told his news.

'De Bracy,' said Prince John, 'what means this?—Speak, I charge thee!—Are the Saxons in rebellion?'

'Speak, De Bracy,' said Fitzurse, almost in the same moment with his master, 'thou wert wont to be a man—Where is the Templar?—where Front-de-Bœuf?'

'The Templar is fled,' said De Bracy; 'Front-de-Bœuf you will never see more. He has found a red grave among the blazing rafters of his own castle, and I alone am escaped to tell you.'*

'Cold news,' said Waldemar, 'to us, though you speak of fire and conflagration.'

'The worst news is not yet said,' answered De Bracy; and, coming up to Prince John, he uttered in a low and emphatic tone—'Richard is in England—I have seen and spoken with him.'

Prince John turned pale, tottered, and caught at the back of an oaken bench to support himself—much like to a man who receives an arrow in his bosom.

'Thou ravest, De Bracy,' said Fitzurse, 'it cannot be.'

'It is as true as truth itself,' said De Bracy; 'I was his prisoner, and spoke with him.'

'With Richard Plantagenet, sayest thou?' continued Fitzurse.

'With Richard Plantagenet,' replied De Bracy, 'with Richard Cœur-de-Lion—with Richard of England.'

'And thou wert his prisoner?' said Waldemar; 'he is then at the head of a power?'

'No—only a few outlawed yeomen were around him, and to these his person is unknown. I heard him say he was about to depart from them. He joined them only to assist at the storming of Torquilstone.'

'Ay,' said Fitzurse, 'such is indeed the fashion of Richard—a true knight-errant he, and will wander in wild adventure, trusting the prowess of his single arm, like any Sir Guy or Sir Bevis,* while the weighty affairs of his kingdom slumber, and his own safety is endangered.—What dost thou propose to do, De Bracy?'

'I?—I offered Richard the service of my Free Lances, and he refused them—I will lead them to Hull, seize on shipping, and embark for Flanders; thanks to the bustling times, a man of action will always find employment. And thou, Waldemar, wilt thou take lance and shield, and lay down thy policies, and wend along with me, and share the fate which God sends us?'

'I am too old, Maurice, and I have a daughter,' answered Waldemar.

'Give her to me, Fitzurse, and I will maintain her as fits her rank, with the help of lance and stirrup,' said De Bracy.

'Not so,' answered Fitzurse; 'I will take sanctuary in this church of Saint Peter—the Archbishop is my sworn brother.'*

During this discourse, Prince John had gradually awakened from the stupor into which he had been thrown by the unexpected intelligence, and had been attentive to the conversation which passed betwixt his followers. 'They fall off from me,' be said to himself, 'they hold no more by me than a withered leaf by the bough when a breeze blows on it!—Hell and fiends! can I shape no means for myself when I am deserted by these cravens?'—He paused, and there was an expression of diabolical passion in the constrained laugh with which he at length broke in on their conversation.

'Ha, ha, ha! my good lords, by the light of Our Lady's brow, I held ye sage men, bold men, ready-witted men; yet ye throw down wealth, honour, pleasure, all that our noble game promised you, at the moment it might be won by one bold cast!'

'I understand you not,' said De Bracy. 'As soon as Richard's return is blown abroad, he will be at the head of an army, and all is then over with us. I would counsel you, my lord, either to fly to France, or take the protection of the Queen Mother.'

'I seek no safety for myself,' said Prince John, haughtily; 'that I could secure by a word spoken to my brother. But although you, De Bracy, and you, Waldemar Fitzurse, are so ready to abandon me, I should not greatly delight to see your heads blackening on Clifford's gate* yonder. Thinkest thou, Waldemar, that the wily Archbishop will not suffer thee to be taken from the very horns of the altar, would it make his peace with King Richard? And forgettest thou, De Bracy, that Robert Estoteville lies betwixt thee and Hull with all his forces, and that the Earl of Essex* is gathering his followers? If we had reason to fear these levies even before Richard's return, trowest thou there is any doubt now which party their leaders will take? Trust me, Estoteville alone has strength enough to drive all thy Free Lances into the Humber.'—Waldemar Fitzurse and De Bracy looked in each other's faces with blank dismay.—'There is but one road to safety,' continued the Prince, and his brow grew black as midnight; 'this object of our terror journeys alone—He must be met withal.'

'Not by me,' said De Bracy, hastily; 'I was his prisoner, and he took me to mercy. I will not harm a feather in his crest.'

'Who spoke of harming him?' said Prince John, with a hardened laugh; 'the knave will say next that I meant he should slay him!—No—a prison were better; and whether in Britain or Austria, what matters it?—Things will be but as they were when we commenced our enterprise—It was founded on the hope that Richard would remain a captive in Germany—Our uncle Robert* lived and died in the castle of Cardiffe.'

'Ay, but,' said Waldemar, 'your sire Henry sate more firm in his seat than your Grace can. I say the best prison is that which is made by the sexton—no dungeon like a church-vault! I have said my say.'

'Prison or tomb,' said De Bracy, 'I wash my hands of the whole matter.'

'Villain!' said Prince John, 'thou wouldst not bewray our counsel?'

'Counsel was never bewrayed* by me,' said De Bracy, haughtily, 'nor must the name of villain be coupled with mine!'

'Peace, Sir Knight!' said Waldemar; 'and you, good my lord, forgive the scruples of valiant De Bracy; I trust I shall soon remove them.'

'That passes your eloquence, Fitzurse,' replied the Knight.

'Why, good Sir Maurice,' rejoined the wily politician, 'start not aside like a scared steed, without, at least, considering the object of your terror.—This Richard—but a day since, and it would have been thy dearest wish to have met him hand to hand in the ranks of battle—a hundred times I have heard thee wish it.'

'Ay,' said De Bracy, 'but that was as thou sayest, hand to hand, and in the ranks of battle! Thou never heardest me breathe a thought of assaulting him alone, and in a forest.'

'Thou art no good knight if thou dost scruple at it,' said Waldemar. 'Was it in battle that Lancelot de Lac and Sir Tristram* won renown? or was it not by encountering gigantic knights under the shade of deep and unknown forests?'

'Ay, but I promise you,' said De Bracy, 'that neither Tristram nor Lancelot would have been match, hand to hand, for Richard Plantagenet, and I think it was not their wont to take odds against a single man.'

'Thou art mad, De Bracy—what is it we propose to thee, a hired and retained captain of Free Companions, whose swords are purchased for Prince John's service? Thou art apprized of our enemy, and then thou scruplest, though thy patron's fortunes, those of thy comrades, thine own, and the life and honour of every one amongst us, be at stake!'

'I tell you,' said De Bracy, sullenly, 'that he gave me my life. True, he sent me from his presence, and refused my homage—so far I owe him neither favour nor allegiance—but I will not lift hand against him.'

'It needs not—send Louis Winkelbrand and a score of thy lances.'

'Ye have sufficient ruffians of your own,' said De Bracy; 'not one of mine shall budge on such an errand.'

'Art thou so obstinate, De Bracy?' said Prince John; 'and wilt thou forsake me, after so many protestations of zeal for my service?'

'I mean it not,' said De Bracy; 'I will abide by you in aught that becomes a knight, whether in the lists or in the camp; but this highway practice comes not within my vow.'

'Come hither, Waldemar,' said Prince John. 'An unhappy prince am I. My father, King Henry, had faithful servants—He had but to say that he was plagued with a factious priest, and the blood of Thomas-a-Becket, saint though he was, stained the steps of his own altar.*—Tracy, Morville, Brito,[43] loyal and daring subjects, your names, your spirit, are extinct! and although Reginald Fitzurse hath left a son, he hath fallen off from his father's fidelity and courage.'

'He has fallen off from neither,' said Waldemar Fitzurse; 'and since it may not better be, I will take on me the conduct of this perilous enterprise. Dearly, however, did my father purchase the praise of a zealous friend; and yet did his proof of loyalty to Henry fall far short of what I am about to afford; for rather would I assail a whole calendar of saints, than put spear in rest against Cœur-de-Lion.—De Bracy, to thee I must trust to keep up the spirits of the doubtful, and to guard Prince John's person. If you receive such news as I trust to send you, our enterprise will no longer wear a doubtful aspect.—Page,' he said, 'hie to my lodgings, and tell my armourer to be there in readiness; and bid Stephen Wetheral, Broad Thoresby, and the Three Spears of Spyinghow, come to me instantly; and let the scout-master, Hugh Bardon, attend me also.—Adieu, my Prince, till better times.' Thus speaking, he left the apartment.

'He goes to make my brother prisoner,' said Prince John to De Bracy, 'with as little touch of compunction, as if it but concerned the liberty of a Saxon franklin. I trust he will observe our orders, and use our dear Richard's person with all due respect.'

De Bracy only answered by a smile.

'By the light of Our Lady's brow,' said Prince John, 'our orders to him were most precise—though it may be you heard them not, as we stood together in the oriel window—Most clear and positive was our charge that Richard's safety should be cared for, and woe to Waldemar's head if he transgress it!'

'I had better pass to his lodgings,' said De Bracy, 'and make him fully aware of your Grace's pleasure; for, as it quite escaped my ear, it may not perchance have reached that of Waldemar.'

'Nay, nay,' said Prince John, impatiently, 'I promise thee he heard me; and, besides, I have farther occupation for thee. Maurice, come hither; let me lean on thy shoulder.'

They walked a turn through the hall in this familiar posture, and Prince John, with an air of the most confidential intimacy, proceeded to say, 'What thinkest thou of this Waldemar Fitzurse, my De Bracy?—He trusts to be our Chancellor. Surely we will pause ere we give an office so high to one who shows evidently how little he reverences our blood, by his so readily undertaking this enterprise against Richard. Thou dost think, I warrant, that thou hast lost somewhat of our regard, by thy boldly declining this unpleasing task—But no, Maurice! I rather honour thee for thy virtuous constancy. There are things most necessary to be done, the perpetrator of which we neither love nor honour; and there may be refusals to serve us, which shall rather exalt in our estimation those who deny our request. The arrest of my unfortunate brother forms no such good title to the high office of Chancellor, as thy chivalrous and courageous de- nial establishes in thee to the truncheon of High Marshal. Think of this, De Bracy, and begone to thy charge.'

'Fickle tyrant!' muttered De Bracy, as he left the presence of the Prince; 'evil luck have they who trust thee. Thy Chancellor, indeed!—He who hath the keeping of thy conscience shall have an easy charge, I trow. But High Marshal of England! that,' he said, extending his arm, as if to grasp the baton of office, and assuming a loftier stride along the antechamber, 'that is indeed a prize worth playing for!'

De Bracy had no sooner left the apartment than Prince John summoned an attendant.

'Bid Hugh Bardon, our scout-master, come hither, as soon as he shall have spoken with Waldemar Fitzurse.'

The scout-master arrived after a brief delay, during which John traversed the apartment with unequal and disordered steps.

'Bardon,' said he, 'what did Waldemar desire of thee?'

'Two resolute men, well acquainted with these northern wilds, and skilful in tracking the tread of man and horse.'

'And thou hast fitted him?'

'Let your grace never trust me else,' answered the master of the spies. 'One is from Hexamshire; he is wont to trace the Tynedale and Teviotdale thieves, as a bloodhound follows the slot of a hurt deer. The other is Yorkshire bred, and has twanged his bowstring right oft in merry Sherwood; he knows each glade and dingle, copse and high-wood, betwixt this and Richmond.'

' 'Tis well,' said the Prince.—'Goes Waldemar forth with them?'

'Instantly,' said Bardon.

'With what attendance?' asked John, carelessly.

'Broad Thoresby goes with him, and Wetheral, whom they call, for his cruelty, Stephen Steel-heart; and three northern men-at-arms that belonged to Ralph Middleton's gang—they are called the Spears of Spyinghow.'

' 'Tis well,' said Prince John; then added, after a moment's pause, 'Bardon, it imports our service that thou keep a strict watch on Maurice de Bracy—so that he shall not observe it, however—And let us know of his motions from time to time— with whom he converses, what he proposeth. Fail not in this, as thou wilt be answerable.'

Hugh Bardon bowed, and retired.

'If Maurice betrays me,' said Prince John—'if he betrays me, as his bearing leads me to fear, I will have his head, were Richard thundering at the gates of York.'

CHAPTER XXXV

Arouse the tiger of Hyrcanian deserts,
Strive with the half-starved lion for his prey;
Lesser the risk, than rouse the slumbering fire
Of wild Fanaticism.

*Anonymous**

OUR tale now returns to Isaac of York.—Mounted upon a mule, the gift of the Outlaw, with two tall yeomen to act as his guard and guides, the Jew had set out for the Preceptory of Templestowe, for the purpose of negotiating his daughter's redemption. The Preceptory was but a day's journey from the demolished castle of Torquilstone, and the Jew had hoped to reach it before nightfall; accordingly, having dismissed his guides at the verge of the forest, and rewarded them with a piece of silver, he began to press on with such speed as his weariness permitted him to exert. But his strength failed him totally ere he had reached within four miles of the Temple-Court; racking pains shot along his back and through his limbs, and the excessive anguish which he felt at heart being now augmented by bodily suffering, he was rendered altogether incapable of proceeding farther than a small market-town, where dwelt a Jewish Rabbi of his tribe, eminent in the medical profession, and to whom Isaac was well known. Nathan Ben Israel received his suffering countryman with that kindness which the law prescribed, and which the Jews practised to each other. He insisted on his betaking himself to repose, and used such remedies as were then in most repute to check the progress of the fever, which terror, fatigue, ill usage, and sorrow, had brought upon the poor old Jew.

On the morrow, when Isaac proposed to arise and pursue his journey, Nathan remonstrated against his purpose, both as his host and as his physician. It might cost him, he said, his life. But Isaac replied, that more than life and death depended upon his going that morning to Templestowe.

'To Templestowe!' said his host with surprise; again felt his pulse, and then muttered to himself, 'His fever is abated, yet seems his mind somewhat alienated and disturbed.'

'And why not to Templestowe?' answered his patient. 'I grant thee, Nathan, that it is a dwelling of those to whom the despised Children of the Promise are a stumbling-block and an abomination;* yet thou knowest that pressing affairs of traffic sometimes carry us among these bloodthirsty Nazarene soldiers, and that we visit the Preceptories of the Templars, as well as the Commanderies of the Knights Hospitallers, as they are called.'[44]

'I know it well,' said Nathan; 'but wottest thou that Lucas de Beaumanoir,* the chief of their Order, and whom they term Grand Master, is now himself at Templestowe?'

'I know it not,' said Isaac; 'our last letters from our brethren at Paris advised us that he was at that city, beseeching Philip for aid against the Sultan Saladine.'

'He hath since come to England, unexpected by his brethren,' said Ben Israel; 'and he cometh among them with a strong and outstretched arm* to correct and to punish. His countenance is kindled in anger against those who have departed from the vow which they have made, and great is the fear of those sons of Belial. Thou must have heard of his name?'

'It is well known unto me,' said Isaac; 'the Gentiles deliver this Lucas Beaumanoir as a man zealous to slaying for every point of the Nazarene law; and our brethren have termed him a fierce destroyer of the Saracens, and a cruel tyrant to the Children of the Promise.'

'And truly have they termed him,' said Nathan the physician. 'Other Templars may be moved from the purpose of their heart by pleasure, or bribed by promise of gold and silver; but Beaumanoir is of a different stamp—hating sensuality, despising treasure, and pressing forward to that which they call the crown of martyrdom—The God of Jacob speedily send it unto him, and unto them all! Specially hath this proud man extended his glove over the children of Judah, as holy David over Edom,* holding the murder of a Jew to be an offering of as sweet savour as the death of a Saracen. Impious and false things has he said even of the virtues of our medicines, as if they were the devices of Satan—The Lord rebuke him!'

'Nevertheless,' said Isaac, 'I must present myself at

Templestowe, though he hath made his face like unto a fiery furnace seven times heated.'*

He then explained to Nathan the pressing cause of his journey. The Rabbi listened with interest, and testified his sympathy after the fashion of his people, rending his clothes, and saying, 'Ah, my daughter!—ah, my daughter!—Alas! for the beauty of Zion!*—Alas! for the captivity of Israel!'

'Thou seest,' said Isaac, 'how it stands with me, and that I may not tarry. Peradventure, the presence of this Lucas Beaumanoir, being the chief man over them, may turn Brian de Bois-Guilbert from the ill which he doth meditate, and that he may deliver to me my beloved daughter Rebecca.'

'Go thou,' said Nathan Ben Israel, 'and be wise, for wisdom availed Daniel in the den of lions* into which he was cast; and may it go well with thee, even as thine heart wisheth. Yet, if thou canst, keep thee from the presence of the Grand Master, for to do foul scorn to our people is his morning and evening delight. It may be if thou couldst speak with Bois-Guilbert in private, thou shalt the better prevail with him; for men say that these accursed Nazarenes are not of one mind in the Preceptory—May their counsels be confounded and brought to shame!* But do thou, brother, return to me as if it were to the house of thy father, and bring me word how it has sped with thee; and well do I hope thou wilt bring with thee Rebecca, even the scholar of the wise Miriam, whose cures the Gentiles slandered as if they had been wrought by necromancy.'

Isaac accordingly bade his friend farewell, and about an hour's riding brought him before the Preceptory of Templestowe.

This establishment of the Templars was seated amidst fair meadows and pastures, which the devotion of the former Preceptor* had bestowed upon their Order. It was strong and well fortified, a point never neglected by these knights, and which the disordered state of England rendered peculiarly necessary. Two halberdiers, clad in black, guarded the drawbridge, and others, in the same sad livery, glided to and fro upon the walls with a funereal pace, resembling spectres more than soldiers. The inferior officers of the Order were thus dressed, ever since their use of white garments, similar to those of the knights and esquires, had given rise to a combination of certain false brethren in the mountains of Palestine, terming themselves Templars, and bringing great dishonour on the Order. A knight was now and then seen to cross the court in his long white cloak, his head depressed on his breast, and his arms folded. They passed each other, if they chanced to meet, with a slow, solemn, and mute greeting; for such was the rule of their Order,* quoting there-upon the holy texts, 'In many words thou shalt not avoid sin,' and 'Life and death are in the power of the tongue.' In a word, the stern ascetic rigour of the Temple discipline, which had been so long exchanged for prodigal and licentious indulgence, seemed at once to have revived at Templestowe under the severe eye of Lucas Beaumanoir.

Isaac paused at the gate, to consider how he might seek entrance in the manner most likely to bespeak favour; for he was well aware, that to his unhappy race the reviving fanaticism of the Order was not less dangerous than their unprincipled licentiousness; and that his religion would be the object of hate and persecution in the one case, as his wealth would have exposed him in the other to the extortions of unrelenting oppression.

Meantime Lucas Beaumanoir walked in a small garden be-longing to the Preceptory, included within the precincts of its exterior fortification, and held sad and confidential communica-tion with a brother of his Order, who had come in his company from Palestine.

The Grand Master was a man advanced in age, as was testified by his long grey beard, and the shaggy grey eyebrows overhang-ing eyes, of which, however, years had been unable to quench the fire. A formidable warrior, his thin and severe features retained the soldier's fierceness of expression; an ascetic bigot, they were no less marked by the emaciation of abstinence, and the spiritual pride of the self-satisfied devotee. Yet with these severer traits of physiognomy, there was mixed somewhat striking and noble, arising, doubtless, from the great part which his high office called upon him to act among monarchs and princes, and from the habitual exercise of supreme authority over the valiant and high-born knights, who were united by the rules of the Order. His stature was tall, and his gait, undepressed by age and toil, was erect and stately. His white mantle was shaped with severe regularity, according to the rule of Saint Bernard himself,* being composed of what was then called Burrel cloth, exactly fitted to the size of the wearer, and bearing on the left shoulder the octangular cross peculiar to the Order, formed of red cloth. No vair or ermine* decked this garment; but in respect of his age, the Grand Master, as permitted by the rules, wore his doublet lined and trimmed with the softest lambskin, dressed with the wool outwards, which was the nearest approach he could regularly make to the use of fur, then the greatest luxury of dress. In his hand he bore that singular *abacus*,* or staff of office, with which Templars are usually represented, having at the upper end a round plate, on which was engraved the cross of the Order, inscribed within a circle or orle, as heralds term it. His companion, who attended on this great personage, had nearly the same dress in all respects, but his extreme deference towards his Superior showed that no other equality subsisted between them. The Preceptor, for such he was in rank, walked not in a line with the Grand Master, but just so far behind that Beaumanoir could speak to him without turning round his head.

'Conrade,' said the Grand Master, 'dear companion of my battles and my toils, to thy faithful bosom alone I can confide my sorrows. To thee alone can I tell how oft, since I came to this kingdom, I have desired to be dissolved and to be with the just. Not one object in England hath met mine eye which it could rest upon with pleasure, save the tombs of our brethren, beneath the massive roof of our Temple Church in yonder proud capital.* O, valiant Robert de Ros! did I exclaim internally, as I gazed upon these good soldiers of the cross, where they lie sculptured on their sepulchres,—O, worthy William de Mareschal! open your marble cells, and take to your repose a weary brother, who would rather strive with a hundred thousand pagans than witness the decay of our Holy Order!'

'It is but true,' answered Conrade Mont-Fitchet; 'it is but too true; and the irregularities of our brethren in England are even more gross than those in France.'

'Because they are more wealthy,' answered the Grand Master. 'Bear with me, brother, although I should something vaunt myself. Thou knowest the life I have led, keeping each point of my Order, striving with devils embodied and disembodied, striking down the roaring lion, who goeth about seeking whom he may devour,* like a good knight and devout priest, wheresoever I met with him—even as blessed Saint Bernard hath prescribed to us in the forty-fifth capital of our rule, *Ut Leo semper feriatur.*[45]* But, by the Holy Temple! the zeal which hath devoured my substance and my life,* yea, the very nerves and marrow of my bones; by that very Holy Temple I swear to thee, that save thyself and some few that still retain the ancient severity of our Order, I look upon no brethren whom I can bring my soul to embrace under that holy name. What say our statutes,* and how do our brethren observe them? They should wear no vain or worldly ornament, no crest upon their helmet, no gold upon stirrup or bridle-bit; yet who now go pranked out so proudly and so gaily as the poor soldiers of the Temple? They are forbidden by our statutes to take one bird by means of another, to shoot beasts with bow or arblast, to halloo to a hunting-horn, or to spur the horse after game. But now, at hunting and hawking, and each idle sport of wood and river, who so prompt as the Templars in all these fond vanities? They are forbidden to read, save what their Superior permitted, or listen to what is read, save such holy things as may be recited aloud during the hours of refection; but lo! their ears are at the command of idle minstrels, and their eyes study empty romaunts. They were commanded to extirpate magic and heresy. Lo! they are charged with studying the accursed cabalistical secrets of the Jews, and the magic of the Paynim Saracens. Simpleness of diet was prescribed to them, roots, pottage, gruels, eating flesh but thrice a-week, because the accustomed feeding on flesh is a dishonourable corruption of the body; and behold, their tables groan under delicate fare! Their drink was to be water, and now, to drink like a Templar, is the boast of each jolly boon companion! This very garden, filled as it is with curious herbs and trees sent from the Eastern climes, better becomes the harem of an unbelieving Emir, than the plot which Christian Monks should devote to raise their homely pot-herbs.—And O, Conrade! well it were that the relaxation of discipline stopped even here!—Well thou knowest that we were forbidden to receive those devout women, who at the beginning were associated as sisters of our Order, because, saith the forty-sixth chapter,* the Ancient Enemy hath, by female society, withdrawn many from the right path to paradise. Nay, in the last capital, being, as it were, the cope-stone which our blessed founder placed on the pure and undefiled doctrine which he had enjoined, we are prohibited from offering, even to our sisters and our mothers, the kiss of affection—*ut omnium mulierum fugiantur oscula*.*—I shame to speak—I shame to think—of the corruptions which have rushed in upon us even like a flood. The souls of our pure founders, the spirits of Hugh de Payen and Godfrey de Saint Omer, and of the blessed Seven who first joined in dedicating their lives to the service of the Temple,* are disturbed even in the enjoyment of paradise itself. I have seen them, Conrade, in the visions of the night—their sainted eyes shed tears for the sins and follies of their brethren, and for the foul and shameful luxury in which they wallow. Beaumanoir, they say, thou slumberest—awake! There is a stain in the fabric of the Temple, deep and foul as that left by the streaks of leprosy on the walls of the infected houses of old.[46] The soldiers of the Cross, who should shun the glance of a woman as the eye of a basilisk, live in open sin, not with the females of their own race only, but with the daughters of the accursed heathen, and more accursed Jew. Beaumanoir, thou sleepest; up, and avenge our cause!— Slay the sinners, male and female!—Take to thee the brand of Phineas!*—The vision fled, Conrade, but as I awaked I could still hear the clank of their mail, and see the waving of their white mantles.—And I will do according to their word, I WILL purify the fabric of the Temple! and the unclean stones in which the plague is, I will remove and cast out of the building.'

'Yet bethink thee, reverend father,' said Mont-Fitchet, 'the stain hath become engrained by time and consuetude; let thy reformation be cautious, as it is just and wise.'

'No, Mont-Fitchet,' answered the stern old man—'it must be sharp and sudden—the Order is on the crisis of its fate. The sobriety, self-devotion, and piety of our predecessors, made us powerful friends—our presumption, our wealth, our luxury, have raised up against us mighty enemies.—We must cast away these riches, which are a temptation to princes—we must lay down that presumption, which is an offence to them—we must reform that license of manners, which is a scandal to the whole Christian world! Or—mark my words—the Order of the

Temple will be utterly demolished—and the place thereof shall no more be known among the nations.'*

'Now may God avert such a calamity!' said the Preceptor.

'Amen,' said the Grand Master, with solemnity, 'but we must deserve his aid. I tell thee, Conrade, that neither the powers in Heaven, nor the powers on earth, will longer endure the wickedness of this generation—My intelligence is sure—the ground on which our fabric is reared is already undermined, and each addition we make to the structure of our greatness will only sink it the sooner in the abyss. We must retrace our steps, and show ourselves the faithful Champions of the Cross, sacrificing to our calling, not alone our blood and our lives—not alone our lusts and our vices—but our ease, our comforts, and our natural affections, and act as men convinced that many a pleasure which may be lawful to others, is forbidden to the vowed soldier of the Temple.'

At this moment a squire, clothed in a threadbare vestment, (for the aspirants after this holy Order wore during their noviciate the cast-off garments of the knights,)* entered the garden, and, bowing profoundly before the Grand Master, stood silent, awaiting his permission ere he presumed to tell his errand.

'Is it not more seemly,' said the Grand Master, 'to see this Damian, clothed in the garments of Christian humility, thus appear with reverend silence before his Superior, than but two days since, when the fond fool was decked in a painted coat, and jangling as pert and as proud as any popinjay?*—Speak, Damian, we permit thee—What is thine errand?'

'A Jew stands without the gate, noble and reverend father,' said the Squire, 'who prays to speak with brother Brian de Bois-Guilbert.'

'Thou wert right to give me knowledge of it,' said the Grand Master; 'in our presence a Preceptor is but as a common compeer of our Order, who may not walk according to his own will, but to that of his Master—even according to the text, "In the hearing of the ear he hath obeyed me."*—It imports us especially to know of this Bois-Guilbert's proceedings,' said he, turning to his companion.

'Report speaks him brave and valiant,' said Conrade.

'And truly is he so spoken of,' said the Grand Master; 'in our valour only we are not degenerated from our predecessors, the heroes of the Cross. But brother Brian came into our Order a moody and disappointed man, stirred, I doubt me, to take our vows and to renounce the world, not in sincerity of soul, but as one whom some touch of light discontent had driven into penitence. Since then, he hath become an active and earnest agitator, a murmurer, and a machinator, and a leader amongst those who impugn our authority; not considering that the rule is given to the Master even by the symbol of the staff and the rod*—the staff to support the infirmities of the weak—the rod to correct the faults of delinquents.—Damian,' he continued, 'lead the Jew to our presence.'

The squire departed with a profound reverence, and in a few minutes returned, marshalling in Isaac of York. No naked slave, ushered into the presence of some mighty prince, could approach his judgment-seat with more profound reverence and terror than that with which the Jew drew near to the presence of the Grand Master. When he had approached within the distance of three yards, Beaumanoir made a sign with his staff that he should come no farther. The Jew kneeled down on the earth, which he kissed in token of reverence; then rising, stood before the Templars, his hands folded on his bosom, his head bowed on his breast, in all the submission of Oriental slavery.

'Damian,' said the Grand Master, 'retire, and have a guard ready to await our sudden call; and suffer no one to enter the garden until we shall leave it.'—The squire bowed and retreated.—'Jew,' continued the haughty old man, 'mark me. It suits not our condition to hold with thee long communication, nor do we waste words or time upon any one. Wherefore be brief in thy answers to what questions I shall ask thee, and let thy words be of truth; for if thy tongue doubles with me, I will have it torn from thy misbelieving jaws.'

The Jew was about to reply, but the Grand Master went on.

'Peace, unbeliever!—not a word in our presence, save in answer to our questions.—What is thy business with our brother Brian de Bois-Guilbert?'

Isaac gasped with terror and uncertainty. To tell his tale might be interpreted into scandalizing the Order; yet, unless he told it, what hope could he have of achieving his daughter's deliverance?

Beaumanoir saw his mortal apprehension, and condescended to give him some assurance.

'Fear nothing,' he said, 'for thy wretched person, Jew, so thou dealest uprightly in this matter. I demand again to know from thee thy business with Brian de Bois-Guilbert?'

'I am bearer of a letter,' stammered out the Jew, 'so please your reverend valour, to that good knight, from Prior Aymer of the Abbey of Jorvaulx.'

'Said I not these were evil times, Conrade?' said the Master. 'A Cistercian Prior sends a letter to a soldier of the Temple, and can find no more fitting messenger than an unbelieving Jew.—Give me the letter.'

The Jew, with trembling hands, undid the folds of his Armenian cap, in which he had deposited the Prior's tablets for the greater security, and was about to approach, with hand extended and body crouched, to place it within the reach of his grim interrogator.

'Back, dog!' said the Grand Master; 'I touch not misbelievers, save with the sword.—Conrade, take thou the letter from the Jew, and give it to me.'

Beaumanoir, being thus possessed of the tablets, inspected the outside carefully, and then proceeded to undo the packthread which secured its folds. 'Reverend father,' said Conrade, interposing, though with much deference, 'wilt thou break the seal?'

'And will I not?' said Beaumanoir, with a frown. 'Is it not written in the forty-second capital, *De Lectione Literarum*,* that a Templar shall not receive a letter, no not from his father, without communicating the same to the Grand Master, and reading it in his presence?'

He then perused the letter in haste, with an expression of surprise and horror; read it over again more slowly; then holding it out to Conrade with one hand, and slightly striking it with the other, exclaimed—'Here is goodly stuff for one Christian man to write to another, and both members, and no inconsiderable members, of religious professions! When,' said he solemnly, and looking upward, 'wilt thou come with thy fanners to purge the thrashing-floor?'*

Mont-Fitchet took the letter from his Superior, and was about to peruse it. 'Read it aloud, Conrade,' said the Grand Master,—

'and do thou' (to Isaac) 'attend to the purport of it, for we will question thee concerning it.'

Conrade read the letter, which was in these words: 'Aymer, by divine grace, Prior of the Cistercian house of Saint Mary's of Jorvaulx, to Sir Brian de Bois-Guilbert, a Knight of the holy Order of the Temple, wisheth health, with the bounties of King Bacchus and of my Lady Venus. Touching our present condition, dear Brother, we are a captive in the hands of certain lawless and godless men, who have not feared to detain our person, and put us to ransom; whereby we have also learned of Front-de-Bœuf's misfortune, and that thou hast escaped with that fair Jewish sorceress, whose black eyes have bewitched thee. We are heartily rejoiced of thy safety; nevertheless, we pray thee to be on thy guard in the matter of this second Witch of Endor; for we are privately assured that your Great Master, who careth not a bean for cherry cheeks and black eyes, comes from Normandy to diminish your mirth, and amend your misdoings. Wherefore we pray you heartily to beware, and to be found watching, even as the Holy Text hath it, *Invenientur vigilantes.** And the wealthy Jew her father, Isaac of York, having prayed of me letters in his behalf, I gave him these, earnestly advising, and in a sort entreating, that you do hold the damsel to ransom, seeing he will pay you from his bags as much as may find fifty damsels upon safer terms, whereof I trust to have my part when we make merry together, as true brothers, not forgetting the wine-cup. For what saith the text, *Vinum lætificat cor hominis*; and again, *Rex delectabitur pulchritudine tua.**

'Till which merry meeting, we wish you farewell. Given from this den of thieves, about the hour of matins,

'AYMER PR. S. M. JORVOLCIENCIS*

'*Postscriptum*. Truly your golden chain hath not long abidden with me, and will now sustain, around the neck of an outlaw deer-stealer, the whistle wherewith he calleth on his hounds.'

'What sayest thou to this, Conrade?' said the Grand Master— 'Den of thieves! and a fit residence is a den of thieves for such a Prior. No wonder that the hand of God is upon us, and that in the Holy Land we lose place by place, foot by foot, before the infidels, when we have such churchmen as this Aymer.—And what meaneth he, I trow, by this second Witch of Endor?' said he to his confident, something apart.

Conrade was better acquainted (perhaps by practice) with the jargon of gallantry, than was his Superior; and he expounded the passage which embarrassed the Grand Master, to be a sort of language used by worldly men towards those whom they loved *par amours*; but the explanation did not satisfy the bigoted Beaumanoir.

'There is more in it than thou dost guess, Conrade; thy simplicity is no match for this deep abyss of wickedness. This Rebecca of York was a pupil of that Miriam of whom thou hast heard. Thou shalt hear the Jew own it even now.' Then turning to Isaac, he said aloud, 'Thy daughter, then, is prisoner with Brian de Bois-Guilbert?'

'Ay, reverend valorous sir,' stammered poor Isaac, 'and whatsoever ransom a poor man may pay for her deliverance'——

'Peace!' said the Grand Master. 'This thy daughter hath practised the art of healing, hath she not?'

'Ay, gracious sir,' answered the Jew, with more confidence; 'and knight and yeoman, squire and vassal, may bless the goodly gift which Heaven hath assigned to her. Many a one can testify that she hath recovered them by her art, when every other human aid hath proved vain; but the blessing of the God of Jacob was upon her.'

Beaumanoir turned to Mont-Fitchet with a grim smile. 'See, brother,' he said, 'the deceptions of the devouring Enemy! Behold the baits with which he fishes for souls, giving a poor space of earthly life in exchange for eternal happiness hereafter. Well said our blessed rule, *Semper percutiatur leo vorans.**—— Upon the lion! Down with the destroyer!' said he, shaking aloft his mystic abacus, as if in defiance of the powers of darkness—— 'Thy daughter worketh the cures, I doubt not,' thus he went on to address the Jew, 'by words and sigils, and periapts,* and other cabalistical mysteries.'

'Nay, reverend and brave Knight,' answered Isaac, 'but in chief measure by a balsam of marvellous virtue.'

'Where had she that secret?' said Beaumanoir.

'It was delivered to her,' answered Isaac, reluctantly, 'by Miriam, a sage matron of our tribe.'

'Ah, false Jew! was it not from that same witch Miriam, the abomination of whose enchantments have been heard of throughout every Christian land?' exclaimed the Grand Master, crossing himself. 'Her body was burnt at a stake, and her ashes were scattered to the four winds; and so be it with me and mine Order, if I do not as much to her pupil, and more also! I will teach her to throw spell and incantation over the soldiers of the blessed Temple.—There, Damian, spurn this Jew from the gate—shoot him dead if he oppose or turn again. With his daughter we will deal as the Christian law and our own high office warrant.'

Poor Isaac was hurried off accordingly, and expelled from the preceptory; all his entreaties, and even his offers, unheard and disregarded. He could do no better than return to the house of the Rabbi, and endeavour, through his means, to learn how his daughter was to be disposed of. He had hitherto feared for her honour, he was now to tremble for her life. Meanwhile, the Grand Master ordered to his presence the Preceptor of Templestowe.

CHAPTER XXXVI

Say not my art is fraud—all live by seeming.
The beggar begs with it, and the gay courtier
Gains land and title, rank and rule, by seeming;
The clergy scorn it not, and the bold soldier
Will eke with it his service.—All admit it,
All practise it; and he who is content
With showing what he is, shall have small credit
In church, or camp, or state—So wags the world.

*Old Play**

ALBERT MALVOISIN, President, or, in the language of the Order, Preceptor of the establishment of Templestowe, was brother to that Philip Malvoisin who has been already occasionally mentioned in this history, and was, like that baron, in close league with Brian de Bois-Guilbert.

Amongst dissolute and unprincipled men, of whom the Temple Order included but too many, Albert of Templestowe might be distinguished; but with this difference from the audacious Bois-Guilbert, that he knew how to throw over his vices and his ambition the veil of hypocrisy, and to assume in his exterior the fanaticism which he internally despised. Had not the arrival of the Grand Master been so unexpectedly sudden, he would have seen nothing at Templestowe which might have appeared to argue any relaxation of discipline. And, even although surprised, and, to a certain extent, detected, Albert Malvoisin listened with such respect and apparent contrition to the rebuke of his Superior, and made such haste to reform the particulars he censured,—succeeded, in fine, so well in giving an air of ascetic devotion to a family which had been lately devoted to license and pleasure, that Lucas Beaumanoir began to entertain a higher opinion of the Preceptor's morals, than the first appearance of the establishment had inclined him to adopt.

But these favourable sentiments on the part of the Grand Master were greatly shaken by the intelligence that Albert had received within a house of religion the Jewish captive, and, as was to be feared, the paramour of a brother of the Order; and

when Albert appeared before him, he was regarded with unwonted sternness.

'There is in this mansion, dedicated to the purposes of the
holy Order of the Temple,' said the Grand Master, in a severe
tone, 'a Jewish woman, brought hither by a brother of religion,
by your connivance, Sir Preceptor.'

Albert Malvoisin was overwhelmed with confusion; for the
unfortunate Rebecca had been confined in a remote and secret
part of the building, and every precaution used to prevent her
residence there from being known. He read in the looks of
Beaumanoir ruin to Bois-Guilbert and to himself, unless he
should be able to avert the impending storm.

'Why are you mute?' continued the Grand Master.

'Is it permitted to me to reply?' answered the Preceptor, in a
tone of the deepest humility, although by the question he only
meant to gain an instant's space for arranging his ideas.

'Speak, you are permitted,' said the Grand Master—'speak,
and say, knowest thou the capital of our holy rule,—*De
commilitonibus Templi in sancta civitate, qui cum miserrimis
mulieribus versantur, propter oblectationem carnis?*'[47]*

'Surely, most reverend father,' answered the Preceptor, 'I
have not risen to this office in the Order, being ignorant of one of
its most important prohibitions.'

'How comes it, then, I demand of thee once more, that thou
hast suffered a brother to bring a paramour, and that paramour
a Jewish sorceress, into this holy place, to the stain and pollution
thereof?'

'A Jewish sorceress!' echoed Albert Malvoisin; 'good angels
guard us!'

'Ay, brother, a Jewish sorceress!' said the Grand Master,
sternly. 'I have said it. Darest thou deny that this Rebecca, the
daughter of that wretched usurer Isaac of York, and the pupil of
the foul witch Miriam, is now—shame to be thought or
spoken!—lodged within this thy Preceptory?'

'Your wisdom, reverend father,' answered the Preceptor,
'hath rolled away the darkness from my understanding. Much
did I wonder that so good a knight as Brian de Bois-Guilbert
seemed so fondly besotted on the charms of this female, whom I
received into this house merely to place a bar betwixt their

growing intimacy, which else might have been cemented at the expense of the fall of our valiant and religious brother.'

'Hath nothing, then, as yet passed betwixt them in breach of his vow?' demanded the Grand Master.

'What! under this roof?' said the Preceptor, crossing himself; 'Saint Magdalene and the ten thousand virgins forbid!*—No! if I have sinned in receiving her here, it was in the erring thought that I might thus break off our brother's besotted devotion to this Jewess, which seemed to me so wild and unnatural, that I could not but ascribe it to some touch of insanity, more to be cured by pity than reproof. But since your reverend wisdom hath discovered this Jewish quean* to be a sorceress, perchance it may account fully for his enamoured folly.'

'It doth!—it doth!' said Beaumanoir. 'See, brother Conrade, the peril of yielding to the first devices and blandishments of Satan! We look upon woman only to gratify the lust of the eye,* and to take pleasure in what men call her beauty; and the Ancient Enemy, the devouring Lion, obtains power over us, to complete, by talisman and spell, a work which was begun by idleness and folly. It may be that our brother Bois-Guilbert does in this matter deserve rather pity than severe chastisement; rather the support of the staff, than the strokes of the rod; and that our admonitions and prayers may turn him from his folly, and restore him to his brethren.'

'It were deep pity,' said Conrade Mont-Fitchet, 'to lose to the Order one of its best lances, when the Holy Community most requires the aid of its sons. Three hundred Saracens hath this Brian de Bois-Guilbert slain with his own hand.'

'The blood of these accursed dogs,' said the Grand Master, 'shall be a sweet and acceptable offering* to the saints and angels whom they despise and blaspheme; and with their aid will we counteract the spells and charms with which our brother is entwined as in a net. He shall burst the bands of this Delilah, as Sampson burst the two new cords with which the Philistines had bound him, and shall slaughter the infidels, even heaps upon heaps.* But concerning this foul witch, who hath flung her enchantments over a brother of the Holy Temple, assuredly she shall die the death.'

'But the laws of England,'—said the Preceptor, who, though

delighted that the Grand Master's resentment, thus fortunately averted from himself and Bois-Guilbert, had taken another direction, began now to fear he was carrying it too far.

'The laws of England,' interrupted Beaumanoir, 'permit and enjoin each judge to execute justice within his own jurisdiction. The most petty baron may arrest, try, and condemn a witch found within his own domain.* And shall that power be denied to the Grand Master of the Temple within a preceptory of his Order?—No!—we will judge and condemn. The witch shall be taken out of the land, and the wickedness thereof shall be forgiven. Prepare the Castle-hall for the trial of the sorceress.'

Albert Malvoisin bowed and retired,—not to give directions for preparing the hall, but to seek out Brian de Bois-Guilbert, and communicate to him how matters were likely to terminate. It was not long ere he found him, foaming with indignation at a repulse he had anew sustained from the fair Jewess. 'The unthinking,' he said, 'the ungrateful, to scorn him who, amidst blood and flames, would have saved her life at the risk of his own! By Heaven, Malvoisin! I abode until roof and rafters crackled and crashed around me. I was the butt of a hundred arrows; they rattled on mine armour like hailstones against a latticed casement, and the only use I made of my shield was for her protection. This did I endure for her; and now the self-willed girl upbraids me that I did not leave her to perish, and refuses me not only the slightest proof of gratitude, but even the most distant hope that ever she will be brought to grant any. The devil, that possessed her race with obstinacy, has concentrated its full force in her single person!'

'The devil,' said the Preceptor, 'I think, possessed you both. How oft have I preached to you caution, if not continence? Did I not tell you that there were enough willing Christian damsels to be met with, who would think it sin to refuse so brave a knight *le don d'amoureux merci*,* and you must needs anchor your affection on a wilful, obstinate Jewess! By the mass, I think old Lucas Beaumanoir guesses right, when he maintains she hath cast a spell over you.'

'Lucas Beaumanoir!'—said Bois-Guilbert reproachfully—'Are these your precautions, Malvoisin? Hast thou suffered the dotard to learn that Rebecca is in the Preceptory?'

'How could I help it?' said the Preceptor. 'I neglected nothing that could keep secret your mystery; but it is betrayed, and whether by the devil or no, the devil only can tell. But I have turned the matter as I could; you are safe if you renounce Rebecca. You are pitied—the victim of magical delusion. She is a sorceress, and must suffer as such.'

'She shall not, by Heaven!' said Bois-Guilbert.

'By Heaven, she must and will!' said Malvoisin. 'Neither you nor any one else can save her. Lucas Beaumanoir hath settled that the death of a Jewess will be a sin-offering sufficient to atone for all the amorous indulgences of the Knights Templars; and thou knowest he hath both the power and will to execute so reasonable and pious a purpose.'

'Will future ages believe that such stupid bigotry ever existed!' said Bois-Guilbert, striding up and down the apartment.

'What they may believe, I know not,' said Malvoisin, calmly; 'but I know well, that in this our day, clergy and laymen, take ninety-nine to the hundred, will cry *amen* to the Grand Master's sentence.'

'I have it,' said Bois-Guilbert. 'Albert, thou art my friend. Thou must connive at her escape, Malvoisin, and I will transport her to some place of greater security and secrecy.'

'I cannot, if I would,' replied the Preceptor; 'the mansion is filled with the attendants of the Grand Master, and others who are devoted to him. And, to be frank with you, brother, I would not embark with you in this matter, even if I could hope to bring my bark to haven. I have risked enough already for your sake. I have no mind to encounter a sentence of degradation, or even to lose my Preceptory, for the sake of a painted piece of Jewish flesh and blood. And you, if you will be guided by my counsel, will give up this wild-goose chase, and fly your hawk at some other game. Think, Bois-Guilbert,—thy present rank, thy future honours, all depend on thy place in the Order. Shouldst thou adhere perversely to thy passion for this Rebecca, thou wilt give Beaumanoir the power of expelling thee, and he will not neglect it. He is jealous of the truncheon which he holds in his trembling gripe, and he knows thou stretchest thy bold hand towards it. Doubt not he will ruin thee, if thou affordest him a pretext so fair as thy protection of a Jewish sorceress. Give him his scope in this matter, for thou canst not control him. When the staff is in thine own firm grasp, thou mayest caress the daughters of Judah, or burn them, as may best suit thine own humour.'

'Malvoisin,' said Bois-Guilbert, 'thou art a cold-blooded'——

'Friend,' said the Preceptor, hastening to fill up the blank, in which Bois-Guilbert would probably have placed a worse word,—'a cold-blooded friend I am, and therefore more fit to give thee advice. I tell thee once more, that thou canst not save Rebecca. I tell thee once more, thou canst but perish with her. Go hie thee to the Grand Master—throw thyself at his feet and tell him'——

'Not at his feet, by Heaven! but to the dotard's very beard will I say'——

'Say to him, then, to his beard,' continued Malvoisin, coolly, 'that you love this captive Jewess to distraction; and the more thou dost enlarge on thy passion, the greater will be his haste to end it by the death of the fair enchantress; while thou, taken in flagrant delict* by the avowal of a crime contrary to thine oath, canst hope no aid of thy brethren, and must exchange all thy brilliant visions of ambition and power, to lift perhaps a mercenary spear in some of the petty quarrels between Flanders and Burgundy.'

'Thou speakest the truth, Malvoisin,' said Brian de Bois-Guilbert, after a moment's reflection. 'I will give the hoary bigot no advantage over me; and for Rebecca, she hath not merited at my hand that I should expose rank and honour for her sake. I will cast her off—yes, I will leave her to her fate, unless'——

'Qualify not thy wise and necessary resolution,' said Malvoisin; 'women are but the toys which amuse our lighter hours—ambition is the serious business of life. Perish a thousand such frail baubles as this Jewess, before thy manly step pause in the brilliant career that lies stretched before thee! For the present we part, nor must we be seen to hold close conversation—I must order the hall for his judgment-seat.'

'What!' said Bois-Guilbert, 'so soon?'

'Ay,' replied the Preceptor, 'trial moves rapidly on when the judge has determined the sentence beforehand.'

'Rebecca,' said Bois-Guilbert, when he was left alone, 'thou art like to cost me dear—Why cannot I abandon thee to thy fate,

as this calm hypocrite recommends?—One effort will I make to
save thee—but beware of ingratitude! for if I am again repulsed,
my vengeance shall equal my love. The life and honour of Bois-
Guilbert must not be hazarded, where contempt and reproaches
are his only reward.'

The Preceptor had hardly given the necessary orders, when he
was joined by Conrade Mont-Fitchet, who acquainted him with
the Grand Master's resolution to bring the Jewess to instant trial
for sorcery.

'It is surely a dream,' said the Preceptor; 'we have many
Jewish physicians, and we call them not wizards though they
work wonderful cures.'

'The Grand Master thinks otherwise,' said Mont-Fitchet;
'and, Albert, I will be upright with thee—wizard or not, it were
better that this miserable damsel die, than that Brian de Bois-
Guilbert should be lost to the Order, or the Order divided by
internal dissension. Thou knowest his high rank, his fame in
arms—thou knowest the zeal with which many of our brethren
regard him—but all this will not avail him with our Grand
Master, should he consider Brian as the accomplice, not the
victim, of this Jewess. Were the souls of the twelve tribes in her
single body, it were better she suffered alone, than that Bois-
Guilbert were partner in her destruction.'

'I have been working him even now to abandon her,' said
Malvoisin; 'but still, are there grounds enough to condemn this
Rebecca for sorcery?—Will not the Grand Master change his
mind when he sees that the proofs are so weak?'

'They must be strengthened, Albert,' replied Mont-Fitchet,
'they must be strengthened. Dost thou understand me?'

'I do,' said the Preceptor, 'nor do I scruple to do aught for
advancement of the Order—but there is little time to find engines fitting.'

'Malvoisin, they *must* be found,' said Conrade; 'well will it
advantage both the Order and thee. This Templestowe is a poor
Preceptory—that of Maison-Dieu is worth double its value—
thou knowest my interest with our old Chief—find those who
can carry this matter through, and thou art Preceptor of Maison-
Dieu* in the fertile Kent—How sayst thou?'

'There is,' replied Malvoisin, 'among those who came hither

with Bois-Guilbert, two fellows whom I well know; servants they
were to my brother Philip de Malvoisin, and passed from his
service to that of Front-de-Bœuf—It may be they know something of the witcheries of this woman.'

'Away, seek them out instantly—and hark thee, if a byzant or
two will sharpen their memory, let them not be wanting.'

'They would swear the mother that bore them a sorceress for
a zecchin,' said the Preceptor.

'Away, then,' said Mont-Fitchet; 'at noon the affair will proceed. I have not seen our senior in such earnest preparation since
he condemned to the stake Hamet Alfagi, a convert who relapsed
to the Moslem faith.'

The ponderous castle-bell had tolled the point of noon, when
Rebecca heard a trampling of feet upon the private stair which
led to her place of confinement. The noise announced the arrival
of several persons, and the circumstance rather gave her joy; for
she was more afraid of the solitary visits of the fierce and passionate Bois-Guilbert than of any evil that could befall her besides.
The door of the chamber was unlocked, and Conrade and the
Preceptor Malvoisin entered, attended by four warders clothed
in black, and bearing halberds.

'Daughter of an accursed race!' said the Preceptor, 'arise and
follow us.'

'Whither,' said Rebecca, 'and for what purpose?'

'Damsel,' answered Conrade, 'it is not for thee to question,
but to obey. Nevertheless, be it known to thee, that thou art to be
brought before the tribunal of the Grand Master of our holy
Order, there to answer for thine offences.'

'May the God of Abraham be praised!' said Rebecca, folding
her hands devoutly; 'the name of a judge, though an enemy to
my people, is to me as the name of a protector. Most willingly do
I follow thee—permit me only to wrap my veil around my head.'

They descended the stair with slow and solemn step, traversed a long gallery, and, by a pair of folding doors placed at the
end, entered the great hall in which the Grand Master had for
the time established his court of justice.

The lower part of this ample apartment was filled with squires
and yeomen, who made way not without some difficulty for
Rebecca, attended by the Preceptor and Mont-Fitchet, and fol-

lowed by the guard of halberdiers, to move forward to the seat appointed for her. As she passed through the crowd, her arms folded and her head depressed, a scrap of paper was thrust into her hand, which she received almost unconsciously, and continued to hold without examining its contents. The assurance that she possessed some friend in this awful assembly gave her courage to look around, and to mark into whose presence she had been conducted. She gazed, accordingly, upon the scene, which we shall endeavour to describe in the next chapter.

CHAPTER XXXVII

Stern was the law which bade its vot'ries leave
At human woes with human hearts to grieve;
Stern was the law, which at the winning wile
Of frank and harmless mirth forbade to smile;
But sterner still, when high the iron-rod
Of tyrant power she shook, and call'd that power of God.

The Middle Ages*

THE tribunal, erected for the trial of the innocent and unhappy
Rebecca, occupied the dais or elevated part of the upper end of
the great hall—a platform, which we have already described as
the place of honour, destined to be occupied by the most distinguished inhabitants or guests of an ancient mansion.

On an elevated seat, directly before the accused, sat the Grand
Master of the Temple, in full and ample robes of flowing white,
holding in his hand the mystic staff, which bore the symbol
of the Order. At his feet was placed a table, occupied by two
scribes, chaplains of the Order, whose duty it was to reduce to
formal record the proceedings of the day. The black dresses, bare
scalps, and demure looks of these churchmen, formed a strong
contrast to the warlike appearance of the knights who attended,
either as residing in the Preceptory, or as come thither to attend
upon their Grand Master. The Preceptors, of whom there were
four present, occupied seats lower in height, and somewhat
drawn back behind that of their superior; and the knights, who
enjoyed no such rank in the Order, were placed on benches still
lower, and preserving the same distance from the Preceptors as
these from the Grand Master. Behind them, but still upon the
dais or elevated portion of the hall, stood the esquires of the
Order, in white dresses of an inferior quality.

The whole assembly wore an aspect of the most profound
gravity; and in the faces of the knights might be perceived traces
of military daring, united with the solemn carriage becoming
men of a religious profession, and which, in the presence of their
Grand Master, failed not to sit upon every brow.

The remaining and lower part of the hall was filled with guards, holding partisans, and with other attendants whom curiosity had drawn thither, to see at once a Grand Master and a Jewish sorceress. By far the greater part of those inferior persons were, in one rank or other, connected with the Order, and were accordingly distinguished by their black dresses. But peasants from the neighbouring country were not refused admittance; for it was the pride of Beaumanoir to render the edifying spectacle of the justice which he administered as public as possible. His large blue eyes seemed to expand as he gazed around the assembly, and his countenance appeared elated by the conscious dignity, and imaginary merit, of the part which he was about to perform. A psalm, which he himself accompanied with a deep mellow voice, which age had not deprived of its powers, commenced the proceedings of the day; and the solemn sounds, *Venite exultemus Domino*,* so often sung by the Templars before engaging with earthly adversaries, was judged by Lucas most appropriate to introduce the approaching triumph, for such he deemed it, over the powers of darkness. The deep prolonged notes, raised by a hundred masculine voices accustomed to combine in the choral chant, arose to the vaulted roof of the hall, and rolled on amongst its arches with the pleasing yet solemn sound of the rushing of mighty waters.*

When the sounds ceased, the Grand Master glanced his eye slowly around the circle, and observed that the seat of one of the Preceptors was vacant. Brian de Bois-Guilbert, by whom it had been occupied, had left his place, and was now standing near the extreme corner of one of the benches occupied by the Knights Companions of the Temple, one hand extending his long mantle, so as in some degree to hide his face; while the other held his cross-handled sword, with the point of which, sheathed as it was, he was slowly drawing lines upon the oaken floor.

'Unhappy man!' said the Grand Master, after favouring him with a glance of compassion. 'Thou seest, Conrade, how this holy work distresses him. To this can the light look of woman, aided by the Prince of the Powers of this world, bring a valiant and worthy knight!—Seest thou he cannot look upon us; he cannot look upon her; and who knows by what impulse from his tormentor his hand forms these cabalistic lines upon the floor?—

It may be our life and safety are thus aimed at; but we spit at and defy the foul enemy. *Semper Leo percutiatur!*'

This was communicated apart to his confidential follower, Conrade Mont-Fitchet. The Grand Master then raised his voice, and addressed the assembly.

'Reverend and valiant men, Knights, Preceptors, and Companions of this Holy Order, my brethren and my children!—you also, well-born and pious Esquires, who aspire to wear this holy Cross!—and you also, Christian brethren, of every degree!—Be it known to you, that it is not defect of power in us which hath occasioned the assembling of this congregation; for, however unworthy in our person, yet to us is committed, with this batoon, full power to judge and to try all that regards the weal of this our Holy Order. Holy Saint Bernard, in the rule of our knightly and religious profession, hath said, in the fifty-ninth capital,[48]* that he would not that brethren be called together in council, save at the will and command of the Master; leaving it free to us, as to those more worthy fathers who have preceded us in this our office, to judge, as well of the occasion as of the time and place in which a chapter of the whole Order, or of any part thereof, may be convoked. Also, in all such chapters, it is our duty to hear the advice of our brethren, and to proceed according to our own pleasure. But when the raging wolf hath made an inroad upon the flock, and carried off one member thereof, it is the duty of the kind shepherd to call his comrades together, that with bows and slings they may quell the invader, according to our well-known rule, that the lion is ever to be beaten down. We have therefore summoned to our presence a Jewish woman, by name Rebecca, daughter of Isaac of York—a woman infamous for sortileges* and for witcheries; whereby she hath maddened the blood, and besotted the brain, not of a churl, but of a Knight—not of a secular Knight, but of one devoted to the service of the Holy Temple—not of a Knight Companion, but of a Preceptor of our Order, first in honour as in place. Our brother, Brian de Bois-Guilbert, is well known to ourselves, and to all degrees who now hear me, as a true and zealous champion of the Cross, by whose arm many deeds of valour have been wrought in the Holy Land, and the holy places purified from pollution by the blood of those infidels who defiled them. Neither have our brother's sagacity and prudence been less in repute among his brethren than his valour and discipline; in so much, that knights, both in eastern and western lands, have named De Bois-Guilbert as one who may well be put in nomination as successor to this batoon, when it shall please Heaven to release us from the toil of bearing it. If we were told that such a man, so honoured, and so honourable, suddenly casting away regard for his character, his vows, his brethren, and his prospects, had associated to himself a Jewish damsel, wandered in this lewd company through solitary places, defended her person in preference to his own, and, finally, was so utterly blinded and besotted by his folly, as to bring her even to one of our own Preceptories, what should we say but that the noble knight was possessed by some evil demon, or influenced by some wicked spell?—If we could suppose it otherwise, think not rank, valour, high repute, or any earthly consideration, should prevent us from visiting him with punishment, that the evil thing might be removed, even according to the text, *Auferte malum ex vobis.** For various and heinous are the acts of transgression against the rule of our blessed Order in this lamentable history.*—1st, He hath walked according to his proper will, contrary to capital 33, *Quod nullus juxta propriam voluntatem incedat.*—2d, He hath held communication with an excommunicated person, capital 57, *Ut fratres non participent cum excommunicatis*, and therefore hath a portion in *Anathema Maranatha.*—3d, He hath conversed with strange women, contrary to the capital, *Ut fratres non conversantur cum extraneis mulieribus.*—4th, He hath not avoided, nay, he hath, it is to be feared, solicited the kiss of woman; by which, saith the last rule of our renowned Order, *Ut fugiantur oscula,** the soldiers of the Cross are brought into a snare. For which heinous and multiplied guilt, Brian de Bois-Guilbert should be cut off and cast out from our congregation, were he the right hand and right eye thereof.'*

He paused. A low murmur went through the assembly. Some of the younger part, who had been inclined to smile at the statute *De osculis fugiendis,** became now grave enough, and anxiously waited what the Grand Master was next to propose.

'Such,' he said, 'and so great should indeed be the punishment of a Knight Templar, who wilfully offended against the rules of his Order in such weighty points. But if, by means of charms and of spells, Satan had obtained dominion over the Knight, perchance because he cast his eyes too lightly upon a damsel's beauty, we are then rather to lament than chastise his backsliding; and, imposing on him only such penance as may purify him from his iniquity, we are to turn the full edge of our indignation upon the accursed instrument, which had so wellnigh occasioned his utter falling away.—Stand forth, therefore, and bear witness, ye who have witnessed these unhappy doings, that we may judge of the sum and bearing thereof; and judge whether our justice may be satisfied with the punishment of this infidel woman, or if we must go on, with a bleeding heart, to the further proceeding against our brother.'

Several witnesses were called upon to prove the risks to which Bois-Guilbert exposed himself in endeavouring to save Rebecca from the blazing castle, and his neglect of his personal defence in attending to her safety. The men gave these details with the exaggerations common to vulgar minds which have been strongly excited by any remarkable event, and their natural disposition to the marvellous was greatly increased by the satisfaction which their evidence seemed to afford to the eminent person for whose information it had been delivered. Thus the dangers which Bois-Guilbert surmounted, in themselves sufficiently great, became portentous in their narrative. The devotion of the Knight to Rebecca's defence was exaggerated beyond the bounds, not only of discretion, but even of the most frantic excess of chivalrous zeal; and his deference to what she said, even although her language was often severe and upbraiding, was painted as carried to an excess, which, in a man of his haughty temper, seemed almost preternatural.

The Preceptor of Templestowe was then called on to describe the manner in which Bois-Guilbert and the Jewess arrived at the Preceptory. The evidence of Malvoisin was skilfully guarded. But while he apparently studied to spare the feelings of Bois-Guilbert, he threw in, from time to time, such hints, as seemed to infer that he laboured under some temporary alienation of mind, so deeply did he appear to be enamoured of the damsel whom he brought along with him. With sighs of penitence, the Preceptor avowed his own contrition for having admitted

Rebecca and her lover within the walls of the Preceptory—'But my defence,' he concluded, 'has been made in my confession to our most reverend father the Grand Master; he knows my motives were not evil, though my conduct may have been irregular. Joyfully will I submit to any penance he shall assign me.'

'Thou hast spoken well, Brother Albert,' said Beaumanoir; 'thy motives were good, since thou didst judge it right to arrest thine erring brother in his career of precipitate folly. But thy conduct was wrong; as he that would stop a runaway steed, and seizing by the stirrup instead of the bridle, receiveth injury himself, instead of accomplishing his purpose. Thirteen paternosters are assigned by our pious founder for matins, and nine for vespers; be those services doubled by thee. Thrice a-week are Templars permitted the use of flesh; but do thou keep fast for all the seven days. This do for six weeks to come, and thy penance is accomplished.'

With a hypocritical look of the deepest submission, the Preceptor of Templestowe bowed to the ground before his Superior, and resumed his seat.

'Were it not well, brethren,' said the Grand Master, 'that we examine something into the former life and conversation of this woman, specially that we may discover whether she be one likely to use magical charms and spells, since the truths which we have heard may well incline us to suppose, that in this unhappy course our erring brother has been acted upon by some infernal enticement and delusion?'

Herman of Goodalricke was the Fourth Preceptor present; the other three were Conrade, Malvoisin, and Bois-Guilbert himself. Herman was an ancient warrior, whose face was marked with scars inflicted by the sabre of the Moslemah, and had great rank and consideration among his brethren. He arose and bowed to the Grand Master, who instantly granted him license of speech. 'I would crave to know, most Reverend Father, of our valiant brother, Brian de Bois-Guilbert, what he says to these wondrous accusations, and with what eye he himself now regards his unhappy intercourse with this Jewish maiden?'

'Brian de Bois-Guilbert,' said the Grand Master, 'thou hearest the question which our Brother of Goodalricke desireth thou shouldst answer. I command thee to reply to him.'

Bois-Guilbert turned his head towards the Grand Master when thus addressed, and remained silent.

'He is possessed by a dumb devil,' said the Grand Master. 'Avoid thee, Sathanas!—Speak, Brian de Bois-Guilbert, I conjure thee, by this symbol of our Holy Order.'

Bois-Guilbert made an effort to suppress his rising scorn and indignation, the expression of which, he was well aware, would have little availed him. 'Brian de Bois-Guilbert,' he answered, 'replies not, most Reverend Father, to such wild and vague charges. If his honour be impeached, he will defend it with his body, and with that sword which has often fought for Christendom.'

'We forgive thee, Brother Brian,' said the Grand Master; 'though that thou hast boasted thy warlike achievements before us, is a glorifying of thine own deeds, and cometh of the Enemy, who tempteth us to exalt our own worship. But thou hast our pardon, judging thou speakest less of thine own suggestion than from the impulse of him whom, by Heaven's leave, we will quell and drive forth from our assembly.' A glance of disdain flashed from the dark fierce eyes of Bois-Guilbert, but he made no reply.—'And now,' pursued the Grand Master, 'since our Brother of Goodalricke's question has been thus imperfectly answered, pursue we our quest, brethren, and with our patron's assistance, we will search to the bottom this mystery of iniquity.*—Let those who have aught to witness of the life and conversation of this Jewish woman, stand forth before us.' There was a bustle in the lower part of the hall, and when the Grand Master enquired the reason, it was replied, there was in the crowd a bedridden man, whom the prisoner had restored to the perfect use of his limbs, by a miraculous balsam.

The poor peasant, a Saxon by birth, was dragged forward to the bar, terrified at the penal consequences which he might have incurred by the guilt of having been cured of the palsy by a Jewish damsel. Perfectly cured he certainly was not, for he supported himself forward on crutches to give evidence. Most unwilling was his testimony, and given with many tears; but he admitted that two years since, when residing at York, he was suddenly afflicted with a sore disease, while labouring for Isaac the rich Jew, in his vocation of a joiner; that he had been unable to stir from his bed until the remedies applied by Rebecca's directions, and especially a warming and spicy-smelling balsam, had in some degree restored him to the use of his limbs. Moreover, he said, she had given him a pot of that precious ointment, and furnished him with a piece of money withal, to return to the house of his father, near to Templestowe. 'And may it please your gracious Reverence,' said the man, 'I cannot think the damsel meant harm by me, though she hath the ill hap to be a Jewess; for ever when I used her remedy, I said the Pater and the Creed, and it never operated a whit less kindly.'

'Peace, slave,' said the Grand Master, 'and begone! It well suits brutes like thee to be tampering and trinketing with hellish cures, and to be giving your labour to the sons of mischief. I tell thee, the fiend can impose diseases for the very purpose of removing them, in order to bring into credit some diabolical fashion of cure. Hast thou that unguent of which thou speakest?'

The peasant, fumbling in his bosom with a trembling hand, produced a small box, bearing some Hebrew characters on the lid, which was, with most of the audience, a sure proof that the devil had stood apothecary. Beaumanoir, after crossing himself, took the box into his hand, and, learned in most of the Eastern tongues, read with ease the motto on the lid,—*The Lion of the Tribe of Judah hath conquered.** 'Strange powers of Sathanas,' said he, 'which can convert Scripture into blasphemy,* mingling poison with our necessary food!—Is there no leech here who can tell us the ingredients of this mystic unguent?'

Two mediciners, as they called themselves, the one a monk, the other a barber, appeared, and avouched they knew nothing of the materials, excepting that they savoured of myrrh and camphire, which they took to be Oriental herbs. But with the true professional hatred to a successful practitioner of their art, they insinuated that, since the medicine was beyond their own knowledge, it must necessarily have been compounded from an unlawful and magical pharmacopeia; since they themselves, though no conjurors, fully understood every branch of their art, so far as it might be exercised with the good faith of a Christian. When this medical research was ended, the Saxon peasant desired humbly to have back the medicine which he had found so salutary; but the Grand Master frowned severely at the request. 'What is thy name, fellow?' said he to the cripple.

'Higg, the son of Snell,' answered the peasant.

'Then Higg, son of Snell,' said the Grand Master, 'I tell thee it is better to be bedridden, than to accept the benefit of unbelievers' medicine that thou mayest arise and walk; better to despoil infidels of their treasure by the strong hand, than to accept of them benevolent gifts, or do them service for wages. Go thou, and do as I have said.'

'Alack,' said the peasant, 'an it shall not displease your Reverence, the lesson comes too late for me, for I am but a maimed man; but I will tell my two brethren, who serve the rich Rabbi Nathan Ben Samuel,* that your mastership says it is more lawful to rob him than to render him faithful service.'

'Out with the prating villain!' said Beaumanoir, who was not prepared to refute this practical application of his general maxim.

Higg, the son of Snell, withdrew into the crowd, but, interested in the fate of his benefactress, lingered until he should learn her doom, even at the risk of again encountering the frown of that severe judge, the terror of which withered his very heart within him.

At this period of the trial, the Grand Master commanded Rebecca to unveil herself. Opening her lips for the first time, she replied patiently, but with dignity,—'That it was not the wont of the daughters of her people to uncover their faces when alone in an assembly of strangers.' The sweet tones of her voice, and the softness of her reply, impressed on the audience a sentiment of pity and sympathy. But Beaumanoir, in whose mind the suppression of each feeling of humanity which could interfere with his imagined duty, was a virtue of itself, repeated his commands that his victim should be unveiled. The guards were about to remove her veil accordingly, when she stood up before the Grand Master and said, 'Nay, but for the love of your own daughters—Alas,' she said, recollecting herself, 'ye have no daughters!—yet for the remembrance of your mothers—for the love of your sisters, and of female decency, let me not be thus handled in your presence; it suits not a maiden to be disrobed by such rude grooms. I will obey you,' she added, with an expression of patient sorrow in her voice, which had almost melted the heart of Beaumanoir himself; 'ye are elders among your people, and at your command I will show the features of an ill-fated maiden.'

She withdrew her veil, and looked on them with a countenance in which bashfulness contended with dignity. Her exceeding beauty excited a murmur of surprise, and the younger knights told each other with their eyes, in silent correspondence, that Brian's best apology was in the power of her real charms, rather than of her imaginary witchcraft. But Higg, the son of Snell, felt most deeply the effect produced by the sight of the countenance of his benefactress. 'Let me go forth,' he said to the warders at the door of the hall,—'let me go forth!—To look at her again will kill me, for I have had a share in murdering her.'

'Peace, poor man,' said Rebecca, when she heard his exclamation; 'thou hast done me no harm by speaking the truth—thou canst not aid me by thy complaints or lamentations. Peace, I pray thee—go home and save thyself.'

Higg was about to be thrust out by the compassion of the warders, who were apprehensive lest his clamorous grief should draw upon them reprehension, and upon himself punishment. But he promised to be silent, and was permitted to remain. The two men-at-arms, with whom Albert Malvoisin had not failed to communicate upon the import of their testimony, were now called forward. Though both were hardened and inflexible villains, the sight of the captive maiden, as well as her excelling beauty, at first appeared to stagger them; but an expressive glance from the Preceptor of Templestowe restored them to their dogged composure; and they delivered, with a precision which would have seemed suspicious to more impartial judges, circumstances either altogether fictitious or trivial, and natural in themselves, but rendered pregnant with suspicion by the exaggerated manner in which they were told, and the sinister commentary which the witnesses added to the facts. The circumstances of their evidence would have been, in modern days, divided into two classes—those which were immaterial, and those which were actually and physically impossible. But both were, in those ignorant and superstitious times, easily credited as proofs of guilt.—The first class set forth, that Rebecca was heard to mutter to herself in an unknown tongue—that the songs she sung by fits were of a strangely sweet sound, which made the ears of the hearer tingle, and his heart throb—that she spoke at times to herself, and seemed to look upward for a reply—that her garments were of a strange and mystic form, unlike those of women of good repute—that she had rings impressed with cabalistical devices, and that strange characters were broidered on her veil.

All these circumstances, so natural and so trivial, were gravely listened to as proofs, or, at least, as affording strong suspicions that Rebecca had unlawful correspondence with mystical powers.

But there was less equivocal testimony, which the credulity of the assembly, or of the greater part, greedily swallowed, however incredible. One of the soldiers had seen her work a cure upon a wounded man, brought with them to the castle of Torquilstone. She did, he said, make certain signs upon the wound, and repeated certain mysterious words, which he blessed God he understood not, when the iron head of a square crossbow bolt disengaged itself from the wound, the bleeding was stanched, the wound was closed, and the dying man was, within the quarter of an hour, walking upon the ramparts, and assisting the witness in managing a mangonel, or machine for hurling stones. This legend was probably founded upon the fact, that Rebecca had attended on the wounded Ivanhoe when in the castle of Torquilstone. But it was the more difficult to dispute the accuracy of the witness, as, in order to produce real evidence in support of his verbal testimony, he drew from his pouch the very bolt-head, which, according to his story, had been miraculously extracted from the wound; and as the iron weighed a full ounce, it completely confirmed the tale, however marvellous.

His comrade had been a witness from a neighbouring battlement of the scene betwixt Rebecca and Bois-Guilbert, when she was upon the point of precipitating herself from the top of the tower. Not to be behind his companion, this fellow stated, that he had seen Rebecca perch herself upon the parapet of the turret, and there take the form of a milk-white swan, under which appearance she flitted three times round the castle of

Torquilstone; then again settle on the turret, and once more assume the female form.

Less than one half of this weighty evidence would have been sufficient to convict any old woman, poor and ugly, even though she had not been a Jewess. United with that fatal circumstance, the body of proof was too weighty for Rebecca's youth, though combined with the most exquisite beauty.

The Grand Master had collected the suffrages, and now in a solemn tone demanded of Rebecca what she had to say against the sentence of condemnation, which he was about to pronounce.

'To invoke your pity,' said the lovely Jewess, with a voice somewhat tremulous with emotion, 'would, I am aware, be as useless as I should hold it mean. To state that to relieve the sick and wounded of another religion, cannot be displeasing to the acknowledged Founder of both our faiths, were also unavailing; to plead that many things which these men (whom may Heaven pardon!) have spoken against me are impossible, would avail me but little, since you believe in their possibility; and still less would it advantage me to explain, that the peculiarities of my dress, language, and manners, are those of my people—I had wellnigh said of my country, but alas! we have no country. Nor will I even vindicate myself at the expense of my oppressor, who stands there listening to the fictions and surmises which seem to convert the tyrant into the victim.—God be judge between him and me! but rather would I submit to ten such deaths as your pleasure may denounce against me, than listen to the suit which that man of Belial has urged upon me—friendless, defenceless, and his prisoner. But he is of your own faith, and his lightest affirmance would weigh down the most solemn protestations of the distressed Jewess. I will not therefore return to himself the charge brought against me—but to himself—Yes, Brian de Bois-Guilbert, to thyself I appeal, whether these accusations are not false? as monstrous and calumnious as they are deadly?'

There was a pause; all eyes turned to Brian de Bois-Guilbert. He was silent.

'Speak,' she said, 'if thou art a man—if thou art a Christian, speak!—I conjure thee, by the habit which thou dost wear, by the name thou dost inherit—by the knighthood thou dost vaunt—by the honour of thy mother—by the tomb and the bones of thy father—I conjure thee to say, are these things true?'

'Answer her, brother,' said the Grand Master, 'if the Enemy with whom thou dost wrestle will give thee power.'

In fact, Bois-Guilbert seemed agitated by contending passions, which almost convulsed his features, and it was with a constrained voice that at last he replied, looking to Rebecca,— 'The scroll!—the scroll!'

'Ay,' said Beaumanoir, 'this is indeed testimony! The victim of her witcheries can only name the fatal scroll, the spell inscribed on which is, doubtless, the cause of his silence.'

But Rebecca put another interpretation on the words extorted as it were from Bois-Guilbert, and glancing her eye upon the slip of parchment which she continued to hold in her hand, she read written thereupon in the Arabian character, *Demand a Champion!* The murmuring commentary which ran through the assembly at the strange reply of Bois-Guilbert, gave Rebecca leisure to examine and instantly to destroy the scroll unobserved. When the whisper had ceased, the Grand Master spoke.

'Rebecca, thou canst derive no benefit from the evidence of this unhappy knight, for whom, as we well perceive, the Enemy is yet too powerful. Hast thou aught else to say?'

'There is yet one chance of life left to me,' said Rebecca, 'even by your own fierce laws. Life has been miserable—miserable, at least, of late—but I will not cast away the gift of God, while he affords me the means of defending it. I deny this charge—I maintain my innocence, and I declare the falsehood of this accusation—I challenge the privilege of trial by combat, and will appear by my champion.'

'And who, Rebecca,' replied the Grand Master, 'will lay lance in rest for a sorceress? who will be the champion of a Jewess?'

'God will raise me up a champion,' said Rebecca—'It cannot be that in merry England—the hospitable, the generous, the free, where so many are ready to peril their lives for honour, there will not be found one to fight for justice. But it is enough that I challenge the trial by combat*—there lies my gage.'

She took her embroidered glove from her hand, and flung it down before the Grand Master with an air of mingled simplicity and dignity, which excited universal surprise and admiration.

CHAPTER XXXVIII

―――There I throw my gage,
To prove it on thee to the extremest point
Of martial daring.

Richard II*

Even Lucas Beaumanoir himself was affected by the mien and appearance of Rebecca. He was not originally a cruel or even a severe man; but with passions by nature cold, and with a high, though mistaken, sense of duty, his heart had been gradually hardened by the ascetic life which he pursued, the supreme power which he enjoyed, and the supposed necessity of subduing infidelity and eradicating heresy, which he conceived peculiarly incumbent on him. His features relaxed in their usual severity as he gazed upon the beautiful creature before him, alone, unfriended, and defending herself with so much spirit and courage. He crossed himself twice, as doubting whence arose the unwonted softening of a heart, which on such occasions used to resemble in hardness the steel of his sword. At length he spoke.

'Damsel,' he said, 'if the pity I feel for thee arise from any practice thine evil arts have made on me, great is thy guilt. But I rather judge it the kinder feelings of nature, which grieves that so goodly a form should be a vessel of perdition. Repent, my daughter—confess thy witchcrafts—turn thee from thine evil faith—embrace this holy emblem, and all shall yet be well with thee here and hereafter. In some sisterhood of the strictest order, shalt thou have time for prayer and fitting penance, and that repentance not to be repented of. This do and live—what has the law of Moses done for thee that thou shouldest die for it?'

'It was the law of my fathers,' said Rebecca; 'it was delivered in thunders and in storms upon the mountain of Sinai, in cloud and in fire.* This, if ye are Christians, ye believe—it is, you say, recalled; but so my teachers have not taught me.'

'Let our chaplain,' said Beaumanoir, 'stand forth, and tell this obstinate infidel'——

'Forgive the interruption,' said Rebecca, meekly; 'I am a maiden, unskilled to dispute for my religion, but I can die for it, if it be God's will.—Let me pray your answer to my demand of a champion.'

'Give me her glove,' said Beaumanoir. 'This is indeed,' he continued, as he looked at the flimsy texture and slender fingers, 'a slight and frail gage for a purpose so deadly!—Seest thou, Rebecca, as this thin and light glove of thine is to one of our heavy steel gauntlets, so is thy cause to that of the Temple, for it is our Order which thou hast defied.'

'Cast my innocence into the scale,' answered Rebecca, 'and the glove of silk shall outweigh the glove of iron.'

'Then thou dost persist in thy refusal to confess thy guilt, and in that bold challenge which thou hast made?'

'I do persist, noble sir,' answered Rebecca.

'So be it then, in the name of Heaven,' said the Grand Master; 'and may God show the right!'

'Amen,' replied the Preceptors around him, and the word was deeply echoed by the whole assembly.

'Brethren,' said Beaumanoir, 'you are aware that we might well have refused to this woman the benefit of the trial by combat—but though a Jewess and an unbeliever, she is also a stranger and defenceless, and God forbid that she should ask the benefit of our mild laws, and that it should be refused to her. Moreover, we are knights and soldiers as well as men of religion, and shame it were to us upon any pretence, to refuse proffered combat. Thus, therefore, stands the case. Rebecca, the daughter of Isaac of York, is, by many frequent and suspicious circumstances, defamed of sorcery practised on the person of a noble knight of our holy Order, and hath challenged the combat in proof of her innocence. To whom, reverend brethren, is it your opinion that we should deliver the gage of battle, naming him, at the same time, to be our champion on the field?'

'To Brian de Bois-Guilbert, whom it chiefly concerns,' said the Preceptor of Goodalricke, 'and who, moreover, best knows how the truth stands in this matter.'

'But if,' said the Grand Master, 'our brother Brian be under the influence of a charm or a spell—we speak but for the sake of precaution, for to the arm of none of our holy Order would we more willingly confide this or a more weighty cause.'

'Reverend father,' answered the Preceptor of Goodalricke, 'no spell can affect the champion who comes forward to fight for the judgment of God.'

'Thou sayest right, brother,' said the Grand Master. 'Albert Malvoisin, give this gage of battle to Brian de Bois-Guilbert.— It is our charge to thee, brother,' he continued, addressing himself to Bois-Guilbert, 'that thou do thy battle manfully, nothing doubting that the good cause shall triumph.—And do thou, Rebecca, attend, that we assign thee the third day from the present to find a champion.'

'That is but brief space,' answered Rebecca, 'for a stranger, who is also of another faith, to find one who will do battle, wagering life and honour for her cause, against a knight who is called an approved soldier.'

'We may not extend it,' answered the Grand Master; 'the field must be foughten in our own presence, and divers weighty causes call us on the fourth day from hence.'

'God's will be done!' said Rebecca; 'I put my trust in Him, to whom an instant is as effectual to save as a whole age.'*

'Thou hast spoken well, damsel,' said the Grand Master; 'but well know we who can array himself like an angel of light.* It remains but to name a fitting place of combat, and, if it so hap, also of execution.—Where is the Preceptor of this house?'

Albert Malvoisin, still holding Rebecca's glove in his hand, was speaking to Bois-Guilbert very earnestly, but in a low voice.

'How!' said the Grand Master, 'will he not receive the gage?'

'He will—he doth, most Reverend Father,' said Malvoisin, slipping the glove under his own mantle. 'And for the place of combat, I hold the fittest to be the lists of Saint George belonging to this Preceptory, and used by us for military exercise.'

'It is well,' said the Grand Master.—'Rebecca, in those lists shalt thou produce thy champion; and if thou failest to do so, or if thy champion shall be discomfited by the judgment of God, thou shalt then die the death of a sorceress, according to doom.—Let this our judgment be recorded, and the record read aloud, that no one may pretend ignorance.'

One of the chaplains, who acted as clerks to the chapter,

immediately engrossed the order in a huge volume, which contained the proceedings of the Templar Knights when solemnly assembled on such occasions; and when he had finished writing, the other read aloud the sentence of the Grand Master, which, when translated from the Norman-French in which it was couched, was expressed as follows:—

'Rebecca, a Jewess, daughter of Isaac of York, being attainted of sorcery, seduction, and other damnable practices, practised on a Knight of the most Holy Order of the Temple of Zion, doth deny the same; and saith, that the testimony delivered against her this day is false, wicked, and disloyal; and that by lawful *essoine*[49] of her body as being unable to combat in her own behalf, she doth offer, by a champion instead thereof, to avouch her case, he performing his loyal *devoir* in all knightly sort, with such arms as to gage of battle do fully appertain, and that at her peril and cost. And therewith she proffered her gage. And the gage having been delivered to the noble Lord and Knight, Brian de Bois-Guilbert, of the Holy Order of the Temple of Zion, he was appointed to do this battle, in behalf of his Order and himself, as injured and impaired by the practices of the appellant. Wherefore the most reverend Father and puissant Lord, Lucas Marquis of Beaumanoir, did allow of the said challenge, and of the said *essoine* of the appellant's body, and assigned the third day for the said combat, the place being the enclosure called the lists of Saint George, near to the Preceptory of Templestowe. And the Grand Master appoints the appellant to appear there by her champion, on pain of doom, as a person convicted of sorcery or seduction; and also the defendant so to appear, under the penalty of being held and adjudged recreant in case of default; and the noble Lord and most reverend Father aforesaid appointed the battle to be done in his own presence, and according to all that is commendable and profitable in such a case. And may God aid the just cause!'

'Amen!' said the Grand Master; and the word was echoed by all around. Rebecca spoke not, but she looked up to heaven, and, folding her hands, remained for a minute without change of attitude. She then modestly reminded the Grand Master, that she ought to be permitted some opportunity of free communication with her friends, for the purpose of making her condition known to them, and procuring, if possible, some champion to fight in her behalf.

'It is just and lawful,' said the Grand Master; 'choose what messenger thou shalt trust, and he shall have free communication with thee in thy prison-chamber.'

'Is there,' said Rebecca, 'any one here, who, either for love of a good cause, or for ample hire, will do the errand of a distressed being?'

All were silent; for none thought it safe, in the presence of the Grand Master, to avow any interest in the calumniated prisoner, lest he should be suspected of leaning towards Judaism. Not even the prospect of reward, far less any feelings of compassion alone, could surmount this apprehension.

Rebecca stood for a few moments in indescribable anxiety, and then exclaimed, 'Is it really thus?—And, in English land, am I to be deprived of the poor chance of safety which remains to me, for want of an act of charity which would not be refused to the worst criminal?'

Higg, the son of Snell, at length replied, 'I am but a maimed man, but that I can at all stir or move was owing to her charitable assistance.—I will do thine errand,' he added, addressing Rebecca, 'as well as a crippled object can, and happy were my limbs fleet enough to repair the mischief done by my tongue. Alas! when I boasted of thy charity, I little thought I was leading thee into danger!'

'God,' said Rebecca, 'is the disposer of all. He can turn back the captivity of Judah,* even by the weakest instrument. To execute his message the snail is as sure a messenger as the falcon. Seek out Isaac of York—here is that will pay for horse and man—let him have this scroll.—I know not if it be of Heaven the spirit which inspires me, but most truly do I judge that I am not to die this death, and that a champion will be raised up for me. Farewell!—Life and death are in thy haste.'

The peasant took the scroll, which contained only a few lines in Hebrew. Many of the crowd would have dissuaded him from touching a document so suspicious; but Higg was resolute in the service of his benefactress. She had saved his body, he said, and he was confident she did not mean to peril his soul.

'I will get me,' he said, 'my neighbour Buthan's good capul,[50] and I will be at York within as brief space as man and beast may.'

But as it fortuned, he had no occasion to go so far, for within a quarter of a mile from the gate of the Preceptory he met with two riders, whom, by their dress and their huge yellow caps, he knew to be Jews; and, on approaching more nearly, discovered that one of them was his ancient employer, Isaac of York. The other was the Rabbi Ben Samuel; and both had approached as near to the Preceptory as they dared, on hearing that the Grand Master had summoned a chapter for the trial of a sorceress.

'Brother Ben Samuel,' said Isaac, 'my soul is disquieted, and I wot not why. This charge of necromancy is right often used for cloaking evil practices on our people.'

'Be of good comfort, brother,' said the physician; 'thou canst deal with the Nazarenes as one possessing the mammon of unrighteousness, and canst therefore purchase immunity at their hands—it rules the savage minds of those ungodly men, even as the signet of the mighty Solomon* was said to command the evil genii.—But what poor wretch comes hither upon his crutches, desiring, as I think, some speech of me?—Friend,' continued the physician, addressing Higg, the son of Snell, 'I refuse thee not the aid of mine art, but I relieve not with one asper* those who beg for alms upon the highway. Out upon thee!—Hast thou the palsy in thy legs? then let thy hands work for thy livelihood; for, albeit thou be'st unfit for a speedy post, or for a careful shepherd, or for the warfare, or for the service of a hasty master, yet there be occupations—How now, brother?' said he, interrupting his harangue to look towards Isaac, who had but glanced at the scroll which Higg offered, when, uttering a deep groan, he fell from his mule like a dying man, and lay for a minute insensible.

The Rabbi now dismounted in great alarm, and hastily applied the remedies which his art suggested for the recovery of his companion. He had even taken from his pocket a cupping apparatus, and was about to proceed to phlebotomy,* when the object of his anxious solicitude suddenly revived; but it was to dash his cap from his head, and to throw dust on his grey hairs. The physician was at first inclined to ascribe this sudden and violent emotion to the effects of insanity; and, adhering to his original purpose, began once again to handle his implements. But Isaac soon convinced him of his error.

'Child of my sorrow,' he said, 'well shouldst thou be called Benoni,* instead of Rebecca! Why should thy death bring down my grey hairs to the grave, till, in the bitterness of my heart, I curse God and die!'*

'Brother,' said the Rabbi, in great surprise, 'art thou a father in Israel, and dost thou utter words like unto these?—I trust that the child of thy house yet liveth?'

'She liveth,' answered Isaac; 'but it is as Daniel, who was called Beltheshazzar,* even when within the den of the lions. She is captive unto those men of Belial, and they will wreak their cruelty upon her, sparing neither for her youth nor her comely favour. O! she was as a crown of green palms to my grey locks; and she must wither in a night, like the gourd of Jonah!*—Child of my love!—child of my old age!—oh, Rebecca, daughter of Rachel! the darkness of the shadow of death hath encompassed thee.'*

'Yet read the scroll,' said the Rabbi; 'peradventure it may be that we may yet find out a way of deliverance.'

'Do thou read, brother,' answered Isaac, 'for mine eyes are as a fountain of water.'*

The physician read, but in their native language, the following words:—

'To Isaac, the son of Adonikam, whom the Gentiles call Isaac of York, peace and the blessing of the promise be multiplied unto thee!—My father, I am as one doomed to die for that which my soul knoweth not—even for the crime of witchcraft. My father, if a strong man can be found to do battle for my cause with sword and spear, according to the custom of the Nazarenes, and that within the lists of Templestowe, on the third day from this time, peradventure our fathers' God will give him strength to defend the innocent, and her who hath none to help her. But if this may not be, let the virgins of our people mourn for me* as for one cast off, and for the hart that is sticken by the hunter, and for the flower which is cut down by the scythe of the mower. Wherefore look now what thou doest, and whether there be any rescue. One Nazarene warrior might indeed bear arms in my behalf, even Wilfred, son of Cedric, whom the Gentiles call Ivanhoe. But he may not yet endure the weight of his armour. Nevertheless, send the tidings unto him, my father; for he hath favour among the strong men of his people, and as he was our companion in the house of bondage, he may find some one to do battle for my sake. And say unto him, even unto him, even unto Wilfred, the son of Cedric, that if Rebecca live, or if Rebecca die, she liveth or dieth wholly free of the guilt she is charged withal. And if it be the will of God that thou shalt be deprived of thy daughter, do not thou tarry, old man, in this land of bloodshed and cruelty; but betake thyself to Cordova, where thy brother liveth in safety, under the shadow of the throne, even of the throne of Boabdil the Saracen;* for less cruel are the cruelties of the Moors unto the race of Jacob, than the cruelties of the Nazarenes of England.'

Isaac listened with tolerable composure while Ben Samuel read the letter, and then again resumed the gestures and exclamations of Oriental sorrow, tearing his garments, besprinkling his head with dust, and ejaculating, 'My daughter! my daughter! flesh of my flesh, and bone of my bone!'*

'Yet,' said the Rabbi, 'take courage, for this grief availeth nothing. Gird up thy loins, and seek out this Wilfred, the son of Cedric. It may be he will help thee with counsel or with strength; for the youth hath favour in the eyes of Richard, called of the Nazarenes Cœur-de-Lion, and the tidings that he hath returned are constant in the land. It may be that he may obtain his letter, and his signet, commanding these men of blood, who take their name from the Temple to the dishonour thereof, that they proceed not in their purposed wickedness.'

'I will seek him out,' said Isaac, 'for he is a good youth, and hath compassion for the exile of Jacob. But he cannot bear his armour, and what other Christian shall do battle for the oppressed of Zion?'

'Nay, but,' said the Rabbi, 'thou speakest as one that knoweth not the Gentiles. With gold shalt thou buy their valour, even as with gold thou buyest thine own safety. Be of good courage, and do thou set forward to find out this Wilfred of Ivanhoe. I will also up and be doing, for great sin it were to leave thee in thy calamity. I will hie me to the city of York, where many warriors and strong men are assembled, and doubt not I will find among them some one who will do battle for thy daughter; for gold is their god, and for riches will they pawn their lives as well as their lands.—Thou wilt fulfil, my brother, such promise as I may make unto them in thy name?'

'Assuredly, brother,' said Isaac, 'and Heaven be praised that raised me up a comforter in my misery. Howbeit, grant them not their full demand at once, for thou shalt find it the quality of this accursed people that they will ask pounds, and peradventure accept of ounces—Nevertheless, be it as thou willest, for I am distracted in this thing, and what would my gold avail me if the child of my love should perish!'

'Farewell,' said the physician, 'and may it be to thee as thy heart desireth.'

They embraced accordingly, and departed on their several roads. The crippled peasant remained for some time looking after them.

'These dog-Jews!' said he; 'to take no more notice of a free guild-brother, than if I were a bond slave or a Turk, or a circumcised Hebrew like themselves! They might have flung me a mancus* or two, however. I was not obliged to bring their unhallowed scrawls, and run the risk of being bewitched, as more folks than one told me. And what care I for the bit of gold that the wench gave me, if I am to come to harm from the priest next Easter at confession, and be obliged to give him twice as much to make it up with him, and be called the Jew's flying post all my life, as it may hap, into the bargain? I think I was bewitched in earnest when I was beside that girl!—But it was always so with Jew or Gentile, whosoever came near her—none could stay when she had an errand to go—and still, whenever I think of her, I would give shop and tools to save her life.'

CHAPTER XXXIX

O maid, unrelenting and cold as thou art,
My bosom is proud as thine own.

Seward*

IT was in the twilight of the day when her trial, if it could be called such, had taken place, that a low knock was heard at the door of Rebecca's prison-chamber. It disturbed not the inmate, who was then engaged in the evening prayer recommended by her religion, and which concluded with a hymn* we have ventured thus to translate into English.

When Israel, of the Lord beloved,
  Out of the land of bondage came,
Her father's God before her moved,
  An awful guide, in smoke and flame.
By day, along the astonish'd lands
  The cloudy pillar glided slow;
By night, Arabia's crimson'd sands
  Return'd the fiery column's glow.

There rose the choral hymn of praise,
  And trump and timbrel answer'd keen,
And Zion's daughters pour'd their lays,
  With priest's and warrior's voice between.
No portents now our foes amaze,
  Forsaken Israel wanders lone;
Our fathers would not know THY ways,
  And THOU hast left them to their own.

But present still, though now unseen;
  When brightly shines the prosperous day,
Be thoughts of THEE a cloudy screen
  To temper the deceitful ray.
And oh, when stoops on Judah's path
  In shade and storm the frequent night,
Be THOU, long-suffering, slow to wrath,
  A burning, and a shining light!

Our harps we left by Babel's streams,
  The tyrant's jest, the Gentile's scorn;

No censer round our altar beams,
    And mute our timbrel, trump, and horn.
But THOU hast said, the blood of goat,
    The flesh of rams, I will not prize;
A contrite heart, an humble thought,
    Are mine accepted sacrifice.

When the sounds of Rebecca's devotional hymn had died away in silence, the low knock at the door was again renewed. 'Enter,' she said, 'if thou art a friend; and if a foe, I have not the means of refusing thy entrance.'

'I am,' said Brian de Bois-Guilbert, entering the apartment, 'friend or foe, Rebecca, as the event of this interview shall make me.'

Alarmed at the sight of this man, whose licentious passion she considered as the root of her misfortunes, Rebecca drew backward with a cautious and alarmed, yet not a timorous demeanour, into the farthest corner of the apartment, as if determined to retreat as far as she could, but to stand her ground when retreat became no longer possible. She drew herself into an attitude not of defiance, but of resolution, as one that would avoid provoking assault, yet was resolute to repel it, being offered, to the utmost of her power.

'You have no reason to fear me, Rebecca,' said the Templar; 'or if I must so qualify my speech, you have at least *now* no reason to fear me.'

'I fear you not, Sir Knight,' replied Rebecca, although her short-drawn breath seemed to belie the heroism of her accents; 'my trust is strong, and I fear thee not.'

'You have no cause,' answered Bois-Guilbert, gravely; 'my former frantic attempts you have not now to dread. Within your call are guards, over whom I have no authority. They are designed to conduct you to death, Rebecca, yet would not suffer you to be insulted by any one, even by me, were my frenzy—for frenzy it is—to urge me so far.'

'May Heaven be praised!' said the Jewess; 'death is the least of my apprehensions in this den of evil.'

'Ay,' replied the Templar, 'the idea of death is easily received by the courageous mind, when the road to it is sudden and open. A thrust with a lance, a stroke with a sword, were to me little—

To you, a spring from a dizzy battlement, a stroke with a sharp poniard, has no terrors, compared with what either thinks disgrace. Mark me—I say this—perhaps mine own sentiments of honour are not less fantastic, Rebecca, than thine are; but we know alike how to die for them.'

'Unhappy man,' said the Jewess; 'and art thou condemned to expose thy life for principles, of which thy sober judgment does not acknowledge the solidity? Surely this is a parting with your treasure for that which is not bread*—but deem not so of me. Thy resolution may fluctuate on the wild and changeful billows of human opinion, but mine is anchored on the Rock of Ages.'*

'Silence, maiden,' answered the Templar; 'such discourse now avails but little. Thou art condemned to die not a sudden and easy death, such as misery chooses, and despair welcomes, but a slow, wretched, protracted course of torture, suited to what the diabolical bigotry of these men calls thy crime.'

'And to whom—if such my fate—to whom do I owe this?' said Rebecca; 'surely only to him, who, for a most selfish and brutal cause, dragged me hither, and who now, for some unknown purpose of his own, strives to exaggerate the wretched fate to which he exposed me.'

'Think not,' said the Templar, 'that I have so exposed thee; I would have bucklered* thee against such danger with my own bosom, as freely as ever I exposed it to the shafts which had otherwise reached thy life.'

'Had thy purpose been the honourable protection of the innocent,' said Rebecca, 'I had thanked thee for thy care—as it is, thou hast claimed merit for it so often, that I tell thee life is worth nothing to me, preserved at the price which thou wouldst exact for it.'

'Truce with thine upbraidings, Rebecca,' said the Templar; 'I have my own cause of grief, and brook not that thy reproaches should add to it.'

'What is thy purpose, then, Sir Knight?' said the Jewess; 'speak it briefly.—If thou hast aught to do, save to witness the misery thou hast caused, let me know it; and then, if so it please you, leave me to myself—the step between time and eternity is short but terrible, and I have few moments to prepare for it.'

'I perceive, Rebecca,' said Bois-Guilbert, 'that thou dost continue to burden me with the charge of distresses, which most fain would I have prevented.'

'Sir Knight,' said Rebecca, 'I would avoid reproaches—But what is more certain than that I owe my death to thine unbridled passion?'

'You err—you err,'—said the Templar, hastily, 'if you impute what I could neither foresee nor prevent to my purpose or agency.—Could I guess the unexpected arrival of yon dotard, whom some flashes of frantic valour, and the praises yielded by fools to the stupid self-torments of an ascetic, have raised for the present above his own merits, above common sense, above me, and above the hundreds of our Order, who think and feel as men free from such silly and fantastic prejudices as are the grounds of his opinions and actions?'

'Yet,' said Rebecca, 'you sate a judge upon me, innocent—most innocent—as you knew me to be—you concurred in my condemnation, and, if I aright understood, are yourself to appear in arms to assert my guilt, and assure my punishment.'

'Thy patience, maiden,' replied the Templar.—'No race knows so well as thine own tribes how to submit to the time, and so to trim their bark as to make advantage even of an adverse wind.'

'Lamented be the hour,' said Rebecca, 'that has taught such art to the House of Israel! but adversity bends the heart as fire bends the stubborn steel, and those who are no longer their own governors, and the denizens of their own free independent state, must crouch before strangers. It is our curse, Sir Knight, deserved, doubtless, by our own misdeeds and those of our fathers; but you—you who boast your freedom as your birth-right, how much deeper is your disgrace when you stoop to soothe the prejudices of others, and that against your own conviction?'

'Your words are bitter, Rebecca,' said Bois-Guilbert, pacing the apartment with impatience, 'but I came not hither to bandy reproaches with you.—Know that Bois-Guilbert yields not to created man, although circumstances may for a time induce him to alter his plan. His will is the mountain stream, which may indeed be turned for a little space aside by the rock, but fails not to find its course to the ocean. That scroll which warned thee to demand a champion, from whom couldst thou think it came, if not from Bois-Guilbert? In whom else couldst thou have excited such interest?'

'A brief respite from instant death,' said Rebecca, 'which will little avail me—was this all thou couldst do for one, on whose head thou hast heaped sorrow, and whom thou hast brought near even to the verge of the tomb?'

'No, maiden,' said Bois-Guilbert, 'this was *not* all that I purposed. Had it not been for the accursed interference of yon fanatical dotard, and the fool of Goodalricke, who, being a Templar, affects to think and judge according to the ordinary rules of humanity, the office of the Champion Defender had devolved, not on a Preceptor, but on a Companion of the Order. Then I myself—such was my purpose—had, on the sounding of the trumpet, appeared in the lists as thy champion, disguised indeed in the fashion of a roving knight, who seeks adventures to prove his shield and spear; and then, let Beaumanoir have chosen not one, but two or three of the brethren here assembled, I had not doubted to cast them out of the saddle with my single lance. Thus, Rebecca, should thine innocence have been avouched, and to thine own gratitude would I have trusted for the reward of my victory.'

'This, Sir Knight,' said Rebecca, 'is but idle boasting—a brag of what you would have done had you not found it convenient to do otherwise. You received my glove, and my champion, if a creature so desolate can find one, must encounter your lance in the lists—yet you would assume the air of my friend and protector!'

'Thy friend and protector,' said the Templar, gravely, 'I will yet be—but mark at what risk, or rather at what certainty, of dishonour; and then blame me not if I make my stipulations, before I offer up all that I have hitherto held dear, to save the life of a Jewish maiden.'

'Speak,' said Rebecca; 'I understand thee not.'

'Well, then,' said Bois-Guilbert, 'I will speak as freely as ever did doting penitent to his ghostly father, when placed in the tricky confessional.—Rebecca, if I appear not in these lists I lose fame and rank—lose that which is the breath of my nostrils,* the esteem, I mean, in which I am held by my brethren, and the hopes I have of succeeding to that mighty authority, which is now wielded by the bigoted dotard Lucas de Beaumanoir, but of which I should make a far different use. Such is my certain doom, except I appear in arms against thy cause. Accursed be he of Goodalricke, who baited this trap for me! and doubly accursed Albert de Malvoisin, who withheld me from the resolution I had formed, of hurling back the glove at the face of the superstitious and superannuated fool, who listened to a charge so absurd, and against a creature so high in mind, and so lovely in form as thou art!'

'And what now avails rant or flattery?' answered Rebecca. 'Thou hast made thy choice between causing to be shed the blood of an innocent woman, or of endangering thine own earthly state and earthly hopes—What avails it to reckon together?—thy choice is made.'

'No, Rebecca,' said the knight, in a softer tone, and drawing nearer towards her; 'my choice is NOT made—nay, mark, it is thine to make the election. If I appear in the lists, I must maintain my name in arms; and if I do so, championed or unchampioned, thou diest by the stake and faggot, for there lives not the knight who hath coped with me in arms on equal issue, or on terms of vantage, save Richard Cœur-de-Lion, and his minion of Ivanhoe. Ivanhoe, as thou well knowest, is unable to bear his corslet, and Richard is in a foreign prison. If I appear, then thou diest, even although thy charms should instigate some hot-headed youth to enter the lists in thy defence.'

'And what avails repeating this so often?' said Rebecca.

'Much,' replied the Templar; 'for thou must learn to look at thy fate on every side.'

'Well, then, turn the tapestry,' said the Jewess, 'and let me see the other side.'

'If I appear,' said Bois-Guilbert, 'in the fatal lists, thou diest by a slow and cruel death, in pain such as they say is destined to the guilty hereafter. But if I appear not, then am I a degraded and dishonoured knight, accused of witchcraft and of communion with infidels—the illustrious name which has grown yet more so under my wearing, becomes a hissing and a reproach.* I lose fame, I lose honour, I lose the prospect of such greatness as scarce emperors attain to—I sacrifice mighty ambition, I destroy schemes built as high as the mountains with which heathens say their heaven was once nearly scaled*—and yet, Rebecca,' he added, throwing himself at her feet, 'this greatness will I sacrifice, this fame will I renounce, this power will I forego, even now when it is half within my grasp, if thou wilt say, Bois-Guilbert, I receive thee for my lover.'

'Think not of such foolishness, Sir Knight,' answered Rebecca, 'but hasten to the Regent, the Queen Mother,* and to Prince John—they cannot, in honour to the English crown, allow of the proceedings of your Grand Master. So shall you give me protection without sacrifice on your part, or the pretext of requiring any requital from me.'

'With these I deal not,' he continued, holding the train of her robe—'it is thee only I address; and what can counterbalance thy choice? Bethink thee, were I a fiend, yet death is a worse, and it is death who is my rival.'

'I weigh not these evils,' said Rebecca, afraid to provoke the wild knight, yet equally determined neither to endure his passion, nor even feign to endure it. 'Be a man, be a Christian! If indeed thy faith recommends that mercy which rather your tongues than your actions pretend, save me from this dreadful death, without seeking a requital which would change thy magnanimity into base barter.'

'No, damsel!' said the proud Templar, springing up, 'thou shalt not thus impose on me—if I renounce present fame and future ambition, I renounce it for thy sake, and we will escape in company. Listen to me, Rebecca,' he said, again softening his tone; 'England,—Europe,—is not the world. There are spheres in which we may act, ample enough even for my ambition. We will go to Palestine, where Conrade, Marquis of Montserrat,* is my friend—a friend free as myself from the doting scruples which fetter our free-born reason—rather with Saladin will we league ourselves, than endure the scorn of the bigots whom we contemn.—I will form new paths to greatness,' he continued, again traversing the room with hasty strides—'Europe shall hear the loud step of him she has driven from her sons!—Not the millions whom her crusaders send to slaughter, can do so much to defend Palestine—not the sabres of the thousands and ten thousands of Saracens can hew their way so deep into that land for which nations are striving, as the strength and policy of me and those brethren, who, in despite of yonder old bigot, will adhere to me in good and evil. Thou shalt be a queen, Rebecca— on Mount Carmel shall we pitch the throne which my valour will gain for you, and I will exchange my long-desired batoon for a sceptre!'

'A dream,' said Rebecca; 'an empty vision of the night, which, were it a waking reality, affects me not. Enough, that the power which thou mightest acquire, I will never share; nor hold I so light of country or religious faith, as to esteem him who is willing to barter these ties, and cast away the bonds of the Order of which he is a sworn member, in order to gratify an unruly passion for the daughter of another people.—Put not a price on my deliverance, Sir Knight—sell not a deed of generosity— protect the oppressed for the sake of charity, and not for a selfish advantage—Go to the throne of England; Richard will listen to my appeal from these cruel men.'

'Never, Rebecca!' said the Templar, fiercely. 'If I renounce my Order, for thee alone will I renounce it—Ambition shall remain mine, if thou refuse my love; I will not be fooled on all hands.—Stoop my crest to Richard?—ask a boon of that heart of pride?—Never, Rebecca, will I place the Order of the Temple at his feet in my person. I may forsake the Order, I never will degrade or betray it.'

'Now God be gracious to me,' said Rebecca, 'for the succour of man is wellnigh hopeless!'

'It is indeed,' said the Templar; 'for, proud as thou art, thou hast in me found thy match. If I enter the lists with my spear in rest, think not any human consideration shall prevent my putting forth my strength; and think then upon thine own fate— to die the dreadful death of the worst of criminals—to be consumed upon a blazing pile—dispersed to the elements of which our strange forms are so mystically composed—not a relic left of that graceful frame, from which we could say this lived and moved!—Rebecca, it is not in woman to sustain this prospect— thou wilt yield to my suit.'

'Bois-Guilbert,' answered the Jewess, 'thou knowest not the heart of woman, or hast only conversed with those who are lost to her best feelings. I tell thee, proud Templar, that not in thy fiercest battles hast thou displayed more of thy vaunted courage, than has been shown by woman when called upon to suffer by affection or duty. I am myself a woman, tenderly nurtured, naturally fearful of danger, and impatient of pain—yet, when we enter those fatal lists, thou to fight and I to suffer, I feel the strong assurance within me, that my courage shall mount higher than thine. Farewell—I waste no more words on thee; the time that remains on earth to the daughter of Jacob must be otherwise spent—she must seek the Comforter,* who may hide his face from his people, but who ever opens his ear to the cry of those who seek him in sincerity and in truth.'

'We part then thus?' said the Templar, after a short pause; 'would to Heaven that we had never met, or that thou hadst been noble in birth and Christian in faith!—Nay, by Heaven! when I gaze on thee, and think when and how we are next to meet, I could even wish myself one of thine own degraded nation; my hand conversant with ingots and shekels, instead of spear and shield; my head bent down before each petty noble, and my look only terrible to the shivering and bankrupt debtor—this could I wish, Rebecca, to be near to thee in life, and to escape the fearful share I must have in thy death.'

'Thou hast spoken the Jew,' said Rebecca, 'as the persecution of such as thou art has made him. Heaven in ire has driven him from his country, but industry has opened to him the only road to power and to influence, which oppression has left unbarred. Read the ancient history of the people of God, and tell me if those, by whom Jehovah wrought such marvels among the nations, were then a people of misers and of usurers!—And know, proud knight, we number names amongst us to which your boasted northern nobility is as the gourd compared with the cedar—names that ascend far back to those high times when the Divine Presence shook the mercy-seat between the cherubim, and which derive their splendour from no earthly prince, but from the awful Voice,* which bade their fathers be nearest of the congregation to the Vision—Such were the princes of the House of Jacob.'

Rebecca's colour rose as she boasted the ancient glories of her race, but faded as she added, with a sigh, 'Such *were* the princes of Judah, now such no more!—They are trampled down like the shorn grass, and mixed with the mire of the ways.* Yet are there those among them who shame not such high descent, and of such shall be the daughter of Isaac the son of Adonikam! Farewell!— I envy not thy blood-won honours—I envy not thy barbarous descent from northern heathens—I envy thee not thy faith, which is ever in thy mouth, but never in thy heart nor in thy practice.'

'There is a spell on me, by Heaven!' said Bois-Guilbert. 'I almost think yon besotted skeleton spoke truth, and that the reluctance with which I part from thee hath something in it more than is natural.—Fair creature!' he said, approaching near her, but with great respect,—'so young, so beautiful, so fearless of death! and yet doomed to die, and with infamy and agony. Who would not weep for thee?—The tear, that has been a stranger to these eyelids for twenty years, moistens them as I gaze on thee. But it must be—nothing may now save thy life. Thou and I are but the blind instruments of some irresistible fatality, that hurries us along, like goodly vessels driving before the storm, which are dashed against each other, and so perish. Forgive me, then, and let us part at least as friends part. I have assailed thy resolution in vain, and mine own is fixed as the adamantine decrees of fate.'

'Thus,' said Rebecca, 'do men throw on fate the issue of their own wild passions. But I do forgive thee, Bois-Guilbert, though the author of my early death. There are noble things which cross over thy powerful mind; but it is the garden of the sluggard,* and the weeds have rushed up, and conspired to choke the fair and wholesome blossom.'

'Yes,' said the Templar, 'I am, Rebecca, as thou hast spoken me, untaught, untamed—and proud, that, amidst a shoal of empty fools and crafty bigots, I have retained the pre-eminent fortitude that places me above them. I have been a child of battle from my youth upward, high in my views, steady and inflexible in pursuing them. Such must I remain—proud, inflexible, and unchanging; and of this the world shall have proof.—But thou forgivest me, Rebecca?'

'As freely as ever victim forgave her executioner.'

'Farewell, then,' said the Templar, and left the apartment.

The Preceptor Albert waited impatiently in an adjacent chamber the return of Bois-Guilbert.

'Thou hast tarried long,' he said; 'I have been as if stretched on red-hot iron with very impatience. What if the Grand Master, or his spy Conrade, had come hither? I had paid dear for my complaisance.—But what ails thee, brother?—Thy step totters, thy brow is as black as night. Art thou well, Bois-Guilbert?'

'Ay,' answered the Templar, 'as well as the wretch who is doomed to die within an hour.—Nay, by the rood, not half so well—for there be those in such state, who can lay down life like a cast-off garment. By Heaven, Malvoisin, yonder girl hath wellnigh unmanned me. I am half resolved to go to the Grand Master, abjure the Order to his very teeth, and refuse to act the brutality which his tyranny has imposed on me.'

'Thou art mad,' answered Malvoisin; 'thou mayst thus indeed utterly ruin thyself, but canst not even find a chance thereby to save the life of this Jewess, which seems so precious in thine eyes. Beaumanoir will name another of the Order to defend his judgment in thy place, and the accused will as assuredly perish as if thou hadst taken the duty imposed on thee.'

' 'Tis false—I will myself take arms in her behalf,' answered the Templar, haughtily; 'and, should I do so, I think, Malvoisin, that thou knowest not one of the Order, who will keep his saddle before the point of my lance.'

'Ay, but thou forgettest,' said the wily adviser, 'thou wilt have neither leisure nor opportunity to execute this mad project. Go to Lucas Beaumanoir, and say thou hast renounced thy vow of obedience, and see how long the despotic old man will leave thee in personal freedom. The words shall scarce have left thy lips, ere thou wilt either be an hundred feet under ground, in the dungeon of the Preceptory, to abide trial as a recreant knight; or, if his opinion holds concerning thy possession, thou wilt be enjoying straw, darkness, and chains, in some distant convent cell, stunned with exorcisms, and drenched with holy water, to expel the foul fiend which hath obtained dominion over thee. Thou must to the lists, Brian, or thou art a lost and dishonoured man.'

'I will break forth and fly,' said Bois-Guilbert—'fly to some distant land, to which folly and fanaticism have not yet found their way. No drop of the blood of this most excellent creature shall be spilled by my sanction.'

'Thou canst not fly,' said the Preceptor; 'thy ravings have excited suspicion, and thou wilt not be permitted to leave the Preceptory. Go and make the essay—present thyself before the gate, and command the bridge to be lowered, and mark what answer thou shalt receive.—Thou art surprised and offended; but is it not the better for thee? Wert thou to fly, what would ensue but the reversal of thy arms, the dishonour of thine ancestry, the degradation of thy rank?—Think on it. Where shall thine old companions in arms hide their heads when Brian de Bois-Guilbert, the best lance of the Templars, is proclaimed recreant, amid the hisses of the assembled people? What grief will be at the Court of France! With what joy will the haughty Richard hear the news, that the knight that set him hard in Palestine, and wellnigh darkened his renown, has lost fame and honour for a Jewish girl, whom he could not even save by so costly a sacrifice!'

'Malvoisin,' said the Knight, 'I thank thee—thou hast touched the string at which my heart most readily thrills!—Come of it what may, recreant shall never be added to the name of Bois-Guilbert. Would to God, Richard, or any of his vaunting minions of England, would appear in these lists! But they will be empty—no one will risk to break a lance for the innocent, the forlorn.'

'The better for thee, if it prove so,' said the Preceptor; 'if no champion appears, it is not by thy means that this unlucky damsel shall die, but by the doom of the Grand Master, with whom rests all the blame, and who will count that blame for praise and commendation.'

'True,' said Bois-Guilbert; 'if no champion appears, I am but a part of the pageant, sitting indeed on horseback in the lists, but having no part in what is to follow.'

'None whatever,' said Malvoisin; 'no more than the armed image of Saint George* when it makes part of a procession.'

'Well, I will resume my resolution,' replied the haughty Templar. 'She has despised me—repulsed me—reviled me— And wherefore should I offer up for her whatever of estimation

I have in the opinion of others? Malvoisin, I will appear in the lists.'

He left the apartment hastily as he uttered these words, and the Preceptor followed, to watch and confirm him in his resolution; for in Bois-Guilbert's fame he had himself a strong interest, expecting much advantage from his being one day at the head of the Order, not to mention the preferment of which Mont-Fitchet had given him hopes, on condition he would forward the condemnation of the unfortunate Rebecca. Yet although, in combating his friend's better feelings, he possessed all the advantage which a wily, composed, selfish disposition has over a man agitated by strong and contending passions, it required all Malvoisin's art to keep Bois-Guilbert steady to the purpose he had prevailed on him to adopt. He was obliged to watch him closely to prevent his resuming his purpose of flight, to intercept his communication with the Grand Master, lest he should come to an open rupture with his Superior, and to renew, from time to time, the various arguments by which he endeavoured to show, that, in appearing as champion on this occasion, Bois-Guilbert, without either accelerating or ensuring the fate of Rebecca, would follow the only course by which he could save himself from degradation and disgrace.

CHAPTER XL

Shadows avaunt!—Richard's himself again.

*Richard III**

WHEN the Black Knight—for it becomes necessary to resume the train of his adventures—left the Trysting-tree of the generous Outlaw, he held his way straight to a neighbouring religious house, of small extent and revenue, called the Priory of Saint Botolph,* to which the wounded Ivanhoe had been removed when the castle was taken, under the guidance of the faithful Gurth, and the magnanimous Wamba. It is unnecessary at present to mention what took place in the interim betwixt Wilfred and his deliverer; suffice it to say, that after long and grave communication, messengers were dispatched by the Prior in several directions, and that on the succeeding morning the Black Knight was about to set forth on his journey, accompanied by the jester Wamba, who attended as his guide.

'We will meet,' he said to Ivanhoe, 'at Coningsburgh, the castle of the deceased Athelstane, since there thy father Cedric holds the funeral feast for his noble relation. I would see your Saxon kindred together, Sir Wilfred, and become better acquainted with them than heretofore. Thou also wilt meet me; and it shall be my task to reconcile thee to thy father.'

So saying, he took an affectionate farewell of Ivanhoe, who expressed an anxious desire to attend upon his deliverer. But the Black Knight would not listen to the proposal.

'Rest this day; thou wilt have scarce strength enough to travel on the next. I will have no guide with me but honest Wamba, who can play priest or fool as I shall be most in the humour.'

'And I,' said Wamba, 'will attend you with all my heart. I would fain see the feasting at the funeral of Athelstane; for, if it be not full and frequent, he will rise from the dead to rebuke cook, sewer, and cupbearer; and that were a sight worth seeing. Always, Sir Knight, I will trust your valour with making my excuse to my master Cedric, in case mine own wit should fail.'

'And how should my poor valour succeed, Sir Jester, when thy light wit halts?—resolve me that.'

'Wit, Sir Knight,' replied the Jester, 'may do much. He is a quick, apprehensive knave, who sees his neighbour's blind side, and knows how to keep the lee-gage* when his passions are blowing high. But valour is a sturdy fellow, that makes all split.* He rows against both wind and tide, and makes way notwithstanding; and, therefore, good Sir Knight, while I take advantage of the fair weather in our noble master's temper, I will expect you to bestir yourself when it grows rough.'

'Sir Knight of the Fetterlock, since it is your pleasure so to be distinguished,' said Ivanhoe, 'I fear me you have chosen a talkative and a troublesome fool to be your guide. But he knows every path and alley in the woods as well as e'er a hunter who frequents them; and the poor knave, as thou hast partly seen, is as faithful as steel.'

'Nay,' said the Knight, 'an he have the gift of showing my road, I shall not grumble with him that he desires to make it pleasant.—Fare thee well, kind Wilfred—I charge thee not to attempt to travel till to-morrow at earliest.'

So saying, he extended his hand to Ivanhoe, who pressed it to his lips, took leave of the Prior, mounted his horse, and departed, with Wamba for his companion. Ivanhoe followed them with his eyes, until they were lost in the shades of the surrounding forest, and then returned into the convent.

But shortly after matin-song, he requested to see the Prior. The old man came in haste, and enquired anxiously after the state of his health.

'It is better,' he said, 'than my fondest hope could have anticipated; either my wound has been slighter than the effusion of blood led me to suppose, or this balsam hath wrought a wonderful cure upon it. I feel already as if I could bear my corslet; and so much the better, for thoughts pass in my mind which render me unwilling to remain here longer in inactivity.'

'Now, the saints forbid,' said the Prior, 'that the son of the Saxon Cedric should leave our convent ere his wounds were healed! It were shame to our profession were we to suffer it.'

'Nor would I desire to leave your hospitable roof, venerable father,' said Ivanhoe, 'did I not feel myself able to endure the journey, and compelled to undertake it.'

'And what can have urged you to so sudden a departure?' said the Prior.

'Have you never, holy father,' answered the Knight, 'felt an apprehension of approaching evil, for which you in vain attempted to assign a cause?—Have you never found your mind darkened, like the sunny landscape, by the sudden cloud, which augurs a coming tempest?—And thinkest thou not that such impulses are deserving of attention, as being the hints of our guardian spirits, that danger is impending?'

'I may not deny,' said the Prior, crossing himself, 'that such things have been, and have been of Heaven; but then such communications have had a visibly useful scope and tendency. But thou, wounded as thou art, what avails it thou shouldst follow the steps of him whom thou couldst not aid, were he to be assaulted?'

'Prior,' said Ivanhoe, 'thou dost mistake—I am stout enough to exchange buffets with any who will challenge me to such a traffic—But were it otherwise, may I not aid him were he in danger, by other means than by force of arms? It is but too well known that the Saxons love not the Norman race, and who knows what may be the issue, if he break in upon them when their hearts are irritated by the death of Athelstane, and their heads heated by the carousal in which they will indulge themselves? I hold his entrance among them at such a moment most perilous, and I am resolved to share or avert the danger; which, that I may the better do, I would crave of thee the use of some palfrey whose pace may be softer than that of my *destrier*.'*

'Surely,' said the worthy churchman; 'you shall have mine own ambling jennet, and I would it ambled as easy for your sake as that of the Abbot of Saint Albans. Yet this will I say for Malkin, for so I call her, that unless you were to borrow a ride on the juggler's steed that paces a hornpipe amongst the eggs,* you could not go a journey on a creature so gentle and smooth-paced. I have composed many a homily on her back, to the edification of my brethren of the convent, and many poor Christian souls.'

'I pray you, reverend father,' said Ivanhoe, 'let Malkin be got ready instantly, and bid Gurth attend me with mine arms.'

'Nay, but fair sir,' said the Prior, 'I pray you to remember that Malkin hath as little skill in arms as her master, and that I warrant not her enduring the sight or weight of your full panoply. O, Malkin, I promise you, is a beast of judgment, and will contend against any undue weight—I did but borrow the *Fructus Temporum*** from the priest of Saint Bees, and I promise you she would not stir from the gate until I had exchanged the huge volume for my little breviary.'

'Trust me, holy father,' said Ivanhoe, 'I will not distress her with too much weight; and if she calls a combat with me, it is odds but she has the worst.'

This reply was made while Gurth was buckling on the Knight's heels a pair of large gilded spurs, capable of convincing any restive horse that his best safety lay in being conformable to the will of his rider.

The deep and sharp rowels with which Ivanhoe's heels were now armed, began to make the worthy Prior repent of his courtesy, and ejaculate,—'Nay, but fair sir, now I bethink me, my Malkin abideth not the spur—Better it were that you tarry for the mare of our manciple* down at the Grange, which may be had in little more than an hour, and cannot but be tractable, in respect that she draweth much of our winter fire-wood, and eateth no corn.'

'I thank you, reverend father, but will abide by your first offer, as I see Malkin is already led forth to the gate. Gurth shall carry mine armour; and for the rest, rely on it, that as I will not overload Malkin's back, she shall not overcome my patience. And now, farewell!'

Ivanhoe now descended the stairs more hastily and easily than his wound promised, and threw himself upon the jennet, eager to escape the importunity of the Prior, who stuck as closely to his side as his age and fatness would permit, now singing the praises of Malkin, now recommending caution to the Knight in managing her.

'She is at the most dangerous period for maidens as well as mares,' said the old man, laughing at his own jest, 'being barely in her fifteenth year.'

Ivanhoe, who had other web to weave than to stand canvassing a palfrey's paces with its owner, lent but a deaf ear to the Prior's grave advices and facetious jests, and having leapt on his mare, and commanded his squire (for such Gurth now called himself) to keep close by his side, he followed the track of the Black Knight into the forest, while the Prior stood at the gate of the convent looking after him, and ejaculating,—'Saint Mary! how prompt and fiery be these men of war! I would I had not trusted Malkin to his keeping, for, crippled as I am with the cold rheum, I am undone if aught but good befalls her. And yet,' said he, recollecting himself, 'as I would not spare my own old and disabled limbs in the good cause of Old England, so Malkin must e'en run her hazard on the same venture; and it may be they will think our poor house worthy of some munificent guerdon—or, it may be, they will send the old Prior a pacing nag. And if they do none of these, as great men will forget little men's service, truly I shall hold me well repaid in having done that which is right. And it is now wellnigh the fitting time to summon the brethren to breakfast in the refectory—Ah! I doubt they obey that call more cheerily than the bells for primes and matins.'

So the Prior of Saint Botolph's hobbled back again into the refectory, to preside over the stockfish* and ale, which was just serving out for the friars' breakfast. Pursy and important, he sat him down at the table, and many a dark word he threw out, of benefits to be expected to the convent, and high deeds of service done by himself, which, at another season, would have attracted observation. But as the stockfish was highly salted, and the ale reasonably powerful, the jaws of the brethren were too anxiously employed to admit of their making much use of their ears; nor do we read of any of the fraternity, who was tempted to speculate upon the mysterious hints of their Superior, except Father Diggory, who was severely afflicted by the toothach, so that he could only eat on one side of his jaws.

In the meantime, the Black Champion and his guide were pacing at their leisure through the recesses of the forest; the good Knight whiles humming to himself the lay of some enamoured troubadour, sometimes encouraging by questions the prating disposition of his attendant, so that their dialogue formed a whimsical mixture of song and jest, of which we would fain give our readers some idea. You are then to imagine this Knight, such as we have already described him, strong of person, tall, broad-shouldered, and large of bone, mounted on his mighty black charger, which seemed made on purpose to bear his weight, so easily he paced forward under it, having the visor of his helmet raised, in order to admit freedom of breath, yet keeping the beaver, or under part, closed, so that his features could be but imperfectly distinguished. But his ruddy embrowned cheek-bones could be plainly seen, and the large and bright blue eyes, that flashed from under the dark shade of the raised visor; and the whole gesture and look of the champion expressed careless gaiety and fearless confidence—a mind which was unapt to apprehend danger, and prompt to defy it when most imminent—yet with whom danger was a familiar thought, as with one whose trade was war and adventure.

The Jester wore his usual fantastic habit, but late accidents had led him to adopt a good cutting falchion,* instead of his wooden sword, with a targe to match it; of both which weapons he had, notwithstanding his profession, shown himself a skilful master during the storming of Torquilstone. Indeed, the infirmity of Wamba's brain consisted chiefly in a kind of impatient irritability, which suffered him not long to remain quiet in any posture, or adhere to any certain train of ideas, although he was for a few minutes alert enough in performing any immediate task, or in apprehending any immediate topic. On horseback, therefore, he was perpetually swinging himself backwards and forwards, now on the horse's ears, then anon on the very rump of the animal,—now hanging both his legs on one side, and now sitting with his face to the tail, moping, mowing,* and making a thousand apish gestures, until his palfrey took his freaks so much to heart, as fairly to lay him at his length on the green grass—an incident which greatly amused the Knight, but compelled his companion to ride more steadily thereafter.

At the point of their journey at which we take them up, this joyous pair were engaged in singing a virelai,* as it was called, in which the clown bore a mellow burden, to the better instructed Knight of the Fetterlock. And thus run the ditty:--

> Anna-Marie, love, up is the sun,
> Anna-Marie, love, more is begun,
> Mists are dispersing, love, birds singing free,

Up in the morning, love, Anna-Marie.
Anna-Marie, love, up in the morn,
The hunter is winding blithe sounds on his horn,
The echo rings merry from rock and from tree,
'Tis time to arouse thee, love, Anna-Marie.

WAMBA

O Tybalt, love, Tybalt, awake me not yet,
Around my soft pillow while softer dreams flit,
For what are the joys that in waking we prove,
Compared with these visions, O, Tybalt, my love?
Let the birds to the rise of the mist carol shrill,
Let the hunter blow out his loud horn on the hill,
Softer sounds, softer pleasures, in slumber I prove,—
But think not I dreamt of thee, Tybalt, my love.

'A dainty song,' said Wamba, when they had finished their carol, 'and I swear by my bauble, a pretty moral!—I used to sing it with Gurth, once my playfellow, and now, by the grace of God and his master, no less than a freeman; and we once came by the cudgel for being so entranced by the melody, that we lay in bed two hours after sunrise, singing the ditty betwixt sleeping and waking—my bones ache at thinking of the tune ever since. Nevertheless, I have played the part of Anna-Marie, to please you, fair sir.'

The Jester next struck into another carol, a sort of comic ditty, to which the Knight, catching up the tune, replied in the like manner.

KNIGHT and WAMBA

There came three merry men from south, west, and north,
    Ever more sing the roundelay;
To win the Widow of Wycombe forth,
    And where was the widow might say them nay?

The first was a knight, and from Tynedale he came,
    Ever more sing the roundelay;
And his fathers, God save us, were men of great fame,
    And where was the widow might say him nay?

Of his father the laird, of his uncle the squire,
    He boasted in rhyme and in roundelay;

She bade him go bask by his sea-coal fire,
    For she was the widow would say him nay.

WAMBA

The next that came forth, swore by blood and by nails,
    Merrily sing the roundelay;
Hur's a gentleman, God wot, and hur's lineage was of Wales,*
    And where was the widow might say him nay?

Sir David ap Morgan ap Griffith ap Hugh
    Ap Tudor ap Rhice, quoth his roundelay;
She said that one widow for so many was too few,
    And she bade the Welshman wend his way.

But then next came a yeoman, a yeoman of Kent,
    Jollily singing his roundelay;
He spoke to the widow of living and rent,
    And where was the widow could say him nay?

BOTH

So the knight and the squire were both left in the mire,
    There for to sing their roundelay;
For a yeoman of Kent, with his yearly rent,
    There never was a widow could say him nay.

'I would, Wamba,' said the Knight, 'that our host of the Trysting-tree, or the jolly Friar, his chaplain, heard this thy ditty in praise of our bluff yeoman.'

'So would not I,' said Wamba—'but for the horn that hangs at your baldric.'

'Ay,' said the Knight,—'this is a pledge of Locksley's good-will, though I am not like to need it. Three mots on this bugle will, I am assured, bring round, at our need, a jolly band of yonder honest yeomen.'

'I would say, Heaven forefend,'* said the Jester, 'were it not that that fair gift is a pledge they would let us pass peaceably.'

'Why, what meanest thou?' said the Knight: 'thinkest thou that but for this pledge of fellowship they would assault us?'

'Nay, for me I say nothing,' said Wamba; 'for green trees have ears as well as stone walls. But canst thou construe me this, Sir Knight—When is thy wine-pitcher and thy purse better empty than full?'

'Why, never, I think,' replied the Knight.

'Thou never deservest to have a full one in thy hand, for so simple an answer! Thou hadst best empty thy pitcher ere thou pass it to a Saxon, and leave thy money at home ere thou walk in the greenwood.'

'You hold our friends for robbers, then?' said the Knight of the Fetterlock.

'You hear me not say so, fair sir,' said Wamba: 'it may relieve a man's steed to take off his mail when he hath a long journey to make; and, certes, it may do good to the rider's soul to ease him of that which is the root of evil;* therefore will I give no hard names to those who do such services. Only I would wish my mail at home, and my purse in my chamber, when I meet with these good fellows, because it might save them some trouble.'

'*We* are bound to pray for them, my friend, notwithstanding the fair character thou dost afford them.'

'Pray for them with all my heart,' said Wamba; 'but in the town, not in the greenwood, like the Abbot of Saint Bees,* whom they caused to say mass with an old hollow oak-tree for his stall.'

'Say as thou list, Wamba,' replied the Knight, 'these yeomen did thy master Cedric yeomanly service at Torquilstone.'

'Ay, truly,' answered Wamba; 'but that was in the fashion of their trade with Heaven.'

'Their trade, Wamba! how mean you by that?' replied his companion.

'Marry, thus,' said the Jester. 'They make up a balanced account with Heaven, as our old cellarer used to call his ciphering, as fair as Isaac the Jew keeps with his debtors, and, like him, give out a very little, and take large credit for doing so; reckoning, doubtless, on their own behalf the seven-fold usury which the blessed text hath promised to charitable loans.'*

'Give me an example of your meaning, Wamba,—I know nothing of ciphers or rates of usage,' answered the Knight.

'Why,' said Wamba, 'an your valour be so dull, you will please to learn that those honest fellows balance a good deed with one not quite so laudable; as a crown given to a begging friar with an hundred byzants taken from a fat abbot, or a wench kissed in the greenwood with the relief of a poor widow.'

'Which of these was the good deed, which was the felony?' interrupted the Knight.

'A good gibe! a good gibe!' said Wamba; 'keeping witty company sharpeneth the apprehension. You said nothing so well, Sir Knight, I will be sworn, when you held drunken vespers with the bluff Hermit.—But to go on. The merry-men of the forest set off the building of a cottage with the burning of a castle,—the thatching of a choir against the robbing of a church,—the setting free a poor prisoner against the murder of a proud sheriff; or, to come nearer to our point, the deliverance of a Saxon franklin against the burning alive of a Norman baron. Gentle thieves they are, in short, and courteous robbers; but it is ever the luckiest to meet with them when they are at the worst.'

'How so, Wamba?' said the Knight.

'Why, then they have some compunction, and are for making up matters with Heaven. But when they have struck an even balance, Heaven help them with whom they next open the account! The travellers who first met them after their good service at Torquilstone would have a woful flaying.—And yet,' said Wamba, coming close up to the Knight's side, 'there be companions who are far more dangerous for travellers to meet than yonder outlaws.'

'And who may they be, for you have neither bears nor wolves,* I trow?' said the Knight.

'Marry, sir, but we have Malvoisin's men-at-arms,' said Wamba; 'and let me tell you, that, in time of civil war, a halfscore of these is worth a band of wolves at any time. They are now expecting their harvest, and are reinforced with the soldiers that escaped from Torquilstone. So that, should we meet with a band of them, we are like to pay for our feats of arms.—Now, I pray you, Sir Knight, what would you do if we met two of them?'

'Pin the villains to the earth with my lance, Wamba, if they offered us any impediment.'

'But what if there were four of them?'

'They should drink of the same cup,' answered the Knight.

'What if six,' continued Wamba, 'and we as we now are, barely two—would you not remember Locksley's horn?'

'What! sound for aid,' exclaimed the Knight, 'against a score

of such *rascaille* as these, whom one good knight could drive
before him, as the wind drives the withered leaves?'

'Nay, then,' said Wamba, 'I will pray you for a close sight of
that same horn that hath so powerful a breath.'

The Knight undid the clasp of the baldric, and indulged his
fellow-traveller, who immediately hung the bugle round his own
neck.

'Tra-lira-la,' said he, whistling the notes; 'nay, I know my
gamut* as well as another.'

'How mean you, knave?' said the Knight; 'restore me the
bugle.'

'Content you, Sir Knight, it is in safe keeping. When Valour
and Folly travel, Folly should bear the horn, because she can
blow the best.'

'Nay but, rogue,' said the Black Knight, 'this exceedeth thy
license—Beware ye tamper not with my patience.'

'Urge me not with violence, Sir Knight,' said the Jester, keeping at a distance from the impatient champion, 'or Folly will
show a clean pair of heels, and leave Valour to find out his way
through the wood as best he may.'

'Nay, thou hast hit me there,' said the Knight; 'and, sooth to
say, I have little time to jangle with thee. Keep the horn an thou
wilt, but let us proceed on our journey.'

'You will not harm me, then?' said Wamba.

'I tell thee no, thou knave!'

'Ay, but pledge me your knightly word for it,' continued
Wamba, as he approached with great caution.

'My knightly word I pledge; only come on with thy foolish
self.'

'Nay, then, Valour and Folly are once more boon companions,' said the Jester, coming up frankly to the Knight's side;
'but, in truth, I love not such buffets as that you bestowed on the
burly Friar, when his holiness rolled on the green like a king of
the nine-pins.* And now that Folly wears the horn, let Valour
rouse himself, and shake his mane; for, if I mistake not, there are
company in yonder brake that are on the look-out for us.'

'What makes thee judge so?' said the Knight.

'Because I have twice or thrice noticed the glance of a
morrion* from amongst the green leaves. Had they been honest

men, they had kept the path. But yonder thicket is a choice chapel for the Clerks of Saint Nicholas.'*

'By my faith,' said the Knight, closing his visor, 'I think thou be'st in the right on't.'

And in good time did he close it, for three arrows flew at the same instant from the suspected spot against his head and breast, one of which would have penetrated to the brain, had it not been turned aside by the steel visor. The other two were averted by the gorget, and by the shield which hung around his neck.

'Thanks, trusty armourer,' said the Knight.—'Wamba, let us close with them,'—and he rode straight to the thicket. He was met by six or seven men-at-arms, who ran against him with their lances at full career. Three of the weapons struck against him, and splintered with as little effect as if they had been driven against a tower of steel. The Black Knight's eyes seemed to flash fire even through the aperture of his visor. He raised himself in his stirrups with an air of inexpressible dignity, and exclaimed, 'What means this, my masters!'—The men made no other reply than by drawing their swords and attacking him on every side, crying, 'Die, tyrant!'

'Ha! Saint Edward! Ha! Saint George!' said the Black Knight, striking down a man at every invocation; 'have we traitors here?'

His opponents, desperate as they were, bore back from an arm which carried death in every blow, and it seemed as if the terror of his single strength was about to gain the battle against such odds, when a knight, in blue armour, who had hitherto kept himself behind the other assailants, spurred forward with his lance, and taking aim, not at the rider but at the steed, wounded the noble animal mortally.

'That was a felon stroke!' exclaimed the Black Knight, as the steed fell to the earth, bearing his rider along with him.

And at this moment, Wamba winded the bugle, for the whole had passed so speedily, that he had not time to do so sooner. The sudden sound made the murderers bear back once more, and Wamba, though so imperfectly weaponed, did not hesitate to rush in and assist the Black Knight to rise.

'Shame on ye, false cowards!' exclaimed he in the blue harness, who seemed to lead the assailants, 'do ye fly from the empty blast of a horn blown by a Jester?'

Animated by his words, they attacked the Black Knight anew, whose best refuge was now to place his back against an oak, and defend himself with his sword. The felon knight, who had taken another spear, watching the moment when his formidable antagonist was most closely pressed, galloped against him in hopes to nail him with his lance against the tree, when his purpose was again intercepted by Wamba. The Jester, making up by agility the want of strength, and little noticed by the men-at-arms, who were busied in their more important object, hovered on the skirts of the fight, and effectually checked the fatal career of the Blue Knight, by hamstringing his horse with a stroke of his sword. Horse and man went to the ground; yet the situation of the Knight of the Fetterlock continued very precarious, as he was pressed close by several men completely armed, and began to be fatigued by the violent exertions necessary to defend himself on so many points at nearly the same moment, when a grey-goose shaft suddenly stretched on the earth one of the most formidable of his assailants, and a band of yeomen broke forth from the glade, headed by Locksley and the jovial Friar, who, taking ready and effectual part in the fray, soon disposed of the ruffians, all of whom lay on the spot dead or mortally wounded. The Black Knight thanked his deliverers with a dignity they had not observed in his former bearing, which hitherto had seemed rather that of a blunt bold soldier, than of a person of exalted rank.

'It concerns me much,' he said, 'even before I express my full gratitude to my ready friends, to discover, if I may, who have been my unprovoked enemies.—Open the visor of that Blue Knight, Wamba, who seems the chief of these villains.'

The Jester instantly made up to the leader of the assassins, who, bruised by his fall, and entangled under the wounded steed, lay incapable either of flight or resistance.

'Come, valiant sir,' said Wamba, 'I must be your armourer as well as your equerry—I have dismounted you, and now I will unhelm you.'

So saying, with no very gentle hand he undid the helmet of the Blue Knight, which, rolling to a distance on the grass, displayed to the Knight of the Fetterlock grizzled locks, and a countenance he did not expect to have seen under such circumstances.

'Waldemar Fitzurse!' he said in astonishment; 'what could urge one of thy rank and seeming worth to so foul an undertaking?'

'Richard,' said the captive Knight, looking up to him, 'thou knowest little of mankind, if thou knowest not to what ambition and revenge can lead every child of Adam.'

'Revenge?' answered the Black Knight; 'I never wronged thee—On me thou hast nought to revenge.'

'My daughter, Richard, whose alliance thou didst scorn—was that no injury to a Norman, whose blood is noble as thine own?'

'Thy daughter?' replied the Black Knight; 'a proper cause of enmity, and followed up to a bloody issue!—Stand back, my masters, I would speak to him alone.—And now, Waldemar Fitzurse, say me the truth—confess who set thee on this traitorous deed.'

'Thy father's son,' answered Waldemar, 'who, in so doing, did but avenge on thee thy disobedience to thy father.'

Richard's eyes sparkled with indignation, but his better nature overcame it. He pressed his hand against his brow, and remained an instant gazing on the face of the humbled baron, in whose features pride was contending with shame.

'Thou dost not ask thy life, Waldemar,' said the King.

'He that is in the lion's clutch,' answered Fitzurse, 'knows it were needless.'

'Take it, then, unasked,' said Richard; 'the lion preys not on prostrate carcasses.—Take thy life, but with this condition, that in three days thou shalt leave England, and go to hide thine infamy in thy Norman castle, and that thou wilt never mention the name of John of Anjou as connected with thy felony. If thou art found on English ground after the space I have allotted thee, thou diest*—or if thou breathest aught that can attaint the honour of my house, by Saint George! not the altar itself shall be a sanctuary. I will hang thee out to feed the ravens, from the very pinnacle of thine own castle.—Let this knight have a steed, Locksley, for I see your yeomen have caught those which were running loose, and let him depart unharmed.'

'But that I judge I listen to a voice whose behests must not be disputed,' answered the yeoman, 'I would send a shaft after the skulking villain that should spare him the labour of a long journey.'

'Thou bearest an English heart, Locksley,' said the Black Knight, 'and well dost judge thou art the more bound to obey my behest—I am Richard of England!'

At these words, pronounced in a tone of majesty suited to the high rank, and no less distinguished character of Cœur-de-Lion, the yeomen at once kneeled down before him, and at the same time tendered their allegiance, and implored pardon for their offences.

'Rise, my friends,' said Richard, in a gracious tone, looking on them with a countenance in which his habitual good-humour had already conquered the blaze of hasty resentment, and whose features retained no mark of the late desperate conflict, excepting the flush arising from exertion,—'Arise,' he said, 'my friends!— Your misdemeanours, whether in forest or field, have been atoned by the loyal services you rendered my distressed subjects before the walls of Torquilstone, and the rescue you have this day afforded to your sovereign. Arise, my liegemen, and be good subjects in future.—And thou, brave Locksley'——

'Call me no longer Locksley, my Liege, but know me under the name, which, I fear, fame hath blown too widely not to have reached even your royal ears—I am Robin Hood of Sherwood Forest.'[51]*

'King of Outlaws, and Prince of good fellows!' said the King, 'who hath not heard a name that has been borne as far as Palestine? But be assured, brave Outlaw, that no deed done in our absence, and in the turbulent times to which it hath given rise, shall be remembered to thy disadvantage.'

'True says the proverb,' said Wamba, interposing his word, but with some abatement of his usual petulance,—

> "When the cat is away,
> The mice will play."*

'What, Wamba, art thou there?' said Richard: 'I have been so long of hearing thy voice, I thought thou hadst taken flight.'

'I take flight!' said Wamba; 'when do you ever find Folly separated from Valour? There lies the trophy of my sword, that good grey gelding, whom I heartily wish upon his legs again, conditioning his master lay there houghed* in his place. It is true, I gave a little ground at first, for a motley jacket does not brook lance-heads, as a steel doublet will. But if I fought not at sword's point, you will grant me that I sounded the onset.'

'And to good purpose, honest Wamba,' replied the King. 'Thy good service shall not be forgotten.'

'*Confiteor!* *Confiteor!*'—exclaimed, in a submissive tone, a voice near the King's side—'my Latin will carry me no farther—but I confess my deadly treason, and pray leave to have absolution before I am led to execution!'

Richard looked around, and beheld the jovial Friar on his knees, telling his rosary, while his quarter-staff, which had not been idle during the skirmish, lay on the grass beside him. His countenance was gathered so as he thought might best express the most profound contrition, his eyes being turned up, and the corners of his mouth drawn down, as Wamba expressed it, like the tassels at the mouth of a purse. Yet this demure affectation of extreme penitence was whimsically belied by a ludicrous meaning which lurked in his huge features, and seemed to pronounce his fear and repentance alike hypocritical.

'For what art thou cast down, mad Priest?' said Richard; 'art thou afraid thy diocesan should learn how truly thou dost serve Our Lady and Saint Dunstan?—Tush, man! fear it not; Richard of England betrays no secrets that pass over the flagon.'

'Nay, most gracious sovereign,' answered the Hermit, (well known to the curious in penny-histories of Robin Hood, by the name of Friar Tuck,) 'it is not the crosier I fear, but the sceptre.—Alas! that my sacrilegious fist should ever have been applied to the ear of the Lord's anointed!'

'Ha! ha!' said Richard, 'sits the wind there?*—In truth I had forgotten the buffet, though mine ear sung after it for a whole day. But if the cuff was fairly given, I will be judged by the good men around, if it was not as well repaid—or, if thou thinkest I still owe thee aught, and will stand forth for another counterbuff'——

'By no means,' replied Friar Tuck, 'I had mine own returned, and with usury—may your Majesty ever pay your debts as fully!'

'If I could do so with cuffs,' said the King, 'my creditors should have little reason to complain of an empty exchequer.'

'And yet,' said the Friar, resuming his demure hypocritical countenance, 'I know not what penance I ought to perform for that most sacrilegious blow!'——

'Speak no more of it, brother,' said the King; 'after having stood so many cuffs from Paynims and misbelievers, I were void of reason to quarrel with the buffet of a clerk so holy as he of Copmanhurst. Yet, mine honest Friar, I think it would be best both for the church and thyself, that I should procure a license to unfrock thee, and retain thee as a yeoman of our guard, serving in care of our person, as formerly in attendance upon the altar of Saint Dunstan.'

'My Liege,' said the Friar, 'I humbly crave your pardon; and you would readily grant my excuse, did you but know how the sin of laziness has beset me. Saint Dunstan—may he be gracious to us!—stands quiet in his niche, though I should forget my orisons in killing a fat buck—I stay out of my cell sometimes a night, doing I wot not what—Saint Dunstan never complains— a quiet master he is, and a peaceful, as ever was made of wood.— But to be a yeoman in attendance on my sovereign the King —the honour is great, doubtless—yet, if I were but to step aside to comfort a widow in one corner, or to kill a deer in another, it would be, "where is the dog Priest?" says one. "Who has seen the accursed Tuck?" says another. "The unfrocked villain destroys more venison than half the country besides," says one keeper; "And is hunting after every shy doe in the country!" quoth a second.—In fine, good my Liege, I pray you to leave me as you found me; or, if in aught you desire to extend your benevolence to me, that I may be considered as the poor Clerk of Saint Dunstan's cell in Copmanhurst, to whom any small donation will be most thankfully acceptable.'

'I understand thee,' said the King, 'and the Holy Clerk shall have a grant of vert and venison* in my woods of Warncliffe. Mark, however, I will but assign thee three bucks every season; but if that do not prove an apology for thy slaying thirty, I am no Christian knight nor true king.'

'Your Grace may be well assured,' said the Friar, 'that, with the grace of Saint Dunstan, I shall find the way of multiplying your most bounteous gift.'

'I nothing doubt it, good brother,' said the King; 'and as

venison is but dry food, our cellarer shall have orders to deliver to thee a butt of sack, a runlet of Malvoisie, and three hogsheads of ale of the first strike, yearly—If that will not quench thy thirst, thou must come to court, and become acquainted with my butler.'

'But for Saint Dunstan?' said the Friar—

'A cope, a stole, and an altar-cloth shalt thou also have,' continued the King, crossing himself—'But we may not turn our game into earnest,* lest God punish us for thinking more on our follies than on his honour and worship.'

'I will answer for my patron,' said the Priest, joyously.

'Answer for thyself, Friar,' said King Richard, something sternly; but immediately stretching out his hand to the Hermit, the latter, somewhat abashed, bent his knee, and saluted it. 'Thou dost less honour to my extended palm than to my clenched fist,' said the Monarch; 'thou didst only kneel to the one, and to the other didst prostrate thyself.'

But the Friar, afraid perhaps of again giving offence by continuing the conversation in too jocose a style—a false step to be particularly guarded against by those who converse with monarchs—bowed profoundly, and fell into the rear.

At the same time, two additional personages appeared on the scene.

CHAPTER XLI

All hail to the lordings of high degree,
Who live not more happy, though greater than we!
    Our pastimes to see,
    Under every green tree,
In all the gay woodland, right welcome ye be.

MACDONALD*

THE new comers were Wilfred of Ivanhoe, on the Prior of Botolph's palfrey, and Gurth, who attended him, on the Knight's own war-horse. The astonishment of Ivanhoe was beyond bounds, when he saw his master besprinkled with blood, and six or seven dead bodies lying around in the little glade in which the battle had taken place. Nor was he less surprised to see Richard surrounded by so many silvan attendants, the outlaws, as they seemed to be, of the forest, and a perilous retinue therefore for a prince. He hesitated whether to address the King as the Black Knight-errant, or in what other manner to demean himself towards him. Richard saw his embarrassment.

'Fear not, Wilfred,' he said, 'to address Richard Plantagenet as himself, since thou seest him in the company of true English hearts, although it may be they have been urged a few steps aside by warm English blood.'

'Sir Wilfred of Ivanhoe,' said the gallant Outlaw, stepping forward, 'my assurances can add nothing to those of our sovereign; yet, let me say somewhat proudly, that of men who have suffered much, he hath not truer subjects than those who now stand around him.'

'I cannot doubt it, brave man,' said Wilfred, 'since thou art of the number—But what mean these marks of death and danger? these slain men, and the bloody armour of my Prince?'

'Treason hath been with us, Ivanhoe,' said the King; 'but, thanks to these brave men, treason hath met its meed—But, now I bethink me, thou too art a traitor,' said Richard, smiling; 'a most disobedient traitor; for were not our orders positive, that thou shouldst repose thyself at Saint Botolph's until thy wound was healed?'

'It is healed,' said Ivanhoe; 'it is not of more consequence than the scratch of a bodkin.* But why, oh why, noble Prince, will you thus vex the hearts of your faithful servants, and expose your life by lonely journeys and rash adventures, as if it were of no more value than that of a mere knight-errant, who has no interest on earth but what lance and sword may procure him?'

'And Richard Plantagenet,' said the King, 'desires no more fame than his good lance and sword may acquire him—and Richard Plantagenet is prouder of achieving an adventure, with only his good sword, and his good arm to speed, than if he led to battle an host of an hundred thousand armed men.'

'But your kingdom, my Liege,' said Ivanhoe, 'your kingdom is threatened with dissolution and civil war—your subjects menaced with every species of evil, if deprived of their sovereign in some of those dangers which it is your daily pleasure to incur, and from which you have but this moment narrowly escaped.'

'Ho! ho! my kingdom and my subjects?' answered Richard, impatiently; 'I tell thee, Sir Wilfred, the best of them are most willing to repay my follies in kind—For example, my very faithful servant, Wilfred of Ivanhoe, will not obey my positive commands, and yet reads his king a homily, because he does not walk exactly by his advice. Which of us has most reason to upbraid the other?—Yet forgive me, my faithful Wilfred. The time I have spent, and am yet to spend in concealment, is, as I explained to thee at Saint Botolph's, necessary to give my friends and faithful nobles time to assemble their forces, that when Richard's return is announced, he should be at the head of such a force as enemies shall tremble to face, and thus subdue the meditated treason, without even unsheathing a sword. Estoteville and Bohun will not be strong enough to move forward to York for twenty-four hours. I must have news of Salisbury from the south; and of Beauchamp, in Warwickshire; and of Multon and Percy in the north. The Chancellor must make sure of London.* Too sudden an appearance would subject me to dangers, other than my lance and sword, though backed by the bow of bold Robin, the quarter-staff of Friar Tuck, and the horn of the sage Wamba, may be able to rescue me from.'

Wilfred bowed in submission, well knowing how vain it was to contend with the wild spirit of chivalry which so often impelled his master upon dangers which he might easily have avoided, or rather, which it was unpardonable in him to have sought out. The young knight sighed, therefore, and held his peace; while Richard, rejoiced at having silenced his counsellor, though his heart acknowledged the justice of the charge he had brought against him, went on in conversation with Robin Hood.—'King of Outlaws,' he said, 'have you no refreshment to offer to your brother sovereign? for these dead knaves have found me both in exercise and appetite.'

'In troth,' replied the Outlaw, 'for I scorn to lie to your Grace, our larder is chiefly supplied with'—— He stopped, and was somewhat embarrassed.

'With venison, I suppose?' said Richard, gaily; 'better food at need there can be none—and truly, if a king will not remain at home and slay his own game, methinks he should not brawl too loud if he finds it killed to his hand.'

'If your Grace, then,' said Robin, 'will again honour with your presence one of Robin Hood's places of rendezvous, the venison shall not be lacking; and a stoup of ale, and it may be a cup of reasonably good wine, to relish it withal.'

The Outlaw accordingly led the way, followed by the buxom* Monarch, more happy, probably, in this chance meeting with Robin Hood and his foresters, than he would have been in again assuming his royal state, and presiding over a splendid circle of peers and nobles. Novelty in society and adventure were the zest of life to Richard Cœur-de-Lion, and it had its highest relish when enhanced by dangers encountered and surmounted. In the lion-hearted King, the brilliant, but useless character, of a knight of romance, was in a great measure realized and revived; and the personal glory which he acquired by his own deeds of arms, was far more dear to his excited imagination, than that which a course of policy and wisdom would have spread around his government. Accordingly, his reign was like the course of a brilliant and rapid meteor, which shoots along the face of Heaven, shedding around an unnecessary and portentous light, which is instantly swallowed up by universal darkness;* his feats of chivalry furnishing themes for bards and minstrels, but affording none of those solid benefits to his country on which history loves to pause, and hold up as an example to posterity. But in his present company Richard showed to the greatest imaginable advantage. He was gay, good-humoured, and fond of manhood in every rank of life.

Beneath a huge oak-tree the silvan repast was hastily prepared for the King of England, surrounded by men outlaws to his government, but who now formed his court and his guard. As the flagon went round, the rough foresters soon lost their awe for the presence of Majesty. The song and the jest were exchanged—the stories of former deeds were told with advantage;* and at length, and while boasting of their successful infraction of the laws, no one recollected they were speaking in presence of their natural guardian. The merry King, nothing heeding his dignity any more than his company, laughed, quaffed, and jested among the jolly band. The natural and rough sense of Robin Hood led him to be desirous that the scene should be closed ere any thing should occur to disturb its harmony, the more especially that he observed Ivanhoe's brow clouded with anxiety. 'We are honoured,' he said to Ivanhoe, apart, 'by the presence of our gallant Sovereign; yet I would not that he dallied with time, which the circumstances of his kingdom may render precious.'

'It is well and wisely spoken, brave Robin Hood,' said Wilfred, apart; 'and know, moreover, that they who jest with Majesty even in its gayest mood, are but toying with the lion's whelp,* which, on slight provocation, uses both fangs and claws.'

'You have touched the very cause of my fear,' said the Outlaw; 'my men are rough by practice and nature, the King is hasty as well as good-humoured; nor know I how soon cause of offence may arise, or how warmly it may be received—it is time this revel were broken off.'

'It must be by your management then, gallant yeoman,' said Ivanhoe; 'for each hint I have essayed to give him serves only to induce him to prolong it.'

'Must I so soon risk the pardon and favour of my Sovereign?' said Robin Hood, pausing for an instant; 'but by Saint Christopher, it shall be so. I were undeserving his grace did I not peril it for his good.—Here, Scathlock, get thee behind yonder thicket, and wind me a Norman blast on thy bugle, and without an instant's delay, on peril of your life.'

Scathlock obeyed his captain, and in less than five minutes the revellers were startled by the sound of his horn.

'It is the bugle of Malvoisin,' said the Miller, starting to his feet, and seizing his bow. The Friar dropped the flagon, and grasped his quarter-staff. Wamba stopt short in the midst of a jest, and betook himself to sword and target. All the others stood to their weapons.

Men of their precarious course of life change readily from the banquet to the battle; and, to Richard, the exchange seemed but a succession of pleasure. He called for his helmet and the most cumbrous parts of his armour, which he had laid aside; and while Gurth was putting them on, he laid his strict injunctions on Wilfred, under pain of his highest displeasure, not to engage in the skirmish which he supposed was approaching.

'Thou hast fought for me an hundred times, Wilfred,—and I have seen it. Thou shalt this day look on, and see how Richard will fight for his friend and liegeman.'

In the meantime, Robin Hood had sent off several of his followers in different directions, as if to reconnoitre the enemy; and when he saw the company effectually broken up, he approached Richard, who was now completely armed, and, kneeling down on one knee, craved pardon of his Sovereign.

'For what, good yeoman?' said Richard, somewhat impatiently. 'Have we not already granted thee a full pardon for all transgressions? Thinkest thou our word is a feather, to be blown backward and forward between us? Thou canst not have had time to commit any new offence since that time?'

'Ay, but I have though,' answered the yeoman, 'if it be an offence to deceive my prince for his own advantage. The bugle you have heard was none of Malvoisin's, but blown by my direction, to break off the banquet, lest it trenched upon hours of dearer import than to be thus dallied with.'

He then rose from his knee, folded his arms on his bosom, and in a manner rather respectful than submissive, awaited the answer of the King,—like one who is conscious he may have given offence, yet is confident in the rectitude of his motive. The blood rushed in anger to the countenance of Richard; but it was the first transient emotion, and his sense of justice instantly subdued it.

'The King of Sherwood,' he said, 'grudges his venison and his wine-flask to the King of England? It is well, bold Robin!—but when you come to see me in merry London, I trust to be a less niggard host. Thou art right, however, good fellow. Let us therefore to horse and away—Wilfred has been impatient this hour. Tell me, bold Robin, hast thou never a friend in thy band, who, not content with advising, will needs direct thy motions, and look miserable when thou dost presume to act for thyself?'

'Such a one,' said Robin, 'is my Lieutenant, Little John, who is even now absent on an expedition as far as the borders of Scotland; and I will own to your Majesty, that I am sometimes displeased by the freedom of his councils—but, when I think twice, I cannot be long angry with one who can have no motive for his anxiety save zeal for his master's service.'

'Thou art right, good yeoman,' answered Richard; 'and if I had Ivanhoe, on the one hand, to give grave advice, and recommend it by the sad gravity of his brow, and thee, on the other, to trick me into what thou thinkest my own good, I should have as little the freedom of mine own will as any king in Christendom or Heathenesse.—But come, sirs, let us merrily on to Coningsburgh, and think no more on't.'

Robin Hood assured them that he had detached a party in the direction of the road they were to pass, who would not fail to discover and apprize them of any second ambuscade; and that he had little doubt they would find the ways secure, or, if otherwise, would receive such timely notice of the danger as would enable them to fall back on a strong troop of archers, with which he himself proposed to follow on the same route.

The wise and attentive precautions adopted for his safety touched Richard's feelings, and removed any slight grudge which he might retain on account of the deception the Outlaw Captain had practised upon him. He once more extended his hand to Robin Hood, assured him of his full pardon and future favour, as well as his firm resolution to restrain the tyrannical exercise of the forest rights and other oppressive laws, by which so many English yeomen were driven into a state of rebellion. But Richard's good intentions towards the bold Outlaw were frustrated by the King's untimely death; and the Charter of the Forest was extorted from the unwilling hands of King John when he succeeded to his heroic brother.* As for the rest of Robin Hood's career, as well as the tale of his treacherous death, they are to be found in those black-letter garlands, once sold at the low and easy rate of one halfpenny,

'Now cheaply purchased at their weight in gold.'*

The Outlaw's opinion proved true; and the King, attended by Ivanhoe, Gurth, and Wamba, arrived, without any interruption, within view of the Castle of Coningsburgh, while the sun was yet in the horizon.

There are few more beautiful or striking scenes in England, than are presented by the vicinity of this ancient Saxon fortress. The soft and gentle river Don sweeps through an amphitheatre, in which cultivation is richly blended with woodland, and on a mount, ascending from the river, well defended by walls and ditches, rises this ancient edifice, which, as its Saxon name implies, was, previous to the Conquest, a royal residence of the kings of England. The outer walls have probably been added by the Normans, but the inner keep bears token of very great antiquity.* It is situated on a mount at one angle of the inner court, and forms a complete circle of perhaps twenty-five feet in diameter. The wall is of immense thickness, and is propped or defended by six huge external buttresses which project from the circle, and rise up against the sides of the tower as if to strengthen or to support it. These massive buttresses are solid when they arise from the foundation, and a good way higher up; but are hollowed out towards the top, and terminate in a sort of turrets communicating with the interior of the keep itself. The distant appearance of this huge building, with these singular accompaniments, is as interesting to the lovers of the picturesque, as the interior of the castle is to the eager antiquary, whose imagination it carries back to the days of the heptarchy. A barrow, in the vicinity of the castle, is pointed out as the tomb of the memorable Hengist; and various monuments, of great antiquity and curiosity, are shown in the neighbouring churchyard.[52]

When Cœur-de-Lion and his retinue approached this rude yet

stately building, it was not, as at present, surrounded by external fortifications. The Saxon architect had exhausted his art in rendering the main keep defensible, and there was no other circumvallation than a rude barrier of palisades.

A huge black banner, which floated from the top of the tower, announced that the obsequies of the late owner were still in the act of being solemnized. It bore no emblem of the deceased's birth or quality, for armorial bearings were then a novelty among the Norman chivalry themselves, and were totally unknown to the Saxons. But above the gate was another banner, on which the figure of a white horse, rudely painted, indicated the nation and rank of the deceased, by the well-known symbol of Hengist* and his Saxon warriors.

All around the castle was a scene of busy commotion; for such funeral banquets were times of general and profuse hospitality, which not only every one who could claim the most distant connexion with the deceased, but all passengers whatsoever, were invited to partake. The wealth and consequence of the deceased Athelstane occasioned this custom to be observed in the fullest extent.

Numerous parties, therefore, were seen ascending and descending the hill on which the castle was situated; and when the King and his attendants entered the open and unguarded gates of the external barrier, the space within presented a scene not easily reconciled with the cause of the assemblage. In one place cooks were toiling to roast huge oxen, and fat sheep; in another, hogsheads of ale were set abroach, to be drained at the freedom of all comers. Groups of every description were to be seen devouring the food and swallowing the liquor thus abandoned to their discretion. The naked Saxon serf was drowning the sense of his half-year's hunger and thirst, in one day of gluttony and drunkenness—the more pampered burgess and guild-brother was eating his morsel with gust, or curiously criticising the quantity of the malt and the skill of the brewer. Some few of the poorer Norman gentry might also be seen, distinguished by their shaven chins and short cloaks, and not less so by their keeping together, and looking with great scorn on the whole solemnity, even while condescending to avail themselves of the good cheer which was so liberally supplied.

Mendicants were of course assembled by the score, together with strolling soldiers returned from Palestine, (according to their own account at least,) pedlars were displaying their wares, travelling mechanics were enquiring after employment, and wandering palmers, hedge-priests, Saxon minstrels, and Welsh bards, were muttering prayers, and extracting mistuned dirges from their harps, crowds, and rotes.[53] One sent forth the praises of Athelstane in a doleful panegyric; another, in a Saxon genealogical poem, rehearsed the uncouth and harsh names of his noble ancestry. Jesters and jugglers were not awanting, nor was the occasion of the assembly supposed to render the exercise of their profession indecorous or improper. Indeed the ideas of the Saxons on these occasions were as natural as they were rude. If sorrow was thirsty, there was drink—if hungry, there was food—if it sunk down upon and saddened the heart, here were the means supplied of mirth, or at least of amusement. Nor did the assistants scorn to avail themselves of those means of consolation, although, every now and then, as if suddenly recollecting the cause which had brought them together, the men groaned in unison, while the females, of whom many were present, raised up their voices and shrieked for very woe.

Such was the scene in the castle-yard at Coningsburgh when it was entered by Richard and his followers. The seneschal or steward deigned not to take notice of the groups of inferior guests who were perpetually entering and withdrawing, unless so far as was necessary to preserve order; nevertheless he was struck by the good mien of the Monarch and Ivanhoe, more especially as he imagined the features of the latter were familiar to him. Besides, the approach of two knights, for such their dress bespoke them, was a rare event at a Saxon solemnity, and could not but be regarded as a sort of honour to the deceased and his family. And in his sable dress, and holding in his hand his white wand of office, this important personage made way through the miscellaneous assemblage of guests, thus conducting Richard and Ivanhoe to the entrance of the tower. Gurth and Wamba speedily found acquaintances in the court-yard, nor presumed to intrude themselves any farther until their presence should be required.

CHAPTER XLII

I found them winding of Marcello's corpse.
And there was such a solemn melody,
'Twixt doleful songs, tears, and sad elegies,—
Such as old grandames, watching by the dead,
Are wont to outwear the night with.

*Old Play**

THE mode of entering the great tower of Coningsburgh Castle is very peculiar, and partakes of the rude simplicity of the early times in which it was erected. A flight of steps, so deep and narrow as to be almost precipitous, leads up to a low portal in the south side of the tower, by which the adventurous antiquary may still, or at least could a few years since, gain access to a small stair within the thickness of the main wall of the tower, which leads up to the third story of the building,—the two lower being dungeons or vaults, which neither receive air nor light, save by a square hole in the third story, with which they seem to have communicated by a ladder. The access to the upper apartments in the tower, which consist in all of four stories, is given by stairs which are carried up through the external buttresses.

By this difficult and complicated entrance, the good King Richard, followed by his faithful Ivanhoe, was ushered into the round apartment which occupies the whole of the third story from the ground. Wilfred, by the difficulties of the ascent, gained time to muffle his face in his mantle, as it had been held expedient that he should not present himself to his father until the King should give him the signal.

There were assembled in this apartment, around a large oaken table, about a dozen of the most distinguished representatives of the Saxon families in the adjacent counties. These were all old, or, at least, elderly men; for the younger race, to the great displeasure of the seniors, had, like Ivanhoe, broken down many of the barriers which separated for half a century the Norman victors from the vanquished Saxons. The downcast and sorrowful looks of these venerable men, their silence and their mournful posture, formed a strong contrast to the levity of the revellers on the outside of the castle. Their grey locks and long full beards, together with their antique tunics and loose black mantles, suited well with the singular and rude apartment in which they were seated, and gave the appearance of a band of ancient worshippers of Woden, recalled to life to mourn over the decay of their national glory.

Cedric, seated in equal rank among his countrymen, seemed yet, by common consent, to act as chief of the assembly. Upon the entrance of Richard (only known to him as the valorous Knight of the Fetterlock) he arose gravely, and gave him welcome by the ordinary salutation, *Waes hael*, raising at the same time a goblet to his head. The King, no stranger to the customs of his English subjects, returned the greeting with the appropriate words, *Drinc hael*, and partook of a cup which was handed to him by the sewer. The same courtesy was offered to Ivanhoe, who pledged his father in silence, supplying the usual speech by an inclination of his head, lest his voice should have been recognised.

When this introductory ceremony was performed, Cedric arose, and, extending his hand to Richard, conducted him into a small and very rude chapel, which was excavated, as it were, out of one of the external buttresses. As there was no opening, saving a very narrow loop-hole, the place would have been nearly quite dark but for two flambeaux or torches, which showed, by a red and smoky light, the arched roof and naked walls, the rude altar of stone, and the crucifix of the same material.

Before this altar was placed a bier, and on each side of this bier kneeled three priests, who told their beads, and muttered their prayers, with the greatest signs of external devotion. For this service a splendid *soul-scat* was paid to the convent of Saint Edmund's by the mother of the deceased; and, that it might be fully deserved, the whole brethren, saving the lame Sacristan, had transferred themselves to Coningsburgh, where, while six of their number were constantly on guard in the performance of divine rites by the bier of Athelstane, the others failed not to take their share of the refreshments and amusements which went on at the castle. In maintaining this pious watch and ward, the good monks were particularly careful not to interrupt their hymns for an instant, lest Zernebock, the ancient Saxon Apollyon, should lay his clutches on the departed Athelstane. Nor were they less careful to prevent any unhallowed layman from touching the pall, which, having been that used at the funeral of Saint Edmund, was liable to be desecrated, if handled by the profane. If, in truth, these attentions could be of any use to the deceased, he had some right to expect them at the hands of the brethren of Saint Edmund's, since, besides a hundred mancuses of gold paid down as the soul-ransom, the mother of Athelstane had announced her intention of endowing that foundation with the better part of the lands of the deceased, in order to maintain perpetual prayers for his soul, and that of her departed husband.

Richard and Wilfred followed the Saxon Cedric into the apartment of death, where, as their guide pointed with solemn air to the untimely bier of Athelstane, they followed his example in devoutly crossing themselves, and muttering a brief prayer for the weal of the departed soul.

This act of pious charity performed, Cedric again motioned them to follow him, gliding over the stone floor with a noiseless tread; and, after ascending a few steps, opened with great caution the door of a small oratory, which adjoined to the chapel. It was about eight feet square, hollowed, like the chapel itself, out of the thickness of the wall; and the loop-hole, which enlightened it, being to the west, and widening considerably as it sloped inward, a beam of the setting sun found its way into its dark recess, and showed a female of a dignified mien, and whose countenance retained the marked remains of majestic beauty. Her long mourning robes, and her flowing wimple of black cypress,* enhanced the whiteness of her skin, and the beauty of her light-coloured and flowing tresses, which time had neither thinned nor mingled with silver. Her countenance expressed the deepest sorrow that is consistent with resignation. On the stone table before her stood a crucifix of ivory, beside which was laid a missal, having its pages richly illuminated, and its boards adorned with clasps of gold, and bosses of the same precious metal.

'Noble Edith,' said Cedric, after having stood a moment silent, as if to give Richard and Wilfred time to look upon the lady of the mansion, 'these are worthy strangers, come to take a part in thy sorrows. And this, in especial, is the valiant Knight who fought so bravely for the deliverance of him for whom we this day mourn.'

'His bravery has my thanks,' returned the lady; 'although it be the will of Heaven that it should be displayed in vain. I thank, too, his courtesy, and that of his companion, which hath brought them hither to behold the widow of Adeling, the mother of Athelstane, in her deep hour of sorrow and lamentation. To your care, kind kinsman, I intrust them, satisfied that they will want no hospitality which these sad walls can yet afford.'

The guests bowed deeply to the mourning parent, and withdrew from their hospitable guide.

Another winding stair conducted them to an apartment of the same size with that which they had first entered, occupying indeed the story immediately above. From this room, ere yet the door was opened, proceeded a low and melancholy strain of vocal music. When they entered, they found themselves in the presence of about twenty matrons and maidens of distinguished Saxon lineage. Four maidens, Rowena leading the choir, raised a hymn for the soul of the deceased,* of which we have only been able to decipher two or three stanzas:—

> Dust unto dust,
> To this all must;
> The tenant hath resign'd
> The faded form
> To waste and worm—
> Corruption claims her kind.
>
> Through paths unknown
> Thy soul hath flown,
> To seek the realms of woe,
> Where fiery pain
> Shall purge the stain
> Of actions done below.
>
> In that sad place,
> By Mary's grace,
> Brief may thy dwelling be!
> Till prayers and alms,
> And holy psalms,
> Shall set the captive free.

While this dirge was sung, in a low and melancholy tone, by the female choristers, the others were divided into two bands, of which one was engaged in bedecking, with such embroidery as their skill and taste could compass, a large silken pall, destined to cover the bier of Athelstane, while the others busied themselves in selecting, from baskets of flowers placed before them, garlands, which they intended for the same mournful purpose. The behaviour of the maidens was decorous, if not marked with deep affliction; but now and then a whisper or a smile called forth the rebuke of the severer matrons, and here and there might be seen a damsel more interested in endeavouring to find out how her mourning-robe became her, than in the dismal ceremony for which they were preparing. Neither was this propensity (if we must needs confess the truth) at all diminished by the appearance of two strange knights, which occasioned some looking up, peeping, and whispering. Rowena alone, too proud to be vain, paid her greeting to her deliverer with a graceful courtesy. Her demeanour was serious, but not dejected; and it may be doubted whether thoughts of Ivanhoe, and of the uncertainty of his fate, did not claim as great a share in her gravity as the death of her kinsman.

To Cedric, however, who, as we have observed, was not remarkably clear-sighted on such occasions, the sorrow of his ward seemed so much deeper than any of the other maidens, that he deemed it proper to whisper the explanation—'She was the affianced bride of the noble Athelstane.'—It may be doubted whether this communication went a far way to increase Wilfred's disposition to sympathize with the mourners of Coningsburgh.

Having thus formally introduced the guests to the different chambers in which the obsequies of Athelstane were celebrated under different forms, Cedric conducted them into a small room, destined, as he informed them, for the exclusive accommodation of honourable guests, whose more slight connexion with the deceased might render them unwilling to join those who were immediately affected by the unhappy event. He assured them of every accommodation, and was about to withdraw when the Black Knight took his hand.

'I crave to remind you, noble Thane,' he said, 'that when we last parted, you promised, for the service I had the fortune to render you, to grant me a boon.'

'It is granted ere named, noble Knight,' said Cedric; 'yet, at this sad moment'——

'Of that also,' said the King, 'I have bethought me—but my time is brief—neither does it seem to me unfit, that, when closing the grave on the noble Athelstane, we should deposit therein certain prejudices and hasty opinions.'

'Sir Knight of the Fetterlock,' said Cedric, colouring, and interrupting the King in his turn, 'I trust your boon regards yourself and no other; for in that which concerns the honour of my house, it is scarce fitting that a stranger should mingle.'

'Nor do I wish to mingle,' said the King, mildly, 'unless in so far as you will admit me to have an interest. As yet you have known me but as the Black Knight of the Fetterlock—Know me now as Richard Plantagenet.'

'Richard of Anjou!' exclaimed Cedric, stepping backward with the utmost astonishment.

'No, noble Cedric—Richard of England!—whose deepest interest—whose deepest wish, is to see her sons united with each other.—And, how now, worthy Thane! hast thou no knee for thy prince?

'To Norman blood,' said Cedric, 'it hath never bended.'

'Reserve thine homage then,' said the Monarch, 'until I shall prove my right to it by my equal protection of Normans and English.'

'Prince,' answered Cedric, 'I have ever done justice to thy bravery and thy worth—Nor am I ignorant of thy claim to the crown through thy descent from Matilda, niece to Edgar Atheling, and daughter to Malcolm of Scotland. But Matilda, though of the royal Saxon blood, was not the heir to the monarchy.'

'I will not dispute my title with thee, noble Thane,' said Richard, calmly; 'but I will bid thee look around thee, and see where thou wilt find another to be put into the scale against it.'

'And hast thou wandered hither, Prince, to tell me so?' said Cedric—'To upbraid me with the ruin of my race, ere the grave has closed o'er the last scion of Saxon royalty?'— His countenance darkened as he spoke.—'It was boldly—it was rashly done!'

'Not so, by the holy rood!' replied the King; 'it was done in the frank confidence which one brave man may repose in another, without a shadow of danger.'

'Thou sayest well, Sir King*—for King I own thou art, and wilt be, despite of my feeble opposition.—I dare not take the only mode to prevent it, though thou hast placed the strong temptation within my reach!'

'And now to my boon,' said the King, 'which I ask not with one jot the less confidence, that thou hast refused to acknowledge my lawful sovereignty. I require of thee, as a man of thy word, on pain of being held faithless, man-sworn, and *nidering*,[54] to forgive and receive to thy paternal affection the good knight, Wilfred of Ivanhoe. In this reconciliation thou wilt own I have an interest—the happiness of my friend, and the quelling of dissension among my faithful people.'

'And this is Wilfred!' said Cedric, pointing to his son.

'My father!—my father!' said Ivanhoe, prostrating himself at Cedric's feet, 'grant me thy forgiveness!'

'Thou hast it, my son,' said Cedric, raising him up. 'The son of Hereward knows how to keep his word, even when it has been passed to a Norman. But let me see thee use the dress and costume of thy English ancestry—no short cloaks, no gay bonnets, no fantastic plumage in my decent household. He that would be the son of Cedric, must show himself of English ancestry.—Thou art about to speak,' he added, sternly, 'and I guess the topic. The Lady Rowena must complete two years' mourning, as for a betrothed husband—all our Saxon ancestors would disown us were we to treat of a new union for her ere the grave of him she should have wedded—him, so much the most worthy of her hand by birth and ancestry—is yet closed. The ghost of Athelstane himself would burst his bloody cerements,* and stand before us to forbid such dishonour to his memory.'

It seemed as if Cedric's words had raised a spectre; for, scarce had he uttered them ere the door flew open, and Athelstane, arrayed in the garments of the grave, stood before them, pale, haggard, and like something arisen from the dead![55]

The effect of this apparition on the persons present was utterly appalling. Cedric started back as far as the wall of the apartment would permit, and, leaning against it as one unable to support himself, gazed on the figure of his friend with eyes that seemed fixed, and a mouth which he appeared incapable of shutting. Ivanhoe crossed himself, repeating prayers in Saxon, Latin, or Norman-French, as they occurred to his memory, while Richard alternately said, *Benedicite*, and swore, *Mort de ma vie!**

In the meantime, a horrible noise was heard below stairs, some crying, 'Secure the treacherous monks!'—others, 'Down with them into the dungeon!'—others, 'Pitch them from the highest battlements!'

'In the name of God!' said Cedric, addressing what seemed the spectre of his departed friend, 'if thou art mortal, speak!—if a departed spirit, say for what cause thou dost revisit us, or if I can do aught that can set thy spirit at repose.—Living or dead, noble Athelstane, speak to Cedric!'

'I will,' said the spectre, very composedly, 'when I have collected breath, and when you give me time—Alive, saidst thou?—I am as much alive as he can be who has fed on bread and water for three days, which seem three ages—Yes, bread and water, Father Cedric! By Heaven, and all saints in it, better food hath not passed my weasand* for three livelong days, and by God's providence it is that I am now here to tell it.'

'Why, noble Athelstane,' said the Black Knight, 'I myself saw you struck down by the fierce Templar towards the end of the storm at Torquilstone, and as I thought, and Wamba reported, your skull was cloven through the teeth.'

'You thought amiss, Sir Knight,' said Athelstane, 'and Wamba lied. My teeth are in good order, and that my supper shall presently find—No thanks to the Templar though, whose sword turned in his hand, so that the blade struck me flatlings,* being averted by the handle of the good mace with which I warded the blow; had my steel-cap been on, I had not valued it a rush, and had dealt him such a counter-buff as would have spoilt his retreat. But as it was, down I went, stunned, indeed, but unwounded. Others, of both sides, were beaten down and slaughtered above me, so that I never recovered my senses until I found myself in a coffin—(an open one, by good luck)—placed before the altar of the church of Saint Edmund's. I sneezed repeatedly—groaned—awakened, and would have arisen, when the Sacristan and Abbot, full of terror, came running at the noise, surprised, doubtless, and no way pleased to find the man alive, whose heirs they had proposed themselves to be. I asked for wine—they gave me some, but it must have been highly medicated, for I slept yet more deeply than before, and wakened not for many hours. I found my arms swathed down—my feet tied so fast that mine ankles ache at the very remembrance—the place was utterly dark—the oubliette,* as I suppose, of their accursed convent, and from the close, stifled, damp smell, I conceive it is also used for a place of sepulture. I had strange thoughts of what had befallen me, when the door of my dungeon creaked, and two villain monks entered. They would have persuaded me I was in purgatory, but I knew too well the pursy short-breathed voice of the Father Abbot.—Saint Jeremy!* how different from that tone with which he used to ask me for another slice of the haunch!—the dog has feasted with me from Christmas to Twelfth-night.'*

'Have patience, noble Athelstane,' said the King, 'take breath—tell your story at leisure—beshrew me but such a tale is as well worth listening to as a romance.'

'Ay but, by the rood of Bromeholm, there was no romance in the matter!' said Athelstane.—'A barley loaf and a pitcher of water—that *they* gave me, the niggardly traitors, whom my father, and I myself, had enriched, when their best resources were the flitches of bacon and measures of corn, out of which they wheedled poor serfs and bondsmen, in exchange for their prayers—the nest of foul ungrateful vipers—barley bread and ditch water to such a patron as I had been! I will smoke them out of their nest, though I be excommunicated!'

'But, in the name of Our Lady, noble Athelstane,' said Cedric, grasping the hand of his friend, 'how didst thou escape this imminent danger?—did their hearts relent?'

'Did their hearts relent!' echoed Athelstane.—'Do rocks melt with the sun?* I should have been there still, had not some stir in the Convent, which I find was their procession hitherward to eat my funeral feast, when they well knew how and where I had been buried alive, summoned the swarm out of their hive. I heard them droning out their death-psalms, little judging they were sung in respect for my soul by those who were thus famishing my body. They went, however, and I waited long for food—no wonder—the gouty Sacristan was even too busy with his own provender to mind mine. At length down he came, with an unstable step and a strong flavour of wine and spices about his person. Good cheer had opened his heart, for he left me a nook of pasty and a flask of wine, instead of my former fare. I ate, drank, and was invigorated;* when, to add to my good luck, the Sacristan, too totty to discharge his duty of turnkey fitly, locked the door beside the staple, so that it fell ajar. The light, the food, the wine, set my invention to work. The staple to which my chains were fixed, was more rusted than I or the villain Abbot had supposed. Even iron could not remain without consuming in the damps of that infernal dungeon.'

'Take breath, noble Athelstane,' said Richard, 'and partake of some refreshment, ere you proceed with a tale so dreadful.'

'Partake!' quoth Athelstane; 'I have been partaking five times to-day—and yet a morsel of that savoury ham were not altogether foreign to the matter; and I pray you, fair sir, to do me reason in a cup of wine.'

The guests, though still agape with astonishment, pledged their resuscitated landlord, who thus proceeded in his story:—He had indeed now many more auditors than those to whom it was commenced, for Edith, having given certain necessary orders for arranging matters within the Castle, had followed the dead-alive up to the stranger's apartment, attended by as many of the guests, male and female, as could squeeze into the small room, while others, crowding the staircase, caught up an erroneous edition of the story, and transmitted it still more inaccurately to those beneath, who again sent it forth to the vulgar without, in a fashion totally irreconcilable to the real fact. Athelstane, however, went on as follows, with the history of his escape:—

'Finding myself freed from the staple, I dragged myself up stairs as well as a man loaded with shackles, and emaciated with fasting, might; and after much groping about, I was at length directed, by the sound of a jolly roundelay, to the apartment where the worthy Sacristan, an it so please ye, was holding a devil's mass with a huge beetle-browed, broad-shouldered brother of the grey-frock and cowl, who looked much more like a thief than a clergyman. I burst in upon them, and the fashion of my grave-clothes, as well as the clanking of my chains, made me more resemble an inhabitant of the other world than of this. Both stood aghast; but when I knocked down the Sacristan with my fist, the other fellow, his pot-companion, fetched a blow at me with a huge quarter-staff.'

'This must be our Friar Tuck, for a count's ransom,' said Richard, looking at Ivanhoe.

'He may be the devil, an he will,' said Athelstane. 'Fortunately he missed the aim; and on my approaching to grapple with him, took to his heels and ran for it. I failed not to set my own heels at liberty by means of the fetter-key, which hung amongst others at the sexton's belt; and I had thoughts of beating out the knave's brains with the bunch of keys, but gratitude for the nook of pasty and the flask of wine which the rascal had imparted to my captivity, came over my heart; so, with a brace of hearty kicks, I left him on the floor, pouched some baked meat, and a leathern bottle of wine, with which the two venerable brethren had been regaling, went to the stable, and found in a private stall mine own best palfrey, which, doubtless, had been set apart for the holy Father Abbot's particular use. Hither I came with all the speed the beast could compass—man and mother's son flying before me wherever I came, taking me for a spectre, the more especially as, to prevent my being recognised, I drew the corpse-hood over my face. I had not gained admittance into my own castle, had I not been supposed to be the attendant of a juggler who is making the people in the castle-yard very merry, considering they are assembled to celebrate their lord's funeral—I say the sewer thought I was dressed to bear a part in the tregetour's* mummery, and so I got admission, and did but disclose myself to my mother, and eat a hasty morsel, ere I came in quest of you, my noble friend.'

'And you have found me,' said Cedric, 'ready to resume our brave projects of honour and liberty. I tell thee, never will dawn a morrow so auspicious as the next, for the deliverance of the noble Saxon race.'

'Talk not to me of delivering any one,' said Athelstane; 'it is well I am delivered myself. I am more intent on punishing that villain Abbot. He shall hang on the top of this Castle of

Coningsburgh, in his cope and stole; and if the stairs be too strait to admit his fat carcass, I will have him craned up from without.'

'But, my son,' said Edith, 'consider his sacred office.'

'Consider my three days' fast,' replied Athelstane; 'I will have their blood every one of them. Front-de-Bœuf was burnt alive for a less matter, for he kept a good table for his prisoners, only put too much garlic in his last dish of pottage. But these hypocritical, ungrateful slaves, so often the self-invited flatterers at my board, who gave me neither pottage nor garlic, nor less, they die, by the soul of Hengist!'

'But the Pope, my noble friend,'—said Cedric——

'But the devil, my noble friend,'—answered Athelstane: 'they die, and no more of them. Were they the best monks upon earth, the world would go on without them.'

'For shame, noble Athelstane,' said Cedric; 'forget such wretches in the career of glory which lies open before thee. Tell this Norman prince, Richard of Anjou, that, lion-hearted as he is, he shall not hold undisputed the throne of Alfred, while a male descendant of the Holy Confessor lives to dispute it.'

'How!' said Athelstane, 'is this the noble King Richard?'

'It is Richard Plantagenet himself,' said Cedric; 'yet I need not remind thee that, coming hither a guest of free-will, he may neither be injured nor detained prisoner—thou well knowest thy duty to him as his host.'

'Ay, by my faith!' said Athelstane; 'and my duty as a subject besides, for I here tender him my allegiance, heart and hand.'

'My son,' said Edith, 'think on thy royal rights!'

'Think on the freedom of England, degenerate Prince!' said Cedric.

'Mother and friend,' said Athelstane, 'a truce to your upbraidings—bread and water and a dungeon are marvellous mortifiers of ambition, and I rise from the tomb a wiser man than I descended into it. One half of those vain follies were puffed into mine ear by that perfidious Abbot Wolfram, and you may now judge if he is a counsellor to be trusted. Since these plots were set in agitation, I have had nothing but hurried journeys, indigestions, blows and bruises, imprisonments and starvation; besides that they can only end in the murder of some thousands of quiet folk. I tell you, I will be king in my own domains, and nowhere else; any my first act of dominion shall be to hang the Abbot.'

'And my ward Rowena,' said Cedric—'I trust you intend not to desert her?'

'Father Cedric,' said Athelstane, 'be reasonable. The Lady Rowena cares not for me—she loves the little finger of my kinsman Wilfred's glove better than my whole person. There she stands to avouch it—Nay, blush not, kinswoman, there is no shame in loving a courtly knight better than a country franklin—and do not laugh neither, Rowena, for grave-clothes and a thin visage are, God knows, no matter of merriment—Nay, an thou wilt needs laugh, I will find thee a better jest—Give me thy hand, or rather lend it me, for I but ask it in the way of friendship.—Here, cousin Wilfred of Ivanhoe, in thy favour I renounce and abjure——Hey! by Saint Dunstan, our cousin Wilfred hath vanished!—Yet, unless my eyes are still dazzled with the fasting I have undergone, I saw him stand there but even now.'

All now looked around and enquired for Ivanhoe, but he had vanished. It was at length discovered that a Jew had been to seek him; and that, after very brief conference, he had called for Gurth and his armour, and had left the castle.

'Fair cousin,' said Athelstane to Rowena, 'could I think that this sudden disappearance of Ivanhoe was occasioned by other than the weightiest reason, I would myself resume'——

But he had no sooner let go her hand, on first observing that Ivanhoe had disappeared, than Rowena, who had found her situation extremely embarrassing, had taken the first opportunity to escape from the apartment.

'Certainly,' quoth Athelstane, 'women are the least to be trusted of all animals, monks and abbots excepted. I am an infidel, if I expected not thanks from her, and perhaps a kiss to boot—These cursed grave-clothes have surely a spell on them, every one flies from me.—To you I turn, noble King Richard, with the vows of allegiance, which, as a liege-subject'——

But King Richard was gone also, and no one knew whither. At length it was learned that he had hastened to the court-yard, summoned to his presence the Jew who had spoken with Ivanhoe, and after a moment's speech with him, had called vehemently to horse, thrown himself upon a steed, compelled the Jew to mount another, and set off at a rate, which, according to Wamba, rendered the old Jew's neck not worth a penny's purchase.

'By my halidome!' said Athelstane, 'it is certain that Zernebock hath possessed himself of my castle in my absence. I return in my grave-clothes, a pledge restored from the very sepulchre, and every one I speak to vanishes as soon as they hear my voice!—But it skills not talking of it. Come, my friends—such of you as are left, follow me to the banquet-hall, lest any more of us disappear—it is, I trust, as yet tolerably furnished, as becomes the obsequies of an ancient Saxon noble; and should we tarry any longer, who knows but the devil may fly off with the supper?'

CHAPTER XLIII

Be Mowbray's sins heavy in his bosom,
That they may break his foaming courser's back,
And throw the rider headlong in the lists,
A caitiff recreant!

*Richard II**

OUR scene now returns to the exterior of the Castle, or Preceptory, of Templestowe, about the hour when the bloody die was to be cast for the life or death of Rebecca. It was a scene of bustle and life, as if the whole vicinity had poured forth its inhabitants to a village wake, or rural feast. But the earnest desire to look on blood and death, is not peculiar to those dark ages; though in the gladiatorial exercise of single combat and general tourney, they were habituated to the bloody spectacle of brave men falling by each other's hands. Even in our own days, when morals are better understood, an execution, a bruising match, a riot, or a meeting of radical reformers, collects, at considerable hazard to themselves, immense crowds of spectators, otherwise little interested, except to see how matters are to be conducted, or whether the heroes of the day are, in the heroic language of insurgent tailors, flints or dunghills.*

The eyes, therefore, of a very considerable multitude, were bent on the gate of the Preceptory of Templestowe, with the purpose of witnessing the procession; while still greater numbers had already surrounded the tiltyard belonging to that establishment. This enclosure was formed on a piece of level ground adjoining to the Preceptory, which had been levelled with care, for the exercise of military and chivalrous sports. It occupied the brow of a soft and gentle eminence, was carefully palisaded around, and, as the Templars willingly invited spectators to be witnesses of their skill in feats of chivalry, was amply supplied with galleries and benches for their use.

On the present occasion, a throne was erected for the Grand Master at the east end, surrounded with seats of distinction for the Preceptors and Knights of the Order. Over these floated the sacred standard, called *Le Beau-seant*, which was the ensign, as its name was the battle-cry, of the Templars.

At the opposite end of the lists was a pile of faggots, so arranged around a stake, deeply fixed in the ground, as to leave a space for the victim whom they were destined to consume, to enter within the fatal circle, in order to be chained to the stake by the fetters which hung ready for that purpose. Beside this deadly apparatus stood four black slaves, whose colour and African features, then so little known in England, appalled the multitude, who gazed on them as on demons employed about their own diabolical exercises. These men stirred not, excepting now and then, under the direction of one who seemed their chief, to shift and replace the ready fuel. They looked not on the multitude. In fact, they seemed insensible of their presence, and of every thing save the discharge of their own horrible duty. And when, in speech with each other, they expanded their blubber lips, and showed their white fangs, as if they grinned at the thoughts of the expected tragedy, the startled commons could scarcely help believing that they were actually the familiar spirits with whom the witch had communed, and who, her time being out, stood ready to assist in her dreadful punishment. They whispered to each other, and enumerated all the feats which Satan had performed during that busy and unhappy period, not failing, of course, to give the devil rather more than his due.

'Have you not heard, Father Dennet,' quoth one boor to another advanced in years, 'that the devil has carried away bodily the great Saxon Thane, Athelstane of Coningsburgh?'

'Ay, but he brought him back though, by the blessing of God and Saint Dunstan.'

'How's that?' said a brisk young fellow, dressed in a green cassock embroidered with gold, and having at his heels a stout lad bearing a harp upon his back, which betrayed his vocation. The Minstrel seemed of no vulgar rank; for, besides the splendour of his gayly broidered doublet, he wore around his neck a silver chain, by which hung the *wrest*, or key, with which he tuned his harp. On his right arm was a silver plate, which, instead of bearing, as usual, the cognizance or badge of the baron to whose family he belonged, had barely the word SHERWOOD engraved upon it.—'How mean you by that?' said the gay Minstrel, mingling in the conversation of the peasants; 'I came to seek one subject for my rhyme, and, by'r Lady, I were glad to find two.'

'It is well avouched,' said the elder peasant, 'that after Athelstane of Coningsburgh had been dead four weeks'——

'That is impossible,' said the Minstrel; 'I saw him in life at the Passage of Arms at Ashby-de-la-Zouch.'

'Dead, however, he was, or else translated,'* said the younger peasant; 'for I heard the Monks of Saint Edmund's singing the death's hymn for him; and, moreover, there was a rich death-meal and dole at the Castle of Coningsburgh, as right was; and thither had I gone, but for Mabel Parkins, who'——

'Ay, dead was Athelstane,' said the old man, shaking his head, 'and the more pity it was, for the old Saxon blood'——

'But, your story, my masters—your story,' said the Minstrel, somewhat impatiently.

'Ay, ay—construe us the story,' said a burly Friar, who stood beside them, leaning on a pole that exhibited an appearance between a pilgrim's staff and a quarter-staff, and probably acted as either when occasion served,—'Your story,' said the stalwart churchman; 'burn not daylight about it—we have short time to spare.'

'An please your reverence,' said Dennet, 'a druken priest came to visit the Sacristan at Saint Edmund's'——

'It does not please my reverence,' answered the churchman, 'that there should be such an animal as a drunken priest, or, if there were, that a layman should so speak him. Be mannerly, my friend, and conclude the holy man only wrapt in meditation, which makes the head dizzy and foot unsteady, as if the stomach were filled with new wine—I have felt it myself.'

'Well, then,' answered Father Dennet, 'a holy brother came to visit the Sacristan at Saint Edmund's—a sort of hedge-priest is the visitor, and kills half the deer that are stolen in the forest, who loves the tinkling of a pint-pot better than the sacring-bell,* and deems a flitch of bacon worth ten of his breviary; for the rest, a good fellow and a merry, who will flourish a quarter-staff, draw a bow, and dance a Cheshire round,* with e'er a man in Yorkshire.'

'That last part of thy speech, Dennet,' said the Minstrel, 'has saved thee a rib or twain.'

'Tush, man, I fear him not,' said Dennet; 'I am somewhat old and stiff, but when I fought for the bell and ram at Doncaster'——

'But the story—the story, my friend,' again said the Minstrel.

'Why, the tale is but this—Athelstane of Coningsburgh was buried at Saint Edmund's.'

'That's a lie, and a loud one,' said the Friar, 'for I saw him borne to his own Castle of Coningsburgh.'

'Nay, then, e'en tell the story yourself, my masters,' said Dennet, turning sulky at these repeated contradictions; and it was with some difficulty that the boor could be prevailed on, by the request of his comrade and the Minstrel, to renew his tale.—— 'These two *sober* friars,' said he at length, 'since this reverend man will needs have them such, had continued drinking good ale, and wine, and what not, for the best part of a summer's day, when they were aroused by a deep groan, and a clanking of chains, and the figure of the deceased Athelstane entered the apartment, saying, "Ye evil shepherds!" '——

'It is false,' said the Friar, hastily, 'he never spoke a word.'

'So ho! Friar Tuck,' said the Minstrel, drawing him apart from the rustics; 'we have started a new hare, I find.'

'I tell thee, Allan-a-Dale,' said the Hermit, 'I saw Athelstane of Coningsburgh as much as bodily eyes ever saw a living man. He had his shroud on, and all about him smelt of the sepulchre— A butt of sack will not wash it out of my memory.'

'Pshaw!' answered the Minstrel; 'thou dost but jest with me!'

'Never believe me,' said the Friar, 'an I fetched not a knock at him with my quarter-staff that would have felled an ox, and it glided through his body as it might through a pillar of smoke!'

'By Saint Hubert,' said the Minstrel, 'but it is a wondrous tale, and fit to be put in metre to the ancient tune, "Sorrow came to the old Friar." '

'Laugh, if ye list,' said Friar Tuck; 'but an ye catch me singing on such a theme, may the next ghost or devil carry me off with him headlong! No, no—I instantly formed the purpose of assisting at some good work, such as the burning of a witch, a judicial combat, or the like matter of godly service, and therefore am I here.'

As they thus conversed, the heavy bell of the church of Saint Michael of Templestowe, a venerable building, situated in a hamlet at some distance from the Preceptory, broke short their argument. One by one the sullen sounds fell successively on the ear, leaving but sufficient space for each to die away in distant echo, ere the air was again filled by repetition of the iron knell. These sounds, the signal of the approaching ceremony, chilled with awe the hearts of the assembled multitude, whose eyes were now turned to the Preceptory, expecting the approach of the Grand Master, the champion, and the criminal.

At length the drawbridge fell, the gates opened, and a knight, bearing the great standard of the Order, sallied from the castle, preceded by six trumpets, and followed by the Knights Preceptors, two and two, the Grand Master coming last, mounted on a stately horse, whose furniture was of the simplest kind. Behind him came Brian de Bois-Guilbert, armed cap-a-pie in bright armour, but without his lance, shield, and sword, which were borne by his two esquires behind him. His face, though partly hidden by a long plume which floated down from his barret-cap,* bore a strong and mingled expression of passion, in which pride seemed to contend with irresolution. He looked ghastly pale, as if he had not slept for several nights, yet reined his pawing war-horse with the habitual ease and grace proper to the best lance of the Order of the Temple. His general appearance was grand and commanding; but, looking at him with attention, men read that in his dark features, from which they willingly withdrew their eyes.

On either side rode Conrade of Mont-Fitchet, and Albert de Malvoisin, who acted as godfathers to the champion. They were in their robes of peace, the white dress of the Order. Behind them followed other Companions of the Temple, with a long train of esquires and pages clad in black, aspirants to the honour of being one day Knights of the Order. After these neophytes came a guard of warders on foot, in the same sable livery, amidst whose partisans might be seen the pale form of the accused, moving with a slow but undismayed step towards the scene of her fate. She was stript of all her ornaments, lest perchance there should be among them some of those amulets which Satan was supposed to bestow upon his victims, to deprive them of the power of confession even when under the torture. A coarse white dress, of the simplest form, had been substituted for her Oriental garments; yet there was such an exquisite mixture of courage and resignation in her look, that even in this garb, and with no other ornament than her long black tresses, each eye wept that looked upon her, and the most hardened bigot regretted the fate that had converted a creature so goodly into a vessel of wrath,* and a waged slave of the devil.

A crowd of inferior personages belonging to the Preceptory followed the victim, all moving with the utmost order, with arms folded, and looks bent upon the ground.

This slow procession moved up the gentle eminence, on the summit of which was the tiltyard, and, entering the lists, marched once around them from right to left, and when they had completed the circle, made a halt. There was then a momentary bustle, while the Grand Master and all his attendants, excepting the champion and his godfathers, dismounted from their horses, which were immediately removed out of the lists by the esquires, who were in attendance for that purpose.

The unfortunate Rebecca was conducted to the black chair placed near the pile. On her first glance at the terrible spot where preparations were making for a death alike dismaying to the mind and painful to the body, she was observed to shudder and shut her eyes, praying internally doubtless, for her lips moved though no speech was heard. In the space of a minute she opened her eyes, looked fixedly on the pile as if to familiarize her mind with the object, and then slowly and naturally turned away her head.

Meanwhile, the Grand Master had assumed his seat; and when the chivalry of his order was placed around and behind him, each in his due rank, a loud and long flourish of the trumpets announced that the Court were seated for judgment. Malvoisin, then, acting as godfather of the champion, stepped forward, and laid the glove of the Jewess, which was the pledge of battle, at the feet of the Grand Master.

'Valorous Lord, and reverend Father,' said he, 'here standeth the good Knight, Brian de Bois-Guilbert, Knight Preceptor of the Order of the Temple, who, by accepting the pledge of battle which I now lay at your reverence's feet, hath become bound to do his devoir in combat this day, to maintain that this Jewish maiden, by name Rebecca, hath justly deserved the doom passed upon her in a Chapter of this most Holy Order of the Temple of Zion, condemning her to die as a sorceress;—here, I say, he standeth, such battle to do, knightly and honourable, if such be your noble and sanctified pleasure.'

'Hath he made oath,' said the Grand Master, 'that his quarrel is just and honourable? Bring forward the Crucifix and the *Te igitur*.'*

'Sir, and most reverend father,' answered Malvoisin, readily, 'our brother here present hath already sworn to the truth of his accusation in the hand of the good Knight Conrade de Mont-Fitchet; and otherwise he ought not to be sworn, seeing that his adversary is an unbeliever, and may take no oath.'

This explanation was satisfactory, to Albert's great joy; for the wily knight had foreseen the great difficulty, or rather impossibility, of prevailing upon Brian de Bois-Guilbert to take such an oath before the assembly, and had invented this excuse to escape the necessity of his doing so.

The Grand Master, having allowed the apology of Albert Malvoisin, commanded the herald to stand forth and do his devoir. The trumpets then again flourished, and a herald, stepping forward, proclaimed aloud,—'Oyez, oyez, oyez.— Here standeth the good Knight, Sir Brian de Bois-Guilbert, ready to do battle with any knight of free blood, who will sustain the quarrel allowed and allotted to the Jewess Rebecca, to try by champion, in respect of lawful essoine* of her own body; and to such champion the reverend and valorous Grand Master here present allows a fair field, and equal partition of sun and wind, and whatever else appertains to a fair combat.' The trumpets again sounded, and there was a dead pause of many minutes.

'No champion appears for the appellant,' said the Grand Master. 'Go, herald, and ask her whether she expects any one to do battle for her in this her cause.' The herald went to the chair in which Rebecca was seated, and Bois-Guilbert suddenly turning his horse's head toward that end of the lists, in spite of hints on either side from Malvoisin and Mont-Fitchet, was by the side of Rebecca's chair as soon as the herald.

'Is this regular, and according to the law of combat?' said Malvoisin, looking to the Grand Master.

'Albert de Malvoisin, it is,' answered Beaumanoir; 'for in this appeal to the judgment of God, we may not prohibit parties from having that communication with each other, which may best tend to bring forth the truth of the quarrel.'

In the meantime, the herald spoke to Rebecca in these terms:—'Damsel, the Honourable and Reverend the Grand Master demands of thee, if thou art prepared with a champion to do battle this day in thy behalf, or if thou dost yield thee as one justly condemned to a deserved doom?'

'Say to the Grand Master,' replied Rebecca, 'that I maintain my innocence, and do not yield me as justly condemned, lest I become guilty of mine own blood. Say to him, that I challenge such delay as his forms will permit, to see if God, whose opportunity is in man's extremity, will raise me up a deliverer; and when such uttermost space is passed, may His holy will be done!' The herald retired to carry this answer to the Grand Master.

'God forbid,' said Lucas Beaumanoir, 'that Jew or Pagan should impeach us of injustice!—Until the shadows be cast from the west to the eastward, will we wait to see if a champion shall appear for this unfortunate woman. When the day is so far passed, let her prepare for death.'

The herald communicated the words of the Grand Master to Rebecca, who bowed her head submissively, folded her arms, and, looking up towards heaven, seemed to expect that aid from above which she could scarce promise herself from man. During this awful pause, the voice of Bois-Guilbert broke upon her ear—it was but a whisper, yet it startled her more than the summons of the herald had appeared to do.

'Rebecca,' said the Templar, 'dost thou hear me?'

'I have no portion in thee, cruel, hard-hearted man,' said the unfortunate maiden.

'Ay, but dost thou understand my words?' said the Templar; 'for the sound of my voice is frightful in mine own ears. I scarce know on what ground we stand, or for what purpose they have

brought us hither.—This listed space—that chair—these faggots—I know their purpose, and yet it appears to me like something unreal—the fearful picture of a vision, which appals my
sense with hideous fantasies, but convinces not my reason.'

'My mind and senses keep touch and time,' answered
Rebecca, 'and tell me alike that these faggots are destined to
consume my earthly body, and open a painful but a brief passage
to a better world.'

'Dreams, Rebecca,—dreams,' answered the Templar; 'idle
visions, rejected by the wisdom of your own wiser Sadducees.*
Hear me, Rebecca,' he said, proceeding with animation; 'a better
chance hast thou for life and liberty than yonder knaves and
dotard dream of. Mount thee behind me on my steed—on
Zamor, the gallant horse that never failed his rider. I won him in
single fight from the Soldan of Trebizond*—mount, I say, behind me—in one short hour is pursuit and enquiry far behind—
a new world of pleasure opens to thee—to me a new career of
fame. Let them speak the doom which I despise, and erase the
name of Bois-Guilbert from their list of monastic slaves! I will
wash out with blood whatever blot they may dare to cast on my
scutcheon.'

'Tempter,' said Rebecca, 'begone!—Not in this last extremity
canst thou move me one hair's-breadth from my resting place—
surrounded as I am by foes, I hold thee as my worst and most
deadly enemy—avoid thee, in the name of God!'

Albert Malvoisin, alarmed and impatient at the duration of
their conference, now advanced to interrupt it.

'Hath the maiden acknowledged her guilt?' he demanded of
Bois-Guilbert; 'or is she resolute in her denial?'

'She is indeed *resolute*,' said Bois-Guilbert.

'Then,' said Malvoisin, 'must thou, noble brother, resume thy
place to attend the issue—The shades are changing on the circle
of the dial—Come, brave Bois-Guilbert—come, thou hope of
our holy Order, and soon to be its head.'

As he spoke in this soothing tone, he laid his hand on the
knight's bridle, as if to lead him back to his station.

'False villain! what meanest thou by thy hand on my rein?'
said Sir Brian, angrily. And shaking off his companion's grasp,
he rode back to the upper end of the lists.

'There is yet spirit in him,' said Malvoisin apart to Mont-Fitchet, 'were it well directed—but, like the Greek fire,* it burns whatever approaches it.'

The Judges had now been two hours in the lists, awaiting in vain the appearance of a champion.

'And reason good,' said Friar Tuck, 'seeing she is a Jewess—and yet, by mine Order, it is hard that so young and beautiful a creature should perish without one blow being struck in her behalf! Were she ten times a witch, provided she were but the least bit of a Christian, my quarter-staff should ring noon on the steel cap of yonder fierce Templar, ere he carried the matter off thus.'

It was, however, the general belief that no one could or would appear for a Jewess, accused of sorcery; and the knights, insti-gated by Malvoisin, whispered to each other, that it was time to declare the pledge of Rebecca forfeited. At this instant a knight, urging his horse to speed, appeared on the plain advancing towards the lists. A hundred voices exclaimed, 'A champion! a champion!' And despite the prepossessions and prejudices of the multitude, they shouted unanimously as the knight rode into the tiltyard. The second glance, however, served to destroy the hope that his timely arrival had excited. His horse, urged for many miles to its utmost speed, appeared to reel from fatigue, and the rider, however undauntedly he presented himself in the lists, either from weakness, weariness, or both, seemed scarce able to support himself in the saddle.

To the summons of the herald, who demanded his rank, his name, and purpose, the stranger knight answered readily and boldly, 'I am a good knight and noble, come hither to sustain with lance and sword the just and lawful quarrel of this damsel, Rebecca, daughter of Isaac of York; to uphold the doom pro-nounced against her to be false and truthless, and to defy Sir Brian de Bois-Guilbert, as a traitor, murderer, and liar; as I will prove in this field with my body against his, by the aid of God, of Our Lady, and of Monseigneur Saint George, the good knight.'

'The stranger must first show,' said Malvoisin, 'that he is good knight, and of honourable lineage. The Temple sendeth not forth her champions against nameless men.'

'My name,' said the Knight, raising his helmet, 'is better known, my lineage more pure, Malvoisin, than thine own. I am Wilfred of Ivanhoe.'

'I will not fight with thee at present,' said the Templar, in a changed and hollow voice. 'Get thy wounds healed, purvey thee a better horse, and it may be I will hold it worth my while to scourge out of thee this boyish spirit of bravade.'

'Ha! proud Templar,' said Ivanhoe, 'hast thou forgotten that twice didst thou fall before this lance? Remember the lists at Acre—remember the Passage of Arms at Ashby—remember thy proud vaunt in the halls of Rotherwood, and the gage of your gold chain against my reliquary, that thou wouldst do battle with Wilfred of Ivanhoe, and recover the honour thou hadst lost! By that reliquary, and the holy relic it contains, I will proclaim thee, Templar, a coward in every court in Europe—in every Preceptory of thine Order—unless thou do battle without farther delay.'

Bois-Guilbert turned his countenance irresolutely towards Rebecca, and then exclaimed, looking fiercely at Ivanhoe, 'Dog of a Saxon! take thy lance, and prepare for the death thou hast drawn upon thee!'

'Does the Grand Master allow me the combat?' said Ivanhoe.

'I may not deny what thou hast challenged,' said the Grand Master, 'provided the maiden accepts thee as her champion. Yet I would thou wert in better plight to do battle. An enemy of our Order hast thou ever been, yet would I have thee honourably met with.'

'Thus—thus as I am, and not otherwise,' said Ivanhoe; 'it is the judgment of God—to his keeping I commend myself.— Rebecca,' said he, riding up to the fatal chair, 'dost thou accept of me for thy champion?'

'I do,' she said—'I do,' fluttered by an emotion which the fear of death had been unable to produce, 'I do accept thee as the champion whom Heaven hath sent me. Yet, no—no—thy wounds are uncured—Meet not that proud man—why shouldst thou perish also?'

But Ivanhoe was already at his post, and had closed his visor, and assumed his lance. Bois-Guilbert did the same; and his esquire remarked, as he clasped his visor, that his face, which had, notwithstanding the variety of emotions by which he had been agitated, continued during the whole morning of an ashy paleness, was now become suddenly very much flushed.

The herald, then, seeing each champion in his place, uplifted his voice, repeating thrice—*Faites vos devoirs, preux chevaliers!** After the third cry, he withdrew to one side of the lists, and again proclaimed, that none, on peril of instant death, should dare, by word, cry, or action, to interfere with or disturb this fair field of combat. The Grand Master, who held in his hand the gage of battle, Rebecca's glove, now threw it into the lists, and pronounced the fatal signal words, *Laissez aller.*

The trumpets sounded, and the knights charged each other in full career. The wearied horse of Ivanhoe, and its no less exhausted rider, went down, as all had expected, before the well-aimed lance and vigorous steed of the Templar. This issue of the combat all had foreseen; but although the spear of Ivanhoe did but, in comparison, touch the shield of Bois-Guilbert, that champion, to the astonishment of all who beheld it, reeled in his saddle, lost his stirrups, and fell in the lists.

Ivanhoe, extricating himself from his fallen horse, was soon on foot, hastening to mend his fortune* with his sword; but his antagonist arose not. Wilfred, placing his foot on his breast, and the sword's point to his throat, commanded him to yield him, or die on the spot. Bois-Guilbert returned no answer.

'Slay him not, Sir Knight,' cried the Grand Master, 'unshriven and unabsolved—kill not body and soul! We allow him vanquished.'

He descended into the lists, and commanded them to unhelm the conquered champion. His eyes were closed—the dark red flush was still on his brow. As they looked on him in astonishment, the eyes opened—but they were fixed and glazed. The flush passed from his brow, and gave way to the pallid hue of death. Unscathed by the lance of his enemy, he had died a victim to the violence of his own contending passions.*

'This is indeed the judgment of God,' said the Grand Master, looking upwards—'*Fiat voluntas tua!*'*

CHAPTER XLIV

So! now 'tis ended, like an old wife's story.

WEBSTER*

WHEN the first moments of surprise were over, Wilfred of Ivanhoe demanded of the Grand Master, as judge of the field, if he had manfully and rightfully done his duty in the combat?

'Manfully and rightfully hath it been done,' said the Grand Master; 'I pronounce the maiden free and guiltless—The arms and the body of the deceased knight are at the will of the victor.'

'I will not despoil him of his weapons,' said the Knight of Ivanhoe, 'nor condemn his corpse to shame—he hath fought for Christendom—God's arm, no human hand, hath this day struck him down. But let his obsequies be private, as becomes those of a man who died in an unjust quarrel.—And for the maiden'——

He was interrupted by a clattering of horses' feet, advancing in such numbers, and so rapidly, as to shake the ground before them; and the Black Knight galloped into the lists. He was followed by a numerous band of men-at-arms, and several knights in complete armour.

'I am too late,' he said, looking around him. 'I had doomed Bois-Guilbert for mine own property.—Ivanhoe, was this well, to take on thee such a venture, and thou scarce able to keep thy saddle?'

'Heaven, my Liege,' answered Ivanhoe, 'hath taken this proud man for its victim. He was not to be honoured in dying as your will had designed.'

'Peace be with him,' said Richard, looking steadfastly on the corpse, 'if it may be so—he was a gallant knight, and has died in his steel harness full knightly. But we must waste no time— Bohun, do thine office!'

A Knight stepped forward from the King's attendants, and, laying his hand on the shoulder of Albert de Malvoisin, said, 'I arrest thee of High Treason.'

The Grand Master had hitherto stood astonished at the appearance of so many warriors.—He now spoke.

'Who dares to arrest a Knight of the Temple of Zion, within the girth of his own Preceptory, and in the presence of the Grand Master? and by whose authority is this bold outrage offered?'

'I make the arrest,' replied the Knight—'I, Henry Bohun, Earl of Essex, Lord High Constable of England.'*

'And he arrests Malvoisin,' said the King, raising his visor, 'by the order of Richard Plantagenet, here present.—Conrade Mont-Fitchet, it is well for thee thou art born no subject of mine.—But for thee, Malvoisin, thou diest with thy brother Philip, ere the world be a week older.'

'I will resist thy doom,' said the Grand Master.

'Proud Templar,' said the King, 'thou canst not—look up, and behold the Royal Standard of England floats over thy towers instead of thy Temple banner!—Be wise, Beaumanoir, and make no bootless opposition—Thy hand is in the lion's mouth.'

'I will appeal to Rome against thee,' said the Grand Master, 'for usurpation on the immunities and privileges of our Order.'

'Be it so,' said the King; 'but for thine own sake tax me not with usurpation now. Dissolve thy Chapter, and depart with thy followers to thy next Preceptory, (if thou canst find one,) which has not been made the scene of treasonable conspiracy against the King of England—Or, if thou wilt, remain, to share our hospitality, and behold our justice.'

'To be a guest in the house where I should command?' said the Templar; 'never!—Chaplains, raise the Psalm, *Quare fremuerunt Gentes?*—Knights, squires, and followers of the Holy Temple, prepare to follow the banner of *Beau-seant!*'

The Grand Master spoke with a dignity which confronted even that of England's king himself, and inspired courage into his surprised and dismayed followers. They gathered around him like the sheep around the watch-dog, when they hear the baying of the wolf. But they evinced not the timidity of the scared flock—there were dark brows of defiance, and looks which menaced the hostility they dared not to proffer in words. They drew together in a dark line of spears, from which the white cloaks of the knights were visible among the dusky garments of their retainers, like the lighter-coloured edges of a sable cloud. The multitude, who had raised a clamorous shout of reprobation, paused and gazed in silence on the formidable and experienced body to which they had unwarily bade defiance, and shrunk back from their front.

The Earl of Essex, when he beheld them pause in their assembled force, dashed the rowels into his charger's sides, and galloped backwards and forwards to array his followers, in opposition to a band so formidable. Richard alone, as if he loved the danger his presence had provoked, rode slowly along the front of the Templars, calling aloud, 'What, sirs! Among so many gallant knights, will none dare splinter a spear with Richard?—Sirs of the Temple! your ladies are but sun-burned, if they are not worth the shiver of a broken lance?'

'The Brethren of the Temple,' said the Grand Master, riding forward in advance of their body, 'fight not on such idle and profane quarrel—and not with thee, Richard of England, shall a Templar cross lance in my presence. The Pope and Princes of Europe shall judge our quarrel, and whether a Christian prince has done well in bucklering the cause which thou hast to-day adopted. If unassailed, we depart assailing no one. To thine honour we refer the armour and household goods of the Order which we leave behind us, and on thy conscience we lay the scandal and offence thou hast this day given to Christendom.'

With these words, and without waiting a reply, the Grand Master gave the signal of departure. Their trumpets sounded a wild march, of an Oriental character, which formed the usual signal for the Templars to advance. They changed their array from a line to a column of march, and moved off as slowly as their horses could step, as if to show it was only the will of their Grand Master, and no fear of the opposing and superior force, which compelled them to withdraw.

'By the splendour of Our Lady's brow!' said King Richard, 'it is pity of their lives that these Templars are not so trusty as they are disciplined and valiant.'

The multitude, like a timid cur which waits to bark till the object of its challenge has turned his back, raised a feeble shout as the rear of the squadron left the ground.

During the tumult which attended the retreat of the Templars, Rebecca saw and heard nothing—she was locked in the arms of her aged father, giddy, and almost senseless, with the rapid change of circumstances around her. But one word from Isaac at length recalled her scattered feelings.

'Let us go,' he said, 'my dear daughter, my recovered treasure—let us go to throw ourselves at the feet of the good youth.'

'Not so,' said Rebecca, 'O no—no—no—I must not at this moment dare to speak to him—Alas! I should say more than—— No, my father, let us instantly leave this evil place.'

'But, my daughter,' said Isaac, 'to leave him who hath come forth like a strong man with his spear and shield, holding his life as nothing, so he might redeem thy captivity; and thou, too, the daughter of a people strange unto him and his—this is service to be thankfully acknowledged.'

'It is—it is—most thankfully—most devoutly acknowledged,' said Rebecca—'it shall be still more so—but not now—for the sake of thy beloved Rachel, father, grant my request—not now!'

'Nay, but,' said Isaac, insisting, 'they will deem us more thankless than mere dogs!'

'But thou seest, my dear father, that King Richard is in presence, and that'——

'True, my best—my wisest Rebecca!—Let us hence—let us hence!—Money he will lack, for he has just returned from Palestine, and, as they say, from prison—and pretext for exacting it, should he need any, may arise out of my simple traffic with his brother John. Away, away, let us hence!'

And hurrying his daughter in his turn, he conducted her from the lists, and by means of conveyance which he had provided, transported her safely to the house of the Rabbi Nathan.

The Jewess, whose fortunes had formed the principal interest of the day, having now retired unobserved, the attention of the populace was transferred to the Black Knight. They now filled the air with 'Long life to Richard with the Lion's Heart, and down with the usurping Templars!'

'Notwithstanding all this lip-loyalty,' said Ivanhoe to the Earl of Essex, 'it was well the King took the precaution to bring thee with him, noble Earl, and so many of thy trusty followers.'

The Earl smiled and shook his head.

'Gallant Ivanhoe,' said Essex, 'dost thou know our Master so well, and yet suspect him of taking so wise a precaution! I was drawing towards York, having heard that Prince John was making head there, when I met King Richard, like a true knight-errant, galloping hither to achieve in his own person this adventure of the Templar and the Jewess, with his own single arm. I accompanied him with my band, almost maugre* his consent.'

'And what news from York, brave Earl?' said Ivanhoe; 'will the rebels bide us there?'

'No more than December's snow will bide July's sun,' said the Earl; 'they are dispersing; and who should come posting to bring us the news, but John himself!'

'The traitor! the ungrateful insolent traitor!' said Ivanhoe; 'did not Richard order him into confinement?'

'O! he received him,' answered the Earl, 'as if they had met after a hunting party; and, pointing to me and our men-at-arms, said, "Thou seest, brother, I have some angry men with me—thou wert best go to our mother, carry her my duteous affection, and abide with her until men's minds are pacified."'

'And this was all he said?' enquired Ivanhoe; 'would not any one say that this Prince invites men to treason by his clemency?'

'Just,' replied the Earl, 'as the man may be said to invite death, who undertakes to fight a combat, having a dangerous wound unhealed.'

'I forgive thee the jest, Lord Earl,' said Ivanhoe; 'but, remember, I hazarded but my own life—Richard, the welfare of his kingdom.'

'Those,' replied Essex, 'who are specially careless of their own welfare, are seldom remarkably attentive to that of others—But let us haste to the castle, for Richard meditates punishing some of the subordinate members of the conspiracy, though he has pardoned their principal.'

From the judicial investigations which followed on this occasion, and which are given at length in the Wardour Manuscript, it appears that Maurice de Bracy escaped beyond seas, and went into the service of Philip of France; while Philip de Malvoisin, and his brother Albert, the Preceptor of Templestowe, were executed, although Waldemar Fitzurse, the soul of the conspiracy, escaped with banishment; and Prince John, for whose behoof it was undertaken, was not even censured by his good-natured brother.* No one, however, pitied the fate of the two Malvoisins, who only suffered the death which they had both well deserved, by many acts of falsehood, cruelty, and oppression.

Briefly after the judicial combat, Cedric the Saxon was summoned to the court of Richard, which, for the purpose of quieting the counties that had been disturbed by the ambition of his brother, was then held at York. Cedric tushed and pshawed more than once at the message—but he refused not obedience. In fact, the return of Richard had quenched every hope that he had entertained of restoring a Saxon dynasty in England; for, whatever head the Saxons might have made in the event of a civil war, it was plain that nothing could be done under the undisputed dominion of Richard, popular as he was by his personal good qualities and military fame, although his administration was wilfully careless, now too indulgent, and now allied to despotism.

But, moreover, it could not escape even Cedric's reluctant observation, that his project for an absolute union among the Saxons, by the marriage of Rowena and Athelstane, was now completely at an end, by the mutual dissent of both parties concerned. This was, indeed, an event which, in his ardour for the Saxon cause, he could not have anticipated, and even when the disinclination of both was broadly and plainly manifested, he could scarce bring himself to believe that two Saxons of royal descent should scruple, on personal grounds, at an alliance so necessary for the public weal of the nation. But it was not the less certain: Rowena had always expressed her repugnance to Athelstane, and now Athelstane was no less plain and positive in proclaiming his resolution never to pursue his addresses to the Lady Rowena. Even the natural obstinacy of Cedric sunk beneath these obstacles, where he, remaining on the point of junction, had the task of dragging a reluctant pair up to it, one with each hand. He made, however, a last vigorous attack on Athelstane, and he found that resuscitated sprout of Saxon royalty engaged, like country squires of our own day, in a furious war with the clergy.

It seems that, after all his deadly menaces against the Abbot of Saint Edmund's, Athelstane's spirit of revenge, what between the natural indolent kindness of his own disposition, what through the prayers of his mother Edith, attached, like most ladies, (of the period,) to the clerical order, had terminated in his keeping the Abbot and his monks in the dungeons of Coningsburgh for three days on a meagre diet. For this atrocity the Abbot menaced him with excommunication, and made out a dreadful list of complaints in the bowels and stomach, suffered by himself and his monks, in consequence of the tyrannical and unjust imprisonment they had sustained. With this controversy, and with the means he had adopted to counteract this clerical persecution, Cedric found the mind of his friend Athelstane so fully occupied, that it had no room for another idea. And when Rowena's name was mentioned, the noble Athelstane prayed leave to quaff a full goblet to her health, and that she might soon be the bride of his kinsman Wilfred. It was a desperate case therefore. There was obviously no more to be made of Athelstane; or, as Wamba expressed it, in a phrase which has descended from Saxon times to ours, he was a cock that would not fight.*

There remained betwixt Cedric and the determination which the lovers desired to come to, only two obstacles—his own obstinacy, and his dislike of the Norman dynasty. The former feeling gradually gave way before the endearments of his ward, and the pride which he could not help nourishing in the fame of his son. Besides, he was not insensible to the honour of allying his own line to that of Alfred, when the superior claims of the descendant of Edward the Confessor were abandoned for ever. Cedric's aversion to the Norman race of kings was also much undermined,—first, by consideration of the impossibility of ridding England of the new dynasty, a feeling which goes far to create loyalty in the subject to the king *de facto*; and, secondly, by the personal attention of King Richard, who delighted in the blunt humour of Cedric, and, to use the language of the Wardour Manuscript, so dealt with the noble Saxon, that, ere he had been a guest at court for seven days, he had given his consent to the marriage of his ward Rowena and his son Wilfred of Ivanhoe.

The nuptials of our hero, thus formally approved by his father, were celebrated in the most august of temples, the noble Minster of York. The King himself attended, and from the countenance which he afforded on this and other occasions to the distressed and hitherto degraded Saxons, gave them a safer and more certain prospect of attaining their just rights, than they could reasonably hope from the precarious chance of a civil war. The Church gave her full solemnities, graced with all the splendour which she of Rome knows how to apply with such brilliant effect.

Gurth, gallantly apparelled, attended as esquire upon his young master whom he had served so faithfully, and the magnanimous Wamba, decorated with a new cap and a most gorgeous set of silver bells. Sharers of Wilfred's dangers and adversity, they remained, as they had a right to expect, the partakers of his more prosperous career.

But besides this domestic retinue, these distinguished nuptials were celebrated by the attendance of the high-born Normans, as well as Saxons, joined with the universal jubilee of the lower orders, that marked the marriage of two individuals as a pledge of the future peace and harmony betwixt two races, which, since that period, have been so completely mingled, that the distinction has become wholly invisible. Cedric lived to see this union approximate towards its completion; for as the two nations mixed in society and formed intermarriages with each other, the Normans abated their scorn, and the Saxons were refined from their rusticity. But it was not until the reign of Edward the Third that the mixed language, now termed English, was spoken at the court of London,* and that the hostile distinction of Norman and Saxon seems entirely to have disappeared.

It was upon the second morning after this happy bridal, that the Lady Rowena was made acquainted by her handmaid Elgitha, that a damsel desired admission to her presence, and solicited that their parley might be without witness. Rowena wondered, hesitated, became curious, and ended by commanding the damsel to be admitted, and her attendants to withdraw.

She entered—a noble and commanding figure, the long white veil, in which she was shrouded, overshadowing rather than concealing the elegance and majesty of her shape. Her demeanour was that of respect, unmingled by the least shade either of fear, or of a wish to propitiate favour. Rowena was ever ready to acknowledge the claims, and attend to the feelings, of others. She arose, and would have conducted her lovely visitor to a seat; but the stranger looked at Elgitha, and again intimated a wish to discourse with the Lady Rowena alone. Elgitha had no sooner retired with unwilling steps, than, to the surprise of the Lady of Ivanhoe, her fair visitant kneeled on one knee, pressed her hands to her forehead, and bending her head to the ground, in spite of Rowena's resistance, kissed the embroidered hem of her tunic.

'What means this, lady?' said the surprised bride; 'or why do you offer to me a deference so unusual?'

'Because to you, Lady of Ivanhoe,' said Rebecca, rising up and resuming the usual quiet dignity of her manner, 'I may lawfully, and without rebuke, pay the debt of gratitude which I owe to Wilfred of Ivanhoe. I am—forgive the boldness which has offered to you the homage of my country—I am the unhappy Jewess, for whom your husband hazarded his life against such fearful odds in the tiltyard of Templestowe.'

'Damsel,' said Rowena, 'Wilfred of Ivanhoe on that day rendered back but in slight measure your unceasing charity towards him in his wounds and misfortunes. Speak, is there aught remains in which he or I can serve thee?'

'Nothing,' said Rebecca, calmly, 'unless you will transmit to him my grateful farewell.'

'You leave England, then?' said Rowena, scarce recovering the surprise of this extraordinary visit.

'I leave it, lady, ere this moon again changes. My father hath a brother high in favour with Mohammed Boabdil, King of Grenada—thither we go, secure of peace and protection, for the payment of such ransom as the Moslem exact from our people.'

'And are you not then as well protected in England?' said Rowena. 'My husband has favour with the King—the King himself is just and generous.'

'Lady,' said Rebecca, 'I doubt it not—but the people of England are a fierce race, quarrelling ever with their neighbours or among themselves, and ready to plunge the sword into the bowels of each other. Such is no safe abode for the children of my people. Ephraim is an heartless dove—Issachar an overlaboured drudge, which stoops between two burdens.* Not in a land of war and blood, surrounded by hostile neighbours, and distracted by internal factions, can Israel hope to rest during her wanderings.'

'But you, maiden,' said Rowena—'you surely can have nothing to fear. She who nursed the sickbed of Ivanhoe,' she continued, rising with enthusiasm—'she can have nothing to fear in England, where Saxon and Norman will contend who shall most do her honour.'

'Thy speech is fair, lady,' said Rebecca, 'and thy purpose fairer; but it may not be—there is a gulf betwixt us. Our breeding, our faith, alike forbid either to pass over it. Farewell—yet, ere I go, indulge me one request. The bridal-veil hangs over thy face; deign to raise it, and let me see the features of which fame speaks so highly.'

'They are scarce worthy of being looked upon,' said Rowena; 'but, expecting the same from my visitant, I remove the veil.'

She took it off accordingly; and, partly from the consciousness of beauty, partly from bashfulness, she blushed so intensely, that cheek, brow, neck, and bosom, were suffused with crimson. Rebecca blushed also, but it was a momentary feeling; and, mastered by higher emotions, past slowly from her features like the crimson cloud, which changes colour when the sun sinks beneath the horizon.

'Lady,' she said, 'the countenance you have deigned to show me will long dwell in my remembrance. There reigns in it gentleness and goodness; and if a tinge of the world's pride or vanities may mix with an expression so lovely, how should we chide that which is of earth for bearing some colour of its original? Long, long will I remember your features, and bless God that I leave my noble deliverer united with'——

She stopped short—her eyes filled with tears. She hastily wiped them, and answered to the anxious enquiries of Rowena— 'I am well, lady—well. But my heart swells when I think of Torquilstone and the lists of Templestowe.—Farewell. One, the most trifling part of my duty, remains undischarged. Accept this casket—startle not at its contents.'

Rowena opened the small silver-chased casket, and perceived a carcanet, or necklace, with ear-jewels, of diamonds, which were obviously of immense value.

'It is impossible,' she said, tendering back the casket. 'I dare not accept a gift of such consequence.'

'Yet keep it, lady,' returned Rebecca—'You have power, rank, command, influence; we have wealth, the source both of our strength and weakness; the value of these toys, ten times multiplied, would not influence half so much as your slightest wish. To you, therefore, the gift is of little value,—and to me, what I part with is of much less. Let me not think you deem so wretchedly ill of my nation as your commons believe. Think ye that I prize these sparkling fragments of stone above my liberty? or that my father values them in comparison to the honour of his only child? Accept them, lady—to me they are valueless. I will never wear jewels more.'

'You are then unhappy!' said Rowena, struck with the manner in which Rebecca uttered the last words. 'O, remain with us— the counsel of holy men will wean you from your erring law, and I will be a sister to you.'

'No, lady,' answered Rebecca, the same calm melancholy reigning in her soft voice and beautiful features—'that may not be. I may not change the faith of my fathers like a garment unsuited to the climate in which I seek to dwell, and unhappy, lady, I will not be. He, to whom I dedicate my future life, will be my comforter, if I do His will.'

'Have you then convents, to one of which you mean to retire?' asked Rowena.

'No, lady,' said the Jewess; 'but among our people, since the time of Abraham downwards, have been women who have devoted their thoughts to Heaven, and their actions to works of kindness to men, tending the sick, feeding the hungry, and relieving the distressed. Among these will Rebecca be numbered. Say this to thy lord, should he chance to enquire after the fate of her whose life he saved.'

There was an involuntary tremour on Rebecca's voice, and a tenderness of accent, which perhaps betrayed more than she would willingly have expressed. She hastened to bid Rowena adieu.

'Farewell,' she said. 'May He, who made both Jew and Christian, shower down on you his choicest blessings! The bark that wafts us hence will be under weigh ere we can reach the port.'

She glided from the apartment, leaving Rowena surprised as if a vision had passed before her. The fair Saxon related the singular conference to her husband, on whose mind it made a deep impression. He lived long and happily with Rowena, for they were attached to each other by the bonds of early affection, and they loved each other the more, from the recollection of the obstacles which had impeded their union. Yet it would be enquiring too curiously* to ask, whether the recollection of Rebecca's beauty and magnanimity did not recur to his mind more frequently than the fair descendant of Alfred might altogether have approved.

Ivanhoe distinguished himself in the service of Richard, and was graced with farther marks of the royal favour. He might have risen still higher, but for the premature death of the heroic Cœur-de-Lion, before the Castle of Chaluz, near Limoges.* With the life of a generous, but rash and romantic monarch, perished all the projects which his ambition and his generosity had formed; to whom may be applied, with a slight alteration, the lines composed by Johnson* for Charles of Sweden—

> His fate was destined to a foreign strand,
> A petty fortress and an 'humble' hand;
> He left the name at which the world grew pale,
> To point a moral, or adorn a TALE.

SCOTT'S NOTES

Notes signed 'L.T.' (Laurence Templeton, the supposed editor of the Wardour Manuscript) appeared as footnotes in the first edition of *Ivanhoe*. The other, longer notes were added by Scott in 1830.

1. The motto alludes to the Author returning to the stage repeatedly after having taken leave.

2. This very curious poem, long a *desideratum* in Scottish literature, and given up as irrecoverably lost, was lately brought to light by the researches of Dr Irvine of the Advocates' Library, and has been reprinted by Mr David Laing, Edinburgh.

3. Vol. ii. p. 167.

4. Like the Hermit, the Shepherd makes havock amongst the King's game; but by means of a sling, not of a bow; like the Hermit, too, he has his peculiar phrases of compotation, the sign and countersign being Passelodion and Berafriend. One can scarce conceive what humour our ancestors found in this species of gibberish; but

    'I warrant it proved an excuse for the glass.'

    [Scott quotes from the chorus to the drinking song in Sheridan's *The School for Scandal*, III, iii: 'I'll warrant she'll prove an excuse for a glass'.]

5. The author had revised this posthumous work of Mr Strutt. See General Preface to the present edition, [editor's note].

6. This anticipation proved but too true, as my learned correspondent did not receive my letter until a twelvemonth after it was written. I mention this circumstance, that a gentleman attached to the cause of learning, who now holds the principal control of the post-office, may consider whether by some mitigation of the present enormous rates, some favour might not be shown to the correspondents of the principal Literary and Antiquarian Societies. I understand, indeed, that this experiment was once tried, but that the mail-coach having broke down under the weight of packages addressed to members of the Society of Antiquaries, it was relinquished as a hazardous experiment. Surely, however, it would be possible to build these vehicles in a form more substantial, stronger in the perch, and

broader in the wheels, so as to support the weight of Antiquarian learning; when, if they should be found to travel more slowly, they would be not the less agreeable to quiet travellers like myself.—L. T.

7. Mr Skene of Rubislaw is here intimated, to whose taste and skill the author is indebted for a series of etchings, exhibiting the various localities alluded to in these novels.

[*Mr Skene of Rubislaw*: Scott's close friend James Skene of Rubislaw (1775–1864), advocate, geologist, and antiquarian, had just published *A Series of Sketches of the Existing Localities in the Waverley Novels* (1829). The contemporary revival of the Society of Antiquaries of Scotland owed much to Skene, who had been appointed Curator in 1819. According to Lockhart (*Life of Scott*, ch. 46), Skene's reminiscences of the German ghettos supplied Scott with the idea of including 'a group of Jews' in *Ivanhoe*.]

8. A most sensible grievance of those aggrieved times were the Forest Laws. These oppressive enactments were the produce of the Norman Conquest, for the Saxon laws of the chase were mild and humane; while those of William, enthusiastically attached to the exercise and its rights, were to the last degree tyrannical. The formation of the New Forest bears evidence to his passion for hunting, where he reduced many a happy village to the condition of that one commemorated by my friend, Mr William Stewart Rose,

> 'Amongst the ruins of the church
> The midnight raven found a perch,
>   A melancholy place;
> The ruthless Conqueror cast down,
> Woe worth the deed, that little town,
>   To lengthen out his chase.'

The disabling dogs, which might be necessary for keeping flocks and herds, from running at the deer, was called *lawing*, and was in general use. The Charter of the Forest, designed to lessen those evils, declares that inquisition, or view, for lawing dogs, shall be made every third year, and shall be then done by the view and testimony of lawful men, not otherwise; and they whose dogs shall be then found unlawed, shall give three shillings for mercy; and for the future, no man's ox shall be taken for lawing. Such lawing also shall be done by the assize commonly used, and which is, that three claws shall be cut off without the ball of the right foot. See on this subject the Historical Essay on the Magna Charta of King John, (a most beautiful volume,) by Richard Thomson.

9. The severe accuracy of some critics has objected to the complexion of the slaves of Brian de Bois-Guilbert, as being totally out of costume and propriety. I remember the same objection being made to a set of sable functionaries, whom my friend, Mat Lewis, introduced as the guards and mischief-doing satellites of the wicked Baron, in his Castle Spectre. Mat treated the objection with great contempt, and averred in reply, that he made the slaves black, in order to obtain a striking effect of contrast, and that, could he have derived a similar advantage from making his heroine blue, blue she should have been.

I do not pretend to plead the immunities of my order so highly as this; but neither will I allow that the author of a modern antique romance is obliged to confine himself to the introduction of those manners only which can be proved to have absolutely existed in the times he is depicting, so that he restrain himself to such as are plausible and natural, and contain no obvious anachronism. In this point of view, what can be more natural, than that the Templars, who, we know, copied closely the luxuries of the Asiatic warriors with whom they fought, should use the service of the enslaved Africans, whom the fate of war transferred to new masters? I am sure, if there are no precise proofs of their having done so, there is nothing, on the other hand, that can entitle us positively to conclude that they never did. Besides, there is an instance in romance.

John of Rampayne, an excellent juggler and minstrel, undertook to effect the escape of one Audulf de Bracy, by presenting himself in disguise at the court of the king, where he was confined. For this purpose, 'he stained his hair and his whole body entirely as black as jet, so that nothing was white but his teeth,' and succeeded in imposing himself on the king, as an Ethiopian minstrel. He effected, by stratagem, the escape of the prisoner. Negroes, therefore, must have been known in England in the dark ages.*

* Dissertation on Romance and Minstrelsy, prefixed to Ritson's Ancient Metrical Romances, p. clxxxvii.

10. The original has *Cnichts*, by which the Saxons seem to have designated a class of military attendants, sometimes free, sometimes bondsmen, but always ranking above an ordinary domestic, whether in the royal household or in those of the aldermen and thanes. But the term cnicht, now spelt knight, having been received into the English language as equivalent to the Norman word chevalier, I have avoided using it in its more ancient sense, to prevent confusion.—L. T.

11. These were drinks used by the Saxons, as we are informed by Mr
    Turner: Morat was made of honey flavoured with the juice of
    mulberries; Pigment was a sweet and rich liquor, composed of wine
    highly spiced, and sweetened also with honey; the other liquors
    need no explanation.—L. T.

    [*drinks used by the Saxons*: see Turner, *History*, iii. 32, whose source
    is Henry's *History*, iii. 396.]

12. There was no language which the Normans more formally
    separated from that of common life than the terms of the chase. The
    objects of their pursuit, whether bird or animal, changed their name
    each year, and there were a hundred conventional terms, to be
    ignorant of which was to be without one of the distinguishing marks
    of a gentleman. The reader may consult Dame Juliana Berners'
    book on the subject. The origin of this science was imputed to the
    celebrated Sir Tristrem, famous for his tragic intrigue with the
    beautiful Ysolte. As the Normans reserved the amusement of hunt-
    ing strictly to themselves, the terms of this formal jargon were all
    taken from the French language.

13. In those days the Jews were subjected to an Exchequer, specially
    dedicated to that purpose, and which laid them under the most
    exorbitant impositions.—L. T.

14. This sort of masquerade is supposed to have occasioned the intro-
    duction of supporters into the science of heraldry.

15. These lines are part of an unpublished poem by Coleridge, whose
    muse so often tantalizes with fragments which indicate her powers,
    while the manner in which she flings them from her betrays her
    caprice, yet whose unfinished sketches display more talent than the
    laboured masterpieces of others.

    [*an unpublished poem by Coleridge*: lines 9–11 of Samuel Taylor
    Coleridge, 'The Knight's Tomb: An experiment for a metre'
    (?1817):

    > The knight's bones are dust,
    > And his good sword rust;—
    > His soul is with the saints, I trust.

    Scott had heard Coleridge recite the lines at a dinner-party, and
    their appearance in these pages made Coleridge sure of the identity
    of the Author of *Waverley*.]

16. This term of chivalry transferred to the law, gives the phrase of
    being attainted of treason.

17. Presumption, insolence.

18. *Beau-seant* was the name of the Templars' banner, which was half black, half white, to intimate, it is said, that they were candid and fair towards Christians, but black and terrible towards infidels.

19. There was nothing accounted so ignominious among the Saxons as to merit this disgraceful epithet. Even William the Conqueror, hated as he was by them, continued to draw a considerable army of Anglo-Saxons to his standard, by threatening to stigmatize those who staid at home, as *nidering*. Bartholinus, I think, mentions a similar phrase which had like influence on the Danes— L. T.

[*nidering*: Scott got the word, and the anecdote (concerning William II rather than his father), from Henry's *History*, vi. 45–8. It is an incorrect form of the old English *nithing*, 'coward', originating in a misprint in an early edition (1596) of William of Malmesbury.]

20. All readers, however slightly acquainted with black letter, must recognise in the Clerk of Copmanhurst, Friar Tuck, the buxom Confessor of Robin Hood's gang, the Curtal Friar of Fountain's Abbey.

[*the Curtal Friar of Fountain's Abbey*: Scott's readers are likelier to have been acquainted with Ritson's *Robin Hood* than with the black-letter originals. 'Jolly friar Tucke' appears in 'The Playe of Robyn Hode' (printed as an appendix in Ritson, ii), while the hero of 'Robin Hood and the Curtall Fryer' (ii. 58) is a formidable fighter and, says Ritson's note, 'no fryer at all, but a monk of Fountains abbey [near Ripon], which was of the Cistercian order'. There were no friars in England until the arrival of the Franciscans in the next century; curtal friars were an inferior order, named for their shorter habit.]

21. The realm of France, it is well known, was divided betwixt the Norman and Teutonic race, who spoke the language in which the word Yes is pronounced as *oui*, and the inhabitants of the southern regions, whose speech bearing some affinity to the Italian, pronounced the same word *oc*. The poets of the former race were called *Minstrels*, and their poems *Lays:* those of the latter were termed *Troubadours*, and their compositions called *sirventes*, and other names. Richard, a professed admirer of the joyous science in all its branches, could imitate either the minstrel or troubadour. It is less likely that he should have been able to compose or sing an English

ballad; yet so much do we wish to assimilate Him of the Lion Heart to the land of the warriors whom he led, that the anachronism, if there be one, may readily be forgiven.

[*Minstrelsy*: Scott amplifies Percy's suggestion that in the reign of Richard I 'the national distinctions must have begun to decline, and both the Norman and English languages . . . be heard in the houses of the great; so that probably about this era, or soon after, we are to date that remarkable intercommunity and exchange of one another's compositions, which we discover to have taken place at some early period between the French and English Minstrels' (*Reliques*, i, 'introduction').]

22. It may be proper to remind the reader, that the chorus of 'derry down' is supposed to be as ancient, not only as the times of the Heptarchy, but as those of the Druids, and to have furnished the chorus to the hymns of those venerable persons when they went to the wood to gather mistletoe.

23. A rere-supper was a night-meal, and sometimes signified a collation, which was given at a late hour, after the regular supper had made its appearance.—L. T.

24. A great topographical blunder occurred here in former editions. The bloody battle alluded to in the text, fought and won by King Harold, over his brother the rebellious Tosti, and an auxiliary force of Danes or Norsemen, was said, in the text, and a corresponding note, to have taken place at Stamford, in Leicestershire, and upon the river Welland. This is a mistake, into which the author has been led by trusting to his memory, and so confounding two places of the same name. The Stamford, Strangford, or Staneford, at which the battle really was fought, is a ford upon the river Derwent, at the distance of about seven miles from York, and situated in that large and opulent county. A long wooden bridge over the Derwent, the site of which, with one remaining buttress, is still shown to the curious traveller, was furiously contested. One Norwegian long defended it by his single arm, and was at length pierced with a spear thrust through the planks of the bridge from a boat beneath.

The neighbourhood of Stamford, on the Derwent, contains some memorials of the battle. Horseshoes, swords, and the heads of halberds, or bills, are often found there; one place is called the 'Danes' well,' another the 'Battle flats.' From a tradition that the weapon with which the Norwegian champion was slain, resembled a pear, or, as others say, that the trough or boat in which the soldier floated under the bridge to strike the blow, had such a shape, the country people usually begin a great market, which is held at Stamford, with an entertainment called the Pear-pie feast, which after all may be a corruption of the Spear-pie feast. For more particulars, Drake's History of York may be referred to. The author's mistake was pointed out to him, in the most obliging manner, by Robert Belt, Esq. of Bossal House. The battle was fought in 1066.

25. *Nota Bene.*—We by no means warrant the accuracy of this piece of natural history, which we give on the authority of the Wardour MS.—L.T.

26. This horrid species of torture may remind the reader of that to which the Spaniards subjected Guatimozin, in order to extort a discovery of his concealed wealth. But, in fact, an instance of similar barbarity is to be found nearer home, and occurs in the annals of Queen Mary's time, containing so many other examples of atrocity. Every reader must recollect, that after the fall of the Catholic Church, and the Presbyterian Church Government had been established by law, the rank, and especially the wealth, of the Bishops, Abbots, Priors, and so forth, were no longer vested in ecclesiastics, but in lay impropriators of the church revenues, or, as the Scottish lawyers called them, *titulars* of the temporalities of the benefice, though having no claim to the spiritual character of their predecessors in office.

Of these laymen, who were thus invested with ecclesiastical revenues, some were men of high birth and rank, like the famous Lord James Stewart, the Prior of St Andrews, who did not fail to keep for their own use the rents, lands, and revenues of the church. But if, on the other hand, the titulars were men of inferior importance, who had been inducted into the office by the interest of some powerful person, it was generally understood that the new Abbot should grant for his patron's benefit such leases and conveyances of the church lands and tithes as might afford their protector the lion's share of the booty. This was the origin of those who were wittily termed Tulchan* Bishops, being a sort of imaginary prelate, whose image was set up to enable his patron and principal to plunder the benefice under his name.

There were other cases, however, in which men who had got grants of these secularised benefices, were desirous of retaining them for their own use, without having the influence sufficient to establish their purpose; and these became frequently unable to protect themselves, however unwilling to submit to the exactions of the feudal tyrant of the district.

Bannatyne, secretary to John Knox, recounts a singular course of oppression practised on one of those titular abbots, by the Earl of Cassilis in Ayrshire, whose extent of feudal influence was so wide that he was usually termed the King of Carrick. We give the fact as it occurs in Bannatyne's Journal, only premising that the Journalist held his master's opinions, both with respect to the Earl of Cassilis as an opposer of the king's party, and as being a detester of the practice of granting church revenues to titulars, instead of their being devoted to pious uses, such as the support of the clergy, expense of schools, and the relief of the national poor. He mingles in the narrative, therefore, a well deserved feeling of execration against the tyrant who employed the torture, with a tone of ridicule towards the patient, as if, after all, it had not been ill bestowed on such an equivocal and amphibious character as a titular abbot. He entitles his narrative,

THE EARL OF CASSILIS' TYRANNY AGAINST A QUICK (*i.e.* LIVING) MAN.

'Master Allan Stewart, friend to Captain James Stewart of Cardonall, by means of the Queen's corrupted court, obtained the Abbey of Crossraguel. The said Earl thinking himself greater than any king in those quarters, determined to have that whole benefice (as he hath divers others) to pay at his pleasure; and because he could not find sic security as his insatiable appetite required, this shift was devised. The said Mr Allan being in company with the Laird of Bargany, (also a Kennedy,) was, by the Earl and his friends, enticed to leave the safeguard which he had with the Laird, and come to make good cheer with the said Earl. The simplicity of the imprudent man was suddenly abused; and so he passed his time with them certain days, which he did in Maybole with Thomas Kennedie, uncle to the said Earl: after which the said Mr Allan passed, with quiet company, to visit the place and bounds of Crossraguel, [his abbacy,] of which the said Earl being surely adver- tised, determined to put in practice the tyranny which long before he had conceaved. And so, as king of the country, apprehended the said Mr Allan, and carried him to the house of Denure, where for a season he was honourably treated, (gif a prisoner can think any entertainment pleasing;) but after that certain days were spent, and that the Earl could not obtain the feus of Crossraguel according to his awin appetite, he determined to prove gif a collation could work that which neither dinner nor supper could do for a long time. And so the said Mr Allan was carried to a secret chamber: with him passed the honourable Earl, his worshipful brother, and such as

were appointed to be servants at that banquet. In the chamber there
was a grit iron chimlay, under it a fire; other grit provision was not
seen. The first course was,—"My Lord Abbot," (said the Earl,) "it
will please you confess here, that with your own consent you remain
in my company, because ye durst not commit yourself to the hands
of others." The Abbot answered, "Would you, my lord, that I
should make a manifest lie for your pleasure? The truth is, my lord,
it is against my will that I am here; neither yet have I any pleasure
in your company." "But ye shall remain with me, nevertheless, at
this time," said the Earl. "I am not able to resist your will and
pleasure," said the Abbot, "in this place." "Ye must then obey me,"
said the Earl,—and with that were presented unto him certain
letters to subscribe, amongst which there was a five years' tack, and
a nineteen years' tack, and a charter of feu of all the lands of
Crossraguel, with all the clauses necessary for the Earl to haste him
to hell. For gif adultery, sacrilege, oppression, barbarous cruelty,
and theft heaped upon theft, deserve hell, the great King of Carrick
can no more escape hell for ever, than the imprudent Abbot escaped
the fire for a season as follows.

'After that the Earl spied repugnance, and saw that he could not
come to his purpose by fair means, he commanded his cooks to
prepare the banquet: and so first they flayed the sheep, that is, they
took of the Abbot's cloathes even to his skin, and next they bound
him to the chimney—his legs to the one end, and his arms to the
other; and so they began to beet [i.e. feed] the fire sometimes to his
buttocks, sometimes to his legs, sometimes to his shoulders and
arms; and that the roast might not burn, but that it might rest in
soppe, they spared not flambing with oil, (basting as a cook bastes
roasted meat); Lord, look thou to sic cruelty! And that the crying of
the miserable man should not be heard, they closed his mouth that
the voice might be stopped. It may be suspected that some partisan
of the King's [Darnley's] murder was there. In that torment they
held the poor man, till that often he cried for God's sake to dispatch
him; for he had as meikle gold in his awin purse as would buy
powder enough to shorten his pain. The famous King of Carrick
and his cooks perceiving the roast to be aneuch, commanded it to be
tane fra the fire, and the Earl himself began the grace in this
manner:—"*Benedicite, Jesus Maria*, you are the most obstinate man
that ever I saw; gif I had known that ye had been so stubborn, I
would not for a thousand crowns have handled you so; I never did
so to man before you." And yet he returned to the same practice
within two days, and ceased not till that he obtained his formost
purpose, that is, that he had got all his pieces subscryvit alsweill as

ane half-roasted hand could do it. The Earl thinking himself sure enough so long as he had the half-roasted Abbot in his awin keeping, and yet being ashamed of his presence by reason of his former cruelty, left the place of Denure in the hands of certain of his servants, and the half-roasted Abbot to be kept there as prisoner. The Laird of Bargany, out of whose company the said Abbot had been enticed, understanding, (not the extremity,) but the retaining of the man, sent to the court, and raised letters of deliverance of the person of the man according to the order, which being disobeyed, the said Earl for his contempt was denounced rebel, and put to the horne. But yet hope was there none, neither to the afflicted to be delivered, neither yet to the purchaser [*i.e.* procurer] of the letters to obtain any comfort thereby; for in that time God was despised, and the lawful authority was contemned in Scotland, in hope of the sudden return and regiment of that cruel murderer of her awin husband, of whose lords the said Earl was called one; and yet, oftener than once, he was solemnly sworn to the King and to his Regent.'

The Journalist then recites the complaint of the injured Allan Stewart, Commendator of Crossraguel, to the Regent and Privy Council, averring his having been carried, partly by flattery, partly by force, to the Black Vault of Denure, a strong fortalice, built on a rock overhanging the Irish channel, where its ruins are still visible. Here he stated he had been required to execute leases and conveyances of the whole churches and parsonages belonging to the Abbey of Crossraguel, which he utterly refused as an unreasonable demand, and the more so that he had already conveyed them to John Stewart of Cardonall, by whose interest he had been made Commendator. The complainant proceeds to state, that he was, after many menaces, stript, bound, and his limbs exposed to fire in the manner already described, till, compelled by excess of agony, he subscribed the charter and leases presented to him, of the contents of which he was totally ignorant. A few days afterwards, being again required to execute a ratification of these deeds before a notary and witnesses, and refusing to do so, he was once more subjected to the same torture, until his agony was so excessive that he exclaimed, 'Fye on you, why do you not strike your whingers into me, or blow me up with a barrel of powder, rather than torture me thus unmercifully?' upon which the Earl commanded Alexander Richard, one of his attendants, to stop the patient's mouth with a napkin, which was done accordingly. Thus he was once more compelled to submit to their tyranny. The petition concluded with stating, that the Earl, under pretence of the deeds thus iniquitously obtained, had taken

possession of the whole place and living of Crossraguel, and enjoyed the profits thereof for three years.

The doom of the Regent and Council shows singularly the total
interruption of justice at this calamitous period, even in the most
clamant cases of oppression. The Council declined interference
with the course of the ordinary justice of the county, (which was
completely under the said Earl of Cassilis' control,) and only
enacted, that he should forbear molestation of the unfortunate
Commendator, under the surety of two thousand pounds Scots.
The Earl was appointed also to keep the peace towards the celebrated George Buchanan, who had a pension out of the same
Abbacy, to a similar extent, and under the like penalty.

The consequences are thus described by the Journalist already
quoted.

'The said Laird of Bargany perceiving that the ordiner justice
could neither help the oppressed, nor yet the afflicted, applied his
mind to the next remedy, and in the end, by his servants, took the
house of Denure, where the poor Abbot was kept prisoner. The
bruit flew fra Carrick to Galloway, and so suddenly assembled herd
and hyre-man that pertained to the band of the Kennedies; and so
within a few hours was the house of Denure environed again. The
master of Cassilis was the frackast [i.e. the readiest or boldest] and
would not stay, but in his heat would lay fire to the dungeon, with
no small boasting that all enemies within the house should die.

'He was required and admonished by those that were within to be
more moderate, and not to hazard himself so foolishly. But no
admonition would help, till that the wind of an hacquebute blasted
his shoulder, and then ceased he from further pursuit in fury. The
Laird of Bargany had before purchest [obtained] of the authorities,
letters, charging all faithfull subjects to the King's Majesty, to assist
him against that cruel tyrant and mansworn traitor, the Earl of
Cassilis; which letters, with his private writings, he published, and
shortly found sic concurrence of Kyle and Cunynghame with his
other friends, that the Carrick company drew back fra the house:
and so the other approached, furnished the house with more men,
delivered the said Mr Allan, and carried him to Ayr, where, pub-
licly at the market cross of the said town, he declared how cruelly he
was entreated, and how the murdered King suffered not sic torment
as he did, excepting only he escaped the death: and, therefore,
publickly did revoke all things that were done in that extremity, and
especially he revoked the subscription of the three writings, to wit,
of a fyve yeir tack and nineteen year tack, and of a charter of feu.
And so the house remained, and remains (till this day, the 7th of

February, 1571,) in the custody of the said Laird of Bargany and of his servants. And so cruelly was disappointed of proffeit present, and shall be eternallie punished, unless he earnestly repent. And this far for the cruelty committed, to give occasion unto others, and to such as hate the monstrous dealing of degenerate nobility, to look more diligently upon their behaviours, and to paint them forth unto the world, that they themselves may be ashamed of their own beastliness, and that the world may be advertised and admonished to abhor, detest, and avoid the company of all sic tyrants, who are not worthy of the society of men, but ought to be sent suddenly to the devil, with whom they must burn without end, for their contempt of God, and cruelty committed against his creatures. Let Cassilis and his brother be the first to be the example unto others. Amen. Amen.'†

This extract has been somewhat amended or modernized in orthography, to render it more intelligible to the general reader. I have to add, that the Kennedies of Bargany, who interfered in behalf of the oppressed Abbot, were themselves a younger branch of the Cassilis family, but held different politics, and were powerful enough in this, and other instances, to bid them defiance.

The ultimate issue of this affair does not appear; but as the house of Cassilis are still in possession of the greater part of the feus and leases which belonged to Crossraguel Abbey, it is probable the talons of the King of Carrick were strong enough, in those disorderly times, to retain the prey which they had so mercilessly fixed upon.

I may also add, that it appears by some papers in my possession, that the officers or Country Keepers on the border, were accustomed to torment their prisoners by binding them to the iron bars of their chimneys, to extort confession.

* A *Tulchan* is a calf's skin stuffed, and placed before a cow who has lost its calf, to induce the animal to part with her milk. The resemblance between such a Tulchan and a Bishop named to transmit the temporalities of a benefice to some powerful patron, is easily understood.

† Bannatyne's Journal.

[*Guatimozin*: Cuauhtemoc, Aztec emperor, nephew of Montezuma (d. 1525); so treated by Cortes's officers of the Treasury in 1521.

Bannatyne, secretary to John Knox: Richard Bannatyne (d. 1605; not to be confused with George Bannatyne, compiler of the Bannatyne MS) wrote a *Journal of Transactions in Scotland, during the contest between the Adherents of Queen Mary and those of her Son, 1570, 1571, 1572, 1573.* Scott had this extract copied from the Edinburgh edition of 1806 (pp. 55–9, 65–7); the spelling and many of the words have been turned into modern English. The incident described took place in October 1570.

put to the horne: proclaimed outlaw for failure to obey a summons.

cruel murderer of her awin husband: Queen Mary Stuart.

whingers: Daggers or short swords.

herd and hyre-man: keepers and hired men, retainers.

27. Henry's Hist. edit. 1805, vol. vii. p. 346.

28. I wish the Prior had also informed them when Niobe was sainted. Probably during that enlightened period when

> 'Pan to Moses lent his pagan horn.'
—L. T.

[*Pan to Moses lent his pagan horn*: 'And Pan to Moses lends his pagan horn', Alexander Pope, *The Dunciad*, iii. 110.]

29. *Surquedy* and *outrecuidance*—insolence and presumption.

30. Mantelets were temporary and movable defences formed of planks, under cover of which the assailants advanced to the attack of fortified places of old. Pavisses were a species of large shields covering the whole person, employed on the same occasions.

31. The bolt was the arrow peculiarly fitted to the crossbow, as that of the long-bow was called a shaft. Hence the English proverb—'I will either make a shaft or bolt of it,' signifying a determination to make one use or other of the thing spoken of.

32. The arblast was a crossbow, the windlace the machine used in bending that weapon, and the quarrell, so called from its square or diamond-shaped head, was the bolt adapted to it.

33. The author has been here upbraided with false heraldry, as having charged metal upon metal. It should be remembered, however, that heraldry had only its first rude origin during the crusades, and that all the minutiæ of its fantastic science were the work of time, and introduced at a much later period. Those who think otherwise must suppose that the Goddess of *Armoirers*, like the Goddess of Arms, sprung into the world completely equipped in all the gaudy trappings of the department she presides over.

[*false heraldry*: See Nassau Senior's unsigned review, *Quarterly Review*, 26 (October 1821); reprinted in John O. Hayden (ed.), *Scott: The Critical Heritage*, 241.

The Goddess of Arms is Athena, or Minerva, who emerged thus from the forehead of Zeus/Jupiter.]

In corroboration of what is above stated, it may be observed, that the arms, which were assumed by Godfrey of Boulogne himself, after the conquest of Jerusalem, was a cross counter patent cantoned with four little crosses or, upon a field azure, displaying thus metal upon metal. The heralds have tried to explain this undeniable fact in different modes—but Ferne gallantly contends, that a prince of Godfrey's qualities should not be bound by the ordinary rules. The Scottish Nisbet, and the same Ferne, insist that the chiefs of the Crusade must have assigned to Godfrey this extraordinary and unwonted coat-of-arms, in order to induce those who should behold them to make enquiries; and hence give them the name of *arma inquirenda*. But with reverence to these grave authorities, it seems unlikely that the assembled princes of Europe should have adjudged to Godfrey a coat armorial so much contrary to the general rule, if such rule had then existed; at any rate, it proves that metal upon metal, now accounted a solecism in heraldry, was admitted in other cases similar to that in the text. See Ferne's *Blazon of Gentrie*, p. 238. Edition 1586. Nisbet's *Heraldry*, vol. i. p. 113. Second Edition.

[Scott enclosed this last-minute addition in a letter to Cadell, 20 April 1830.]

34. Every Gothic castle and city had, beyond the outer-walls, a fortification composed of palisades, called the barriers, which were often the scene of severe skirmishes, as these must necessarily be carried before the walls themselves could be approached. Many of those valiant feats of arms which adorn the chivalrous pages of Froissart took place at the barriers of besieged places.

35. The author has some idea that this passage is imitated from the appearance of Philidaspes, before the divine Mandane, when the city of Babylon is on fire, and he proposes to carry her from the flames. But the theft, if there be one, would be rather too severely punished by the penance of searching for the original passage through the interminable volumes of the Grand Cyrus.

[Madeleine de Scudéry's *Artamène, ou le Grand Cyrus* (10 vols., 1649–53) was the most famous of those *romans héroïques* that plunged from the heights of literary fashion in the late seventeenth century to the depths of critical contempt in the eighteenth. Charlotte Lennox's *The Female Quixote* (1752) satirizes them as the idle reading of young ladies, and Scott has his heroine Edith

Bellenden engrossed in *The Grand Cyrus* at the beginning of *Old Mortality*. In fact the influence of these romances on later novelists such as Richardson is considerable, although neglected by scholars. The incident Scott refers to occurs in Part 2, Book 2 of the English translation (*Artamenes, or the Grand Cyrus*, 1690). The King of Assyria, assuming the name Philidaspes, kidnaps the fair Mandana; when her lover Artamenes besieges Babylon the king sneaks her out of the city, dressing his retinue in white for camouflage against the snow. Scott conflates this escape with Philidaspes's earlier appearance to Mandana covered in dust and blood from the battlefield, with his plume shorn and his armour hacked. (The conflagration occurs in yet another episode.)]

36. It will readily occur to the antiquary, that these verses are intended to imitate the antique poetry of the Scalds—the minstrels of the old Scandinavians—the race, as the Laureate so happily terms them,

> 'Stern to inflict, and stubborn to endure,
> Who smiled in death.'

The poetry of the Anglo–Saxons, after their civilisation and conversion, was of a different and softer character; but in the circumstances of Ulrica, she may be not unnaturally supposed to return to the wild strains which animated her forefathers during the time of Paganism and untamed ferocity.

37. The notes upon the bugle were anciently called mots, and are distinguished in the old treatises on hunting, not by musical characters, but by written words.

38. The interchange of a cuff with the jolly priest is not entirely out of character with Richard I, if romances read him aright. In the very curious romance on the subject of his adventures in the Holy Land, and his return from thence, it is recorded how he exchanged a pugilistic favour of this nature, while a prisoner in Germany. His opponent was the son of his principal warder, and was so imprudent as to give the challenge to this barter of buffets. The King stood forth like a true man, and received a blow which staggered him. In requital, having previously waxed his hand, a practice unknown, I believe, to the gentlemen of the modern fancy, he returned the box on the ear with such interest as to kill his antagonist on the spot.— *See, in Ellis's Specimens of English Romance, that of Cœur-de-Lion.*

[(Ellis, *Specimens* ii. 200–1.) Characteristically, Scott conflates this episode with one in the Robin Hood ballads, in which Robin exchanges buffets with the King, who is disguised as a friar; when

Robin recognizes him he kneels and swears allegiance. See Ritson, *Robin Hood*, i. 72 and ii. 162–70. The *modern fancy* is contemporary slang for boxing. In 1819 *Blackwood's Edinburgh Magazine* ran a series of articles on *Tom Crib's Memorial to Congress. By One of the Fancy* (March) and Pierce Egan's *Boxiana; or Sketches of Pugilism. By One of the Fancy* (July–September).]

39. A commissary is said to have received similar consolation from a certain Commander-in-chief, to whom he complained that a general officer had used some such threat towards him as that in the text.

40. Borghs, or borrows, signifies pledges. Hence our word to borrow, because we pledge ourselves to restore what is lent.

41. *Dortour*, or dormitory.

42. It is curious to observe, that in every state of society, some sort of ghostly consolation is provided for the members of the community, though assembled for purposes diametrically opposite to religion. A gang of beggars have their Patrico, and the banditti of the Apennines have among them persons acting as monks and priests, by whom they are confessed, and who perform mass before them. Unquestionably, such reverend persons, in such a society, must accommodate their manners and their morals to the community in which they live; and if they can occasionally obtain a degree of reverence for their supposed spiritual gifts, are, on most occasions, loaded with unmerciful ridicule, as possessing a character inconsistent with all around them.

Hence the fighting parson in the old play of Sir John Oldcastle, and the famous friar of Robin Hood's band. Nor were such characters ideal. There exists a monition of the Bishop of Durham against irregular churchmen of this class, who associated themselves with Border robbers, and desecrated the holiest offices of the priestly function, by celebrating them for the benefit of thieves, robbers, and murderers, amongst ruins and in caverns of the earth, without regard to canonical form, and with torn and dirty attire, and maimed rites, altogether improper for the occasion.

43. Reginald Fitzurse, William de Tracy, Hugh de Morville, and Richard Brito, were the gentlemen of Henry the Second's household, who, instigated by some passionate expressions of their sovereign, slew the celebrated Thomas-a-Becket.

44. The establishments of the Knight Templars were called Preceptories, and the title of those who presided in the Order was Preceptor; as the principal Knights of Saint John were termed

Commanders, and their houses Commanderies. But these terms were sometimes, it would seem, used indiscriminately.

45. In the ordinances of the Knights of the Temple, this phrase is repeated in a variety of forms, and occurs in almost every chapter, as if it were the signal-word of the Order; which may account for its being so frequently put in the Grand Master's mouth.

46. See the 13th chapter of Leviticus.

[Leviticus 13 gives a detailed diagnosis for leprosy in the body. Beaumanoir's words seem rather to allude to Leviticus 14: 37: 'behold, if the plague be in the house with hollow strakes, greenish or reddish, which in sight are lower than the wall'.]

47. The edict which he quotes, is against communion with women of light character.

48. The reader is again referred to the Rules of the Poor Military Brotherhood of the Temple, which occur in the Works of St Bernard.—L. T.

49. *Essoine* signifies excuse, and here relates to the appellant's privilege of appearing by her champion, in excuse of her own person on account of her sex.

50. *Capul*, i.e. horse; in a more limited sense, work-horse.

51. From the ballads of Robin Hood, we learn that this celebrated outlaw, when in disguise, sometimes assumed the name of Locksley, from a village where he was born, but where situated we are not distinctly told.

52. When I last saw this interesting ruin of ancient days, one of the very few remaining examples of Saxon fortification, I was strongly impressed with the desire of tracing out a sort of theory on the subject, which, from some recent acquaintance with the architecture of the ancient Scandinavians, seemed to me peculiarly interesting. I was, however, obliged by circumstances to proceed on my journey, without leisure to take more than a transient view of Coningsburgh. Yet the idea dwells so strongly in my mind, that I feel considerably tempted to write a page or two in detailing at least the outline of my hypothesis, leaving better antiquaries to correct or refute conclusions which are perhaps too hastily drawn.

Those who have visited the Zetland Islands, are familiar with the description of castles called by the inhabitants Burghs; and by the Highlanders—for they are also to be found both in the Western Isles and on the mainland—Duns. Pennant has engraved a view of the famous Dun-Dornadilla in Glenelg; and there are many others, all of them built after a peculiar mode of architecture, which argues a people in the most primitive state of society. The most perfect specimen is that upon the island of Mousa, near to the mainland of Zetland, which is probably in the same state as when inhabited.

It is a single round tower, the wall curving in slightly, and then turning outward again in the form of a dice-box, so that the defenders on the top might the better protect the base. It is formed of rough stones, selected with care, and laid in courses or circles, with much compactness, but without cement of any kind. The tower has never, to appearance, had roofing of any sort; a fire was made in the centre of the space which it encloses, and originally the building was probably little more than a wall drawn as a sort of screen around the great council fire of the tribe. But, although the means or ingenuity of the builders did not extend so far as to provide a roof, they supplied the want by constructing apartments in the interior of the walls of the tower itself. The circumvallation formed a double enclosure, the inner side of which was, in fact, two feet or three feet distant from the other, and connected by a concentric range of long flat stones, thus forming a series of concentric rings or stories of various heights, rising to the top of the tower. Each of these stories or galleries has four windows, facing directly to the points of the compass, and rising of course regularly above each other. These four perpendicular ranges of windows admitted air, and, the fire being kindled, heat, or smoke at least, to each of the galleries. The access from gallery to gallery is equally primitive. A path, on the principle of an inclined plane, turns round and round the building like a screw, and gives access to the different stories, intersecting each of them in its turn, and thus gradually rising to the top of the wall of the tower. On the outside there are no windows; and I may add, that an enclosure of a square, or sometimes a round form, gave the inhabitants of the Burgh an opportunity to secure any sheep or cattle which they might possess.

Such is the general architecture of that very early period when the Northmen swept the seas, and brought to their rude houses, such as I have described them, the plunder of polished nations. In Zetland there are several scores of these Burghs, occupying in every case, capes, headlands, islets, and similar places of advantage singularly well chosen. I remember the remains of one upon an island in a small lake near Lerwick, which at high tide communicates with the sea, the access to which is very ingenious, by means of a causeway or dike, about three or four inches under the surface of the water. This causeway makes a sharp angle in its approach to the Burgh. The inhabitants, doubtless, were well acquainted with this, but strangers, who might approach in a hostile manner, and were ignorant of the curve of the causeway, would probably plunge into the lake, which is six or seven feet in depth at the least. This must have been the device of some Vauban or Cohorn of those early times.

The style of these buildings evinces that the architect possessed neither the art of using lime or cement of any kind, nor the skill to throw an arch, construct a roof, or erect a stair; and yet, with all this ignorance, showed great ingenuity in selecting the situation of Burghs, and regulating the access to them, as well as neatness and regularity in the erection, since the buildings themselves show a style of advance in the arts scarcely consistent with the ignorance of so many of the principal branches of architectural knowledge.

I have always thought, that one of the most curious and valuable objects of antiquaries has been to trace the progress of society, by the efforts made in early ages to improve the rudeness of their first expedients, until they either approach excellence, or, as is most frequently the case, are supplied by new and fundamental discoveries, which supersede both the earlier and ruder system, and the improvements which have been ingrafted upon it. For example, if we conceive the recent discovery of gas to be so much improved and adapted to domestic use, as to supersede all other modes of producing domestic light; we can already suppose, some centuries afterwards, the heads of a whole Scoiety of Antiquaries half turned by the discovery of a pair of patent snuffers, and by the learned theories which would be brought forward to account for the form and purpose of so singular an implement.

Following some such principle, I am inclined to regard the singular Castle of Coningsburgh—I mean the Saxon part of it—as a step in advance from the rude architecture, if it deserves the name, which must have been common to the Saxons as to other Northmen. The builders had attained the art of using cement, and of roofing a building,—great improvements on the original Burgh. But in the round keep, a shape only seen in the most ancient castles—the chambers excavated in the thickness of the walls and buttresses—the difficulty by which access is gained from one story to those above it, Coningsburgh still retains the simplicity of its origin, and shows by what slow degrees man proceeded from occupying such rude and inconvenient lodgings, as were afforded by the galleries of the Castle of Mousa, to the more splendid accommodations of the Norman castles, with all their stern and Gothic graces.

I am ignorant if these remarks are new, or if they will be confirmed by closer examination; but I think, that, on a hasty observation, Coningsburgh offers means of curious study to those who may wish to trace the history of architecture back to the times preceding the Norman Conquest.

It would be highly desirable that a cork model should be taken of the Castle of Mousa, as it cannot be well understood by a plan.

The Castle of Coningsburgh is thus described:—

'The castle is large, the outer walls standing on a pleasant ascent from the river, but much overtopt by a high hill, on which the town stands, situated at the head of a rich and magnificent vale, formed by an amphitheatre of woody hills, in which flows the gentle Don. Near the castle is a barrow, said to be Hengist's tomb. The entrance is flanked to the left by a round tower, with a sloping base, and there are several similar in the outer wall; the entrance has piers of a gate, and on the east side the ditch and bank are double and very steep. On the top of the churchyard wall is a tombstone, on which are cut in high relief, two ravens, or such-like birds. On the south side of the churchyard lies an ancient stone, ridged like a coffin, on which is carved a man on horseback; and another man with a shield encountering a vast winged serpent, and a man bearing a shield behind him. It was probably one of the rude crosses not uncommon in churchyards in this county. The name of Coningsburgh, by which this castle goes in the old editions of the Britannia, would lead one to suppose it the residence of the Saxon kings. It afterwards belonged to King Harold. The Conqueror bestowed it on William de Warren, with all its privileges and jurisdiction, which are said to have extended over twenty-eight towns. At the corner of the area, which is of an irregular form, stands the great tower, or keep, placed on a small hill of its own dimensions, on which lie six vast projecting buttresses, ascending in a steep direction to prop and support the building, and continued upwards up the side as turrets. The tower within forms a complete circle, twenty-one feet in diameter, the walls fourteen feet thick. The ascent into the tower is by an exceeding deep flight of steep steps, four feet and a half wide, on the south side leading to a low doorway, over which is a circular arch crossed by a great transom stone. Within this door is the staircase which ascends straight through the thickness of the wall, not communicating with the room on the first floor, in whose centre is the opening to the dungeon. Neither of these lower rooms is lighted except from a hole in the floor of the third story; the room in which, as well as in that above it, is finished with compact smooth stonework, both having chimney-pieces, with an arch resting on triple clustered pillars. In the third story, or guard-chamber, is a small recess with a loop-hole, probably a bedchamber, and in that floor above a niche for a saint or holy-water pot. Mr King imagines this a Saxon castle of the first ages of the Heptarchy. Mr Watson thus describes it. From the first floor to the second story, (third from the ground,) is a way by a stair in the wall five feet wide. The next staircase is approached by a ladder, and ends at the fourth story from the ground. Two yards from the door, at the head of this stair, is an opening nearly east, accessible by treading on the ledge of the wall, which diminishes eight inches each story; and this last opening leads into a room or chapel ten feet by twelve, and fifteen or sixteen high, arched with freestone, and supported by small circular columns of the same, the capitals and arches Saxon. It has an east window, and on each side in the wall, about four feet from the ground, a stone basin, with a hole and iron pipe to convey the water into or through the wall. This chapel is one of the buttresses, but no sign of it without, for even the window, though large within, is only a long narrow loop-hole, scarcely to be seen without. On the left side of this chapel is a small oratory, eight by six in the thickness of the wall, with a niche in the wall, and enlightened by a like loop-hole. The fourth stair from the ground, ten feet west from the chapel door, leads to the top of the tower through the thickness of the wall, which at top is but three yards. Each story is about fifteen feet high, so that the tower will be seventy-five feet from the ground. The inside forms a circle, whose diameter may be about twelve feet. The well at the bottom of the dungeon is piled with stones.'—GOUGH's *Edition of Camden's Britannia*. Second Edition, vol. iii. p. 267.

[*Pennant*: Thomas Pennant, the naturalist, whose *A Tour in Scotland and Voyage to the Hebrides* (1774–6) was the most thorough of the eighteenth-century Scottish travelogues.

Vauban or Cohorn: Sebastien Le Prestre de Vauban and the Baron van Cohorn, or Coehorn, military engineers active in the seventeenth century.

the recent discovery of gas: In 1823 Scott installed gaslight, a modern innovation, at Abbotsford; the following year he became president of the Edinburgh Oil Gas Company.]

53. The crowth, or crowd, was a species of violin. The rote a sort of guitar, or rather hurdy-gurdy, the strings of which were managed by a wheel, from which the instrument took its name.

[*from which the instrument took its name*: A false etymology; both words share the same Celtic root, and so probably designated the same plucked or bowed instrument (Tulloch, *The Language of Walter Scott*, 57). Compare Chaucer, 'General Prologue' i. 236: 'Wel koude he synge and pleyen on a rote'.]

54. Infamous.

55. The resuscitation of Athelstane has been much criticised, as too violent a breach of probability, even for a work of such fantastic character. It was a *tour-de-force*, to which the author was compelled to have recourse, by the vehement entreaties of his friend and printer, who was inconsolable on the Saxon being conveyed to the tomb.

[For Scott's original intention see editorial note to chapter xxxi, below. Many critics did indeed deplore the proof-stage decision to revive the gluttonous thane: e.g. *Edinburgh Review*, 3 (1820) 1–54; *Edinburgh Magazine*, 6 (1820) 7–16; *Edinburgh Monthly Review*, 3 (1820) 163–95; *Monthly Review*, 91 (1820) 71–89. Reading over *Ivanhoe* in 1828 Scott confided to Ballantyne that 'the resurrection of Athelstane was a botch' (*Letters* xii. 458). However, last-minute resurrections belong to the decorum of the mixed genres of romance and tragi-comedy, and Scott might have cited such distinguished precedents as Shakespeare's *Pericles* and *The Winter's Tale*.]

EDITOR'S NOTES

Scott composed *Ivanhoe* out of the quarry of his extensive reading in English literature, from the Middle-English romances and old ballads to Shakespeare and the King James Bible. Accounting for all of the novel's sources and allusions is beyond the scope of the present edition; these notes attempt to indicate the range and kinds of Scott's sources, and how he used them. I am indebted to three previous editions of *Ivanhoe*: the Dryburgh edition (1893), A. N. Wilson's Penguin Classics edition (1982), and, in particular, an earlier Oxford University Press edition (1921) by F. A. Cavenagh. References to Shakespeare's plays are to the Riverside edition; references to Chaucer's *Canterbury Tales* are to F. N. Robinson's edition of *The Works of Geoffrey Chaucer* (1957). Among other sources cited frequently in these notes, 'Cavenagh' refers to F. A. Cavenagh's notes to his edition of *Ivanhoe* (1921); 'Henry, *History*' refers to Robert Henry, *The History of Great Britain, from the First Invasion of it Under Julius Caesar* (1800); 'Ritson, *Robin Hood*' refers to Joseph Ritson (ed.), *Robin Hood: A Collection of all the Poems, Songs, and Ballads* (2 vols., 1796); 'Strutt, *Dress and Habits*' refers to Joseph Strutt, *A Complete View of the Dress and Habits of the People of England* (2 vols., 1796–9); 'Strutt, *Sports and Pastimes*' refers to Joseph Strutt, *The Sports and Pastimes of the People of England* (1830); and 'Turner' refers to Sharon Turner, *The History of England, from the Earliest Times to the Death of Elizabeth* (1839).

1 *epigraph*: Matthew Prior, *The Thief and the Cordelier, A Ballad* (lines 23–4), reading 'was loath' for 'seem'd loath'.

3 *L'Enfant Gâté*: 'the spoilt child'.

Edwin, in Parnell's Tale: Thomas Parnell, 'A Fairy Tale, in the Ancient English Style' (1729), lines 97–9, reading 'my charm' for 'the spell'.

4 *Men bless their stars and call it luxury*: Thomas Addison, *Cato* (1713), I. iv. 70; original reads, 'Blesses his stars and thinks it luxury'.

5 *wonder that they please no more*: Samuel Johnson, 'The Vanity of Human Wishes' (1749), line 263, 'He views, and wonders that they please no more'.

Logan's tragedy of Runnamede: John Logan (1748–88), popular preacher and miscellaneous writer, had to give up his ministry in the Church of Scotland, partly because of his alcoholism and partly because of the kirk's disapproval of the playhouse. The Saxon and Norman nobles do indeed 'enter at opposite doors' in the first act of *Runnamede* (1783).

6 *attempted by a stranger*: Scott's *Tales of My Landlord, Third Series*, comprising *The Bride of Lammermoor* and *A Legend of Montrose*, appeared in June 1819, just as he was starting work on *Ivanhoe*. Like the preceding two series, the work appeared in the guise of oral and manuscript tales collected and edited by a couple of country schoolmasters, rather than as an invention of 'the Author of *Waverley*'. *Tales of My Landlord, New Series, containing Pontefract Castle* was advertised by the publisher William Fearman on 14 October 1819, and published at the end of the year (3 vols., dated 1820) after an acrimonious exchange in the press with Scott's agent John Ballantyne. So long as the author of *Tales of My Landlord* saw fit to preserve his incognito, Fearman argued, no one could prove that this new series was inauthentic. Constable and his London partner Cadell, jealous of Longman for already advertising Scott's next novel *The Monastery* concurrently with *Ivanhoe*, suspected their rival of having planted the fake *Tales* in order to spoil their market.

'trick upon trick': Dr Wheeler actually says, 'sham upon sham is too much for any man': Maria Edgeworth, *Tales of Fashionable Life*, iii (1802), 95.

7 *Il Bondocani*: 'Il Bondocani, or the Caliph Robber' appears in the series *New Arabian Nights*, rather than the *Thousand and One Nights*; see Henry Weber, *Tales of the East* (3 vols., 1812), i. 475. Haroun Alraschid is the Caliph of Baghdad, Mesrour his chief eunuch, and Giafar his grand vizier. The adventures of James V in disguise occupy much of Scott's *The Lady of the Lake* (1810); for anecdotes of 'the Goodman of Ballengiech', see Scott's note 74 to the poem.

Rauf Colziar: 'The Taill of Rauf Coilzear', printed by David Laing in *Select Remains of the Ancient Popular Poetry of Scotland*, 1822, 'from a printed copy discovered in 1821 in the Library of the Faculty of Advocates'.

the same topic: Thomas Percy, *Reliques of Ancient English Poetry* (1765; 4th edn., 1794) II. i, no. 15 and III. ii, no. 20.

the British Bibliographer: 'The Kyng and the Hermite' is in vol. iv (1814), 81–95. It is not mentioned, however, in Hartshorne's *An-*

cient Metrical Tales (1829). Scott modernizes some of the spelling, grammar, and diction.

10 *High Jinks*: see Scott's *Guy Mannering* (1815), chapter 36.

Mr Hartshorne's collection: *Ancient Metrical Tales*, 35–80.

11 *a commodity of good names*: *1 Henry IV*, I. ii. 93: 'I would to God thou and I knew where a commodity of good names were to be bought'.

Tring, Wing, and Ivanhoe: villages between Aylesbury and Luton in Buckinghamshire, hundreds of miles from the novel's Yorkshire setting. It seems these manors never belonged to the Hampden family (*Notes and Queries*, 5 (1864), 176). Another *Notes and Queries* correspondent (5 (1852), 619) records the doggerel:

> Tring, Wing, and Ivinghoe,
> Three dirty villages all in a row,
> And never without a rogue or two.
> Would you know the reason why?
> Leighton Buzzard is hard by.

12 *Front-de-Bœuf*: Scott cites the name as 'Front-de-buffe', from a list of 'romantic epithets', in the description of the Auchinleck MS in his edition of *Sir Tristrem* (1804).

the freedom of the Rules: the liberty granted to a Scots advocate to plead at the English bar. Scott may also have had in mind another sense. On provision of a security, imprisoned debtors were sometimes allowed to live within 'the rules', a circumscribed area in the neighbourhood of the prison; this was known as enjoying the freedom of the rules. (For a more extended treatment of authorship and financial ruin compare *Chronicles of the Canongate*, 1827, where Scott's narrator finds sanctuary from his creditors in the Edinburgh precinct of that name.)

Wilfred to Rebecca: see editor's introduction.

13 *The Rev. Dr Dryasdust, F.A.S.*: (i.e. F.S.A.: Fellow of the Society of Antiquaries.) Scott had mentioned Dr Dryasdust in *The Antiquary* (1816) as the 'literary friend in York' of the titular hero, Jonathan Oldbuck of Monkbarns. He later appears in the frame matter of *The Fortunes of Nigel* (1822), *Peveril of the Peak* (1822), *Quentin Durward* (1823), and *Redgauntlet* (1824).

the patrimony of St Peter: in chapter 35 of *The Antiquary* Oldbuck refers to his correspondence with Dr Dryasdust 'on the subject of the Saxon horn that is preserved in the minster' at York, a carved

elephant's tusk that supposedly belonged to Ulphus, lord of West
Deira in the reign of Canute. Fearful that his sons might fight over
their inheritance, Ulphus rode to the cathedral of St Peter's at
York, filled his horn with wine, knelt before the altar and pledged
all his property to 'God and the blessed St Peter'. Scott would have
read about this in editions he owned of Francis Drake's *Erboracum:
History and Antiquities of the City of York* (1788) and Camden's
Britannia (1806).

13 *Detur digniori*: 'let it be dedicated to one who is more worthy'.

14 *M'Pherson*: James Macpherson's (1736–96) purported translations
of heroic poetry by Ossian, a third-century Gaelic bard, achieved
sensational popularity throughout late-eighteenth-century Europe
and provoked a furious critical debate about their authenticity.
Scott took the sceptical view: see *Edinburgh Review*, 6 (1805), 429–
62 and *Letters of Sir Walter Scott* i. 320–4.

Mohawks and Iroquois: in the decades following the 1745 Jacobite
rising, analogies between Highland clan society and North American Indian tribes became a commonplace of Scottish Enlightenment 'conjectural history'. Indian tribes were 'our good allies'
(alongside two Highland regiments) against the French in the
Seven Years War, 1756–63.

Kendal green: green woollen cloth, originally manufactured at
Kendal in Westmoreland. For its association with outlaws, see
1 Henry IV, II. iv. 246: 'three misbegotten knaves in Kendal green
came at my back and let drive at me'.

if duly conjured with, should raise a spirit: compare *Julius Caesar*, I. ii.
145: 'Conjure with 'em: | "Brutus" will start a spirit as well as
"Caesar".'

the Bruces and Wallaces of Caledonia: Scots patriots, leaders of the
resistance to English invasions under Edward I. Both were the
heroes of popular modern romances: Sir William Wallace (1272–
1305) of Jane Porter's *The Scottish Chiefs*, 1810, and Robert Bruce
(1274–1329), King of Scotland and victor of Bannockburn, of
Scott's own *The Lord of the Isles*, 1815. Scott had also popularized
Rob Roy McGregor, the eighteenth-century Highland outlaw, in
his 1817 novel of that name.

15 *rivers of Israel*: 2 Kings 5: 12, reading 'waters of Israel'; the 'patriotic Syrian' is Naaman.

The Scottish magician . . . like Lucan's witch: the Author of
Waverley ('the Northern Warlock', below); and Erictho, the
Thessalian witch of Lucan's *Pharsalia*, vi.

in corpore quærit: *Pharsalia*, vi. 629–31. Nicholas Rowe's translation (1718):

> To various carcases by turns she flies,
> And, griping with her gory fingers, tries,
> Till one of perfect organs can be found,
> And fibrous lungs uninjur'd by a wound.

(The necromancer needs a corpse with vocal apparatus intact for the transmission of ghostly speech.)

valley of Jehoshaphat: conflation of 'the valley which was full of bones' of Ezekiel 37: 1 with the valley of Jehoshaphat of Joel 3: 2.

16 *vie privée*: domestic life.

Mr Sharon Turner: author of *The History of the Anglo-Saxons* (4 vols., 1799–1805). *Dr Henry* is Robert Henry (1718–90), the author of *The History of Great Britain, from the first invasion by the Romans* (1771–85); and *the late Mr Strutt* is Joseph Strutt (1749–1802), the author of *A Complete View of the Dress and Habits of the People of England* (2 vols., 1796–9) and *Glig-Gamena Angel-Deod; or the Sports and Pastimes of the People of England* (1801). These are the main historical sources for *Ivanhoe*. Scott tends to rely on Strutt and Turner for information about the Anglo-Saxons and on Henry for the Normans. Strutt and Turner especially represent a new, nationalist historiography based on an antiquarian interest in social and cultural forms; a departure from the 'conjectural history' of the Scottish Enlightenment, which was concerned with finding universal scientific laws of historical evolution. For more detail see the Introduction.

17 *thrilled through many a bosom*: Scott described Walpole's *The Castle of Otranto* (1764) as 'the first modern attempt to found a tale of amusing fiction upon the basis of the ancient romances of chivalry' (*Sir Walter Scott on Novelists and Fiction*, ed. Ioan Williams, 1970: 84).

Abridgement of the Ancient Metrical Romances: George Ellis, *Specimens of Early English Metrical Romances, chiefly written during the early part of the fourteenth century* (3 vols., 1805): urbane prose summaries, interspersed with lightly modernized extracts from the originals.

the types of Caxton or Wynken de Worde: black-letter or Gothic type. William Caxton (1422?–92) introduced printing to Britain; Jan van Wynkyn, or Wynken de Worde (d. 1534?), was his apprentice and successor. Both are associated with important sources for *Ivanhoe*:

Caxton printed Chaucer, Malory, and other vernacular romances, while Wynken (in addition to later editions of the same) published the romance of *Richard Cœur de Lion*, the 'Lytell Geste of Robyn Hode' (reprinted by Ritson) and Juliana Berners's *Book of St Albans*.

18 *Mr Galland's first translation of the Arabian Tales*: made 1704–12; Scott's library at Abbotsford has a later edition, vols. 7–11 of Mayer's 41-volume *Cabinet des Fées*.

Mr Strutt, in his romance of Queen-Hoo-Hall: Scott's completion of which (1808) was his first substantial essay in prose fiction; Strutt's turgid tusheries set off the fleet and modern style of *Ivanhoe*. The chapters by Scott were reprinted in an appendix to the 'General Preface' of the Magnum Opus edition of the Waverley novels, 1829.

19 *the 'well of English undefiled'*: Spenser's tribute to 'Dan *Chaucer*, well of English vndefyled', *Faerie Queene*, IV. ii. 32.

the unfortunate Chatterton: the 'marvellous boy' Thomas Chatterton (1752–70) composed a series of poems in a synthetic medieval style, which he claimed were the productions of a fifteenth-century Bristol monk called Rowley. He sent them to Horace Walpole, who after some prevarication rejected them as forgeries. Chatterton committed suicide in London.

20 *'winter and summer'*: *Merchant of Venice*, III. i. 59–60; see Chapter V, epigraph.

the same general proportion to our own: compare the first chapter of *Waverley*: 'those passions common to men in all stages of society, and which have alike agitated the human heart, whether it throbbed under the steel corslet of the fifteenth century, the brocaded coat of the eighteenth, or the blue frock and white dimity waistcoat of the present day'.

Persepolis: Persian city, a type of barbaric splendour, as in Christopher Marlowe's *Tamburlaine the Great I*, II. v: 'to ride in triumph through Persepolis'. *Inch-Merrin* or Inchmurrin is an island in Loch Lomond.

21 *Ingulphus*: abbot Ingulf of Croyland, not Croyden (1085–1109), later secretary to William I. Although long attributed to him, the *Historia Croylandensis* is now believed to be a later medieval forgery.

Geoffrey de Vinsauff: poet (*fl.* 1200) and adherent of Richard I, whom he is supposed to have accompanied on the Third Crusade.

But he is probably not the author of the *Itinerarium peregrinorum et gesta regis Ricardi* (Rolls chronicles series 34: 1), one of the sources cited in Henry's *History*.

22 *Froissart*: Jean Froissart's (?1337–?1410) *Chronicles of England, France, and Spain*, with its glamorous evocations of chivalry, was one of Scott's favourite books, especially in the translation (1523–5) by John Bourchier, Baron Berners.

Bristol stones and paste: Bristol (or Bristow) stones or diamonds were a kind of transparent rock-crystal from the Clifton limestone, near Bristol; proverbial (from the 1590s) for fake gems.

Sir Arthur Wardour: foolish and obstinate Tory antiquarian, Jonathan Oldbuck's neighbour and rival, in *The Antiquary*.

the Bannatyne MS, the Auchinleck MS: important sources of early Scottish and northern English poetry, which Scott consulted in the library of the Faculty of Advocates, Edinburgh. The Auchinleck MS, donated to the library in 1744 by Alexander Boswell, Lord Auchinleck (father of the biographer), contains *Sir Tristrem* and a fragment of *Richard Cœur de Lyon*; Scott describes its contents in an appendix to his edition of *Sir Tristrem*. The Bannatyne MS was compiled in 1568 by Edinburgh burgess and minor poet George Bannatyne.

Robin of Redesdale: an ancient relief of a huntsman wearing a Phrygian cap, popularly supposed to represent a giant, found near the Roman station of Habitancum at modern Risingham, Northumberland. The local farmer, annoyed by tourists, blew up the relief and used the rubble for gate-posts. See Scott's *Rokeby*, I. xix, and note 9:

> And near the spot that gave me name,
> The moated mound of Risingham . . .
> Some ancient sculptor's art has shown
> An outlaw's image on the stone;
> Unmatch'd in strength, a giant he,
> With quiver'd back and kirtled knee.

'Robin of Redesdale' was also a historical figure, the leader of a northern rising against the Lancastrians in 1469, and thus an avatar of Robin Hood.

23 *fit of the stone*: as Scott was beginning work on *Ivanhoe* he suffered a last attack of gallstones, so severe that at its crisis (June 1819) rumours of his death circulated in Edinburgh.

23 *Tell this not in Gath*: 2 Samuel 1: 20: 'Tell it not in Gath, publish it not in the streets of Askelon'.

Arthur's Oven: or O'on, mentioned in the chronicle of Nennius, was a beehive-shaped antiquity of undetermined (Picto-Roman?) origins, in Stirlingshire. Eighteenth-century Scots historians interpreted it as a shrine to the boundary-god Terminus, marking the limits of Roman rule in Britain, and thus the largely successful (in contrast to England) Scottish resistance; see Colin Kidd, *Subverting Scotland's Past: Scottish Whig Historians and the Creation of an Anglo-British Identity* (1993), 75. In 1743 the local laird, Sir Michael Bruce of Stonehouse, demolished it and used the debris for a mill-dam.

vale tandem, non immemor mei: 'so farewell, and do not forget me'.

25 *epigraph*: Alexander Pope's translation of *The Odyssey*, xiv. 453–6. The original reads 'their several sties'. 'These' are the secretly returned Odysseus and his loyal swineherd Eumaeus (foreshadowing the alliance of Ivanhoe and Gurth).

Dragon of Wantley: See Percy, *Reliques of Ancient English Poetry*, III. iii, no. 13, for the mock-heroic ballad of that name: 'More of More-Hall, with nothing at all, | He slew the Dragon of Wantley'. Wantley was the local pronunciation of Warncliffe.

the date of our story: strictly speaking, the summer of 1193, i.e. some time between the negotiations for Richard I's ransom and his official return to England in March 1194. But many details do not correspond, and Scott refrains from an exact date; this is the chronology of romance rather than of history.

the English Council of State: the Great Council of landowners, the successor to the Anglo-Saxon Witanagemote, established by William I.

28 *their dress and appearance*: here as elsewhere Scott's descriptions of costume derive from Strutt, *Dress and Habits*; see esp. i. 5–6. The Saxons adhere to the traditional, by now archaic, fashion of their pre-Conquest forefathers. The famous brass and silver serfs' collars appear to be Scott's own invention.

29 *Sheffield whittle*: a large knife; compare Chaucer, *Reeve's Tale* i. 3933, 'A Sheffeld thwitel baar he'.

Gurth: one of the valiant and loyal brothers of king Harold, slain with him at Hastings. *Beowulph*: Scott learnt about the poem from Sharon Turner, who noticed it in his *History*, 1805, and would publish modern English extracts in the third edition in 1820. The *Catalogue of the Library at Abbotsford* (1838) includes G. J.

Thorkelin's *De Danorum Rebus Gestis . . . Poema Danicum dialecto Anglo-Saxonico* (Copenhagen, 1815), the first published text of *Beowulf*; but we have no evidence that Scott studied it. A complete version was not published in Britain until 1833. *Cedric* is named after Cerdic, the sixth-century king of Wessex, and *Wamba* (below) after the seventh-century king of Visigothic Spain.

30 *jelly-bag, or the head-gear of a modern hussar*: Scott had just purchased a Cornetship in the Eighteenth Hussars for his son and heir, Walter jun., and was much preoccupied with the expense of outfitting him in the months when he was writing *Ivanhoe*. Indeed, this was a principal reason for his impatience that the novel be published quickly. See *Letters of Sir Walter Scott*, v. 403, 424. A jelly-bag was a bag for straining jelly. Other details of the jester's costume (motley, bells, wooden sword) suggest an Elizabethan rather than twelfth-century figure.

31 *St Withold*: Scott got the name from Edgar's mad song in *King Lear*, III. iv, as emended (from the original 'Swithold') in the edition of Shakespeare by Johnson, Steevens, and Reed (1803): 'Saint Withold footed thrice the wold'. St Withold was St Vitalis of Ravenna.

true man: as opposed to a thief. Compare *Cymbeline* II. iii. 68–72: '[gold] makes | Diana's rangers false themselves, yield up | Their deer to th' stand o' th' stealer; and 'tis gold | Which makes the true man kill'd and saves the thief; | Nay, sometimes hangs both thief and true man'.

malice prepense: malice aforethought, legal term for deliberate wrongdoing.

thou'st got the weather-gage: your opponent is downwind of you, and you therefore have the advantage (nautical).

32 *a Norman name when he becomes matter of enjoyment*: according to Lockhart, Scott got the idea for this celebrated passage from a conversation with his friend William Clerk (*Life of Scott*, ch. 46), who was drawing in turn on a passage in Thomas Fuller's *History of the Worthies of England* (1622): 'our cattle for food are English when feeding in the field, but French when fed on in the family . . . after the Norman Conquest, the French so tyrannized over the English tenants, that they forced them to keep and feed their cattle; but the Monsieurs ate all their good meat after it was slaughtered'.

St Dunstan: Archbishop of Canterbury, Benedictine monk and reformer (909–88), who restored the English monasteries after the

Danish invasions. One of the most popular of the Anglo-Saxon
saints, he was often shown pinching the devil's nose with a pair of
tongs (see p. 194, below).

32 *standing in the gap*: Chaucer, 'Knight's Tale', i. 1638–9: 'Right as
the hunters in the regne of Trace, | That stondeth at the gappe
with a spere'.

33 *a message from King Oberon*: alludes to the thirteenth-century romance *Huon of Bordeaux* (not translated into English until 1534)
rather than *A Midsummer Night's Dream*. See the essay 'On the
Fairies of Popular Superstition' (introduction to 'The Young
Tamlane') in Scott's *Minstrelsy of the Scottish Border* (1802–3, II. ii):
'the ringing of the bridles, and the wild unearthly sound which
accompanied the cavalcade'.

murrain: plague. Shakespeare, *The Tempest*, III. ii. 80: 'A murrain
on your monster'.

Eumæus: the faithful and doughty swineherd of Odysseus.

34 *epigraph*: Chaucer, 'General Prologue', i. 165–71; spelling lightly
modernized.

Cistercian Monk: the Cistercian order, with its (supposedly) strict
application of the Benedictine rule, was the ascendant force in
twelfth-century monastic life. The first English foundation was
at Waverley, in Surrey (1129); but the order flourished most
in the north, with several great abbeys in Yorkshire. In MS
and earlier editions Scott sometimes wrote 'Benedictine' for
'Cistercian'.

penthouse: sloping brow; compare *Macbeth*, I. iii. 20, 'penthouse
lid'.

35 *sumpter mule*: carrying baggage and supplies. A jennet is a small
Spanish horse and a palfrey a small saddle-horse for civilian riders.

36 *a cross of a peculiar form*: the eight-pointed or Maltese cross. Scott
mistakes the costume. Permanent knights of the Order of the
Temple wore the Cistercians' white robe (signifying purity) with a
scarlet cross.

37 *the former were naked . . . to ankle*: no doubt the anatomical reversal
of 'former' and 'latter' (so printed in all editions) reflects the de-
monic nature of these attendants.

El Jerrid: 'the javelin'; a short wooden one was cast from horseback
in these mock combats.

38 *the Prior of Jorvaulx Abbey*: the Cistercian abbey of Jorvaulx or
Jervaulx in the North Riding of Yorkshire, built in 1156 and pulled

down in 1537. Scott gives Aymer the titles of Abbot and Prior (the second rank to Abbot) indiscriminately.

covereth a multitude of sins: 1 Peter 4: 8.

39 *benedicite, mes filz*: 'bless you, my sons.' (Scott reproduces the Old French spelling.)

seneschals: chief steward or major-domo of a noble household.

40 *Clerus clericum non decimat*: a churchman doesn't take tithes from a churchman.

Tush: an exclamation ('pshaw'), common in Shakespeare. Scott was not the first to revive it (Cowper used it in his translation of the *Iliad*) but he certainly popularized it, to the extent that it became a trope for the synthetic style of 'modern antique romance', as in Robert Louis Stevenson's term 'tushery': 'I turned me to—what thinkest 'ou?—to Tushery, by the mass! Ay, friend, a whole tale of tushery [*The Black Arrow*]' (to W. E. Henley, May 1883: *Letters*, i. 316).

demivolte: a half-turn made with the forelegs raised.

41 *chasteneth whom she loveth*: compare Hebrews 12: 6: 'whom the Lord loveth he chasteneth'.

Knights Templars: founded in 1118 to protect the pilgrimage routes to Jerusalem, and given papal sanction eleven years later at the Council of Troyes, the Order of the Temple spread rapidly throughout Western Europe. Its headquarters occupied the site of the Temple of Solomon, at the palace of the King of Jerusalem, until the fall of that city in 1187. Involvement in the Crusades only increased the power and wealth of the Templars, who became as prominent in international finance as they were in military enterprise.

42 *fool speaking according to his folly*: Proverbs 26: 4, 5. 'Answer not a fool according to his folly, lest thou also be like unto him'.

Odin: or Woden; chief of the pagan Norse and Anglo-Saxon pantheon.

43 *Hereward . . . Heptarchy*: the seven Anglo-Saxon kingdoms before the Danish invasions and the reign of Alfred; nothing to do with Hereward's later guerrilla war against the Normans in East Anglia.

vae victis: woe to the vanquished, Livy, *History*, v. xlviii. 9.

arrets of love: decrees of the 'Court of Love', according to the troubadour-based cult of *amor courteois*. For Scott's dismissive comment see his 'Essay on Chivalry' (1818; *Miscellaneous Prose Works*, 1834, vi), 39.

43 *the houris of old Mahound's paradise*: damsels supposed to pleasure the blessed. 'Mahound' is a corruption of 'Mohammed'.

  weighed in the balance and found wanting: the writing on the wall at Belshazzar's feast, Daniel 5: 27.

44 *as meekly as a maiden*: an ironical echo of Chaucer's description of his knight: 'of his port as meeke as is a mayde', 'General Prologue', i. 69.

45 *A Palmer*: a professional pilgrim who signified his vocation by carrying a palm-branch from the Holy Land. The knight disguised in a palmer's habit is an old romance convention. Jerome Mitchell (*Scott, Chaucer, and Medieval Romance*, 1987), cites numerous examples from popular romances such as *Richard Cœur de Lion*, *Bevis of Hampton*, and *Guy of Warwick* (127–9). Scott uses the device in *Marmion* (1808) and again in *The Betrothed* (1825).

47 *epigraph*: James Thomson, *Liberty*, iv. 668–70.

48 *Dividers of Bread*: the etymon of 'lord' is the Old English *hlaford*, a derivation of *hlafweard*, loaf-ward or keeper of bread, expressing the relation between the head of the household and the dependants who ate his bread.

49 *grey squirrel*: Scott's earlier note, in *Sir Tristrem*, is more accurate: 'miniver (*menu vair*), an inferior kind of vair, made from the skins of the small weazel and martin'. Vair 'appears to have been the skin of the Hungarian squirrel' (rather than the Grey squirrel, *Sciurus carolinensis*, introduced much later from the New World).

  now called terriers: *OED* records this name from the mid-fifteenth century. *Slow-hounds*, also called sleuth-hounds or slot-hounds, were a kind of bloodhound, formerly used in Scotland for tracking game and fugitives.

50 *Balder*: the radiant second son of Odin in Norse mythology.

51 *curfew*: popularly supposed to be an innovation of the Conqueror; but Turner attributes its institution to William Rufus, *History*, iv. 138–9.

52 *Wilfred*: Scott originally named his hero Harold, before deciding that 'Harold is over-scutched in this our generation', no doubt thanks to Byron and *Childe Harold's Pilgrimage* (*Letters*, v. 448). The new name was that of the noted Anglo-Saxon archbishop of York and saint (*c.*635–709), whose cult centred on Ripon and Hexham. Scott himself credited Wilfred with converting and civilizing the savages of southern England (Scott, *The Border Antiquities of England and Scotland*, 1814, 'introduction').

hership: Pillage [Scott's note]. An archaism, often used in the context of Border raids.

a tournament: after being forbidden by Henry I, tournaments were revived in England by Richard I. He designated five sites at which they could be held, but Ashby was not one of them (Strutt, *Sports and Pastimes*, 133).

54 *thy tongue outruns thy discretion*: proverbial variant: 'your tongue runs before your wit'.

55 *epigraph*: Pope's *Odyssey*, xx (not xxi), 314–17, 322–4. The original reads 'brimmy' for Scott's 'brimming', 'appoints' for 'assigns'.

56 *sclaveyn*: or 'slavin', recorded in *OED* from 1290; Scott probably got his spelling from a note by Joseph Ritson in *Ancient Engleish Metrical Romancëes* (1802), iii. 278.

cockle-shells: Scott confuses the pilgrim's token of the Holy Land, the scallop-shell, with that of the shrine of St James at Compostella in Spain, the cockle-shell.

horns of the altar: Psalm 118: 27, 'bind the sacrifice with cords, even to the horns of the altar'.

57 *Saint Hilda of Whitby*: a member of the Northumbrian royal family and abbess of Whitby, on the Yorkshire coast. The abbey, which she founded in 657, is the setting of canto ii of *Marmion*.

uncle Cedric: as A. N. Wilson points out, the fool addresses Lear as 'uncle' in Shakespeare's play. In tone rather than in detail, the banter between Wamba and Cedric recalls that between Lear's fool and his master, while Cedric's speech at the end of the chapter evokes the play's wild night and disruptions of kinship and degree—compare *King Lear*, III. vii. 62–3; 'If wolves at thy gate howl'd that dern time, | Thou shouldst have said, "Good porter, turn the key" '. As is often the case, Scott's allusions set up a screen against which we judge his characters and events. Here, although Cedric has quarrelled (like Gloucester) with his son, and despite the alienation of the Saxon kingdom, the local bonds of hospitality remain intact. (We even hear of an Oswald: this time, presumably, a good steward.)

58 *on the bow-hand of fair justice*: i.e. the left hand; the wrong side. (Compare *Love's Labours Lost*, IV. i. 132: 'Wide a' the bow-hand!')

61 *the lac dulce or the lac acidum*: 'Lac acidum, perhaps butter-milk or whey, was used in a monastery in very handsome vessels, called creches, from Hokeday to Michaelmas, and lac dulce from Michaelmas to Martinmas' (Turner, *History*, iii. 27).

61 *shipwreck of his honour and his kingdom*: Strutt, *Sports and Pastimes*: 'The wassail is said to have originated from the words of Rowena, the daughter of Hengist; who, presenting a bowl of wine to Vortigern, the king of the Britons, said, Waes hael, or, Health to you, my Lord the King' (363). The story comes from Nennius, who goes on to tell how the infatuated Vortigern surrendered part of his kingdom to Hengist in exchange for Rowena's hand, thus facilitating the Saxon conquest. A later tradition (from Geoffrey of Monmouth and the *Brut* of Wace and of Layamon) holds that the exchange of toasts, *Waes-hael, Drink-hael* (see below, Chapter XVI), was introduced into Britain at this banquet. Turner's *History* transmits the detail that Rowena was 'fair and blue-eyed', i. 259–60.

a truce with Saladin: after taking the citadel of Acre in 1191, but failing to reach Jerusalem, Richard negotiated a three-year peace with Saladin prior to his departure for England in October 1192. This treaty brought to an end the Third Crusade.

63 *epigraph*: *Merchant of Venice*, III. i. 63.

Isaac of York: perhaps based on Aaron of Lincoln, who dominated banking in the north of England until his death in 1186; his clients included the king of Scotland, the archbishop of Canterbury, and numerous peers and lesser prelates, and his capital helped finance the construction of Lincoln cathedral and several abbeys and monasteries.

Mahound and Termagaunt: Mahound = Mohammed. Conventional Saracen oaths in the ballads and vernacular romances, e.g. *Richard Cœur de Lion*, *Guy of Warwick*, Chaucer's 'Tale of Sir Thopas' (vii. 810). They were also the names of devils in the Mystery plays.

66 *jargon of . . . Sir Tristrem*: Scott's long note in *Sir Tristrem*, 260–70, cites 'the most respectable testimony' of Dame Juliana Berners, Abbess of St Albans (d. 1388?), whose *The Book of St Albans*, a collection of treatises on hawking, hunting, fishing, and heraldry, was printed in 1486 by Wynken de Worde (and reprinted by Joseph Haslewood, 1810). Scott comments on the medieval belief that Sir Tristrem 'was the first by whom the chace was reduced into a science', and glosses the terms: *arber*, the cut by which the deer was disembowelled; *numbles*, the innards; *curée*, or quarry, the hide, heart, liver, lights, and blood, fed to the hounds. The *morte* or tokening is the horn-call sounded at the death of the stag; the *recheat* is a signal to the hounds to return from a false scent.

the field of Northallerton, upon the day of the Holy Standard: the so-called Battle of the Standard, when the northern English barons defeated an invading Scottish host under King David, took place on 22 August 1138—rather more than thirty years before the period of *Ivanhoe*.

A Saxon bard: Scott imitates the manner of the *Battle of Brunanburgh* ('The wall of shields they cleaved, | They hewed the noble banners': Turner, *History*, iii. 280).

67 *Knights Hospitallers*: the Knights Hospitallers of St John of Jerusalem, from 1120 the rival military religious order to the Knights Templars.

a tournament after the taking of St John-de-Acre: the arrival of Richard with his host finally ended the terrible siege of the coastal city of Acre, 1189–91. The tournament is a fictitious event, as Scott's names for the main contenders would tell the reader adept in old romance. In *Richard Cœur de Lyon* the king chooses Sir Fulk Doyley and Sir Thomas de Multon to be his crusading companions by testing them at a tournament at Salisbury; Sir Robert de Tourneham and Sir Robert of Leycester appear later in the story, in Palestine. See the abridgement in Ellis, *Metrical Romances*, ii. 192, 251. (Thomas de Multon, Lord of Gilsland, reappears as Richard's master of horse in *The Talisman*, 1825.) Ivanhoe's reluctance to name himself in the catalogue of feats of arms derives from an episode in the fifteenth-century Catalan romance (mentioned in *Don Quixote*) *Tirant lo Blanch* (Mitchell, *Scott, Chaucer and Medieval Romance*, 127–9).

68 *guerdon*: reward.

69 *a portion of the true cross, brought from the Monastery of Mount Carmel*: the original foundation (1154) of the Carmelite order, south of Acre. St Helena, mother of the emperor Constantine, is supposed to have unearthed the remains of the cross on which Christ was crucified.

70 *the rood of Bromholme*: a relic of the true cross was brought to Bromholme in Norfolk, but not until 1223. It is mentioned in Chaucer's 'Reeve's Tale', i. 4286.

71 *Exchequer of the Jews*: in Richard I's reign committees were set up in the principal English towns to supervise the business transactions of the Jews. These in turn were overseen by a division of the Court of Exchequer at Westminster devoted exclusively to Jewish affairs. The Crown exploited English Jewry in return for royal protection well before the institution of this exchequer—Henry II

took a quarter of their property to finance the crusade to regain Jerusalem in 1187.

71 *gaberdine*: smock or cloak of coarse material, associated with Jews since Shakespeare's Shylock: 'you . . . spit upon my Jewish gaberdine', *Merchant of Venice*, I. iii. 103.

72 *epigraph*: *Merchant of Venice*, I. iii. 168–70.

solere chamber: an upper room or apartment; usually reserved for the use of the lord and his family.

77 *the dream is not dreamed for nought*: perhaps alludes to episodes of dream and interpretation in Genesis 37, 40–1, and Daniel 2.

men of Rabbah . . . children of Ammon: see 2 Samuel 11: 1.

78 *Lazarus*: the beggar at the rich man's gate in Luke 16: 20–1. Although sojourn among Christians has familiarized Isaac with their Testament, he misinterprets it—he is the rich man in the parable, presumably.

gird up our loins: 2 Kings 4: 29, Job 38: 3, etc.

80 *en croupe*: on the rump, behind the saddle.

81 *except perhaps the flying fish*: 'all animated nature seems combined against this little fish, which seems possessed of double powers, only to be subject to greater dangers. For though it should escape from its enemies of the deep, yet the tropic bird and the albatross are for ever on the wing to seize it': Oliver Goldsmith, *An History of the Earth, and Animated Nature* (1776), vi. 342–3.

the Jews of this period: banned from other trades and occupations, Jews in early modern Europe often provided the financial services that Christians were forbidden to practise by the Church edicts against usury. William I and his successors gave royal protection to the Jews, who settled in England after the conquest, in return for exorbitant demands upon their capital. The series of atrocities that marred the opening of Richard I's reign, 1189–90, exposed the uncertain efficacy of that protection. In the words of David Hume, the king's 'zeal against infidels, being communicated amongst his subjects, broke out in London on the day of his coronation, and made them find a crusade less dangerous, and attended with more immediate profit' (*History of England*, i. 397). Mobs attacked and murdered Jews and looted their property in towns all over the country, including Stamford and Lincoln. The worst massacre occurred the following year at York, when rioting townsfolk besieged 150 Jews in the castle and drove them to commit mass suicide. Although these events would have taken place just a few years before the action of *Ivanhoe*, Scott suppresses them in favour of a generalized account of persecution. John, after his accession to the throne, resorted to systematic extortion of his Jewish subjects. The tooth-pulling incident took place in 1210, when he had all the Jews in England held under arrest until they paid him a ransom of 66,000 marks; 10,000 came from the Bristol community, whose leader suffered the torture described. An official policy of persecution was not endorsed, however, until the reign of Edward I, who expelled the Jews after a series of pogroms in 1290.

82 *the host of Pharaoh*: Exodus 14: 25.

83 *Zareth*: Scott appears to have taken this name and *Kirjath Jairam* (below) from Christopher Marlowe, *The Jew of Malta*, I. i. They are garbled versions of biblical place-names: Zareth-Shahar and Kirjathaim, Joshua 13: 19, and Kirjath-jearim, Joshua 18: 14–15.

84 *Milan harnesses*: the fame of the Milanese armourers dates from the fourteenth and fifteenth centuries, rather later than the period of *Ivanhoe*. See Scott's note 7 to *Marmion*.

85 *good youth*: the phrase 'good youth' is typically addressed to the cross-dressing heroines of Shakespearian romantic comedy: Rosalind/Ganymede in *As You Like It*, III. ii. 433, IV. iii. 163; Viola/Cesario in *Twelfth Night*, I. iv. 15, III. i. 131; Imogen/Fidele in *Cymbeline*, IV. ii. 374, IV. ii. 394, V. v. 118.

Gramercy . . . it will go hard with me but I will requite it: a standard example of Scott's synthetic, in this case Shakespearian, antique style: combining 'Gramercy' (frequent in Shakespeare) with 'I'll requite it in the highest degree' (*Twelfth Night*, IV. ii. 119) and 'It shall go hard but I will better the instruction' (*Merchant of Venice*, III. i. 72).

86 *epigraph*: John Dryden's modern version of Chaucer, *Palamon and Arcite; Or, The Knight's Tale*, iii. 453–63.

The condition of the English nation . . . miserable: returning from Palestine in disguise, Richard fell into the hands of Leopold, Duke of Austria, whom he had antagonized during the crusade. (Their quarrel forms one of the central incidents in *The Talisman*.) Richard was released in February 1194 on payment of an enormous ransom. England was racked by riots and rebellions in his absence.

lawless resolutes: like the adherents of young Fortinbras in *Hamlet*, I. i. 98.

87 *spread through the land*: this outbreak occurred in 1196.

real: small silver coin (Spanish).

87 *Passage of Arms*: Scott's translation of *Pas d'armes*; see the account of tournaments in the 'Essay on Chivalry' (*Miscellaneous Prose Works*, vi. 43–5, 82–5). Scott combines a number of sources in his description of the tournament at Ashby, which in detail and in spirit evokes the fourteenth rather than the twelfth century. Chief among these is Froissart, whose account of the thirty days' deeds of arms against all comers at St Inglebert is cited by Scott (Johnes's translation, iv. 413) in the 'Essay on Chivalry'. Scott also draws on Chaucer (part IV of 'The Knight's Tale'), Malory (especially book IX, chapters 26–35 of the *Morte D'Arthur*), and Sydney (book III of *Arcadia*).

88 *salvage or silvan man*: wild man of the woods or green man; a figure of heraldry as well as folklore.

Richard de Malvoisin: elsewhere in these pages called Philip. Malvoisin = 'bad neighbour'.

Hugh de Grantmesnil: fictitious descendant of the Conqueror's companion, who was not, however, Lord High Steward.

90 *triumphs of Cupid*: conventional figures of Courtly Love; memorably anatomized by Spenser, in the *Faerie Queene*, III. xii.

91 *Lincoln-green*: the traditional costume of Robin Hood and his band, as in the 'Lytell Geste of Robyn Hode' (Joseph Ritson, *Robin Hood*, i. 1–80). Scott's description otherwise recalls Chaucer's yeoman: 'And he was clad in cote and hood of grene . . . And in his hand he baar a myghty bowe. | A not heed hadde he, with a broun visage. | . . . A Christofre on his brest of silver sheene. | An horn he bar, the bawdryk was of grene': 'General Prologue', i. 103, 108–9, 115–16. The famous longbow ('a bow of six feet length') dates from the following century, however.

bottled spider: compare *Richard III*, I. iii. 241: 'Why strews't thou sugar on that bottled spider'; and IV. iv. 81: 'That bottled spider, that foul hunch-back toad'.

92 *out-heroding*: wildly overdoing. From *Hamlet*, III. ii. 14, 'it out-Herods Herod', referring to the ranting tyrant of the miracle plays.

93 *caracoled*: technically, a series of half-turns or wheels alternately to the right and left; here, more loosely, prancing about.

rheno: a short, hooded cape of luxurious furs; see Strutt, *Dress and Habits*, i. 97–8.

maroquin: morocco-leather.

Rebecca: Scott is supposed to have based his heroine on Rebecca Gratz of Philadelphia (1781–1869), whose story was told to him in

1817 by Washington Irving. Rich, beautiful, and much courted, she renounced the man she loved and devoted her life to philanthropy and nursing (and incidentally recorded her own admiration of Scott's character; W. S. Crockett, *The Scott Originals*). Both Rebekah and Isaac are, of course, biblical figures. Scott translates the fair and resourceful wife and the rather vague and ineffectual husband of Genesis 24–5 into a strong daughter and weak father (who will later fall into the son's role of sacrificial victim).

94 *agraffe*: an ornamental clasp made of a hook and ring.

the very Bride of the Canticles: the wise king is Solomon, supposed author of the Canticles, or Song of Songs, in which the bride declares: 'I am the rose of Sharon, and the lily of the valleys', 2: 1.

Mammon of unrighteousness: Luke 16: 9, 'Make to yourselves friends of the mammon of unrighteousness'. A *byzant* was a Byzantine gold coin, worth nine shillings; a *mark* was worth thirteen shillings and fourpence (silver) or six pounds (gold). Although accounts were reckoned in pounds, shillings, and silver and gold marks, the only practical currency at the time was the silver penny. Most of the coins Scott mentions are exotic or anachronistic.

not a single cross in their pouches to keep the devil from dancing there: proverb, 'the devil dances in an empty pocket'. *The Oxford Dictionary of English Proverbs* records versions close to Scott's from the early fifteenth century, including Erasmus, *Two Dialogues*: 'The Deuyll (God saue vs) maye daunce in thy purse for euer a crosse that thou hast to kepe him forthe'. Coins were often stamped with a cross (obnoxious to the devil) on the obverse.

congee: bow, made at leave-taking or (as here) in salutation.

95 *the high places of the synagogue*: Matthew 23: 6, 'the uppermost rooms at feasts, and the chief seats in the synagogues', occupied by the Pharisees.

Athelstane: named after the Saxon king, the successor of Alfred and victor of Brunanburgh; he makes an appearance in the popular romance *Sir Guy of Warwick*.

Athelstane the Unready: from King Ethelred the Unready, whose epithet was actually 'redeless', i.e. without counsel, ill-advised. The popular form was retained in standard histories such as those by Hume, Henry, and Turner.

vis inertiæ: the force of inertia. A technical scientific term, in metaphoric use from the mid-eighteenth century.

97 *the fate of William Rufus*: William II was shot while hunting in the New Forest; his companion, Walter Tyrrel, fled abroad and the murder was never proved.

St Grizzel: Grizzel is the Scots form of Griselda, the type of female patience (although never canonized) in a legend recounted by Boccaccio, Petrarch, and Chaucer.

99 *epigraph*: Dryden, *Palamon and Arcite*, iii. 580–6.

by my halidom: by all I hold sacred (halidom = holiness).

dog or hog: echoes the proverbial 'make a hog or dog of it', i.e. bring to one use or another.

Waldemar Fitzurse: fictitious son of Reginald Fitzurse, one of the knights who assassinated Becket.

101 *at outrance*: to the uttermost, i.e. to the surrender or death of one of the combatants. The phrase occurs in Berners's Froissart (e.g. vol. i, chs. lxi–lxii).

102 *cap-a-pie*: head to foot. *Hamlet*, I. ii. 200, 'Armed at point exactly, cap-a-pe'.

the place that once knew them, knows them no more: conflation of Job 7: 10, 'neither shall his place know him any more', and Psalms 103: 16, 'the place thereof shall know it no more'.

106 *Desdichado*: unfortunate, ill-fated.

107 *sleep in Paradise*: Luke 23: 43, 'To day shalt thou be with me in Paradise'.

Templars . . . suppression: himself a major client of the Templar bank, Pope Alexander III had felt moved to regulate abuses of the Order's privileges at the Third Lateran Council of 1179. By the end of the century it was one of the most powerful corporations in Europe. Suppression of the Templars on charges of heresy and depravity followed their formal denunciation in 1305, and culminated in 1314 with the public burning of the Grand Master. The device of two knights mounted on one horse appeared on the Templar seal. Cavenagh suggests that 'the general device of his rider' must be a misprint for '. . . of his order'.

Gare le Corbeau: beware the raven.

109 *Cave, Adsum*: look out, I am here.

111 *epigraph*: *The Flower and the Leaf; Or, The Lady in the Arbor. A Vision*, 175–7, 184–9. Dryden's version of a fifteenth-century poem once (now no longer) attributed to Chaucer. Original reads 'sceptre' for Scott's 'symbol' in the last line. The *Agnus Castus* is a

tree, *Vitex agnus castus* or 'Solomon's Balm', once believed to be a talisman of chastity; it is prominent in medieval herbals.

112 *the Earl of Salisbury*: hero of a precursor modern chivalric romance, Thomas Leland's *Longsword: Earl of Salisbury* (1762). *Richard Cœur de Lyon* describes how he won his epithet *Longespée* (see Ellis, *Metrical Romances*, ii. 218). The historical earl was one of Henry II's illegitimate sons.

Over God's forbode: God forbid. As in the ballad 'Adam Bell, Clym of the Clough, and William Cloudesley', in Percy, *Reliques*, i. ii, no. 1: ' "Over Gods forbode," sayde the kinge'.

116 *zecchins*: or sequins; Venetian or Ottoman gold coins, from a later period.

Og the King of Bashan, and Sihon, King of the Amorites: see Numbers 32: 33.

119 *The forests of Needwood and Charnwood*: Ritson (*Robin Hood*, I. xv) notes Needwood Forest in Staffordshire as the site of a village called Loxley, the traditional name of Robin Hood's birthplace. Charnwood, in northern Leicestershire, has associations with Little John. See Stephen Knight, *Robin Hood: a Complete Study of the English Outlaw* (1994), pp. xii, 29.

120 *distant hum*: compare (for the general context) Milton, *L'Allegro*, 117–24:

> Towered cities please us then,
> And the busy hum of men,
> Where throngs of knights and barons bold
> In weeds of peace high triumphs hold,
> With store of ladies, whose bright eyes
> Rain influence, and judge the prize
> Of wit or arms, while both contend
> To win her grace whom all commend.

121 *epigraph*: Marlowe, *The Jew of Malta*, II. i. 1.

barbed steed: with armour on the head and flanks; a corruption (recorded since the sixteenth century) of 'barded', caparisoned with metal plates or metal-studded leather bands. Scott probably got the usage from *Richard III*, I. i. 10, 'instead of mounting barbed steeds'.

124 *estrada*: properly, estrado or estrade: a carpeted dais or shallow platform.

125 *the blotch of Egypt*: Exodus 9: 9, 'a boil breaking forth with blains upon man, and upon beast, throughout all the land of Egypt'.

125 *robed the seething billows in my choice silks*: *Merchant of Venice*, I. i. 33–4: 'scatter all her spices on the stream, | Enrobe the roaring waters with my silks'.

the herb which flourisheth most when it is most trampled on: 'the camomile, the more it is trodden on, the faster it grows', *1 Henry IV*, II. iv. 390.

126 *Daughter . . . thou hast harped upon*: compare *Hamlet*, II. ii. 185, 'Still harping on my daughter'.

Sabaoths: error for *Sabbaths* (Romans 9: 29, 'Lord of Sabaoth' = 'Lord of Hosts').

127 *draff*: dregs of malt left over after brewing.

128 *wild bulls of Bashan*: Psalm 22: 12, 'strong bulls of Bashan have beset me round'.

129 *clipt within the ring*: before 1205, when they were stamped with an outer circle, coins could be easily clipped or pared. Scott also echoes John Dryden, *The Medal*, l. 229: 'clip his regal rights within the ring'; see also *Hamlet*, II. ii. 457.

weaver's beam: 1 Samuel 17: 7, 'the staff of his spear was like a weaver's beam'.

130 *superstitions . . . from the wilds of Germany*: on Northern traditions of 'satyrs and other subordinate deities of the wood and wild' see Scott, *Letters on Demonology and Witchcraft* (1830), Letter iii. The White Lady of Avenel is an intrusive supernatural agent in Scott's contemporaneous romance *The Monastery*.

132 *epigraph*: *Two Gentlemen of Verona*, IV. i. 3.

133 *St Nicholas's clerks*: footpads, highwaymen. *1 Henry IV*, II. i. 61–2, 'if they meet not with St Nicholas' clerks, I'll give thee this neck'. See note to p. 449, below.

135 *the stream which relieved his fathers in the wilderness*: see Exodus 15: 23–7, 17: 6.

136 *Gandelyn*: named after the hero of a non-canonical Robin Hood ballad, 'Robyn and Gandelyn'. See Francis Child, *The English and Scottish Popular Ballads* (1888), iii. 12.

137 *toll-dish*: used for measuring the share of grain allotted the miller as payment for grinding. Here, his head.

faire le moulinet: a circular or twirling stroke in fencing; like a mill-wheel, from diminutive of French *moulin*, mill.

miller's thumb . . . doubly a thief: the ironical association of the two proverbs, 'an honest miller has a golden thumb' and 'many a miller, many a thief', occurs as early as Chaucer, 'General Prologue', i. 562–3: 'Wel koude he stelen corn and tollen thries; | And yet he hadde a thombe of gold, pardee'.

for want of a sacred poet: Horace, *Odes*, IV. ix. 28, 'carent quia vate sacro': the heroes who lived before Agamemnon are forgotten because 'they lack a sacred poet'.

138 *night-walkers*: thieves (common sixteenth- and seventeenth-century usage).

140 *epigraph*: Chaucer, 'The Knight's Tale', i. 2599–610. Spelling and diction are modernized, obliterating Chaucer's metre, which was not well understood at the time.

141 *fifty knights*: there are one hundred on each side in Chaucer's 'Knight's Tale', from which, as Mitchell points out, Scott derives many of the details of the Ashby tournament: the *mêlée*, restraints on violence such as the prohibition of daggers, the obligation of a knight to retire once overcome (*Scott, Chaucer, and Medieval Romance*, 130). For other regulations see Strutt, *Sports and Pastimes*, 134–5.

144 *Laissez aller!*: 'Laisseir les aler', let them go: Strutt, *Sports and Pastimes*, 135.

145 *Beau-seant!*: *baucent*, pied; the standard of the Templars was called the *gonfanon baucent*.

. . . *terror or compassion*: an essay on Scott's sources in the *Retrospective Review*, 2nd series, i (1827), 25, pointed out the derivation of this paragraph from Sir Philip Sidney's *Arcadia*, III. viii: 'And now the often-changing Fortune began also to chaunge the hewe of the battailes. For at the first, though it were terrible, yet Terror was deckt so brauelie with rich furniture, guilte swords, shining armours, pleasant pensils, that the eye with delight had scarce leasure to be afraide: But now all universally defiled with dust, bloud, broken armours, mangled bodies, tooke away the maske, and sette foorth Horror in his owne horrible manner' (1590 edn., 271–2). See also *The Bridal of Triermain* (1813) II. xxiii–xxiv.

147 *warder*: the official staff or truncheon used to signal the commencement or interruption of a combat. Recorded, like most of the details of Scott's tournament, from the mid-fifteenth century. Compare Walpole, *The Castle of Otranto*, chapter 3: 'So saying, the herald cast down his warder'.

springal: youth. Common usage around 1500–1650; *OED* credits Scott with its modern revival.

148 *the Black Sluggard*: the hero of *Richard Cœur de Lyon* disguises
himself as a knight-errant in black armour on the first day of the
tournament at Salisbury; Musidorus appears in the lists as a Black
Knight in Sidney's *Arcadia*, III. viii.

chamfron: frontlet of a barded or armed horse. Most of Scott's terms
for armour, like this one, date from the mid-fifteenth century.

152 *epigraph*: these lines are a pastiche of the *Iliad* rather than a quotation from it; the context is the funeral games, book 24.

innate attractions and antipathies: believed to inform all matter,
organic and inorganic, in the old physiology.

153 *Askalon*: Richard passed through the coastal town of Askalon (the
present-day Ashqelon, Israel), on the way to and from Jerusalem
(1192).

154 *a bundle of myrrh, and a cluster of camphire*: Song of Solomon, 1: 13–
14 (similes applied to a male lover).

pearls before swine: Matthew 7: 6. 'By the bones of Becket' is a pious
oath in the mouth of prince John, whose father had instigated the
murder of the archbishop in his own cathedral of Canterbury.

Take heed to yourself, for the Devil is unchained!: the letter was sent
in July 1193. Scott would have read about it in Henry's *History*, v.
215. Richard did not reach England until March 1194.

155 *St Hubert, the patron of silvan sport*: he was converted while out
hunting; a stag bearing a crucifix between its antlers preached to
him.

157 *a shot at rovers*: originally, a mark selected at will or random, not at
any fixed distance; but Scott seems to adopt the later usage meaning a mark for long-distance shooting, in contrast to *at butts* (*OED*).

159 *in the clout!*: on target, bullseye; from the piece of canvas fixed to
the butt as a mark. *2 Henry IV*, III. ii. 45: ''A would have clapp'd
i'th' clout at twelve score'.

160 *his arrow split the willow rod against which it was aimed*: 'cleaving the
wand' is a standard feat of archery in ballads celebrating Robin
Hood and other outlaws; see examples in Ritson, *Robin Hood*, i. 27,
71 and ii. 167; and Percy, *Reliques*, I. ii, no. 1, 'Adam Bell, Clym of
the Clough, and William of Cloudesley'. Locksley's feat of splitting
the arrow already stuck in the target echoes that of the Douglas in
Scott's *The Lady of the Lake*, v. xxii ('His second split the first in
twain').

162 *epigraph*: Thomas Warton, the younger, *Ode XVIII: For the New
Year, 1787*; opening lines.

Castle of Ashby: the castle at Ashby (demolished during the Civil War) was built in around 1474. For the execution of Lord Hastings, see *Richard III*, III. iv. It is not known whether Ashby belonged to the De Quincey family during the period of *Ivanhoe*.

163 *golden opinions*: *Macbeth*, I. vii. 32: 'I have bought | Golden opinions from all sorts of people'.

English domination in Ireland: this took place in April 1185.

164 *Charlemagne . . . damp or the frost*: Scott bowdlerizes the anecdote from Strutt, *Dress and Habits*, i. 40, which concludes: 'and when we retire to ease nature they will not secure our legs from the cold and frost'.

simnel-bread and wastle cakes: a rich cake of saffron and currants, eaten at mid-Lent in Cheshire and Lancashire, and loaves baked of the finest flour. Chaucer's Prioress feeds 'wastel breed' to her lapdogs, 'General Prologue', i. 147.

165 *instead of . . . waving them gracefully in the air*: Scott had already recounted the story (from an old romance) of the page who exhibited his high breeding by waving his hands in the air to dry them rather than wiping them on a towel: 'Essay on Chivalry', *Miscellaneous Prose Works*, vi. 52.

beccaficoes: Henry's *History* (which also expounds the contrast between Saxon and Norman table manners) mentions 'karumpie' as a delicacy of unknown composition, vi. 364. Of the ingredients supplied by Scott, *beccaficoes* (Italian, 'fig-peckers'—because good to eat when fattened on figs in the early autumn) are blackcaps or ortolans.

166 *the British crown*: 'this use of the word "British" did not arise till about the time of Henry VIII' (Cavenagh).

167 *head and front of the offence*: *Othello*, I. iii. 80: 'the very head and front of my offending'.

170 *handwriting on the wall*: Daniel 5: 27.

172 *epigraph*: Joanna Baillie, *Basil: A Tragedy*, II. iii. 169–75. Scott held her *Series of Plays in which it is attempted to delineate the Stronger Passions of the Mind* (1798–1812) in high esteem. Volume II of the first edition (1820) began here.

173 *the Conqueror's eldest son*: the feckless Robert inherited Normandy while his younger brother William succeeded to the English throne. He sold his domains to William at a bargain in order to finance his participation in the First Crusade, rebelled against William's successor Henry I, and was defeated by him in 1106.

Robert lived for twenty-eight more years in a captivity that was not especially harsh by the standards of the time.

174 *kirtle*: a man's tunic or coat; Anglo-Saxon.

Christmas gambols and quaint maskings: Christmas was the time of the Feast of Misrule (Strutt, *Sports and Pastimes*, 339–43). The Norman knights are typically unseasonable in their co-option of English festivities.

175 *without the consent either of their brides or their brides' families*: with characteristic carelessness, De Bracy confounds profane history (Livy's rape of the Sabine women) with sacred (Judges 21).

176 *Saint Wittol*: a wittol is a fool or cuckold; compare *Merry Wives of Windsor*, II. iii. 313. Scott uses the word to mean cuckold in *Kenilworth* (1821), ch. 36, and to mean fool in *The Pirate* (1822), ch. 36.

178 *epigraph*: opening lines of Thomas Parnell, *The Hermit* (1729).

184 *parish pinfold*: a pound for stray livestock.

185 *win the ram at a wrestling match*: see Strutt, *Sports and Pastimes*, 82–3; and compare Chaucer, 'General Prologue', i. 548 ('At wrastlynge he wolde have alwey the ram') and 'Sir Thopas', vii. 740–1.

Shadrach, Meshech, and Abednego: 1 Daniel 3. The 'King of the Saracens' is Nebuchadnezzar.

187 *horn of the urus*: the aurochs (*Bos urus*), an extinct wild ox once native to Britain and continental Europe; mentioned by Julius Caesar.

188 *trencher-man*: *Much Ado About Nothing*, I. i. 50, 'He is a very valiant trencherman'.

189 *scissors of Delilah*: with which she enfeebled Samson by cutting off his hair, Judges 16: 19; *nail of Jael*: which she banged through the forehead of the sleeping Sisera, Judges 4: 21; *scimitar of Goliath*: ineffectual against the slingshot of the boy David, 1 Samuel 17: 40–51.

190 *epigraph*: Thomas Warton, *Inscription in a Hermitage, at Ansley Hall in Warwickshire* (1777), 25–30, reading 'blameless' for 'peaceful'.

Allan-a-Dale, the northern minstrel: in 'Robin Hood and Allin A Dale' Robin rescues the lady-love of the disconsolate Allin from marriage to a rich old knight. But Robin, not Allin, disguises himself as 'a bold harper, ... the best in the north country'

(Ritson, *Robin Hood*, ii. 49). Minstrels in the old ballads and romances came traditionally from the north.

191 *The cross upon his shoulders borne . . . | Was token of a foughten field*: compare Spenser's Red-Cross Knight, in the *Faerie Queene*, I. i. 1–2:

> Y cladd in mightie armes and silver shielde,
> Wherein old dints of deepe wounds did remaine,
> The cruell markes of many a bloudy fielde . . .
> But on his brest a bloudie Crosse he bore,
> The deare remembrance of his dying Lord.

Tekla's smile: St Thecla, whose story is told in the apocryphal *Acts of Paul and Thecla*, came from Iconium (Konya) in Asia Minor.

192 *Iconium's turban'd Soldan*: the splendid capital of the Selcuk Turks fell in 1190 to the Emperor Barbarossa, on his way to the Third Crusade.

194 *exceptis excipiendis*: with the necessary exceptions. Compare *Twelfth Night*, I. iii. 6, 'except before excepted'.

Saint . . . Willick: St Dubric is better known as Dubricius or Dyfrig; St Swibert as Swithbert; and St Willick as Willigis.

195 *come cut and long tail*: proverbial: 'come what may'. Compare *Merry Wives of Windsor*, III. iv. 47: 'that I will, come cut and long-tail, under the degree of a squire'.

like old Ariosto: compare *The Heart of Mid-Lothian* (1818), opening of chapter 16: 'Like the digressive poet Ariosto, I find myself under the necessity of connecting the branches of my story, by taking up the adventures of another of the characters, and bringing them down to the point at which we have left those of Jeanie Deans.' In the 'Essay on Romance' (1822) Scott describes Ariosto's narrative technique: 'although he torments the reader's attention by digressing from one adventure to another, [he] delights us, upon frequent perusals, by the extreme ingenuity with which he gathers up the broken ends of his narrative, and finally weaves them all handsomely together in the same piece' (*Miscellaneous Prose Works*, vi. 195). Byron called Scott 'the Ariosto of the North' in *Childe Harold's Pilgrimage*, IV. xl.

196 *epigraph*: *Ettrick Forest* is probably by Scott himself; it is the ancient name of the Border territory near his estate at Abbotsford. See note to epigraph to Chapter XXX, p. 319, below.

197 *the good old weapons of his country*: a *glaive* was originally a lance or spear, but by the fifteenth century it had come to mean a sword. A

EDITOR'S NOTES

bill, conversely, meant a sword in Old English and afterwards a halberd; a *brown bill* was one painted brown, typically carried by infantrymen and sentries. Compare Spenser, *Faerie Queene*, V. xi. 58, 'bills and glaives', anticipating Scott's modern usage.

199 *Burton*: famous for its abbey ale since the fourteenth century; the commercial brewery dates from the early eighteenth century.

200 *St Edward the Confessor*: Edmund and Edward are Saxon royal saints; Edmund was martyred by the Danes in 870, and Edward died in 1066, the last of the royal line.

By the hog dear to St Anthony: St Anthony was the patron saint of swineherds.

203 *like Hotspur*: disgusted by Archbishop Scroop's reluctance to join the Northern rebellion, *1 Henry IV*, II. iii. 33–4.

205 *epigraph*: Joanna Baillie, *Orra: A Tragedy* , III. i. 44–8.

smite them, hip and thigh: Judges 15: 8, 'he smote them hip and thigh with a great slaughter'.

208 *St George for merry England!*: compare Spenser, *Faerie Queene*, I. x. 61, 'Saint George of mery England'. The cult of St George attained its nationalist development only in the Crusades, thanks in large part to Richard I, who declared himself and his army under George's protection. Saxon patriots would more likely have cried allegiance to St Edward the Confessor, who remained the popular national patron well into the next century.

212 *in the lion's mouth*: Psalm 22: 21, 'Save me from the lion's mouth'.

213 *epigraph*: probably by Scott.

Watling-street: the old Roman road, running from Dover through London and York to the Northumbrian border.

214 *there's game afoot*: compare *1 Henry IV*, I. iii. 278, 'Before the game is afoot thou still letst slip'.

the nearer the church the farther from·God: recorded by the *Oxford Dictionary of English Proverbs* from 1303. Compare Spenser, *Shepheardes Calender* (1579): 'To Kerke the narre, from God more farre, | has bene an old-sayd sawe' ('Iulye', 97–8).

black sanctus: Satanic parody of the Roman Catholic mass; as in the sixteenth-century dog-Latin 'Black Sanctus, or monke's hymne to Saunte Satane', published (with a bowdlerized translation) in Thomas Evans, *Old Ballads: Historical and Narrative* (4 vols., 1784), iii. 242–4.

old drinking song: Cavenagh notes the similarity between this and the soldier's song in *The Lady of the Lake*, VI. v, and the derivation of both from 'The Second Three-Man's Song' in Thomas Dekker, *The Shoe-Maker's Holiday*, scene xviii:

> Troll the bowl, the jolly nut-brown bowl,
> And here, kind mate, to thee,
> Let's sing a dirge for Saint Hugh's soul,
> And down it merrily.

215 *De profundis clamavi*: Psalm 130: 1, 'Out of the depths have I cried unto thee'.

216 *church militant*: The Church on earth, considered as warring against the powers of evil.

217 *transmew*: Scott gets the word from Spenser, *Faerie Queene*, I. vii. 35 ('Men into stones therewith he could transmew'), who got it from Chaucer, *Troilus and Criseyde*, iv. 439.

219 *get behind me*: Matthew 16: 23, 'Get thee behind me, Satan'.

Clerk me no Clerks: compare *Richard II*, II. iii. 87: 'Grace me no grace, nor uncle me no uncle'.

221 *epigraph*: Joanna Baillie, *Orra* III. ii. 13–19.

226 *the tale*: Harold of England's embittered brother Tosti and the Norwegian king Harald Halfagar, egged on by William of Normandy, led an invasion fleet up the Humber in September 1066. They were both killed and their force routed at Stamford bridge. Harold received news of the Norman invasion in the south while he was celebrating the victory in York, and he was killed at Hastings less than three weeks later (14 October).

quaffing the blood-red wine: compare the 'Ballad of Sir Patrick Spens', l. 2, 'Drinking the blude-red wine' (*Minstrelsy of the Scottish Border*, I. i).

227 *descended of Harold's blood*: one of Scott's strategic prevarications about historical names, dates, and generations. Here he makes Athelstane the descendant of Harold, who was not part of the royal Saxon bloodline; earlier in the chapter he is 'the descendant of the Confessor', who left no children; 'he is, in fact, the child of a barren stock' (Clare A. Simmons, *Reversing the Conquest*, 1990: 82).

the art of making glass, or of staining it: according to Turner's *History*, glass-making was unknown in England until an abbot imported French artisans in the seventh century; even then its diffusion was slow (iii. 112–13).

228 *Hardicanute*: although he died while boozing at a banquet, Hardicanute, Danish king of England (1039–41), was more notorious for rashness and violence than for gluttony.

228 *sewer*: butler responsible for service at table. See *Macbeth*, I. vii, stage direction.

229 *as if it had been blown before an enchanted castle by the destined knight*: Astolfo's terrific horn-blast, in Ariosto's *Orlando Furioso*, xxii, dissolves the spell that binds the knights in Atalante's magic castle.

230 *epigraph*: *Merchant of Venice*, II. viii. 15–17.

231 *from the fowler*: Psalm 91: 3, 'Surely he shall deliver thee from the snare of the fowler'.

    wiry and broken light . . . period: OED records a contemporary technical usage of 'wiry' to denote strongly marked pictorial lines, as in etching or engraving, citing examples from William Blake (*A Descriptive Catalogue of Pictures, Poetical and Historical Inventions*, 1809) and James Smith (*The Panorama of Science and Art*, 1815). I surmise that Scott's description assisted George Cruikshank's famous illustration for *Oliver Twist*, 'Fagin in the Condemned Cell' (1839). *Rembrandt* was often cited as the master of character-painting and *chiaroscuro* technique; compare Scott, *The Antiquary*, chapter 32: 'Falling in a stream upon the chimney, the rays illuminated, in the way that Rembrandt would have chosen, the features of the unfortunate nobleman and those of the old sybil'.

    frayed and soiled with the stains of his armour: compare Chaucer's knight, 'General Prologue', i. 75–6: 'Of fustian he wered a gypon | Al bismotered with his habergeon'.

233 *just measure and weight of the Tower of London*: the Saxon or Tower pound was named after the mint pound in the Tower of London. A national standard of weights and measures was established at Magna Carta.

    the keys which are given her to bind and to loose: See Matthew 16: 19: 'And I will give thee the keys of the kingdom of heaven: and whatsoever thou shalt bind on earth shall be bound in heaven; and whatsoever thou shalt loose on earth shall be loosed in heaven'.

236 *Fitzdotterel*: 'son of a fool'.

239 *epigraph*: *Two Gentlemen of Verona*, v. iv. 55. Scott added 'force you' in 1830; original reads 'force ye'.

240 *the dress of a gallant of the period*: in fact, like Prince John and Prior Aymer at the tournament, De Bracy wears the extravagant fashions (long hair, elaborately curled shoes) of the reign of William Rufus, John's grandfather: Strutt, *Dress and Habits*, i. 100, 106.

241 *vile crowder*: fiddler. Echoes the famous passage in Sir Philip Sidney's *An Apology for Poetry* (1595) on hearing 'the old song of

Percy and Douglas': 'yet is it sung but by some blind crowder, with no rougher voice than rude style'.

in set terms, and in courtly language: according to the conventions of the troubadour-based Courts of Love.

245 *'hoarse-winded blowing far and keen'*: I have been unable to trace this quotation.

the industrious Henry: Scott lifts the entire paragraph that follows from Henry's *History*, vi. 346, including the quotation from the *Anglo-Saxon Chronicle*. The paragraph after that is paraphrased from Henry, who cites the monkish chronicler Eadmer's (d. 1124) *Historia Novorum* for the story of the princess Matilda.

246 *the Empress Matilda*: Scott confuses (as Henry does not) mother and daughter. The Matilda of the anecdote was born Edith, daughter of the Scottish king Malcolm Canmore, and took the name Matilda when she married Henry I; her formidable daughter, Matilda or Maud, was Empress of Germany by her marriage to Henry V, and mother of Henry II by her second marriage to Geoffrey of Anjou. (A third Matilda, the wife of King Stephen, was niece and cousin to these two.)

247 *epigraph*: John Home, *Douglas* (1759) I. i, reading 'brides' for Scott's 'bride'. Volume 2 of the 1830 edition begins here.

Zernebock: Scott got the name from Turner: 'Zernebogus, or the black, malevolent, ill-omened deity', i. 220. The word is Slavic: 'Chorny [Czerny] Bog', Black God. 'In his conceited romance of Ivanhoe, he couples Thor and Tzernebock together, and calls them gods of the heathen Saxons', sneers a character in George Borrow's *The Romany Rye* (1857); 'Tzernebock was no god of the Saxons, but one of the gods of the Sclaves, on the southern side of the Baltic' (ii. 118–19). As Scott well knew: his *Harold the Dauntless* (II. xvii) includes this invocation to 'a God of heathen days':

> From thy Pomeranian throne,
> Hewn in rock of living stone,
> Where, to thy godhead faithful yet,
> Bend Esthonian, Finn, and Lett, . . .
> Hear me! sovereign of the rock,
> Hear me! mighty Zernebock!

248 *Egyptian*: gypsy.

men know a fox by the train: proverb, 'A fox is known by his brush'; recorded in the *Oxford Dictionary of English Proverbs* from 1545.

249   *my thread is spun out*: by the Norns, the Fatal Sisters of the Norse mythology.

     by a single hair: Dionysus, tyrant of Syracuse, forced Damocles to sit under a dangling sword as an example of the precariousness of worldly enjoyment.

250   *an embattled space*: fortified with battlements.

     bartisan: Scots usage, meaning a battlement or parapet, from the sixteenth and seventeenth centuries ('barteseine', 1558), according to the *Dictionary of the Older Scottish Tongue* (1931). *OED* erroneously declares it to be Scott's own coinage, from 'a misconception of a seventeenth-century illiterate Scots spelling . . . a spurious "modern antique" which had no existence in the time to which it is attributed'. As he worked on *Ivanhoe* Scott was also busy superintending his dear 'romance in limestone', Abbotsford: 'The addition to my house is completed with battlement and bartisan' (*Letters*, v. 421).

     called in with the fulness of the Gentiles: Romans 11: 25, 'that blindness in part is happened to Israel, until the fulness of the Gentiles be come in'.

251   *bright lily of the vale of Baca!*: conflation of Psalm 84: 6, 'Baca', with Song of Solomon 2: 1, 'lily of the valleys'.

     alembic: a still.

252   *witch of Endor*: she appears in 1 Samuel 28.

     Despardieux!: by the gods.

     par amours: as a mistress; courtly love jargon.

     daughter of Sirach . . . gentle Ecclesiastica: Bois-Guilbert twits Rebecca with being a female version of Jesus, son of Sirach, author of the apocryphal *Ecclesiasticus* or book of Wisdom, which contains lengthy homilies on social conduct.

254   *the final plunge*: Nassau Senior, reviewing Scott's novels in the *Quarterly Review*, October 1821, noted that this episode 'is borrowed from the celebrated scene in which Clarissa (vi, letter 13) awes Lovelace by a similar menace of suicide' (reprinted in John O. Hayden (ed.), *Scott: The Critical Heritage*, 1970: 238).

255   *It was woman that taught me cruelty*: 'Here, surely, is a romanticised version of Gerard of Ridefort's anger over the loss of the heiress of Botron, while the Templar arrogance bears more than a passing resemblance to Odo of Saint-Armand' (Malcolm Barber, *The New Knighthood: A History of the Order of the Temple*, 1994: 327).

257 *wrench the sceptre from their gripe*: compare *Macbeth*, III. i. 61, 'hold a barren sceptre in my gripe'.

259 *epigraph*: Oliver Goldsmith, *She Stoops to Conquer*, iv. 680.

St Niobe: another symptomatic confusion of sacred and profane. Niobe's twelve children were killed by Apollo and Diana when she boasted of their beauty, and she continued to weep for them even after grief had turned her into stone (see Ovid, *Metamorphoses*, vi).

Apollyon: Revelations 9: 11: 'the angel of the bottomless pit . . . in the Greek tongue hath his name Apollyon', i.e. Destroyer. 'By Apolyn' is a stock Paynim oath in romances such as *Richard Cœur de Lyon* and *Bevis of Hampton*.

261 *sign-manual*: signature, usually of a lord or sovereign, serving to authenticate a document.

262 *fork-headed shafts of a cloth-yard in length*: the yard (36 inches) by which cloth was measured; see *Marmion*, note 61. 'Cloth-yard shaft' is a ballad epithet for an arrow. Compare Percy, *Reliques*, I. i, no. 1, 'Chevy-Chase', and Scott, *The Lay of the Last Minstrel* (1805) IV. xv: 'faster still a cloth-yard shaft'. *French crown* was the English term for the French *couronne* or *écu*; not current before the fourteenth century.

266 *mammocks*: scraps, shreds; from the sixteenth century.

267 *Pax vobiscum*: 'peace be with you' (Ordinary of the Mass).

268 *epigraph*: see note to epigraph to Chapter XXX p. 319.

Order of St Francis: the Order of Friars Minor was founded in 1209 and the first Franciscans came to England in 1224.

a grey-goose shaft: ballad epithet; compare Ritson, *Robin Hood*, ii. 166, 'grey-goose-wing'.

269 *quidam viator incidit in latrones*: 'a certain traveller fell among thieves'; paraphrasing Luke 10: 30, *homo quidam descendebat ab Hierusalem in Hiericho et incidit in latrones*: 'A certain man went down from Jerusalem to Jericho, and fell among thieves'.

nomen illis legio: Luke 8: 30 reads, *quod tibi nomen est? at ille dixit Legio*: 'What is thy name? And he said, Legion'.

cor meum eructavit: Psalm 45 (Vulgate): 1, *Eructavit cor meum verbum bonum*, 'my heart is inditing a good matter'.

270 *a higher tribunal*: compare Luke 12: 20, 'this night thy soul shall be required of thee'.

270 *leap in the dark*: proverbial combination: 'look before you leap' + 'leap in the dark'. Compare John Vanbrugh, *The Provoked Wife*, V. vi: 'Now I am in for Hobbes's voyage, a great leap in the dark'.

272 *John-a-Duck*: I have not been able to find the source of this; but as Cavenagh remarks, many of Wamba's proverbial sayings appear to be nonce coinages.

basta: Italian, 'enough'. *Taming of the Shrew*, I. i. 203, 'Basta, content thee'.

stool-ball: an ancestor of rounders or baseball, with stools for bases: Strutt, *Sports and Pastimes*, 97–8.

Watch and ward: night-time and day-time guards.

273 *Et vobis—quæso, domine reverendissime, pro misericordia vestra*: 'and with you—I beseech you, most reverend sir, for your mercy'.

274 *Ifrin*: 'Ifurin, the Celtic name for hell, which survives in the Welsh Uffern ('hell'). The Scandinavian gods seem rather out of place there' (Cavenagh).

275 *epigraph*: Thomas Crabbe, 'The Hall of Justice', i. 5–8, 27–32.

276 *gone to render an account of his stewardship*: died and gone to justify his conduct to God. See Luke 16: 2.

277 *bodkin*: dagger; *Hamlet*, III. i. 75, 'he himself might his quietus make | With a bare bodkin'.

279 *power to cleanse the ulcers of the body*: Edward the Confessor instituted touching for the King's Evil, or the royal laying-on of hands to cure scrofula, which was revived by James VI/I (see *Macbeth*, IV. iii) and continued until the death of Queen Anne (1714). Samuel Johnson remembered being taken as a child to be touched by the queen in 1712.

the Gods of our yet unbaptized ancestors: *Hertha* is identified by Turner (who cites Tacitus, *Germania*, xl) as 'mother Earth', *History*, i. 219. '*Mista* black, terrific Maid' is invoked in Thomas Gray's 'The Fatal Sisters: An Ode', line 17. *Skogula* derives from the Valkyrie 'Scogul' ('Battle'), named in Turner's translation of the *Voluspa* from the poetic *Edda*, i. 244.

I bid thee avaunt: *Macbeth*, III. iv. 92: 'Avaunt, and quit my sight'.

280 *donjon*: the castle's central tower or inner keep.

mangonel: a giant catapult for hurling rocks. Common in the vernacular romances, such as *Richard Cœur de Lyon* (Ellis, *Metrical Romances*, ii. 265, where arrowblasts and the quarrel are also mentioned). Tulloch (*The Language of Walter Scott*, 33) suggests Scott may have been influenced by Southey's *Joan of Arc* (1795), which revives many of the same terms for weaponry and siege-armaments.

281 *war-song of Rollo*: Rollo, or Hrolf, father of the Normans, led the first Viking settlement in France. But Scott is probably thinking of the *Song of Roland*, chanted in the van of the Norman attack at Hastings by the minstrel Taillefer. In the debate over the origins of romance, scholars cited this as the first recorded instance of Norman minstrelsy, but disagreed as to whether Rollo imported his scalds with him to Normandy.

bear a burden: sound an accompaniment.

283 *compelled to sing . . . his wallets*: for analogues see Ritson, *Robin Hood*, i. 132 ('A True Tale of Robin Hood'); ii. 23 ('Robin Hood and the Bishop'):

> Then Robin Hood took the bishop by the hand,
>> And bound him fast to a tree,
> And made him sing a mass, God wot,
>> To him and his yeomandree.

284 *St Dennis*: St Denis, patron saint of France.

doit: a Dutch coin of trifling value; not recorded before the sixteenth century.

ever since the biggin was bound first round my head: compare *2 Henry IV*, IV. v. 27: 'he whose brow with homely biggen bound'. A biggin is a child's cap or a nightcap.

St Genevieve: patroness of Paris.

286 *a cardinal*: the red cap was not granted to secular cardinals until 1245, nor to sacred ones until 1591.

Norman yoke: see Introduction. I can find no instance of the phrase in English poetry before 1715. Wamba's 'proverb' is Scott's composition, with the pun on 'saw' no doubt intended.

287 *man of mould*: mortal man. *Henry V*, III. ii. 21, 'Be merciful, great Duke, to men of mould'. Sometimes misinterpreted to mean 'of might'.

288 *Saint Bennet, the prince of these bull-beggars*: St Benedict, patriarch of Western monasticism and patron of Europe. *Bull-beggars* means bullying sturdy beggars, with a pun on the papal bull or licence; but this was originally a kind of goblin (compare Scott's later citation from Reginald Scot, *Discovery of Witchcraft*, in his *Letters on Demonology and Witchcraft*, 1830; Letter vi).

289   *De Civitate Dei*: *Concerning the City of God against the Pagans*, 413–27.

    Si quis, suadente Diabolo: 'if any man, at the tempting of the devil'.

290   *men of Belial*: worthless men; see 1 Samuel 30: 22.

    touch not mine anointed, and do my prophets nought of evil: 1 Chronicles 16: 22, Psalm 105: 15, reading 'do my prophets no harm'.

292   *Some hilding fellow he must be*: base, low-born; compare *2 Henry IV*, I. i. 57: 'He was some hilding fellow that had stol'n | The horse he rode on'.

293   *epigraph*: by Scott. MS title is 'The Lore of Avicenna'. Scott begins the third volume here in the MS of *Ivanhoe*.

    hacqueton: a 'wadded or quilted waistcoat' (Ellis, *Metrical Romances*, ii. 114) worn under the mail; fourteenth-century.

    Rabbi Jacob Ben Tudela: perhaps named after the famous Rabbi Benjamin of Tudela, whose travels (1159–73) took him as far as the borders of China.

294   *dogs of Ishmael and of Edom*: Christians and Saracens.

    Beard of Aaron: Psalm 133: 2. Isaac does well to fear the imputation of blood-guilt, often used to justify attacks on Jewish populations.

    Rabbi Manasses of Byzantium: named after the wizard and idolater in Chronicles 33: 6–7.

    whose eyes had yet more deeply penetrated his heart: Mitchell, *Scott, Chaucer and Medieval Romance* (133–4), lists romance analogues of heroes cured by female and Jewish or Pagan physicians, e.g. Josyan, the daughter of the Saracen king Ermyn, in *Bevis of Hampton* (Ellis, *Metrical Romances*, ii. 108–9). Cervantes satirized the convention in *Don Quixote*, Part 1, chapter iii. The most celebrated English example, no doubt, is Belphebe's cure of the wounded Timias in Spenser, *Faerie Queene*, III. v. As Mitchell points out, Scott's treatment is remarkable for its refusal of the conventional outcome, in which the fair physician's love for the hero drives her to convert to Christianity.

297   *keepeth the day which he appointeth*: echoes the Lord's commandment to keep the Passover, Numbers 9: 3: 'In the fourteenth day of this month, at even, ye shall keep it in his appointed season'.

303   *their horn was most highly exalted*: Psalm 89: 10, 17, 'thou hast scattered thine enemies with thy strong arm', 'for in thy favour our horn shall be exalted'.

Juvenal's tenth satire: the most popular of Juvenal's satires among moralists in early modern Europe. At the end of *Ivanhoe* Scott quotes from Johnson's celebrated imitation, 'The Vanity of Human Wishes'. Lines 37–44 (19–22 in Juvenal) describe the terrors of the enriched traveller:

> Nor Light nor Darkness bring his Pain Relief,
> One shews the Plunder, and one hides the Thief.

304 *feeding upon the wealthy Jew*: *Merchant of Venice*, II. v. 14–15: 'But yet I'll go in hate, to feed upon | The prodigal Christian'. Scott set the phrase in quotation-marks in MS.

307 *epigraph*: Schiller, *Die Jungfrau von Orleans*, V. xi:

> Steig auf die Warte dort, die nach dem Feld
> Hin sieht, und sag' uns, wie die Schlacht sich wendet.

309 *the captains and the shouting*: Job 39: 23, 25, 'The quiver rattleth against him, the glittering spear and the shield', 'the thunder of the captains, and the shouting'.

310 *singular novelty*: MS reads 'selcouth': Old English, 'rare, wonderful, strange'. Scott had used the word, which he got from Spenser (*Faerie Queene*, IV. viii), in *The Lord of the Isles*, IV. xii.

311 *nakers*: Chaucer, 'Knight's Tale', i. 2511: 'Pypes, trompes, nakers, clariounes, | That in the bataille blowen blody sounes'.

En avant De Bracy! . . . Front-de-Bœuf à la rescousse!: 'Forward De Bracy! . . . Front-de-Bœuf to the rescue!'

'wholly together': a recollection of Froissart's *Chronicles*, in Berners's translation: 'the englysshe archers . . . lette fly their arowes so holly and so thycke that it semed snow' (I. cxxx).

315 *derring-do*: 'desperate courage' [Scott's footnote]. Another 'modern antique' given currency by *Ivanhoe*. Scott got the phrase from Spenser, whose *Shepheardes Calender* ('October') glosses it as a substantive, 'manhoode and chevalrie'. Spenser's usage was based on a sixteenth-century misprint of a passage in Lydgate, imitated from Chaucer ('In dorryng-don that longeth to a knyght', *Troilus and Criseyde*, v. 837). In Middle English it is a verbal phrase meaning 'daring to do [deeds]'.

assoilzie: Scots: to absolve from sin, usually after confession or by posthumous intercession; also a legal term.

316 *Moloch*: the idol of the Ammonites in Leviticus 18: 21.

hatchment: escutcheon, shield with quarterings. Compare *Hamlet*, IV. v. 215: 'No trophy, sword, nor hatchment o'er his bones'.

317 *a second Gideon, or a new Maccabeus*: for Gideon see Judges 6–7; for Judas Maccabeus (d. 161 BCE) see Maccabees I and II, in the Apocrypha.

318 *But I will tear this folly from my heart*: compare *1 Henry IV*, III. ii. 152: 'I will tear the reckoning from his heart'.

319 *epigraph*: 'we take it for granted', wrote Francis Jeffrey in his review of *Ivanhoe*, 'that the charming extracts from 'Old Plays' . . . are original compositions of the author whose prose they garnish' (*Edinburgh Review*, 33, 1820: 54). This is usually the case, but not always: compare Chapter XLII, below. Scott began the practice while working on *The Antiquary*. According to Lockhart, when John Ballantyne failed to locate a desired passage from Beaumont and Fletcher, Scott exclaimed: ' "Hang it, Johnny . . . I believe I can make a motto sooner than you can find one." He did so accordingly; and from that hour, whenever memory failed to suggest an appropriate epigraph, he had recourse to the inexhaustible mines of "old play" or "old ballad", to which we owe some of the most exquisite verses that ever flowed from his pen' (*Life of Scott*, 1896 edn., chapter 37). This usage was imitated by, among others, George Eliot.

320 *parish-butt on a holyday even*: see Strutt, *Sports and Pastimes*, 56, 63; such holidays included Bartholomew-tide and May-morning.

322 *'with a great sum'*: Acts 22: 28: 'And the chief captain answered, With a great sum obtained I this freedom'—referring, however, to Roman citizenship.

   hard as a nether millstone: Job 41: 24, 'as hard as a piece of the nether millstone'.

323 *unshriven and unhouseled*: without having received the sacrament, as in *Hamlet*, I. v. 77: 'Cut off even in the blossoms of my sin, | Unhousel'd, disappointed, unanel'd'.

326 *Hateful hag, thou liest!*: conflation of *King Lear*, I. iv. 262, 'Detested kite, thou liest!', and *Richard III*, I. iii. 214, 'Have done thy charm, thou hateful wither'd hag'.

327 *May each stone of this vaulted roof find a tongue*: compare *Macbeth*, II. i. 57–8: 'for fear | The very stones prate of my whereabout'.

   Foul spirit, avoid!: *2 Henry VI*, I. iv. 40: 'False fiend, avoid!'

328 *epigraph*: *Henry V*, III. i. 1–2, 25–8. Volume 3 of the first edition (1820) began here.

   by the Saint Christopher at my baldric: image of the patron saint of foresters, often worn as a talisman. Chaucer's yeoman wears 'A Christofre on his brest of silver sheene' (i. 115).

jeopard: to risk or hazard; a back-formation from 'jeopardy'. *OED* records examples from Chaucer and Lydgate, and credits Scott with its modern revival.

329 *trysting-tree*: a fixture of the Robin Hood ballads, as in the 'Lytell Geste': 'And welcome be thou, gentill knyght, | Under my trystell tree' (Ritson, *Robin Hood*, i. 49). /

332 *Mount joye Saint Dennis*: the battle-cry of the kings of France. St Denis's mount of joy was the site of his glorious decollation.

sendal: a thin rich silken material. Chaucer, 'General Prologue', i. 440: 'Lyned with taffata and with sendal'.

333 *Saint Nicholas of Limoges*: a characteristic garble: none of the St Nicholases in the calendar has an association with Limoges.

334 *dagger of mercy*: so-called, according to the 'Essay on Chivalry', 'because, when unsheathed, it behoved the antagonist to crave mercy or to die' (*Miscellaneous Prose Works*, vi. 75). In fact, as A. N. Wilson notes, this was the misericord, named for its function of delivering the *coup-de-grâce*. The Black Knight's ultimatum is taken from Berners's Froissart: 'Sir, yelde you my prisonere: rescue or no rescue, or else ye be but deed' (i. cccxlii).

338 *hasty hand catches frog for fish*: proverbial variant; compare John Heywood, *Dialogue*, i. xi (1562): 'But now he hath well fisht and caught a frog'. The other saws appear to be Scott's inventions; Wamba's speech here imitates the style of Sancho Panza in *Don Quixote*, part I, chapter 25.

demi-courbette: a half-leap or rearing action of the horse with forelegs together.

339 *descending on his head, levelled him with the earth*: MS reads here: 'descending on his head, fairly cleft it in twain. Thus died Athelstane of Conigsburgh and with him a train of ambitious hopes and lofty pretensions ill assorted to the indolent mind in which they had taken deep root.' At James Ballantyne's insistence Scott changed this in proof. See Scott's note 55.

340 *Fatal Sisters*: Gray's 'The Fatal Sisters' (1761) is one of the first and most famous of the imitations of Scaldic poetry: 'Sisters, weave the web of death' (line 51).

343 *epigraph*: by Scott.

344 *abidden*: obsolete past participle of 'abide'; *OED* notes a revival in
nineteenth-century poetic diction, no doubt influenced by Scott.

345 *liard*: a French coin of trifling value.

THEOW and ESNE . . . FOLK-FREE and SACLESS: 'Thrall and bondsman', 'A lawful freeman' (Scott's footnote, 1830). Scott got the
terms from Sir Henry Spelman's *Feuds and Tenures by Knightly
Service* (1641), in *The English Works of Sir Henry Spelman . . . Re-
lating to the Laws and Antiquities of England* (1723). See Tulloch,
The Language of Walter Scott, 52–3.

346 *Oldhelm of Malmsbury*: St Aldhelm, seventh-century Abbot of
Malmesbury and Bishop of Sherbourne, author of florid Latin
treatises (including one in praise of virginity). Rather than any of
those, Wamba appears to be citing one of the vernacular rhymes
Aldhelm composed to draw folk to church, which have not
survived.

349 *soul-scat*: mortuary dues, payed on behalf of the deceased to the
church of the parish. See Turner, *History*, iii. 146: 'SAUL-SCEAT, or
payment of the clergy on death'.

350 *three mots upon the horn . . . helpers and rescue*: many of the Robin
Hood ballads feature a crisis in which the outlaw instantly sum-
mons fifty or a hundred of his bowmen by sounding his horn; see
Ritson, *Robin Hood*, ii. 50, 127, etc.

352 *Saint Hermangild*: Hermenegild, martyred son of the Gothic king
of Spain.

353 *wild thunder-dint and levin-fire*: lightning. Compare Chaucer, 'Wife
of Bath's Prologue', iv. 276: 'With wilde thonder-dynt and firy
levene'. See also *Marmion*, I. xxiii: 'Mid thunder-dint, and flashing
levin'.

sown in good soil: alludes to the parable of the sower: Mark 4: 20,
'sown on good ground'.

354 *the Promise*: see Genesis 12: 1–3 ('I will make of thee a great
nation').

355 *brazen helmet*: 1 Samuel 17: 5, 'And he had an helment of brass
upon his head'.

Genam meam dedi vapulatori: Scott appears to have back-translated
(as he often does with his Vulgate citations) from Lamentations 3:
30, which reads: *Dabit percutienti se maxillam*, 'He giveth his cheek
to him that smiteth him'.

the piper plays ill that wants the nether chops: proverbial. As Tulloch
notes, Scott recalls the Scots version, 'the piper wants mickle that

wants the nether chaft' ('*Ivanhoe* and Bibles'); but compare also Heywood, *Dialogue*, II. ix: 'He can ill pipe that lacketh his upper lip'.

356 *the leopard will not change his spots*: Jeremiah 13: 23, 'Can the Ethiopian change his skin, or the leopard his spots?'.

Clement: a lapse. He was so called in MS, but rechristened in proof (presumably to distinguish him from the attendant of Front-de-Bœuf) to 'Gilbert', the name he bears earlier in this scene.

totty: unsteady, fuddled, usually with drink. Spenser, *Mutabilitie Cantoes* (*Faerie Queene*, VII), ii. 39: 'his noule was totty of the must'.

cardecu: old French silver coin of moderate value ('*quart d'écu*').

pyet: magpie (Scots).

357 *epigraph*: *Coriolanus*, I. vi. 32–6.

manus imponere in servos Domini: 'to lay hands on the servants of the Lord'.

excommunicabo vos: 'I shall excommunicate you'.

nebulo quidam: 'a worthless fellow'.

358 *crisping-tongs*: it was high fashion at the end of the twelfth century for men to have their hair curled, according to Strutt (*Dress and Habits*, i. 101). A *pouncet-box* is a small box with a perforated lid containing perfume; *OED* credits Scott with reviving this Shakespearian usage (compare *1 Henry IV*, I. iii. 38; also *The Monastery*, chapter 26). *Gymmal rings* are rings made of two rings interlinked.

the gospel of Saint Nicodemus: part of the Apocryphal New Testament, also called the Acts of Pilate; it contains an account of Christ's harrowing of Hell after the Crucifixion.

Deus faciat salvam benignitatem vestram: 'God save your reverence.'

morris-dancer: Morris or 'Moorish' dances, associated with May-day festivities and featuring representations of Robin Hood and Maid Marian, are not recorded before about 1450.

taking our tithes: St Andrew's day is 30 November, thus close to the end of the year, when tithes were due.

359 *facite vobis amicos de Mammone iniquitatis*: Luke 16: 9. The Vulgate reads *mamona*.

set thee free for a blast: 'Free for a blast' was the motto on the family shield of the Clerks of Penicuik. (Cavenagh, citing information supplied by W. S. Crockett.)

hold a candle to the devil: proverb, meaning to assist in wrongdoing;

the *Oxford Dictionary of English Proverbs* cites examples from the mid-fifteenth century.

359 *they do live upon the fat, and drink the sweet wines upon the lees*: Isaiah 25: 6: 'a feast of fat things, a feast of wines on the lees, of fat things full of marrow'.

360 *propter necessitatem, et ad frigus depellendum*: 'in case of need, and to keep out the cold'.

A sentence!—a sentence!: compare *Merchant of Venice*, IV. i. 304: 'Most learned judge, a sentence!'

361 *assuage your choler*: Isaac's speech closely recalls Shylock's in *Merchant of Venice*, I. iii. 106–29.

The curse of Egypt: see Numbers 22 ('Behold, there is a people come out of Egypt . . . curse me this people').

latro famosus: 'a notorious thief'. In his own note to this chapter Scott mentions the decree of excommunication issued against Border outlaws by Richard Fox, Bishop of Durham under Henry VII, *Monitio contra famosos latrones de Tyndall et Rydsdall*. Scott reprinted the text in *Minstrelsy of the Scottish Border* (introduction, appendix no. vii).

362 *the glory hath departed from my house*: 1 Samuel 4: 21: 'And she named the child Ichabod, saying, The glory is departed from Israel'.

364 *verbum Domini projecerunt . . . treasures to others*: Jeremiah 8: 9–10. The Vulgate reads, *verbum enim Domini proiecerunt, et sapientia nulla est in eis* and *propterea dabo mulieres eorum exteris, agros eorum heredibus*: 'therefore I will give their women and their fields [rather than treasures] to strangers'.

365 *maravedi*: Spanish copper coin of small value; recorded from the fifteenth century.

367 *inter res sacras*: 'accounted sacred'.

lapides pro pane condonantes iis: Matthew 7: 9. The Vulgate reads: *Aut quis est ex vobis homo quem si petierit filius suus panem, numquid lapidem porriget ei*; 'which of you, if his son asks him for bread, will give him a stone'.

368 *a lawful spoiling of the Egyptians*: Exodus 3: 22: 'ye shall spoil the Egyptians'.

Ossa ejus perfringam: garbled from Isaiah 38: 13, *sic contrivit omnia ossa mea*, 'so will he break all my bones'.

370 *Thus parted that fair fellowship*: compare Malory, *Morte d'Arthur* XX. 9: 'Such a fellowship of good knights shall never be together in no company'.

371 *epigraph*: *King John*, III. iii, 60–2.

372 *Ahithophel*: counsellor of Absalom in his plot against King David, 2 Samuel 15–17. The 1820 and 1822 spelling, 'Achitophel', evokes Dryden's famous poem *Absalom and Achitophel*.

373 '*bloody with spurring, fiery red with speed*': *Richard II*, II. iii. 58, which reads 'with haste'.

and I alone am escaped to tell you: Job 1: 15–19.

374 *Sir Guy or Sir Bevis*: heroes of two popular Middle English romances; Ellis, *Specimens of Early English Metrical Romances*, epitomizes them under the category 'Saxon Romances' on the grounds that 'they may possibly be founded on some Saxon tradition', i. 4. Chaucer mentions 'Beves and sir Gy' in the burlesque 'Tale of Sir Thopas', vii. 899.

my sworn brother: Archbishop Geoffrey of York (d. 1212) was an illegitimate son of Henry II, and no ally of John's at the time of *Ivanhoe*. The 'church of Saint Peter' is York Minster.

375 *Clifford's gate*: in Clifford's Tower, next to the castle of York.

Robert Estoteville . . . the Earl of Essex: Robert's son, William de Stuteville (d. 1203), is meant. Geoffrey Fitzpeter (d. 1213), Earl of Essex, was one of the council of judges who held the regency in Richard's absence.

Our uncle Robert: Robert of Normandy was a great-uncle.

376 *bewrayed*: to bewray is to expose by divulging secrets.

Lancelot de Lac and Sir Tristram: heroes of the Arthurian romances.

377 *stained the steps of his own altar*: Becket was murdered in 1170 and canonized three years later.

380 *epigraph*: by Scott. Compare *1 Henry VI*, I. iv. 155, 'tigers of Hyrcania'; *Hamlet*, II. ii. 450, 'th' Hyrcanian beast'; *Macbeth*, III. iv. 100, 'th' Hyrcan tiger'.

381 *a stumbling-block and an abomination*: Ezekiel 7: 19 (stumbling-block); Leviticus 7: 18 (abomination).

Lucas de Beaumanoir: Scott's invention (named from Berners's Froissart, IV. xx). The Grand Master of the Order at the time would have been Robert de Sablé (1191–3) or Gilbert Erail (1194–1200).

381 *outstretched arm*: Psalm 136: 12, 'With a strong hand, and with a stretched out arm'.

as holy David over Edom: in 2 Samuel 8: 14.

382 *fiery furnace seven times heated*: Daniel 3: 19.

beauty of Zion: Lamentations 1: 6, 'from the daughter of Zion all her beauty is departed'.

Daniel in the den of lions: Daniel 6: 16–24.

confounded and brought to shame: Psalm 40: 14, 'Let them be ashamed and confounded together'.

the former Preceptor: MS reads 'former proprietor', which seems more likely.

383 *the rule of their Order*: the original Latin rule of the Templars, based on the rule of St Benedict, was formulated after papal recognition of the Order at the Council of Troyes (1129). Laurent Dailliez, *La Règle des Templiers* (1977), prints the Latin text with variants and a French version made later in the twelfth century. Scott's text differs in some respects from the rule, no doubt because of his own creative adaptations; his numbering of the articles corresponds more closely to the version cited in the notes of Henri du Curzon, *La Règle du Temple* (1886). I have followed Curzon's numbering. The article of the rule here referred to is no. 17, which cites the 'holy texts' *In multiloquio non effugies peccatum* (Proverbs 10: 19) and *Mors et vita in manibus lingue* (Proverbs 18: 14). Article 21 contains the monition against 'certain false brethren in the mountains': *Surrexerunt namque in ultramontanis partibus quidam pseudo fratres et coniugati at alii dicentes se esse de Templo, cum sint de mundo.*

384 *according to the rule of Saint Bernard-himself*: it is likelier that St Bernard of Clairvaux advised and edited rather than actually composed the Templars' rule. He did, however, promote the new Order vigorously, lobbying on its behalf at the Council of Troyes and writing a panegyric, *De laude novae militiae* ('In praise of the new knighthood', 1129–36). *Burrel cloth*, prescribed in article 20, was 'one of the coarsest species of woollen cloth' (Strutt, *Dress and Habits*, ii. 137); compare Chaucer, 'Wife of Bath's Prologue', iv. 356: 'my borel for to shewe'.

vair or ermine: 'any of the finer kinds of furs, when their colours were diversified and opposed to each other upon the same garment': Strutt, *Dress and Habits*, ii. 139. Lambskin is sanctioned in article 23 of the rule, *Ut pellibus agnorum utantur.*

that singular abacus: an error for *baculus* (article 68). Cavenagh observes that 'when the Templars of the U.S.A. adopted this staff of office in 1859, they followed Scott's error in naming it the *abacus*'.

our Temple Church in yonder proud capital: the round church of St Mary the Virgin in London, consecrated in 1185. *Robert de Ros* (Robert, Lord of Ros) and *William de Mareschal* (William the Marshall, Earl of Pembroke) were benefactors rather than knights of the Order; their sepulchral effigies, lying with the crusaders' crossed legs, can still be seen today.

385 *the roaring lion, who goeth about seeking whom he may devour*: 1 Peter 5: 8, 'your adversary the devil, as a roaring lion, walketh about, seeking whom he may devour'.

Ut Leo semper feriatur: article 48, 'that the lion is ever to be beaten down'. As a type of the devil (see previous note) the lion was exempted from the Order's general ban on hunting.

the zeal which hath devoured my substance and my life: Psalm 69: 9, 'the zeal of thine house hath eaten me up'.

What say our statutes . . . ?: the prohibitions that follow are all in the rule except that against magic, which Scott inserts under the head of heresy for the convenience of his plot. (Charges of black magic were made at the suppression of the Order, more than a century later.)

the forty-sixth chapter: article 56: *quia antiquis hostis femineo consortio complores expulit a recto tramite paradisi*.

386 *ut omnium mulierem fugiantur oscula*: article 72, 'that they flee the kisses of all women'.

the service of the Temple: the Order was founded by Hugues de Payns (d. 1136), who would become the first Grand Master, and Godfrey de Saint-Omer. According to tradition only nine members had been recruited by the time of the Council of Troyes.

the brand of Phineas: Numbers 25: 7–8. When an Israelite and a Midianitish woman lay together, Phinehas, to avert the wrath of God, took up a javelin 'and thrust both of them through, the man of Israel, and the woman through her belly'.

387 *the place thereof shall no more be known*: Psalm 103: 16.

the cast-off garments of the knights: article 24.

popinjay: parrot. MS reads 'as loud and pert' rather than 'as proud and as pert', which is more apt to the context.

387 *In the hearing of the ear he hath obeyed me*: article 33, which cites Psalm 18: 44, *Ob auditu auris obedivit mihi*: 'As soon as they hear of me, they shall obey me'.

388 *the staff and the rod*: article 68, *baculus et virga*.

389 *De Lectione Literarum*: 'on the reading of letters': article 41, *De Legatione Litterarum*.

   to purge the thrashing-floor: Matthew 3: 12: 'Whose fan is in his hand, and he will thoroughly purge his floor'.

390 *Invenientur vigilantes*: Luke 12: 37 reads *invenerit vigilantes*, 'shall find watching'.

   Vinum lætificat cor hominis . . . Rex delectabitur pulchritudine tua: 'wine [that] maketh glad the heart of man': Psalm 104: 15 (reading *lætificet*); "The king shall rejoice in thy beauty": Scott back-translates Psalm 45: 11, Vulgate: *et concupiscet rex decorum tuum*, 'so shall the king greatly desire thy beauty'.

   Pr. S. M. *Jorvolciensis*: Prior of St Mary (Sanctae Mariae) of Jorvaulx.

391 *Semper percutiatur leo vorans*: 'the devouring lion is ever to be crushed'. A paraphrase of article 48 (see note to p. 385 above).

   sigils, and periapts: magical signs and charms. Compare *1 Henry VI*, v. iii. 2: 'Now help, ye charming spells and periapts'.

393 *epigraph*: by Scott.

394 *. . . propter oblectationem carnis*: 'concerning brethren in arms of the Temple in the holy city, who have congress with fallen women for the gratification of their carnal lusts'. This article does not occur in the Rule, which Scott embellishes to suit his theme. Punished by degradation rather than expulsion, dalliance with women was not among the very gravest infractions of the Order.

395 *Saint Magdalene and the ten thousand virgins forbid!*: Albert gives himself away. St Ursula was supposed to have been martyred with 11,000 virgins at Cologne, not St Mary Magdalene, the fallen woman.

   quean: strumpet; in Scots, less severely, a lass or wench.

   the lust of the eye: compare Matthew 5: 28, 'whosoever looketh on a woman to lust after her hath committed adultery with her already in his heart'.

   a sweet and acceptable offering: Philippians 4: 18, 'an odour of a sweet smell, a sacrifice acceptable'.

   heaps upon heaps: Judges 15: 16.

396 *within his own domain*: barons had power of life and death over felons in their domains; but no statutes against witchcraft were passed in England until the sixteenth century. See Scott's *Demonology*, letter vii. The rules of the Order enjoin the Templars to stamp out heresy rather than sorcery.

le don d'amoureux merci: see 'Essay on Chivalry' (*Miscellaneous Prose Works*, vi. 31): 'the boon of amorous mercy from the lady whom he loved *par amours*'. Scott cites the romance *Petit Jehan de Saintré*, his principal source for the protocols of *amor courtois*.

398 *flagrant delict*: *In flagrante delicto*, 'in the act of committing the crime'. The 1820 and 1822 editions endowed Albert de Malvoisin with another revealing slip, 'fragrant delict', by a felicitous misreading of Scott's holograph.

399 *Maison-Dieu*: 'Godshouse' (MS reading), a common name for hospitals; Cavenagh suggests that Scott may have confused the famous Maison-Dieu of St Mary at Dover, founded in 1227, with the Preceptory of the Templars at Swingfield, near Dover.

402 *epigraph*: by Scott. MS title, *Superstition: A Fragment*.

403 *Venite exultemus Domino*: Psalm 94 (Vulgate 95): 'O come, let us sing unto the Lord'. Prescribed to be sung in chapel, article 7 of the rule.

rushing of mighty waters: Isaiah 17: 12.

404 *the fifty-ninth capital*: *Ut omnes fratres ad secretum consilium non vocentur*, 'That all brethren not be called to the secret council'. The Grand Master translates *Non semper omnes fratres ad consilium convocare jubemus sed quos idoneos et in consilio provideo magister cognovit*.

sortileges: divination by drawing lots.

405 *Auferte malum ex vobis*: article 68 quotes 1 Corinthians 5: 13: *auferte malum ex vobis ipsis*, 'put away from yourselves that wicked person'.

this lamentable history: article 33 is cited accurately; article 57 should read *Ut fratres cum excommunicatis non participentur*; the third article, 'That brethren have no congress with strange women', appears to be Scott's invention. *Anathema Maranatha*: see 1 Corinthians 16: 22, 'If any man love not the Lord Jesus Christ, let him be Anathema Maranatha'. *Anathema* is from the Greek, 'accursed one'; *Maranatha* is a Syriac word meaning 'our Lord cometh'.

Ut fugiantur oscula: that kisses be avoided.

405 *right hand and right eye thereof*: compare Matthew 5: 29–30: 'And if thy right eye offend thee, pluck it out, and cast it from thee ... And if thy right hand offend thee, cut it off, and cast it from thee'.

De osculis fugiendis: on avoiding kisses.

408 *mystery of iniquity*: 2 Thessalonians 2: 7.

409 *The Lion of the Tribe of Judah hath conquered*: Revelations 5: 5, 'the Lion of the tribe of Juda ... hath prevailed to open the book'. A New Testament motto is unlikely.

Scripture into blasphemy: compare *Merchant of Venice*, I. iii. 93, 96: 'The devil can cite Scripture for his purpose. ... A goodly apple rotten at the heart'.

410 *Rabbi Nathan Ben Samuel*: previously Nathan Ben Israel.

414 *trial by combat*: see Scott's remarks in the 'Essay on Chivalry' (*Miscellaneous Prose Works*, vi. 46). Mitchell, *Scott, Chaucer and Medieval Romance* (132–3), notes episodes in *Amadis of Gaul* (book III in Rose's version) and the *Morte d'Arthur* (book xviii) that may have influenced Scott. Patricia C. Hodgell ('The Nonsense of Ancient Days', Ph.D. Diss., 1987, 110–11) points out that Logan's *Runnamede* supplied Scott with the plot in which the heroine's captor stands as her champion and the hero appears as challenger at the last minute.

416 *epigraph*: *Richard II*, IV. i. 46–8, reading 'mortal breathing' for 'martial daring'.

in cloud and in fire: compare Exodus 19: 16, 'thunders and lightnings, and a thick cloud upon the mount'.

418 *as a whole age*: paraphrase of Psalm 90: 4, 'For a thousand years in thy sight are but as yesterday when it is past'.

like an angel of light: 2 Corinthians 11: 14: 'Satan himself is transformed into an angel of light'.

420 *the captivity of Judah*: compare Psalm 126: 1, 'the Lord turned again the captivity of Zion'; also Zephanaiah 3: 20.

421 *signet of the mighty Solomon*: mentioned in the Koran, chapter 38, and the Arabian Nights.

asper: a small Turkish silver coin of trifling value.

phlebotomy: Scott himself had undergone tremendous applications of blood-letting during his long and agonizing bout of gallstones.

422 *Benoni*: Genesis 35: 18. The name given by Rachel to her son with her dying breath; Jacob renamed him Benjamin.

curse God and die: Job 2: 9.

Beltheshazzar: Daniel 1: 7.

gourd of Jonah: Jonah 4: 7: 'But God prepared a worm when the morning rose the next day, and it smote the gourd that it withered'.

the darkness of the shadow of death hath encompassed thee: compare Job 3: 5, 'Let darkness and the shadow of death stain it'; also Job 10: 21–2.

as a fountain of water: Jeremiah 9: 1, 'mine eyes a fountain of tears'.

let the virgins of our people mourn for me: compare Judges 11: 40, 'the daughters of Israel went yearly to lament'.

423 *the throne of Boadbil the Saracen*: Cordoba was the capital of Moorish Spain until 1216, and in the late twelfth century a major European centre of learning, the residence of Averroes and Maimonides. Abu Abdullah, or Boadbil, was the last Moorish king of Granada (1482–92), three centuries later than the period of *Ivanhoe*. Islamic Spain accommodated the Sephardic Jews until the Christian re-conquest and expulsion of 1492, when many accepted an offer of sanctuary from the Ottoman Sultan.

bone of my bone: echoes Adam's salutation of Eve, Genesis 2: 23.

424 *mancus*: an Anglo-Saxon coin.

425 *epigraph*: Anna Seward, Song, 'From thy waves, stormy Lannow, I fly'. Line 6 apostrophizes 'Ah, nymph!' rather than 'O maid'.

hymn: as Tulloch notes ('*Ivanhoe* and Bibles'), Scott imitates the manner of the metrical psalms of the Scottish Presbyterian church to show the ecumenical breadth of Rebecca's faith. The hymn includes allusions to Exodus 13: 21 ('By day . . . fiery column's glow'), Psalm 137: 1–2 ('Our harps we left . . .'), Isaiah 1: 11 ('the blood of goat . . . I will not prize'), and Psalm 51: 17 ('A contrite heart . . . accepted sacrifice').

427 *parting with your treasure for that which is not bread*: compare Matthew 6: 19–21.

Rock of Ages: a literal translation from the Hebrew of Isaiah 26: 4, popularized in eighteenth-century hymnody; e.g. Augustus Montagu Toplady, 'A Living and Dying Prayer for the Holiest Believer in the World', 1776 ('Rock of ages, cleft for me'); John Newton, 'Zion, or the City of God', 1779 ('On the rock of ages founded').

bucklered: shielded, as in *3 Henry VI*, III. iii. 98–9: 'Can Oxford, that did ever fence the right, | Now buckler falsehood with a pedigree?'

429 *the breath of my nostrils*: compare Lamentations 4: 20, 'The breath
of our nostrils, the anointed of the Lord', for the Templar's idola-
try here.

430 *a hissing and a reproach*: Jeremiah 29: 18.

431 *heaven was once nearly scaled*: in the war of the Titans against the
Olympian gods; see book i of Ovid's *Metamorphoses*.

the Regent, the Queen Mother: the regency during Richard's absence
was held not by his mother but by a justiciary committee headed by
the Bishop of Durham and the Earl of Essex. In the MS Rebecca
bids Bois-Guilbert go 'to the King or to Prince John'.

Conrade, Marquis of Montserrat: properly Montferrat; one of the
leaders of the Third Crusade, ally of Philip of France and enemy of
Richard I. He had recently (1192) been assassinated in the streets of
Tyre, a deed some suspected Richard of having instigated. He is
one of the villains in *The Talisman*.

433 *the Comforter*: Lamentations 1: 16 mentions 'the comforter that
should relieve my soul'; the New Testament amplifies the figure to
represent the third person of the Trinity, as in John 14: 16, 'I will
pray the Father, and he shall give you another Comforter', and 14:
26: 'the Comforter, which is the Holy Ghost, whom the Father will
send in my name, he shall teach you all things, and bring all things
to your remembrance, whatsoever I have said unto you'.

the awful Voice: Numbers 7: 89, 'he heard the voice of one speaking
unto him from off the mercy seat that was upon the ark of testimony, from between the two cherubims'; see also Exodus 25: 17–
22.

434 *trampled down like the shorn grass, and mixed with the mire of the
ways*: combination of Psalm 37: 2, 'cut down like the grass', and
Isaiah 10: 6, 'tread them down like the mire of the streets'.

the garden of the sluggard: see Isaac Watts, 'The Sluggard', *Divine
Songs for the Use of Children* (1715), lines 9–10: 'I pass'd by his
Garden, and saw the wild Brier, | The Thorn and the Thistle grow
broader and higher'. Compare Proverbs 24: 30–1 ('the field of the
slothful').

436 *the armed image of Saint George*: (MS, 'armour of St George').
Strutt, *Sports and Pastimes* ('introduction', p. xxv), describes
effigies of the Nine Worthies carried at civic pageants and
processions.

438 *epigraph*: this is not Shakespeare's *Richard III* but Colley Cibber's
notorious 'alteration', 'The Tragicall History of King Richard III'

(1700), which held the stage into the nineteenth century. The original reads 'Conscience' for Scott's 'Shadows'.

Saint Botolph: the cult of St Botulf was primarily East Anglian.

439 *lee-gage*: to the leeward of, i.e. on the sheltered side.

makes all split: compare *A Midsummer Night's Dream*, I. ii. 30: 'I could play Ercles rarely, or a part to tear a cat in, to make all split'.

440 *destrier*: 'war-horse' (Scott's footnote), so called for being led by the squire's right hand.

the juggler's steed that paces a hornpipe amongst the eggs: (MS reads 'prances'). Scott combines Strutt's description of the 'egg-dance', in which a blindfolded (human) dancer performed a hornpipe among a dozen eggs without breaking any (*Sports and Pastimes*, 225–6), with the account of dancing horses in the following chapter (243). *Malkin*, diminutive of Maud or Matilda, was a generic name for servant-women and she-cats.

441 *Fructus Temporum*: *The Fruit of the Times*, an account of sacred and foreign history, printed as a supplement to *The Chronicles of England* by Wynken de Worde at St Albans in 1483. These *Chronicles*, also called *Caxton's Chronicles*, were a continuation of John of Trevisa's famous *Polychronicon*. Clearly the Prior has a much earlier manuscript chronicle with the same title.

maniple: steward or purveyor, responsible for procuring the monastery's supplies; compare Chaucer, 'General Prologue', i. 567–86.

442 *stockfish*: cod dried in the air, without salt.

443 *good cutting falchion*: short sword; compare *King Lear*, v. iii. 277, 'my good biting falchion'. A *targe* is a light shield or buckler.

moping, mowing: making faces. Compare *King Lear*, IV. i. 61–2, 'Flibbertigibbet, of mopping and mowing'.

virelai: properly, a lyric form of short two-rhymed stanzas, not current until the fourteenth century. The songs appear to be by Scott.

445 *Hur's a gentleman, God wot, and hur's lineage was of Wales*: Scott appears to be imitating the literary version of West Country dialect in Spenser's *Shepheardes Calender*, 'September': 'But now her is a most wretched wight', etc.

Heaven forefend: compare *1 Henry VI*, v. iv. 64, 'Now Heaven forfend, the holy Maid with child!'

446 *the root of evil*: properly, 'the love of money': 1 Timothy 6: 10.

446 *Abbot of Saint Bees*: 'he of St Ives' in the version of the anecdote we heard in Chapter XXVII.

the seven-fold usury which the blessed text hath promised to charitable loans: Wamba conflates Matthew 18: 22, 'I say not unto thee, Until seven times: but, until seventy times seven' (on forgiveness of a brother's offence), with Luke 6: 35: 'lend, hoping for nothing again; and your reward shall be very great'.

447 *neither bears nor wolves*: bears were extinct in England at this time, but wolves roamed as close to London as Northamptonshire and Buckinghamshire; during his reign John raised the bounty on them to five shillings a head.

448 *gamut*: the 'Great Scale', comprising all the notes of medieval music; supposedly codified by Guido d'Arezzo (d. 1050?).

nine-pins: the game is described by Strutt, *Sports and Pastimes*, 272–3, who does not mention a 'king'.

morrion: helmet without beaver or visor; sixteenth-century usage.

449 *Clerks of Saint Nicholas*: MS has a footnote here, never published: 'Robbers were anciently called Saint Nicholas's clerks, probably in allusion to Old Nick. They were also called *good fellows* the reason for which is not so obvious.' 'Robin Goodfellow' is a sobriquet of the wood-demon Puck in *A Midsummer Night's Dream*; Richard addresses Robin Hood as 'Prince of good fellows' later in the chapter.

451 *thou diest*: echoes Lear's banishment of Kent, *King Lear*, I. i. 173–4.

452 *Robin Hood of Sherwood Forest*: While Ritson was Scott's main source for Robin Hood, he was also familiar with other literary, legendary, and historical components of the tradition (for which see Knight, *Robin Hood*, esp. chapters 2–4). Scott's Note no. 10 to *The Abbot* (1821) discusses the carnivalesque representation of Robin Hood in the May Games. In making Robin a Saxon yeoman, Scott discarded the gentrifying 'Earl of Huntingdon' pedigree adopted by Ritson from the eighteenth-century antiquarian William Stukeley (and reproduced by Thomas Love Peacock in *Maid Marian*, 1822). The association with Sherwood Forest comes from Michael Drayton's *Poly-Olbion* (1622); the 'Lyttel Geste' locates the outlaw in Barnsdale, near Doncaster.

The mice will play: the earliest citation in the *Oxford Dictionary of English Proverbs* is from the 1530s.

453 *houghed*: hamstrung.

Confiteor: 'I confess'; from the Ordinary of the Mass.

sits the wind there?: compare *Much Ado About Nothing*, II. iii. 98, 'Sits the wind in that corner?'

454 *a grant of vert and venison*: the right to cut green trees or shrubbery and to kill deer; legal formula. *OED* cites examples from the *Rolls of Parliament* (1455) and Holinshed's *Chronicles* (1577).

455 *we may not turn our game into earnest*: compare Chaucer, 'Miller's Prologue', i. 3186: 'men shal nat maken ernest of game'.

456 *epigraph*: Andrew MacDonald (1755–88), *Love and Loyalty: An Opera*, II, air xi. Original reads:

> Hail, ladies and lordings, of courtly degree,
> Who live not more happy, tho' higher, than we!
> Our pastimes to see,
> Beneath each green tree,
> In all the gay woodlands, most welcome ye be!

The opera, set vaguely in the time of the Crusades, features heroic archers resisting the king in the forests of Bohemia.

457 *bodkin*: here, a pin rather than a dagger.

Estoteville and Bohun . . . London: Bohun, Beauchamp (later Earl of Warwick) and Percy (Earl of Northumberland) were among the barons who later opposed John over the Magna Carta. The Chancellor, William de Longchamp (d. 1197), was one of Richard's staunchest allies; he helped raise his ransom and returned with him to England.

458 *buxom*: jolly, well-favoured.

a brilliant and rapid meteor . . . universal darkness: recalls lines (634, 656) from the end of Pope's *Dunciad*:

> The meteor drops, and in a flash expires . . .
> And Universal Darkness buries all.

459 *the stories of former deeds were told with advantage*: MS reads 'feats' for 'deeds'; compare *Henry V*, IV. iii. 50, 'he'll remember with advantages | What feats he did that day'.

toying with the lion's whelp: compare *Antony and Cleopatra* III. xiii. 93, ' 'Tis better playing with a lion's whelp'.

462 *succeeded to his heroic brother*: the clauses of Magna Carta liberalizing the forest laws were not expanded into a separate Charter of the Forest until the following reign. Far from being disposed to anticipate such a development, Richard I had renewed the

forest laws and their penalties, which included blinding and castration.

462 *'Now cheaply purchased at their weight in gold'*: John Ferriar, 'The Bibliomania, an Epistle to Richard Heber, Esq.' (1809; reprinted in Ferriar's *Illustrations of Sterne*, 1812). The original reads: 'dismal ballads, sung to crouds of old, | Now cheaply bought for thrice their weight in gold'. The 'black-letter garlands' are the collections of broad-sheet ballads, illustrated with crude wood-cuts, bound and printed in the seventeenth and eighteenth centuries under the generic title of *Robin Hood's Garland*. See Ritson's introduction to *Robin Hood*, vol. i. p. lxxxv. For Robin Hood's death from a botched phlebotomy, administered by his treacherous kinswoman the prioress of Kirklees, see *Robin Hood*, ii. 183–7.

very great antiquity: despite Scott's assertions here and in the voluminous note he added in 1830, the castle was built by Hameline Plantagenet in the 1170s and 1180s. Designed after his castle of Mortemer in Normandy, it was however one of the earliest examples of a cylindrical keep in Britain. The name (from the Old English, 'king's stronghold') suggests a Saxon settlement, and the site may well have accommodated an earlier fortified earthwork.

463 *symbol of Hengist*: his name (*hengst*) means 'stallion'.

465 *epigraph*: John Webster, *The White Devil*, v. iv. 53–7: reading 'corse' for 'corpse', 'there is' for 'there was', ' 'Tween' for ' 'Twixt', and: 'Were wont t' out-wear the nights with'.

467 *flowing wimple of black cypress*: coverchief or veil of fine cloth, worn around the head and neck; later adapted for the nun's habit. See Strutt, *Dress and Habits*, i. 111. For cypress, a transparent kind of crape, see *Winter's Tale*, IV. iv. 216, 'Cypress black as e'er was crow'.

468 *hymn for the soul of the deceased*: compare the Dirge in *Cymbeline*, IV. ii. 258.

471 *Thou sayest well, Sir King . . .* : a condensation of themes from *Macbeth*, Cedric's speech typifies Scott's more syncretic and allusive use of his sources. We understand that Cedric, with the king his guest and at his mercy, is no Macbeth.

burst his bloody cerements: compare *Hamlet*, I. iv. 48, 'thy canoniz'd bones, hearsed in death, | Have burst their cerements'.

472 *Mort de ma vie!*: 'death of my life'. Compare *Henry V*, III. v. 10, 'Norman bastards! | Mort Dieu, ma vie!'

weasand: gullet (Old English).

flatlings: with the flat of the blade; used in Malory, *Morte d'Arthur*, VIII. xxxii; Harington's translation of Ariosto, *Orlando Furioso*, xxxliv.

473 *oubliette*: Scott's MS inserts a footnote, never published: '*Oubliette* or cell of forgetfulness, in which those were imprisoned who were doomed never to revisit the day light. Such horrid dungeons were common both in the convents and the feudal castles of former times.—L. T.'

Saint Jeremy: properly Jerome, one of the Doctors of the Church.

Twelfth-night: 6 January, the feast of the Epiphany, which marked the end of the Christmas season.

Do rocks melt with the sun?: compare Robert Burns, 'My Love is like a Red, Red Rose': 'And the rocks melt wi' the sun'.

474 *I ate, drank, and was invigorated*: compare Ecclesiastes 8: 15, 'to eat, and to drink, and to be merry'.

475 *tregetour*: juggler, conjuror, mountebank: see Chaucer, 'Franklin's Tale', v. 1143, and Strutt, *Sports and Pastimes*, 197–8.

479 *epigraph*: *Richard II*, I. ii. 50.

flints or dunghills: 'Flints. Journeymen taylors, who on a late occasion refused to work for the wages settled by law. Those who submitted, were, by the mutineers, styled dungs, i.e. dunghills': Francis Grose, *A Classical Dictionary of the Vulgar Tongue* (3rd edn., 1796). In this paragraph Scott refers to the so-called Peterloo or Manchester Massacre of 16 August 1819, when yeoman cavalry charged a crowd assembled to hear the Radical orator Henry Hunt at St Peter's Fields, Manchester, killing eleven people and injuring hundreds. For a contemporary objection to this passage see William Hazlitt, *The Spirit of the Age* (1825): 'And it is at this moment (when the heart is kindled and bursting with indignation at the revolting abuses of self-constituted power) that Sir Walter *stops the press* to have a sneer at the people, and to put a spoke (as he thinks) in the wheel of upstart innovation!' (First published in the *New Monthly Magazine*, April 1824; reprinted in John O. Hayden (ed.), *Scott: The Critical Heritage*, 288.) A *bruising match* is a prize fight. Public *execution* was a controversial issue of the day, thanks to such scandals as the riot that attended the botched hanging of the thief Robert Johnston from a scaffold erected on the wall of St Giles's cathedral, Edinburgh, in December 1818 (see the *Edinburgh Weekly Journal*, 6 January 1819).

481 *translated*: compare Hebrews 11: 5: 'By faith Enoch was translated

that he should not see death; and was not found, because God had
translated him'.

481 *sacring-bell*: small bell rung at the elevation of the host during
Mass.

Cheshire round: compare Farquhar, *The Recruiting Officer* (1706), v.
ii, 'He shall box, wrestle, or dance the Cheshire round with any
man in the country'.

483 *barret-cap*: small flat cap, beret; as military attire, compare Scott's
The Fair Maid of Perth, chapter 2: 'steel caps, barrets, and plumes'.

484 *vessel of wrath*: Romans 9: 22.

485 *Te igitur*: the opening prayer in the canon of the Mass; by met-
onymy, the liturgical book itself.

essoine: literally, an excuse for non-appearance in a court of law.

487 *wiser Sadducees*: see Matthew 22: 23, 'the Saducees, which say there
is no resurrection'; also Acts 23: 8.

Soldan of Trebizond: Trebizond, modern Trabzon, on the Black
Sea coast of Asia Minor, was part of the Byzantine empire until
1461, and so would not have had a 'Soldan'.

488 *Greek fire*: a combustible fluid like napalm, supposed to consist of
sulphur, bitumen, and naphtha, developed as a secret weapon by
the Byzantine navy. Greek fire was used at the siege of Acre, and
introduced into England from the Third Crusade; Richard himself
used it to reduce Nottingham on his return in 1194. It is described
in Henry's *History*, vi. 211–12, and mentioned in *Richard Coeur de
Lyon*.

490 *Faites vos devoirs, preux chevaliers!*: 'Do your duty, proud knights!'

mend his fortune: compare *King Lear*, I. i. 94: 'Mend your speech a
little, | Lest you may mar your fortunes'.

victim to . . . his own contending passions: as Mitchell points out
(*Scott, Chaucer, and Medieval Romance*, 133), Scott imitates the
death of Arcite in Chaucer's 'Knight's Tale'. Victorious at the
tournament in Thebes, Arcite is thrown by his horse when a fury
starts up from the earth; 'As blak he lay as any cole or crowe, | So
was the blood yronnen in his face', i. 2692–3.

Fiat voluntas tua: 'thy will be done'.

491 *epigraph*: Webster, *The White Devil*, IV. i, reading 'wives'' for
'wife's'.

492 *Henry Bohun, Earl of Essex, Lord High Constable of England*: in MS
he calls himself 'Humphrey De Bohun Earl of Hereford'. Scott

apparently confused (or conflated) two separate de Bohuns: Henry (1176–1220), first Earl of Hereford (in 1199), Constable of England at the time of *Ivanhoe*; and Humphrey (d. 1274), second Earl of Hereford and first Earl of Essex. It is likely that a third figure compounds the matter: Henry, Earl of Essex, a previous constable (impeached for cowardice in 1157).

Quare fremuerunt Gentes?: Psalm 2: 1, 'Why do the heathen rage?'

495 *maugre*: despite; used in a like context in *King Lear*, v. iii. 132, 'maugre thy strength'.

496 *not even censured by his good-natured brother*: after Richard put down the remains of John's rebellion the brothers were reconciled by their mother in Normandy, May 1195; however Richard did not restore any of John's lands (or any of his castles) until the following year.

497 *a cock that would not fight*: according to *OED* and the *Oxford Dictionary of English Proverbs*, a nineteenth-century saying. Perhaps this is a philological joke.

498 *spoken at the court of London*: in 1367 Edward III became the first monarch to address parliament in English rather than in French; after that date English replaced French in the courts of law.

499 *two burdens*: Hosea 7: 11, 'Ephraim also is like a silly dove without heart'; Genesis 49: 14, 'Issachar is a strong ass couching down between two burdens'.

502 *too curiously*: *Hamlet*, V. i. 205, ' 'Twere to consider too curiously, to consider so'.

near Limoges: this happened in 1199. Richard was besieging the castle in order to get his hands on a treasure-trove, when a crossbow bolt struck him in the neck. Despite his dying instructions, the soldier who shot him was flayed alive.

Johnson: 'On the Vanity of Human Wishes', lines 219–22:

> His Fall was destin'd to a barren Strand,
> A petty Fortress, and a dubious Hand;
> He left the Name, at which the World grew pale,
> To point a Moral, or adorn a Tale.

(Scott's MS accurately quoted 'barren strand'.) This verse refers to Charles XII of Sweden, who was fatally wounded by a musket-shot while besieging Frederikshald in Norway in 1718.

ANTHONY TROLLOPE

An Autobiography
The American Senator
Barchester Towers
Can You Forgive Her?
The Claverings
Cousin Henry
Doctor Thorne
The Duke's Children
The Eustace Diamonds
Framley Parsonage
He Knew He Was Right
Lady Anna
The Last Chronicle of Barset
Orley Farm
Phineas Finn
Phineas Redux
The Prime Minister
Rachel Ray
The Small House at Allington
The Warden
The Way We Live Now

The
Oxford
World's
Classics
Website

www.worldsclassics.co.uk

- Information about new titles
- Explore the full range of Oxford World's Classics
- Links to other literary sites and the main OUP webpage
- Imaginative competitions, with bookish prizes
- Peruse the Oxford World's Classics Magazine
- Articles by editors
- Extracts from Introductions
- A forum for discussion and feedback on the series
- Special information for teachers and lecturers

www.worldsclassics.co.uk

American Literature

British and Irish Literature

Children's Literature

Classics and Ancient Literature

Colonial Literature

Eastern Literature

European Literature

History

Medieval Literature

Oxford English Drama

Poetry

Philosophy

Politics

Religion

The Oxford Shakespeare

A complete list of Oxford Paperbacks, including Oxford World's Classics, Oxford Shakespeare, Oxford Drama, and Oxford Paperback Reference, is available in the UK from the Academic Division Publicity Department, Oxford University Press, Great Clarendon Street, Oxford OX2 6DP.

In the USA, complete lists are available from the Paperbacks Marketing Manager, Oxford University Press, 198 Madison Avenue, New York, NY 10016.

Oxford Paperbacks are available from all good bookshops. In case of difficulty, customers in the UK can order direct from Oxford University Press Bookshop, Freepost, 116 High Street, Oxford OX1 4BR, enclosing full payment. Please add 10 per cent of published price for postage and packing.